THE DODD FAMILY ABROAD.

BY
CHARLES LEVER.

BOSTON.
LITTLE, BROWN, & COMPANY.

THE NOVELS OF CHARLES LEVER.

With an Introduction by Andrew Lang.

THE

DODD FAMILY ABROAD.

TO WHICH IS ADDED,

THAT BOY OF NORCOTT'S.

WITH ILLUSTRATIONS BY PHIZ AND
W. CUBITT COOKE.

IN TWO VOLUMES.
VOL. I.

BOSTON:
LITTLE, BROWN, AND COMPANY.
1895.

Copyright, 1895,

By Little, Brown, and Company.

TO

SIR EDWARD LYTTON BULWER LYTTON,

BART., M.P.

MY DEAR SIR EDWARD, — While asking you to accept the
dedication of this volume, I feel it would be something very
nigh akin to the Bathos were *I* to say one word of Eulogy of
those powers which the world has recognised in *you*.

Let me, however, be permitted, in common with thousands,
to welcome the higher development which your Genius is hourly
attaining, to say God speed to the Author of "The Caxtons"
and "My Novel," and cry "Hear!" to the Eloquent Orator
whose words have awakened an enthusiasm that shows Chivalry
still lives amongst us.

Believe me, in all admiration and esteem,

Your faithful friend,

CHARLES LEVER.

CASA CAPPONI, FLORENCE,
March, 1854.

PREFACE.

ALTHOUGH the faulty judgment of authors on their own productions has assumed something like the force of a proverb, I am ready to incur the hazard of avowing that the present volume is, to my own thinking, better than anything else I have done. I am not about to defend its, numerous shortcomings and great faults. I will not say one word in extenuation of a plan which, to many readers, forms an insuperable objection, — that of a story in letters. I wish simply to record the fact that the book afforded me much pleasure in the writing, and that I felt an amount of interest in the character of Kenny Dodd such as I have never before nor since experienced for any personage of my own creation.

The reader who is at all acquainted with the incidents of foreign travel, and the strange individuals to be met with on every European highway, will readily acquit me of exaggeration either in describing the mistaken impressions conceived of Continental life, or the difficulties of forming anything like a correct estimate of national habits by those whose own sphere of observation was so limited in their own country. In Kenny Dodd, I attempted to portray a man naturally acute and intelligent, sensible and well judging where his prejudices did not pervert his reason, and singularly quick to appreciate the ridicule of any absurd situation in which he did not figure himself. To all the pretentious ambitions of his family, — to their exaggerated sense of themselves and their station, — to their inordinate desire to figure in a rank above their own, and appear to be something they had never hitherto attempted, — I have made him keenly and sensitively alive. He sees Mrs. Dodd's perils, — there is not a sunk rock nor a shoal before her that he has not noted, and yet for the life of him he can't help booking himself for the voyage. There is an Irishman's love of drollery, — that passion for what gives him a hearty laugh, even though he come in for his share of the ridicule, which repays him for every misadventure. If he is momentarily elated by the high and distinguished company in which he finds himself, so far from being shocked when he discovers them to be swindlers and blacklegs, he chuckles over the blunders of Mrs. D. and Mary Anne, and writes off to his friend Purcell a letter over which he laughs till his eyes run.

Of those broad matters to which a man of good common-sense can apply his faculties fairly, his opinions are usually just and true; he likes truth, he wants to see things as they are. Of everything conventional he is almost invariably in error; and it is this struggle that in a manner reflects the light and shade of his nature, showing him at one moment clear-headed and observant, and at the next absurdly mistaken and ignorant.

It was in no spirit of sarcasm on my countrymen that I took an Irishman to represent these incongruities; nay, more, I will say that in the very liability to be so strongly impressed from without, lies much of that unselfishness which forms that staple of the national character which so greatly recommends them to strangers.

If I do not speak of the other characters of the book,

it is because I feel that whatever humble merit the volume may possess is ascribable to the truthfulness of this principal personage. It is less the Dodd family for which I would bespeak the reader's interest, than for the trials of Kenny Dodd himself, his thoughts and opinions.

Finally, let me observe that this story has had the fortune to be better liked by my friends, and less valued by the public, than any other of my books.

I wrote it, as I have said, with pleasure; well satisfied should I be that any of my readers might peruse it with as much. It was planned and executed in a quiet little cottage in the Gulf of Spezia, something more than six years ago. I am again in the same happy spot; and, as I turn over the pages, not altogether lost to some of the enjoyment they once afforded me in the writing, and even more than before anxious that I should not be alone in that sentiment.

It is in vain, however, for an author to bespeak favor for that which comes not recommended by merits of its own; and if Kenny Dodd finds no acceptance with you on his own account, it is hopeless to expect that he will be served by the introduction of so partial a friend as

Your devoted servant,

CHARLES LEVER.

MAROLA, GULF OF SPEZIA,
October 1, 1859.

A WORD FROM THE EDITOR.

THE Editor of the Dodd Correspondence may possibly be
expected to give the Public some information as to the manner by which these Letters came into his possession, and the
reasons which led him to publish them. Happily he can do
both without any breach of honorable confidence. The circumstances were these : —

Mr. Dodd, on his returning to Ireland, passed through the
little watering-place of Spezzia, where the Editor was then
sojourning. They met accidentally, formed acquaintanceship, and then intimacy. Amongst the many topics of
conversation between them, the Continent and its habits
occupied a very wide space. Mr. D. had lived little abroad ;
the Editor had passed half of a life there. Their views and
judgment were, as might be surmised, not always alike ;
and if novelty had occasionally misled one, time and habit
had not less powerfully blunted the perceptions of the other.
The old resident discovered, to his astonishment, that the
very opinions which he smiled at from his friend, had been
once his own ; that he had himself incurred some of the mistakes, and fallen into many of the blunders, which he now
ridiculed, and that, so far from the Dodd Family being the
exception, they were in reality no very unfair samples of a
large class of our travelling countrymen. They had come
abroad with crude and absurd notions of what awaited them
on the Continent. They dreamed of economy, refinement,
universal politeness, and a profound esteem for England
from all foreigners. They fancied that the advantages of
foreign travel were to be obtained without cost or labor ;
that locomotion could educate, sight-seeing cultivate them ;

that in the capacity of British subjects every society should
be open to them, and that, in fact, it was enough to emerge
from home obscurity to become at once recognized in the
fashionable circles of any Continental city.

They not only entertained all these notions, but they held
them in defiance of most contradictory elements. They
practised the most rigid economy when professing immense
wealth; they affected to despise the foreigner while shunning
their own countrymen; they assumed to be votaries of art
when merely running over galleries; and lastly, while laying
claim, and just claim, for their own country to the highest
moral standard of Europe, they not unfrequently outraged
all the proprieties of foreign life by an open and shameless
profligacy. It is difficult to understand how a mere change
of locality can affect a man's notions of right and wrong,
and how Cis-Alpine evil may be Trans-Alpine good. It is
very hard to believe that a few parallels of latitude can
affect the moral thermometer; but so it is, and so Mr. Dodd
honestly confessed he found it. He not only avowed that
he could do abroad what he could not dare to do at home,
but that, worse still, the infraction cost no sacrifice of self-
esteem, no self-reproach. It was not that these derelictions
were part of the habits of foreign life, or at least of such of
it as met the eye; it was, in reality, because he had come
abroad with his own preconceived ideas of a certain latitude
in morals, and was resolved to have the benefit of it. Such
inconsistency in theory led, naturally, to absurdity in action,
and John Bull became, in consequence, a mark for every
trait of eccentricity that satirists could describe, or carica-
turists paint.

The gradations of rank so rigidly defined in England are
less accurately marked out abroad. Society, like the face
of the soil, is not enclosed by boundaries and fenced by
hedgerows, but stretches away in boundless undulations of
unlimited extent. The Englishman fancies there are no
boundaries, because he does not see the landmarks. Since
all seems open, he imagines there can be no trespass. This
is a serious mistake! Not less a one is, to connect title
with rank. He fancies that nobility represents abroad the
same pretensions which it maintains in England, and indig-

nantly revenges his own blunder by calumniating in common every foreigner of rank.

Mr. Dodd fell into some of these errors; from others he escaped. Most, indeed, of his mistakes were those inseparable from a false position; and from the acuteness of his remarks in conversation, it is clear that he possessed fair powers of observation, and a mind well disposed to receive and retain the truth. One quality certainly his observations possessed, — they were "his own." They were neither worked out from the Guide-book, nor borrowed from his *Laquais de Place*. They were the honest convictions of a good ordinary capacity, sharpened by the habits of an active life. It was with sincere pleasure the Editor received from him the following note, which reached him about three weeks after they parted : —

"DODSBOROUGH, BRUFF.

"MY DEAR HARRY LORREQUER, — I have fished up all the Correspondence of the Dodd Family during our *Annus Mirabilis* abroad, and send it to you with this. You have done some queer pranks at Editorship before now, so what would you say to standing Sponsor to us all, foundlings as we are in the world of letters? I have a notion in my head that we were n't a bit more ridiculous than nine-tenths of our travelling countrymen, and that, maybe, our mistakes and misconceptions might serve to warn such as may come after us over the same road. At all events, use your own discretion on the matter, but say nothing about it when you write to me, as Mrs. D. reads all my letters, and if she knew we were going to print her, the consequences would be awful!

"You 'll be glad to hear that we got safe back here, — Tuesday was a week, — found everything much as usual, — farming stock looking up, pigs better than ever I knew them. I have managed to get James into the Police, and his foreign airs and graces are bringing him into the tip-top society of the country. Purcell tells me that we 'll be driven to sell Dodsborough in the Estates Court, and I suppose it 's the best thing after all, for we can buy it in, and clear off the mortgages that was the ruin of us.

"When everything is settled, I have an idea of taking a run through the United States, to have a peep at Jonathan. If so, you shall hear from me.

"Meanwhile, I am yours, very faithfully,

"KENNY I. DODD.

"Do you know any Yankees, or could you get me a few letters to some of their noticeable men? for I 'd like to have an opportunity of talk with them."

The Editor at once set about the inspection of the documents forwarded to him, and carefully perused the entire
correspondence; nor was it until after a mature consideration that he determined on accepting the responsible post
which Mr. Dodd had assigned to him.

He who edits a Correspondence, to a certain extent is assumed to be a concurring party, if not to the statements
contained in it, at least to its general tone and direction. It
is in vain for him to try and hide his own shadow behind
the foreground figure of the picture, or merge his responsibility in that of his principal. The reader will hold him
chargeable for opinions that he has made public, and for
sentiments which, but for his intervention, had slept within
the drawer of a cabinet. This is more particularly the case
where the sentiments recorded are not those of any great
thinker or high authority amongst men whose *dicta* may be
supposed capable of standing the test of a controversy, on
the mere strength of him who uttered them. Now, unhap-
pily, the Dodd Family have not as yet produced one of these
gifted individuals. Their views of the world, as they saw it
in a foreign tour, are those of persons of very moderate
capacity, with very few special opportunities for observation.
They wrote in all the frankness of close friendship to those
with whom they were most intimately allied. They uttered
candidly what they felt acutely. They chronicled their sorrows, their successes, their triumphs, and their shame. And
although experience did teach them something as they went,
their errors tracked them to the last. It cannot be expected,
then, that the Editor is prepared to back their opinions and
uphold their notions, nor is he blamable for the judgments
they have pronounced on many points. It is true, it was
open to him to have retrenched this and suppressed that.
He might have cancelled a confession here, or blotted out
an avowal there; but had he done so in one Letter, the allusion contained in some other might have been pointless, —
the distinctive character of the writer lost; and what is of
more moment than either, a new difficulty engendered, viz.,
what to retain where there was so much to retrench. Besides this, Mrs. D. is occasionally wrong where K. I. is
right, and it is only by contrasting the impressions that the
value of the judgments can be appreciated.

It is not in our present age of high civilization that an Editor need fear the charge of having divulged family secrets, or made the private history of domestic life a subject for public commentary. Happily, we live in a period of enlightenment that can defy such petty slanders. Very high and titled individuals have shown themselves superior to similar accusations, and if the " Dodds " can in any wise contribute to the amusement or instruction of the world, they may well feel recompensed for an exposure to which others have been subjected before them.

As in all cases of this kind, the Editor's share has been of the very lightest. It would not have become him to have added anything either of explanation or apology to the contents of these Letters. Even when a word or two might have served to correct a mistaken impression, he has preferred to leave the obvious task to the reader's judgment to obtrusively making himself the means of interpretation. In fact, he has had little to do beyond opening the door and announcing the company, and his functions cease when this duty is accomplished. It would be alike ungracious and ungrateful in him, however, were he to retire without again thanking those kind and indulgent friends who have so long and so warmly welcomed him.

With no higher ambition in life than to be the servant of that same Public, nor any more ardent desire than to merit well at their hands, he writes himself, as he has so often had occasion to do before, but at no time more sincerely than now,

Their very devoted and faithful servant,

THE EDITOR.

CONTENTS.

ILLUSTRATIONS BY PHIZ IN VOL. I.

Etchings.

Illustrations in the Text.

THE

DODD FAMILY ABROAD.

LETTER I.

TO MR. THOMAS PURCELL, OF THE GRANGE, BRUFF.

Hôtel des Bains, Ostend.

DEAR TOM, — Here we are at last, — as tired and seasick a party as ever landed on the same shore! Twenty-eight hours of it, from the St. Katharine Docks, six of them bobbing opposite Margate in a fog, — ringing a big bell all the time, and firing minute-guns, lest some thumping India-man or a homeward-bound Peninsular should run into us, — and five more sailing up and down before Ostend, till it was safe to cross the bar, and enter the blackguard little harbor. The "Phœnix" — that was our boat — started the night before the "Paul Jones" mail-packet, and we only beat her by a neck, after all! And this was a piece of Mrs. Dodd's economy: the "Phœnix" only charges "ten-and-six" for the first cabin; but, what with the board for a day and night, boats to fetch you out, and boats to fetch you in, brandy-and-water against the sickness, — much good it was! — soda-water, stewards, and the devil knows what of broken crockery, — James fell into the "cuddy," I think they call it, and smashed two dozen and three wine-glasses, the most of a blue tea-service, and a big tureen, — the economy turned out a "delusion and a snare," as they say in the House. It 's over now, thank God! and, except some bruises against the bulkheads and a touch of a jaundice, I 'm nothing the

worse. We landed at night, and were marched off in a gang
to the Custom House. Such a time I never spent before!
for when they upset all our things on the floor, there was no
getting them into the trunks again; and so we made our
way through the streets, with shawls and muffs and silk
dresses all round us, like a set of play-actors. As for me,
I carried a turban in one hand, and a tray of artificial
flowers in the other, with a toque on my head and a bird-of-
paradise feather in my mouth. James fell, crossing the
plank, with three bran-new frocks and a bonnet of the girls',
and a thing Mrs. D. calls a "visite," — egad, they made a
visite of it, sure enough, and are likely to stay some time
there, for they are under some five feet of black mud, that
has lain there since before the memory of man. This was n't
the worst of it; for Mrs. D., not seeing very well in the
dark, gave one of the passport people a box on the ear that
she meant for poor Paddy, and we were hauled up before
the police, and made pay thirty francs for "insulting the
authorities," with something written on our passport, besides, describing my wife as a dangerous kind of woman,
that ought to be looked after. Poor Mathews had a funny
song, that ran, —

> "If ever you travel, it must n't seem queer
> That you sometimes get rubs that you never get here."

But, faith, it appears to me that we have fallen in with a
most uncommon allowance of friction. Perhaps it 's all for
the best; and by a little roughing at first, we 'll the sooner
accustom ourselves to our new position.

You know that I never thought much of this notion of
coming abroad, but Mrs. D. was full of it, and gave me
neither peace nor ease till I consented. To be sure, if it
only realizes the half of what she says, it 's a good speculation, — great economy, tip-top education for Tom and the
girls, elegant society without expense, fine climate, and
wine for the price of the bottles. I 'm sorry to leave Dodsborough. I got into a way of living there that suited me;
and even in the few days I spent in London I was missing
my morning's walk round the big turnip-field, and my little
gossip with Joe Moone. Poor Joe! don't let him want while

I 'm away, and be sure to give him his turf off our own bog.
We won't be able to drain the Lough meadows this year,
for we 'll want every sixpence we can lay our hands on for
the start. Mrs. D. says, " 'T is the way you begin abroad
decides everything;" and, faith, our opening, up to this,
has not been too prosperous.

I thought we 'd have got plenty of letters of recommendation for the Continent while we were in London; but it is
downright impossible to see people there. Vickars, our
member, was never at home, and Lord Pummistone — I
might besiege Downing Street from morning till night, and
never get a sight of him! I wrote as many as twenty
letters, and it was only when I bethought me of saying that
the Whigs never did anything except for people of the
Grey, Elliott, or Dundas family, that he sent me five lines,
with a kind of introduction to any of the envoys or plenipo-
tentiaries I might meet abroad, — a roving commission after
a dinner, — sorrow more or less! I believe, however, that
this is of no consequence; at least, a most agreeable man,
one Krauth, the sub-consul at Mœlendrach, somewhere in
Holland, and who came over in the same packet with us,
tells me that people of condition, like us, find their place in
the genteel society abroad as naturally as a man with moustaches goes to Leicester Square. That seems a comfort; for,
between me and you, the fighting and scrambling that goes
on at home about *who* we 'll have, and who 'll have *us*, makes
life little better than an election shindy! K. is a mighty
nice man, and full of information. He appears to be rich,
too, for Tom saw as many as thirteen gold watches in his
room; and he has chains and pins and brooches without
end. He was trying to persuade us to spend the winter at
Mœlendrach, where, besides a heavenly climate, there are
such beautiful walks on the dikes, and elegant society! Mrs.
D. does n't like it, however, for, though we 've been looking
all the morning, we can't find the place on the map; but that
does n't signify much, since even our post town of Kelly-
unaignabacklish is put down in the "Gazetteer" "a small
village on the road to Bruff," and no mention whatever of
the police-station, nor Hannagin's school, nor the Pound.
That 's the way the blackguards make books nowadays!

Mary Anne is all for Brussels, and, afterwards, Germany and the Rhine; but we can fix upon nothing yet. Send me the letter of credit on Brussels, in any case, for we 'll stay there, to look about us, a few weeks. If the two townlands cannot be kept out of the "Encumbered Estates," there's no help for it; but sure any of our friends would bid a trifle, and not see them knocked down at seven or eight years' purchase. If Tullylicknaslatterley was drained, and the stones off it, and a good top dressing of lime for two years, you 'd see as fine a crop of oats there as ever you 'd wish; and there has n't been an "outrage," as they call it, on the same land since they shot M'Shea, last September; and when you consider the times, and the way winter set in early, this year, 't is saying a good deal. I wish Prince Albert would take some of these farms, as they said he would. Never mind enclosing the town parks, we can't afford it just now; but mind that you look after the preserves. If there 's a cock shot in the boundary-wood, I 'll turn out every mother's son of the barony.

I was going to tell you about Nick Mahon's holding, but it 's gone clean out of my head, for I was called away to the police-office to bail out Paddy Byrne, the dirty little spalpeen; I wish I never took him from home. He saw a man running off with a yellow valise, — this is his story, — and thinking it was mine, he gave him chase; he doubled and turned, — now under an omnibus, now through a dark passage, — till Paddy overtook him at last, and gave him a clippeen on the left ear, and a neat touch of the foot that sent him sprawling. This done, Paddy shouldered the spoil, and made for the inn; but what d' ye think? It turned out to be another man's trunk, and Paddy was taken up for the robbery; and what with the swearing of the police, Pat's yells, and Mrs. D.'s French, I have passed such a half-hour as I hope never to see again. Two "Naps." settled it all, however, and five francs to the Brigadier, as well-dressed a chap as the Commander of the Forces at home; but foreigners, it seems, are the devil for bribery. When I told Pat I 'd stop it out of his wages, he was for rushing out, and taking what he called the worth of his money out of the blackguard; so that I had to lock him into my room, and

there he is now, crying and screeching like mad.   This will
be my excuse for anything I may make in way of mistakes;
for, to say truth, my head is fairly moidered!   As it is,
we 've lost a trunk; and when Mrs. D. discovers that it was
the one containing all her new silk dresses, and a famous
red velvet that was to take the shine out of the Tuileries,
we 'll have the devil to pay!   She 's in a blessed humor,
besides, for she says she saw the Brigadier wink at Mary
Anne, and that it was a good kicking he deserved, instead
of a five-franc piece; and now she 's turning on me in the
vernacular, in which, I regret to say, her fluency has no
impediment.   I must now conclude, my dear Tom, for it 's
quite beyond me to remember more than that I am, as
ever,

Your sincere friend,

KENNY I. DODD.

Betty Cobb insists upon being sent home; this is more of
it!   The journey will cost a ten-pound note, if Mrs. D. can't
succeed in turning her off of it.   I 'm afraid the economy, at
least, begins badly.

LETTER II.

MRS. DODD TO MISTRESS MARY GALLAGHER, AT DODSBOROUGH.

HOTEL OF THE BATHS, OSTEND.

DEAR MOLLY, — This is the first blessed moment of quiet
I've had since I quitted home; and even now there's the
table d'hôte of sixty-two in the next room, and a brass band
in the lobby, with, to be sure, the noisiest set of wretches
as waiters ever I heard, shouting, screaming, knife-jingling,
plate-crashing, and cork-drawing, till my head is fairly
turned with the turmoil. The expense is cruel, besides, —
eighteen francs a day for the rooms, although James sleeps
in the *salon;* and if you saw the bed, — his father swears
it was a mignonette-box in one of the windows! The
eating is beautiful; that must be allowed. Two soups,
three fishes, five roast chickens, and a piece of veal, stewed
with cherries; a dish of chops with chiccory, and a meat-pie
garnished with cock's-combs, — you may be sure I did n't
touch them; after them there was a carp, with treacle, and
a big plate of larks and robins, with eggs of the same, all
round. Then came the heavy eating: a roast joint of beef,
with a batter-pudding, and a turkey stuffed with chestnuts,
ducks ditto, with olives and onions, and a mushroom tart,
made of grated chickens and other condiments. As for the
sweets, I don't remember the half of them, nor do I like to
try; for poor dear James got a kind of surfeit, and was
obliged to go to bed and have a doctor, — a complaint, they
tell me, mighty common among the English on first coming
abroad. He was a nice man, and only charged five francs.
I wish you'd tell Peter Belton that; for though we subscribe
a pound a year to the dispensary, Mr. Peter thinks to get
six shillings a visit every time he comes over to Dodsborough, — a pleasant ride of eleven miles, — and sure of some-

thing to eat, besides; and now that I think of it, Molly, 't is what 's called the learned professions in Ireland is eating us all up, — the attorneys, the doctors, the parsons. Look at them abroad: Mr. Krauth, a remarkably nice man, and a consul, told me, last night, that for two-and-sixpence of our money you 'd have the best advice, law or medical, the Continent affords; and even that same is a comfort!

The *table d'hôte* is not without some drawbacks, however, my dear Molly, for only yesterday I caught an officer, the Brigadier of the Gendarmerie they call him, throwing sly glances at Mary Anne across the table. I mentioned it to K. I., but like all fathers that were a little free-and-easy when young, he said, "Pooh! nonsense, dear. 'T is the way of foreigners; you 'll get used to it at last." We dined to-day in our own room; and just to punish us, as I suppose, they gave us a scrag of mutton and two blue-legged chickens; and by the bill before me, — for I have it made up every day, — I see "dîner particulier" put down five francs a head, and the *table d'hôte* is for two!

K. I. was in a blessed passion, and cursed my infernal prudery, as he called it. To be sure, I did n't know it was to cost us a matter of fifteen francs. And now he 's gone off to the *café*, and Mary Anne is crying in her own room, while Caroline is nursing James; for, to tell you the truth, Betty Cobb is no earthly use to us; and as for Paddy Byrne, 't is bailing him out of the police-office and paying fines for him we are, all day.

We 'll scarcely save much this first quarter, for what with travelling expenses and the loss of my trunk, — I believe I told you that some villain carried away the yellow valise, with the black satin trimmed with blonde, and the peach-colored "gros de Naples," and my two elegant ball-dresses, one covered with real Limerick lace, — these losses, and the little contingencies of the road, will run away with most of our economies; but if we live we learn, and we 'll do better afterwards.

I never expected it would be all pure gain, Molly; but is n't it worth something to see life, — to get one's children the polish and refinement of the Continent, to teach them foreign tongues with the real accent, to mix in the very highest circles, and learn all the ways of people of fashion? Besides, Dodsborough was dreadful; K. I. was settling down to a common farmer, and in a year or two more would never have asked any higher company than Purcell and Father Maher; as for James, he was always out with the greyhounds, or shooting, or something of the kind; and lastly, you saw yourself what was going on between Peter Belton and Mary Anne! . . . She might have had the pride and decency to look higher than a Dispensary doctor. I told her that her mother's family was M'Carthys, and, indeed, it was nothing but the bad times ever made me think of Kenny Dodd. Not that I don't think well of poor Peter, but sure it's hard to dress well, and keep three horses, and make a decent appearance on less than eighty pounds a year, — not to talk of a wife at all!

I hope you'll get Christy into the Police; they are just the same as the Hussars, and not so costly. Be sure that you send off the two trunks to Ostend with the first sailing-vessel from Limerick; they'll only cost one-and-fourpence a cubic foot, whatever that is, and I believe they'll come just as speedy as by steam. I'm sorry for poor Nancy Doran; she'll be a loss to us in the dairy; but maybe she'll recover yet. How can you explain Brindled Judy not being in calf? I can scarce believe it yet. If it be true, however, you must sell her at the spring fair. Father Maher had a conceit out of her. Try if he is disposed to give ten pounds, or guineas, — guineas if you can, Molly.

There's no curing that rash in Caroline's face, and it's making her miserable. I've lost Peter's receipt; and it was the only thing stopped the itching. Try and get a copy of it from him; but say it's for Betty Cobb.

I was interrupted, my dear Molly, by a visit from a young gentleman whose visiting-card bears the name of Victor de Lancy, come to ask after James, — a very nice piece of attention, considering that he only met us once at the *table d'hôte*. He and Mary Anne talked a great deal together; for, as he does n't speak English, I could only smile and say "We-we" occasionally. He's as anxious about James as if he was his brother, and wanted to sit up the night with him; though what use would it be? for poor J. does n't know a word of French yet. Mary Anne tells me that he 's a count, and that his family was very high under the late King; but it 's dreadful to hear him talk of Louis Philippe and the Orleans branch. He mentioned, too, that they set spies after him wherever he goes; and, indeed, Mary Anne saw a gendarme looking up at the window all the time he was with us.

He spent two hours and a half here; and I must say, Molly, foreigners have a wonderful way of ingratiating themselves with one: we felt, when he was gone away, as if we knew him all our life. Don't pay any attention to Mat, but sell the fruit, and send me the money; and as for Bandy Bob, what 's the use of feeding him now we 're away? Take care that the advertisement about Dodsborough is in the "Mail" and the "Packet" every week: "A Residence fit for a nobleman or gentleman's family, — most extensive out-offices, and two hundred acres of land, more if required," ought to let easy! To be sure, it's in Ireland, Molly; that 's the worst of it. There is n't a little bit of a lodging here on the sands, with rush-bottom chairs and a painted table, does n't bring fifty francs a week!

I must conclude now, for it 's nigh post-hour. Be sure you look after the trunks and the pony. Never mind sending the Limerick paper; it costs three sous, and has never anything new. K. I. sees the "Times" at the rooms, and they give all the outrages just as well as the Irish papers. By the way, who was the Judkin Delaney that was killed at Bruff? Sure it is n't the little creature that collected the county-cess: it would be a disgrace if it was; he was n't five foot high!

Tell Father Maher to send me a few threatening lines for Betty Cobb; 't is nothing but the priest's word will keep her down.

Your most affectionate friend,

JEMIMA DODD.

LETTER III.

MISS DODD TO MISS DOOLAN, OF BALLYDOOLAN.

Hôtel de Bellevue, Brussels.

Dearest Kitty, — If anything could divert the mind from sorrow, — from the "grief that sears and scalds," — it would be the delightful existence of this charming city, where associations of the past and present pleasure divide attention between them. We are stopping at the Bellevue, the great hotel of the upper town; but my delight, my ecstasy, is the old city, — the Grande Place, especially, with its curious architecture, of mediæval taste, its high polished roofs, and carved architraves. I stood yesterday at the window where Count Egmont marched forth to the scaffold; I touched the chair where poor Horn sat for the last time, whilst his fainting wife fell powerless at his knees, and I thought, — yes, dearest Kitty, I own it, — I thought of that last dreadful parting in the summer-house with poor Peter. My tears are blotting out the words as I write them. Why, — why, I ask, must we be wretched? Why are we not free to face the humble destiny which more sordid spirits would shrink from? What is there in narrow fortune, if the heart soars above it? Papa is, however, more inexorable than ever; and as for mamma, she looks at me as though I were the disgrace of our name and lineage. Cary never did — never could understand me, poor child! — may she never know what it is to suffer as I do! But why do I distress you with my sorrows? — "let me tune my harp to lighter lays," as that sweet poet, Haynes Bailey, says. We were yesterday at the great ball of Count Haegenstroem, the Danish Ambassador here. Papa received a large packet of letters of introduction on Monday last, from the Foreign

Office. It would seem that Lord P. thought pa was a member, for he addressed him as M.P.; but the mistake has been so far fortunate, that we are invited on Tuesday to dine at Lord Gledworth's, our ambassador here, and we have his box for to-night at the Opera, — not to speak of last night's invitation, which came from him. I wore my amber gauze over the satin slip, with the "jonquilles" and white roses, two camellias in my hair, with mamma's coral chain twined through the roll at the back. Count Ambrose de Roncy called me a "rose-cameo," and I believe I *did* look my best. I danced with "Prince Sierra d'Aguila Nero," a Sicilian that ought to be King of Sicily, and will, they say, if the King of Naples dies without leaving seven sons. What a splendid man, Kitty! not tall, rather the reverse; but such eyes, and such a beard, and so perfumed, — the very air around him was like the garden of Attarghul! He spoke very little English, and could not bear to talk French; he said the French betrayed "la sua carissima patria;" and so, my dear Kitty, I did my best in the syllables of the sweet South. *He*, at least, called my accent "divina," and said that he would come and read Petrarch with me tomorrow. Don't let Peter be a fool when he hears this. The Prince is in a very different sphere from poor Mary Anne! he always dances with Queen Victoria when he's at Windsor, and called our Prince Consort "Il suo diletto Alberto;" and, more than all, he's married, but separated from the Princess. He told me this himself, and with what terrible emotion, Kitty! I thought of Charles Kean in Claude Melnotte, as he spoke in a low guttural voice, with his hand on his bosom. It was very dreadful, but these temperaments, moulded alike by southern climes and ancient descent, are awful in their passionate vehemence. I assure you, it was a relief to me when he stopped one of the trays and took a pineapple ice. I felt that it was a moment of peril passed in safety. You can form no notion, dearest, of the fascination of foreign manners; something there is so gently insinuating, so captivating, so bewitching, and withal so natural, Kitty, — that's the very strangest thing of all. There is absolutely nothing a foreigner cannot say to you. I almost blush as I think of what I now know must have been the veriest commonplace of society, but which to my ears, in all their untutored ignorance, sounded very odd.

Mamma — and you know her prudery — is actually in ecstasy with them. The Prince said to me last night, "Savez-vous, Mademoiselle! Madame votre mère est d'une beauté classique?" and I assure you ma was delighted with the compliment when she heard it. Papa is not so tractable: he calls them the most atrocious names, and has all the old prejudices about the Continent that we see in the old farces. Cary is, however, worse again, and thinks their easy elegance is impertinence, and all the graceful charm of their manner nothing but — her own words — "egregious vanity." Shall I whisper you a bit of a secret? Well, then, Kitty, the reason of this repugnance may be that she makes no impression whatever, notwithstanding her beauty; and there is no denying that she does not possess the gift — whatever it be — of fascination. She has, besides, a species of antipathy to everything foreign, that she makes no effort to disguise. A rather unfortunate acquaintance ma made, on board the steam-packet, with a certain Mr. Krauth, who called himself sub-consul of somewhere in Holland, but who turned out to be a Jew pedler, has given Cary such an opportunity of inveighing against all foreigners that she is positively unendurable. This Krauth, I must say, was atrociously vulgar, and shockingly ugly; but as he could talk some broken English, ma rather liked him, and we had him to tea; after which he took James home to his lodgings, to show him some wonderful stuffed birds that he was bringing to the Royal Princesses. I have not patience to tell you all the narrative; but the end of it was that poor dear James, having given all his pocket-money and his silver pencil-case for a tin musical snuff-box that won't play Weber's last waltz, except in jerks like a hiccough, actually exchanged two dozen of his new shirts for a box of Havannah cigars and a cigar-case with a picture of Fanny Elssler on it! Papa was in a towering passion when he heard of it, and hastened off to K.'s lodgings; but he had already decamped. This unhappy incident threw a shade over our last few days at Ostend; for James never came down to dine, but sat in his own room smoking the atrocious cigars, and contemplating the portrait of the charming Fanny, — pursuits which, I must say, seemed to have conduced to a most melancholy and despondent frame of mind.

There was another *mésaventure*, my dearest Kitty. My thanks to that sweet language for the word by which I characterize it! A certain Count Victor de Lancy, who made acquaintance with us at the *table d'hôte*, and was presuming enough to visit us afterwards, turned out to be a common thief! and who, though under the surveillance of the police, made away with ma's workbox, and her gold spectacles, putting on pa's paletot, and a new plaid belonging to James, as he passed out. It is very shocking; but confess, dearest, what a land it must be, where the pedlers are insinuating, and the very pickpockets have all the ease and breeding of the best society. I assure you that I could not credit the guilt of M. de L., until the Brigadier came yesterday to inquire about our losses, and take what he called his *signalement*. I thought, for a moment or two, that he had made a mistake, Kitty, and was come for *mine;* for he looked into my eyes in such a way, and spoke so softly, that I began to blush; and mamma, always on the watch, bridled up, and said, "Mary Anne!" in that voice you must so well remember; and so it is, my dear friend, the thief and the constable, and I have no doubt, too, the judge, the jury, and the jailer, are all on the same beat!

I have just been called away to see such a love of a rose tunic, all *glacé*, to be worn over a dull slate-colored jupe, looped up at one side with white camellias and lilies of the valley. Think of me, Kitty, with my hair drawn back and slightly powdered, red heels to my shoes, and a great fan hanging to my side, like grave Aunt Susan in the picture, wanting nothing but the love-sick swain that plays the flageolet at her feet! — Madame Adèle, the modiste, says, "not long to wait for a dozen such," — and this not for a fancy ball, dearest, but for a simple evening party, — a "danceable tea," as papa will call it. I vow to you, Kitty, that it greatly detracts from the pictorial effect of this taste, to see how obstinately men will adhere to their present ungainly and ungraceful style of dress, — that shocking solecism in

costume, a narrow-tailed coat, and those more fearful outrages on shape and symmetry for which no name has been
invented in any language. Now, the levelling effect of this
black-coat system is terrific; and there is no distinguishing
a man of real rank from his tailor, — amongst English at
least, for the crosses and decorations so frequent with
foreigners are unknown to us. Talking of these, Kitty, the
Prince of Aguila Nero is splendid. He wears nearly every
bird and beast that Noah had in the ark, and a few others
quite unknown to antediluvial zoölogy. These distinctions
are sad reflections on the want of a chivalric feeling in our
country; and when we think of the heroic actions, the
doughty deeds, and high achievements of these Paladins, we
are forced to blush for the spirit that condemns us to be a
nation of shopkeepers.

How I run on, dearest, from one topic to another! just as
to my mind is presented the delightful succession of objects
about me, — objects of whose very existence I did not know
till now! And then to think of what a life of obscurity and
darkness we were condemned to, at home! — our neighborhood, a priest, a miller, and those odious Davises; our
gayeties, a detestable dinner at the Grange; our theatricals,
"The Castle Spectre," performed in the coach-house; and
instead of those gorgeous and splendid ceremonials of our
Church, so impressive, so soul-subduing, Kitty, the little
dirty chapel at Bruff, with Larry Behan, the lame sacristan,
hobbling about and thrashing the urchins with the handle of
the extinguisher! his muttered "If I was near yeez!"
breaking in on the "Oremus, Domine." Shall I own it,
Kitty, there is a dreadful vulgarity about our dear little
circle of Dodsborough; and "one demoralizes," as the
French say, by the incessant appeal of low and too familiar
associations.

I have been again called away to interpret for papa, with
the police. That graceless little wretch, Paddy Byrne, who
was left behind by the train at Malines, went to eat his
dinner at one of the small restaurants in the town, called the
"Cheval Pie," and not finding the food to his satisfaction,
got into some kind of an altercation with the waiter, when
the name of the hostel coming up in the dispute, suggested

to Paddy the horrid thought that it was the "Horse Pie-house" he had chanced upon, — an idea so revolting to his culinary prejudices that he smashed and broke everything before him, and was only subdued at last by a corporal's party of the gendarmerie, who handcuffed and conveyed him to Brussels; and here he is, now, crying and calling himself a "poor boy that was dragged from home," and, in fact, trying to persuade himself and all around him that he has

been sold into slavery by a cruel master. Betty Cobb, too, has just joined the chorus, and is eloquently interweaving a little episode of Irish wrongs and sorrows into the tissue of Paddy's woes!

Betty is worse than him. There is nothing good enough for her to eat; no bed to sleep upon; she even finds the Belgians deficient in cleanliness. This, after Bruff, is a little too bad; mamma, however, stands by her in every-thing, and in the end she will become intolerable. James intends to send a few lines to your brother Robert; but if he should fail — not improbable, as writing, with him, com-

bines the double difficulties of orthography and manuscript
— pray remember us kindly to him, and believe me ever, my
dearest Kitty,

Your heart-devoted

MARY ANNE DODD.

P. B. must not think of writing; but you may tell him
that I'm unchanged, unchangeable. The cold maxims of
worldly prudence, the sordid calculations of worldly interests affect me not. As Metastasio says, —

> " O, se ragione intende
> Subito amor, non è."

I know it, — I feel it. There is what Balzac calls *une per-
versité divine* in true affection, that teaches one to brave
father and mother and brother, and this glorious sentiment is the cradle of true martyrdom. May my heart
cherish this noble grief, and never forget that if there is no
struggle, there is no victory!

Do you remember Captain Morris, of the 25th, the little
dark officer that came down to Bruff, after the burning of
the Sheas? I saw him yesterday; but, Kitty, how differently he looked here in his *passé* blue frock, from his air
in "our village!" He wanted to bow, but I cut him
dead. "No," thought I, " times are changed, and we with
them!" Caroline, who was walking behind me with James,
however, not only saluted, but spoke to him. He said, " I
see your sister forgets me; but I know how altered ill-health
has made me. I am going to leave the service." He asked
where we were stopping, — a most unnecessary piece of
attention; for after the altercation he had with pa on the
Bench at Bruff, I think common delicacy might keep him
from seeking us out.

Try and persuade your papa to take you abroad, Kitty, if
only for a summer ramble; believe me, there is no other
refining process like it. If you only saw James already —
you remember what a sloven he was — you'd not know
him; his hair so nicely divided and perfumed; his gloves
so accurately fitting; his boots perfection in shape and
polish; and all the dearest little trinkets in the world —

pistols and steam-carriages, death's-heads, ships and ser-
pents — hanging from his watch-chain; and as for the top
of his cane, Kitty, it is paved with turquoise, and has a
great opal in the middle. Where, how, and when he got
all this "elegance," I can't even guess, and I see it must
be a secret, for neither pa nor ma have ever yet seen him
en gala. I wish your brother Robert was with him. It
would be such an advantage to him. I am certain Trinity
College is all that you say of it; but confess, Kitty, Dublin
is terribly behind the world in all that regards civilization
and "ton."

LETTER IV.

JAMES DODD TO ROBERT DOOLAN, ESQUIRE, TRINITY COLLEGE, DUBLIN.

HÔTEL DE BELLEVUE, BRUSSELS.

DEAR BOB, — Here we are, living another kind of life from our old existence at Dodsborough! We have capital quarters at the "Bellevue," — a fine hotel, excellent dinners, and, what I think not inferior to either, a most obliging Jew money-changer hard by, who advances "moderate loans to respectable parties, on personal security," — a process in which I have already made some proficiency, and with considerable advantage to my outward man. The tailors are first-rate, and rig you out with gloves, boots, hat, even to your cane, — they forget nothing. The hairdressers are also incomparable. I thought, at first, that capillary attraction was beyond *me;* but, to my agreeable surprise, I discover that I boast a very imposing *chevelure*, and a bright promise of moustache which, as yet, is only faintly depicted by a dusky line on my upper lip.

It's all nonsense to undervalue dress: I'm no more the same man in my dark-green paletot, trimmed with Astracan, that I was a month ago in my fustian shooting-jacket, than a well-plumed eagle is like a half-moulted turkey. There is an inseparable connection between your coat and your character; and few things so react on the morality of a man as the cut of his trousers. Nothing more certainly tells me this than the feeling with which I enter any public place now, compared to what I experienced a few weeks back. It was then half shame, half swagger, — a conflict between modesty and defiance. Now, it is the easy assurance of being "all right," — the conviction that my hat, my frock, my cravat, my vest, can stand the most critical examina-

tion; and that if any one be impertinent enough to indulge
in the inquiry through his eye-glass, I have the equal privilege to return stare for stare, with, mayhap, an initiatory
sneer into the bargain. By the way, the habit of looking
unutterably fierce seems to be the first lesson abroad. The
passport people, as you land, the officers of the Customs,
the landlord of your inn, the waiters, the railroad clerks,
all "get up" a general air of sovereign contempt for everybody and everything, rather puzzling at first, but quite reassuring when you are trained to reciprocity. For the time,
I rather flatter myself to have learned the dodge well; not
but, I must confess to you, Bob, that my education is prosecuted under difficulties. During the whole of the morning
I'm either with the governor or my mother, sight-seeing and
house-hunting, — now seeking out a Rubens, now making
an excursion into the market, and making exploratory researches into the prices of fish, fowl, and vegetables; cheap-
ening articles that we don't intend to buy, — a process my
mother looks upon as a moral exercise; and climbing up
"two-pair," to see lodgings we have no intention to take:
all because, as she says, "we ought to know everything;"
and really the spirit of inquiry that moves her will have its
reward, — not always, perhaps, without some drawbacks, as
witness what happened to us on Tuesday. In our rambles
along the Boulevard de Waterloo, we saw a smart-looking
house, with an *affiche* over the door, "A louer;" and, of
course, mother and Mary Anne at once stopped the carriage
for an exploration. In we went, asked for the proprietor,
and saw a small, rosy-cheeked little man, with a big wig, and
a very inquiet, restless look in his eyes. "Could we see the
house? Was it furnished?" "Yes," to both questions.
"Were there stables?" "Capital room for four horses;
good water, — two kinds, and both excellent." Upstairs we
toiled, through one *salon* into another, — now losing ourselves in dark passages, now coming abruptly to unlock-
able doors, — everlastingly coming back to the spot we had
just left, and conceiving the grandest notions of the number of rooms, from the manner of our own perambulations.
Of course you know the invariable incidents of this tiresome process, where the owner is always trying to open

impracticable windows, and the visitors will rush into inscrutable places, in despite of all advice and admonition. Our voyage of discovery was like all preceding ones; and we looked down well-staircases and up into skylights, — snuffed for possible smells, and suggested imaginary smoke, in every room we saw. While we were thus busily criticising the domicile, its owner, it would seem, was as actively engaged in an examination of *us*, and apparently with a less satisfactory result, for he broke in upon one of our consultations by a friendly " No, no, ladies; it won't do, — it won't do at all. This house would never suit; " and while my mother stared, and Mary Anne opened wide her eyes in astonishment, he went on: " We're only losing time, ladies; both your time and mine will be wasted. This is not the house for *you*." " I beg to observe, sir, that I think it is," interposed my mother, who, with a very womanly feeling, took a prodigious fancy to the place the moment she discovered there was a difficulty about it. The owner, however, was to the full as decided; and in fact hurried us out of the rooms, downstairs, and into the street, with a degree of haste savoring far more of impatience than politeness. I rather was disposed to laugh at the little man's energetic rejection of us; but my mother's rage rendered any " mirthful demonstration inopportune," as the French would say; and so I only exchanged glances with Mary Anne, while our eloquent parent abused the " little wretch " to her heart's content. Although the circumstance was amply discussed by us that evening, we had well-nigh forgotten it in the morning, when, to our astonishment, our little friend of the Boulevard sent in his name, " Mr. Cherry," with a request to see papa. My mother was for seeing him herself; but this amendment was rejected, and the original motion carried.

After about five minutes' interview, we were alarmed by a sudden noise and violent cries; and on rushing from the drawing-room, I just caught sight of Mr. Cherry making a flying leap down the first half of the staircase, while my father's uplifted foot stood forth to evidence what had proved the " vis à tergo." His performance of the next flight was less artistic, for he rolled from top to bottom, when, by an almost preternatural effort, he made his escape into the street. The governor's passion made all inquiries perilous for some minutes; in fact, this attempt to make "Cherry-bounce," as Cary called it, seemed to have got into his head, for he stormed like a madman. At last the *causa belli* came out to be, that this unhappy Mr. Cherry had come with an apology for his strange conduct the day before, — by what think you? By his having mistaken my mother and sister for what slang people call "a case of perhaps," — a blunder which certainly was not to be remedied by the avowal of it. So at least thought my father, for he cut short the apology and the explanation at once, ejecting Mr. Cherry by a more summary process than is recognized in the law-courts.

My mother had hardly dried up her tears in crying, and I mine in laughing over this strange incident, when there came an emissary of the gendarmerie to arrest the governor for a violent assault, with intent, &c. &c., and it is only by the intervention of our Minister here that bail has been accepted; my father being bound to appear before the "Court of Correctional Police" on Monday next. If we remain much longer here, we are likely to learn something of the laws, at least in a way which people assure you is always most indelible, — practically. If we continue as we have commenced, a little management on the part of the lawyers, and a natural desire on the part of my father to obtain justice, may prolong our legal affairs far into the spring; so that we may possibly not leave this for some months to come, which, with the aid of my friend, Lazarus Simrock, may be made pleasurable and profitable.

It's all very well to talk about "learning French, seeing galleries and studying works of art," my dear Bob, but where's the time? — that's the question. My mother and the girls poach my entire morning. It's the rarest thing in the world for me to get free of them before five o'clock; and then I have just time to dash down to the club, and have a "shy" at the écarté before dinner. Smart play it is, sometimes seventy, ay, a hundred Naps. on a game; and such players too! — fellows that sit for ten minutes with a card on their knee, studying your face, watching every line and lineament of your features, and reading you, by Jove, — reading you like a book. All the false air of ease and indifference, all the brag assurance you may get up to conceal a " bad hand," is n't worth six-pence. They laugh at your puerile efforts, and tell you " you are voled" before you 've played a card. We hear so much about genius and talent, and all that kind of thing at home, and you, I have no doubt, are full of the high abilities of some fellowship or medallist man of Trin-ity; but give *me* the deep penetration, the intense powers of calculation, the thorough insight into human nature, of some of the fellows I see here; and for success in life, I 'll back them against all your conic section and x plus y geniuses, and all the double first classes that ever breathed. There 's a splendid fellow here, a Pole, called Koratinsky; he commanded the cavalry at Ostrolenca, and, it is said, rode down the Russian Guard, and sabred the Imperial Cuirassiers to a man. He 's the first écarté and piquet player in Europe, and equal to Deschapelles at whist. Though he is very distant and cold in his manner to strangers, he has been most kind and good-natured to me; has given me some capital advice, too, and warned me against several of the fellows that frequent the club. He tells me that he detests and abhors play, but resorts to it as a distraction. " Que voulez-vous ? " said he to me the other day; " when a man who calls himself Ladislaus Koratinsky, who has the blood of three monarchs in his veins, who has twice touched the crown of his native land, sees himself an exile and a ' proscrit,' it is only in the momentary excitement of the gaming-table he can find a passing relief for crushing and withering recollections." He could be in all the highest circles here. The greatest among the nobles are constantly begging and entreating him to come to their houses, but he sternly refuses. " Let me know one family," says he, " one domestic circle, where I can go uninvited, when I will, — where I can repose my confidence, tell my sorrows, and speak of my poor country; give me one such, and I ask for no more; but as for dukes and grand seigneurs, princesses and duchesses, I 've

had but too much of them." I assure you, Bob, it's like a
page out of some old story of chivalry to listen to him. The
splendid sentiments, the glorious conceptions, and the
great plans he has for the regeneration of Europe; and
how he abhors the Emperor of Russia! "It's a 'duel à
mort entre Nicholas et moi,'" said he to me yesterday.

"The terms of the conflict were signed on the field of
Ostrolenca; for the present the victory is his, but there is a
time coming!" I have been trying all manner of schemes
to have him invited to dine with us. Mother and Mary
Anne are with me, heart and hand; but the governor's late
mischances have soured him against all foreigners, and I
must bide my time. I feel, however, when my father sees
him, he'll be delighted with him; and then he could be

invaluable to us in the way of introductions, for he knows every crowned head and prince on the Continent.

After dinner, pretending to take an evening lesson in French, I'm off to the Opera. I belong to an omnibus-box, — all the fast fellows here, — such splendid dressers, Bob, and each coming in his brougham. I'm deucedly ashamed that I've nothing but a cabriolet, which I hire from my friend Lazarus at twelve pounds a month. They quiz me tremendously about my "rococo" taste in equipage, but I turn off the joke by telling them that I'm expecting my cattle and my "traps" from London next week. Lazarus promises me that I shall have a splendid "Malibran" from Hobson, and two grays over by the Antwerp packet, if I give him a bill for the price, at three months; and that he'll keep them for me at his stables till I'm quite ready to pay. Stickler, the other job-master here, wanted the governor's name on the bills, and behaved like a scoundrel, threatening to tell my father all about it. It cost me a "ten-pounder" to stop him.

After the theatre we adjourn to Dubos's to supper, and I can give you no idea, Bob, of what a thing that supper is! I remember when we used to fancy it was rather a grand affair to finish our evening at Jude's or Hayes's with a vulgar set-out of mutton-chops, spatchcocks, and devilled kidneys, washed down with that filthy potation called punch. I shudder at the vile abomination of the whole when I think of our delicate lobster *en mayonnaise*, or *crouton aux truffes*, red partridges in Rhine wine, and maraschino jelly, with Moët frappé to perfection. We generally invite some of the "corps," who abound in conversational ability, and are full of the pleasant gossip of the stage. There is Mademoiselle Léonine, too, in the ballet, the loveliest creature ever was seen. They say Count Maerlens, aide-de-camp of the King, is privately married to her, but that she won't leave the boards till she has saved a million, — but whether of francs or pounds, I don't remember.

When our supper is concluded, it is generally about four o'clock, and then we go to D'Arlaen's rooms, where we play chicken-hazard till our various houses are accessible.

I'm not much up to this as yet; my forte is écarté, at which I am the terror of these fellows; and when the races come on next month, I think my knowledge of horseflesh will teach them a thing or two. I have already a third share in a splendid horse called Number Nip, bred out of Barnabas by a Middleton mare; he's engaged for the Lacken Cup and the Salle Sweepstakes, and I'm backing him even against the field for everything I can get. If you'd like to net a fifty without risk, say so before the tenth, and I'll do it for you.

So that you see, Bob, without De Porquet's Grammar and "Ollendorff's Method," my time is tolerably full. In fact, if the day had forty-eight hours, I have something to fill every one of them.

There would be nothing but pleasure in this life, but for certain drawbacks, the worst of which is that I am not alone here. You have no idea, Bob, to what subterfuges I'm reduced, to keep my family out of sight of my grand acquaintances. Sometimes I call the governor my guardian; sometimes an uncle, so rich that I am forced to put up with all his whims and caprices. Egad! it went so far, t' other day, that I had to listen to a quizzing account of my aunt's costume at a concert, and hear my mother shown up as a *précieuse ridicule* of the first water. There's no keeping them out of public places, too; and how they know of all the various processions, Te Deums, and the like I cannot even guess. My own metamorphosis is so complete that I have cut them twice dead, in the Park; and no later than last night, I nearly ran over my father in the Allée Verte with my tandem leader, and heard the whole story this morning at breakfast, with the comforting assurance that "he'd know the puppy again, and will break every bone in his body if he catches him." In consequence of which threat, I have given orders for a new beard and moustache of the Royal Albert hue, instead of black, which I have worn heretofore. I must own, though, it is rather a bore to stand quietly by and see fellows larking your sister; but Mary Anne is perfectly incorrigible, notwithstanding all I have said to her. Cary's safety lies in hating the Continent and all foreigners, and that is just as absurd.

The governor, it seems, is perpetually writing to Vickars, our member, about something for *me*. Now, I sincerely hope that he may not succeed; for I own to you that I do not anticipate as much pleasure and amusement from either a " snug berth in the Customs " or a colonial situation; and after all, Bob, why should I be reduced to accept of either? Our estate is a good one, and if a little encumbered or so, why, we 're not worse off than our neighbors. If I must do something, I 'd rather go into a Light Cavalry Regiment — such as the Eleventh, or the Seventeenth — than anything else. I say this to you, because your uncle Purcell is bent on his own plans for me, which would be nothing short of utter degradation; and if there 's anything low-bred and vulgar on earth, it 's what they call a " Profession." You know the old adage about leading a horse to the water; now I frankly declare to you that twenty shall not make me drink any of the springs of this knowledge, whether Law, Medicine, or Divinity lie at the bottom of the well.

It does not require any great tact or foresight to perceive that not a man of my " set " would ever know me again under such circumstances. I have heard their opinions often enough on these matters not to be mistaken; and whatever we may think in Ireland about our doctors and barristers, they are what Yankees call " mighty small potatoes " abroad.

Lord George Tiverton said to me last night, " Why does n't your governor put you into ' the House '? You 'd make a devilish good figure there." And the notion has never left me since. Lord George himself is Member for Hornby, but he never attends the sittings, and only goes into Parliament as a means of getting leave from his regiment. They say he 's the " fastest " fellow in the service; he has already run through seventeen thousand a year, and one hundred and twenty thousand of his wife's fortune. They are separated now, and he has something like twelve hundred a year to live on; just enough for cigars and brandy and water, he calls it. He 's the best-tempered fellow I ever saw, and laughs and jokes about his own misfortunes as freely as possible. He knows the world — and he 's not yet five-and-twenty — perhaps better than any man I ever saw. There is not a bill-discounter, not a betting-man, nor a ballet-dancer, he is not acquainted with; and such amusing stories as he tells of his London life and experiences. When he found that he had run through everything — when all his horses were seized at Ascot, and his house taken in execution in London, he gave a splendid *fête* at Hornby, and invited upwards of sixty people down there, and half the county to meet them. "I resolved," said he, "on a grand finish; and I assure you that the company did not enjoy themselves the less heartily because every second fellow in my livery was a sheriff's officer, and that all the forks and spoons on the table were under seizure. There was a 'caption,' as they term it, on everything, down to the footmen's bag-wigs and knee-buckles. We went to supper at two o'clock; and I took in the Duchess of Allington, who assuredly never suspected that there was such a close alliance between my drawing-room and the Queen's Bench. The supper was exquisite; poor Marriton had exhausted himself in the devices of his art, and most ingeniously intimated his appreciation of my situation by a plate of ortolans *en salmi, sautés à la Fonblanque,* — a delicate allusion to the Bankrupt Commissioner. I nearly finished the dish myself, drank off half a bottle of champagne, took out Lady Emily de Maulin for the cotillon, and then, slipping away, threw myself into a post-chaise, arrived at Dover for the morning mail-packet, and landed at Boulogne free as William Tell, or that eagle which he is so enthusiastic in describing as a most remarkable instance of constitutional liberty." These are his own words, Bob; but without you saw his manner, and heard his voice, you could form no notion whatever of the careless, happy self-satisfaction of one who calls himself irretrievably ruined.

From all that I have been jotting down, you may fancy the set I am moving in, and the class with whom I associate. Then there is a German Graf von Blumenkohl, and a Russian Prince Kubitzkoy, two tremendous swells; a young French Marquis de Tregues, whose mother was granddaughter, I believe, of Madame du Barri, and a large margin of inferior dons, Spanish, Italian, and Belgian. That your friend Jemmy Dodd should be a star, even a little one, in such a galaxy, is no small boast; and such, my dear Bob, I am bound to feel it. Each of these fellows has a princely fortune, as well as a princely name, and it is not without many a clever dodge and cunning artifice that, weighted as I am, I can keep pace with them. I hope you 'll succeed, with all my heart, for the scholarship or fellowship. Which is it? Don't blame me for the blunder, for I have never, all my life through, been able to distinguish between certain things which I suppose other persons find no resemblance in. Thus I never knew exactly whether the word "people" was spelled " eo " or " oe." I never knew the Derby from the Oaks, nor shall I ever, I 'm certain, be able to separate in my mind Moore O'Ferral from Carew O'Dwyer, though I am confidently informed there is not a particle of similarity in the individuals, any more than in the names.

Write to me when your match is over, — I mean your examination, — and say where you 're placed. I 'll take you against the field, at the current odds, in " fives."

And believe me, ever your attached friend,

J. DODD.

LETTER V.

KENNY DODD TO THOMAS PURCELL, ESQ.

HÔTEL DE BELLEVUE, BRUSSELS.

DEAR TOM, — Yours did not reach me till yesterday, owing
to some confusion at the Post-office. There is another Dodd
here, who has been receiving *my* letters, and I *his*, for the
last week; and I conclude that each of us has learned more
than was quite necessary of the other's affairs; for while *he*
was reading of all the moneyed distresses and embarrassments of your humble servant, *I* opened a letter dated
Doctors' Commons, beginning, "Dear sir, we have at last
obtained the most satisfactory proofs against Mrs. Dodd,
and have no hesitation in now submitting the case to a jury."
We met yesterday, and exchanged credentials, with an expression of face that I'm sure "Phiz" would have given a
five-pound note to look at. Peachem and Lockit were nothing to it. We agreed that either of us ought to leave this, to
prevent similar mistakes in future, although, in my heart, I
believe that we now know so much of each other's affairs,
that we might depute one of us to conduct both correspond-
ences. In consequence, we tossed up who was to go. *He*
won; so that we take our departure on Wednesday next, if
I can settle matters in the mean while. I'm told Bonn, on
the Rhine, is a cheap place, and good for education, — a
great matter as regards James, — so that you may direct
your next to me there. To tell you the truth, Tom, I'm
scarcely sorry to get away, although the process will be anything but a cheap one. First of all, we have taken the
rooms for three months, and hired a job-coach for the same
time. Moving is also an expensive business, and not over-
agreeable at this season; but against these there is the set-
off that Mrs. D. and the girls are going to the devil in

expense for dress. From breakfast-time till three or four o'clock every day, the house is like a fair with milliners, male and female, hairdressers, perfumers, shoemakers, and trinket-men. I thought we'd done with all this when we left London; but it seems that everything we bought there is perfectly useless, and Mrs. D. comes sailing in every now and then, to make me laugh, as she says, at a bit of English taste by showing me where her waist is too short, or her sleeves too long; and Mary Anne comes down to breakfast in a great stiff watered silk, which for economy she has converted into a house-dress. Caroline, I must say, has not followed the lead, and is quite satisfied to be dressed as she used to be. James I see little of, for he's working hard at the languages, and, from what the girls say, with great success. Of course, this is all for the best; but it's little use French or even Chinese would be to him in the Customs or the Board of Trade, and it's there I'm trying to get him. Vickars told me last week that his name is down on no less than four lists, and it will be bad luck but we'll hit upon something. Between ourselves, I'm not over-pleased with Vickars. Whenever I write to him about James, his reply is always what he's doing about the poor laws, or the Jews, or the grant to Maynooth; so that I had to tell him, at last, that I'd rather hear that my son was in the Revenue, than that every patriarch in Palestine was in Parliament, or every papist in Ireland eating venison and guinea-hens. Patriotism is a fine thing, if you have a fine fortune, and some men we could mention have n't made badly out of it, without a sixpence; but for one like myself, the wrong side of fifty, with an encumbered estate, and no talents for agitation, it's as expensive as horse-racing, or yachting, or any other diversion of the kind. So there's no chance of a tenant for Dodsborough! You ought to put it in the English papers, with a puff about the shooting and the trout-fishing, and the excellent neighborhood, and all that kind of thing. There's not a doubt but it's too good for any Manchester blackguard of them all! What you say about Tully Brack is quite true. The encumbrances are over eleven thousand; and if we bought in the estate at three or four, there would be so much gain to us. The "Times" little knew the good it was doing us when it was blackguarding the Irish landlords, and depreciating Irish property. There's many a one has been able to buy in his own land for one-fifth of the mortgages on it; and if this is n't repudiation, it's not so far off Pennsylvania, after all.

I don't quite approve of your plan for Ballyslevin. Whenever a property's in Chancery, the best thing is to let it go to ruin entirely. The worse the land is, the more miserable the tenants, the cheaper will be the terms you'll get it on; and if the boys shoot a receiver once or twice, no great harm. As for the Government, I don't think they'll do anything for Ireland except set us by the ears about education and church matters; and we're getting almost tired of quarrelling, Tom; for so it is, the very best of dispositions may be imposed on too far!

Now, as to "education," how many amongst those who insist on a particular course for the poor, ever thought of stipulating for the same for their own children? or do they think that the Bible is only necessary for such as have not an independent fortune? And as to Maynooth, is there any man such a fool as to believe that £30,000 a year would make the priests loyal? You gave the money well knowing what for, — to teach Catholic theology, not to instil the oath of allegiance. To expect more would be like asking a market-gardener to raise strawberries with fresh cream round them! The truth is, they don't wish to advance our interests in England. They're afraid of us, Tom. If we ever were to take a national turn, like the Scotch, for instance, we might prove very dangerous rivals to them in many ways. I'm sick of politics; not, indeed, that I know too much of what's doing, for the last "Times" I saw was cut up into a new pattern for a polka, and they only kept me the supplement, which, as you know, is more varied than amusing. In reply to your question as to how I like this kind of life, I own to you that it does n't quite suit me. Maybe I'm too old in years, maybe too old in my notions, but it does n't do, Tom. There is an everlasting bowing and scraping and introducing, — a perpetual prelude to acquaintanceship that never seems to begin. It appears to me like an orchestra that never got further than the tuning of the

instruments! I'm sure that, at the least, I've exchanged
bows and grins and leers with fifty gentlemen here, whom
I should n't know to-morrow, nor do *they* care whether I did
or no. Their intercourse is like their cookery, and you are
always asking, "Is there nothing substantial coming?"
Then they're frivolous, Tom. I don't mean that they are
fond of pleasure, and given up to amusement, but that their
very pleasures and amusements are contemptible in themselves. No such thing as field-sports; at least, nothing
deserving the name; no manly pastimes, no bodily exercises; and lastly, they all, even the oldest of them, think
that they ought to make love to your wife and daughters,
just as you hand a lady a chair or a cup of tea in our
country, — a mere matter of course. I need not tell you
that my observations on men and manners are necessarily
limited by my ignorance of the language; but I have acquired the deaf man's privilege, and if I hear the less, I
see the more.

I begin to think, my dear Tom, that we all make a great
mistake in this taste we've got into for foreign travel, foreign languages, and foreign accomplishments. We rear up
our families with notions and habits quite inapplicable to
home purposes; and we are like the Parisian shopkeepers,
that have nothing on sale but articles of luxury; and, after
all, we have n't a genius for this trifling, and we make very
ungraceful idlers in the end. To train a man for the Continent, you must begin early; teach him French when a
child; let him learn dominoes at four, and to smoke cigars
at six, wear lacquered boots at eight, and put his hair in
paper at nine; eat sugar-plums for dinner, and barley-water
for tea; make him a steady shot with the pistol, and a cool
hand with the rapier; and there he is finished and fit for the
Boulevard, — a nice man for the *salons.*

It is cheap, there is no doubt; but it costs a great deal of
money to come at the economy. You'll perhaps say that's
my own fault. Maybe it is. We'll talk of it more another
time.

I ought to confess that Mrs. D. is delighted with everything; she vows that she is only beginning to live; and to
hear her talk, you'd think that Dodsborough was one of the

new model penitentiaries. Mary Anne's her own daughter, and she raves about princes and dukes and counts, all day long. What they'll say when I tell them that we're to be off on Wednesday next, I can't imagine. I intend to dine out that evening, for I know there will be no standing the row!

The Ambassador has been mighty polite and attentive: we dined there last week. A grand dinner, and fine company; but, talking French, and nothing but French, all the time, Mrs. D. and your humble servant were rather at a nonplus. Then we had his box at the opera, where, I must say, Tom, anything to equal the dancing I never saw, — indecency is no name for it. Not but Mrs. D. and Mary Anne are of a contrary opinion, and tauntingly ask me if I prefer a "Tatter Jack Walsh," at the cross-roads, to Taglioni. As for the singing, it's screeching, — that's the word for it, screeching. The composer is one Verdi, — a fellow, they tell me, that cracks every voice in Europe; and I can believe it. The young woman that played the first part grew purple in the face, and strained till her neck looked like a half-unravelled cable; her mouth was dragged sideways; and it was only when I thought she was off in strong convulsions that the audience began to applaud. There's no saying what their enthusiasm might not have been had she burst a blood-vessel.

I intended to have despatched this by to-day's post, but it is Saint Somebody's day, and the office closes at two o'clock, so that I'll have to keep it over, perhaps till Saturday, for to-morrow, I find, we're to go to Waterloo, to see the field of battle. There's a prince — whose name I forget, and, indeed, I couldn't spell, if I remembered it — going to be our "Cicerone." I'm not sure if he says he was there at the battle; but Mrs. D. believes him as she would the Duke of Wellington. Then there's a German count, whose father did something wonderful, and two Belgian barons, whose ancestors, I've no doubt, sustained the national reputation for speed. The season is hardly suitable for such an excursion; but even a day in the country — a few hours in the fields and the free air — will be a great enjoyment. James is going to bring a Polish friend of his, — a great Don he calls him, — but I'm so overlaid with nobility, the Khan of Tartary would not surprise me now. I'll keep this open to add a few lines, and only say good-bye for the present.

Saturday.

Waterloo's a humbug, Tom. I don't mean to say that Bony found it so some thirty-odd years back, but such it now appears. I assure you they've cut away half the field to commemorate the battle, — a process mighty like slicing off a man's nose to establish his identity. The result is that you might as well stand upon Hounslow Heath or Salisbury Plain, and listen to a narrative of the action, as visit Waterloo for the sake of the localities. La Haye Sainte and Hougoumont stand, certainly, in the old places, but the deep gorge beside the one, and the ridge from whence the cannonade shattered the other, are totally obliterated. The guides tell you, indeed, where Vivian's brigade stood, where Picton charged and fell, where Ney's column halted, faltered, and broke; they speak of the ridge behind which the guard lay in long expectancy; they describe to you the undulating swell over which our line advanced, cheering madly: but it's like listening to a description of Killarney in a fog, and being informed that Turk Mountain is yonder, and that the waterfall is down a glen to your right. One thing is clear, Tom, however, — we beat the French; and when I say "We," I mean what I say. England knows, and all Europe knows, who won the battle, and more's the disgrace for the way we're treated. But, after all, it's our own fault in a great measure, Tom; we take everything that comes from Parliament as a boon and a favor, little guessing often how it will turn out. Our conduct in this respect reminds me of poor Jack Whalley's wife. You remember Jack, that was postboy at the Clanbrazil Arms. Well, his wife one day chanced to find an elegant piece of white leather on the road, and she brought it home with her in great delight, to mend Jack's small clothes, which she did very neatly. Jack set off the next day, little suspecting what was in store for him; but when he trotted about five miles, — it was in the month of July, — he began to feel mighty uneasy in the saddle, — a feeling that continued to increase at every moment, till at last, as he said, "It was like taking a canter on a beehive in swarming time;" and well it might, for the piece of leather was no other than a blister that the apothecary's boy had dropped that morning on the road; and so it is, Tom. There's many a thing we take to be a fine patch for our nakedness that's only a blister, after all. Witness the Poor Law and the "Cumbrous Estates Court," as Rooney calls it. But I'm wandering away from Waterloo all this time. You know the grand controversy is about what time the Prussians came up; because that mainly decides who won the battle. I believe it's nearly impossible to get at the truth of the matter; for though it seems clear enough they were in the wood early in the day, it appears equally plain they stayed there — and small blame to them — till they saw the Inniskillings cutting down the Cuirassiers and sabring all before them. They waited, as you and I often waited in a row, till the enemy began to run, and then they were down on them. Even that same was no small help; for, by the best accounts, the French require a deal of beating, and we were dreadfully tired giving it to them! Sergeant Cotton, the guide, tells me it was a grand sight just about seven o'clock, when the whole line began cheering; first, Adam's brigade, then Cooke's battalion, all taking it up and cheering madly; the general officers waving their hats, and shouting like the rest. I was never able to satisfy myself whether we gained or lost most by that same victory of Waterloo; for you see, Tom, after all our fighting in Spain and Portugal, after all Nelson's great battles, all our triumphs and votes of thanks, Europe is going back to the old system again, — kings bullying their people, setting spies on them, opening their letters, transporting the writers, and hanging the readers. If they'd have let Bony alone when he came back from Elba, the chances were that he'd not have disturbed the peace of the world. He had already got his bellyful of fighting; he was getting old, falling into flesh, and rather disposed to think more of his personal ease than he used to do. Are you aware that the first thing he said on entering the Tuileries from Elba was, "Avant tout, un bon dîner"? One of the marshals, who heard the speech, whispered to a friend,

"He is greatly changed; you 'll see no more campaigns." I
know you 'll reply to me with your old argument about legit-
imacy and divine right, and all that kind of thing. But,
my dear Tom, for the matter of that, have n't I a divine
right to my ancestral estate of Tullylicknaslatterley; and
look what they 're going to do with it, to-morrow or next
day! 'T is much Commissioner Longfield would mind, if I
begged to defer the sale, on the ground of "my divine
right." Kings are exactly like landlords; they can't do
what they like with their own, hard as it may seem to say
so. They have their obligations and their duties; and if
they fail in them, they come into the Encumbered Estates
Court, just like us, — ay, and, just like us, they "take very
little by their motion."

I know it 's very hard to be turned out of your "holding."
I can imagine the feelings with which a man would quit such
a comfortable quarter as the Tuileries, and such a nice
place for summer as Versailles; Dodsborough is too fresh in
my mind to leave any doubt on this point; but there 's another side of the question, Tom. What were they there for?
You 'll call out, "This is all Socialism and Democracy,"
and the devil knows what else. Maybe I 'll agree with you.
Maybe I 'll say I don't like the doctrine myself. Maybe
I 'll tell you that I think the old time was pleasantest, when,
if we pressed a little hard to-day, why, we were all the
kinder to-morrow, and both ruler and ruled looked more
leniently on each other's faults. But say what we will, do
what we will, these days are gone by, and they 'll not come
back again. There 's a set of fellows at work, all over the
world, telling the people about their rights. Some of these
are very acute and clever chaps, that don't overstate the
case; they neither go off into any flights about universal
equality, or any balderdash about our being of the same
stock; but they stick to two or three hard propositions, and
they say, "Don't pay more for anything than you can get
it for, — that 's free-trade; don't pay for anything you don't
want, — that 's a blow at the Church Establishment; don't
pay for soldiers if you don't want to fight, — that 's at ' a
standing army; ' and, above all, when you have n't a pair of
breeches to your back, don't be buying embroidered small-

clothes for lords-in-waiting or gentlemen of the bedchamber." But here I am again, running away from Waterloo just as if I was a Belgian.

When we got to Hougoumont, a dreadful storm of rain came on, — such rain as I thought never fell out of Ireland. It came swooping along the ground, and wetting you through and through in five minutes. The thunder, too, rolled awfully, crashing and cannonading around these old walls, as if to wake up the dead by a memory of the great artillery. Mrs. D. took to her prayers in the little chapel, with Mary Anne and the Pole, James's friend. Caroline stood with me at a little window, watching the lightning; and James, by way of airing his French, got into a conversation, or rather a discussion, about the battle with a small foreigner with a large beard, that had just come in, drenched to the skin. The louder it thundered, the louder they spoke, or rather screamed at each other; and though I don't fancy James was very fluent in the French, it's clear the other was getting the worst of the argument, for he grew terribly angry, and jumped about and flourished a stick, and, in fact, seemed very anxious to try conclusions once more on the old field of conflict.

James carried the day, at last; for the other was obliged, as Uncle Toby says, "to evacuate Flanders," — meaning, thereby, to issue forth into the thickest of the storm rather than sustain the combat any longer. When the storm passed over, we made our way back to the little inn at the village of Waterloo, kept in the house where Lord Anglesey suffered amputation, and there we dined. It was neither a very good dinner nor a very social party. Mrs. D.'s black velvet bonnet and blue ribbons had got a tremendous drenching; Mary Anne contrived to tear a new satin dress all down the back, with a nail in the old chapel; James was unusually grave and silent; and as for the Pole, all his efforts at conversation were so marred by his bad English that he was a downright bore. It is a mistake to bring one of these foreigners out with a small family party! they neither understand *you* nor *you them*. Cary was the only one that enjoyed herself; but she went about the inn, picking up little curiosities of the battle, — old buttons, bullets, and the like;

and it was a comfort to see that one, at least, amongst us
derived pleasure from the excursion.

I have often heard descriptions of that night march from
Brussels to the field; and truly, what with the gloomy pine-
wood, the deep and miry roads, and the falling rain, it must
have been a very piteous affair; but for downright ill-
humor and discontent, I'd back our own journey over the
same ground against all. The horses, probably worn out
with toiling over the field all day, were dead beat, and came
gradually down from a trot to a jog, and then to a sham-
ble, and at last to a stop. James got down from the box,
and helped to belabor them; it was raining torrents all this
time. I got out, too, to help; for one of the beasts, although
too tired to go, contrived to kick his leg over the pole, and
couldn't get it back again; but the Count contented himself with uttering most unintelligible counsels from the
window, which when he saw totally unheeded, he threw
himself back in the coach, lighted his meerschaum, and
began to smoke.

Imagine the scene at that moment, Tom. The driver
was undressing himself coolly on the roadside, to examine a
kick he had just received from one of the horses; James was
holding the beasts by the head, lashing, as they were, all
the time; I was running frantically to and fro, to seek for a
stone to drive in the linch-pin, which was all but out; while
Mrs. D. and the girls, half suffocated between smoke and
passion, were screaming and coughing in chorus. By dint
of violent bounding and jerking, the wheel was wrenched
clean off the axle at last, and down went the whole conveniency on one side, our Polish friend assisting himself out of
the window by stepping over Mrs. D.'s head, as she lay
fainting within. I had, however, enough to do without
thinking of him, for the door being jammed tight would
not open, and I was obliged to pull Mrs. D. and the girls
out by the window. The beasts, by the same time, had
kicked themselves free of everything but the pole, with
which appendage they scampered gayly away towards Brussels; James shouting with laughter, as if it was the best
joke he had ever known. When we began to look about us
and think what was best to be done, we discovered that the

Count had taken a French leave of us, or rather a Polish one; for he had carried off James's cloak and umbrella along with him.

We were now all wet through, our shoes soaked, not a dry stitch on us,— all except the coachee, who, having taken off a considerable portion of his wearables, deposited them in the coach, while he ran up and down the road, wringing his hands, and crying over his misfortune in a condition that I am bound to say was far more pictorial than decent. It was in vain that Mrs. D. opened her parasol as the last refuge of offended modesty. The wind soon converted it into something like a convolvulus, so that she was fain once more to seek shelter inside the conveyance, which now lay pensively over on one side, against a muddy bank.

Such little accidents as these are not uncommon in our own country; but when they do occur, you are usually within reach of either succor or shelter. There is at least a house or a cabin within hail of you. Nothing of the kind was there here. This "Bois de Cambre," as they call it, is a dense wood of beech or pine trees, intersected here and there by certain straight roads, without a single inhabitant along the line. A solitary diligence may pass once in the twenty-four hours, to or from Wâvre. A Waterloo tourist party is occasionally seen in spring or summer, but, except these, scarcely a traveller is ever to be met with along this dreary tract. These reassuring facts were communicated to us by the coachee, while he made his toilet beside the window.

By great persuasions, much eloquence, French and English, and a Napoleon in gold, our driver at length consented to start on foot for Brussels, whence he was to send us a conveyance to return to the capital. This bargain effected, we settled ourselves down to sleep or to grumble, as fancy or inclination prompted.

I will not weary you with any further narrative of our sufferings, nor tell of that miserable attempt I made to doze, disturbed by Mrs. D.'s unceasing lamentations over her ruined bonnet, her shocked feelings, and her shot-silk. A little before daybreak, an empty furniture-van came accidentally by, with the driver of which we contracted for our return to Brussels, where we arrived at nine o'clock this morning, almost as sad a party as ever fled from Waterloo!

I thought I 'd jot down these few details before I lay down for a sleep, and it is likely that I may still add a line or two before post-hour.

Monday.

MY DEAR TOM, — We 've had our share of trouble since I wrote the last postscript. Poor James has been "out," and was wounded in the leg, above the knee. The Frenchman with whom he had a dispute at Hougoumont sent him a message on Saturday last; but as these affairs abroad are always greatly discussed and argued before they come off, the meeting did n't take place till this morning, when they met near Lacken. James's friend was Lord George Tiverton, Member for Hornby, and son to some Marquis, — that you 'll find out in the "Peerage," for my head is too confused to remember.

He stood to James like a trump; drove him to the ground in his own phaeton, lent him his own pistols, — the neatest tools ever I looked at, I wonder he could miss with them, — and then brought him back here, and is still with him, sitting at the bedside like a brother. Of course it 's very distressing to us all, and poor James is in terrible pain, for the leg is swelled up as thick as three, and all blue, and the doctors don't well know whether they can save it; but it 's a grand thing, Tom, to know that the boy behaved beautifully. Lord G. says: "I 've been out something like six-and-twenty times, principal or second, but I never saw anything cooler, quieter, or in better taste than young Dodd's conduct." These are his own words, and let me tell you, Tom, that 's high praise from such a quarter, for the English are great sticklers for a grave, decorous, cold-blooded kind of fighting, that we don't think so much about in Ireland. The Frenchman is one Count Roger, — not pronounced Roger, but Rogee, — and, they say, the surest shot in France. He left his card to inquire after James, about half an hour ago, — a very pretty piece of attention, at all events. Mrs. D. and the girls are not permitted to see James yet, nor would it be quite safe, for the poor fellow is wandering in his mind. When I came into the room he told Lord George that I was his uncle! and begged me not to alarm his aunt on any account!

I can't as yet say how far this unlucky event will interfere with our plans about moving. Of course, for the present, this is out of the question; for the surgeon says that, taking the most favorable view of his case, it will be weeks before J. can leave his bed. To tell you my mind frankly, I don't think they know much about gunshot wounds abroad; for I remember when I hit Giles Eyre, the bullet went through his chest and came out under the bladebone, and Dr. Purden just stopped up the hole with a pitch-plaster, and gave him a tumbler of weak punch, and he was about again, as fresh as ever, in a week's time. To be sure, he used to have a hacking kind of a short cough, and complained of a pain now and then; but everybody has his infirmities!

I mentioned what Purden did, to Baron Seutin, the surgeon here; but he called him a barbarian, and said he deserved the galleys for it! I thought to myself, "It's lucky old Sam does n't hear you, for he's just the boy would give you an early morning for it!"

I was called away by a message from the Commissary of the Police, who has sent one of his sergeants to make an inquiry about the duel.

If it was to Roger he went, it would be reasonable enough; but why come and torment us that have our own troubles? I was obliged to sit quiet and answer all his questions, giving my Christian name and my wife's, our ages, what religion we were, if we were really married, — egad, it's lucky it was n't Mrs. D. was under examination, — what children we had, their ages and sex, — I thought at one time he was going to ask how many more we meant to have. Then he took an excursion into our grandfathers and grandmothers, and at last came back to the present generation and the shindy.

If it was n't for Lord George, we'd never have got through the business; but he translated for me, and helped me greatly,— for what with the confusion I was in, and the language, and the absurdity of the whole thing, I lost my tem-

per very often; and now I discover that we 're to have a kind
of prosecution against us, though of what kind, or at whose
suit, or why, I can't find out. This will be, therefore, number three in my list of law-suits here, — not bad, considering
that I 'm scarce as many weeks in the country! I have n't
mentioned this to you before, for I don't like dwelling on it;
but it 's truth, nevertheless. I must close this at last, for
we have Lord G. to dinner; and I must go and put Paddy
Byrne through his facings, or there 'll be all kinds of blundering. I wish I 'd never brought him with us, nor the
jaunting-car. The young chaps — the dandies here — have
a knack of driving, as if down on us, just to see Mary
Anne trying to save her legs; but I 'll come across them one
day with the whip, in a style they won't like. Betty Cobb,
too, was no bargain, and I wish she was back at Dodsborough. We 're always reading in the newspapers how well
the Irish get on out of Ireland, — how industrious they become, how thrifty, and so on; don't believe a word of it,
Tom. There 's Betty, the same lazy, good-for-nothing,
story-telling, complaining, discontented devil ever she
was; and as for Paddy Byrne, his fists have never been out
of somebody's features, except when there were handcuffs
on them, — *semper eadem!* Tom, as we used to say at
Dr. Bell's. Whatever we may be at home, — and the
"Times" won't say much for us there, — it 's *there* we 're
best, after all. The doctors are here again to see James;
so that I must conclude with love to all yours, and

Remain ever faithfully your friend,

KENNY I. DODD.

DEAREST KITTY, — What a dreadful fortnight have we passed through! We thought that poor dear James must have lost his leg; the inflammation ran so high, and the pain and the fever were so great, that one night the Baron Seutin actually brought the horrid instruments with him, and I believe it was Lord George alone persuaded him to defer the operation. What a dear, kind, affectionate creature he is! He has scarcely ever left the house since it happened; and although he sits up all night with James, he seems never tired nor sleepy, but is so full of life all day long, playing on the piano, and teaching us the mazurka! I should rather say teaching *me*, for Cary, bless the mark, has taken a prudish turn, and says she has no fancy for being pulled about, even by a lord! I may as well mention here, that there is nothing less like romping than the mazurka, when danced properly; and so Lord George as much as told her. He scarcely touches your waist, Kitty; he only " gives you support," as he says himself, and he never by any chance squeezes your hand, except when there 's something droll he wants you to remark.

I must say, Kitty, that in Ireland we conceive the most absurd notions about the aristocracy. Now, here, we have one of the first, the very first young nobleman of the day actually domesticated with us. For the entire fortnight he has never been away, and yet we are as much at home with him, as easy in his presence, and as unconstrained as if it were your brother Robert, or anybody else of no position. You can form no idea how entertaining he is, for, as he says himself, " I 've done everything," and I 'm certain so he has; such a range of knowledge on every subject, — such a mass of acquaintances! And then he has been all over the world in his own yacht. It's like listening to the "Arabian Nights," to hear him talk about the Bosphorus and the Golden Horn; and I'm sure I never knew how to relish Byron's poetry till I heard Lord G.'s description of Patras and Salamis. I must tell you, as a great secret though, that he came, the other evening, in his cloak to the drawing-room door, to say that James wanted to see me; and when I went out, there he was in full Albanian dress, the most splendid thing you ever beheld, — a dark violet velvet jacket all braided with gold, white linen jupe, like the Scotch kilt, but immensely full, — he said, two hundred ells wide, — a fez on his head, embroidered sandals, and such a scimitar! it was a mass of turquoises and rubies. Oh, Kitty! I have no words to describe him; for, besides all this, he has such eyes, and the handsomest beard in the world, — not one of those foppish little tufts they call imperials, nor that grizzly clothes-brush Young France affects, but a regular "Titian," full, flowing, and squared beneath. Now, don't let Peter fancy that he ought to get up a "*moyen âge* look," for, between ourselves, these things, which sit so gracefully on my Lord, would be downright ridiculous in the dispensary doctor; and while I'm on the topic, let me say that nothing is so thoroughly Irish as the habit of imitating, or rather of mimicking, those of stations above our own. I'll never forget Peter's putting the kicking-straps on his mare just because he saw Sir Joseph Vickars drive with them; the consequence was that the poor beast, who never kicked before, no sooner felt the unaccustomed encumbrance than she dashed out, and never stopped till she smashed the gig to atoms. In the same way, I'm certain that if he only saw Lord George's dress, which is a kind of black velvet paletot, braided, and very loose in the sleeves, he'd just follow it, quite forgetting how inconvenient it might be in what he calls "the surgery." At all events, Kitty, do not say that I said so. I'm too conscious how little power I have to serve him, to wish to hurt his feelings.

You could not believe what interest has been felt about James in the very highest circles here. We were at last obliged to issue a species of bulletin every morning, and leave it with the porter at the hotel door. I own to you I thought it did look a little pretentious at first to read these documents, with the three signatures at the foot; but Lord George only laughed at my humility, and said that it was "expected from us." From all this you may gather that poor James's misfortune has not been unalloyed with benefit. The sympathy — I had almost said the friendship — of Lord G. is indeed priceless, and I see, from the names of the inquiries, that our social position has been materially benefited by the accident. In the little I have seen of the Continent, one thing strikes me most forcibly. It is that to have any social eminence or success you must be notorious. I am free to own that in many instances this is not obtained without considerable sacrifice, but it would seem imperative. You may be very rich, or very highly connected, or very beautiful, or very gifted. You may possess some wonderful talent as a painter or a musician or as a dramatist. You may be the great talker of dinner-parties, — the wit who never wanted his repartee. A splendid rider, particularly if a lady, has always her share of admiration. But apart from these qualities, Kitty, you have only to reckon on eccentricities, and, I am almost ashamed to write it, on follies. Chance — I never could call it good fortune, when I think of poor James — has achieved for us what, in all likelihood, we never could have accomplished for ourselves, and by a turn of the wheel we wake and find ourselves famous. I only wish you could see the list of visitors, beginning with princes, and descending by a sliding scale to barons and chevaliers; such flourishing of hats, too, as we receive whenever we drive out! Papa begins to complain that he might as well leave his at home, as he is perpetually carrying it about in his hand. But for Lord George, we should never know who one-half of these fine folk were; but he is acquainted with them all, and such droll histories as he has of them would convulse you with laughter to listen to.

I need not say that so long as poor dear James continues to suffer, we do not accept of any invitation whatever; we just receive a few intimates — say fifteen or twenty very dear friends — twice a week. Then it is merely a little music, tea, and perhaps a polka, always improvised, you understand, and got up without the slightest forethought. Lord G. is perfect for that kind of thing, and whatever he does seems to spring so naturally from the impulse of the moment. Yesterday, however, just as we were dressing for dinner, papa alone was in the drawing-room, the servant announced Monsieur le Général Comte de Vanderdelft, aide-de-camp to the King, and immediately there entered a very tall and splendidly dressed man, with every order you can think of on his breast. He saluted pa most courteously, who bowed equally low in return, and then began something which pa thought was a kind of set speech, for he spoke so fluently and so long, and with such evident possession of his subject, that papa felt it must have been all got up beforehand.

At last he paused, and poor papa, whose French never advanced beyond the second page of Cobbett's Grammar, uttered his usual "Non comprong," with a gesture happily more explanatory than the words. The General, deeming, possibly, that he was called upon for a recapitulation of his discourse, began it all over again, and was drawing towards the conclusion when mamma entered. He at once addressed himself to her, but she hastily rang the bell, and sent for *me*. I, of course, did not lose a moment, but, arranging my hair in plain bands, came down at once. When I came into the drawing-room, I saw there was some mystification, for papa was sitting with his spectacles on, busily hunting out something in the little Dialogue Book of five languages, and mamma was seated directly in front of the General, apparently listening to him with the utmost attention, but as I well knew, from her contracted eyebrows and pursed-up mouth, only endeavoring to read his sentiments from the expression of his features. He turned at once towards me as I saluted him, showing how unmistakably he rejoiced at the sound of his own language. "I come, Mademoiselle," said he, "on the part of the King"—and he paused and bowed at the word as solemnly as if he were in a church. "His Majesty having obtained from the English Legation here the names of the most distinguished visitors of your countrymen, has graciously commanded me to wait upon the Honorable Monsieur —" Here he paused again, and, taking out a slip of paper from his pocket, read the name — "Dodd. I am right, am I not, Mademoiselle Dodd?" At the mention of his name, papa bowed, and placed his hand on his waistcoat as if to confirm his identity; while mamma smiled a bland assent to the partnership. "To wait upon Monsieur Dodd," resumed the General, "and invite him and Madame Dodd to be present at the grand ceremony of the opening of the railroad to Mons." I could scarcely believe my ears, Kitty, as I listened. The inauguration ceremony has been the stock theme of the newspapers for the last month. Archbishops and bishops — cardinals, for aught I know — have been expected, regardless of expense, to bless everything and everybody, from the sovereign down to the stokers. The programme included a High Mass, military bands, the presence of the whole Court, and a grand déjeûner. To have been deemed worthy of an invitation to such a festival was a very legitimate reason for pride. "I have not his Majesty's commands, Mademoiselle," said the General, "to include you in the invitation; but as the King is always pleased to see his Court distinguished by beauty, I may safely promise that you will receive a card within the course of this day or to-morrow." I suppose I must have looked very grateful, for the General dropped his eyes, placed his hand on his heart, and said, "Oh, Mademoiselle!" in a tone of voice the most touching you can conceive. I believe, from watching my emotion, and the General's acknowledgment of it, mamma had arrived at the conclusion that the General had come to propose for me. Indeed, I am convinced, Kitty, that such was the impression on her mind, for she whispered in my ear, "Tell him, Mary Anne, that he must speak to papa first." This suggestion at once recalled me to myself, and I explained what he had come for, — apologizing, of course, to the General for having to speak in a foreign language before him. I am certain mamma's satisfaction at the royal invitation totally obliterated any disappointment she might have felt from baffled expectations, and she courtesied and smiled, and papa bowed and simpered so much, that I felt quite relieved when the General withdrew, — having previously kissed

ma's hand and mine, with an air of respectful homage only
acquired in Courts.

Perhaps this scene did not occupy more space than I have
taken to describe it, and yet, Kitty, it seems to me as
though we had been inhaling the atmosphere that surrounds
royalty for a length of time! From my revery on this theme
I was aroused by a lively controversy between papa and
mamma.

"Egad!" says papa, "Pummistone's blunder has done us
good service. They 've surely taken us for something very
distinguished. Look out, Mary Anne, and see if there 's
any Dodds in the peerage."

"Fudge!" cried mamma; "there 's no blunder whatever
in the case! We are beginning to be known, that 's all; nor
is there anything very astonishing in the fact, seeing that
King Leopold is the uncle to our own Queen. I should like
to know what is there more natural than that we should
receive attention from his Court?"

"Maybe it 's James's accident," muttered papa.

"It 's no such thing, I 'm certain," replied mamma,
angrily, "and it 's downright meanness to impute to a mere
casualty what is the legitimate consequence of our position."

Now, Kitty, whenever mamma uses the word "position,"
she has generally come to the end of her ammunition, which
is of the less consequence that she usually contrives with
this last shot to explode the enemy's magazine, and blow
him clean out of the water! Papa knows this so well, that
the moment he hears it, he takes to the long boat, or, to
drop the use of metaphor, he seizes his hat and decamps;
which he did on the present occasion, leaving ma and myself in the field.

"A Dodd, indeed, in the peerage!" said she, contemptuously; "I 'd like to know where you 'd find it! If it was a
M'Carthy, there would be some difference; M'Carthy More
slew Shawn Bhuy na Tiernian in the year ten thousand and
six, and was hanged for it at his own gate, in a rope of silk
of the family colors, green and white; and I 'd like to know
where were the Dodds then? But it 's the way with your
father always, Mary Anne; he quite forgets the family he
married into."

Though this was somewhat of unjust reproach, Kitty, I did not reply to it, but turned ma's attention to the King's gracious message, and the approaching *déjeûner*. We agreed that as Cary would n't and indeed could n't go, that ma and I should dress precisely alike, with our hair in bands in front, with two long curls behind the ears, white tarletan dresses, three jupes, looped up with marigolds; the only distinction being that ma should wear her carbuncles, and I nothing but moss-roses. It sounds very simple costume, Kitty, but Mademoiselle Adèle has such taste we felt we might rely upon its not being too plain. Papa, of course, would wear his yeomanry uniform, which is really very neat, the only ungraceful part being the white shorts and black gaiters to the knee; and these he insists on adhering to, as well as the helmet, which looks exactly like a gigantic caterpillar crawling over a coal-box! However, it 's military; and abroad, my dearest Kitty, if not a soldier, you are nothing. The English are so well aware of this that not one of them would venture to present himself at a foreign court in that absurd travesty of footmen called the "corbeau" coat. Even the lawyers and doctors, the newspaper editors, the railroad people, the civil engineers, and the solicitors, all come out as Yorkshire Hussars, Gloucestershire Fencibles, Hants Rifles, or Royal Archers; these last, very picturesque, with kilt, filibeg, and dirk, much handsomer than any other Highland regiment! We also discussed a little plot about making pa wear a coronation-medal, which would pass admirably as an "order," and procure him great respect and deference amongst the foreigners; but this, I may as well mention here, he most obstinately rejected, and swore at last that if we persisted, he 'd have his commission as a justice of the peace fixed on a pole, and carry it like a banner before him. Of course, in presence of such a threat, we gave up our project. You may smile, Kitty, at my recording such trivial circumstances; but of such is life. We are ourselves but atoms, dearest, and all around us are no more! As eagerly as *we* strive upwards, so determinedly does *he* drag us down to earth again, and ma's noblest ambitions are ever threatened by papa's inglorious tastes and inclinations.

I'm so full of this delightful *fête*, my dear Kitty, that I can think of nothing else; nor, indeed, are my thoughts very collected even on that,— for that wild creature, Lord George, is thumping the piano, imitating all the opera people, and occasionally waltzing about the room in a manner that would distract any human head to listen to! He has just been tormenting me to tell him what I'm saying to you, and bade me tell you that he's dying to make your acquaintance; so you see, dearest, that he has heard of those deep-blue eyes and long-fringed lids that have done such marvels in our western latitudes! It is really no use trying to continue.   He is performing what he calls a "Grand March, with a full orchestral accompaniment," and there is a crowd actually assembling in front of the house. I had something to say, however, if I could only remember it.

I have just recalled what I wanted to mention.   It is this: P. B. is most unjust, most ungenerous.   Living, as he does, remote from the world and its exciting cares, he can form no conception of what is required from those who mingle in its pleasures, and, alas! partake of its trials! To censure me for the sacrifices I am making to that world, Kitty, is then great injustice.   I feel that he knows nothing of these things!   What knew I myself of them till within a few weeks back!   Tell him so, dearest.   Tell him, besides, that I am ever the same, save in that expansion of the soul which comes of enlarged views of life,— more exalted notions and more ennobling emotions!   When I think of what I was, Kitty, and of what I am, I may indeed shudder at the perils of the present, but I blush deeply for the past!   Of course you will not permit him to think of coming abroad; "settling as a doctor," as he calls it, "on the Continent," is too horrid to be thought of!   Are you aware, Kitty, what place the lawyer and the physician occupy socially here?   Something lower than the courier, and a little higher than the cook!   Two or three, perhaps, in every capital city are received in society, wear decent clothes, and wash their hands occasionally, but there it ends! and even they are only admitted on sufferance, and as it were by a tacit acknowledgment of the uncertainty of human life, and that it is good to have a "learned leech" within call. Shall I avow it, Kitty, I think they are right! It is, unquestionably, a gross anomaly to see everlastingly around one in the gay world those terrible remembrancers of dark hours and gloomy scenes. We do not scatter wills and deeds and settlements amongst the prints and drawings and light literature of our drawing-room tables, nor do we permit physic-bottles to elbow the odors and essences which deck our "consoles" and chimney-pieces; and why should we admit the incarnation of these odious objects to mar the picturesque elegance of our *salons?* No, Kitty; they may figure upon a darker canvas, but they would ill become the gorgeous light that illumines the grand "tableau" of high life! Peter, too, would be quite unsuited to the habits of the Continent. Wrapped up as he is in his profession, he never could attain to that charming negligence of manner, that graceful trifling, that most insinuating languor, which distinguish the well-bred abroad. If they fail to captivate, Kitty, they at least never wound your susceptibilities, nor hurt your prejudices. The delightful maxim that pronounces "Tous les goûts sont respectables," is the keystone of this system. No, no, Peter must not come abroad!

Let me not forget to congratulate you on Robert's success. What is it he has gained? for I could not explain to Lord George whether he is a "double first" or a something else.

You are quite mistaken, my dear friend, about lace. It is fully as dear here as with us. At the same time I must say we never do see real "Brussels point" in Ireland; for even the Castle folk are satisfied with showing you nothing but their cast-off London finery; and as to lace, it is all what they call here "application," — that is, the flowers and tracery are worked in upon common net, and are not part of the fabric, as in real "point de Bruxelles." After all, even this is as superior to "Limerick lace" as a foreign ambassador is, in manner, to a Dublin alderman.

I should like to keep this over till the *déjeûner* at Mons; but as it goes by "the Messenger," — Lord Gledworth having given pa the privilege of the "bag," — I cannot longer defer writing myself my dearest Kitty's most attached friend,

MARY ANNE DODD.

I open my letter to send you the last bulletin about James: —

"Monsieur James Dodd has passed a tranquil night, and is proceeding favorably. The wound exhibits a good appearance, and the general fever is slight.

(Signed)   "Baron DE SEUTIN.
                  "EUSTACHE DE MORNAYE, Méd. du Roi.
                  "SAMUEL MOSSIN, M.R.C.S.L."

We 're in another mess with that wretch Paddy Byrne. The gendarmes are now in the house to inquire after him. It would seem that he has beaten a whole hackney-coach stand, and set the vehicles and horses off full speed down the "Montagne de la Cour," one of the steepest streets in Europe. When will papa see it would be cheaper to send him home by a special steamer than to keep him here and pay for all his "escapades"?

Paddy, who got on to the roof to escape the police, has just fallen through a skylight, and has been conveyed to hospital, terribly injured. He fell upon an old gentleman of eighty-two, who says he will look to papa for compensation. The tumult the affair has caused is dreadful, and pa is like a madman.

The General Count Vanderdelft has come back to say that I am invited.

LETTER VII.

MRS. DODD TO MISTRESS MARY GALLAGHER, DODSBOROUGH.

DEAR MOLLY, — I scarcely have courage to take up my pen, and, maybe, if it was n't that I 'm driven to the necessity of writing, I could n't bring myself to the effort. You have already heard all about poor dear James's duel. It was in the "Post" and "Galignani," and got copied into the French papers; and, indeed, I must say that so far as notoriety goes, it was all very gratifying to our feelings, though the poor boy has had to pay dearly for the honor. His sufferings were very great, and for ten days he did n't know one of us; even to this time he constantly calls me his aunt! He 's now out of danger at last, and able to sit up for a few hours every day, and take a little sustenance, and hear the papers read, and see the names of the people that have called to ask after him; and a proud list it is, — dukes, counts, and barons without end!

This, of course, is all very pleasing, and no one is more ready to confess it than myself; but life is nothing but trials, Molly; you 're up to-day, and you 're down to-morrow; and maybe 't is when you think the road is smoothest and best, and that your load is lightest, 't is just at that very moment you see yourself harnessed between the "shafts of adversity." We never think of these things when all goes well with us; but what a shock we feel when the hand of fate turns the tables on us, with, maybe, the scarlatina or the sheep-rot, the smut in the wheat, or a stain on your reputation! When I wrote last, I mentioned to you the high station we were in, the elegant acquaintances we made, and the fine prospect before us; but I 'm not sure you got my letter, for the gentleman that took charge of it thought of going home by Norway, so that perhaps it has not reached you. It's little matter; maybe 't is all the better, indeed, if it never does come to hand! The last three weeks has been nothing but troubles; and as for expense, Molly, the money goes in a way I never witnessed before, though, if you knew all the shifts I'm put to, you'd pity me, and the sacrifices I make to keep our heads above water would drown you in tears.

I don't know where to begin with our misfortunes, though I believe the first of them was Wednesday week last. You must know, Molly, that we were invited by the King, who sent his own aide-de-camp, in full fig, with crosses and orders all over him, to ask us to a breakfast, or, as they call it, a *déjeûner*, in honor of the opening of a new railroad at Mons. It was, as you may believe, a very great honor to pay us, nothing being invited but the very first families, — the embassies and the ministers; and we certainly felt it well became us not to disgrace either the country we came from or the proud distinction of his Majesty; and so Mary and I had two new dresses made just the same, like sisters, very simple, but elegant, Molly, — a light stuff that cost only two-and-five a yard, thirty-two yards of which would make the two, leaving me a breadth more in the skirt than Mary Anne, — the whole not coming to quite four pounds, without the making. That was our calculation, Molly, and we put it down on paper; for K. I. insists on our paying for everything when it comes home, as he is always saying, "We never know how suddenly we may have to leave this place yet."

Low as the price was, it took a day and a half before he gave in. He stormed and swore about all the expenses of the family, — that there was no end of our extravagant habits, and what with hairdressers, dancing-masters, and doctors, it cost five-and-twenty pounds in a week.

"And if it did, K. I.," said I, — "if it did, is four pounds too much to spend on the dress of your wife and daughter, when they're invited to Court? If you can squander in handfuls on your pleasures, can you spare nothing for the wants of your family?"

I reminded him who *he* was and *I* was. I let him know

what was the stock I came from, and what we were used to, Molly; and, indeed, I believe he 'd rather than double the money not have provoked the discussion.

The end of it was, we carried the day; and early on Wednesday morning the two dresses came home; Mademoi-

selle Adèle herself coming with them to try them on. I have n't words to tell you how mine fitted; if it was made on me, it could n't be better. I need n't say more of the general effect than that Betty — and you know she is no flatterer — called me nothing but "miss" till I took it off. Conscious of how it became me, I too readily listened to her suggestion to "go and show it to the master," and accordingly walked into the room where he was seated reading the newspaper.

"Ain't you afraid of catching cold?" says he, dryly.

"Why so?" replied I.

"Hadn't you better put on your gown, going about the passages?" says he, in a cross kind of way.

"What do you mean, K. I.? Is not this my gown?"

"That!" cried he, throwing down the newspaper on the floor. "*That!*"

"And why not, pray, Mister Dodd?"

"Why not?" exclaimed he; "because you're half-naked, madam, — because it wouldn't do for a bathing-dress, — because the Queen of the Tonga Islands wouldn't go out in it."

"If my dress is not high enough for your taste, K. I., maybe the bill is," says I, throwing down the paper on the table, and sweeping out of the room. Oh, Molly, little I knew the words I was saying, for I never had opened the bill at all, contenting myself with Mademoiselle Adèle's promise that making would be a "bagatelle of some fifteen or twenty francs!" What do you think it came to? Eight hundred and thirty-three francs five sous. Thirty-three pounds six and tenpence-halfpenny! as sure as I write these lines. I was taken with the nerves, — just as I used to be long ago, — screeching and laughing and crying altogether, when I heard it; and the attack lasted two hours, and left me very weak and exhausted after it was over. Oh, Molly dear, what a morning it was! for what with ether and curaçoa, strong sherry and aniseed cordial, my head was splitting; and Betty ran downstairs into the *table-d'hôte* room, and said that "the master was going to murder the mistress," and brought up a crowd of gentlemen after her. K. I. was holding my hands at the time, for they say that I wanted to make at Mademoiselle Adèle to tear her eyes out; so that, naturally enough, perhaps, they believed Betty's story; however that might be, they rushed in a body at K. I., who, quitting hold of me, seized the poker. I needn't tell you what he is like when in a passion! I'm told the scene was awful; for they all made for the stairs together, — K. I.

after them! The appearance of the place afterwards may
give you some notion of what it witnessed: all the orange-
trees in the tubs thrown down, two lamps smashed, the bust
of the King and Queen on the landing in shivers, several
of the banisters broken; while tufts of hair, buttons, and
bits of cloth were strewn about on all sides. The head-
waiter is wearing a patch over his eye still, and the Swiss
porter, one of the biggest men I ever saw, has cut his face
fearfully by a fall into a glass globe with gold-fish. It was
a costly morning's work, Molly! and if twenty pounds
sees us through it, we 're lucky! Mr. Proffles, too, the
landlord, came up to request we 'd leave the hotel; that
there was nothing but rows and disturbances in the house
since we entered it; and much more of the same sort. K. I.
flared up at this, and they abused each other for an hour.
This is very unfortunate, for I hear that P. is a baron, and
a great friend of the King; for abroad, Molly dear, the
nobles are not above anything, and sell cigars, and show the
town to strangers to turn a penny, without any one thinking
the worse of them! All this, as you may suppose, was a
blessed preparation for the Court breakfast; but yet, by
two o'clock we got away, and reached the Allée Verte, when
we heard that all the special trains were already off, and had
to take our places in the common conveyances meant for
the public, and, worse again, to be separated from K. I.,
who had to go into a third-class, while Mary Anne and I
were in a second. There we were, dressed up in full style
in the noonday, with bare necks and arms, in a crowd of
bagmen, officers, and clerks, who, you may be sure, had their
own thoughts about us; and, indeed, there 's no saying
what they might n't have done as well as thought, if K. I.
did n't come to the window every time we stopped, with a
big stick in his hand, and by a very significant gesture gave
the company to comprehend that he 'd make mince veal of
the man that molested us.

You may think, Molly, of what a two hours we spent, for
the women in the train were worse than the men; and
although I did not understand what they said, their looks
were quite intelligible; but I have not patience to tell you
more. We reached Mons at four o'clock; a great part of

the ceremony was over.   The High Mass and Benediction pronounced by the Cardinal of Malines; the rail was blessed; and the deputation had addressed the King, and his Majesty had replied, and all kinds of congratulations were exchanged, orders and crosses given to everybody, from the surveyors to the stokers, and now the procession was forming to the royal pavilion, where there were tables laid out for eight hundred people.

K. I.'s scarlet uniform, though a little the worse for wear, and so tight in the waist that the last three buttons were left unfastened, procured him immediate respect, and we passed through sentries and patrols as if we were royalty itself; indeed, the military presented arms to K. I. at every step, and such clinking of muskets and bayonets I never heard before.

All this time, Molly, we were going straight on, without knowing where to; for K. I. said to me in a whisper, "Let us put a bold face on it, or they'll ask us for tickets or something of the kind;" and so we went, hoping every moment to see our friend the Count, who would take us under his protection.   If it was n't for our own anxieties, the scene would have amused us greatly, for there was all manner of elegant females, and men in fine uniforms, and the greatest display of jewels I ever saw; but for all that, we were getting uneasy, for we saw that they each carried cards in their hands, and that the official came and asked for them as they passed on.

"We'll be in a nice way if Vanderdelft does n't turn up," says K. I.; and as he said it, there was the General himself beside us.   He was greatly heated, as if he had been running or walking fast, and, although dressed in full uniform, his stock was loose, and his cocked-hat was without the feather. "I was afraid I should have missed you," said he, in a hurried voice to Mary Anne, "and I'm half-killed running about after you.   Where's the Queen-Mother?"   This was n't very ceremonious, my dear, but I did n't know what he said at the time; indeed, he spoke so fast, it was all Mary Anne could do to follow him! for he talked of everything and everybody in a breath.   "We've not a minute to lose," cried he, drawing Mary Anne's arm inside his own.   "If

Leopold once sits down to table, I can't present you. Come
along, and I'll get you a good place."

How we pierced the crowd the saints alone can tell! but
the General went at them in a way of his own, and they fell
back as they saw him coming, in a style that made us think
we had no common guide to conduct us. At last, by dint
of crushing, driving, and pushing everybody out of our

way, we reached a kind of barrier, where two fine-looking
men in blue and gold were taking the tickets. As Mary
Anne and the General were in advance of us, I didn't see
what happened first; but when we came up, we found
Vanderdelft in a flaring passion, and crying out, "These
scullions don't know me; this canaille never heard of my
name?"

"We're in a mess, Mrs. D.," said K. I. to me, in a
whisper.

"How can that be?" said I.

"We 're in a mess," says he, again, "and a pretty mess,
too, or I 'm mistaken; " but he had n't time for more, for
just then the General kicked up the bar with his foot, and
passed in with Mary Anne, flourishing his drawn sword in
the air, and crying out, "Take them in flank — sabre them,
every man — no prisoners! — no quarter! " Oh, Molly, I
can't continue, though I 'll never forget the scene that followed. Two big men in gray coats burst through the
crowd and laid hands on the General, who, it seems, had
made his escape out of a madhouse at Ghent a week before,
and was, as they said, the most dangerous lunatic in all
Belgium. It appeared that he had gone down to his own
country-house near Brussels, and stolen his uniform and his
orders, for he was once on a time aide-de-camp to the Prince
of Orange, and went mad after the Revolution.

Just think of our situation as we stood there, among all
the nobles and grandees, suffocated with laughter; for, as
they tore the poor General away, he cried out "to take care
of the Queen-Mother, and to be sure and get something to
eat for the Aga of the Janissaries," meaning K. I.!

The mob at this time began screeching and hooting, and
there 's no knowing how it might have ended, if it was n't
for the little Captain — Morris is his name — that was once
quartered at Bruff, and who happened to be there, and knew
us, and he came up and explained who we were, and got us
away to a coach, more dead than alive, Molly.

And so we got back to Brussels that night, in a state of
mind and body I leave you to imagine, K. I. abusing us all
the way about the milliner's bill, the expense of the trip, and
the exposure! "It 's clear," says he, "we may leave this
city now, for you 'll never recover what you call your ' position' here, after this day's exploit!" You may conceive
how humbled and broken I was when he dared to say that to
me, Molly, and I did n't so much as give him a word back!

You 'll see from this that life is n't all roses with us; and
indeed, for the last two days I 've done nothing but cry, and
Mary Anne the same; for how we 're ever to go to court
and be presented now, nobody can tell! Morris advises
K. I. to go into Germany for the summer, and maybe he is
right; but, to tell you the truth, Molly, I can't bear that

little man, — he has a dry, sneering kind of way with him that is odious to me. Mary Anne, too, hates him.

So Father Maher won't buy " Judy," because she 's not in calf. It 's just like him, — he must have everything in this life his own way! Send me the price of the wool by Purcell; he can get a post-bill for it; and be sure to dispose of the fruit to the best advantage. Don't make any jam this year, for I 'd rather have the money than be spending it on sugar. You 'd not believe the straits I 'm put to for a pound or two. It was only last week I sold four pair of K. I.'s drab shorts and gaiters, and a brown surtout, to a hawker for a trifle of fifteen francs, and persuaded him they were stolen out of his drawers! and I believe he has spent nearly double the money in handbills, offering a reward for the thief! That 's the fruits of his want of confidence, and the secret and mysterious way he behaves to me! Many 's the time I told him that his underhand tricks cost him half his income!

I tell him every day it 's " no use to be here if we don't live in a certain style ; " and then he says, " I 'm quite ready to go back, Mrs. D. It was never my will that we came here at all." And there he is right, for it 's just Ireland he 's fit for! Father Maher and Tom Purcell and Sam Davis are exactly the company to suit him ; but it 's very hard that me and the girls are to suffer for his low tastes!

The " Evening Mail," I see, puts Dodsborough down at the bottom of a column, as if it was Holloway's Ointment. That 's what we get by having dealings with an Orange newspaper. They could murder us, — that 's their feeling. They know in their hearts that they 're heretics, and they hate the True Church. There is nothing I detest so much as bigotry. Go to heaven *your own* way, and let the Protestants go to the other place *theirs*. Them 's my sentiments, Molly, and I believe they 're the sentiments of a good Christian!

I 'm sorry for Peter Belton, but what business has he to think of a girl like Mary Anne? If Dr. Cavanagh was dead himself, the whole practice of the country would n't be three hundred a year. Try and get an opportunity to tell him what I think, and say that he ought to look out for one of the Davises ; though what a dispensary doctor wants with a wife the Lord only knows! K. I. civilly says he ought to be content making blisters for the neighbors, without wanting one on his own back! That's the way he talks of women. Father Maher never sent me the lines for Betty Cobb, and maybe I'll be driven to have her cursed by a foreign priest after all. She and Paddy are the torment of our lives. I saved up five pounds to send them both back by a sailing-ship, but by good luck I discovered the vessel was going to Cuba instead of Cork, and so here they are still; maybe it would have been better if I had sent them off, though the way was something of a roundabout. There's no use in my speaking to K. I. about Christy, for he can get nothing for James. We may write to Vickars every week, but he never answers; he knows Parliament won't be dissolved soon, and he does n't mind us. If I 'd my will, there would be a general election every year, at least, and then we 'd have a chance of getting something. I don't know which is worst, the Whigs or the Tories, nor is there much difference between them. K. I. supported each of them in turn, and never got bit nor sup from one or other, yet!

I was sounding K. I. about Christy last night, and *he* thinks you ought to send him to the gold diggings; he wants nothing but a pickaxe and a tin cullender and a pair of waterproof boots, to make a fortune there; and that 's more than we can say of the County Limerick. There 's nothing so hard to provide for as a boy in these times, except a girl!

The trunks have not arrived yet: I hope you despatched them.

Your attached and sincere friend,

JEMIMA DODD.

LETTER VIII.

BETTY COBB TO MRS. SHUSAN O'SHEA, PRIEST'S HOUSE, BRUFF.

DEAR MISSES SHUSAN, — This comes with my heart's sorrow that I'm not at home where I was bred and born, but livin' abroad like a pelican on a dissolute island, more by token that I never wanted to come, but was persuaded by them that knew nothin' about what they wor talking; but thought it was all figs and lemons and raisins, with green pays and the sun in season all the year round; but, on the contrahery, sich rain and wind I never seen afore; and as for the eating, the saints forgive me if it's not true, but I b'l'eve I ate more rats since I've come, than ever ould Tib did since she was kittened. The drinkin''s as bad or worse. What they call wine is spoilt vinegar; and the vegables has no bone nor eatin' in them at all, but melts away in the mouth like butter in July. But 't is the wickedness is the worst of all. O Shusan! but the men is bad, and the women worse. Of all the devils ever I heerd of, they bate them. 'T is n't a quiet walk to mass on Sunday, with maybe a decent boy beside you, discoorsin' or the like, and then sitting under a hedge for the evening, with your apron afore you, talkin' about the praties, or the price of pigs, or maybe the polis; but here 't is dancin' and rompin' and eatin', with merry-go-rounds, swing-swongs, and skittles all the day long. The dancin''s dreadful! they don't stand up fornent other, like a jig, where anything of a dacent partner would n't so much as look hard at you, but keep minding his steps and humorin' the tune; but they catch each other round the waist — 't is true I am saying — and go huggin' and tearin' about like mad, till they can't breathe nor spake; and then, the noise! for 't is n't one fiddle they have, but maybe twenty, with horns and flutes and a murderin' big brown tube, that a

man blows into at one side, that makes a sound like the
sea among the rocks at Kelper; and that's dancin', my
dear! I got lave from the mistress last Sunday to go out
in the evening with Mr. Francis, the currier, as they call
him, — a mighty nice man, but a little free in his manners;
and we went to the Moelenbeck Gardens, an iligant place,
no doubt, with a hundred little tables under the trees, and
a flure for dancin' and fireworks and a boat on a lake, with
an island in it, where there was a hermit, — a fine-looking
ould man, with a beard down to his waist, but, for all that,
no better than he ought to be, for he made an offer to kiss
me when I was going into the boat, and Mr. Francis laughed
at me bekase I was angry. No matter, we went off to a
place they call the Temple of Bakis, where there was a fat
man, as I thought, stark nakit; but it was flesh-colored web
he had on, and he was settin' on a beer-barrel, with a wreath
of roses round his head, and looking as drunk as ever I seen;
and for half a franc apiece, Bakis pulled out the spiget, and
gave you a glassful of the nicest drink ever was tasted, —
warm wine, with nutmeg in it, and cloves, and a taste of
mint. I was afeerd to do more nor sup, seein' the place
and the croud; but indeed, Shusan, little as I took, it got
into my head; and I sat down on the steps of the Temple,
and begun to cry about home and Dodsborough; and something came over me that Mr. Francis did n't mane well; and
so I told everybody that I was a poor Irish girl, and that he
was a wicked blaguard; and then the polis came, and there
was a shindy! I don't know how far my head was wrong
all the time; and they said that I sung the "Croniawn
Dhubh;" maybe I did; but I know that I bate off the
polis; and at last they took me away home, when every
stitch on me was in ribbins; my iligant bonnet with the
green bows as flat as a halfpeny; and the bombazine the
mistress gave me, all rags; one of my shoes, too, was lost;
and except a handful of hair I tore out of the corporal's
beard, 't was all loss to me. This was n't the worst; for
little Paddy Byrne, that was in bed for a baiting he got
'mong the hackney-coachmen, jumped up and flew at Mister
Francis for the honor of ould Ireland; and they fit for
twenty minutes in the pantry, and broke every bit of glass

and chaney in the house, forbye three lamps and some alybastard figures that was put there for safety; and the end of it was, Mr. Francis was discharged, but would n't take his wages, if the master did n't pay him half a year in advance, with diet and washing, and his expenses home to Swisserland, wherever that is; and there it is now, and master is in a law-shute, that everybody says will go agin him; for there's one good thing abroad, Shusan dear, the

coorts stands by poor sarvants, and won't see them wronged by any cruel masters; and maybe it would be taching ould Mister Dodd something, if they made him smart for this!

Ye may think, from all this, that I'd be glad to be back again, and so it is. I cry all day and night, and sorrow stich I do for either the mistress or the young ladies, and maybe at last they'll see 't is best to send me home. They need n't begrudge me the thrifle 't would cost, for they're spending money like mad; and even the mistress, that would skin a flay in Ireland, thinks nothing of layin' out ten or fifteen pounds here of a day. Miss Mary Anne is as bad as the mother, and grown so proud and stand off that I never spake to her. Miss Caroline is what she used to be, barrin' the spirits; to be sure, she has no divarsion and no horse to ride, nor does n't be out in the fields as she used, but for all that she bears it better than myself. Mister James is grown a young man in three weeks, and never passes me on the stair without a wink or a look of the same kind; that's the way the Continent taches good manners! Mrs. Shusan! oh dear! oh dear! but 't is wishing it I am, the day I come on this incontential tour. If I can't get back, — though it's not my fault if I don't, — send me the pair of strong shoes you 'll find in my hair trunk, and the two petticoats in the corner. If you could get a blade in the big scissors, send it too, and the two bits of dimity I want for mendin'. There was some Dandy Lion in a paper, I'd like; for there's none here, they say, has strength in it. You 'll be able to send me these by somebody coming this way, for I heerd mistress say everybody is travellin' these times. What was it Father Tom used to take for the redness in his nose? mine is tormentin' me dreadful, and though I'm poulticin' it every night with ash-bark, earthworms, and dragon's blood, I think it's only worse it's gettin'. Mr. Francis said that I must larn to sleep with my nose higher than my head, though how I'm to do it, the saints alone can tell! No time for more than to say your loving friend,

BETTY COBB.

LETTER IX.

KENNY DODD TO THOMAS PURCELL, ESQ.

BELLEVUE, BRUSSELS.

DEAR TOM, — It's no use in talking; I can't go over to
Ireland now, and you know that as well as myself.
Besides, what's the good of me taking a part in the elections? Who can tell which side will be uppermost, after
all? And if one is "to enter, it's as well to ride the
winning horse." Vickars has behaved so badly that I
don't think I'd support him; but there's a fortnight yet
before the elections, and perhaps he may see the errors
of his ways before that!

I've little heart or spirits for politics, for my life is fairly
bothered out of me with domestic troubles. James is going
on very slowly. There was a bit of glove-leather round the
ball — a most inexcusable negligence on the part of his
second — that has given much uneasiness; and he has a
kind of night fever that keeps him low and weak. With
that, too, he has too many doctors. Three of them come
every morning, and never go away without a dispute.

It strikes me forcibly, Tom, that medical science is one
of the things that makes little progress, considering all the
advantages of our century. I don't mean to say that they
don't know better what's inside of you, what your bones
are made of, that they haven't more hard names for everything than formerly; but that when it comes to cure you of
a toothache, or a colic, or a fit of the gout, my sure belief
is they made just as good a hand of it two hundred years
ago. I won't deny that they'll whip off your leg, tie one
of your arteries, or take your hip out of the socket quicker
than they used long ago; but how few of us, thank God,
have need of that kind of skill! and if we have, what sig-

nifies a quarter of a minute more or less? Tim Hackett,
that was surgeon to our County Infirmary forty years, never
used any other tools than an old razor and a pair of pincers,
and I believe he was just as successful as Astley Cooper;
and yet these fellows that come to see James cover the table
every day with instruments that would puzzle the Royal
Society, — things like patent corkscrews, scissors with teeth
like a saw, and one little crankum for all the world like a
landing-net: James is more afraid of that than all the rest.
When I saw it first, I thought it was a new contrivance for
taking the fees in.   The Pharmacopœia — I hope I spell it
right — is greater, to be sure, than long ago, but what's the
advantage of that?   We never discover a new kind of beast
for food, and I see little benefit in multiplying what only
disgusts you.   'T is with medicine as with law, Tom; the
more precedents we have, the more confused we get; and
where our ignorant ancestors saw their way clearly, we,
with all our enlightenment, never can hit on the right track
at all.   The mill-owner and the engineer, the tanner, the
dyer, the printer, ay, even the farmer, picks up something
every day that helps him in his craft.   It's only the learned
professions that never learn anything; maybe that's how
they got the name "lucus à non," Tom, as Dr. Bell would
say.

You keep preaching to me about economy and making
"both ends meet," and all that kind of balderdash; and if
you only saw the way we're living, you'd be surprised at
our cheapness.   Whenever a five-pound note sees me through
our bill for the day, I give myself a bottle of champagne at
night out of gratitude!   You remember all Mrs D.'s promises about thrift and saving; and, faith, I must say that so
far as cutting "down the estimates" for the rest of the
family, she's worthy of the Manchester school; but whenever it touches herself, her liberality becomes boundless.

I believe it would be cheaper to give the milliner a room
in the house than pay her coach-hire, for she's here every
morning, and generally in my room when I'm shaving,
sometimes before I'm up.   Not that this trifling circumstance ever disconcerted her.   On my conscience, I believe
she'd have taken Eve's measure before Adam, without a

blush at the situation! So far as I have seen of foreign life, Tom, shamelessness is the grand characteristic, and I grieve to say that one picks up the indecency much easier than the irregular verbs. I wish, however, I had nothing to complain of but this.

I told you in one of my late letters that I was getting into law here; the plot is thickening since that, and I have now, I believe, four actions — I hope it is not five — pending in four different courts; in some I'm the plaintiff, in some the defendant, and in another I'm something between the two; but what that may be, or what consequences it entails, I know as much as I do about calculating the next eclipse! Indeed, to distinguish between the several suits and the advocates I have engaged is no small difficulty, and a considerable part of every conference is occupied with purely introductory matter. These foreign lawyers have a mysterious kind of way with them, too, that always gives you the impression that a law-suit is something like the Gunpowder Plot! There's a fellow comes to me every morning for instructions, as he calls it, muffled up in a great cloak, and using as many precautions against being seen by the servants as if he were going to blow up the Government. I'd not be so sensitive on the subject, if it hadn't provoked a species of annoyance, at which, perhaps, you'll be more disposed to laugh than sympathize.

For the last week Mrs. D. has adopted a kind of warfare at which she, I'll be bound to say, has few equals and no superior, — a species of irregular attack, at all times and on all subjects, by innuendo and insinuation, so dexterously thrown out as to defy opposition; for you might as well take your musket to keep off the mosquitoes! What she was driving at I never could guess, for the assault came on every flank, and in all manner of ways. If I was dressed a little more carefully than usual, she called attention to my "smartness;" if less so, she hinted that I was probably going out "on the sly." If I stayed at home, I was "waiting for somebody;" if I went out, it was to "meet them." But all this guerilla warfare gave way at last to a grand attack, when I ventured to remonstrate about some extravagance or other. "It came well from *me*," she burst forth,

with indignant anger, — "it came well from *me* to talk of
the little necessary expenses of the family, — the bit they
ate, and the clothes on their backs." She spoke as if they
were Mandans or Iraquois, and lived in a wigwam! "It
came well from *me*, living the life I did, to grudge them the
commonest requirements of decency!" "Living the life
I did!" I avow to you, Tom, the words staggered me.
Warren Hastings tells us that when Burke concluded his
terrible invective, that he actually sat for five minutes
overwhelmed with a sense of guilt; and so stunning was
this charge that it took me full double as long to rally! for
though Mrs. D.'s eloquence may not possess all the splendor
or sublimity of the great Edmund, there is a homely significance, a kind of natural impressiveness, about it not
to be despised. "Living the life I did," rang in my ears
like the words of a judge in a charge. It sounded like —
"Kenny Dodd, you have been fairly convicted by an honest
and impartial jury!" and I confess I sat there expecting
to hear "the last sentence of the law." It was only after
some interval I was able to ask myself, "what was really
the kind of life I had been leading." My memory assured
me it was a very stupid, tiresome existence, — very good-
for-nothing and uninstructive. It was by no means, however, one of flagrant vice or any outrageous wickedness; and
I could n't help muttering with honest Jack, —

> " If sack and sugar be a sin,
> God help the wicked ! "

The only things like personal amusements I had indulged in
being gin-and-water and dominoes, — cheap pleasures, if
not very fascinating ones!

"Living the life I did!" Why, what does the woman
mean? Is she throwing in my teeth the lazy, useless,
unprofitable course of my daily existence, without a pursuit,
except to hear the gossip of the town, — without an object,
except to retail it? "Mrs. D.," said I, at last, "you are,
generally speaking, comprehensible. Whatever faults may
attach to your parts of speech, it must be owned they usually convey your meaning. Now, for the better mainte-
nance of this characteristic, will you graciously be pleased

to explain the words you have just spoken? What do you mean by the ' life I am leading '? " "Not before the girls, certainly, Mr. D.," said she, in a Lady Macbeth whisper that made my blood curdle.

The mischief was out at once, Tom, — I know you are laughing at it already; it 's quite true, she was jealous, — mad jealous! Ah, Tom, my boy, it 's all very good fun to laugh at Keeley, or Buckstone, or any other of those diverting vagabonds who can convulse the house with such a theme; but in real life the farce is downright tragedy. There is not a single comfort or consolation of your life that is not kicked clean from under you! A system of normal agitation is a fine thing, they tell us, in politics, but it is a cruel adjunct of domestic life! Everything you say, every look you give, every letter you seal, or every note you receive, are counts in a mysterious indictment against you, till at last you are afraid to blow your nose, lest it be taken for a signal to the fat widow lady that is caressing her poodle at the window over the way!

You may be sure, Tom, that I repelled the charge with all the indignation of injured innocence. I invoked my thirty years' good character, the gravity of my demeanor, the gray of my whiskers; I confessed to twenty other minor misdemeanors, — a taste for practical jokes, a love of cribbage and long whist; I went further, — I expressed a kind of St. Kevenism about women in general; but she cut me short with, "Pray, Mr. D., make one exception; do be gallant enough to say that there is one, at least, not included in this category of horrors."

"What are you at now?" cried I, almost losing all patience.

"Yes, sir," said she, in a grand melodramatic tone that she always reserves for the peroration, — as postilions keep a trot for the town, — "yes, sir, I am well accustomed to your perfidy and dissimulation. I know perfectly for what infamous purposes abroad your family are treated so ignominiously at home; I 'm no stranger to your doings." I tried to stop her by an appeal to common-sense; she despised it. I invoked my age, — egad! I never put my foot in it till then. That was exactly what made me the great-

est villain of all! Whatever veneration attaches to white
hairs, it must be owned they get mighty ill treated in discussions like the present; at least, Mrs. D. assured me so,
and gave me to understand that one pays a higher premium
for their morality, as they do for their life-assurance, as
they grow older. "Not," added she, as her eyes glittered
with anger, and she sidled near the door for an exit, — "not
but, in the estimation of others, you may be quite an
Adonis, — a young gentleman of wit and fashion, — a beau
of the first water; I have no doubt Mary Jane thinks so, —
you old wretch!" This, in alt, and a bang of the door that
brought down an oil picture that hung over it, closed the
scene.

"Mary Jane thinks so!" said I, with my hand to my
temples to collect myself. Ah, Tom! it would have required a cooler head than mine was at that moment to go
hunting through the old archives of memory! Nor will I
torment you with even a narrative of my struggles.   I
passed that evening and the night in a state of half distraction; and it was only when I was giving one of our lawyers
a check the next morning that I unravelled the mystery,
for, as I wrote down his name, I perceived it was Marie
Jean de Rastanac, — a not uncommon Christian name for
men, though, considering the length and breadth of the
masculine calendar, a very needless appropriation.

This was "Mary Jane," then, and this the origin of as
pretty a conjugal flare-up as I remember for the last twelve-
month!

Mrs. D. reminds me of the Opposition, and the Opposition
of Vickars. I suppose he wants to be a Lord of the Treasury. It's very like what old Frederick used to call making
a "goat a gardener." What rogues the fellows are! You
write to them about your son or your nephew, and they
answer you with some tawdry balderdash about their principles, as if any one of us ever believed they were troubled
with principles! I'm all for fair straightforward dealing.
Put James in the Board of Trade, and you may cut up the
Caffres for ten years to come. Give us something in the
Customs, and I don't care if New Zealand never has a constitution! 'T is only the fellows that have no families ask

questions at the hustings! Show me a man that wants
pledges from his *representative*, and I'll show you one that
has got none from his *wife!*

And there's Vickars writing to me, as if I was a fool,
about all the old clap-traps that we used to think were kept
for the election dinner; and these chaps, like him, always
spoil a good argument when they get hold of it. Now,
when a parson hasn't tact enough to write his sermons, he
buys a volume of Tillotson or Blair, or any other, and
reads one out as well as he can; but your member — God
bless the mark! — must invent his own nonsense. How
much better if he'd give you Peel, or Russell, or Ben Disraeli in the original! There are skeleton sermons for
drowsy curates; I wish any one would compose skeleton
speeches for the county members. You'll say that I'm
unreasonably testy about these things; but I've got a letter
this instant from Vickers, expressing his hope that I'll be
satisfied with the view he has taken on the "question of free-
labor sugar." Did I ever dispute it, Tom? I drink no
tea, — I hate sweet things, and, except a lump, and that a
small one, that I take in my tumbler of punch, I never use
sugar; and I care no more what's the color of the man that
raises it than I do for the name of the supercargo that
brought it over. Don't put cockroaches in it, and sell it
cheap, and I don't care a brass farthing whether it grew
in Barbary or Barbadoes! Not, my dear Tom, but it's all
gammon, the way they discuss the question; for the two
parties are always debating two different issues; one crying
out cheap sugar, the other no slavery! and the consequence
is, they never meet in argument. As to the preference
Vickars insists should be given to free-labor sugar, carry
out the principle and see what it comes to. I ought to receive eight or ten shillings a barrel more for my wheat than
old Joe M'Curdy, because *I* always gave my laborers eight-
pence a day, and *he* never went higher than sixpence, more
often fourpence. Is not that free labor and slavery, just as
well exemplified as if every man in the barony was a black?

They tell me the niggers won't work if you don't thrash
them, and I don't wonder, when I think of the heat of the
climate; but sure if they've more idleness, they ought to

get less money; and lastly, I take the Abolitionists —
bother it for a long word! — on their own ground, and are
they prepared to say that if you impose a duty on slave
sugar, the Cubans and the rest of them won't only take
more out of the niggers to meet "the exigency of the market," as the newspapers call it? If they do so, they'll only
be imitating our own farmers since the repeal of the corn
law. "You must bestir yourselves," says Lord Stanley;
"competition with the foreigner will demand all your activity. It won't do to go on as you used. You must buy
guano, take to drainage, study Smith of Deanstown, and
mind the rotation of your crops." Don't you think that
some enlightened Cuban will hit upon the same train of
argument, and make a fresh investment in whipcord? Ah,
Tom! these are only party squabbles, after all; and so I
told Vickars. I don't know why, but it always seemed to
me that the blacks absorb a very unfair amount of our loose
sympathies; whether it's the color of them, or that they're
so far away, or because they're naked, I never knew; but
certain it is, we pity them far more than our own people,
and I back myself to get up a ladies' committee for a nigger
question, before you collect three people to hear you discuss
a home grievance.

I have just been interrupted to receive Monsieur Jellicot,
my defender in action No. 3, a suit preferred by my late
courier, "François Tehetuer, born in the canton of Zug,
aged thirty-seven years, single, and a Protestant, against
Monsieur Kenyidod, natif d'Irlande, près de Dublin, dans
le Royaume de la Grande Bretagne," &c., &c.; the demand
being for a year's wages, bed, board, and travelling expenses to his native country. He, the aforesaid François,
having been sent away for a disgraceful riot in my house,
in which he beat Pat, the other servant, and smashed
about five-and-twenty pounds' worth of glass and china.
A very pretty claim, Tom, — the preliminary resistance to
which has already cost me about one hundred and fifty
francs to remove the litigation into an upper court, where
the bribery is higher, and consequently deemed more within
the reach of *my* finances than those of honest Francis!

To tell you all that I think of the rascality of the admin-

istration of justice here, would lead me into a diffusiveness
something like that of the pleasant "Mémoire" which my
advocate has just left me to read, and in which, as a measure of defence against an iniquitous demand, I'm obliged
to give a short history of my life, with some account of my
father and grandfather. I made it as brief as I could, and
said nothing about the mortgages nor Hackett's bond; but
even with all my conciseness, the thing is very voluminous.
The greatest difficulty of all is the examination of Paddy
Byrne, who, imagining that a law process cannot have any
other object than either to hang or transport *him*, has
already made two efforts at escape, and each time been
brought back by the police. His repugnance to the course
of justice has already damaged my case with my own defender, who, naturally enough, thinks if *my own* witnesses
are so little to my credit, what will be the *opposite* evidence?

Another of my " causes célèbres," as Cary calls them, —
she is the only one of us has a laugh left in her, — is for
the assault and battery of a certain Mr. Cherry, a little
rascal that came one day to tell me that Mrs. D.'s appearance struck him as being more fascinating than respectable!
I kicked him downstairs into the street, and in return he
has dragged me into the Court of the Correctional Police,
where I'm told they'll maul *me* far worse than I did him;
besides this, I have a small interlude suit for a breach of
contract, in not taking a lodging next an Anatomy School;
and lastly, James's duel! I have compromised fully double
the number, and have received vague threats from different
quarters, that may either mean being waylaid or prosecuted,
as the case may be.

So far, therefore, as economy goes, this Continentalizing
has not succeeded up to this. Instead of living rent free at
Dodsborough, with our own mutton and turnips, the ducks
and peas, that cost us, I may say, nothing, here we are,
keeping up the price of foreign markets, and feeding the
foreigners at the expense of our own poor people. If,
instead of excluding British manufactures from the Continent, Bony had only struck out the notion of seducing over
here John Bull himself and his family, let me assure you,
Tom, that he'd have done us far more lasting and irrep-

arable mischief.   We can do without their markets.   What
between their Zollvereins, their hostile tariffs, and trouble-
some trade restrictions, they have themselves taught us to
do without them; and, indeed, except when we get up a row
at Barcelona, and smuggle five or six hundred thousand
pounds' worth of goods into Spain, we care little for the
old Continent; but I'll tell you what we cannot do without,
— we cannot do without their truffled turkeys, their tenors,
their men-cooks, and their dancing-women.   French novels
and Italian knavery have got a fast hold of us; and I
doubt much if the polite world of England would n't rather
see this country cut off from all the commerce of America
than be themselves excluded from the wicked old cities of
Europe!

When I think of myself holding these opinions, and still
living abroad, I almost fancy I was meant for a Parliamentary life; for assuredly my convictions and my actions are
about as contradictory as any honorable or right honorable gentleman on either side of the House.   But so it is,
Tom.   Whatever's the reason of it I can't tell, but I believe in my heart that every Irishman is always doing something or other that he does n't approve of; and that this
is the real secret of that want of conduct, deficient steadi-
ness, uncertainty of purpose, and all the other faults that
our polite neighbors ascribe to us, and what the "Times"
has a word of its own for, and sets shortly down as "Celtic
barbarism."   And between ourselves, the "Times" is too
fond of blackguarding us.   What's the use of it?   What
good does it ever do?   I may throw mud at a man every
day till the end of the world, but I'll never make his face
the cleaner for it!

The same system we used to follow once with America;
and at last, what with sneering and jibing, we got up a
worse feeling between the two countries than ever existed
in the heat of the war.   No matter how stupid the writer,
how little he saw, or how ill he told it, let a fellow come
back from the United States with a good string of stories
about whittling, spitting, and chewing, interlard the narrative with a full share of slang, show up Jonathan as a vulgar, obtrusive, self-important animal, boastful and ignorant,

and I'll back the book to run through its two or three edi-
tions with a devouring and delighted public. But what
would you think of a man that went down to Leeds or
Manchester, to look at some of our great factories at full
work; who saw the evidences of our enterprise and industry, that are felt at the uttermost ends of the earth; who
knew that every bang of that big piston had its responsive
answer in some far-away land over the sea, where British
skill and energy were diffusing comfort and civilization,—
what, I say, would you think of him if, instead of standing
amazed at the future before such a people, he sat down to
chronicle how many fustian jackets had holes in them, how
many shaved but twice a week, whether the overseer made
a polite bow, or the timekeeper talked with a strong Yorkshire accent?

I tell you, Tom, our travellers in the States did little
other than this. I don't mean to say that it would n't be
pleasanter and prettier to look at, if all the factory-folk
were dressed like Young England, with white waistcoats
and cravats, and all the young ladies wore silk petticoats
and white satin shoes; but I'm afraid that, considering
the work to do, that's scarcely practicable; and so with
regard to America, considering the work to do, — ay, Tom,
and the way they are doing it, — I'm not over-disposed to
be critical about certain asperities that are sure to rub off
in time, particularly if we don't sharpen them into spikes
by our own awkward attempts to polish them.

If I was able, I'd like to write a book about America.
I'd like to inquire, first, if, seeing the problem that the
Yankees are trying to solve, the way they have set about
it is the best and the shortest? I'd like, too, to study
what secret machinery combines a weak government and
a strong people, — the very reverse of what we see in the
Old World, where the governments are strong and the
people weak? I'd like to find out, if I could, why people
that, for the most part, have formed the least subordinate
populations of the Old World, behave so remarkably well
in the New?

In running off into these topics, Tom, I suppose I'm
like every one else, who, in proportion as his own affairs

become embarrassed, takes a wonderful interest in those of his neighbors. Half the patriotism in the world comes out of the bankruptcy courts.

And here's Monsieur Gabriel Dulong " for my instructions *in re* Cherry," as if to recall me from foreign affairs, and once more bring back my wandering thoughts to the Home Office.

Write to me, Tom, and send me money. You have no idea how it goes here; and as for the bankers, I never met the like of them! The exchange is always against you, and if you want a ten-pound English note, they 'll make you smart for it.

The more I see of this foreign life, the less I like it. I know that we have been unfortunate in one or two respects. I know that it is rash in me to speak on so brief an acquaintance with it, but I already dread our being more intimate. Mrs. D. is not the woman you knew her. No more thrift, no more saving, — none of that looking after trifles that, however we may laugh at in our wives, we are right glad to profit by. She has taken a new turn, and fancies, God forgive her! that we have an elegant estate, and a fine, thriving, solvent tenantry. Wherever the delusion came from, I cannot guess; but I'm certain that the little slip of sea between Dover and Calais is the origin of more false notions and extravagant fancies than the wide Atlantic.

I have been thinking for some days back that you ought to write me a strong letter, — you know what I mean, Tom, — a strong letter about matters at home. There's no great difficulty, when a man lives in Ireland, to make out a good list of grievances.

Give it to us, then, and let us have our fill of rotten potatoes, blighted wheat, runaway tenants, and workhouse riots. Throw in a murder if you like, and make it "strong," Tom. Say that, considering the cheapness of the Continent, we draw a terrible sight of money, and add that you can't imagine what we do with the cash. Put "Strictly PRIVATE and CONFIDENTIAL" on the outside, and I 'll take care to be out of the way when it comes. You can guess that Mrs. D. will soon open it, and perhaps

it may give her a shock. Is n't it hard that I have to go
about the bush in this way? but that's what we 're come to.
If I hint a word about expense, they look on me as if I
was Shylock; and I believe they 'd rather hear me blaspheme
than say the phrase " economy." I think, from what I see
in James, that he 's fretting about this very same thing. He
did n't say exactly *that*, but he dropped a remark the other
day that showed me he was grieved by the turn for dress
and finery that Mrs. D. and Mary Anne have taken up; and
one of the nurses that sat up with him told me that he used
to sigh dreadfully at times, and mutter broken expressions
about money.

To tell you the truth, Tom, I 'd go back to-morrow, if
I could. " And why can't you? — what prevents you,
Kenny?" I hear you say. Just this, then, I have n't the
pluck! I could n't stand the attack of Mrs. D. and her
daughter. I 'm not equal to it. My constitution is n't
what it used to be, and I 'm afraid of the gout. At my
time of life, they say it always flies to the heart or to the
head, — maybe because there 's a vacancy in these places
after fifty-six or seven years of age! I see, too, by the
looks Mrs. D. gives Mary Anne occasionally, that they
know this; and she often gives me to understand that she
does n't wish to dispute with me, for reasons of her own.
This is all very well, and kindly meant, Tom, but it throws
me into a depression that is dreadful.

I see by the papers that you 've taken up all kinds of
" Sanitary Questions" at home. As for the health of
towns, Tom, the grand thing is not to suffer them to grow
too big. You 're always crying out about twelve people
sleeping in one room somewhere, and you gave the ages of
each of them in the " Times," and you grow moral and
modest, and I don't know what else, about decency, destitution, and so forth; but what 's London itself but the very
same thing on an enlarged scale? It 's nonsense to fret
about a wart, when you have a wen in the same neighborhood. Not that I 'm sorry to see fine folk taking trouble
about what concerns the poor, particularly when they go
about it sensibly and quietly, without any balderdash of
little books, and, above all, without a ladies' committee. If

there's anything chokes me, it's a ladies' committee. Three married women on bad terms with their husbands, four widows, and five old maids, all prying, pedantic, and impertinent, — going loose about the world with little subscription-cards, decrying innocent pleasures, and decoying your children's pocket-money, — turning benevolence into a house-tax, and making charity like the "Pipe-water." You remark, too, that the pretty women won't join these gangs at all. Now and then you may see one take out a letter of marque, and cruise for herself, but never in company. Seeing the importunity of these old damsels, I often wondered why the Government never thought of employing ladies as tax-collectors. He'd be a hardy man who'd make one or two I could mention call twice.

I have been turning over in my mind what you said about Dodsborough; and though I don't like the notion of giving a lease, still it's possible we might do it without much danger. "He is an Englishman," you say, "that has never lived in Ireland." Now, my notion is, Tom, that if he be as old as you say, it's too late for him to try. They're a mulish, obstinate, unbending kind of people, these English; and wherever you see them, they never conform to the habits of the people. After thirty years' experience of Ireland, you'll hear them saying that they cannot accustom themselves to the "lies and the climate"! If I have heard that same remark once, I've heard it fifty times. And what does it amount to but a confession that they won't take the world as they find it. Ireland is rainy, there's no doubt, and Paddy is fond of telling you what he thinks is agreeable to you, — a kind of native courtesy, just like his offering you his potato when he knows in his heart that he can't spare it, — but he gives it, nevertheless.

I'd say, then, we might let him have Dodsborough, on the chance that he'd never stay six months there, and perhaps in the mean while we'd find out another Manchester gentleman to succeed him. I remember poor old Dycer used to sell a little chestnut mare every Saturday, — nobody ever kept her a fortnight, — and when she died, by jumping over Bloody Bridge into the Liffey, and killed herself and her rider, Dycer said, "There's four-and-twenty pounds a

year lost to *me*," — and so it was too! Think over this,
and tell me your mind on it.

I believe I told you of the Polish Count that we took with
us to Waterloo. I met him yesterday with my cloak on
him; but really the number of my legal embroilments here
is so great that I was shy of arresting him. We hear a
great deal of talk about the partition of Poland, and there
is an English lord keeps the subject for his own especial
holdings forth; but I am convinced that the greatest evil of
that nefarious act lies in having thrown all these Polish
fellows broadcast over Europe. I wish it was a kingdom
to-morrow, if they'd only consent to stay there. To be
well rid of them and their sympathizers, whom I own I like
even less, would be a great blessing just now. I wish the
"Times" would stop blackguarding Louis Napoleon. If
the French like being bullied, what is that to us? My own
notion is that the people and their ruler are well met; besides, if we only reflect a little on it, we'll see that anything
is better for *us* than a Bourbon, — I don't care what branch!
They are under too deep obligations to us, and have too
often accepted of English hospitality, not to hate us; and
hate us they do. I believe the first Frenchman that cher-
ishes an undying animosity to England is your Legitimist;
next to him comes the Orleanist.

It's a strange thing, but the more I have to think of about
my own affairs, and the worse they are going with me, the
more my thoughts run after politics and the newspapers. I
suppose that's all for the best, and that if people dwelled
too much on their own troubles, their heads would n't stand
it. You've seen a trick the horse jockeys have when a
horse goes lame of one foot, — to pinch him a little with
the shoe of the opposite one; and it's not bad philosophy
to practise mentally, and you may preserve your equanimity just by putting on the load fairly. And so it is I try
to divert my thoughts from mortgages, creditors, and Chancery, by wondering how the King of Naples will contrive
to keep his throne, and how the Austrians will save themselves from bankruptcy! I know it would be more to the
purpose if I turned my thoughts to getting Mary Anne
married, and James into the Board of Trade; at least, so

Mrs. D. tells me, and although she is always repeating the old saw about "marriages being made in heaven," she evidently does n't wish to give too much trouble in that quarter, and would like to lend a hand herself to the work.

Jellicot has sent his clerk here to tell me that I have been pronounced "Contumacious," for not appearing somewhere, and before somebody that I never heard of! Egad! these kind of proceedings are scarcely calculated to develop the virtues of humanity! They sent me something I thought was a demand for a tax, and it turns out a judge's warrant; for aught I know, there may be an order to seize the body of Kenny James Dodd, and consign him to the dungeons of the Inquisition! Write to me at once, Tom, and above all don't forget the money.

Yours, most faithfully,

K. I. DODD.

Why does Molly Gallagher keep pestering me about Christy? She wants me to get him into the "Grand Canal." I wish they were both there, with all my heart.

I open this to say that Vickars has just sent me a copy of his address to the "Independent Electors of Bruff." I'd like to see one of them, for the curiosity of the thing. He asks me to give him my opinion of the document, and the "benefit of my advice and counsel," as if I had not been reading the very same productions since I was a child. The very phraseology is unaltered. Why can't they hit on something new? He "hopes that he restores to them, unsullied, the high trust they had committed to his keeping." Egad! if he does so, he ought to get a patent for taking out spots, stains, and discolorations, for a dirtier garment than our representative mantle has been, would be hard to find. Like all our patriots that sit in Whig company, he is sorely puzzled between his love for Ireland and his regard for himself, and has to limit his political line to a number of vague threats about overgrown Church Establishments and Landlord tyranny, not being quite sure how far his friends in power are disposed to worry the Protestants and grind the gentry.

Of course he butters up the pastors of the people; but he might as well leave *that* alone; the priests are too cunning for all that balderdash nowadays. They'll insist on something real, tangible, and substantial. What they say is this: "The landlords used to have it all their own way at one time. *Our* day is come now." And there they're right, Tom; there's no doubt of it. O'Connell said true when he told the English, "Ye're always abusing me, — and call me the 'curse of Ireland' and the destroyer of the public peace, — but wait a bit. I'll not be five years in my grave till you'd wish me back again." There never was anything more certain. So long as you had Dan to deal with, you could make your bargain, — it might be, it often was, a very hard one, — but when it was once made, he kept the terms fairly and honestly! But with whom will you treat *now?* Is it with M'Hale, or Paul Cullen, or Dr. Meyler? Sure each of them will demand separate and specific conditions, and you might as well try to settle the Caffre war by a compact with Sandilla, who, the moment he sells himself to you, enters into secret correspondence with his successor.

I'm never so easy in my mind as when I see the English in a row with the Catholics. I don't care a brass farthing how much it may go against us at first, — how enthusiastically they may yell "No Popery," burn cardinals in effigy, and persecute the nuns. Give them rope enough, Tom, and see if they don't hang themselves! There never came a fit of rampant Protestantism in England that all the weak, rash, and ridiculous zealots did n't get to the head of the movement. Off they go at score, subsidizing renegade vagabonds of our Church to abuse us, raking up bad stories of conventual life, and attacking the confessional. There never were gulls like them! They swallow all the cases of cruelty and persecution at once, — they foster every scoundrel, if he's only a deserter from us, — ay, and they even take to their fireplaces the filthiest novels of Eugène Sue, if he only satisfies their rancorous hate of a Jesuit. And where does it end? I'll tell you. Their converts turn out to be scoundrels too infamous for common contact; their prosecutions fail, — why would n't they, when we get them up ourselves? — John Bull gets ashamed of himself; round comes the Press, and that's the moment when any young rising Catholic barrister in the House can make his own terms, whether it be to endow the true Church or to smash the false one!

As for John Bull, he never can do mischief enough when he's in a passion, but he's always ready to pay double the damage in the morning. And as for putting " salt on our tails," let him try it with the " Dove of Elphin," that's all.

I was forgetting to tell you that I sent back Vickars's address, only remarking that I was sorry not to know his sentiments about the Board of Trade. *Ver. sap.*

LETTER X.

CAROLINE DODD TO MISS COX, AT MISS MINCING'S ACADEMY, BLACK ROCK, IRELAND.

MY DEAR MISS COX, — I have long hesitated and delib-
erated with myself whether it were not better to appear
ungrateful for my silence, than by writing inflict you with
a very tiresome, good-for-nothing epistle; and if I have
now taken the worst counsel, it is because I prefer anything rather than seem forgetful of one to whom I owe so
much as to my dear, kind governess. Were I only to tell
you of our adventures and mishaps since we came abroad,
there might, perhaps, be enough to fill half a dozen letters;
but I greatly doubt if the theme would amuse you. You
were always too good-natured to laugh at anything where
there was even one single feature that suggested sorrow;
and I grieve to say that, however ludicrously many of our
accidents might read, there is yet mixed with them too much
that is painful and distressing. You will say this is a very
gloomy opening, and from one whom you had so often to
chide for the wild gayety of her spirits; but so it is: I am
sad enough now, — sadder than ever you wished to see me.
It is not that I am not in the very midst of objects full of
deep interest, — it is not that I do not recognize around me
scenes, places, and names, all of which are imbued with great
and stirring associations. I am neither indifferent nor cal-
lous, but I see everything through a false medium, and I
hear everything with a perverted judgment; in a word, we
seem to have come abroad, not to derive the advantages that
might arise from new sources of knowledge in language,
literature, and art, but to scramble for a higher social
position, — to impose ourselves on the world for something
that we have no pretension to, and to live in a way that we

cannot afford. You remember us at Dodsborough, — how happy we were, how satisfied with the world; that is, with our world, for it was a very little one. We were not very great folk, but we had all the consideration as if we were; for there were none better off than ourselves, and few had so many opportunities of winning the attachment of all classes. Papa was always known as the very best of land-lords, mamma had not her equal for charity and kindness, James was actually adored by the people, and I hesitate not to say that Mary Anne and myself were not friendless. There was a little daily round of duties that brought us all together in our cares and sympathies; for, however different our ages or tastes, we had but one class of subjects to discuss, and, happily, we saw them always with the same light and shadow. Our life was, in short, what fashionable people would have deemed a very vulgar, inglorious kind of exist-ence; but it was full of pleasant little incidents, and a thousand little cares and duties, that gave it abundant variety and interest. I was never a quick scholar, as you know too well. I have tried my dear Miss Cox's patience sorely and often, but I loved my lessons; I loved those calm hours in the summer-house, with the perfume of the rose and the sweetbrier around us, and the hum of the bee mingling its song with my own not less drowsy French. That sweet "Telemachus," so easy and so softly sounding; that good Madame de Genlis, so simple-minded when she thought herself most subtle! Not less did I love the little old schoolroom of a winter's day, when the pattering rain streamed down the windows, and gave, by contrast, all the aspect of more comfort within. How pleasant was it, as we gathered round the turf fire, to think that we were surrounded with such appliances against gloomy hours, — the healthful exercise of happy minds! Ah, my dear Miss Cox, how often you told us to study hard, since that, once launched upon the great sea of life, the voyage would exact all our cares; and yet see, here am I upon that wide ocean, and already longing to regain the quiet little creek, — the little haven of rest that I quitted!

I promised to be very candid with you, to conceal noth-ing whatever; but I did not remember that my confessions,

to be thus frank, must necessarily involve me in remarks
on others, in which I may be often unjust,— in which I am
certain to be unwarranted,— since nothing in my position
entitles me to be their censor. However, I will keep my
pledge this once, and you will tell me afterwards if I
should continue to observe it. And now to begin. We are
living here as though we were people of vast fortune. We
occupy the chief suite of apartments at the first hotel, and
we have a carriage, with showy liveries, a courier, and are
quite beset with masters of every language and accomplishment you can fancy, — expensive kind of people, whose
very dress and style bespeak the terms on which their services are rendered. Our visitors are all titled: dukes,
princes, and princesses shower amongst our cards. Our invitations are from the same class, and yet, my dear Miss Cox,
we feel all the unreality of this high and stately existence.
We look at each other and think of Dodsborough! We
think of papa in his old fustian shooting-jacket, paying the
laborers, and higgling about half a day to be stopped
here, and a sack of meal to be deducted there. We think of
mamma's injunctions to Darby Sloan about the price he is
to get for the "boneens," — have you forgotten our vernacular for little pigs?— and how much he must "be sure to
ask" for the turkeys. We think of Mary Anne and myself taking our lesson from Mr. Delaney, and learning the
Quad—drilles as he pronounced it, as the last new discovery of the dancing art, and dear James hammering away at
the rule of three on an old slate, to try and qualify himself for
the Board of Trade. And we remember the utter consternation of the household — the tumult dashed with a certain
sense of pride — when some subaltern of the detachment at
Bruff cantered up to the door and sent in his name! Dear
me, how the little words 25th Regiment, or 91st, used to
make our hearts beat, suggestive as they were of gay balls
at the Town-hall with red-coated partners, the regimental
band, and the colors tastefully festooning the whitewashed
walls. And now, my dear Miss Sarah, we are actually
ashamed of the contact with one of those whom once it was
our highest glory to be acquainted with! You may remember a certain Captain Morris, who was stationed at Bruff,

— dark, with very black eyes, and most beautiful teeth; he was very silent in company, and, indeed, we knew him but slightly, for he chanced to have some altercation with pa on the bench one day, and, as I hear he was all in the right, pa did not afterwards forgive him. Well, here he is now, having left the army, — I don't know if on half-pay, or sold out altogether, — but here he is, travelling for the benefit of his mother's health, — a very old and infirm lady, to whom he is dotingly attached. She fretted so much when she discovered that his regiment was ordered abroad to the Cape, that he had no other resource than to leave the service! He told me so himself.

"I had nobody else in the world," said he, "who felt any interest in my fortunes; *she* had made a hundred sacrifices for me. It was but fair I should make one for *her*."

He knew he was surrendering position and prospect forever, — that to him no career could ever open again; but he had placed a duty high above all considerations of self, and so he parted with comrades and pursuit, with everything that made up his hope and his object, and descended to a little station of unobtrusive, undistinguished humility, satisfied to be the companion of a poor, feeble old lady! He has as much as confessed to me that their means are very small. It was an accidental admission with reference to something he thought of doing, but which he found to be too expensive; and the avowal was made so easily, so frankly, so free from any false shame on one side, or any unworthy desire to entrap sympathy on the other! It was as if he spoke of something which indeed concerned him, but in no wise gave the mainspring to his thoughts or actions! He came to visit us here; but his having left the service, coupled with our present taste for grand acquaintance, were so little in his favor that I believed he would not have repeated his call. An accidental service, however, that he was enabled to render mamma and Mary Anne at a railroad station the other day, and where but for him they might have been involved in considerable difficulties, has opened a chance of further intimacy, for he has already been here two mornings, and is coming this evening to tea.

You will, perhaps, ask me how and by what chain of

circumstances Captain Morris is linked with the earlier portion of this letter, and I will tell you. It was from him that I learned the history of those high and distinguished individuals by whom we are surrounded; from him I heard that, supposing us to be people of immense wealth, a whole web of intrigue has been spun around us, and everything that the ingenuity and craft of the professional adventurer could devise put in requisition to trade upon our supposed affluence and inexperience! He has told me of the dangerous companions by whom James is surrounded; and if he has not spoken so freely about a certain young nobleman — Lord George Tiverton — who is now seldom or never out of the house, it is because that they have had something of a personal difference, — a serious one, I suspect, and which Captain Morris seems to reckon as a bar to anything beyond the merest mention of his name. It is not impossible, too, that though he might not make any revelations to *me* on such a theme, he would be less guarded with papa or James. Whatever may be the fact, he does not advance at all in the good graces of the others. Mamma calls him a dry crust, — a confirmed old bachelor. Mary Anne and Lord George — for they are always in partnership in matters of opinion — have set him down as a "military prig;" and papa, who is rarely unjust in the long run, says that "there's no guessing at the character of a fellow of small means, who never goes in debt." This may or may not be true; but it is certainly hard to condemn him for an honorable trait, simply because it does not give the key to his nature. And now, my last hope is what James may think of him, for as yet they have not met. I think I hear you echo my words, "And why your 'last hope,' Miss Cary? What possible right have you to express yourself in these terms?" Simply because I feel that one man of true and honorable sentiments, one right-judging, right-feeling gentleman, is all-essential to us abroad! and if we reject this chance, I'm not so sure we shall meet with another.

How ashamed I am not to be able to tell you of all I have seen! But so it is, — description is a very tame performance in good hands; it is a lamentable exhibition in weak ones! As to painters, I prefer Vandyk to Rubens; not that I have

even the pretence of a reason for my criticism. I know
nothing, whatever, of what constitutes excellence in color,
drawing, or design. I understand in a picture only what it
suggests to my own mind, either as a correct copy of nature,
or as originating new trains of thought, new sources of feeling; and by these tests Vandyk pleases me more than his master. But, shall I own it, there is a class of pictures of a far
inferior order that gives me greater enjoyment than either,
—I mean those scenes of real life, those representations of
some little uneventful incident of the every-day world,— an
old chemist at work in his dim old laboratory; an old house
Vrow knitting in her red-tiled chamber, the sunlight slant-
ing in, and tipping with an azure tint the tortoiseshell cat
that purrs beside her; a lover teaching his mistress the
guitar; an old cavalier giving his horse a drink at a fountain. These, in all the lifelike power of Gerard Dow, Teer-
burgh, or Mieris, have a charm for me I cannot express.
They are stories, and they are better than stories; for oftentimes the writer conveys his meaning imperfectly, and oftentimes he overlays you with his explanations, stifling within
you those expansive bursts of sentiment that ought to have
been his aim to evoke, and thus, by elaborating, he obliter-
ates. Now, your artist — I mean, of course, your great
artist — is eminently suggestive. He gives you but one
scene, it is true, but how full is it of the past, and the
future too! Can you gaze on that old alchemist, with his
wrinkled forehead, and dim, deep-set eyes, his threadbare
doublet, and his fingers tremulous from age? Can you
watch that countenance, calm but careworn, where every
line exhibits the long struggle there has been between the
keen perceptions of science and the golden dreams of
enthusiasm, where the coldest passions of a worldly nature
have warred with the most glorious attributes of a poetic
temperament? Can you see him, as he sits watching the
alembic wherein the toil of years is bubbling, and not
weave within your own mind the life-long conflict he has
sustained? Have you him not before you in his humble
home, secluded and forgotten of men, yet inhabiting a
dream-world of crowded images? What beautiful stories —
what touching little episodes of domestic life — lie in the

quiet scenes of those quaint interiors; and how deep the charm that attaches one to these peaceful spots of home happiness! The calm intellectuality of the old, the placid loveliness of the young, the air of cultivated enjoyment that pervades all, are in such perfect keeping that you feel as though they imparted to yourself some share of that gentle, tranquil pleasure that forms their own atmosphere!

Oh, my dear Miss Cox! if there be "sermons in stones," there are romances in pictures, — and romances far more truthful than the circulating libraries supply us with. And, to turn back to real life, shall I own to you that I am sadly disappointed with the gay world? I am fully alive to all the value of the confession. I appreciate perfectly how double-edged is the weapon of this admission, and that I am in reality but pleading guilty to my own unfitness for its enjoyments; but as I never tried to evade or deny that fact, I may be suffered to give my testimony with so much of qualification. When I compare the little gratification that society confers on the very highest classes, with the heartfelt delight intercourse imparts to the humble, I am at a loss to see wherein lies the advantage of all the exclusive regulations of fashionable life. Of one thing I feel assured, and that is, that one must be born in a certain class, habituated from the earliest years to its ideas and habits, filled with its peculiar traditions, and animated by its own special hopes, to conform gracefully and easily to its laws. *We* go into society to perform a part, — just as artificial a one as any in a genteel comedy, — and consequently are too much occupied with "our character" to derive that benefit from intercourse which is so attainable by those less constrained by circumstances. If all this amounts to the simple confession that I am by no means at home in the great world, and far more at my ease with more humble associates, it is no more than the fact, and comes pretty near to what you often remarked to me, — that "in criticising external objects one is very frequently but delineating little traits and lineaments of one's own nature."

I am unable to answer your question about our future plans; for, indeed, they appear anything but fixed. I believe if papa had his choice he would go back at once.

This, however, mamma will not hear of; and, indeed, the word Ireland is now as much under ban amongst us as that name that is never "syllabled to ears polite." The doctors say James ought to pass a month or six weeks at Schwalbach, to drink the waters and take the baths; and, from what I can learn, the place is the perfection of rural beauty and quietude. Captain Morris speaks of it as a little paradise. He is going there himself; for I have learned — though not from him — that he was badly wounded in the Afghan war. I will write to you whenever our destination is decided on; and, meanwhile, beg you to believe me my dear Miss Cox's

Most attached and faithful pupil,

CAROLINE DODD.

LETTER XI.

MR. DODD TO THOMAS PURCELL, ESQ., OF THE GRANGE,
BRUFF.

DEAR TOM, — I got the bills all safe, and cashed two of
them yesterday. They came at the right moment, — when
does not money? — for we are going to leave this for Germany, one of the watering-places there, the name of which
I cannot trust myself to spell, being recommended for
James's wound. I suppose I'm not singular, but somehow
I never was able to compute what I owed in a place till I
was about to leave it. From that moment, however, in come
a shower of bills and accounts that one never dreamed of.
The cook you discharged three months before has never
paid for the poultry, and you have as many hens to your
score as if you were a fox. You've lost the fishmonger's
receipts, and have to pay him over again for a whole
Lent's consumption. Your courier has run up a bill in
your name for cigars and curaçoa, and your wife's maid has
been conducting the most liberal operations in perfumery
and cosmetics, under the title of her mistress. Then comes
the landlord, for repairs and damages. Every creaky sofa
and cracked saucer that you have been treating for six
months with the deference due to their delicate condition
must be replaced by new ones. Every window that
wouldn't shut, and every door that would not open, must be
put in perfect order; keys replaced, bells rehung. The
saucepans, whose verdigris has almost killed you with colic,
must be all retinned or coppered; and, lastly, the pump is
sure to be destroyed by the housemaid, and vague threats
about sinking a new well are certain to draw you into a
compromise. Nor is the roguery the worst of it; but all the
sneaking scoundrels that wouldn't "trouble you with their

little demands " before, stand out now as sturdy creditors
that would not abate a jot of their claims. Lucky are ye
if they don't rake up old balances, and begin the score with
"Restant du dernier compte."

The moralists say that a man should be enabled to visit
the world after his death, if he would really know the opinion entertained of him by his fellows. Until this desirable
object be attainable, one ought to be satisfied with the experience obtained by change of residence. There is no disguise, no concealment then! The little blemishes of your
temper, once borne with such Christian charity, are remembered in a more chastening spirit; and it is half hinted that
your custom was more than compensated for by your complaining querulousness. Is not the moral of all this that
one should live at home, in his own place, where his father
lived before him, and his son will live after him; where the
tradespeople have a vested interest in your welfare, and are
nearly as anxious about your wheat and potatoes as you are
yourself? Unlike these foreign rascals, that think you have
a manufactory of "Herries and Farquhar's circular notes,"
and can coin at will, your neighbors know when and at
what times it's no use to tease you,— that asking for money
at the wrong season is like expecting new peas in December, or grouse in the month of May.

I make these remarks in all the spirit of recent suffering,
for I have paid away two hundred pounds since yesterday
morning, of which I was not conscious that I owed fifty.
And, besides, I have gone through more actual fighting — in
the way of bad language, I mean — than double the money
would repay me for. In these wordy combats, I feel I
always come off worst; for as my knowledge of the language
is limited, I'm like the sailor that for want of ammunition crammed in whatever he could lay hands on into his
gun, and fired off his bag of doubloons against the enemy
instead of round shot. Mrs. D., too, whom the sounds of
conflict always "summon to the field," does not improve
matters; for if her vocabulary be limited, it is strong, and
even the most roguish shopkeeper does not like to be called
a thief and a highwayman! These diversions in our parts
of speech have cost me dearly, for I have had to compromise

about six cases of "defamation," and two of threatened
assault and battery, though these last went no further than
demonstrations on Mrs. D.'s part, which, however, were
quite sufficient to terrify our grocer, who is a colonel in the
National Guard, and a gigantic hairdresser, whose beard is
the glory of a "*Sapeur* company." I have discovered,
besides, that I have done something, but what it is — in
contravention to the laws — I do not know, and for which I
am fined eighty-two francs five centimes, plus twenty-
seven for contumacy; and I have paid it now, lest it should
grow into more by to-morrow, for so the Brigadier has just
hinted to me; for that formidable functionary — with tags
that would do credit to a general — is just come to "invite
me," as he calls it, to the Prefecture. As these invitations
are like royal ones, I must break off now abruptly.

Here I am again, Tom, after four hours of ante-chamber
and audience. I had been summoned to appear before the
authorities to purge myself of a contempt, — for which, by
the way, they had already fined me; my offence being that
I had not exchanged some bit of paper for another bit of
paper given me in exchange for my passport, the purport of
which was to show that I, Kenny Dodd, was living openly
and flagrantly in the city of Brussels, and not following out
any clandestine pursuit or object injurious to the state, and
subversive of the monarchy. Well, I hope they're satisfied
now; and if my eighty-two francs five centimes gave any
stability to their institutions, much good may it do them!
This, however, seems but the beginning of new troubles;
for on my applying to have the aforesaid passport *viséd* for
Germany, they told me that there were two "detainers" on
it, in the shape of two actions at law yet undecided, although
I yesterday morning paid up what I understood to be the
last instalment for compromising all suits now pending
against said Kenny I. Dodd. On hearing this, I at once
set out for the tribunal to see Vanhoegen and Draek, my
chief lawyers. Such a place as the tribunal you never set
eyes on. Imagine a great quadrangle, with archways all
round crammed full of dirty advocates, — black-gowned,
black-faced, and black-hearted; peasants, thieves, jailers,
tip-staffs, and the general public of fruit-sellers and lucifer-

matches all mixed up together, with a turmoil and odor that would make you hope Justice was as little troubled with nose as eyesight. Over the heads of this mob you catch glimpses of the several courts, where three old fellows, like the figures in a Holbein, sit behind a table covered with black cloth, administering the law, — a solemn task that loses some of its imposing influence when you think that these reverend seigniors, if wanting in the wisdom, are not free from one of the weaknesses of Bacon! By dint of great pressing, pushing, and perseverance, I forced my way forward into one of these till I reached a strong wooden rail, or barrier, within which was an open space, where the accused sat on a kind of bench, the witness under examination being opposite to him, and the procureur hard by in a little box like a dwarf pulpit. I thought I saw Draek in the crowd, but I was mistaken, — an easy matter, they all look so much alike. Once in, however, I thought I 'd remain for a while and see the proceedings. It was a trial for murder, as well as I could ascertain the case. The prisoner, a gentlemanlike young fellow of six or seven and twenty, had stabbed another in some fit of jealousy. I believe they were at supper, or were going to sup together when the altercation occurred. There was a waiter in the witness-box giving evidence when I came up; and really the tone of deference he exhibited to the prisoner, and the prisoner's own off-hand, easy way of interrogating him, were greatly to be admired. It was easy to see that he had got many a half-crown from the accused, and had not given up hope of many more in future. His chief evidence was to the effect that Monsieur de Verteuil, the accused, had ordered a supper for two in a private room, the bill of fare offering a wide field for discussion, one of the points of the case being whether the guest who should partake of the repast was a lady or the deceased; and this the advocates on each side handled with wonderful dexterity, by inferences drawn from the *carte*. You see, Verteuil's counsel wanted to show that Bretigny was an intruder, and had forced himself into the company of the accused. The opposite side were for implying that he came there on invitation, and was murdered of malice aforethought. I don't

think the point would have been so very material with us;
or, at all events, that we should have tried to elicit it in this
manner; but they have their own way of doing things, and
I suppose they know what suits them. After half an hour's
very animated skirmishing, the president, with a sudden
flash of intelligence, bethought him of asking the accused
for whom he bespoke the entertainment.

"You must excuse me, Monsieur le Président," said he,
blandly; "but I'm sure that your nice sense of honor will
show that I cannot answer your question."

"Très bien, très bien," rang through the crowded court, in
approbation of this chivalrous speech, and one young lady
from the gallery flung down her bouquet of moss-roses to the
prisoner, in token of her enthusiastic concurrence. The
delicate reserve of the accused seemed to touch every one.
Husbands and wives, sons and daughters, all appeared to
feel that they had a vested interest in the propagation of
such principles; and the old judge who had propounded the
ungracious interrogatory really seemed ashamed of himself.

The waiter soon after this retired, and what the newspapers next day called a *sensation prononcée* was caused by
the entrance of a very handsome and showy-looking young
lady, — no less a personage than Mademoiselle Catinka
Lövenfeld, the prima donna of the opera, and the Dido of
this unhappy Æneid. With us, the admiration of a pretty
witness is always a very subdued homage; and even the
reporters do not like venturing beyond the phrase, "here a
person of prepossessing appearance took her place on the
table." They are very superior to us here, however, for the
buzz of admiration swelled from the lowest benches till it
rose to the very judicial seat itself, and the old president,
affecting to look at his notes, wiped his glasses afresh, and
took a sly peep at the beauty, like the rest of us.

Though, as Macheath says, "Laws were made for every
degree," the mode of examining witnesses admits of considerable variety. The interrogatories were now no longer
jerked out with abruptness; the questions were not put
with the categorical sternness of that frowning aspect
which, be the lawyer Belgian, French, or Irish, seems an
instinct with him; on the contrary, the pretty witness was

invited to tell her name, she was wheedled out of her birth-
place, coaxed out of her peculiar religious profession, and
joked into saying something about her age.

I must say, if she had rehearsed the part as often as she
had that of Norma, she could n't be more perfect. Her
manner was the triumph of ease and grace. There was an
almost filial deference for the bench, an air of respectful
attention for the bar, courtesy for the jury, and a most
touching shade of compassion for the prisoner, and all this
done without the slightest seeming effort. I do not pretend
to know what others felt; but as for me, I paid very little
attention to the matter, so much more did the manner of the
inquiry engage me: still, I heard that she was a Saxon by
birth, of noble parentage, born with the highest expectations, but ruined by the attachment of her father to the cause
of the Emperor Napoleon. The animation with which she
alluded to this parental trait elicited a most deafening burst
of applause, and the tip-staff, a veteran of the Imperial
Guard, was carried out senseless, overcome by his emotions. Ah, Tom! we have nothing like this in England,
and strange enough that they should have it here; but the
fact is, these Belgians are only "second-chop" Frenchmen,
— a kind of weak "after grass," with only the weeds luxu-
riant! It 's pretty much as with ourselves, — the people
that take a loan of a language never take a lease of the
traditions! They catch up just some popular clap-traps of
the mother country, but there ends the relationship!

But to come back to Mademoiselle Catinka. She now
had got into a little narrative of her youth, in some old
chateau on the Elbe, which held the Court breathless; to be
sure, it had not a great deal to do with the case in hand;
but no matter for that: a more artless, gifted, lovely, and
loving creature than she appeared to have been never existed.
On this last attribute she laid considerable stress. There
was, I think, a little rhetorical art in the confession; for
certainly a young lady who loved birds, flowers, trees,
water, clouds, and mountains so devotedly, might possibly
have a spare corner for something else; and even the old
judge could n't tell if he had not chanced on the lucky ticket
in that lottery. I wish I could have heard the case out;

I'd have given a great deal to see how they linked all that Paul and Virginia life with the bloody drama they were there to investigate, and what possible connection existed between Tieck's romances and sticking a man with a table-knife. This gratification was, however, denied me; for just as I was listening with my greediest ears, Vanhoegen placed his hand on my shoulder, and whispered, "Come along — don't lose a minute — *your* cause is on!"

"What do you mean? Have n't I compro—"

"Hush!" said he, warningly; "respect the majesty of the law."

"With all my heart; but what's *my* cause? — what do you mean by *my* cause?"

"It's no time for explanation," said he, hurrying me along; "the judges are in chamber,— you'll soon hear all about it."

He said truly; it was neither the fitting time nor place for much converse, for we had to fight our way through a crowd that was every moment increasing; and it took at least twenty minutes of struggle and combat to get out, my coat being slit up to the collar, and my friend's gown being reduced to something like bell-ropes.

He did n't seem to think much about his damaged costume, but still dragged me along, across a courtyard, up some very filthy stairs, down a dark corridor, then up another flight, and, passing into a large ante-room, where a messenger was seated in a kind of glass cage, he pushed aside a heavy curtain of green baize, and we found ourselves in a court, which, if not crowded like that below, was still sufficiently filled, and by persons of respectable exterior. There was a dead silence as we entered. The three judges were examining their notes, and handing papers back and forward to each other in dumb show. The procureur was picking his teeth with a paper-knife, and the clerk of the court munching a sandwich, which he held in his hat. Vanhoegen, however, brushed forward to a prominent place, and beckoned me to a seat beside him. I had but time to obey, when the clerk, seeing us in our places, bolted down an enormous mouthful, and, with an effort that nearly choked him, cried out, "L'affaire de Dodd fils est en audience." My heart drooped as I heard the words. The "affaire de Dodd fils" could mean nothing but that confounded duel of which I have already told you. All the misfortune and all the criminality seemed to fall upon us. For at least four times a week I was summoned somewhere or other, now before a civil, now a military auditor; and though I swore repeatedly that I knew nothing about the matter till it was all over, they appeared to think that if I was well tortured, I might make great revelations. They were not quite wrong in their calculations. I would have turned "approver" against my father rather than gone on in this fashion. But the difficulty was, I had really nothing to tell. The little I knew had been obtained from others. Lord George had told me so much as I was acquainted with; and, from my old habits of the bench at home, I was well aware that such could not be admitted as evidence.

Still it was their good pleasure to pursue me with warrants and summonses, and there was nothing for it but to appear when and wherever they wanted me.

"Is this confounded affair the cause of my passport being detained?" whispered I to Van.

"Precisely," said he; "and if not very dexterously handled, the expense may be enormous."

I almost lost all self-possession at these words. I had been a mark for legal pillage and robbery from the first moment of my arrival, and it seemed as if they would not suffer me to leave the country while I had a Napoleon remaining. Stung nearly to madness, I resolved to make one desperate effort at rescue, and, like some of those woebegone creatures in our own country who insist on personal appeals to a Chief Justice, I called, "Monsieur le Président —" There, however, my French left me, and, after a terrible struggle to get on, I had to continue my address in the vernacular.

"Who is this man?" asked he, sternly.

"Dodd père, Monsieur le Président," interposed my lawyer, who seemed most eager to save me from the consequences of my rashness.

"Ah! he is Dodd père," said the president, solemnly; and now he and his two colleagues adjusted their spectacles, and gazed at me long and attentively; in fact, with such earnestness did they stare that I began to feel my character of Dodd père was rather an imposing kind of performance. "Enfin," said the president, with a faint sigh, as though the reasoning process had been rather a fatiguing one,—"enfin! Dodd père is the father of Dodd fils, the respondent."

Vanhoegen bowed submissive assent, and muttered, as I thought, some little flattery about the judicial acuteness and perspicuity.

"Let him be sworn," said the president; and accordingly I held up my hand, while the clerk recited something with a humdrum rapidity that I guessed must mean an oath.

"You are called Dodd père?" said the Attorney-General, addressing me.

"I find I am so called here, but I never was so before," said I, tartly.

"He means that the appellation is not usual in his own country," said one of the judges, — a small, red-eyed man, with pock-marks.

"Put it down," observed the president, gravely. "The witness informs us that he is only called Dodd."

"Kenny James Dodd, Monsieur," cried I, interrupting.

"Dodd — dit Kenny James," dictated the small judge; and the amanuensis took it down.

"And you swear you are the father of Dodd fils?" asked the president.

I suppose that the adage of a wise child knowing his own father cuts both ways; but I answered boldly, that I'd swear to the best of my belief, — a reservation, however, that excited a discussion of three-quarters of an hour, the point being at last ruled in my favor.

I am bound to say that there was a great deal of legal learning displayed in the controversy, — a vast variety of authorities cited, from King David downwards; and although at one time matters seemed going against me, the red-eyed man turned the balance in my favor, and it was agreed that I was the father of my own son. If I knew but all, it might have been better for me there had been a hitch in the case. But I am anticipating.

There now arose another dispute, on a point of law, I

believe, and which was, what degree of responsibility —
there were fourteen degrees, it seems, in the Pandects — I
stood in as regarded the present suit. From the turn the
debate took, I began to suspect we might all of us have
to plead to our responsibilities in the other world ere it could
be finished; but the red-eyed man, who seemed the shrewdest of them all, cut the matter short by proposing that I
should be invited — that's the phrase — to say so much as
I pleased in the question before the Court.

"Yes, yes," assented the president. "Let him relate the
affair." And the whole bar and the audience seemed to re-
echo the words.

You know me well, Tom, and you can vouch for it that
I never had any objection to telling a story. It was, in
truth, a kind of weakness with me, and some used to say
that I was getting into the habit of telling the same ones
too often. Be that as it may, I never was accused of relat-
ing a garbled, broken, and disjointed tale, and for the honor
of my anecdotic powers, I resolved not to do so.

"My Lord," said I, "I'm like the knife-grinder, — I have
no story!"

Bad luck to my illustration, it took half an hour to show
that my identity was not somehow mixed up with a wheel
and a grinding-stone!

"Let him relate the affair," said the president, once
more; and this time his voice and manner both proclaimed
that his patience was not to be trifled with.

"Relate what?" asked I, tartly.

"All that you know, — anything you have heard," whispered Van, who was trembling for my rashness.

"My Lord," said I, "of myself I know nothing; I was
in bed all the time."

"He was in bed all the time," said the president to the
others.

"In bed," said red eyes; "let us see;" and he turned
over a file of documents before him for several minutes.
"Dodd père swears that he was in bed from the 7th of
February, which is the first entry here, to the 19th of May,
inclusive."

"I swear no such thing, my Lord," cried I.

" What does he swear, then?" asked the small judge.

" Let us hear his own version; tell us unreservedly all that you know," said the president, who really spoke as if he compassionated my embarrassment.

" My Lord," said I, " there is nothing would give me more pleasure than to display the candor you require; but when I assure you that I actually know nothing — "

" Know nothing, sir!" interposed the president. " Do you mean to tell this Court that you are, and were, in total ignorance of every part of your son's conduct, — that you never heard of his difficulties, nor of his efforts to meet them?"

" If hearsay be sufficient, then," said I, " you shall have it;" and so, taking a long breath, for I saw a weary road before me, I began thus, the amanuensis occasionally begging of me a slight halt to keep up: —

" It was about five or six weeks ago, my Lord, we — that is, Mrs. D., the girls, James, and myself — made an excursion to the field of Waterloo, filled by the very natural desire to see a spot so intimately associated with our country's glory. I will not weary you with any detail of disappointment, nor deplore the total absence of everything that could revive recollections of that great day. In fact, except the big lion with his tail between his legs, there is nothing symbolic of the nations engaged."

I waited a moment here, Tom, to see how they took this; but they never winced, and so I perceived my shell exploded harmlessly.

" We prowled about, my Lord, for two or three hours, and at last reached Hougoumont, in time to take shelter against a tremendous storm which just then broke over us; and there it was that James accidentally came in contact with the young gentleman whom I may not wrongfully call the cause of all our misfortunes. It would appear that they began discussing the battle, with all the natural prejudices of the two conflicting sides. I will not affirm that James was very well read on the subject; indeed, my impression is that his stock of information was principally derived from a representation he had witnessed by an equestrian troop at home, and where Bony, after galloping twice round the circus, throws himself on his knees and begs for mercy, — a fact so strongly impressed upon his memory that he insisted the Frenchman should receive it as historical. The dispute, it would seem, was not conducted within the legitimate limits of debate; they waxed angry, and the Frenchman, after a fierce provocation, set off into the thickest of the storm rather than endure the further discussion."

"This seems to me, sir," interposed the president, "to be perfectly irrelevant to the matter before us. The Court accords the very widest latitude to explanations, but if they really have no bearing on the case in hand, — if, as it appears to my learned brethren and myself, this polemic on a battle has no actual connection with your son's difficulties — "

"It's the very source and origin of them, my Lord," broke I in. "He has no embarrassment which does not date from that incident and that hour."

"In that case you may proceed, sir," said he, blandly; and I went on.

"I do not mean to say, my Lord, that all that followed was inevitable; nor that, with cooler heads and calmer tempers, the whole affair could not have been arranged; but James is hot, mighty hot, — the Celt is strong in him. He really likes a 'shindy,' not like some chaps for the notoriety of it, — not because it gets into the newspapers, and makes a noise, — but he likes it for itself, and for its own intrinsic merits, as one might say. And I may remark here, my Lord, that the Irishman is, perhaps, the only man in Europe that understands fighting in this sense; and this trait, if rightly considered, will give a strong clew to our national character, and will explain the general failure of all our attempts at revolution. We take so much diversion in a row that we quite forget it's only the means to an end. We have, so to say, so much fun on the road that we lose sight of the place we were going to.

"I don't know, Tom, how much further I might have gone on in my analytical researches into our national character; but the interpreter cut me short, by assuring the Court that he was totally unable to follow me. In the nar-

rative parts of my discourse he was good enough; but it
seemed that my reflections, and my general remarks on
men and manners, were a cut above him. I was therefore
warned to " try back " to the line of my story, which I did
accordingly.

" As for the affair itself, my Lord," resumed I, " I understand from eyewitnesses that it was most respectably and
discreetly conducted. James was put up with his face to
the west, so that Roger had the sun on him. The tools
were beauties. It was a fine May morning, mellow, and
not too bright. There was nothing wanting to make the
scene impressive, and, I may add, instructive. Roger's
friend gave the word — one, two, three — bang went both
pistols together, and poor James received the other's fire
just here, — between the bone and the artery, so Seutin
described it, — a critical spot, I 'm sure."

" Dodd père," said the president, solemnly, " you are trifling with the patience of the tribunal! " A grave edict,
which the other judges responded to by a majestic inclination of the head.

" If you are not," resumed he, slowly, and with great
emphasis, — " if you are not a man of weak intellects and
deficient reasoning powers, the conduct you have pursued
is inexcusable, — it is a high contempt! "

" And we shall teach you, sir," said the red-eyed, " that
no pretence of national eccentricity can weigh against the
claims of insulted justice."

" Ay, sir," chimed in number three, who had not spoken
before, " and we shall let you feel that the majesty of the
law in this country is neither to be assailed by covert impertinence nor cajoled by assumed ignorance."

" My Lords," said I, " all this rebuke is a riddle to me.
You asked me to tell you a story; and if it be not a very
connected and consistent one, the fault is not mine."

" Let him stand committed for contempt," said the president. " The Petits Carmes may teach him decorum."

Now, Tom, the Petits Carmes is Newgate, no less! and
you may imagine my feelings at this announcement, particularly as I saw the clerk busily taking down, from dic-
tation, a little history of my offence and its penalty. I

turned to look for Van in my sore distress, and there he
was, searching the volumes, briefs, and records, to find,
as he afterwards said, "some clew to what I had been
saying."

"By Heaven!" cried I, losing all patience, "this is too
bad. You urge me into a long account of what I know
nothing, and then to rescue *your* own ignorance, you declare
me impertinent. There is not a lawyer's clerk in Ireland,
there is no pettifogging practitioner for half-crown fees,
there's not a brat that carries a blue bag down the Bachelor's Walk, could n't teach you all three. You go through
some of the forms, but you know nothing of the facts of
justice. You sit up there, like three stucco-men in mourning, — a perfect mockery of — "

I was not suffered to finish, Tom, for, at a signal from
the president, two gendarmes seized me on either side, and,
notwithstanding some demonstrations of resistance, led me
off to prison. Ay, I must write the word again — to prison!
Kenny I. Dodd, of Dodsborough, Justice of the Peace, and
chairman of the Union of Bruff, committed to jail like a
common felon!

I'm sorry I suffered my feelings to get the better — perhaps I ought to say the worse — of me. Now that it's all
over, it were better that I had not knocked down the turnkey, and kicked Vanhoegen out of my cell. It would have
been both more discreet and more decorous, to have submitted patiently. I know it's what *you* would have done, Tom,
and trusted to your action for damages to indemnify you;
but I'm hasty, that's the fact; and if I wanted to deny
it, the state of the jailer's nose, and my own sprained
thumb, would give evidence against me. But are there
no allowances to be made for the provocation? Perhaps
not for a simple assault; but if I had killed the turnkey,
I'm certain the jury would discover the "circonstances
attenuantes."

Partly out of respect to my own feelings, partly out of
regard to yours, I have not put the words "Petits Carmes"
at the top of this letter; but truth will out, Tom, and
the real fact is that I date the present from cell No. 65, in
the common prison of Brussels! Is not that a pretty con-

fession? Is not that a new episode in this Iliad of enjoyment, cultivation, and Heaven knows what besides, that
Mrs. D. projected by our tour on the Continent? But I
swear to you, solemnly, as I write this, that, if I live to get
back, I'll expose the whole system of foreign travel. I
don't think I could write a book, and it's hard nowadays to
find a chap to put down one's own sentiments fairly and
honestly, neither overlaying them with bits of poetry, nor

explaining them away by any garbage of his own; so that,
maybe, I'll not be able to come out hot-pressed and lettered;
but if the worst comes to it, I'll go about the country giving
lectures. I'll hire an organ-man to play at intervals, and
I'll advertise, "Kenny Dodd on Men and Manners abroad
— Evenings with Frenchmen, and Nights with Distinguished
Belgians." I'll show up their cookery, their morals, their
modesty, their sense of truth, and their notions of justice.
And though I well know that I'll expose myself to the everlasting hate of a legion of hairdressers, dancing-masters, and
white-mice men, I'll do it as sure as I live. I have heard

you and Peter Belton wax warm and eloquent about the disgrace to our laws in permitting every kind of quackery to prevail unhindered; but what quackery was ever the equal to this taste for the Continent? If people ate Morison's pills like green peas, they would n't do themselves as much moral injury as by a month abroad! And if I were called before a committee of the House to declare, on my conscience, what I deemed the most pernicious reading of the day, I 'd say — Murray's Handbooks! I give you this under my hand and seal. That fellow — Murray, I mean — has got up a kind of Pictorial Europe of his own, with bits of antiquarianism, history, poetry, and architecture, that serves to convince our vulgar, vagabondizing English that they are doing a refined thing in coming abroad. He half persuades them that it is not for cheap champagne and red partridges they 're come, but to see the Cathedral of Cologne and the Dome of St. Peter's, till he breeds up a race of conceited, ill-informed, prating coxcombs, that disgrace us abroad and disgust us at home.

I think I see your face now, and I half hear you mutter, "Kenny's in one of his fits of passion;" and you 'd be right, too, for I have just upset my ink-bottle over the table, and there 's scarcely enough left to finish this scrawl, as I must reserve a little for a few lines to Mrs. D. Apropos to that same, Tom, I don't know how to break it to her that I 'm in a jail, for her feelings will be terribly shocked at first; not but, between you and me, before a year 's over, she 'll make it a bitter taunt to me whenever we have a flareup, and remind me that, for all my justiceship of the peace, I was treated like a common felon in Brussels!

I believe that the best thing I can do is to send for Jellicot, since Vanhoegen and Draek have sent to say that they retire from my cause, "reserving to themselves all liberty of future action as regards the injury personally sustained;" which means that they require ten pounds for the kicking. Be it so!

When I have seen Jellicot, I 'll give you the result of the interview, that is, if there be any result; but my friend J. is a lawyer of the lawyers, and it is not only that he keeps his right hand on terms of distance with his left, but I don't

believe that the thumb and the forefinger of the same side
are ever acquainted.   He is very much that stamp of man
your English Protestants call a Jesuit.   God help them,
little they know what a real Jesuit is!

It's now a quarter to two in the morning, and I sit down
to finish this with a heavy heart, and certainly no inclination
for sleep.   I don't know where to begin, nor how to tell
you, what has happened; but the short of it is, Tom, I'm
half ruined.   Jellicot has been here for hours and gone over
the whole case; he received the papers from D. and V.;
and, indeed, everything considered, he has done the thing
kindly and feelingly.   I'm sure my head would n't stand the
task of telling you all the circumstances; the matter resolves
itself simply into this: The "affaire de Dodd fils," instead
of being James's duel, as I thought, is a series of actions
against him for debt, amounting to upwards of two thousand
pounds sterling!   There is not an extravagance, from the
ballet to the betting-book, that he has not tasted; and
saddle-horses, suppers, velvet waistcoats, jewelry, and
gimcracks are at this moment dancing an infernal reel
through my poor brain.
He has contrived, in less than three months, to condense
and concentrate wickedness enough for a lifetime; this is
technically called "going fast."   Egad, I should say it's a
pace far too quick to last with any man, much less with the
son of a broken-down Irish gentleman!   You would not believe that the boy could know the very names of the things
that he appears to have reckoned as mere necessaries of
daily life; and how he contrived to raise money and contract loans — a thing that has been a difficulty to myself all
my life long — is clean beyond me to explain.   I'll get a
copy of the "claims" and send it over to you, and I feel
that your astonishment will equal my own.   It would appear
that the young vagabond talked as if the Barings were his
next of kin, and actually took delight in squandering money!
Only think!   all the time I believed he was hard at work at
his French lessons, it was rattling a dice-box he was, and
his education for the Board of Trade was going on in the
side-scenes of the opera!   Vickars has been the cause of

all this. If he'd have kept his promise, the boy would n't
have been ruined with rascally companions and spendthrift
associates.

Where's the money to come from, Tom? Have you any
device in your head to get us out of this scrape? I suppose
some, at least, of the demands will admit of abatement, and
Lazarus, they say, always takes a fourth of his claim. You
can estimate the pleasant game of cross-purposes I was playing all yesterday with the Court of Cassation, and what a
chaotic mass of rubbish the field of Waterloo and the duel
must have appeared in an action for debt! But why did n't
they apprise me of what I was there for? Why did they go
on with their ridiculous demand, "Racontez l'affaire"?
Recount what? What should I know of the nefarious dealings of Shadrach, Meshach, and Abed-nego? They torment
me for six weeks by a daily examination, till it would be
nothing singular if I became monomaniac, and could discuss
no other theme than a duel and a gunshot wound, and then,
without the slightest suggestion of a change, they launch me
into a thing like a Court of Bankruptcy!

It appears that I have been committed for three days for
my "contempt," and before that time elapses, there is no
resource in Belgian law to compel them to bring up the body
of Kenny Dodd; so that here I must stay, "chewing," as
the poet says, "the cud of sweet and bitter fancy." Not
that I have not a great deal of business to transact in this
interval. Jellicot's papers would fill a cart; besides which,
I have in contemplation a letter for Mrs. D. that will, I suspect, astonish her. I mean briefly, but clearly, to place
before her the state we are in, and her own share in bringing
us to it. I'll let her feel that her own extravagance has
given the key-note to the family, and that she alone is to
blame for this calamity. Among the many fine things
promised me for coming abroad, she forgot to say that I was
to be like Silvio Pellico; but *I*'ll not forget it, Tom!

Then, I have an epistle special for James. He shall feel
that he has a share in the general ruin; for I will write to
Vickars, and ask for a commission for him in a black regiment, or an appointment in the Cape Mounted Rifles, — what
old Burrowes used to call the Blessed Army of Martyrs. I

don't care a jot where he goes! But he'll find it hard to give suppers at four pound a head in the Gambia, and ballet-dancers will scarcely be costly acquaintances on the banks of the Niger! And lastly, I mean to threaten a return to Ireland! "Only threaten," you say: "why not do it in earnest?" As I told you before, I'm not equal to it! I've pluck for anything that can be done by one effort, but I have not strength for a prolonged conflict. I could better jump off the Tarpeian rock than I could descend a rugged mountain! Mrs. D. knows this so well that whenever I show fight, she lays down her parallels so quietly, and prepares for a siege with such deliberation, that I always surrender before she brings up her heavy guns. Don't prate to me of pusillanimity and cowardice! Nobody is brave with his wife. From the Queen of Sheba down to the Duchess of Marlborough, ay, and to our own days, if I liked to quote instances, history teaches the same lesson. What chance have you with one that has been studying every weak point, and every frailty of your disposition, for, maybe, twenty years? Why, you might as well box with your doctor, who knows where to plant the blow that will be the death of you.

I have another "dodge," too, Tom,—don't object to the phrase, for it's quite parliamentary; see Bernal Osborne, *passim*. I'll tell Mrs. D. that I'll put an advertisement in "Galignani," cautioning the public against giving credit to her, or her son, or her daughters; that the Dodd family is come abroad especially for economy, and has neither pretension to affluence, nor any claim to be thought rich. If that won't frighten her, my name is not Kenny! The fact is, Tom, I intend to pursue a very brave line of action for the three days I'm "in," since she cannot have access to me without my own request. You understand me.

I cannot bring my mind to answer your questions about Dodsborough; my poor head is too full of its own troubles. They've just brought me my breakfast,— prison fare,— for in my indignation I have refused all other. Little I used to think, while tasting the jail diet at home, as one of the visitors, that I'd ever be reduced to eating it on less experimental grounds!

I must reserve all my directions about home affairs for

my next; but bestir yourself to raise this money for us. Without some sort of a compromise we cannot leave this; and I am as anxious to " evacuate Flanders" as ever was Uncle Toby! Captain Morris told me, the other day, of a little town in Germany where there are no English, and where everything can be had for a song. The cheapness and the isolation would both be very advisable just now. I 'll get the name of it before I write next.

By the way, Morris is a better fellow than I used to think him: a little priggish or so, but good-hearted at bottom, and honest as the sun. I think he has an eye on Mary Anne. Not that at present he 'd have much chance in that quarter. These foreign counts and barons give a false glitter to society that throws into the shade all untitled gentility; and your mere country gentleman beside them is like your mother's old silver teapot on a table with a show specimen of Elkington's new galvanic plate. Not but if you wanted to raise a trifle of money on either, the choice would be very difficult.

I 'll keep anything more for another letter, and now sign myself

Your old and attached friend,

KENNY I. DODD.

PETITS CARMES, BRUSSELS, Tuesday Morning.

LETTER XII.

MRS. DODD TO MISTRESS MARY GALLAGHER, DODSBOROUGH.

DEAR MOLLY, — The blessed Saints only can tell what sufferings I have gone through the last two days, and it's more
than I'm equal to, to say how it happened! The whole
family has been turned topsy and turvy, and there's not
one of us is n't upside down; and for one like me, that loves
to live in peace and enmity with all mankind, this is a sore
trial!

Many's the time you heard me remark that if it was n't
for K. I.'s temper, and the violence of his passion, that we'd
be rich and well off this day. Time, they say, cures many
an evil; but I'll tell you one, Molly, that it never improves,
and that is a man's wilful nature; on the contrary, they
only get more stubborn and cross-grained, and I often think
to myself, what a blessed time one of the young creatures
must have had of it, married to some patriarch in the Old
Testament; and then I reflect on my own condition, — not
that Kenny Dodd is like anything in the Bible! And now
to tell you, if I'm able, some of my distresses.

You have heard about poor dear James, and how he was
shot; but you don't know that these last six weeks he has
never been off his back, with three doctors, and sometimes
five-and-thirty leeches on him; and what with the torturing
him with new-fashioned instruments, and continued "reple-
tion," as they call it, — if it had n't been for strong wine-
gruel that I gave him, at times, "unknownst," — my sure
belief is that he would n't have been spared to us. This has
been a terrible blow, Molly; but the ways of Providence is
unscrupulous, and we must submit.

Here it is, then. James, like every boy, spent a little
more money than he had, and knowing well his father's

temper, he went to the Jews to help him. They smarted
the poor dear child, who, in his innocent heart, knew nothing of the world and its wicked ways. They made him take
all kinds of things instead of cash, — Dutch tiles, paving-
stones, an altar-piece, and a set of surveying-tools, amongst
the rest; and these he had to sell again to raise a trifle of
cash. Some of them he disposed of mighty well, — particularly the altar-piece, — but on others he lost a good deal,
and, at the end, was a heavy balance in debt. If it had n't
been for the duel, however, he says he 'd have no trouble at
all in "carrying on," — that 's his own word, and I suppose
alludes to the business. Be that as it may, his wound was
his ruin. Nobody knew how to manage his affairs but
himself. It was the very same way with my grandfather,
Maurice Lynch M'Carthy; for when he died there was n't
a soul left could make anything of his papers. There was
large sums in them, — thousands and thousands of pounds
mentioned, — but where they were, and what 's become of
them, we never discovered.

And so with James. There he was, stretched on his bed,
while villains and schemers were working his ruin! The
business came into the courts here, which, from all I can
learn, Molly, are not a bit better than at home with ourselves. Indeed, I believe, wherever one goes, lawyers is
just the same for roguery and rampacity. To be sure, it 's
comfort to think that you can have another, to the full as
bad as the one against you; and if there is any abuse or bad
language going, you can give it as hot as you get it; that 's
equal justice, Molly, and one of the proudest boasts of the
British constitution! And you 'd suppose that K. I., sitting
on the bench for nigh four-and-twenty years, would know
that as well as anybody. Yet what does he do? — you 'll
not believe me when I tell you! Instead of paying one of
these creatures to go in and torment the others, to pick holes
in all he said, and get fellows to swear against them, he
must stand out, forsooth, and be his own lawyer! And a
blessed business he made of it! A reasonable man would
explain to the judges how it all was, — that James was a
child; that it was the other day only he was flying a kite
on the lawn at home; that he knew as much about wicked-

ness as K. I. did of paradise; that the villains that led
him on ought to be publicly whipped! Faith, I can fancy,
Molly, it was a beautiful field for any man to display every
commotion of the heart; but what does he do? He gets
up on his legs, — I did n't see, but I 'm told it, — he gets up
on his legs and begins to ballyrag and blackguard all the
courts of justice, and the judges, and the attorneys, down to
the criers, — he spares nobody! There is nothing too dreadful for him to say, and no words too bad to express it in;
till, their patience being all run out, they stop him at last,
and give orders to have him taken from the spot, and
thrown into a dungeon of the town jail, — a terrible old
place, Molly, that goes by the name of the "Petit Carême!"
and where they say the diet is only a thin sheet of paper
above starving.

And there he is now, Molly; and you may picture to
yourself, as the poet says, "what frame he 's in"! The
news reached me when we were going to the play. I was
under the hands of the hairdresser, and I gave such a
screech that he jumped back, and burned himself over the
mouth with the curling-irons. Even that was a relief to
me, Molly; for Mary Anne and myself laughed till we
cried again!

I was for keeping the thing all snug and to ourselves
about K. I.; but Mary Anne said we should consult Lord
George, that was then in the house, and going with us to the
theatre. They are a wonderful people, the great English
aristocracy; and if it 's anything more than another distin-
guishes them, 't is the indifference to every kind and description of misfortune. I say this, because, the moment Lord
George heard the story, he lay down on the sofa, and
laughed and roared till I thought he 'd split his sides. His
only regret was that he had n't been there, in the courts, to
see it all. As for James's share of the trouble, he said it
"did n't signify a rush!"

He made the same remark I did myself, — that James was
the same as an infant, and could, consequently, know nothing of the world and its pompous vanities.

"I 'll tell you how to manage it all," said he, "and how
you 'll not only escape all gossip, but actually refute even

the slightest scandal that may get abroad. Say, first of all, that Mr. Dodd is gone over to England — we'll put it in the 'Galignani' — to attend his Parliamentary duties. The Belgian papers will copy it at once. This being done, issue invitations for an evening at home, 'tea and dance,' — that's the way to do it. Say that the governor hates a ball, and that you are just taking the occasion of his absence to see your friends without disturbing *him*. The people that will come to you won't be too critical about the facts. Believe me, the gay company will be the very last to inquire where is the head of the house. I'll take care that you'll have everybody worth having in Brussels, and with Latour's band, and the supper by Dubos, I'd like to see who'll have a spare thought for Mr. Dodd the absent."

I own to you, Molly, the counsel shocked my feelings at first, and I asked my heart, "What will the world say, if it ever comes out that we had our house full of company, and the height of gayety going on, when the head of the family was, maybe, in chains in a dungeon?" "Don't you perceive," says Lord G., "that what I'm advising will just prevent the possibility of all that, — that you are actually rescuing your family, by a master-stroke, from the evil consequences of Mr. D.'s rashness? As to the boldness of the policy," added he, "that is the only merit it possesses." And then he said something about the firing at St. Sebastian above somebody's head, that I didn't quite rightly understand. The upshot was, Molly, I was convinced, not, you may be sure, that I felt any pleasure or gratification in the prospect of a ball under such trying circumstances, but just as Lord G. said, I felt I was "rescuing the family."

When we came home from the play, — for we went with heavy hearts, I assure you, though we afterwards laughed a great deal, — we set about writing the invitations for "Our Evening;" and although James and Mary Anne assisted Lord G., it was nigh daybreak when we were done. You'll ask, where was Caroline? And you might well ask; but as long as I live I'll never forget her unnatural conduct! It isn't that she opposed everything about the ball, but she had the impudence to say to my face "that hitherto we had been only ridiculous, but that this act would be one of down-right shame and disgrace." Her language to Lord George was even worse, for she told him that his "counsel was a very sorry requital for the generous hospitality her father had always extended to him." Where the hussey got the words so glibly, I can't imagine; but she, that rarely speaks at all, talked away with the fluency of a lawyer. As to helping us to address the notes, she vowed she'd rather cut her fingers off; and what made this worse was, that she's the only one of them knows the genders in French, and whether a *soirée* is a man or a woman!

You may imagine the trouble of the next day; for in order to have the ball come off before K. I. was out, we were only able to give two days' notice. Little the people that come to your house to dance or to sup know or think what a deal of trouble — not to say more — it costs to give a ball. Lord George tells me that even the Queen herself always gives it in another house, so she's not put out of her way with the preparations, — and, to be sure, what is more natu-ral? — and that she wouldn't like to be exposed to the tur-moil of taking down beds, hanging lustres, fixing sconces, raising a platform for the music, and settling tables for the supper. I'm sure and certain, if she only knew what it was to pass such a day as yesterday was with me, she'd never have a larger party than that lord that's always in waiting, and the ladies of the bedroom! As for regular meals, Molly, we had none. There was a ham and cold chickens in the lobby, and a veal pie and some sherry on the back stairs; and that's the way we breakfasted, dined, and supped. To be sure, we laughed heartily all the time, and I never saw Mary Anne in such spirits. Lord George was greatly struck with her, — I saw it by his manner, — and I wouldn't be a bit surprised if something came of it yet!

I have little time to say more now, for I'm called down to see the flowerpots and orange-trees that's to line the hall and the stairs; but I'll try and finish this by post hour.

As I see that this cannot be despatched to-day, I'll keep it over, to give you a "full and true" account of the ball, which Lord George assures me will be the greatest *fête* Brussels has seen this winter; and, indeed, if I am to judge from the preparations, I can well believe him! There are seven men cooks in the kitchen making paste and drinking sherry in a way that's quite incredible, not to speak of an elderly man in my own room that's doing the M'Carthy arms in spun-sugar for a temple that is to represent Dodsborough, in the middle of the table, with K. I. on the top of it, holding a flag, and crying out something in French that means welcome to the company. Poor K. I., 'tis something else he's thinking of all the time!

Then, the whole stairs and the landing is all one bower of camellias and roses and lilies of the valley, brought all the way from Holland for another ball, but, by Lord George's ingenuity, obtained by us. As for ice, Molly, you'd think my dressing-room was a Panorama of the North Pole; and there's every beast of that region done in strawberries or lemon, with native creatures, the color of life, in coffee or chocolate. The music will be the great German Brass Band, fifty-eight performers, and two Blacks with cymbals. They're practising now, and the noise is dreadful! Carts are coming in every moment with various kinds of eatables, for I must tell you, Molly, they don't do things here the way we used at Dodsborough. Plenty of cold roast chickens, tongues, and sliced ham, apple-pies, tarts, jelly, and Spanish flummery, with Naples biscuits and a plum-cake, is a fine supper in Ireland; and if you begin with sherry, you can always finish with punch: but here there's nothing that ever was eaten they won't have. Ice when they're hot, soup when they're chilly, oyster patties and champagne continually during the dancing, and every delicacy under the sun afterwards on the supper-table.

There's nothing distresses me in it all but the Polka, Molly. I can't learn it. I always slide when I ought to hop, and where there's a hop I duck down in spite of me! And whether it's the native purity of an Irishwoman, or that I never was reared to it, I can't say; but the notion of a man's arm round me keeps me in a flutter, and I'm always looking about to see how K. I. bears it. I suppose, however, I'll get through it well enough, for Lord George is to be my partner; and as I know K. I.'s "safe," my mind is more easy.

Perhaps it 's the shortness of the invitation, but there 's a
great many apologies coming in.   The English Ambassador
won't come.   Lord G. says it 's all the better, for the Tories
are going out, and it will be a great service to K. I. with
the Whigs if it 's thought he did n't invite him!   This may
be true, but it 's no reason in life for the Austrian, the
French, the Prussian, and the Spanish Ministers sending
excuses.   Lord George, however, thinks it 's the terrible
state of the Continent explains it all, and the Despotic
Powers are so angry with Lord Dudley Stuart and Roebuck
that they like to insult the English!   If it be so, they
have n't common-sense.   Kenny James has taken a turn
with all their parties, and much good it has done him!

Lord G. and Mary Anne are in high spirits, notwithstanding these disappointments, for "the Margravine" is
coming, — at least, so he tells me; but whether the Margravine be a man or woman, Molly, or only something to eat,
I don't rightly know, and I 'm ashamed to ask.

I have just been greatly provoked by a visit from Captain
Morris, who called twice this morning, and at last insisted
on seeing me.   He came to entreat me, he says, "if not to
abandon, at least to put off, our ball till Mr. Dodd's return."
I tried to browbeat him, Molly, for his impertinent interference, but it would n't do; and he showed me that he knew
perfectly well where K. I. was, — a piece of information
that, of course, he obtained from Caroline.   Oh, Molly
dear, when one's own flesh and blood turns against them, —
when children forget all the lessons you 've been teaching
them from infancy, — it 's a sore, sore trial!   Not but I have
reason to be thankful.   Mary Anne and James are like part
of myself; nothing mean or little-minded about *them*, but
fine, generous, confiding creatures, — happy for to-day,
hopeful for to-morrow!

When I mentioned to Lord G. what Morris came about,
he only laughed, and said, "It was a clever dodge of the
half-pay, — he wanted an invitation;" and I see now that
such must have been his object.   The more one sees of
mankind, the greater appears their meanness; and in my
heart I feel how unsuited guileless, simple-hearted creatures
like myself are to combat against the stratagems and

ambuscades of this wicked world. Not that little Morris
will gain much by his morning's work, for Mary Anne says
that Lord George will never suffer him to get on full pay as
long as he lives. "A friend in need is a friend indeed,"
Molly, more particularly when he's a lord.

The Margravine is a princess, Molly. I've just found it
out; for James is to receive her at the foot of the stairs,
Mary Anne and myself on the lobby. Lord G. says she
must have whist at half-"Nap." points, and always play
with her own "Gentleman-in-Waiting." She never goes
out on any other conditions. But he says, "She's cheap
even at that price, for an occasion like the present;" and
maybe he's right.

No more now, for my gown is come to be tried on.

    *   *   *   *   *   *   *   *   *

    *   *   *   *   *   *   *   *   *

Dear Molly, I'll try and finish this, since, maybe, it's
the last lines you'll ever receive from your attached friend.
Three days have elapsed since I put my hand to paper, and
three such days, I'll be bound, no human creature ever
passed. Out of one fit of hysterics into another, and taking the strongest stimulants, with no more effect than if
they were water! My screeches, I am told, were dreadful,
and there's scarcely one of the family can't show the mark
of my nails; and this is what K. I. has brought me to.
You know well what I used to suffer from him at Dodsborough, and the terrible scenes we always had when the
Christmas bills came in; but it's all nothing, Molly, to
what has happened here. But as my Uncle Joe said, no
good ever came out of a "mess-alliance."

My moments are few, so I'll be brief. The ball was
beautiful, Molly; there never was the like of it for elegance
and splendor! For great names, rank, fashion, beauty,
and jewels, it was, they tell me, far beyond the Court, because we had a great many people who, from political reasons, refuse to go to Leopold, but who had no prejudices
against your humble servant; for, strange enough, they
have Orangemen here as well as in Ireland! Princes, dukes,
counts, and generals came pouring in, all shining with stars
and crosses, blue and red ribbons, and keys worked on

their coat-tails, till nearly twelve o'clock. There were, then, nigh seven hundred souls in the house, eating, dancing, drinking, and enjoying themselves; and a beautiful sight it was: everybody happy, and thinking only of pleasure. Mary Anne looked elegant, and many remarked that we must be sisters. Oh dear, if they only saw me now!

There was a mazurka that lasted till half-past one, for it's a dance that everybody must take out each in turn, and you'd fancy there was no end to it, for, indeed, they never do seem tired of embracing and holding each other round the waist; but Lord George came to say that the Margravine had finished her whist and wanted her supper, so down we must go at once.

James was to take her Supreme Highness, and the Prince of Dammiseisen — a name that always made me laugh — was to take *me ;* but he is a great man in Germany, and had a kingdom of his own till he was ."modified " by Bonaparte, which means, as Lord George says, that "he took it out in money." But why do I dwell on these things? Down we went, Molly, — down the narrow stairs, — for the supper was laid out below; and a terrible crush it was, for, strange as it may seem, your grand people are just as anxious to get good places as any; and I saw a duke fighting his way in, just like old Ted Davis at Dodsborough!

When we came to the last flight of stairs, the crowd was awful, and the banisters creaked, and the wood-work groaned, so that I thought it was going to give way; and instead of James moving on in front, he pressed back upon us, and increased the confusion, for we were forced forward by hundreds behind us.

"What's the matter, James?" said I. "Why don't you go on?"

"I'd rather be excused," said he. "It's like Donnybrook Fair, down there, — a regular shindy!"

It was no less, Molly; for although the hall was filled with servants, there were two men armed with sticks, laying about them like mad, and fighting their way towards the supper-room.

"Who are those wretches?" cried I; "why don't they turn them out?"

The words were n't well out, my dear Molly, when the door gave way, and the two, trampling down all before them, passed into the room. From that moment it was crash after crash! Lamps, lustres, china, glass, plates, dishes, fruit, and confectionery flying on all sides! In less time than I 'm writing it, the table was cleared, and of the elegant temple there was n't a bit standing. I just got inside the door to see the M'Carthy arms in smithereens! and K. I. — for it was *him!* — dancing over them, with that little blackguard Paddy Byrne smashing everything round him! I went off into fits, Molly, and never saw more; and, indeed, I wish with all my heart that I never came to again, if what they tell me be only true. K. I., it seems, no sooner demolished the supper than he set to work on the company. He snatched off the Margravine's wig, and beat her with it, kicking Dammiseisen and two other princes into the street. They say that many of the nobility leaped out of the first-pair windows, and one fat old gentleman, a chamberlain to the King of Bavaria, was caught by a lamp iron, and hung there for twenty minutes, with a mob shouting round him!

This all came of the Belgians letting out K. I. at one o'clock, which, according to their reckoning, was the end of his three days.

I 'm getting another attack, so I must conclude. We left Brussels the next morning, and arrived here the same night. I don't know where we are going, and I don't care. K. I. has never had the face to come near me since his infamous conduct, and I hope, for the little time I may be spared on this side of the grave, not to see him again. Mary Anne is in bed, too, and nearly as bad as myself; and as for Caroline, I would n't let her into the room! Lord George took James away to his own lodgings till K. I. learns to behave more like a Christian; but when that may be is utterly beyond

Your afflicted and disgraced friend,
JEMIMA DODD.

HÔTEL D'ANGLETERRE, LIÈGE.

* * * * * * * * *
* * * * * * * * *

Dear Molly, I open this to say that I have made my will; for, if Divine Providence does n't befriend me, your poor Jemima will be in paradise before this reaches you! I have left you my black satin with the bugles, and my brown bombazine, which, when it is dyed, will be very nice mourning for common wear. I also bequeath to you the things you'll find in the oak press in my own room, and ten silver spoons, and a fish-knife marked with the M'Carthy arms, which, not to be too particular, I have put down in the will as "plate and linen." I leave you, besides, my book of "Domestic Cookery," "The Complete Housewife," and the "Way to Glory," by St. Francis Xavier. There are marks all through them with my own pen; and be particular to observe the receipt for snow pancakes, and the prayers for a "Plenary" after Candlemas.

It will be a comfort to your feelings to know that I am departing from this life in peace and charity with every one. Tell Mat I forgive him the fleece he stole out of the hayloft; and though he swears still he never laid hand on it, who else was there, Molly? You can give Kitty Hogan the old shoes in the closet, for, though she never wears any, she'd like to have them for keepsakes! K. I. cared too little for my peace here to suppose that he will think of my repose hereafter, so that Father John can take the yearling calf and the two ewes out in masses! My feelings is overcoming me, Molly, and I can't go on! — breathing my last, as I am, in a far-away land, and sinking under the cruelty of a hard-hearted man!

I think it would only be a decent mark of respect to my family if the M'Carthy arms was hung up over the door, to show I was n't a Dodd. The crest is an angel sheltering a fox, or a beast like a fox, under his wing; but you'll see it on the spoons. When you sell the piggs — maybe I ought n't to put two g's in them, but my head is wandering — pay old Judy Cobb two-and-sevenpence for the yarn, and say that I won't stop the ninepence out of Betty's wages. Maybe, when I'm gone, they'll begin to see what they've lost, and maybe K. I. will feel it too, when he finds no buttons on his shirts and the strings out of his waistcoat; and what's far worse, nobody to contradict him, and control his wilful nature! That's the very struggle that's killing me now! Nobody knows, nor would believe, the opposition I've given him for twenty years. But *he*'ll feel it, Molly, and that before I'm six weeks in the grave.

I don't know my age to a day or a month, but you can put me down at thirty-nine, and maybe the " Blast of Freedom" would say a word or two about my family. I'd like that far better than to be " deeply regretted," or " to the inexpressible grief of her bereaved relations."

I have made it a last request that my remains are to be sent home, and as I know K. I. won't go to the expense, he'll have to bear all the disgrace of neglecting my dying entreaty. That's my legacy to him, Molly; and if it's not a very profitable one, the " duty " will not be heavy.

Remember me affectionately to everybody, and say that to the last my heart was in my own country; and indeed, Molly, I never did hear so much good about Ireland as since we left it!

I have just taken a draught that has restored me wonderfully. It has a taste of curaçoa, and evidently suits my constitution. Maybe Providence, in his mercy, means to reserve me for more trials and misfortunes; for I feel stronger already, and am going to taste a bit of roast duck, with sage and onions. Betty has done it for me herself.

If I do recover, Molly, I promise you K. I. won't find me the poor submissive worm he has been trampling upon these more than twenty years! I feel more like myself already; the " mixture " is really doing me good.

You may write to me to this place, with directions to be opened by Mary Anne, if I'm no more. The very thought of it overwhelms me. The idea of one's own death is the most terrible of all afflictions; and as for me, I don't think I could ever survive it.

I mean to send for K. I., to take leave of him, and forgive him, before I go. I'm not sure that I'd do so, Molly, if it was n't for the opportunity of telling him my mind about all his cruelty to me, and that I know well what he's at, and that he'll be married again before six months. That's the treachery of men; but there's one comfort, — they are well paid off for it when they marry — as they always do — some young minx of nineteen or twenty. It's exactly what K. I. is capable of; and I mean to show him that I see it, and all the consequences besides.

The mixture is really of service to me, and I feel as if I could take a sleep. Mary Anne will seal this if I'm not awake before post hour.

LETTER XIII.

FROM K. I. DODD TO THOMAS PURCELL, ESQ., OF THE GRANGE, BRUFF.

Liège, Tuesday Evening.

My dear Tom, — Your reproaches are all just, but I really have not had courage to wield a pen these last three weeks, nor have I now patience to go back on the past. Perhaps when we meet — if ever that good time is to come round again — I may be able to tell you something of my final exit from Brussels; but now with the shame yet fresh, and the disgrace recent, I cannot find pluck for it.

Here we are at what they call the "Pavilion," having changed from the Hôtel d'Angleterre yesterday. You must know, Tom, that this same city of Liège is the noisiest, most dinning, hammering, hissing, clanking, creaking, welding, smelting, and furnace-roaring town in Europe. Something like a hundred thousand tinkers are at work every day; and from an egg saucepan to a steam-boiler there is something to be hammered at by every capacity!

You would say that tumult like this might satisfy the most craving appetite for uproar; but not so: the Liègeois are regular gluttons for noise, and they insist upon having Verdi's new opera of "Nabuchodonosor" performed at their great theatre. Now, this same theatre is exactly in front of the Hôtel d'Angleterre, so that when, by dint of time, patience, and a partial dulness of the acoustic nerves, we were getting used to steam-factories and shot-foundries, down comes Verdi on us, with a din and clangor to which even the works of Seraing were like an Æolian harp! Now, of all the Pretenders of these days of especial humbug, with our "Long ranges," Morison's pills and Louis Napoleons, I don't think you could show me a greater charlatan than this same Verdi. I don't pretend to know a bit about music; I only knew two tunes all my life, "God save the King" and "Patrick's Day," and these only because we used to stand up and take off our hats to them in the Dublin theatre; but modulated, soft sounds have always had their effect on me, and I never heard a country girl singing as she beetled her linen beside a river's bank, or listened to the deep bay of an old fox-hound of a clear winter's morning, without feeling that there was something inside of me somewhere that responded to the note. But this fellow is all marrow-bones and cleavers! Trumpets, drums, big fiddles, and bassoons are the softest things he knows. I take it as a providential thing that his music cracks every voice after one season; for before long there will be nobody left in Europe to sing him, except it be the steam-whistle of an express-train!

But we live in strange times, Tom, that's the fact. The day was when our operas used to be taken from real life, — or what authors and poets thought was real life. We had the "Maid of the Mill," and the "Duenna," and "Love in a Village," and a score more, pleasant and amusing enough; and except that there was nothing wrong or incomprehensible in them, perhaps they might have stood their ground. There was the great failure, Tom; everybody could understand them, and nobody need be shocked. Now, the taste is, puzzle a great many, and shock every one!

A grand opera now must be from the Old Testament. Not even drums and kettle-drums would save you, if you have n't Moses or Melchisedek to sit down in white raiment, and see some twenty damsels, with petticoats about as long as a lace ruffle, capering and attitudinizing in a way that ought to make even a patriarch blush. Now, this is all wrong, Tom. The public might be amused without profanity, and even the most inveterate lover of dancing need n't ask David and Uriah for a *pas de deux*. And now, let me remark to you, that a great deal of that so-much-vaunted social liberty abroad is neither more nor less than this same latitude with respect to any and every thing. We at home were bred up to believe that good-breeding mainly consists in a certain reserve, — a cautious deference not alone for the feelings, but even the prejudices of others; that you have no right to offend your neighbor's sense of respect for fifty things that you held cheaply yourself. They reverse all this here. Everybody talks to you of yourself, ay, and of your wife and your mother, as frankly as though they were characters of the heathen mythology: they treat you like a third party in these discussions, and very likely it was a practice of this kind originally suggested the phrase of being "beside oneself."

You'll perhaps remark that my tone is very low and depressed, Tom; and I own to you I feel so. For a man that came abroad to enjoy himself, I am, to say the least, going a mighty strange way about it. The most rigid moralist couldn't accuse me of my epicurism, for I seem to be husbanding my Continental pleasures with a laudable degree of self-denial. Would you like a peep at us? Well, Mrs. D. is over there in No. 19, in bed with fourteen leeches on her temples, and a bottle as big as a black jack of camphor and sal-volatile beside her as a kind of table beverage; Mary Anne and Caroline are somewhere in the dim recesses of the same chamber, silent, if they're not sobbing; James is under lock and key in No. 17, with Ollendorff's Method, and the Gospel of St. John in French; and here am I, trying to indite a few lines, with blast furnaces and brass instruments baying around me, and Paddy Byrne cleaning knives outside the door!

Mrs. D.'s attack is not serious, but it is very distressing. She has got the notion into her head that foreign apothecaries have a general pardon for poisoning, and so she requires that some of us should always take part of her physic before she touches it. The consequence is that I have been going through a course of treatment that would have pushed an elephant rather hard. I can stand some things pretty well; but what they call réfrigérants, Tom, play the devil with me! and I am driven to brandy and water to an extent that I can scarcely call myself quite sober at any time of the day. Were we at home in Dodsborough, there would be none of this; so that here, again, is another of the blessings of our foreign experiences! Ah, Tom! it's all a mistake from beginning to end. You would n't know your old friend if you saw him; and although they 've padded me out, and squeezed me in, I 'm not the man I used to be!

You tell me that I 'm not to expect any more money till November; but you forgot to tell me how I 'm to live without it. We compromised with the Jews for fifteen hundred.

Our "extraordinaries," as the officials would call them, amounted to three more; so that, taking all things into account, we have been living since April last at a trifle more than eleven thousand a year. It 's a mercy that when they sell a man out by the Encumbered Estates Court, they ask no impertinent questions about how he contracted his debts. I 'd cut a sorry figure under such an examination.

We have begun the economy, Tom, and I hope that even you will be satisfied; for although this place is detestable to me, here I 'll stay, if my hearing can stand it, till winter. Mary Anne says we might as well be in Birmingham, and my reply is, I'm quite ready to go there! I own to you I have a kind of diabolical delight in seeing them all nonplussed. There are neither dukes nor marquises here, neither princesses nor ballet-dancers! The most reckless spendthrift could only ruin himself in steam-boilers, gunbarrels, and kitchen-ranges; there's nothing softer than cast-iron in the whole town.

Our rooms are in the third story. James and I dine at the public table. Our only piece of extravagance is the doctor that attends Mrs. D.; and if you saw him, you'd scarcely give him the name of a luxury! I needn't say that there is very little pleasure in all this; indeed, for anything *I* see, I think we might be leading the same kind of life in Kilmainham Jail; and perhaps at last they'll see this themselves, and consent to return home.

I go out for an hour's walk every day, but it does me little good. My usual stroll is to a shot factory, and back by a patent bolt and rivet establishment; but this avoids the theatre, for I own to you Nabucco, as they call him for shortness, shouts in a manner that makes me quite irritable.

James never leaves his room; he's studying hard at last; and although his health would be the better for a little exercise, I'll just leave him to himself. It's right he should pay some penalty for his late conduct. As for the girls, Mary Anne is indignant with me, and only comes to say good-morning and good-night; and Cary, though she tries to look cheerful and happy, is evidently fretting in secret. Betty Cobb takes less trouble to repress her feelings, and goes howling about the hotel like a dog run over by the mail, and is always getting accompanied by strange and inquisitive travellers, who insist upon hearing her sorrows, and occasionally push their inquiries even as far as my room!

Paddy Byrne alone appears to have taken a philosophical view of his position, for he has been drunk ever since we arrived. He usually sleeps in the hall, on the stairs, or the lobbies; and although this saves the cost of a bedroom, the economy is counterbalanced by occasional little reprisals he takes, as stray gentlemen stumble over him with their bed-room candles. At such moments he smashes lamps and china ornaments, for which his wages will require a long sequestration to clear off. And now a word about home. Our English tenant, you tell me, is getting tired of Dods-borough; we guessed how it would be already. "He thinks the people lazy"! Ask him, did he ever try to cut turf, with two meals of wet potatoes per diem? "They are bigoted and superstitious too." How much better would they be if they knew all about Lord Rosse's telescope? "They won't give up their old barbarous ways." Is n't that the very boast of the Conservative party? Is n't that what Disraeli is preaching every day and every hour? — "Fall back upon this, — fall back upon that, — think of the spirit of your ancestors." Now they say, our ancestors yoked their horses by the tails to save a harness. It's rather hard that all the "progress," as they call it, must begin with the poor. It's a dead puzzle to me, Tom, to explain one thing. All the moralists, from the earliest ages, keep crying up humility, and telling you that true nobility of soul consists in self-denial and moderation, simple tastes, and so on; and yet, what is the great reproach they bring against Paddy? Is n't it that he is satisfied with the potato? There's the head and front of his offence. That he does n't want beef, like the Englishman, — nor soup and three courses, like "Mounseer" — nor sauerkraut and roast veal, like a German; "cups and cold water" being the food of a fellow that could thrash the whole three of them all round, and think it mighty good fun besides.

Poor Dan used to say that he was the best abused man in Europe; but I'll tell you that the potato is the best abused vegetable in the universal globe. From the "Times" down to the Scotch farmers, it's one hue-and-cry after it, — "The filthy root" — "The disgusting tuber," — "The source of all Irish misery," — "The father of famine, and mother of fever," — on they go, blackguarding the only food of the people, till at last, as if it were a judgment on their bad tongues, it took to rot in the ground, and left us with noth-ing to eat. Now, Tom, you know as well as myself, Ireland is not a wheat country; it's one year in three that we can raise a crop of it; for our climate is as treacherous as the English Government. I hope you would n't have us live on oats, like the Scotch; nor on Indian corn, like the savages; so what is there like the potato? And then, how easy the culture, and how simple the cookery! It does well in every soil, and agrees well with every constitution. It feeds the peasant, it fattens the pig, it rears the children, and supports the chickens. What can compare with that?

Do you know that there's no cant of the day annoys me more than that cry about model farming, and green crops, and rotations, and subsoiling, and so on. The whole ingenuity of mankind would seem devoted to ascertaining how much a bullock can eat, and how little will feed a laborer. Stuff one and starve the other, and you may be the President of an Agricultural Society, and Chairman of your Union. What treatises we have upon stock, and improving the breed of boars! Will you tell me who ever thought of turning the same attention to the condition of the people? and I 'm sure, if you go into the county Galway, you 'll soon acknowledge that they need it. "Look at that lanky pig," calls out the Scotch steward, in derision; "his snout and his legs are fit for a greyhound!" But I say, "Look at Paddy, there. His neck is shrivelled and knotted, like an old vine-tree; his back rounded, and his legs crooked; all for want of care and nourishment. Is all your sympathy to be kept for the sheep, and have you none for the shepherd?"

I made some memorandums for you about Belgian farming, but Mary Anne curled her hair with them. It 's no loss to you, however, for their system would n't do with us. Small tenures and spade husbandry do mighty well here, because there are great cities within a few miles of each other, and agriculture takes somewhat the character of market gardening; but their success would be far different were there long distances to be traversed with the produce.

This country is certainly prospering; but I 'm not so certain that it can continue to do so. Their industry is now stimulated to a high state of productiveness, because they are daily extending their railroads; but there must come an end to that, and it strikes me that a country that only deals with itself is pretty much what the adage says

of the "man that is his own doctor." They are now, however, enjoying what your political economists all agree in
pronouncing to be the great test of prosperity. Everything
has nearly doubled in price: house rent, meat, vegetables,
wages, clothes, luxuries of all kind, and, of course, taxation. I own to you I never clearly understood this problem; it always seemed to me as if a whole population took
to walk upon stilts, for the pleasure of thinking themselves
nine feet high.

These matters put me in mind of Vickars. I now see
that I was wrong in not going over to the election. His
tone is quite changed, and he writes to me as if I were a
deputation from the distressed hand-loom weavers. He
acknowledges mine of the 5th ult., and he deplores, and
regrets, and feels constrained to remind me, and so on,
ending with being "humble and obedient," — two things
that I believe his own mother never found him. The fact
is, Tom, he's in Parliament, and he is a Lord of the Treasury, and he does n't care a brass farthing for one of us.
Do you remark how the Ministerial papers praise the Government for promoting Irishmen? It is not on the ground
of their superior capacity for office, their readiness and
natural ability. Nothing of the kind; it is simply the
unbounded generosity of the administration, and perhaps as
a proof of their humility! They put an Irishman in the
Cabinet, just as the Roman Conqueror took a slave in his
chariot, to show that they don't intend to forget themselves!

I wish "Punch" would make a picture of it. Pat with
his pipe in his mouth beside the Premier; the roguish leer
of the eye, the careless ease of his crossed legs, and small-
clothes open at the knee, would be a grand contrast to the
high-bred air of his companion.

Don't bother me any more about the salmon weirs; make
the best bargain you can, and I'll be satisfied. It appears
to me, however, the more laws we have, the less fish we
catch. In my father's time there was no legislation at all,
and salmon was a penny a pound. The fish seem to hate
Acts of Parliament just as much as ourselves. And, talking
of that, I'm glad we're out of our scrape with the Yankees.

Depend upon it, all the cod that ever was salted would n't
pay for one collision.   It would n't be like any other war,
Tom, for French and Russians, Austrians and Italians, have
each their separate peculiarities, — giving certain advantages in certain situations; but we — that is, English and
Americans — fight exactly in the same way.   Each knows
every dodge of the other, — long sixty-fives and thirty-twos,
boarders, riflemen, riggers, — all alike.   It 's the old story
of the Kilkenny cats, and I 'm greatly afraid our "tail"
would be nearly as much mauled as Jonathan's.

The longer I live, the nearer I find myself drawing to
these Yankees; and I 've some notion of going over there to
have a look at them.   They tell me that the worst thing
about them is the air of gravity, even of depression, that
prevails, — a strange fault, considering how many Irish
there are amongst them; but I suppose Paddy is like the
rest of the world, and he loses his fun when he gets prosperous.   There was Tom Martin, that went our circuit, and
there was n't as pleasant a fellow at the bar till he got into
business.   There was no good asking him to dinner after
that; as he owned himself, "he kept his jokes for his
clients."   Now, there may be something like this the case
in America; at all events, Tom, I 'd have one advantage
there, — I 'd know the language, what I 'm never likely to do
here; not but I 'm doing my best every day at the *table
d'hôte;* occasionally, perhaps, with some sacrifice of the
"propers;" but as a foreigner is too polite to laugh, the
stranger has little chance to learn.   For my own part, I 'd
rather they 'd tell me when I was wrong, and give me some
hope of going right.   I 'd think it more friendly of a man
to say, "Kenny Dodd, you 're going into a hole," than if he
smiled and simpered, and assured me that I was in the
middle of the path, and getting on beautifully.

And there is n't any good-nature in it; not a bit.   It 's
not good-heartedness, nor kindness, nor amiability.   I don't
believe a word of it; because the chap that does it is n't
thinking of you at all, — he 's only minding himself; he 's
fancying how he 's delighting you, or captivating your wife
or your sister-in-law; or, if it 's a woman, she wants to
fascinate or make a fool of you.

The real and essential difference between us and all foreigners is that they are always thinking of what effect they
are producing; they never for a single moment forget that
there is an audience. Now we, on the contrary, never
remember it. Life with them is a drama, in all the blaze
of wax-lights and a crowded house; with us, it's a day-
rehearsal, and we slip about, mumbling our parts, getting
through the performance, unmindful of all but our own share
in it.

More than half of what is attributed to rudeness and
unsociality in us, springs out of the simple fact that we
do not care to obtrude even our politeness when there seems
no need of it. *Our* civilities are like a bill of exchange,
that must represent value one day or other. *Theirs* are
like the gilt markers on a card-table: they have a look of
money about them, but are only counterfeit. Perhaps this
may explain why our women like the Continent so much
better than ourselves. All this mock interchange of courtesy amuses and interests *them ;* it only worries *us.*

To come back to Vickars. He'll do nothing for James.
His "own list is quite full;" he "has mentioned his name,"
he says, "to the Secretary for the Colonies," and will speak
of him "at the Home Office." But I know what that means.
The party is safe for the present, and don't need our dirty
voices for many a day to come. It's distressing me to find
out what to do with him. Can you get me any real information about the gold diggings? Is it a thing that would
suit him? His mother, I know well, would never consent
to the notion of his working with his hands; but, upon my
conscience, if it's his head he's to depend on, he'll fare
worse! He is very good-looking, six foot one and a half,
strong as a young bull; and to ride an unbroken horse,
drive a fresh team, to shoot a snipe, or hook a salmon, I'll
back him against the field. I hear, besides, he's a beautiful
cue at billiards. But what's the use of all these at the
Board of Trade, if he had even the luck to get there?
Many's the time I've heard poor old Lord Kilmahon say
that an Irish education was n't worth a groat for England;
and I now see the force of the remark.

Not but he's working hard every day, with French and

fortification and military surveying, with a fine old officer
that served in the wars of the Empire, — Captain de la
Bourdonaye, — a regular old soldier of Bony's day, that
hates the English as much as any Irishman going. He
comes and sits with me now and then of an evening, but
there's not much society in it, since we can't understand
each other. We have a bottle of rum and some cigars between us, and our conversation goes on somewhat in this
fashion: —

"Help yourself, Mounseer."

A grin and bow, and something mumbled between his
teeth.

"Take a weed?"

We smoke.

"James is getting on well, I hope? Mon fils James
improving, eh? Grand general one of these days, eh?"

"Oui, oui." Fills and drinks.

"Another Bonaparte, I suppose?"

"Ah! le grand homme!" Wipes his eyes, and looks up
to the ceiling.

"Well, we thrashed him for all that! Faith, we made
him dance in Spain and Portugal. What do you say to
Talavera and Vittoria?"

Swears like a trooper, and rattles out whole volumes of
French, with gestures that are all but blows. I wait till
it's over, and just say "Waterloo!"

This nearly drives him crazy, and he forgets to put water
in his glass; and off he goes about Waterloo in a way that's
dreadful to look at. I suppose, if I understood him, I'd
break his neck; but as I don't, I only go on saying "Waterloo" at intervals; but every time I utter it, he has to blow
off the steam again. When the rum is finished, he usually
rushes out of the room, gnashing his teeth, and screaming
something about St. Helena. But it's all over the next
day, and he's as polite as ever when we meet, — grins, and
hands me his tin snuff-box with the air of an emperor.
They're a wonderful people, Tom; and though they'd murder you, they'd never forget to make a bow to your corpse.

You may imagine, from what I tell you, that I am very
lonely here; and so I am. I never meet anybody I can

speak to; I never see any newspaper I can read! I eat
things without knowing the names of them, or, what's
worse, what they are; and all this I must do for economy,
while I could live for less than one-half the expense at
Dodsborough!

Mary Anne has just come to say that the doctors are
agreed Mrs. D. must be removed; the noise of the town will
destroy her. My only surprise is that she did n't discover
it sooner. They speak of a place called Chaude Fontaine,
seven miles away, and of a little watering-place called Spa.
But I 'll not budge an inch till I have all the particulars, for
I know well they 're all dying to be at the old work again,
— tea-parties, and hired horses, and polkas, in the evening,
and the rest of it. Lord George has arrived at Liège, and
I would n't be astonished if he was at the bottom of it all;
not but he behaved well in James's business. To deal with
a Jew there 's nothing in the world like one of your young
sprigs of nobility! Moses does n't care a bulrush for you
or me; but when he hears of a Lord Charles or Lord Augustus, he alters his tone. It is that class which supplies his
customers, and he dares not outrage them.

I wish you saw the way he managed our friend Lazarus!
He would n't look into his statement, read one of his accounts, or even bestow a glance at the bills.

"I 'm up to all those dodges, Lazzy," said he; "it 's no
use coming that over *me*. What 'll you do it for?"

"Ah, my good Lord Shorge, you know better as me,
that we cannot give away our moneys. Here are all the
bills — "

"Don't care for that, Lazzy, — won't look at 'em.
What 'll you do it for?"

"If I lend my moneys at a fair per shent — "

"Well, what 's the figure to be? Say it at once, or
I 'm off."

"You 'll shurely look at my claims — "

"Not one of them."

"Nor the bills."

"No."

"Nor the vouchers?"

"No."

"Oh dear! oh dear! how hard you are grown; and you so young and so handsome, so little like — "

"Never mind the resemblance, but answer me.   How much?"

"It's impossible, my Lord Shorge!"

"Will two hundred do?   Well, two fifty?"

"No, nor twelve fifty, my Lord.   I will have my claim."

"That's what I want to come at, Lazzy.   How much?" This process goes on for half an hour, without any apparent result on either side; when, at last, Lord George, taking out his pocket-book, proceeds to count various bank-notes on the table.   The effect is magical; the sight of the money melts Lazarus, — he hesitates, and gives in.   Of course his compliance does not cost him much; fifty per cent is the very lowest we escape for!   But even at this, Tom, our bargain is a good one.

I see it all, Tom; they are bent on getting to a watering-place, and that's exactly the very thing I won't stand.   Our Irish notions on these subjects are all taken from Bundoran, or Kilkee, or Dunmore, or some such localities; and where, to say the least, there is not a great deal to find fault with. Tiresome they are enough; and, after a week or so, one gets wearied of always walking over ankles in deep sand, listening to the plash of the tide, or the less musical squall of some half-drowned baby, or sitting on a rock to watch some miraculous draught of fishes, that is sure to be sent off some twenty miles into the interior.   These, and occasional pictorial studies of your acquaintances, in all the fascinations of oil-skin caps and wet drapery, tire at last.   But they are cheap pleasures, Tom; and, as the world goes, that is something.

Now, from all I can learn, for I know nothing of them myself, your foreign watering-place is just a big city taking an airing.   The self-same habits of dress, late hours, play, dancing, debt, and dissipation; the great difference being that wickedness is cultivated in straw hats and Russia-duck, instead of its more conventional costume of black coat and trousers!   From my own brief experience of life, I think a garden by moonlight is just as dangerous as a conservatory with colored lamps; and a polka in public is less peril-

ous than a mountain excursion, even on donkeys! They'll
not catch me at that game, Tom!

I have just discovered in "Cochrane's Guide " — for I
have burned my "John Murray" — the very place to suit
me, — Bonn on the Rhine.   He says it has a pleasant appearance, and contains 1,300 houses and 15,000 inhabitants,
and that the Star, kept by one Schmidt, is reasonable, and
that he speaks English, and takes in the "Galignani," —
two evidences of civilization not to be despised.

I think I see you smile; but that's the fact, — we come
abroad to hunt after somebody we can talk to, or find a
newspaper we can read, making actual luxuries of what we
had every day at home for nothing.

Besides these, Bonn has a university, and that will be a
great thing for James, and masters of various kinds for the
girls; but, better than all this, there's no society, no balls,
no dinners, no theatre.   The only places of public amusement are the Cathedral and the Anatomy House; and even
Mrs. D. will be puzzled to get up a jinketing in them.

I'll write to Schmidt this evening about rooms, and I'll
show him that we are not to be "done," like your newly
arrived Bulls; for I won't pay more than "four-and-six " a
head for dinner; and plenty it is too.   I wish we could
have remained here; but now that the doctors have decided
against it, there's no help.   It is not that I liked the place,
— Heaven knows I have no right to be pleased with it, —
but I'll tell you one great advantage about it: it was actually "breaking them all in to hate the Continent; " another
month of this tinkering din, this tiresome *table d'hôte,* and
wearisome existence, and I'd wager a trifle they'd agree to
any terms to get away.   You'd not believe your eyes if you
saw how they are altered.   The girls so thin, and no color
in their cheeks; James as lank as a greyhound, and always
as if half asleep; and myself, pluffy and full and short-
winded, irascible about everything, and always thirsty,
without anything wholesome to drink.   But I'd bear it all,
Tom, for the result, or for what I at least expect the result
would be.   I'd submit to it like a course of physic, looking
to the cure for my recompense.

Shall I now tell you, Tom, that I have my misgivings

about Mrs. D.'s illness? I was passing the lobby last night, and I heard her laughing as heartily as ever she did in her life, though it was only two hours before she had sent down for the man of the house to witness her will. To be sure, she always does make a will whenever she takes to bed; but this time she went further, and had a grand leave-taking of us all, which I only escaped by being wrapped up in blankets, under the "influence," as the doctors call it, of "tartarized antimony," of which I partook, to satisfy her scruples, before she would taste it. If I have to perform much longer as a pilot balloon, Tom, I'm thinking I'm very likely to explode.

As for one word of truth from the doctors, I'm not such a fool as to expect it. The priest or the physician that attends your wife always seems to regard *you* as a natural enemy.. If he happen to be well bred, he conducts himself with all the observance due to a distinguished opponent; but no confidence, Tom, — nothing candid. He never forgets that he is engaged for the "opposite party."

Your foreign doctor, too, is a dreadful animal. He has not the bland look, the soft smile, the noiseless slide, the snowy shirt-frill, and the tender squeeze of the hand, of our own fellows, every syllable of whose honeyed lips seems like a lenitive electuary made vocal. He is a mean, scrubby, little, damp-looking chap, not unlike the bit of dirty cotton in the bottom of an ink-bottle, the incarnation of black draught and a bitter mixture. He won't poison you, however, for his treatment ranges between dill-water and syrup of gum; in fact, to use the expressive phrase of the French, he only comes to "assist" at your death, and not to cause it. I have remarked that homœopathic fellows are more attentive to the outward man than the others, whatever be the reason. Their beards and whiskers are certainly not cut on the infinitesimal principle, and, assuredly, flattery is one of the medicaments they never administer in small doses. By the way, Tom, I wish this same theory could be applied to the distresses of a man's estate as well as that of his body. It would be a right comfortable thing to pay off one's mortgagees with fractional parts of a halfpenny, and get rid of one's creditors on the "decillionth" scale.

I have now finished my paper, and I have just discovered
that I have not answered one of your questions about home
affairs; but, after all, does it matter much, Tom? Things
in Ireland go their own way, however we may strive to direct
and control them. In fact, I am half disposed to think we
ought to manage our business on the principle that our
countryman drove his pig, — turning his head towards Cork
because he wanted him to go to Fermoy! Look at us at this
moment. We never were so thoroughly divided as since we
have enjoyed the benefits of a united education!

If Tullylicknaslatterley must be sold, see that it is soon
done; for if we put it off till November, the boys will be
shooting somebody, or doing some infernal folly or other,
that will take five years off the purchase-money. These
Manchester fellows are always so terrified at what is called
an outrage! Sure, if they had the least knowledge of the
doctrine of chances, they'd see that the estate where a man
was shot was exactly the place there would be no more mischief for many a year to come. The only spot where accidents are always recurring is the drop in front of a jail.

Try and persuade the Englishman to take Dodsborough
for another year. Tell him Ireland is looking up, prices are
improving, &c. If he be Hibernian in his leanings, show
him how teachable Paddy is, — how disposed to learn,
and how grateful for instruction. If he be bitten by the
"Times," tell him that the Irish are all emigrating, and that
in three years there will neither be a Pat, a priest, nor a
potato to be seen. As old Fitzgibbon used to say on our
circuit, "I wish I had a hundred pounds to argue it either
way!"

I can manage to keep afloat for a couple of weeks, but be
sure to remit me something by that time.

Yours, ever sincerely,

KENNY I. DODD.

LETTER XIV.

JAMES DODD TO ROBERT DOOLAN, ESQ., TRINITY COLLEGE, DUBLIN.

Liège, Tuesday Morning.

MY DEAR BOB, — A thousand pardons for not answering either of your two last letters. It was not, believe me, that I have not felt the most sincere interest in all that you tell me about yourself and your doings. Far from it: I finished two bottles of Hock in honor of your Science Premium, and I have called a short-tailed hack Bob, after you, though, unfortunately, she happens to be a mare.

Mine has been rather a varied kind of existence since I wrote last. A little in the draught-board style, only that the black checkers have rather predominated! I got "hit hard" at the Brussels races, lost twelve hundred at écarté, and had some ugly misadventures arising out of a too liberal use of my autograph. The governor, however, has stumped up, and though the whole affair was serious enough at one time, I fancy that we are at length over the stiff country, and with nothing but grass fields and light cantering land before us.

The greatest inconvenience of the whole has been that we 've been laid up here, "dismasted and in ordinary," for the last three weeks, during which my mother has made a steeple-chase through the Pharmacopœia, and the governor finished all the Schiedam in the town. In fact, there has been nothing very serious the matter with her; but as we left the capital under rather unpleasant circumstances, we came in here to "blow off our steam," and cool down to a reasonable temperature. To reduce the budget and retrench expenditure, the choice was probably not a bad one, since we are housed, fed, and done for on the most reasonable

terms; but the place is a perfect disgust, and there is actually nothing for a man to do, except to poke into steam-
engines and prove gun-barrels.

As for me, I never leave my room from breakfast till
table d'hôte hour. My French master comes at eleven and
stays till four. This sounds all very diligent and studious,
and so thinks the governor, Bob. The real state of the case
is, however, different. The distinguished officer of the
Old Guard engaged to instruct me in military science and
mathematics is an old hairdresser, who combines with his
functions of barber the honorable duties of *laquais de place*
and police spy, occasionally taking a turn at the "scho-
lastic" whenever he is lucky enough to find any English
illiterate enough to be his dupes. The governor heard of
him from the master of the hotel, and took him especially
for his cheapness. Such is the Captain de la Bourdonaye,
who swaggers upstairs every morning with a red ribbon in
his button-hole, and a curling-iron in his pocket; for I take
good care, Bob, that as he cannot furnish the inside of my
head, he shall at least decorate it without.

I must say this is a most nefarious old rascal, and I have
heard of more villany from him than I ever knew before.
He knows all the scandal and gossip of the town, and retails
it with an almost diabolical raciness. As I have already
made use of him in various ways, we are bound to each
other in the very heaviest of recognizances. He brought
me yesterday a note from Lord George, who had just
arrived here, but judged better not to see me till he had
called on the governor. The Captain was once Lord G.'s
courier, and, I believe, the chief mentor of his earlier
Continental experiences.

Lord George has behaved like a trump to me. He has
brought away from Brussels all my traps, which, in the haste
of my retreat, I had fancied fallen into the hands of the
enemy. The brown mare Bob, a neatish dennet, two sets
of single harness, a racing saddle, a lady's ditto, three
chests of toggery, all my pipes and canes, and a bull-
terrier, — the whole of which would have to-day been the
chattels of Lazarus, had not Lord G. made out a bill of sale
of them to himself, and got two "respectable" advocates to

swear they were witnesses to it. The fun of this is, Lazarus saw all the knavery, and Tiverton never denied it! The
most rascally transactions are dashed with such an air of
frankness and candor, that, hang me! if one can regard
them as transportable offences! I know all this would be
infamous in England, — it would n't be quite right even in
Ireland, Bob, — but here we are abroad, and the latitude
warps morality just as the vicinity to the pole affects the
compass.

I have learned from Lord George that there are to be races
at a place called Spa, about twelve miles off, and that if
Bob were in training we might do a good thing among
"les gentlemen riders," who certainly ride like neither gents
nor jocks. George slipped his knee-cap at a gate the other
day, and cannot ride; and how I am to get away from this
for an entire day without the governor's knowledge, is more
than I can see. I have told the Captain, however, that he
must manage it somehow, or I 'll turn king's evidence and
betray him; so that the case is not yet hopeless. Bob is
exactly the kind of thing to walk into these fellows. She 's
very nearly thoroughbred, but has a cock-tailed look about
her, and, with a hogged mane and a short dock, is only, to
all appearance, a clever hackney. I know well that these
foreigners have got first-rate cattle,— they buy the very
best of horses, and the smartest carriages of London; but
what avails it? They can neither ride nor drive! They curb
up a thoroughbred so that he 's thrown clean out of his
stride, and they clap the saddle on his withers so that he is
certain to come smash down if he tries to cross a furrow.
You can imagine what hands they have, when I tell you
that they all hold on by the head! Lord G., however, who
knows them well, says that there 's no use in bringing over
a good horse against them. They are confoundedly cautious, and what they lack in skill they make up in cunning;
and if they heard of anything that ran second at Goodwood
or Chester, they 'd "shut up" at once. It 's only a "dodge"
will do, he says, and I am certain nobody knows better than
he does.

Whenever they get pluck enough for hurdle-racing, there
will be some money to be picked up abroad; but the pros-

perity won't last, for when one fellow breaks his neck there will be an end of it.

I'll not close this till I can tell you the success of our scheme for the races. Meanwhile to your questions, which, to make short work of, I'll answer all at once. It's all very fine to talk about studying, and the learned professions; but how many succeed in them? Three or four swells carry off the stakes, and the rest are nowhere! Let me tell you, Bob, that the fellows that really do best in life never knew trade nor profession, except you can call Tattersall's yard a lecture-room, and short-whist a calling. There's Colling-wood's got two hundred thousand with his wife; Upton, he's netted thirty on the last Derby, and stands to win at least twelve more on the Spring Meeting. Brook — Shallow Brook, as you used to call him at school — has been deep enough to break the bank at Hamburg! I just wish you'd show me one of your University dons who could do any one of the three! If it came to a trial of wits, the heads of houses would n't have houses over their heads. Believe me, Bob, the poet was right, — "The proper study of mankind is man!" and if he add thereto a little knowledge of horse-flesh, there's no fear of him in this life!

Look at the thing in another light too. The Church is only open to the Protestants; the bar is, then, the sole pro-fession with great rewards; for as to the army and navy, they may do to spend money in and leave when you're sick of them, but nothing else. Now the bar is awful labor, — ten or twelve hours a day for three or four years, as many more in a special pleader's office, six years after that report-ing for the newspapers; and, perhaps, after three or four struggling terms you drop off out of the course altogether, and are only heard of as writing a threatening letter to Lord John Russell, or as our "own Correspondent at Tahiti"!

As to physic, "I throw it to the dogs." It's not a gentle-manly calling! So long as a fellow can rout you out of bed at night for a guinea, it's all nonsense to talk about independence. Your doctor has n't even the cabman's priv-ilege to higgle for a trifle more. Real liberty, Bob, con-sists in having no craft whatsoever. Like the free lances in the sixteenth century, take a turn of service wherever it

suits you, but wear no man's livery. As Lord George remarks, whenever a fellow takes to that line of life the men
are all afraid, and the women all delighted with him; he's
so sure with his pistol and so lax in his principles, nothing
obstructs his progress.

This same glorious independence I am like enough to
attain, since up to this moment I am a perfect gentleman,
according to Lord George's definition; nor could I, by any
means that I know of, support myself for twenty-four hours.
You would probably remark that so blank a prospect ought
to alarm me. Not a bit of it! I never felt more thoroughly confident and at ease than now as I write these lines.
George's theory is this: Life is a round game, with some
skill and a vast amount of hazard; the majority of the
players are dupes, who, some from inattention, some from
deficient ability, and others, again, from utter indifference,
are easy victims to the few shrewd and clever fellows that
never neglect a chance, and who know when to back their
luck. "Do not be too eager," says George, — "do not be
over-anxious to play, but just walk about and watch the
game for a year or so, and only cut in when it suits you.
By that time you have mastered the peculiar style of every
man's play. You are up to all their weaknesses, and aware
of where their strength lies; and if you can only afford to
lose a little cash yourself at the start, and pass for a pigeon,
your fortune is made!" This, of course, is but a sorry
sketch of his system; for, after all, it requires his own
dashing description, his figurative manner, and his flow of
illustration, to make the thing intelligible. He is, in reality,
a first-rate fellow, and may be what he chooses. All that
I know of life I owe to his teaching; and I own to you I
was in the "lowest form" when he began with me.

The only thing that distresses me now, is the fear that
Vickars may yield to the governor's solicitations, and give
or get me something, — some confounded official appointment that would shut me up all day in a Government office,
on mayhap one hundred and twenty per annum, with a
promised increase of ten pounds when I attain the age of
fifty. I'd nearly as soon be in the hulks as the Home Office,
and I'm certain that pounding oyster-shells is just as intel-

lectual, and a far more salubrious occupation than *précis* writing! The dread of such a destiny has induced me to take a rather bold step, and one which it is possible you will not exactly approve of. I have written myself a "private and strictly confidential" note to Vickars, to say that my father's application to him on my behalf never had my sanction nor approval; that I despise the Board of Trade, and hold the Customs uncommon cheap; and that although there are some gentlemen in what they call the diplomatic service, that all the juniors are snobs, and the grade above them — what George calls snoozers — old red-tapery fellows, that label their washing-bills "soap question," and send out their boots to be new soled in an old despatch-bag.

I have added a few lines, by way of showing that my repugnance does not proceed from any disinclination to exertion or an active life, that I am quite ready to accept of a commission in the Guards, or any good post in the house-hold, where my natural advantages might be seen and appreciated.

I have not told Lord George about this, because he is tremendously opposed to my taking anything like office. He says it 's not only "bad style," but a positive throwing away of oneself; since, whenever they do get a regularly clever fellow amongst them, they always keep him in some subordinate position. "They 'll just treat you the way they did Edmund Burke," he says; and though I 'm not aware how that was, I am quite satisfied that it was a rascally shame! Our name, too, I own to you, in all frankness, is awfully against us. Lord George has advised me over and over to add a syllable or two to it; so I should, perhaps, if I were not living with the governor; but for the present I must submit.

The Captain has just dropped in to tell me that all is arranged, — I am to have a fearful toothache, and be con-fined to bed for two days; and this, with heavy blankets and nitre whey, will take at least seven pounds off me. The governor is to be seduced into an excursion, to see the works of Seraing. We have contrived to have his card of admis-sion dated for a particular day, and the hackney coachman has been bribed to break down on the way home, and detain him several hours.   Lord George is to have a drag ready for me at the outside of Liège at eight o'clock and I hope to figure on the course by twelve!   Mary Anne alone is in the secret.   I was obliged to tell her, since without her aid I should have had no jacket; but she has cut up a splendid green satin of my mother's, which, with white sleeves and cap to match, will turn me out rather smart, and national to boot.   Bob is already gone, and has had her canters for the last four mornings, so that who knows but that we shall do something?

You describe to me the trepidation of heart you felt on going up for honors at college, — the fits of heat and cold, the tremblings, the sighings, the throbbings, and faintishness; trust me, Bob, it 's all nothing to what one experiences on the eve of a race!   *Your* contest is conducted in secret; your success or failure is witnessed by a few; *ours* is an open tournament, with thousands of spectators, who are, or who at least fancy that they are, most competent judges of the performance; and if it be a glorious thing to come sweeping past the grand stand amidst the vociferous cheers of a mighty host, to catch the fitful glance of waving hats and floating handkerchiefs as you dash by, it is a sorry affair to come hobbling along dead-lame or broke down, three hundred yards behind, greeted only by the scoffs of the multitude and the jokes of the greasy populace.

Which of these fortunes is to be mine you shall hear before I seal this epistle; and now, for the present, adieu!

Friday Evening.

I have just an hour before the post closes to announce to you my safe return here, though I greatly doubt if my swelled and still trembling fingers will make me legible. We started at cock-crow, and reached Spa for an early breakfast, having " tooled along" with a spicy tandem the thirteen miles in an hour.   Before eight o'clock I had taken a hot bath, and reduced my weight nine pounds, having taken seven rounds of the race-course in a heavy fur pelisse of Lord George's.   Twenty minutes more toiling, and some hot lemonade, completed my training, and left me by twelve o'clock somewhat groggy in gait and white about the gills, and, as George said, very much like a chicken boiled down for broth!

Our game was not to bet on the general race, but to look on as mere spectators and see what could be done in a private match. This was not so easy, since these Belgian fellows were so intent on the " Liège St. Leger " and the " Spa Derby," and twenty other travesties of the like kind, that they would not listen to anything but what sounded at least like English sport. We had therefore to wait with all due patience for their tiresome races, — " native horses and native jockeys," as the printed programme very needlessly informed us. " Flemish mares and fat riders " would have been the suitable description.

I had almost despaired of doing anything, when near five o'clock George came up to say that he had made a match for a hundred Naps. a side, — Bob against Bronchitis, twice round the course, — I to ride my own horse, and Count Amédée de Kaerters the other, he giving me twelve pounds and a distance. Not too much odds, I assure you, since Bronchitis is out of Harpsichord by a Bay Middleton mare.

Before I had reached the stand, George had made a very pretty book, taking five, and even seven to two, against Bob, and an even fifty on her being distanced. Still I was far from comfortable when I saw Bronchitis; a splendid-looking horse, with a great slapping stride, light about the head, and strong in the quarters; just the kind of horse that wants no riding whatever, only to be let do his own work his own way.

" The mare can't gallop with that horse, George! " said I, in a whisper. " She 'll never see him after the first time round! "

" I 'm half afraid of that," said he, in the same low voice. " They told me he was n't all right, but he 's in top condition. We must see what 's to be done." He smoked his cigar quite coolly for a minute or two, and then said, " Ah, here comes the Count! I have it, ' Jim!' " — he always calls me " Jim," — " just mind me, and it will all come right."

I was by no means convinced that everything was so safe,

however; and had I been possessed of the fifty Naps. required, I should gladly have paid the forfeit. Fortunately, as it turned out, I had n't so much money; so into the scale I went, my heart being the heaviest spot about me!

"Eleven two," said George; "we'll say eleven."

The Count weighed eleven stone four, which, with his added weight, brought him to upwards of twelve stone.

"It's exactly as I suspected," whispered George to me. "The Belgian has weighed himself as if he was a gold guinea. He has been so anxious not to give you an ounce too much, that he has outwitted himself. All that you've to do, Jim, is, ride at him every now and then; tease and worry the fellow wherever you can, and try if you can't take some of that loose flesh off him before it's over."

I saw the scheme at once, Bob. I had nothing whatever to do but to save my distance to win the race; for it was clearly impossible that the Count could go twice round a mile course, and come in as heavy as he started.

I must be brief, for my minutes are few. Would that you could have seen us going round! — I lying always on his quarter, making a rush whenever I got a bit of ugly ground, and, though barely able to keep up with him, just being near enough to worry him. He was n't much of a rider, it is true, but he knew quite enough to see that he could run away from me whenever he liked; and so he did when he came to the last turn near home. Off he went at speed, pitching the mud behind him, and making my smart jacket something like a dirty draught-board. It was only by dint of incessant spurring and tremendous punishment that I was able to get inside the distance-post just as the cheering in front announced to me that he had passed the grand stand.

My canter in — for I was so dead-beat it was only a canter — was greeted with a universal yell of derision. To have a laugh against the Englishman on a race-course was a national triumph of no mean order. "It was a 'set-off' against Waterloo," George said.

In I came, splashed, splattered, and scorned, but not crestfallen, Bob, for one glance at my victorious rival satisfied me that all was safe. The Count was so completely fagged that he could scarcely get down from his horse, and when he did so, he staggered like a drunken man.

" Come now, Count, into the scale ! " cried Lord George ; " show your weight, and let us pay our money ! "

" I have weighed already," said the other. " I weighed before the start."

" Very true," rejoined George, " but let us see that you are the same weight still."

It required considerable explanation and argument to show the justice of this proposition, nor was it till a jury of English jocks decided in its favor that the Belgians were convinced.

At last he did consent to get into the scale, and to the utter wonderment of all but the few English present, it was discovered that he had lost something like six pounds, and consequently lost the race.

It was capital fun to see the consternation of the Belgians at the announcement. They had been betting with such perfect certainty; they had been giving any odds to tempt a wager; and there they were ! — " in," as George said, " for a whole pot of money."

While they were counting down the cash, too, George kept assuring them that the lesson they had just received was " cheap as dirt; " " that it ought by right to have cost them thousands instead of hundreds, but that we preferred doing the thing in an amicable way." At such times, I must say, George is perfect. He is so cool, so courteous ; so apparently serious, too, that even his sharpest cuts seem like civil speeches and kindly counsel. I never admired him more than when, having bought a courier's leather-bag to stuff the gold in, he slung it round his neck, and, taking leave of the party with a polite bow, said, —

" There are times, gentlemen, when one goes all the lighter for a little additional weight ! "

I scarcely remember how we reached Liège. It was almost one roar of laughter between us the whole road ! And then such plans and schemes for the future !

Luck stood by me to the last. I reached home before the governor, and in time to resume my bandages and my toothache.   Mary Anne had taken care to have a very tidy bit of dinner ready; and now, while I sip my Bordeaux, I dedicate to you the last moments of my long and eventful day.

I do not ask of you to write to me till you hear again, for there is no guessing where I may be this day fortnight.   Vickars may possibly respond to my request; or I may find some complaisant doctor to order me to a distant watering-place, in which case I may get free of the Dodd family, who, I own to you, Bob, are a serious drawback on the progress and advancement of your

Attached, but now wide-awake friend,

JAMES DODD.

Dodd père has just come home with a sprained ankle. The scoundrel of a coachee overdid his instructions, and upset the " conveniency " into a lime-kiln.   I suppose I'll have to pay two or three Naps. additional for the damage.

One good result, however, has followed : the governor is in such a rage that he has determined to leave this to-morrow.

LETTER XV.

My dearest Kitty, — I do not, indeed, deserve your reproaches. Mine is not a heart to forget the fondest ties
of early affection, nor would you charge me with this were
you near me. But how can *you*, lying peacefully in the
calm haven of domestic quiet, " sleeping on your shadow,"
as the poetess says, sympathize with one storm-tossed, and
all but shipwrecked on the wild, wide ocean of life?

Of the past I cannot trust myself to speak, and I must
say, Kitty, if there be one lesson which the Continent
teaches above all others, it is not to go over the bygone.
A week ago, in foreign acceptation, is half a century; and
he who remembers the events of yesterday rather verges
on being a " bore " for his pains. Probably it is the intensity with which they throw themselves into the " present "
that imparts to foreigners their incontestable superiority in
all that constitutes social distinction, — their glowing enthusiasm even about what we should call trifles, — their
ardor to attain what we should deem of little moment !

If you were not to witness it, Kitty, you could n't believe
what an odious thing your regular untravelled Englishman
is. His pride, his stiffness, his self-conceit, his contempt
for everybody and everything, from good breeding to grammar. Contrast him with your pliant Frenchman, your
courteous German, or your devoted Italian ; so smiling and
so submissive, so grateful for the slightest mark of your
favor, that you feel all the power of riches in the wealth of
your smiles or the resources of your wit !

, And they are so ingenious in discovering your perfec-
tions ! It is not alone the rich color of your hair, the arch
of your eyebrow, or the symmetry of your instep, Kitty,

but even the secret workings of your fancy, the fitful playings of your imagination: these they understand by a kind of magic. I really believe that the reason Englishmen do not comprehend women is that they despise and look down upon them. Foreigners, on the other hand, adore and revere them! There is a kind of worship paid to the sex abroad that is most fascinating.

One reason for all this may be that in England there are so many roads to ambition quite separated from female influence. Now, here this is not the case. We are everything abroad, Kitty. Political, literary, artistic, fashionable, — as we will. We can be fascinating and go everywhere, or exclusive and only admit a chosen few. We can be deep in all the secrets of State, and exhausted with all the cares of the cabinet, or can be *lionnes*, and affect cigars and men society, talk scandal and *coulisses*, wear all the becoming caprices of costume, and be even more than men in independence.

I see — or I fancy that I see — your astonishment at all that I am telling you, and that you half exclaim, "Where and how did Mary Anne learn all this?" I'll tell you, my dearest Kitty, since even the expansion of heart to my oldest friend is not sweeter to me than the enjoyment of speaking of one whose very name is already a spell to me.

You must know, then, that after various incidents, too numerous to recount, we left Brussels for Liège, where poor mamma was taken so ill that we were forced to remain several weeks. This, of course, threw a gloom over our party, and deprived me of the inestimable pleasure I should have felt in visiting the scenes so graphically described in Scott's delightful " Quentin Durward." As it was, I did contrive to make acquaintance with the old palace of the prince bishops, and brought away, as souvenir, a very pretty lace lappet and a pair of gold earrings of antique form, which I wanted greatly to suit a *moyen âge* costume that I have just completed, and of which I shall speak hereafter.

Liège, however, did not agree with any of us. Mamma never slept at night; papa did little else than sleep day and night; poor James overworked himself at study; and

Cary and myself grew positively plain! so that we started at last for Aix-la-Chapelle, intending to proceed direct to the Rhine. On arriving, however, at the "Quatre Saisons" Hotel, pa found an excellent stock of port wine, which an Englishman, just deceased, had brought over for his own drinking, and he resolved to remain while it lasted. There were fortunately only seven dozen, or we should not have got away, as we did, in three weeks.

Not that Aix was entirely devoid of amusement. In the morning there is a kind of promenade round the bath-house, where you drink a sulphur spa to soft music; but, as James says, a solution of rotten eggs in ditch water is scarcely palatable, even with Donizetti. After that, you breakfast with what appetite you may; then you ride out in large parties of fifteen or twenty till dinner, the day being finished with a kind of half-dress, or no dress, ball at "the rooms." The rooms, my dear Kitty, require a word or two of description. They are a set of six or seven *salons* of considerable size, and no mean pretension as to architecture; at least, the ceilings are very handsome, and the architraves of doors and windows display a vast deal of ornament, but so dirty, so shamefully, shockingly dirty, it is incredible to say! In some there are newspapers; in others they talk; in one large apartment there is dancing; but the rush and recourse of all seem to two chambers, where they play at rouge-et-noir and roulette.

I only took a passing peep at this pandemonium, and was shocked at the unshaven and ill-cared-for aspect of the players, who really, to my eyes, appeared like persons in great poverty; and, indeed, Lord George informs me that the frequenters of this place are a very inferior class to those who resort to Ems and Baden.

I was not very sorry to get away from this; for, independently of other reasons, pa had made us very remarkable — I had almost said very ridiculous — before the first week was over. In order to prevent James from frequenting the play-room, papa stationed himself at the door, where he sat, with a great stick before him, from twelve o'clock every day till the same hour at night, — a piece of eccentricity that of course drew public attention to him, and made us all the subject of impertinent remarks, and indeed of some practical jokes: such as sudden alarms of fire, anonymous letters, and other devices, to seduce him from his watch.

It was, therefore, an inexpressible relief to me to hear that we were off for Cologne, — that city of sweet waters and a glorious cathedral! — though I must own to you, Kitty, that in the first of these two attractions the place is disappointing. The manufacturers of the far-famed perfume would seem so successfully to have extracted the odor of the richly gifted flowers, that they have actually left nothing endurable by human nose! Of all the towns in Europe, it is, they tell, the very worst in this respect; and even papa, who between snuff and nerves long inured to Irish fairs and quarter sessions, is tolerably indifferent, — even he said that he felt it "rather close and stuffy."

As for the cathedral, dearest, I have no words to convey my sensations of awe, wonderment, and worship. Yes, Kitty, it was a sense of soft devotional bewilderment, — a kind of deliciously pious rapture I felt come over me, as I sat in a dark recess of this glorious building, the rich organ notes pealing through the vaulted aisles, and floating upwards towards the fretted roof. Even Lord George — that volatile spirit — could not resist the influence of the spot, and he pressed my hand in the fervor of his feelings, — a liberty, I need scarcely tell you, he never would have ventured on under less exciting circumstances.

Shall I own to you, Kitty, that this sign of emotion on his part emboldened me to a step that you will call one of daring heroism? I could not, however, resist the temptation of contrasting the solemn grandeur and gorgeous sublimity of *our* Church with the cold, unimpressive nakedness of *his*. The theme, the spot, the hour, — all seemed to inspire me, Kitty; and I suppose I must have pleaded eloquently, for his hand trembled, his head drooped, and almost fell upon my shoulder. I told him repeatedly that it was his reason I wished to convince, — that I neither desired to captivate his imagination nor engage his heart.

" And why not my heart?" cried he, passionately. " Is it that — "

Oh, Kitty, who can tell what he would have said next, if a dirty little acolyte had not whisked round the corner and begged of us to move away and let him light two tapers beside a skull in a glass case? The officious little wretch might, at least, have waited till we had gone away; but no, nothing would do for him but he must illuminate his bones that very instant, and thus, probably, was lost to me forever the un speakable triumph I had all but accomplished.

We arose and set out in search of our party, who were, it appeared, in quest of papa: nor was it for two hours that we found him. He had ascended the tower with us all, but instead of coming down when we did, he took a short turn on the leads, and, finding the door closed on his return, remained a prisoner there during all the time we were in search of him. There is no saying how much longer he might have passed in this captivity — for all his cries and shouts were unheard — had he not hit upon an expedient, not entirely devoid of danger, for his rescue. This was to tear off any loose tiles he could find, and hurl them over into the street beneath. Why and how nobody was killed by it we cannot guess, for it is a most crowded thoroughfare, and actually crammed with stalls of fruit and vegetables. The buttresses and projections of the cathedral probably arrested many of the missiles in their flight; but one, thrown I con- jecture with extraordinary force, came bang on the roof of the archbishop's carriage, just as his Grace had got in, the noise and the shock almost depriving him of consciousness! Papa, however, knew nothing of all this, and was actually hard at work detaching a lead gutter when they rushed up and apprehended him.

It was almost an hour before we could come to anything like a reasonable explanation of the incident, for papa insisted that he was the aggrieved person throughout, and raved about his action for false imprisonment. The dean of the cathedral demanded a handsome sum for reparation, and threw in a sly word about " sacrilege " if we demurred. Mamma, still weak and delicate, took to hysterics, while a considerable mob outside gave token of preparation to maltreat us on our exit. Under all these adverse conjunctures we thought it wiser to remain where we were till night; so we sent for something to the hotel, and made ourselves comfortable in the sacristan's room, where, the first shock over, we grew both merry and happy, Lord G., as usual, being the life of our party, by that buoyant exhilaration that really, Kitty, is the first of all nature's gifts.

I already guess whither your thoughts are carrying you, Kitty! Have I not divined aright? You are calling to mind the night we passed at the old windmill at Gariff, when the bridge was carried away by the flood! I vow to you it was uppermost in my own thoughts too! It was there Peter first told me of his love! Never till that moment had I the slightest suspicion of his feeling towards me. I was young, artless, and confiding, — a mere child of nature! Indeed, I must say that he was not blameless in taking the advantage he did of my fresh and unsuspecting heart! What knew I of the world? How could I anticipate the position I was yet to hold in society, or how measure the degree of presumption by which he aspired to my hand?

He has many excellent qualities of head and heart. I do not deny it; but the deceit he thus practised on me I can never forget. I do not desire that you should tell him so. No, Kitty. The likelihood is that we may never meet again; and I do not wish that one harsh thought should mar the memory of the past! It may be that at some future time I can befriend and serve him; and he may rest assured that no station of life, however exalted and brilliant, will separate me from the ties of early friendship. Even now, I am certain, Lord George would oblige me on his behalf. Do you think, or could you ascertain, whether he would like to go out as surgeon to a convict ship? They tell me that these are excellent appointments, and admirably suited to young men of enterprising habits and no friends; and that, if they settle in the colony, they get several thousand acres of land, and as many natives as they can catch. From what I can learn, it would suit P. B., for he was always of a romantic turn, and fond of mutton.

How my wandering fancies have led me away! Where was I? Oh, in the little vaulted chamber of the sacristan,

A Sacrilegious Monster!

with its quaint old wainscot and its one narrow window, dim
and many-paned! It was midnight before we left it to
return to our hotel, and then the streets were quite deserted,
and we walked along in silent thoughtfulness, I leaning on
Lord G.'s arm, and wishing — I know not well why — that
we had two miles to go!

We are stopping at the "Emperor," a very fine hotel that
looks out upon the Rhine, and, as my window overhangs the
river, I sat and gazed upon the rushing waters till nigh
daybreak, occasionally adding a line to this scrawl to my
dearest Kitty, and then wafting a sigh to the night-breeze
as it stole along.

And now, at length, and after all these windings and
digressions, I come to what I promised to speak of in
the early part of this rambling epistle. We were at breakfast on the morning after what Lord G. calls our "cathedral service," — for he persists in quizzing about it, and
says that pa was practising to become a "minor canon,"
when a very handsome travelling-carriage drove up to the
hotel door, attracting us all to the windows by the noise and
clatter. It was one of those handsome britschkas, Kitty,
that at once bespeak the style of their owner; scrupulously
plain and quiet, — almost Quaker-like in simplicity, but
elegant in form, and surrounded with all that luxury of
cases and imperials that show the traveller carries every
indulgence and comfort along with him.

There was no courier, but a very smartly dressed maid,
evidently French, occupied the rumble. While we stood
speculating as to the new arrival, Lord George broke out
with a sudden exclamation of astonishment and delight,
and rushed downstairs. The next moment he was at the
side of the carriage, from which a very fair, white hand was
extended to him. It was very easy to see, by his air and
manner, that he was on the most intimate terms with the
fair traveller; nor was it difficult to detect, by the gestures
of the landlord, that he was deploring the crowded state of
the hotel, and the impossibility of affording accommodation.
As is usual on such occasions, a considerable crowd had
gathered, — beggars, loungers, luggage-porters, waiters, and
stablemen, who all eagerly poked their heads into the car-

riage, and seemed to take a lively interest in what was going forward, to escape from whose impertinent curiosity Lord G. entreated the lady to alight.

To this she consented, and we saw a very elegant-looking person, in a kind of half-mourning, descend from the carriage, displaying what James called a "stunning foot and ankle" as she alighted. We had no time to resume our seats at the breakfast-table, when Lord George rushed in, saying, "Only think, there's Mrs. Gore Hampton arrived, and not a place to put her head in! Her stupid courier has, they say, gone on to Bonn, although she told him she meant to stay some days here."

Now, my dearest Kitty, I blush to own that not one of us had ever heard of Mrs. Gore Hampton till that hour, although unquestionably, from the way Lord George announced the name, she was as well known in the great world as Albert Prince of Wales and the rest of the Royal Family. We, of course, however, did not exhibit our ignorance, but deplored and regretted and sorrowed over her misfortune, as though it had been what the "Times" calls "a shocking case of destitution."

"It just shows," said Lord George, as he walked hurriedly to and fro, rubbing his hands through his hair in distraction, "that with every accident of fortune that can befall human beings, — rank, wealth, beauty, and accomplishment, — one is not exempt from the annoyances of life. If a man were to have laid a bet at Brookes's, that Mrs. Gore Hampton would be breakfasting in the public room of an hotel on the Rhine on such a day, he'd have netted a pretty smart sum by the odds."

"And is she?" cried three or four of us together. "Is that possible?"

"It will be an accomplished fact, as the French say, in about ten minutes," cried he, "for there is really not a corner unoccupied in the hotel."

We looked at each other, Kitty, for some seconds in silence, and then, as if by a common impulse, every eye was turned towards papa. Whatever his feelings, I cannot pretend to guess, but he evidently shrank from our scrutiny, for he opened the "Galignani," and entrenched himself behind it.

"I'm sure that either Mary Anne or Cary," broke in mamma, "would willingly give up her room."

"Oh! delighted,—but too happy too oblige," cried we together. But Lord George stopped us. "That's the worst of it; she is so timid, so fearful of giving trouble, and especially when she is not acquainted, that I'm certain she could not bring herself to occasion all this inconvenience."

"But it will be none whatever. If she could be content with one room—"

"One room!" cried he,—"one room is a palace at such a moment. But that is precisely the value of the sacrifice."

We assured him, again and again, that we thought nothing of it; that the opportunity of serving any friend of his —not to speak of one so worthy of every attention—was an ample recompense for such a trifling inconvenience. We became eloquent and entreating, and at last, I actually believe, we had to importune him at least to give the lady herself the choice of accepting our proposition.

"Be it so," cried he, suddenly; and, starting up, hurried downstairs to convey our message.

When he had left the room, we sat staring at each other, as if profoundly conscious that we had done something very magnanimous and very splendid, and yet at the same time not quite satisfied that we had done it in the right way. Mamma suggested that papa ought to have gone down himself with our offer. *He*, on the contrary, said that it was *her* business, or that of one of the girls. James was of opinion that a civil note would be the proper thing. "Mrs. Kenny James Dodd, of Dodsborough, presents her respectful compliments," and so forth,—thus giving us the opportunity of mentioning our ancestral seat, not to speak of the advantage of rounding off a monosyllabic name with a sonorous termination. James defended his opinion so successfully that I actually fetched my writing-desk and opened it on the breakfast-table, when Lord George flung wide the door, and announced "Mrs. Gore Hampton."

You may judge of our confusion, when I tell you that mamma was in her dressing-gown and without her cap; papa in his shocking old flannel *robe de chambre*, with the brown spots, which he calls his "Leprosy," and a pair of

fur boots that he wears over his trousers, giving him the look
of the Russian ferryman we see in the vignette of "Eliza-
beth, or the Exiles of Siberia;" Cary and I in curl-papers,
and "not fastened;" and James in a sailor's check shirt and
Russia-duck trousers, with a red sash round him, and an
enormous pipe in his hand, — a picturesque group, if not
a pleasing one. I mention these details, dearest Kitty, less
as to any relation they bear to ourselves, than for the sake
of commemorating the inimitable tact of our accomplished
visitor. To any one of less perfect breeding the situation
might have seemed awkward, — almost, indeed, ludicrous.
Mamma's efforts to make her scanty drapery extend to the
middle of her legs; papa's struggles to hide his feet;
James's endeavors to escape by an impracticable door; and
Cary and myself blushing as we tried to shake out our curls,
— made up a scene that anything short of courtly good manners might have laughed at.

In this trying emergency she was perfect. The easy
grace of her step, the elegant quietude of her manner, the
courtesy with which she acknowledged what she termed
"our most thoughtful kindness," were actual fascinations.
It seemed as if she really carried into the room with her an
atmosphere of good breeding, for we, magically as it were,
forgot all about the absurdities of our appearance. Mamma
thought no more of her almost Highland costume, papa
crossed his legs with the air of an old elephant, and James
leaned over the back of a chair to converse with her, as if
he had been a captain of the Coldstreams in full uniform.
To say that she was charming, Kitty, is nothing; for,
besides being almost perfectly beautiful, there is a grace, a
delicacy, a feminine refinement in her manner, that make
you feel her loveliness almost secondary to her elegance.
It seemed, besides, like an instinct to her, the way she fell
in with all our humors, enjoying with keen zest papa's acute
and droll remarks about the Continent and the habits of foreigners, mamma's opinions on the subject of dress and
domestic economy, and James's notions of "fast men"
and "smart people" in general.

She repeatedly assured us that she concurred in everything we said, and gave exactly the same reasons for pre-

ferring the Continent to England that we did, instancing
the very fact of our making acquaintance in this uncere-
monious manner, as a palpable case in point. "Had we
been at the Star and Garter at Windsor, or the Albion at
Brighton," said she, "you had certainly left me to my fate,
and I should not have been now enjoying the privilege of an
acquaintance that I trust is not destined to end here."

Oh, Kitty! if you could but have heard the tone of winning softness with which she uttered words simple as these.
But, indeed, the real charm of manner is to invest commonplaces with interest, and impart to the mere nothings of
intercourse a kind of fictitious value and importance. She
congratulated us so heartily on travelling *without* a courier,
— the very thing we were at the moment ashamed of, and
that mamma was trying all manner of artifices to conceal.
"It is so sensible of you," said she, "so independent, and
shows that you thoroughly understand the Continent.
Travelling as *I* do," — there was a sorrowful tenderness as
she said this, that brought the tears to my eyes, — "travelling as I do," — she paused, and only resumed after a
moment of difficulty, — "a courier is indispensable; but *you*
have no such necessity."

"And Grégoire apparently wants to show you how well
you could do without him," cried Lord George. "He has
gone on to Bonn, and left you here to your destiny."

"Oh, but he is such a good, careful old creature," said
she, "that, though he *does* make fearful mistakes, I cannot
be angry with him."

"It's very kind of you to say so," resumed he; "but if *I*
told him that I meant to stop at Cologne, and *he* went forward to order rooms at Bonn, I'd break his neck when we
met."

"Then I assure you I shall do no such thing," added she,
taking off her gloves, as if to show how unsuited her beautifully taper fingers, all glittering with gems, would be to
any such occupation.

"And now you'll have to wait here for Fordyce?" said
he, half angrily.

"Of course I shall!" said she, with a sweet smile.

Lord George made some rejoinder, but I could not hear

it, to this; and so, Kitty, we all determined that instead of at once setting out for Bonn, we should stay and dine with Mrs. Gore Hampton, and not leave her till evening, — a kindness at which she really seemed overjoyed, thanking each of us again and again for our "dear good-nature."

And now, Kitty, I have just left her to hasten off these lines by post hour. My heart is yet fluttering with the delight of her charming conversation, and my hand trembles as I write myself

> Your ever attached and fascinated friend,
>
> MARY ANNE DODD.

HÔTEL DE L'EMPEREUR, COLOGNE.

P. S. Mrs. G. H. has just slipped into my dressing-room to say that she is *so* sorry that we are going away; that she feels as if we were actually old friends already. She has, evidently, some secret sorrow; would that I knew how to console her!

We are to write to each other; but I am not to show her letters to Cary: this she made an express stipulation. She thinks Cary "a sweet girl, but volatile;" and I believe, Kitty, that there is something of levity in her character, which is its greatest defect.

LETTER XVI.

KENNY I. DODD TO THOMAS PURCELL, ESQ., OF THE GRANGE, BRUFF.

MY DEAR TOM, — There's an old Turkish proverb, to the effect that, whenever a man finds himself happy, he should immediately sit down and write word of it to his friends; for the great likelihood is, that if he loses a post, he'll have to change his note. Depend upon it, the adage has some truth in it! If, for example, I'd have finished and sent off a letter I began to you last Wednesday, I'd have given you a very favorable account of myself and our prospects here. The place seemed very much what we were looking for, — a quiet little University town on the bank of this fine river, — snug and comfortable, and yet, at the same time, not shut in, but with glorious expansive views on every side; shady walks for noonday, and hill rambles for sunset; museums and collections for bad weather occupation, and that kind of simple, unostentatious living that bespeaks a community of small fortunes and as small ambitions.

A quaint-looking, half-shy, half-defiant look in the faces showed that if not very great or very rich folk, they still had other and perhaps not less sterling claims to worldly reverence; and so they have too! There are some of the first men, not only in Germany but in Europe, here, living on the income of a London butler, and letting the "first floor furnished" to people like the Dodd family.

It is a great privation to me that I don't speak German, for something tells me we should suit each other wonderfully! Don't mistake me, Tom, and fancy that I am saying this out of any conceit in my abilities, or any false notion of my education. I believe, in my heart, I have as little of one thing as the other; and the only wise thing my father

ever did was to take me away from Dr. Bell's when I
was thirteen, and when he saw that putting Latin and
Greek into me was like sowing barley in a bog, — a waste
of good seed in a soil not fit for it.   But I'll tell you why
I think I'd get on well with these Germans.   They seem to
be a kind of dreamy, thoughtful, imaginative creatures, that
would relish the dry, commonplace thoughts, and hard, practical hints of a man like myself.   I could n't discuss a clas-
sical subject with them, nor talk about the varieties of the
Greek dialects; but I could converse pleasantly enough
about the difference between the ancients and ourselves in
points of government and on matters of social life.   I know
little of books, but I've seen a good deal of men; and if it
be objected that they were chiefly of my own country, I
answer at once, that, however strongly impressed with his
nationality, there's not a man in any country of Europe so
versatile, so many-sided, and so difficult to understand, as
Paddy.   Don't be frightened, Tom; I'm not going off into
the "ethnologies," and not a word will you hear from me
about the facial angle, or frontal development!   I'm not
speaking of Pat as if he were a plaster cast to be measured
with a rule and marked with a piece of charcoal; I'm talking of him as he is, in a frieze coat or one of broadcloth,
— a sceptical, credulous, patient, headlong, calculating, impulsive, miserly spendthrift; a species of bull incarnate,
that never prospers till he is ruined outright, and only has
real success in life when all the odds are against him.

Ireland's birdlime to me, — I stick fast if I only touch it;
and why ain't I back there, growling about the markets,
cursing the poor-rates, and enjoying myself as I used to do?
Does n't it strike you, Tom, that we take more "out" of
ourselves in Ireland — in the way of temper, I mean — than
any other people we hear of in history?   Paddy often reminds me of those cutters on the American lakes, where they
saw across the timbers to give them greater speed; we go fast,
it is true, but we strain ourselves terribly for the sake of it.

And now to come back to Bonn: there is really much to
like in it.   It is cheap, it is quiet without seclusion, and
there's no snobbery.   You know what I mean, Tom.
There's not a tilbury, nor a tiger, nor a genteel tea-party

in the town. I don't know of a single waistcoat with more than five colors in it; and, except James and the head waiter, there's nobody wears diamond shirt buttons. In fact, if we must live out of our country, I thought that this was about the best spot we could fix upon. We made an excellent bargain at our hotel; ten pounds a week was to cover everything; no extras of any kind after that; so that at last I began to see my way before me, and perceive some chance of solving that curious problem that torments alike chancellors and country gentlemen, — how to meet expenditure by income.

Masters in German, music, and mathematics, and other little odds and ends, took a couple of pounds more; and I allowed myself ten shillings a week for what the doctor calls "my little charities," that now resolve themselves into threepenny whist, or a game of ninepins with the Professor of Oriental languages. Even *you*, Tom — "Joe" as you are about the budget — could n't pick a hole in this! Not that I want to give myself credit for a measure absolutely imperative; for, to say the truth, our late performances in Brussels were of the very costliest, and even Liège ran away with a deal of money. Doctors have about the same ideas respecting your cash account as your constitution. They never leave either in a state of plethora! Now, as I was saying, my letter, begun on Wednesday last, had all these details, and might have concluded with a flattering picture of James hard at his studies, and the girls not less diligently occupied with their music and embroidery, — the two resources by which modern ingenuity fancies it keeps female minds employed! As if Double-Bass or Berlin wool were disinfecting liquors! I could also have added that Mrs. D. had fallen into that peculiar condition which is natural to her whenever she finds a place stupid and unexciting, and what she fondly fancies to be a religious frame of mind; in other words, she took to reading her breviary, and worrying Betty Cobb about her duties; got up for five o'clock mass, and insisted upon Friday coming three times a week. I could bear all this for quietness' sake; and if fish diet could insure peace, I'd be content to live upon isinglass for the rest of my days.

Mrs. D., however, is not a woman to do things by halves; there's no John Russellism about her; and now that she had taken this serious turn, I saw clearly enough what was in store for us. I had actually ordered a small silk skull-cap, as a protection to my head, not knowing when I might be sent to do duty in a procession, when suddenly the wind veered round, and began to blow very fresh in exactly the opposite quarter. You must know, Tom, that just before we left Cologne we chanced to make acquaintance with a certain very fashionable person, — a Mrs. Gore Hampton. She was standing disconsolately to be rained on, in the street, when Lord George brought her upstairs to our rooms, and introduced her to us. She was, I must say, what is popularly called a very splendid woman, — tall, dark-eyed, and dashing, with a bewitching smile, and that kind of voice that somehow makes commonplaces very graceful. She had, too, that wonderful tact — wherever it comes from I can't guess — to suit us all, without seeming to take the slightest trouble about the matter.

She talked to Mrs. D. about London fashionable life, just as if they had both been going out together for the last three or four seasons; ay, and stranger still, without even once puzzling her, or making her feel astray in the geography of this *terra incognita*. I conclude she was equally successful with the girls; and though she scarcely addressed a word to James, I suppose she must have made up for it by a look, for he has never ceased raving of her since.

I haven't told you how she "landed" me, for I'm not above confessing that I was as bad as the rest; but the truth is, Tom, I don't really know how I was caught. I am too old for these blandishments; they no more suit me now than a tight boot or a runaway hack; one gets too rheumatic and too stiff in the joints for homage after fifty; and besides that, there's a kind of croaking conscience that whispers, "Don't be making a fool of yourself, Kenny James!" and, between you and me, Tom, 'tis well for us when we're not too deaf to hear it.

Besides this, Tom, it is only the fellows that never were in love when they were young that become irretrievably entangled in after life. If you want to see a true sexagenarian victim, look out for some hang-dog, downcast, mopish creature, or some suspectful, wary, crafty, red-haired rascal, that thought every woman had a trap laid for him. These are your hopeless cases; these are the men that always die in some mysterious manner, and leave wills behind them to be litigated for half a century.

The Kenny Dodds of this world come into another category. They knew that love and the measles are mildest in young constitutions, and so they began early. Maybe it was in a firm reliance on this that I felt so easy about the widow, — if widow she be; for, to tell the truth, I don't yet know if Mr. Gore Hampton be to the fore or only has left her a memory of his virtues.

I leave you to guess what impression she made upon me; for the more I go on trying to explain and refine upon it the less intelligible do I become. One thing, however, I must say, — these charming women are the ruin of Irishmen! Our own fair creatures, with a great share of good looks, and far more than ordinary agreeability, are not so dangerous as the English, and for this reason: in their demands for admiration they are too general; they — so to say — fire at the whole covey; now, your Englishwoman marks her bird, and never goes home till she bags it!

We were to have left Cologne that morning for Bonn, but so agreeably did the time pass, that we did n't start till evening, and even then it was quite tearing ourselves away; for the delightful widow — for widow I must call her till she shows cause to the contrary — hourly gained on us.

She was obliged to wait there for some lawyers or men of business that were to follow her with papers to sign; and although Lord George did his best to persuade her that she might as well come on with us, — that Bonn was only fifteen miles farther, — she was firm, and said that "Old Mr. Fordyce was a great prig, and when she had once named Cologne for their meeting, she would have travelled from Naples rather than break the appointment." I own to you, there was a tenacity and determination in all that which pleased me. Maybe the great charm of it was that it was very unlike what I 'd have done myself!

The whole way to Bonn we talked of nothing but her, the

discussion being all the more unconstrained that Lord
George had stayed behind, and was only to come up the
next morning. We were agreed upon a number of points:
her beauty, her elegance, the grace and fascination of her
manner, and her high breeding; but we took different views
as to her condition, — Mrs. D. and the girls thinking that
she was married, James and I standing out for widowhood.
Lord George joined us the next day; and although he could
have resolved our doubts at once, Mary Anne stopped all
inquiry, by assuring us that nothing was so hopelessly
vulgar as to display any ignorance about the family or
connections of people of rank. "If she be in the peerage,
we ought to know her, and all about her. She is, of course,
some Augusta Louisa, b. 18 and dash; m. to the Honorable
Leopold Conway Gore Hampton, third son, and so on."
In a word, Tom, we had the whole family tree before us,
from its old gnarled root to its last bud, and ours the shame
if we were ignorant of its botanical properties!

A few quiet humdrum days of Bonn existence had almost
obliterated our memory of the charming widow, and we
were beginning to "train off " our attachments to fashionable life, when, in all the splashing and whip-cracking of
foreign posting, up dashes the dark green britschka to our
hotel one fine evening; and before we could well recognize
the carriage, the fair owner herself was making the tour of
the Dodd family, embracing and hand-shaking, as age and
sex dictated!

I wish any physiologist would explain why the English,
that are so proverbial for a cold and chilling demeanor at
home, grow at once so cordial when they come abroad.
Whether it be the fear of the damp, or the swell mob, I
can't tell, but everybody in England goes about with his
hands in his pockets, and only nods to a friend when he
meets him; whereas here you start with a grin at fifty yards
off, then off goes your hat with a flourish, that, if you
have any tact, what with shaking your head, and looking
overcome with delight, occupies you till you come up with
him, when your greeting grows more enthusiastic, — lucky if
it does not finish with a kiss on both cheeks.

I suppose it was the influence of habit betrayed me, for,

in a fit of abstraction, I took the charming widow into my
arms, and saluted her as if she were Mrs. Dodd. If this
was in London, Tom, or even in Dublin, there's no saying
what mischief might not have grown out of it. I might
have been fighting duels every day for the last week, not
to mention still more formidable encounters of a domestic nature; but just to show you what the Continent does
for us, — how instinctively, as it were, we rise above the

little narrow prejudices of our insular situation, — she threw
herself into a chair and laughed immoderately. Ay, and
droller again, so did Mrs. D.! To tell you the truth, Tom,
I could n't well believe my senses when I saw it. It would
seem to be the same in morals as in murder, — you can
dignify the offence by the rank of your victim; for if it had
been one of the maids at home, Mrs. D. would have left my
face like a piece of music paper!

There's a great deal in how you open an acquaintance!
You may be card-leaving, and bowing, and how-d'ye-doing
for years, and never get farther; or, on the other hand, by

some lucky accident, you come plump down into the right place, just as a chance shell will now and then drop into a magazine, and finish an engagement at once.

In less than an hour after her arrival, Mrs. Gore Hampton was one of ourselves. It was not that she was calling the girls dearest Cary, and darling Mary Anne, but she had got a regular sisterly tone with Mrs. D. and myself — treating James all the while as if he was about twelve years old, and at home for the holidays. She had not only done all this, but before luncheon was on the table we had ratified a solemn league and covenant that she was to travel with us, and be one of us, going wherever we went, and living as we did. How the treaty was ever mooted, who proposed, and who signed it, I know no more than the man in the moon. It was done in a kind of rattling, bantering fashion; and when we rose from table it was all settled. Mrs. Gore Hampton was to take Cary and Mary Anne with her in the britschka; the "dear boy" — viz. James — would be the "guard in the rumble." There was a place for everybody and everything; and I believe, if any one had proposed that I should ride the leader, it would have been carried without opposition. Never was there such unanimity! The whole arrangement was huddled up like a road-presentment on a Grand Jury, or a private bill before the House on a Wednesday afternoon. As for myself, if I had even the will, I could not have summoned the shamelessness to offer any opposition to the measure.

"Devilish good thing for *you*, Dodd!" whispered Lord George. "Mrs. G. knows everybody in the world, and does n't care for money." — "Oh, papa! she is delightful; there never was such a piece of good fortune as our meeting with her," cried Mary Anne. And Mrs. D. assured me that, for the very first time in her life, she had met a person thoroughly companionable to her in all respects; in fact, a "kindred soul," though not a "blood relation."

Now, Tom, considering that we came abroad to enjoy the advantages of high society, fashionable habits, and refined associations, this accident did indeed seem a propitious one; for, disguise it how we may, the great world is a dangerous ocean to venture upon without a pilot. Our own little experiences might teach that lesson. We sailed out in all the confidence of a stout crew and a safe vessel, and a pretty voyage we made of it! Perhaps we did not make more mistakes than our neighbors, but assuredly our blunders were neither few nor insignificant!

Mrs G., however, would soon rectify all this. "No more making acquaintance with wrong people, K. I." says Mrs. D.; "no more getting into vulgar intimacies at the *café*, and cementing friendships over a game of dominos. James will know the class of young men that he ought to mix with, and the girls will only dance with suitable partners." It sounded well, Tom! It was a grand protective policy, that really secured the Dodd family in the possession of all home advantages, and relieved them of all aggressions "from the foreigner."

If we had fallen on a prize in the lottery, I don't think the joy of our circle could have been greater. I am not going to pretend that I did n't join in it! I make no affectation of prudent reserve and caution, and Heaven knows what other elegant qualities, that, however natural to other people, very seldom fall to the lot of an Irishman. I vow to you, Tom, I went off full cry like the rest of the pack. She is a fine woman, this Mrs. Gore Hampton; she has a low, soft voice, a very bewitching smile, and a way of looking at you while you are talking to her, that somehow half suggests to yourself that you must be making love without knowing it. Now, don't misunderstand me, Tom, and come out with one of your long whistles, as much as to say, "Kenny James is as great a fool as ever!" No such thing! a suit in Chancery, the repeal of the corn laws, and the Estates Court, have made me an altered man. The very nature of me is changed, and changed so much that many 's the time I ask myself, "Is this Kenny Dodd? Where upon earth is that light-hearted, careless, hopeful vagabond, that always took the sunny road in life, though maybe it was n't exactly the way to the place he was going?" I 'm another man now; I 'm wiser, as they call it; and, upon my conscience, I 'm mighty sorry for it!

But I hear you say, "Have n't you just confessed that you were — what shall I call it? — fascinated by the widow?"

And if I did, Tom Purcell, do you mean to tell me that you would have escaped her? Not a bit of it. The brown wig would have been set a little more forward, so as to bring one of those silky curls over your right eye. I think I see you exchanging your spectacles for a double eye-glass, and turning out your toes so as to display to the best advantage that shapely calf in its trim brown silk stocking. Ah, Tom! not even quarter sessions and a rate in aid will drive these thoughts out of an Irishman's head.

From the moment that this new alliance was signed, we entered upon a new existence. Bonn, as I have told you, was a quiet little collegiate place, with primitive habits of no very expensive kind. The chief pleasures were weak wine in a garden, or small whist in a summer-house, with now and then an " æsthetic tea," as they phrase it, at the Pro-Rector's; of which, of course, I understand nothing, but sincerely hope the discourse was better than the beverage. It was, I own it, Tom, a strange kind of life, that seemed to me always like a moral convalescence, when you were only strong enough for small virtues. One undoubted advantage it had, — it was inexpensive, Tom. We were living, with few comforts and some privations, I confess, at only one-third more than we used to spend at Dodsborough; and, considering that we know nothing of the language, I conclude that we were enjoying the Continent as cheaply as was practicable.

I won't pretend that it suited me. I don't want you to believe that I was taking a scientific or a studious turn. Still I liked the place for one thing, which was this, — its quiet monotony, its placid, unvarying simplicity was telling upon Mrs. D. and the children in an astonishing manner. It was exactly the way that the water-cure works its wonders with old drunkards; the mountain air, the light diet, and the early hours being the best of the remedy. They were getting into a healthy state of mind without ever suspecting it.

Our grand junction, as Cary calls it, finished this; from the day Mrs. G. arrived our reforms began. First, we had to change our hotel, and betake ourselves to one on the river-side, three times as dear, and not one-fourth as good.

The second story was fine enough for us before; now we have the whole "premier," taking two rooms more than we want, lest anybody should live on the same floor with us. Instead of the *table d'hôte*, that was cheap and cheerful, we were to dine upstairs, — "a particular dinner," as they call what is particularly bad, and costly besides. Then we have had to hire two lackeys, one of whom sits in an ante-room all day reading the newspaper, and only rises to make me a grand bow as I pass; which worries me so much that I usually go down by the back stairs to escape him.

We have two job coaches, for we are too many for one, and a boat hired by the week, with a considerable retinue of mountain ponies and donkeys, guides, goats, whey-sellers, and geological specimen-folk without end. If Mrs. G. was only fashionable, we could n't be more than ruined; but she is learned and literary, and given to the "ologies," Tom, and that's what I fear will drive us clean mad. She has an eternal restlessness in her to be at something; one day, it's the date of a medal; the next, it is the family connec-tions of a "moss," or the chemistry of a meteoric stone; and, shall I own to you, my dear friend, that I don't be-lieve she either understands or cares one jot about them all? There's a big herbarium bound in green, and a grand book of autographs in blue and gold, on the drawing-room table; there's a bit of "gneiss," a big beetle, and a fossil frog on the chimney-piece; but my name is n't Kenny Dodd if she has n't more sympathies with modern dandies than antediluvian monsters. That's my private opinion; and, of course, I mention it in confidence. You'll say, "What matter is that to you?" and, true enough, it is not, as regards her; but what will become of us, if Mrs. D. takes a turn for entomology or comparative anatomy, and worse, maybe? She's just the kind of woman to do it. She'd learn the tight-rope if she thought it was fashion-able, or, as the newspapers say, "patronized by the aris-tocracy." Now, Tom, you can fancy the unknown sea upon which we have embarked. For, however unadapted we may be to fashionable life, one thing is quite clear, — we never were made for the abstract sciences; and it strikes me for-cibly that the great lesson of Continental life is that every-

body can do everything. I am not going to say that it is
not a pleasant and a very flattering theory, but is it quite
safe, Tom? That's the question. The highest step I ever
attained in chemistry was how to concoct a tumbler of
punch; and my knowledge of botany does not go far beyond distinguishing "greens" from geraniums; and it's
not at my time of life that I'm to drive myself crazy with
hard names and classifications; and if I know anything of
Mrs. D., her intellectual faculties have attained all the vigor
that nature meant for them many a year ago.

My own private opinion about these sciences is, they're
capital things for employing young people, and keeping
them out of wickedness! The fellows that teach them,
too, are musty, snuff-taking, prosy old dogs, with heavy
shoes and greasy cravats, — the very reverse of your race
of dancing and music masters, who are a pestilent crew!
So that, for a man who has daughters abroad, my advice
is — stick to the sciences. Gray sandstone is safer than
the polka, and there's not as dangerous an experiment in
all chemistry as singing duets with some black-bearded
blackguard from Naples or Palermo. Now mind, Tom,
this counsel of mine applies to the education of the young;
for when people come to the forties, you may rely upon
it, if they set about learning anything, they'll have the
devil for a schoolmaster. What does all the geology
mean? Junketing, Tom, — nothing but junketing! Primitive rock is another name for picnic, and what they call
quartz is a figurative expression for iced champagne.
Just reflect for a moment, and see what it comes to. You
can enter a protest against family extravagances when
they take the shape of balls and soirées, but what are
you to do against botanical excursions and antiquarian
researches? It's like writing yourself down Goth at once
to oppose these. "Oh, papa hates chemistry; he despises
natural history," that's the cry at once, and they hold me
up to ridicule, just in the way the rascally Protestant
newspapers did Dr. Cullen for saying that he did n't believe
the world was round. If the liberty of the subject be worth
anything, — if the right for which the same Protestants are
always prating, private judgment, be the great privilege they

deem it, — why should n't Dr. Cullen have his own opinion
about the shape of the earth? He can say, " It suits *me* to
think I 'm walking erect on a flat surface, and not crawling
along with my head down, like a fly on the ceiling ! I 'm happier when I believe what does n't puzzle my understanding,
and I don't want any more miracles than we have in the
Church." He may say that, and I 'd like to know what
harm does that do you or me? Does it endanger the
Protestant succession or the State religion? Not a bit of
it, Tom. The real fact is simply this : private judgment
is a boon they mean to keep for themselves, and never
share with their neighbors. So far as I have seen of life,
there 's no such tyrant as your Protestant, and for this
reason : it 's bad enough to force a man to believe something that he does n't like, but it 's ten times worse to
make him disbelieve what he 's well satisfied with ; and that 's
exactly what they do. Even on the ground of common humanity it is indefensible. If my private judgment goes in
favor of saints' toe-nails and martyrs' shin-bones, I have a
right to my opinion, and you have no right to attack it.
Besides, I won't be badgered into what may suit somebody
else to think. My opinion is like my flannel waistcoat,
that I 'll take off or put on as the weather requires ; and
I think it very cruel if I must wear *mine* simply because
you feel cold.

I get warm — I almost grow angry — when I think of these
things ; and I wonder within myself why our people don't
expose them as they might. Not that some are not doing
the duty well and manfully, Tom. M'Hale is a glorious
fellow ; and for blackguarding a Prime Minister, for a real
good effective slanging, it 's hard to find his equal. He
never embarrasses himself with logic, — he wastes no time
in arguing, but " goes in " at once, and plants his blow
between the eyes ! That 's what the English can't stand.
They want discussion. They are always fishing for evidence for this, and a proof of that ; but come down on
them with a strong torrent of foul abuse, and you sweep
them away like mud in a mill-race.

That 's where we always beat them in our controversial
discussions, Tom ; and we never failed so long as we relied

on this superiority.   It was like the bayonet in the hands of
our infantry.

Is n't it strange how I get back to Ireland in spite of me?
I 'm like that madman in the story that can't keep Charles
the First out of his memorial?   And, after all, why should
I?   Is there anything more natural than to think of my
country, if I can't manage to live in it?   And this reminds
me to ask you about home matters.   What was it you wrote
at the end of your letter about Jones M'Carthy?   I can't
make out the word, whether it is his "death," or his "debts;"
though, from my experience of the family, I surmise it to
be the latter.   If it 's dead he is, I suppose we 'll come in
for that blessed legacy that Mrs. D. has been talking about
every day for the last twenty-five years, the history of
which I have heard so often that I actually know nothing
about it, except that it was the only bit of property possessed by my wife's relations they could n't make away
with.   It was so strictly "tied up," as they call it in law,
that nobody could ever get the use of it, — pretty much like
the silver sixpence given to a schoolboy, with the express
stipulation that he is never to change it.

I am rather curious to know what Mrs. D. will think of
these "wise provisions" of her ancestors, if she succeeds to
the bequest.   To tell you the plain truth, Tom, I don't
know a greater misfortune for a man that has married a wife
without money, than to discover at the end of some fifteen
or twenty years that somebody has left her a few hundred
pounds!   It is not only that she conceives visions of unbounded extravagance, and raves about all manner of expense, but she begins to fancy herself an heiress that was
thrown away, and imagines wonderful destinies she might
have arrived at, if she had n't had the bad luck to meet you.
For a real crab-apple of discord, I 'll back a few hundreds
in the Three per Cents against all the family jars that ever
were invented.   Save us then from this, if you can, Tom.
There must surely be twenty ways to avoid the legacy; and
so that Mrs. D. does n't hear of it, I 'd rather you 'd prove her
illegitimate than allow her to succeed to this bequest.   I 'll
not enlarge upon all I feel about this subject, hoping that
by your skill and address we may never hear more of it;

but I tell you, frankly, I'd face the small-pox with a stouter heart than the news of succeeding to the M'Carthy inheritance.

There are many other matters I intended to write about, but I believe I must keep them for the next time; such as the plan for taking away the Church property, and the income-tax for Ireland; and that business of the Madiais, that I read of in the papers. So far as I have seen, Tom, the King of Tuscany — if that be his name — was right. There were plenty of books the Madiais might have read without breaking the laws. There are translations of all the rascally French novels of the day, from Georges Sand down to Paul de Kock; and if they wanted mischief, might n't these have satisfied them? But the truth is, Protestants are never easy without they are attacking the true Church, and if there were more of them sent to tne galleys, the world would be all the quieter.

You amaze me about the Great Exhibition for this year in Dublin. Faith! I remember when I used to think that the less we exhibited ourselves the better! I suppose times are changed. I think, if I could send Mrs. D. over as a specimen of Continental plating on Irish manufacture, she 'd deserve a place, and maybe a prize.

Well, well! it 's a queer world we live in. They 've just come to tell me that the man of the post-office has shut up an hour earlier, as he is engaged out to dine, so that I 'll keep this open till to-morrow's mail.

Wednesday Morning.

I suspect that the mischief is done, Tom, — I mean about the legacy. Mrs. D. received a strange-looking, square-shaped, formally addressed epistle this morning, the contents of which, not being a demand for money, she did not communicate to me. She and Mary Anne both retired to peruse it in secret, and when they again appeared in the drawing-room, it was with an air of conscious pride and self-possession that smacked terribly of a bequest. I own to you, the prospect alarms me; it may be that my fears take an exaggerated shape, but I can't shake off the impression that this is the hardest trial I had ever to go through.

I know her in most of her moods, Tom, and have got a kind of way of managing her in each of them, — not very successful, perhaps, but sufficiently so to get on with. I have seen her in straits about money; I have seen her in her jealous fits; I have seen her in her moments of family pride; and I have repeatedly seen her on what she calls "her dying couch," — an opportunity she always seizes to say the most disagreeable things she can think of, so that I often speculate what she 'd say if she was really going off: but all these convey no notion to me of how she 'd behave if she thought herself rich. As for our poverty, we never knew anything else; the jealousy I 'm getting used to; the family pride often gives me a hearty laugh when I 'm alone; and I am as hardened about death-bed scenes as if I was an undertaker. It 's the prosperity I have n't strength for, Tom; and I feel it.

Maybe, after all, it 's only false terror alarms me. I hope it may turn out so; and in this last wish I am sure of your hearty sympathy and good feeling.

Ever yours, most sincerely,

KENNY I. DODD.

LETTER XVII.

MRS. DODD TO MISTRESS MARY GALLAGHER, DODSBOROUGH.

THE RHINE HOTEL, BONN.

MY DEAR MOLLY, — If my well-known hand did not strike you, the sight of all the black around this letter, and the mourning seal, might suggest the thought that your poor Jemima was no more. Your next impression will be that Providence had sent for K. I. No, my dear Molly, I am still reserved for more trials in this vale of tears. I must bear my burden further! As for K. I., he's just as he used to be, — croaking away about the pain in his toe, or a gouty cramp in his stomach. He's always taking things that disagrees with him, and what he calls the "correctives" makes him worse. I cannot give you the least notion of how irritable he's grown. You know as well as anybody the blessings he has about him. I don't speak of myself, nor the stock I came from. I don't want to revive the dreadful mistake that I made in my youth, nor to mention the struggles I've had with him on every subject for more than five-and-twenty years, — struggles, my dear Molly, that would have killed any one that had n't the constitution of a horse; but that now, thanks to the goodness of Providence, have become a part of my nature, so that there is n't an hour of the day or night that I'm not able and willing to dispute and argue with him on any question whatsoever. I don't want to mention these blessings, — but is n't there James and Mary Anne, and, indeed, except for some things, Caroline, — was there ever a father with more reason to be proud? And so you'd say if you only saw them. As a dear friend of mine, Mrs. Gore Hampton, said this morning, "Where will you see such natural advantages?" And I must own, Molly, it's not flattery; for the way they talk

French and waltz, even how they come into a room, salute, or sit down, has something in it that shows them to be brought up in the top of fashion.

Any other man than K. I. would overflow with gratitude for all this, but you'd scarcely believe, Molly, he only ridicules it!

"If we meant her for the stage," says he, — this is the way he talks of Mary Anne, — "if we meant her for the stage, I think she has effrontery enough to stand before a full house, and I don't say it would discompose her; but for the wife of some respectable man of the middle rank, I see no use in all this flouncing about here, and flourishing there, whisking through a room, upsetting small tables and crockery by way of gracefulness, and never sitting down on a chair till she has spread out her petticoats like a peacock!"

If I've said it once to him, Molly, I've said it fifty times, there's nothing I despise so much as a respectable man in the middle rank. There's no refinement about them, — no elegance! They may be what's called estimable in their families; but what's the use of all that for the world at large? A man can only have one wife, but he may have a thousand acquaintances. We don't ask how amiable he is at home; what we want is, that he should be delightful abroad. "That," says Lord George, "is true, both socially and economically; it's the grand principle that everybody stands up for, 'the greatest happiness of the greatest number!'"

And talking of this, I'd strenuously advise your cultivating your mind on matters of political economy. It appears dry and uninteresting at first, but as you get on it improves wonderfully, and takes a great hold of the mind. I don't think I was ever more unhappy than since I read a chapter describing what would become of us when the population got too thick; and if the unthinking creatures in Ireland don't take warning, it's exactly what will happen. When my mind was full of it, I ordered up Betty Cobb, and gave her such a lecture about it she'll never forget.

But you'll say it's not for this I'm gone into black; neither is it, Molly, — it's for my poor relative, the late Jones M'Carthy, of the Folly, one of the last surviving

members of the great M'Carthy stock, in the west of Ireland. Grief and sorrow for the miserable condition of his
country preyed upon him, and made him seek obliteration
in drink; and more's the pity, for he was a man of enlarged
understanding and capacious mind. My heart overflows
when I think of the beautiful sentiments I've heard from
him at various times. He loved his country, and it was a
treat to hear him praise it. "Ah!" he would say, "there's
but one blot on her, — the judges is rogues, the Government's rogues, the grand jury's rogues, and the people is
villains!"

He died as he lived, a little in drink, but a true patriot.
"Tell Jemima," says he, "I forgive her. She was a child
when she married, and she never meant to disgrace us; but
as she now succeeds to the estate, I hope she'll have the
pride to resume the family name."

Yes, Molly, the M'Carthy property, that once extended
from Gorramuck to Knocksheedownie, with seventeen
townlands and four baronies, descends now to me. To be
sure, it was all mortgaged over and over again, and 't is
little there's left but the parchments and the maps; and,
except the property in the funds, there's not a great deal
coming to me. This is all that I know at present, for
Waters, the attorney, writes in such a confused way, I can
make nothing of it, and I don't wish to show the letter to
K. I. That seems strange to you, Molly, but you'll think
it stranger when I tell you that the bare notion of my succeeding to the estate drives him half crazy. He thinks that
all the money being on his side makes up for his low birth,
and makes a Dodd equal to a M'Carthy, and that now when
I get my fortune the tables will be turned. Maybe he's
right there; I won't say that he is not; but sure it would
be time enough to show this feeling when my manner was
changed to him.

I suppose he must have heard something from Purcell
about the matter, for when I came into the room, with my
eyes red from crying, he said, "Is it for old Jones M'Carthy
you're crying? Begad, then, you must have a feeling heart,
for you never saw him since you were three years old!"

Did you ever hear a more barbarous speech, Molly, not

to say a more ignorant one? Twenty or thirty years might
be a very long time in a family called Dodd, but is it more
than a week or so in one with the name of M'Carthy? And
so I told him.

"You don't pretend that you 're sorry after him?" says
he. And I could only answer him with my sobs. "If it
was Giles Moore, the distiller," says he, "that went into
mourning, one could understand the sense of it, for *he* has
lost a friend indeed!"

"They 're to bury him in Cloughdesman Abbey," says I,
not wishing to let his sarcastic remarks provoke me.

"They need n't take much trouble about embalming him,
anyway," says he, "for there 's more whiskey soaked into
him than could preserve a whole family!"

You may think, Molly, how far I was overcome by grief
when he ventured to talk this way to me; and, indeed, I
left the room in a flood of tears. When I grew more composed, I went over Waters's letter again with Mary Anne,
but without any great success. There is so much law in
it, and so many words that we never saw before, and to
which, indeed, our pocket dictionary gave us little help:
Administer being set down, — to perform the duty of an
administrator; and for Administrator, we are told to see
Administer, — a kind of hide-and-go-seek that one does n't
expect in books like this.

The lawyers and the doctors, my dear Molly, go on the
same plan, — they never let us know the hard names they
have for everything. If we once come to do that, we 'll
know what 's the matter with ourselves and our affairs, and
neither need one nor the other. Mary Anne thinks that
administering means going to show the will to somebody
that 's to pay the money; but my private opinion is that
it 's something about Ministers' Money, for I remember my
poor cousin Jones never would consent to pay it, nor, indeed, anything else that went to the Established Church.
It was against his conscience, he used to say; and the Government that coerces a man's conscience is worthy of "Grim
Tartary." My notion is, then, that they 're coming against
me for the arrears, as if I had n't any conscience too!

At all events, Molly, the property is to come to *me ;* and

the very thought of it gives me a feeling of independence and pride that is really overwhelming. K. I.'s temper was, indeed, becoming a sore trial, and how I was to go on bearing it was more than I could imagine. He may now return to Ireland and his dear Dodsborough whenever he pleases. Mary Anne and I are determined to live abroad. Fortunately for us we have made acquaintance with a very distinguished English lady — a Mrs. Gore Hampton — who can introduce us everywhere. She is in the very height of the fashion, and knows all the great people of Europe. She took a sudden liking — I might call it an affection — for me and Mary Anne, and actually proposed our all travelling together as one party. There never was luck like it, Molly! She has a beautiful barouche of her own, with the arms on it, and a French maid and a courier, and such heaps of luggage, you would n't believe it could be carried. K. I. was afraid of the expense, and gave, as you may believe, every kind of opposition to the plan. He said it would "lead us into this," and "lead us into that;" the great thing he dreaded being led into — as I told him — being good society and high company."

So far from costing us anything, I believe it will be a considerable saving; for, as Lord George says, "You can always make a better bargain at the hotels when you're a strong party." And he has kindly taken the whole of this on himself.

He is a wonderful young man, Lord George; and, considering his tip-top rank and connections, he's never above doing anything to serve, or be useful to us. He knows K. I. as well, too, as I do myself. "Let me alone," says he, "to manage the governor; I know him. He's always grumbling about expense and moaning over his poverty; but you may remark that he does get the money somehow." And the observation is remarkably just, Molly; for no matter what distress or distraction he's in, he does contrive to rub through it; and this convinces me that he is only deceiving us in talking about his want of means, and so forth. Since I have discovered this, I never fret the way I used about expense.

It was Lord George that arranged our compact with

Mrs. G. "You had better leave all to me," said he to K. I., "for Mrs. Gore Hampton is a perfect child about money. She tells that old fool of a courier to put a hundred pounds in his bag, and he pays away till it's all gone, or till he says it's gone; and then she gives him another check for the same amount. So that she's not bored with accounts, nor ever hears of them, she never cares."

"Of course, then," said I, "her expenses are very great."

"I should say enormous," replied he; "for though personally the simplest creature on earth, she never objects to the cost of anything."

I hinted that, with our moderate fortune, we should never be able to maintain a style of living equal to hers; but he stopped me short, saying, "Don't let that distress you; besides, she has taken such a fancy for you and Miss Dodd that it would be a downright cruelty to deny her your companionship; and at this moment, too, when really she requires sympathy." I was dying to ask on what account, Molly, — was it that she is a widow, or is she separated, and what? — but I had n't the courage; nor, indeed, did he give me time, for he went on so fast: "Let her pay half the expense, it's only fair; she has plenty of tin, and nothing to do with it. Even then she will be a gainer, for old Grégoire pockets as much as he pays away."

You'd suppose, Molly, that an arrangement so liberal as this might have satisfied K. I. Not a bit of it. His only remark was, "What's to be the amount of the other half?"

"Do you expect to travel about the Continent for nothing, K. I.?" said I. "Does your experience say that it costs so little?"

"No, faith!" replied he, with that sardonic grin that almost kills me, "I can't say that."

"Well, then," said I, "is it better for us to go about the world unnoticed and unknown, or to be visited and received, and made much of everywhere? The name of Dodd," said I, "is n't a great recommendation; and there's some of us, at least, that have n't the exterior of the first fashion." I wish you saw how he fidgeted when I said this. "And as the great question is, What did we come abroad for? — "

"Ay, that's exactly it!" cried he, thumping his clenched

fist on the table with a smash that made me scream out. "What did we come abroad for?"

"There's no need to drive all the blood to my head, Mr. Dodd," said I, "to ask that. Though I am accustomed to your violence, my constitution may sink under it at last; but if you wish to know seriously and calmly why we came abroad, I'll tell you."

"Do, then," said he, folding his arms in front of him, "and I'll be mighty thankful for the information."

"We came abroad," said I, "first of all, for — "

"It wasn't economy," said he, with a grin.

"No, not exactly."

"I'm glad of that," cried he. "I'm glad that we've got rid of one delusion, at least. Now, then, go on."

"Maybe you'll call refinement a delusion, Mr. Dodd," said I. "Maybe politeness and good-breeding, the French language and music are delusions? Is high society a delusion? Is the sphere we move in a delusion?"

"I am disposed to think it is, Mrs. D.," said he, "and a very great delusion too. It's like nothing we were ever used to. It is not social, and it is not friendly. It has nothing to say, nor any concern with a single topic, or any one theme that we can care for. Do you know one, or can you even remember the names of any of the princes and princesses you are always discussing? Do you really care whether Mademoiselle Zephyrini's pirouette was steadier than Miss Angelina's? Does it concern you that somebody with a hard name has given the first-class order of the Pig and Whistle to somebody else, with a harder? Is it the meat stewed to rags you like, or the reputations with morality boiled out of them? Is it pleasant to think that, wherever you go, you meet nothing wholesome for mind or for body? I can stand scandal and wickedness as well as my neighbors, but I can't spend my life upon them, nor can I give up the whole day to dominos. You ask me what are delusions, and I tell you now some things that are not."

But I wouldn't listen to more, Molly. I stopped him short by saying, "You, at least, Mr. D., have little reason for your regrets; for really, in all that regards your manner, language, dress, and demeanor, no one would ever suspect you had been a day out of Dodsborough."

"I wish to my heart my bank account could tell the same story," says he; and with that he takes down a file of bills, and begins to read out some of what he calls his anti-delusions.

"Do you know, Mrs. D.," says he, "that your milliner has got more money in the last four months than I have spent on my estate for the last eight years? That Genoa velvet and Mechlin lace have run away with what would have drained the Low Meadows! Ay, the price of that red turban, that made you look like Bluebeard, would have put a roof on the school-house. The priest of our parish at home did n't get as much for his dues as you gave for a seat to look at a procession in honor of Saint — Saint — "

"If you 're going to blaspheme, Mr. D.," said I, "I 'll leave you;" and so I did, Molly, banging the door after me in a way that I know well his gouty ankle is not the better for.

I mention these particulars to show you the difficulties I have to contend against, and the struggles it costs me to give my children the benefits of the Continent. I intended to tell you something about this place where we are stopping, too; but my head is rambling now on other matters, so that, maybe, I 'll not be able to say much.

It 's a university, just like Trinity College in Dublin, only they don't wear gowns, nor keep within certain buildings, but scatter about over the whole town. We know several of the young men who are princes, and more or less related to crowned heads; but for all that, very simple, quiet, inoffensive creatures as ever you met. Billy Davis, after he was articled to that attorney in Abbey Street, had more impudence in him than them all put together.

The place itself is pretty, but I think it does n't suit my constitution. Maybe it 's the running water, for there 's a big river under the windows, but I am never free from cold in my head, and weak eyes. To be sure, we are always doing imprudent things, such as sitting out till after midnight in a summer-house, where the young Germans come to sing for us, — for singing and smoking, Molly, is their two passions. It's a melancholy kind of music they have, that has no tune whatever, nor anything like a tune in it; but as Mrs. G. and my daughters agree that it's beautiful, why, of course, I give in, and say the same. But, in confidence to you, Molly, I own that it puts me to sleep at once; and, indeed, most of our other amusements here are of the same kind. We are either botanizing, or looking for stones and shells, to tell us the age of the world. Faith! you may well stare, Molly, but it's truth I'm saying, that is what they

pretend to find out. They got an elephant's jawbone the other day, that gave them great delight, and K. I. said, "I could tell a horse's age by his teeth, but for guessing how old the earth is by an elephant's grinders is clear beyond me."

When it rains and we can't go out, we have chemistry at home; but I'm always in a fright about the combustibles, and I'm sure one of these days we'll pay for our curiosity. That man that comes to lecture has n't a bit of eyebrows, and only two fingers on one hand, and half a thumb on the other; not to say that he sat down one day on a pocketful of crackers, and blew himself up in a dreadful manner.

If the weather be fine, — and I was near saying, God

grant it may n't — we are to have a course of astronomy
every night next week. I can stand everything, however,
better than "moral philosophy and economics." As to the
first of the two, it's not even common-sense. It was only
two evenings ago, they laughed at me for twenty minutes
about a remark that's as true as the Bible.

"What relations does Locke say are least regarded?"
says the professor to me.

"Faith! I know nothing about Locke," says I; "but
I know well that the relations least regarded are poor
relations."

As to the economics, if they could enliven it a bit by
experiments, as they do the chemistry, I could bear it well
enough; but it's awfully dry to be always listening to what
you can't understand.

This is the way we live at Bonn; and though it's very
elevating, I find it's very depressing to the spirits. But I
don't think we'll remain much longer here, for K. I. is
beginning to find out that the sciences are just as dear as
silks and satins; and, as he remarked the other day, "it
would be cheaper to have a dish of asparagus on the table
than them dirty weeds that they are gathering only for the
sake of their hard names."

Of course, when all is settled about the legacy, I'll not
be obliged to submit to his humors, as I have been up to
this. I'll have a voice, Molly, and I'll take care that it
is heard too. I suppose it will come to a separation yet
between us. I own to you, Molly, the "impossibility" of
our tempers will do it at last. Well, when the time comes,
I'll be, as Mrs. G. says, equal to the occasion. I can
say, "I brought you rank, name, and fortune, Kenny Dodd,
and I leave you with my character unvarnished; and maybe
both is more than you deserved!"

When I think of where and what I might be, Molly, and
see what I am, I fret for a whole livelong day. And now
a word about home before I conclude. Don't mention a
syllable about the legacy to Mat, or he'll be expecting a
present at Candlemas, and I really can spare nothing.
You can say to Father John that Jones M'Carthy is dead,
but that nobody knows how the estate will go. He'll

maybe say some masses for him, in the hope of being paid hereafter by the heir. I'd advise you to keep the wool back, for they say prices will rise in Ireland, by reason of all the people leaving it, just as it's described in the Book of Genesis, Molly, only that Ireland is not Paradise,—that's the difference.

Mary Anne unites in her affectionate love to you, and I am your attached

JEMIMA DODD.

LETTER XVIII.

MARY ANNE DODD TO MISS DOOLAN, OF BALLYDOOLAN.

GRAND HÔTEL DU RHIN, BONN.

DEAREST CATHERINE,— Forgive me if I substitute for the loved appellation of infancy the more softly sounding epithet which is consecrated to verse in every language of Europe. Yes, thou mayst be Kate of all Kates to the rest of Christendom, but to me thou art Catherine,— " Catrinella mia," as thou wilt.

Here, dearest, as I sit embowered beside the wide and winding Rhine, the day-dream of my childhood is at length realized. I live, I breathe, in the land glorified by genius. Reflected in that stream is the castled crag of Drachenfels, mirrored as in my heart the image of my dearest Catherine. How shall I tell you of our existence here, fascinated by the charms of song and scenery, elevated by the strains of immortal verse? We are living at the Grand Hôtel du Rhin, my sweet child; and having taken the entire first floor, are regarded as something like an imperial family travelling under the name of Dodd.

I told you in my last of our acquaintance with Mrs. Gore Hampton. It has, since then, ripened into friendship. It is now love. I feel the dangerous captivation of speaking of her, even passingly. Her name suggests all that can fascinate the heart and inthrall the imagination. She is perfectly beautiful, and not less gifted than she is lovely. Perhaps I cannot convey to my dearest Catherine a more accurate conception of this charming being than by mentioning some — a few — of the changes wrought by her influence on the habits of our daily life.

Our mornings are scientific,— entirely given up to botany, chemistry, natural history, and geology, with occasional readings in political economy and statistics. We all attend these except papa. Even James has become a most attentive student, and never takes his eyes off Mrs. G. during the lecture. At three we lunch, and then mount our horses for a ride; since, thanks to Lord George's attentive politeness, seven saddle-horses have been sent down from Brussels for our use. Once mounted, we are like a school released from study, so full of gayety, so overflowing with spirits and animation.

Where shall we go? is then the question. Some are for Godesberg, where we dismount to eat ice and stroll through the gardens; others, of whom your Mary Anne is ever one, vote for Rolandseck, that being the very spot whence Roland the bravo — the brave Roland — sat to gaze upon those convent walls that enclosed all that he adored on earth.

And oh! Catherine dearest, is there amongst the very highest of those attributes which deify human nature any one that can compare with fidelity? Does it not comprise nearly all the virtues, heroic as well as humble? For my part, I think it should be the great theme of poets, blending as it does some of the tenderest with some of the grandest traits of the heart. From Petrarch to Paul — I mean Virginia's Paul — there is a fascination in these examples that no other quality ever evokes. My dearest Emily — I call Mrs. G. H. by her Christian name always — joined me the other evening in a discussion on this subject against Lord George James, and several others, our only cavalier being the Ritter von Wolfenschäfer, a young German noble, who is studying here, and a remarkable specimen of his class. He is tall, and what at first seems heavy-browed, but, on nearer acquaintance, displays one of those grand heads which are rarely met with save on the canvas of Titian; he wears a long beard and moustache of a reddish brown, which, accompanied by a certain solemnity of manner and a deep-toned voice, impress you with a kind of awe at first. His family is, I believe, the oldest in Germany, having been Barons of the Black Forest, in some very early century. "The first Hapsburg," he says, was a "knecht," or vassal, of one of his ancestors. His pride is, therefore, something indescribable.

Lord George met him, I fancy, first at some royal table, and they renewed their acquaintance here, shyly at the beginning, but after a while with more cordiality; and now he is here every day singing, sketching, reciting Schiller and Goethe, talking the most delightful rhapsodies, and raving about moonlights on the Brocken, and mysticism in the Hartzwald, till my very brain turns with distraction.

Don't you detest the " positif," — the dreary, tiresome, tame, sad-colored robe of reality? and do you not adore the prismatic-tinted drapery, that envelops the dream-creatures of imagination? I know, dearest Catherine, that you do. I feel by myself how you shrink from the stern aspect of reality, and love to shroud yourself in the graceful tissues of fancy! How, then, would you long to be here, — to discuss with us themes that have no possible relation to anything actually existing, — to talk of those visionary essences which form the creatures of the unreal world? The " Ritter " is perfectly charming on these subjects; there is a vein of love through his metaphysics, and of metaphysics through his love, that elevates while it subdues. You will say it is a strange transition that makes me flit from these things to thoughts of home and Ireland; but in the wilful wandering of my fancy a vision of the past rises before me, and I must seize it ere it depart. I wish, in fact, to speak to you about a passage in your last letter which has given me equal astonishment and suffering. What, dearest Kitty, do you mean by talking of a certain person's " long-tried and devoted affection," — " his hopes, and his steadfast reliance on my truthfulness "? Have I ever given any one the right to make such an appeal to me? I do really believe that no one is less exposed to such a reproach than I am! I have the right, if I please, to misconstrue your meaning, and assume a total ignorance as to whom you are referring. But I will not avail myself of the privilege, Kitty, — I will accept your allusion. You mean Dr. Belton. Now, I own that I write this name with considerable reluctance and regret. His many valuable qualities, and the natural goodness of his disposition, have endeared him to all of that humble circle in which his lot is cast, and it would grieve me to write one single word which should pain him to hear. But I ask you, Kitty, what is there in our relative stations in society which should embolden him to offer me attentions? Do we move in the same sphere? have we either thoughts, ideas, or ambitions — have we even acquaintances — in common? I do not want to magnify the position I hold. Heaven knows that the great world is not a sea devoid of rocks and quicksands. No one feels its perils more acutely than myself. But I repeat it: Is there not a wide gulf between us? Could *he* live, and move, think, act, or plan, in the circle that I associate with? Could *I* exist, even for a day, in *his?* No, dearest, impossible, — utterly impossible. The great world has its requirements, — exactions, if you will; they are imperative, often tyrannical: but their sweet recompense comes back in that delicious tranquillity of soul, that bland imperturbability that springs from good breeding, — the calm equanimity that no accident can shake, from which no sudden shock can elicit a vibration. I do not pretend, dearest friend, that I have yet attained to this. I know well that I am still far distant from that great goal; but I am on the road, Kitty, — my progress has commenced, and not for the wealth of worlds would I turn back from it.

With thoughts like these in my heart, — instincts I should perhaps call them, — how unsuited should I be to the humble monotony of a provincial existence! Were I even to sacrifice my own happiness, should I secure his? My heart responds, No, certainly not.

As to what you remark of the past, I feel it is easily replied to. The little chapel at Bruff once struck me as a miracle of architectural beauty. I really fancied that the doorway was in the highest taste of florid Gothic, and that the east window was positively gorgeous in tracery. As to the altar, I can only say that it appeared a mass of gold, silver, and embroidery, such as we read of in the "Arabian Nights." Am I to blame, Kitty, that, after having seen the real splendors of St. Gudule, and the dome of Cologne, I can recant my former belief, and acknowledge that the little edifice at Bruff is poor, mean, and insignificant; its architecture a sham, and its splendor all tinsel? and yet it is precisely what I left it.

You will then retort, that it is *I* am changed! I own it, Kitty. I am so. But can you make this a matter of reproach? If so, is not every step in intellectual progress, every stage of development, a stigma? Your theory, if carried out, would soar beyond the limits of this life, and dare to assail the angelic existences of the next!

But you could not intend this; no, Kitty, I acquit you at once of such a notion; even the defence of your friend could not make you so unjust. Dr. Belton must, surely, be in error as to any supposed pledges or promises on my part. I have taxed my memory to the utmost, and cannot recall any such. If, in the volatile gayety of a childish heart, — remember, sweetest, I was only eighteen when I left home, — I may have said some silly speech, surely it is not worth remembering, still less recording, to make me blush for it. Lastly, Kitty, I have learned to know that all real happiness is based upon filial obedience; and whatever sentiments it would be possible for me to entertain for Dr. B. would be diametrically opposed to the wishes of my papa and mamma.

I have now gone over this question in every direction I could think of, because I hope that it may nevermore recur between us. It is a theme which I advert to with sorrow, for really I am unable to acquit of presumption one whose general character is conspicuous for a modest and retiring humility. You will acquaint him with as much of the sentiments I here express as you deem fitting. I leave everything to your excellent delicacy and discretion. I only beg that I may not be again asked for explanations on a matter so excessively disagreeable to discuss, and that I may be spared alluding to those peculiar circumstances which separate us forever. If the time should come when he will take a more reasonable and just view of our respective conditions, nothing will be more agreeable to me than to renew those relations of friendship which we so long cultivated as neighbors; and if, in any future state I may occupy, I can be of the least service to him, I beg you to believe that it will be both a pride and a pleasure to me to know it.

It is needless, after this, to answer the question of your postscript. Of course he must not write to me. Nothing could induce me to read his letter. That he should ever have thought of such a thing is a proof — and no slight one — of his utter ignorance of all the conventional rules which regulate social intercourse. But a truce to a theme so painful.

I answer your brief question of the turn-down of your letter as curtly as it is put. No; I am not in love with Lord George, nor is he with *me*. We regard each other as brother and sister; we talk in the most unreserved confidence; we say things which, in the narrower prejudices of England, would be infallibly condemned. In fact, Kitty, the sway of a conscientious sense of right, the inward feeling of purity, admit of many liberties here, which are denied to us at home. Here I tell you, in one word, what it is that constitutes the superiority in tone of the Continent over our own country, — I should say it was this very same freedom of thought and action.

The language is full of a thousand graceful courtesies that mean so much or so little. The literature abounding in analysis of emotions, — that secret anatomy of the heart, so fascinating and so instructive; the habits of society so easy and so natural; and then that chivalrous homage paid to the sex,— all contribute to extend the realms of conversational topics, and at the same time to admit of various ways of treating them, such as may suit the temper, the talent, or the caprice of each. How often does it happen from this that one hears the gravest themes of religion and politics debated in a spirit of the most sparkling wit and levity, while subjects of the most trivial kind are discussed with a degree of seriousness and a display of learning actually astounding! This wonderful versatility is very remarkable in another respect; for, strange enough, it is the young people abroad who are the gravest in manner, the most reserved and most saturnine.

The high-spirited, the buoyant, and most daring talkers are the elderly. In a word, Kitty, everything here is the reverse of that at home; and, I am forced to confess, possesses a great superiority over our own notions.

I am dying to tell you more of the Ritter, which, I must explain to you, is the German for "Chevalier." If you

want a confession, too, I will make one; and that is that
he is desperately in love with a poor friend of yours, who
feels herself quite unworthy of the devotion of this scion of
thirty-two quarterings.

In a worldly point of view, Kitty, the possibility of such
an event would be brilliant beyond conception. His estates
are a principality, and his Schloss von Wölfenberg one of
the wonders of the Black Forest. Does not your heart
swell and bound, dearest, at the thought of a real castle, in
a real forest, with a real baron, Kitty? — one of those cruel
creatures, perhaps, who lived in feudal times, and always
killed a child, to warm their feet in his heart's blood? Not
that our Ritter looks this. On the contrary, he is gentle,
low-voiced, and dreamy, — a little too dreamy, — if I must
say it, and not sufficiently alive to the rattling drolleries of
Lord George and James, who torment him unceasingly.

Mamma likes him immensely, though their intercourse is
limited to mere bows and greetings; and even papa, whose
prejudice against foreigners increases with every day,
acknowledges that he is very amiable and good-tempered.
Cary appears to me to be greatly taken with him, but he
never notices her, nor pays her the slightest attention. I'm
sure I wish he would, and I should be delighted to contribute towards such a conjuncture. Who knows what may
happen later, for he has invited us all to the Schloss for the
shooting-season, — some time, I believe, in autumn, — and
papa has said "Yes."

I now come to another secret, dearest Kitty, depending
on all your discretion not to divulge it, at least for the
present. Mamma has received a confidential note from
Waters, the attorney, informing her that she is to succeed
to the M'Carthy estates and property of the late Jones
M'Carthy, of M'Carthy's Folly. The amount is not yet
known to us, and we are surrounded by such difficulties,
from our desire to keep the matter secret, that we cannot
expect to know the particulars for some time. The estates
were considerable; but, like those of all the Irish aristocracy, greatly encumbered. The personal property, mamma
thinks, could not have been burdened, so that this alone
may turn out handsomely.

By some deed of settlement, or something of the kind, executed at papa's marriage with mamma, he voluntarily abandoned all right over any property that should descend to her, so that she will possess the unlimited control over this bequest. Mr. Waters mentions that the testator desired — I am not certain that he did not require as a condition — that we should take the name of M'Carthy. I hope so with all my heart. I do not believe that anything could offer such obstacles to us abroad as this terrible and emphatic monosyllable; now, Dodd M'Carthy has a rhythm in it, and a resonance also.

It sounds territorially, too; like the *de* of French nobility. We should figure in fashionable "Arrivals and Departures" with a certain air of distinction that is denied to us at present; and I really do not see why we should not be "The M'Carthy." You know, dearest, that the Herald's office never interferes about Celtic nobility, inasmuch as its origin utterly defies investigation; and there are, consequently, no pains nor penalties attached to the assumption of a native title. How I should be delighted to hear us announced as "The M'Carthy, family and suite," with an explanatory paragraph about papa being the blue or the black knight. The English are always impressed with these things, and foreigners regard them with immense devotion. There is another incalculable advantage, Kitty, not to be overlooked. All little eccentricities of manner, little peculiarities of accent, voice, and intonation, of which neither pa nor ma are totally exempt, instead of being criticised, as some short-sighted folk might criticise them, as vulgar, low, and commonplace, rise at once to the dignity of a national trait.

They are like Breton French, or certain Provençal expressions in use amongst the ancient "Seigneurie" of the land. They actually dignify station, instead of disgracing it, so that a "brogue" seems to seal the very patent of your nobility, and the mutilations of your parts of speech stand for quarterings on your escutcheon.

It might seem invidious were I to quote the instances which support my theory; but I assure you, seriously, that social success, to be rapid, requires aids like these. There was a time when being a Villiers, a Stanley, or a Seymour gave you a kind of illusory nobility. You were a species of human shot-silk, that turned blue in one light, and brown in another; but now that Burke is read in the national schools, and the "Almanach de Gotha" in the godless colleges, deception on this head is impossible. They take you "to book" at once. You can't be one of the Howards of Ettinham, for Lady Mary died childless; nor one of the Worseley branch, for the present Marquis, who married Lady Alice de Courtenaye, had only two children, — one, British envoy at the Court of Prince of Salms und Schweinigen; the other, &c. In fact, Kitty, you are voted nobody. They will not allow you father nor mother, uncle nor aunt, nor even any good·friends. Better be Popkins, or Perkins, Snooks, or even Smith, than this! The Celtic *noblesse*, however, is a safe refuge against all impertinent curiosity. Tracing the Dodd M'Carthy to his parent stem would be like keeping count of the sheep in Sancho's story. Besides, matters of succession are made matters of faith in the Church, and why shouldn't they be in the M'Carthy family? I don't suppose we want to be more infallible than the Pope?

I have not forgotten what you mentioned about your brother Robert; nor was it at all necessary, my dear Kitty, for you to speak of his talents and acquirements, which I well know are first-rate. I took an opportunity the other day of alluding to the matter to Lord George, who has influence in every quarter. I told him pretty much in the words of your letter, that he was equally distinguished in science as in classics, had taken honors in both, and was in all other respects fully qualified to be a tutor. That, being a gentleman by birth, though of small fortune, his desire was to obtain the advantages of foreign travel, and the opportunity of acquiring modern languages, for which he was quite willing to assume all the labor and fatigue of a teacher. He stopped me short here by saying, "I'm afraid it's no go. They've made a farce, and a devilish good one, too, of the 'Irish Tutor;' and I half suspect that Dr. O'Toole, as he is called, has spoiled the trade."

I tried to introduce a word about Robert's attainments,

but he broke in with, — "That's all very well; I'm quite
sure of everything you say. But who takes a ' coach'?" —
That's the slang for tutor, Kitty! — "No one takes a
' coach' for his learning nowadays. What's wanted —
particularly when travelling — is a sharp, wide-awake fellow, that knows all the dodges of the Continent as well as
a courier, can bully the police, quiz the custom-house, and
slang the waiters. He ought to be up to the opera and the
ballet; be a dead hand at écarté, and a capital judge of
cigars. After these, his great requisites are never ceasing
good-humor, and a general flow of high spirits, to stand all
the bad jokes and vapid fun of young college men; a yielding disposition to go anywhere, with any one, and for anything that may be proposed; and, finally, a ready tact never
to suppose himself included in any invitation with his
'Bear,' who, however well he may treat him, will always
prefer leaving him at home when he dines at an ' Embassy.' "

This is a rapid sketch of a tutor's life and habits, as practised abroad, Kitty; and I more than suspect Robert would
not like it. Should I be in error, however, and that such
would suit his views, I'm sure I can reckon on Lord
George's kindness to find him an appointment. Meanwhile let him "accustom himself to much smoking and
occasional brandy-and-water, lay in a good stock of droll
anecdotes, and if he can acquire any conjuring knowledge,
or tricks on the cards, it will aid him greatly." These
hints are Lord G.'s, and, I am sure, invaluable.

A thunderstorm has just broken over the valley of the
Rhine, and the dread artillery of heaven comes pealing
down from the "Lurlie" like a chorus of demons in a modern opera. Our excursion being impossible, I once more
resume my task, and again seat myself to hold communion
with my dearest Kitty.

I find, besides, innumerable questions still unanswered
in your last dear letter. You ask me if, on the whole, I am
happier than I was at Dodsborough? How could you ever
have penned such a quære? The tone of seriousness which
you tell me of, in my letters, admits perhaps of a softer
epithet. May it not be that soul-kindled elevation that

comes of daily association with high intelligences? If I were but to tell you the names of the illustrious writers and great thinkers whom we meet here almost every evening, Kitty, you would no longer be amazed at the soaring flight my faculties have taken. Not that they appear to us, my dearest friend, in the mystic robes of science, but in the humble garb of common life, playing "groschen" whist, or a game of tric-trac. Just fancy, if you can, Professor Faraday playing "petits jeux," or Wollaston engaged at "hunt the slipper."

These are the intimacies, this the kind of intercourse, which imperceptibly cultivate the mind, and enlarge the understanding; for, as Mrs. Gore Hampton beautifully observes, "The charm of high-bred manner is not to be acquired by attendance on a ' levee ' or a ' drawing-room,' it is imbibed in the atmosphere that pervades a court, in the daily, hourly association with that harmonious elegance that surrounds a sovereign." So, dearest Kitty, from intercourse with great minds is there a perpetual gain to our stock of knowledge. "They are," as Mrs. G. says, "the charged machines from which the electric sparks of genius are eternally disengaging themselves." What a privilege to be the receivers!

There is a wondrous charm, too, in their simplicity, as well as in that habit they have of mystically connecting the most trivial topics with the most astounding speculations. A fairy tale becomes to *them* a metaphysical allegory. You would scarcely credit what curious doctrines of socialism lie veiled under "Jack the Giant Killer," or that the Marquis of Carabas, in the tale of "Puss in Boots," is meant to illustrate the oppression of the landed aristocracy. Nor is this all, Kitty; but they go further, and they are always speculating on something beyond the actual catastrophe of a story; as, the other evening, I heard a learned argument to show that had Bluebeard not been killed, he would have inevitably formed an alliance with "Sister Anne," just for the sake of supporting the cause of "marriage with a deceased wife's sister." I only mention these as passing instances of that rich imaginative fertility which is as much their characteristic as is their wonderful power of argumentation.

Lord George and James worry me greatly for my admiration of Germany and the Germans. They talk, in slang, on themes that require a high strain of intelligence to comprehend or even appreciate. No wonder, then, if their frivolity offend and annoy me! The Ritter von Wolfenschäfer is an unspeakable relief to me, after this tiresome quizzing. Shall I own that Cary is their ally in the same ignoble warfare? Indeed, nothing surprises, and at the same time depresses me more than to remark the little benefit derived by Caroline from foreign travel. She would seem to sit down perfectly contented with the information derived from books, as though the really substantial advantages of a residence abroad were not all dependent on direct intercourse with the people. "Why not read Uhland and Tieck at home at Dodsborough?" say I to her. "To what end do you come hundreds of miles away from your country, to do what might so easily have been accomplished at home?" What do you think was her reply? It was this: "That is exactly what I should like to do. Having seen some parts of the Continent, having enjoyed the spectacle of those wonderful things of nature and of art which a tour abroad would display, and having acquired that facility in languages which comes so rapidly by their daily use, I should like to go home again, adding to the pleasures my own country supplies, stores of knowledge and resources from other lands. I neither want to think that Frenchmen and Germans are better bred than my own countrymen, nor that the rigid decorum of English manners is only a flimsy veil of hypocrisy thrown over the coarse vices of a coarse people."

Now, my dear Kitty, be as national and patriotic as one will; play "Rule Britannia" every morning, with variations, on the piano; wear a Paisley shawl and a Dunstable bonnet; make yourself as hideous and absurd as the habits of your native country will admit of, — and that is a wide latitude,— you will be obliged to own the startling fact, the Continent *is* more civilized than England. Daily life is surrounded with more of elegance and of refinement, for the simple reason that there is more leisure for both. There is none of that vulgarity of incessant occupation so observable with us.   Men do not live here to be Poor-law guardians and Quarter Sessions chairmen, directors of railroads, or members of select committees.   They choose the nobler ambition of mental cultivation and intellectual polish.   They study the arts which adorn social intercourse, and acquire those graceful accomplishments which fascinate in the great world, and, in the phrase of the newspapers, "make home happy."

I have now come to the end of my paper, and perhaps of your patience, but not of my arguments on this theme, nor the wish to impress them upon my dearest Kitty. Adieu!   Adieu!

I can understand your astonishment at reading this, Kitty; but is it not another proof that Ireland is far behind the rest of the world in civilization?   The systems exploded everywhere are still pursued there, and the unprofitable learning that all other countries have abandoned is precisely the object of hardest study and ambition.

There are twenty other things that I wished to consult my dearest Kitty about, but I must conclude.   It is now nigh eleven o'clock, the moon is rising, and we are off on our excursion to the Drachenfels, — for you must know that one of the stereotyped amusements of the Continent is to ascend mountains for the sake of seeing daybreak from the "summit."   It is frequently a failure as regards the picturesque; but never so with respect to the pleasure of the trip. Think of a mountain path by moonlight, Kitty; your mule slowly toiling up the steep ascent, while some one near murmurs "Childe Harold" in your ear, the perils of the way permitting a hundred little devotional attentions so suggestive of dependence and protection.   I must break off, — they are calling for me; and I have but time to write myself my dearest Kitty's dearest friend,

MARY ANNE DODD.

LETTER XIX.

BETTY COBB TO MRS. SHUSAN O'SHEA, PRIEST'S HOUSE, BRUFF.

DEAR MISSES SHUSAN, — I thought before this I'd be back again in Bruff, but I leave it all to Providence, that maybe, all the time, is thinkin' little about me. It's not out of any unpiety I say this, but bekase the longer I live the more I see how sarvants are trated in this world; and the next I'm towld is much the same.

If the mistress would let me alone, I'd get used to the ways of the place at last, for there's some things isn't so bad at all; since we came to this we have four males every day, but, if you mind grace, you might as well have none. They've a puddin' for everything, fish — flesh — fowl — vegebles, it's all alike; but the hardest thing is to eat blackberries with beef, or stewed pork with rasberries; not to spake of a pike with pine-apple, that we had yesterday.

There is always an abundance and a confusion at dinner that's plazing to one's feelin's; for, indeed, in Ireland there is no great variety in the servants' hall, and polatics has a sameness in them that's very tiresome.

We are livin' now at an elegant hotel, where we sit down forty-seven of us every day, at the sound of a big bell at one o'clock. They call it the table doat, and I don't wonder they do, for it's the pleasantest place I ever see. We goes down, linked arm-in-arm, me and Lord George's man, Mister Slipper, and the Frinsh made lanin' on Mounseer Gregory, the currier; and there's as much bowin' and scrapin', or more, than upstairs in the parlor. Mr. Slipper takes the head of the table, and I am on his rite, and mamsel on his left, and the dishes all cums to us first, and we tumble the things about, and helps ourselves to the best before the others, and we laff so loud, Shusan, for Mr. Slipper is uncommon drol, and tells a number of stories that makes me cry for lafflin'; and he is just as polite, too, for whinever he tells anything wrong he says it in French. And if you only heerd the way masters and mistresses is spoke of, Shusan, you 'd pity poor sarvants that has to live with them, and put up with their bad 'umors. Mr. Slipper himself is trated like a dog, on eighty pounds a year, and what he calls the spoils, — that 's the close that 's spoiled. Many the day he never sees the newspaper, for Lord G. sticks it in his pocket, and carries it out with him; and when he went out to tay, the other evenin', there was n't an embroidered shirt of his master's to put on, and he was obleeged to take a plain cambric to make a clane breast of it! "Faix," says he, "there 's no sayin' what will happen soon, and maybe the day 'll cum I 'll have to buy my own cigars." He had an iligant place before this one, — Sir Michael Bexley, — but tho' the wagis was high, and the eating first-rate, he could n't stay. "We wore in Vi-enna," says he, "where they dance a grate dale in sosiety, and Sir Michael's hands and feet was smaller than mine, and I could n't wear either his kid gloves or his dress-boots, and goin' out every night the expense was krushin'."

Mamsel is trated just as bad. It 's maybe three when she gets to bed; her mistress, Mrs. G., would n't take a flour out of her head herself, but must have the poor crayture waitin' there, like a centry. And maybe it 's at that time o' night she 'll take the notion of seein' how it bekomes her to have her hare, this way or that, or to see if she 'd look better with more paint on her, or if her eyebrows was blacker.

Sometimes, too, she takes a fit of tryin' ball dresses, five or six, one after another; but mamsel says, she thinks she cured her of that by dropping some lamp oil over a bran new white satin, with Brussels lace, that was never worn at all. As Mr. Slipper says, "Our ingenuity is taxed to a degree that destroys our dispositions;" and I may here observe, Shusan, that all sarvants ever I heerd of get somehow worse trated than Irish. I don't mane in regard to wagis, bekase the Irish cartainly gets laste, but I spake of tratement; and the rayson is this, Shusy, the others do their work as a kind of duty, a thing they 're paid for, and that they ought to do;

we, the Irish I mane, do everything as if it was out of our own
goodness, and that we would n't do it if we did n't like;
and that's the real way to manage a master or a mistress.
If he asks for a knife at diner, sure he can't deny it's a
knife bekase it's dirty, there would n't be common sense
in that. There's two ways of doin' everything, Shusan;
but, easy as it is, the Irish is the only people profits by
the lesson! It's only ourselves, Shusan dear, knows how
to make a master or mistress downright miserable!

It is true we seldom have good wagis, but we take it out
in temper. If ye seen the life I sometimes lead the mistress
you'd pity her; but why would you after all? was n't I
taken away from my home and country, and put down here
in a strange place; and if I did n't spend the day now and
then cryin', would she ever think of razing my sperits with a
new bonnet, or a pare of shoes, or a ticket for the play?
Take *them* azy, Shusy, and they'll take *you* the same. But
if you show them they're in your power, take to your bed,
sick, when they're in a hot hurry, and want you most, be
sulky and out of sperits when they're all full of fun, and
go singin' about the house the day they've got a distressin'
letter by the post, — keep to that, and my shure and sartain
beleef is, that you'll break down the sperit of the wickidest
master and mistress that ever breathed.

Is n't my mistress, I ask you, as hard to dale with as any?
Well, many's the time, when I'm listenin' at the doore, I
heerd her say, "Betty can't bear me in that shawl, — Betty
put it somewhere, and I'm afraid to ask for it, — Betty's
in one of her tantrums to-day, so I must not cross her. I
wish I knew how to put Betty Cobb in good humor."
"Faix, ma'am," says I to myself, "I believe you well, and
it would puzzle wiser heads nor you!"

And now, Misses Shusan dear, is it any wonder that our
tempers get spoiled? seein' the lives we lade, and the dreadful turns and twists we are obleeged to give our natral dispositions. It's for all the world like play-actin'.

There's many things different betune this and home, and
first and foremost religion, Shusan. Religion is n't the same
at all. To begin, there's no fastin' at all, or next to none;
maybe that's bekase, by the nature of the cookery, nobody

could tell what it was he was eatin'. Then, there's little penance, — and the little there is ye can get off of it by a thrifle. Ye go to confessin' whin ye like, and ye keep anything back for another time that ye don't wish to tell just then. In fact, my dear, it comes to this, — it's harder to go to Heaven in Ireland than any place ever I heerd of, and costs more money into the bargain!

The priests has n't half the power they have in Ireland, they're not as well paid, and they can't curse a congregation, nor do any other good action that is n't set down in their duty. It's the polis, Shusy, that makes ye tremble abroad, and that's the great difference between the two countries.

As to morils, my dear, I'm afraid we're not supariar, for it's the women always makes love to the men, which, till you get used to it, has a mighty ugly appearance. I b'l'eve it's the smokin' leads to this, for a German would n't take his pipe out of his mouth for anything; so that courtin' is n't what it is at home.

These is my general remarks on the habits of furriners, which I give you as free as you ask for them. As to the family, nobody knows where the money comes from, but that they're spendin' it in lashins, is true as I'm here. And they're broke up, Shusy, and not the way they used to be. The master walks out alone, or with Miss Caraline. Miss Mary Anne stays with the mother; and Master James, that's now a grone man, and as bowld as brass besides, is always phelanderin' about with Mrs. G., the lady that lives with us. I mistrust her, Shusan dear, and Mamsel Virginy, her made, too, though she's mighty kind and polite to *me*, and says she has so many "bounties" for the whole family.

Paddy Byrne is exactly what you suspect. There's nothin' would put the least polish on him. The very way he ates at the table doat disgraces us; whenever he gets a thing he likes, instead of helpin' himself and passin' it on, he takes the whole dish before him, and conshumes it all. As he is always ready to fite, they let him do as he likes, and he is become now the terror of the place. I have towld ye now about everybody but the ould currier, Mounseer Gregory, an invetherate ould Frinsh bla'guard, that never has a dacent word in his mouth, though he has n't a good tooth in it, and ye 'd say 't was at his prayers the ould hardened sinner should be. The very laff he has, and the way his bleery eyes twinkle, is a shame to see! It 's nigh to fifty years since he took to the road, so that you may think, Shusan dear, what a dale of innequity he 's seen in that time. It 's dreadful sometimes to listen to him.

If I was n't ashamed to write them, I 'd tell you two or three of his stories, but I will when we meet; and now with my

hearty blessin' and love, I remane yours

to command, BETTY COBB.

What 's this I heer about one of the M'Carthys dyin', and levin' his money to the mistress? Get the news right for me, Shusan dear, for I mane to ask for more wagis if it 's true, and if Mrs. D. won't decrease them, I 'll lave the sarvis. Mamsel Virginy towl me last nite there was a duches here that wants a confidenshal made to tache her only daughter English, and that 's exactly the thing to shoot me; five hundred franks a year is equal to twenty pounds, all eatin' and washin', not to mention the hoith of respect from all the men-ials in the house. I 'm takin' Frinsh lessons from ould Gregory every evenin', and he says I 'll be in my "accidents" next week.

LETTER XX.

JAMES DODD TO ROBERT DOOLAN, ESQUIRE, TRINITY COLLEGE,
DUBLIN.

You guessed rightly, my dear Bob; my letter to Vickars has
turned out confoundedly ill, though I must say, all from his
total want of gentlemanlike feeling. To my ineffable horror
the other morning, the post arrived with a large packet for
the governor, containing my "strictly private and confidential" epistle, which this infernal son of a pen-wiper sends
coolly back to be read by my father.

Matters were not going on exactly quite smooth before.
We had had a rather stormy sitting of the Cabinet the
evening previous on the estimates, which struck the President of the Council as out of all bounds; and yet, all
things considered, were reasonable enough. You know,
Bob, we are a strongish party. Mrs. G. H., with maid and
courier; Lord George and man; the Dodd family five, with
two native domestics, and two foreign supernumeraries;
occupying the first floor of the first hotel at Bonn, with a
capital table, and a considerable quantity of wine, of one
kind or other; these — without anything that one can call
extravagance — swell up a bill, and at the end of a month
give it an actually formidable look.

"What are these?" said the governor, peering through
his glasses at a long battalion of figures at the foot of the
score, — "what are these? Groschen, eh?"

"Pardon, Monsieur le Comte," said the other, bowing,
"dey are Prussian thalers!"

I wish you saw his face when he heard it! George and
I were obliged to bolt out of the room, or we should have
infallibly exploded.

"You'd better go back," said George to me, after we had our laugh out; "I'll take a stroll with the womenkind till you smooth him down a bit."

A pleasant office this for me; but there was no help for it, so in I went.

The first shock of his surprise was not over as I entered, for he stood holding the bill in one hand, while he pressed the other on his forehead, with a most distracted expression of face.

"Do you suspect," said he — "have you any notion of what rate we are living at, James?"

"Not the slightest," replied I.

"Do you think it's of any consequence?" asked he again, in a harsher tone.

"Why, of course, sir, it — is — of some con — "

"I mean," broke he in, "does it signify whether I go to jail, and the rest of you to the workhouse, — if there be a workhouse in this rascally land?"

Seeing that he had totally forgotten the landlord's presence, I now motioned to that functionary to leave the room. The noise of the door shutting roused up the governor again. He looked wildly about him for an instant, and then snatching up the poker he aimed a blow at a large mirror over the chimney. He struck it with such violence that it was smashed in a dozen pieces, four or five of which came clattering down upon the floor.

"I'll be a maniac," cried he. "They shall never say that I ran into this extravagance in my sober senses; I'll finish my days in a madhouse first." And with these words he made a rush over to a marble table, where a large porcelain vase was standing; by a timely spring I overtook him, and pressed him down on an ottoman, where, I assure you, it required all my force to hold him. After a few minutes, however, there came a reaction; he dropped the poker from his grasp, and said, in a low, faint voice, "There — there — I'll do nothing now — you may release me."

There's not a doubt of it, Bob, but he really was insane for a few moments, though, fortunately, it passed away as rapidly as it came.

"That," said he, with a motion towards the looking-glass,
— "that will cost twenty or twenty-five pounds, eh?"

"Not so much, perhaps," said I, though I knew I was
considerably below the mark.

"Well, I'm sure it saved me from a fit of illness, anyhow," rejoined he, sighing. "If I hadn't smashed it, I
think my head would have burst. Go over that, James,
and see what it is in pounds."

I sat down to a table, and after some calculation made
out the total to be two hundred and seven pounds sterling.

"And with the looking-glass, about two hundred and
thirty," said he, with a sigh. "That's about — taking
everything into consideration — five thousand a year."

"You must remember," said I, trying to comfort him,
"that these are not our expenses solely. There's Tiverton and his servant, and Mrs. Gore Hampton and her
people also."

"So there is," added he, quickly; "but they had nothing
to do with *that ;*" and he pointed to the confounded
looking-glass, which somehow or other had taken a fast
hold of his imagination. "Eh, James, that was a luxury
we had for ourselves!" There was a bitter, sardonic laugh
that accompanied these words, indescribably painful to
hear.

"Come now," said he, in a more composed and natural
voice, "let us see what's to be done. This is a joint
account, James; why not have sent it to Lord George — ay,
to the widow also? They may as well frank the Dodd
family as *we* pay for *them*, — of course, omitting the
looking-glass."

I hinted that this was a step requiring some delicacy in
its management; that, if not conducted with great tact, it
might be the occasion of deep offence. In a word, Bob,
I surmised, and conjectured, and hinted a hundred things,
just to gain a little time, and turn him, if possible, into
another channel.

"Well, what do you advise?" said he, as if wishing to
fix me to some tangible project.

For a moment I was bent on adopting the grand parliamentary tactic of stating that there were "three courses

open to the House," and then going on to show that one of
these was absurd, the second impracticable, and the last
utterly impossible; but I saw that the governor could not
be so easily put down as the Opposition, and so I said,
"Give it till to-morrow morning, and I'll see what can be
done."

Here I felt I was on safe ground, for throughout life I
have ever remarked that whenever an Irishman is in difficulties, a reprieve is as good as a free pardon to him; for
so is it, the land which seems so thoroughly hopeless in its
destinies, contains the most hopeful population of Europe!

The delay of a few hours made all the difference in the
governor's spirits, and he rallied and came down to supper
just as usual, only whispering, as we left the room, with a

peculiar low chuckle in his voice, "I would n't wonder if the fire there cracked that chimney-glass."

"Nothing more likely," added I, gravely; and down we went.

It might possibly be out of utter recklessness, or perhaps from some want of a stimulant to cheer him, but he insisted on having two extra bottles of champagne, and he toasted Mrs. Gore Hampton with a zest and fervor that certainly my mother did n't approve of. On the whole, however, all passed off well, and we wished each other good-night, with the pleasantest anticipations for the morrow.

All was well; and we were at breakfast the next morning, merrily discussing the plans for the day, when the post arrived, with that ominous-looking packet I have already mentioned.

"Shall I guess what that contains?" cried Lord George, pointing to the words, "on her Majesty's service," printed in the corner. "They 've made you Lord-Lieutenant of your county, Dodd! You shake your head. Well, it 's something in the colonies they 've given you."

"Perhaps it 's the Civil Cross of the Bath," said Mrs. Gore Hampton. "They told me, before I left town, they were going to select some Irishman for that distinction."

"I 'd rather it was a baronetcy," interposed my mother.

"You are all forgetting," broke in my father, "that it 's the Tories are in power, and they 'll give me nothing. I was always a moderate politician, and, for the last ten or fifteen years, there was nothing so unprofitable. Violence on either side met its reward, but the quiet men, like myself, were never remembered."

"Then hang me if I should have been quiet!" cried Lord George.

"Well, you see," said my father, breaking his egg slowly with the back of his spoon, "it suited me! I 've seen a great deal of Ireland; I 'm old enough to remember the time when the Beresfords governed the country, — if you can call that government that was done with pitched-caps and cat-o'-nine-tails, — and I remember Lord Whitworth's Administration, and Lord Wellesley's, and latterly, Lord Normanby's. But, take my word for it, they were wrong, every one of them, and the reason was this: the English had a notion in their heads that Ireland must always be ruled through the intervention of some leadership or other. One time it was the Protestants, then it was the landlords, then came Dan O'Connell, and, lastly, it was the priests. Now, every one of these failed, because they could n't perform a tithe of what they promised; but still they all had that partial kind of success that saved the Administration a deal of trouble, and imposed upon the English the notion that they were at last learning how to govern Ireland. Meanwhile I 'll tell you what was happening. The Government totally forgot there was such a thing as a people in Ireland, and, what's worse, the people forgot it themselves; and the consequence was, they sank down to the level of a mean party following — a miserable, shabby herd — to shout after an Orange or a Green Demagogue, as the case might be. It was a faction, and not a nation; and England saw that, but she had not the honesty to own it was her own doing made it such. It was seeing all this made me a moderate politician, or, in other words, one who reposed a very moderate confidence in either of the parties that pretended to rule Ireland."

"But you supported your friend, Vickars, notwithstanding," said Lord George, slyly.

"Very true, so I did; but I never put forward any mock patriotism as the reason. What I said was, ' Ye 're all rogues and vagabonds alike, and as I know you 'll do nothing for Ireland, at least do something for the Dodd family; ' and now let us see if he has, for I perceive that this address is in his handwriting."

I own to you, Bob, I quaked somewhat as I saw him smash the seal. My mind misgave me in fifty ways. "Vickars," thought I, "has given me some infernal storekeepership in the Gambia, or made me inspector of yellow fever in Chusan." I surmised a dozen different promotions, every one of which was several posts on the road to the next world. Nor were my anticipations much brightened by watching the workings of the governor's face as he perused the epistle; for it grew darker and darker, the angles of the mouth were drawn down, till that expressive feature put on

the semblance of a Saxon arch, while his eyes glistened with
an expression of fiend-like malice.

"Well, K. I.," said my mother, in whom the Job-like
element was not of a high development, — "well, K. I.,
what does he say? Is it the old story about his list being
full, or has he done it at last?"

"Yes, ma'am," said my father, as though echoing her
words. "He has done it at last!"

"And what is it to be, papa? Is it something that a
gentleman can suitably accept?" cried Mary Anne.

"Done it at last, you may well say!" muttered my father,
half aloud.

"Better late than never," cried Lord George, gayly.

"Well, I don't know *that*, my Lord," said my father,
turning upon him with an abruptness little short of offensive; "I am not so sure that I quite coincide with you. If
a young fellow enters life totally uneducated and unpro-
vided for, his only certain heritage being the mortgages on
his father's property, and perhaps," he added with a sneer,
— "and perhaps some of his mother's virtues, I say I am
not exactly convinced that he has improved his chances of
worldly success by such a production as *that!*"

And with these words, every one of which he delivered
with a terrible distinctness, he handed a letter across the
table to Lord George, who slowly perused it in silence.

"As for *you*, sir," continued my father, turning towards
me, "I grieve to inform you that no vacancy at present
offers itself in the Guards, nor in the household, where your
natural advantages could be remarked and appreciated. It
will be, however, a satisfaction to you to know that your
high claims are already understood, and well thought of, in
the proper quarter. There's Mr. Vickars's letter." And
he presented me with the note, which ran thus: —

"DEAR MR. DODD, — By the enclosed letter, bearing your
son's signature, I have discovered how totally below his just
expectations would be any of those official appointments
which are within the limits of my humble patronage to
bestow.

"I have, consequently, cancelled the minute of his nomi-

nation to a place in the Treasury, which was yesterday
conferred upon him, and having myself no influence in
either of those departments to which his wishes incline, I
have but to express the regret I feel at my inability to serve
him, and the great respect with which I beg to remain,

"Your very faithful servant,

"HADDINGTON VICKARS.

" Board of Trade, London.
" To Mr. James K. Dodd, Bonn."

I am able to give you the precious document word for
word; for, if I went over it once, I did so twenty times.

"Perhaps you might like to refresh your memory by a
glance at the enclosure," said my father. "My Lord George
will kindly hand it to you."

"It is a devilish good letter, though, I must say," broke
in George; who, to do him justice, Bob, never deserts a
friend in difficulties. "It's all very fine of this fellow to
talk of his inability to do this, that, and t' other. Sure,
we all know how they chop and barter their patronage with
one another. One says, you may have that thing at Per-
nambuco, and then another says, ' Very well, there's an
ensigncy in the Fifty-ninth.' And that's only gammon
about the appointment made out yesterday; he wants to
ride off on that. A sharp fellow your friend Vickars!
He'd look a bit surprised, however, if you were to say that
this letter of ' Jem's ' was a forgery, and that you most
gratefully accept the nomination he alludes to, and which,
of course, is not yet filled up."

"Eh, what! how do you mean?" cried my father, eagerly,
for he caught at the very shadow of a chance with desperate
avidity.

"I was only in jest," said Lord George, who merely
wanted, as he afterwards said, "to hustle the governor
through the deep ground" of his anger. "I was in jest
about them, for ' Jem's ' letter is so good, so exceedingly
well put, that it would be downright folly to disavow it.
You have no idea," continued he, gravely, "what excellent
policy it is always to ask for a high thing. They respect
you for it, even when they give you nothing; and then,

when you do at last receive some appointment, it is so certain to be beneath what you solicited, it establishes a claim for your perpetual discontent. You go on eternally boring about neglect, and so on. You accepted the humble post of Envoy at Stuttgard, for instance, under an implied pledge about Vienna or Constantinople. Besides these advantages, it is also to be remembered that every now and then they actually do take a fellow at his own valuation, and give him what he asks for."

"Lord George is quite right," chimed in Mrs. Gore Hampton; "half of these things are purely accidental. I remember so well my uncle writing to beg that the tutor of his boys might get some small thing in the Church, just at the moment when the bishop of the diocese had died, and the minister, reading the letter carelessly, — my uncle's hand is very hard to decipher, — mistook the object of the request, and appointed him to the bishopric."

"In that case," remarked my father, dryly, "I think Mrs. D. had better indite an epistle to the Home Office."

And, although this was said in a sneer, the laughter. that followed went far to restore us all to good-humor, particularly as Lord George took the opportunity of explaining to Mrs. Gore Hampton what had occurred, bespeaking her aid and influence in our behalf.

"It is so absurd," said she, "that one should have any difficulty about these things, but such is the case. The Duchess will be certain to make excuses; she cannot ask for something, because she *is* 'in waiting,' or she is not in waiting. Lord Harrowcliff is sure to tell me that he has just been refused a request, and cannot subject himself to another humiliation; but I always reply, these are most selfish arguments, and that I really must have what I want; that a refusal always attacks my nerves, and that I will not be ill merely to indulge a caprice of theirs. What is it Mr. James wants?"

There was something so practical in this short question, Bob, something so decisive, that had she been talking the rankest absurdity but the moment before, we should have forgotten it all in an instant.

"A mere nothing," replied Lord George. "You'll smile

when you hear what we 're making such a fuss about." As he said these words, he muttered in the governor's ear, "It's all right now; she detests asking a favor, but, if she *will* stoop to it — " An expressive gesture implied that success was certain.

"Well, you have n't told me what it is," said she again.

Lord George passed round to the back of her chair, and whispered a few words. She replied in the same low tone, and then they both laughed.

"You don't mean to say," cried she, turning to my father, "that you have experienced any difficulty about this trifle?"

The governor blundered out some bashful confession, that he had encountered the most extraordinary obstacles to his wishes.

"I really think," said she, sighing, "they do these things just to provoke people. They wanted Augustus t' other day to go out to the Cape, and I assure you it was as much as Lady Mary could do to have the appointment changed. They said his 'regiment' was there. ' *Tant pis* for his regiment!' replied she. 'It must be a most disgusting station.' And that is, I must say, the worst of the Horse Guards; they are always so imperative, — so downright cruel. Don't you agree with me, Mrs. Dodd?"

"They could n't be worse than the regiment I 've heard my father speak of," replied my mother. "They were called the 'North Britains,' and were the wickedest set of wretches in the rebellion of '98."

This unhappy blunder set my father into a roar of laughter, for latterly it is only on occasions like this that he is moved to any show of merriment. Mrs. Gore Hampton, of course, never noticed the mistake, but saying, "Now for my letters," ordered her writing-desk to be brought: a sign of promptitude that at once diverted all our thoughts into another channel.

"Shall I write to the Duke or to Lady Mary first?" said she, pondering; and her eyes, accidentally falling upon my mother, she thought herself the person addressed, and replied, —

"Indeed, ma'am, if you ask *me*, I 'd say the Duke."

"I'm for Lady Mary," interposed Lord George. "There's nothing like a woman to ferret out news, and find a way to profit by it. The duke will just say, casually, 'I've got a letter somewhere — I hope I have not mislaid it — about a vacancy in the "Coldstreams;" if you hear of anything, just drop me a hint. By the way — is Fox in the Fusiliers still?' — or, 'I hope they'll change that shako, it's monstrous!' Now, my Lady Mary will go another way to work. She'll remember the name of everybody that can be possibly useful. She'll drive about, and give little dinners, and talk, and flatter, and cajole, and intrigue, and, growing distant here, and jealous there, she'll bring into action a thousand forces that mere men-creatures know nothing of."

"I'm for the Duke still," said my mother; and Mary Anne, by an inclination of her head, showed that she seconded the motion.

It became now an actual debate, Bob, and you would be amazed were I to tell you what strong expressions and angry feelings were evoked by mere partisanship, on a subject whereupon not one of us had the slightest knowledge whatsoever. My father and I were with Tiverton, and as "Caroline walked into the lobby," as George phrased it, we carried the question. Mrs. G., however, declared that, beside the casting voice, she had a right to a vote, and, giving it to my mother's side, we were equal. In this stage of the proceedings a compromise alone could be resorted to, and so it was agreed that she should write to both by the same post; but the discussion had already lost us a day, for the mail went out while my mother was "left speaking."

I have probably been prolix, my dear friend, in all this detail, but it will at least show you how the Dodd family conduct questions of internal policy; and teach you, besides, that Cabinets and Councils of State have no special prerogative for folly and absurdity, since even small and obscure folk like ourselves can contest the palm with them.

Neither could you well believe what small but bitter animosities, what schisms, and what divisions grew out of a matter so insignificant as this. The remainder of the day was passed gloomily enough, for we each of us avoided the other, with that misgiving that belongs to those who have uneasy consciences.

They say that a good harvest often saves a bad administration; certainly a fine day will frequently avert a domestic broil. Had the morning which followed our debate been a favorable one, the chances are we should have been away to the Seven Mountains, or the village of Königswinter, or some such place; bad luck would have it that the rain came down in torrents from daybreak, heavy clouds gathered over the Rhine, shutting out the opposite bank from view, so that nothing remained to us but home resources, which is but too often a brief expression for row and recrimination.

Breakfast over, each of us, as if dreading a "call of the House," affected some peculiarly pressing duty that he had to perform. The governor retired to pore over his accounts, and tried to make out that the debit against him in his bank-book was a balance in his favor. My mother retreated to her room to hold a grand inspection of her wardrobe; a species of review that always discovers several desertions, and a vast amount of "unserviceables." Leaving her and Mary Anne in court-martial over Betty Cobb, who, as usual, when brought up for sentence, claimed the right to be sent home, I pass on to Lord George, whose wet days are generally devoted to practising some new "hazard off the cushion," or the investigation of that philosopher's stone, a martingale at Rouge-et-Noir, and I arrive at my own case, which invariably resolves itself into a day of gun and pistol cleaning, — an occupation mysteriously linked with gloomy weather, as though one ought to have everything in readiness to blow his brains out, if the mercury continued to fall.

Mrs. G. had a headache, and Caroline was in pursuit of one over the pages of the "Thirty Years' War." Such was the tableau of the Dodd family on this agreeable day. I don't give myself much up to reflection, Bob. I have always thought that as life is a road to be travelled, one step forward is worth any number in the opposite direction; but I vow to you that, on this occasion, I did begin to ponder a little over the past and the present, with a half-glance

at the future. What the governor had said the day before
was no more than the truth, — we *were* living at a tremendous rate. If all belonging to us were sold, the capital
would scarcely afford six or seven years of such expenditure. These were serious, if not stunning reflections, and
I heartily wished they had occupied any other head than
my own.

To *you* — who have always given your brains their own
share of work — thinking is no labor. It's like a gallop to
a horse in hard hunting condition, and only serves to keep
him in wind; but to *me*, whose faculties are, so to say,
fresh from grass, the fatigue of thought is no trifling inflic-
tion. Slow men, I take it, suffer more than your clever
fellows on these occasions, since their minds are not suggestive of expedients, and they go on plodding over the same
ground, till they make a beaten course in their poor brains,
like an old race-ground. Something in this fashion must
have occurred to me; for by dint of that dreary morning's
rumination, I half made up my mind to emigrate somewhere,
and if I did n't exactly know where, the fault lies more in
my geography than my spirit of enterprise.

The only book I could lay my hands on likely to give
me any information was "Cook's Voyages;" and this, I
remembered, was in the governor's room. I at once descended the stairs, and had just reached the little conservatory outside of it, when I caught sight of a woman's dress
beneath the thick foliage of the orange-trees. I crept noiselessly onward, and after a very devious series of artful
dodges, I detected Mrs. D. playing eavesdropper at the
governor's door.

I tried to persuade myself that I was mistaken. I did
my best to fancy that she was botanizing or "bouquet"
gathering; but no, the stubborn fact would not be denied.
There she was, bent down, with ear and eye alternately at
the keyhole. Neither the act nor the situation were very
dignified, and determining that she should not be detected by
any other in this predicament, I kicked down a flower-pot,
and, before I had well time to replace it, she was gone.

I'm quite prepared for the laugh you'll give, Bob, when
I own to you that no sooner had I seen her vanish from the

horizon than I deliberately took my place exactly where she had been. Of course, my sense of honor and delicacy suggested that I had no other object in view than to ascertain what it was that had drawn her to the spot. Any curiosity that possessed me was strictly confined to this.

I accordingly bent my ear to the keyhole, and had just time to recognize Mrs. Gore Hampton's voice, when the noise of chairs being drawn back, and the scuffling sounds of feet, showed that the interview had come to an end. Scarcely a moment was left me to shelter myself among the leaves, when the door opened, "discovering," as stage directions would say, Mr. Dodd and Mrs. Gore Hampton in conversation.

There was really a dramatic look in the situation too. The governor's flowered dressing-gown and velvet skull-cap, decorated in front by his up-raised spectacles, like a portcullis over his nose, contrasted so well with the graceful morning robe of Mrs. G., all floating and gauzy, and to which her every gesture imparted some new character of vapory lightness.

"Dear Mr. Dodd," said she, pressing his hand with extreme cordiality, "you have been so very, very kind, I really have no words to express what I feel towards you. I have long felt that I owed you this explanation — I have tried to summon courage for it for weeks past — then I sometimes doubted how you might receive it."

"Oh, madam!" interrupted he, gracefully closing his drapery with one hand, while he pressed the other on his heart.

"You kind creature!" cried she, enthusiastically. "I can now wonder at myself that I should ever have admitted a doubt on the question. But if you only knew what sorrows I have seen — if you only knew with what severe lessons mistrust and suspicion have become graven on this heart, young as it is — "

"Ah, madam!" murmured he, as though the last few words had made the deepest impression upon him.

"Well, it's over now," cried she, in her more natural tone of gayety. "The weary load is off me, and I am myself again, — thanks to you, dear, dear kind friend."

Faith, Bob, from the enthusiasm of the utterance of

this last speech, I thought that a stage embrace ought to have followed; and I believe that the governor was of my mind too, and only restrained by some real or fancied necessity to keep his toga closed in front of him. Mrs. G., however, as though fearing that he might ultimately forget the " unities," again pressed his hand with both her own, and murmuring, " With you, then, my secret is safe, — to *you* all is confided," she hurried away, as if overcome by her feelings.

I could not guess what might have reached my mother's ears, but I thought to myself, if she only had heard even this much, and witnessed the fervor with which it was uttered, the governor's life for the next few weeks needs not be envied by any one out of a condemned cell. Not that to *me* the scene admitted of any interpretation which should warrant her suspicions; but so it is, she takes a jealous turn every now and then, and he can't take a pinch of snuff without her peering over his shoulder to see if he has not got a miniature in the lid of the box. He used to try to reason her out of these notions, — his vindications even took the dangerous length of certain abstract opinions about the sex in general, very far from complimentary; but latterly he has sought refuge in drink, which usually ends in an illness, so that an attack of jealousy was the invariable premonitory symptom of one of gout; and my mother's temper and tincture of colchicum seemed inseparably connected by some unseen link.

From these thoughts I followed on to others about the scene itself, and what possible circumstance could have led Mrs. G. H. to visit the governor in his own room, and what was the prodigious mystery she had just confided to his keeping. Probability, I fear, takes up little space in any speculation about a woman. I am sure that if I were to recount to you one-half of the absurd and extravagant fancies that occurred to me on this occasion, you would infallibly set me down as mad. I 'll not tax your patience with the recital, but frankly confess to you that I have not a clew, even the slightest, to the mystery; nor from the manner in which I have learned its existence, can I venture to ask Lord George to aid me.

The incident had one effect, — it totally banished emigration, clearings, and log huts from my mind, and set my thoughts a rambling upon all the strange people and extraordinary events that travelling abroad introduces one to; and with this reflection I strolled back to my room, and sat brooding over the fire till it was time to dress for dinner. Although you may not have the vaguest notion of what is passing in the minds of certain people, the very fact that they are fully occupied with certain strong feelings is a reason for observing them with an extraordinary interest; and so was it that our party at table that day was full of meaning to me. There was a kind of languid repose about Mrs. Gore Hampton's manner which seemed especially assumed towards the governor, and a certain fidgety consciousness in *his*, sufficiently noticeable; while my mother, dressed in one of her war turbans, looked unutterably fierce things on every side. It was easy enough to see that all this additional weight upon the safety-valves of her temper threatened a terrible explosion at last, and it required all the tact I could muster to my aid to defer the catastrophe. Lord George gave me, too, his willing aid, and by the help of an old Professor of Oriental Languages, we made up her rubber of whist in the evening.

Alas, Bob! even four by honors could n't console her for the "odd trick" she suspected the governor was playing her; and she broke up the card-table, and retired with that swelling dignity of manner that is the accompaniment of injured feelings.

It had been our plan to proceed from this place direct to Baden-Baden, which, from everything I can learn, must be a perfect paradise; but now, to my great surprise, I discovered that for some secret reason we should first go to Ems, and remain there a week or two before proceeding further. This arrangment was Mrs. G.'s, and Lord George seemed to give it his hearty concurrence; alleging, but for the first time, that it was absurd to think of Baden before the middle of July. I could easily perceive that this change of purpose contained some mysterious motive; but, as Tiverton persisted in averring that it was "all on the square," and "no double," I had to accept it as such.

Such is, therefore, our position as I write these lines; and although to-morrow might develop the first movement of the campaign, I cannot keep my letter open to communicate it.   You will see that we are as divided as a Ministerial Cabinet.   Some of us, doubtless, have their honest convictions, and others are, perhaps, plastic enough to receive impressions from without, but how we are to work together, and how, as the great authority said, the "Government is to be carried on," is more than yet appears to

Your ever attached friend,

JAMES DODD.

I open my letter to say that Lord G. has just dropped in to tell me what is the plan of procedure.   The Grand Duchess of Hohenschwillinghen is to arrive at Ems this week, and Mrs. G. H. is anxious to wait upon her at once.   They were dear friends once, but something or other interposed a coolness between them of late years.   Lord G. endeavored to explain this, but I could n't follow the story.   It was something about one of our royal family wanting to marry, or not to marry, somebody else, and that Mrs. G. H. or the Duchess had promoted or opposed the match.   Suffice, it was a regular kingly shindy, and all engaged in it were of the blood royal.

The really important thing at the moment is that the governor is to conduct Mrs. G. H. to-morrow to Ems, and we are to follow in a day or two.   How my mother will receive this information, or who is to communicate it to her, are questions not so easily solved.

LETTER XXI.

MY DEAR MOLLY, — If it was n't that I am supported in a
wonderful way, and that my appetite keeps good for the bit
I eat, I would n't be able to sit down here and relate the
sufferings of my afflicted heart. There has been nothing
but trials and tribulations over me since I wrote last, and
I knew it was coming, too, for that dirty beast, Paddy
Byrne, upset the lamp, and spilled all the oil over the sofa
the other evening; and whilst the others were scouring and
scrubbing with spirit of soap and neumonia, I sat down to
cry heartily, for I foresaw what was coming; and I knew
well that spilt oil is the unluckiest thing that ever happens
in a family.

Maybe I was n't right. The very next morning Betty
Cobb goes and cuts my antic lace flounce down the middle,
to make borders for caps; and that was n't enough, but she
puts the front breadth of my new flowered satin upside down,
so that, "to make the roses go right," as James says, "I
ought to walk on my head." That's spilt oil for you!

Whilst I was endeavoring to bear up against these with
all Christian animosity, in comes the post-bag. The very
sight of it, Molly, gave me a turn; and, I declare to you,
I knew as well there was bad news in it as if I was inside
of it. You've often heard of a "presentment," Molly, and
that's what I had; and when you have that, it's no matter
what it's about, whether it's a road that's broke up, or a
bridge that's broke down, take my advice, and never listen
to what they call "reason," for it's just flying in the face
of Providence. I had one before Mary Anne was born.
I thought the poor baby would have the mark of a snail on
her neck; and true enough, the very same week K. I. was

shot through the skirts of his coat, and came home with five
slugs in him; and when you think, as Father Maher said,
"Slugs and snails are own brothers," or, at least, have a
strong anomaly between them, my dream came true; not
but I acknowledge, gratefully, that in this case the fright
was worse than the reality.

Well, to come back to the bag; I looked at it, and said
to myself, as I often said to K. I., "Smooth and slippery
as you seem without, there's bad inside of you;" and
you'll see yourself if I was n't right both ways.

The first letter they took out was for myself, and in
Waters's handwriting. It began with all the balderdash
and hard names the lawyers have for everything, trying to
confuse and confound, just as, Father Maher says, the
"scuttle-fish" muddies the water before he runs away; but
towards the end, my dear, he grew plainer and more conspicuous, for he said, "You will perceive, by the subjoined
account, that after the payment of law charges, and other
contingent expenses, the sum at your disposal will amount
to twelve hundred and thirty-four pounds six and ninepence-
halfpenny." I thought I'd drop, Molly, as I read it; I
shook and I trembled, and I believe, indeed, ended with a
strong fit of screeching, for my nerves was weak before,
and really this shock was too much for any constitution.
Twelve hundred and thirty-six! when I expected, at the
very least, fifteen or sixteen thousand pounds! It was
only that very blessed morning that I was planning to myself
about a separation from K. I. I calculated that I'd have
about six hundred a year of my own; and, out of decency
sake, he could n't refuse me three or four more, and with
this, and my present knowledge of the Continent, I thought
I'd do remarkably well. For I must observe to you, Molly,
that there's no manner of disgrace, or even unpleasantness,
in being separated abroad. It is not like in Ireland, where
everybody thinks the worse of you both; and, what between your own friends and your husband's friends, there
is n't an event of your private life that's not laid bare before
the world, so that, at last, the defence of you turns out to
be just as dreadful as the abuse. No, Molly, here it's all
different. Next to being divorced, the most fashionable

thing is a separation, and for one woman, in really high life, that lives with her husband, you 'll find three that does not. I suppose, like everything else in this sinful world, there 's good and there 's bad in this custom. When I first came abroad, I own, I disliked to see it. I fancied that, no matter how it came about, the women was always wrong. But that was merely an Irish prejudice, and, like many others, I have lived to get rid of it. There 's nothing convinces you of this so soon as knowing intimately the ladies that are in this situation.

Of all the amiable creatures I ever met, I know nothing to compare with them. It is not merely of manners and good breeding that I speak, but the gentle, mild quietness of their temper, — a kind of submissive softness that, I own to you, one can't have with their husbands, and maybe that 's the reason they 've left them. I merely mention this to show you that if I had a reasonably good income, and was separated from K. I., there 's no society abroad that I might n't be in; and, in fact, my dear Molly, I may sum all up by saying that living with your husband may give you some comfort when you 're at home, but it certainly excludes you from all sympathy abroad; and for one friend that you have in the former case, you 'll have, at the least, ten in the latter.

This will explain to you why and how my thoughts ran upon separation, for if I had stayed in Ireland, I 'm sure I 'd never have thought of it; for I own to you, with shame and sorrow, Molly, that we know no more about civilization in our poor Ireland "than," as Lord George says, "a prairie bull does about oil-cake."

You may judge, then, of what my feelings was when I read Waters's letter, and saw all my elegant hopes melting like jelly on a hot plate. Twelve hundred pounds! Was it out of mockery he left it to me? Faith, Molly, I cried more that night than ever I thought to do for old Jones M'Carthy! Myself and Mary Anne was as red in the eyes as two ferrets.

The first, and of course the great shock was the loss of the money, and after that came the thought of the way K. I. would behave when he discovered my disappointment. For

I must tell you that the bare idea of my being independent drove him almost crazy. He seemed, somehow, to have a kind of lurking suspicion that I'd want to separate, and now, when he'd come to discover the trifle I was left, there would be no enduring his gibes and his jeers. I had it all before me how he'd go on, tormenting and harassing me from daylight to dark. This was dreadful, Molly, and overcame me completely. I knew him well; and that he would n't be satisfied with laughing at my legacy, but he'd go on to abuse the M'Carthy family and all my relations. There's nothing a low man detests like the real old nobility of a country.

Mary Anne and I talked it all over the whole night, and turned it every way we could think. If we kept the whole secret, it would save "going into black" for ourselves and the servants, and that was a great object; but then we could n't take the name of M'Carthy after that of Dodd, quartering the arms on our shield, and so on, without announcing the death of poor Jones M'Carthy. There was the hitch; for Mary Anne persisted in thinking that the best thing about it all was the elegant opportunity it offered of getting rid of the name of Dodd, or, at the least, hiding it under the shadow of M'Carthy.

Ah, my dear Molly, you know the proverb, "Man proposes, but fate opposes." While we were discoursing over these things, little I guessed the mine that was going to explode under my feet. I mentioned to you in my last, I think, a lady with whom we agreed to travel in company, — a Mrs. Gore Hampton, a very handsome, showy woman, — though I own to you, Molly, not what I call "one of *my* beauties."

She is tall and dark-haired, and has that kind of soft, tender way with men that I remark does more mischief than any other. We all liked her greatly at first, — I suppose she determined we should, and spared no pains to suit herself to our various dispositions. I'm sure I tried to be as accommodating as she was, and I took to arts and sciences that I could n't find any pleasure in; but I went with the stream, as the saying is, and you'll see where it left me! I vow to you I had my misgivings that a handsome, fine-

looking young woman was only thinking of dried frogs and
ferns. They were n't natural tastes, and so I kept a sharp
eye on her. At one time I suspected she was tender on Lord
George, and then I thought it was James; but at last,
Molly darling, the truth flashed across me, like a streak of
lightning, making me stone blind in a minute! What was
it I perceived, do you think, but that the real "Lutherian"
was no other than K. I. himself? I feel that I 'm blushing
as I write it. The father of three children, grown-up, and
fifty-eight in November, if he 's not more, but he won't
own to it.

There 's things, Molly, "too dreadful," as Father Maher
remarks, "for human credulity," and when one of them
comes across you in life, the only thing is to take up the
Litany to St. Joseph, and go over it once or twice, then
read a chapter or two of Dr. Croft's "Modern Miracles of
the Church," and by that time you're in a frame to believe
anything. Well, as I had n't the book by me, I thought
I 'd take a solitary ramble by myself, to reflect and consider, and down I went to a kind of greenhouse that is full
of orange and lemon trees, and where I was sure to be
alone.

K. I. has what he calls his dressing-room — it 's little
trouble dressing gives him — at the end of this; but I was n't
attending to that, but sitting with a heavy heart under a
dwarf fig-tree, like Nebuchadnezzar, and only full of my
own misfortunes, when I heard through the trees the rustling
sound of a woman's dress. I bent down my head to see,
and there was Mrs. G. in a white muslin dressing-gown,
but elegantly trimmed with Malines lace, two falls round
the cape, and the same on the arm, just as becoming a thing
as any she could put on.

"What 's this for?" said I to myself; for you may guess
I knew she did n't dress that way to pluck lemons and green
limes; and so I sat watching her in silence. She stood,
evidently listening, for a minute or two; she then gathered
two or three flowers, and stuck them in her waist, and, after
that, she hummed a few bars of a tune, quite low, and as if
to herself. That was, I suppose, a signal, for K. I.'s door
opened; and there he stood himself, and a nice-looking

article he was, with his ragged *robe de chambre*, and his greasy skull-cap, bowing and scraping like an old monkey. "I little knew that such a flower was blooming in the conservatory," said he, with a smirk I suppose he thought quite captivating.

"You do not pretend that you selected your apartment here but in the hope of watching the unfolding buds," replied she; and then, with something in a lower voice, to which he answered in the same, she passed on into his room, and he closed the door after her.

I suppose I must have fainted, Molly, after that. I remembered nothing, except seeing lemon and orange trees all sliding and flitting about, and felt myself as if I was shooting down the Rhine on a raft. Maybe it's for worse that I'm reserved. Maybe it would have been well for me if I was carried away out of this world of woe, wickedness, and artful widows. When I came to myself, I suddenly recalled everything; and it was as much as I could do not to scream out and bring all the house to the spot and expose them both. But I subdued my indigent feelings, and, creeping over to the door, I peeped at them through the keyhole.

K. I. was seated in his big chair, she in another close beside him. He was reading a letter, and she watching him, as if her life depended on him.

"Now read this," said she, thrusting another paper into his hand, "for you'll see it is even worse."

"My heart bleeds for you, my dear Mrs. Gore," said he, taking off his spectacles and wiping his eyes, and red enough they were afterwards, for there was snuff on his handkerchief, — "my heart bleeds for you!"

These were his words; and why I didn't break open the door when I heard them, is more than I can tell.

"I was certain of your sympathy; I knew you'd feel for me, my dear Mr. Dodd," said she, sobbing.

"Of course you were," said I to myself. "He was the kind of old fool you wanted. But, faith, he shall feel for *me*, too, or my name is not Jemima."

"I don't suppose you ever heard of so cruel a case?" said she, still sobbing.

"Never, — never," cried he, clasping his hands. "I did n't believe it was in the nature of man to treat youth, beauty, and loveliness with such inhumanity. One that could do it must be a Creole Indian."

"Ah, Mr. Dodd!" said she, looking up into his eyes.

"In Tartary, or the Tropics," said he, "such wretches may be found, but in our own country and our own age—"

"Ah, Mr. Dodd," ·said she, again, "it is only in an Irish heart such generous emotions have their home!"

The artful hussey, she knew the tenderest spot of his nature by an instinct! for if there was anything he could n't resist, it was the appeal to his being Irish. And to show you, Molly, the designing craft of her, *she* knew that weakness of K. I. in less than a month's acquaintance, that *I* did n't find out till I was eight or nine years married to him.

For a minute or two my feelings overcame me so much that I could n't look or listen to them; but when I did, she had her hand on his arm, and was saying in the softest voice, —

"I may, then, count upon your kindness, — I may rest assured of your friendship."

"That you may, — that you may, my dear madam," said he.

Yes, Molly, he called her "madam" to her own face.

"If there should be any cruel enough, ungenerous enough, or base enough," sobbed she, "to calumniate me, *you* will be my protector; and beneath *your* roof shall I find my refuge. *Your* character — your station in society — the honorable position you have ever held in the world — your claims as a father — your age — will all give the best contradiction to any scandal that malevolence can invent. Those dear venerable locks — "

Just as she said this, I heard somebody coming, and in haste too, for a flower-pot was thrown down, and I had barely time to make my escape to my own room, where I threw myself on my bed, and cried for two hours.

I have gone through many trials, Molly. Few women, I believe, have seen more affliction and sorrow than myself; from the day of my ill-suited marriage with K. I. to the present moment, I may say, it has been out of one misery into another with me ever since. But I don't think I ever cried as hearty as I did then, for, you see, there was no delusion or confusion possible! I heard everything with my own ears, and saw everything with my own eyes.

I listened to their plans and projects, and even heard them rejoicing that, because he was stricken in years, and the father of a grown family, nobody would suspect what he was at. "Those dear venerable locks," as she called them, were to witness for him!

Oh, Molly, was n't this too bad; could you believe that there was as much duplicity in the world as this? *I* own, *I* never did. I thought I saw wickedness enough in Ireland. I know the shameless way I was cheated in wool, and that Mat never was honest about rabbit-skins. But what was all that compared to this?

When I grew more composed, I sent for Mary Anne, and told her everything; but just to show you the perversity of human nature, she would n't agree to one word I said. It was law papers, she was sure, that Mrs. G. was showing; she had something in Chancery, maybe, or perhaps it was a legacy " tied up," like our own, " and that she wanted advice about it." But what nonsense that was! Sure, he need n't be the father of a family to advise her about all that. And there I was, Molly, without human creature to support or sustain me! For the first time since I came abroad, I wished myself back in Dodsborough. Not, indeed, that K. I. would ever have behaved this way at home in Ireland, with the eyes of the neighborhood on him, and Father Maher within call.

I passed a weary night of it, for Mary Anne never left me, arguing and reasoning with me, and trying to convince me that I was wrong, and if I was to act upon my delusions, that I 'd be the ruin of them all. " Here we are now," said she, " with the finest opportunity for getting into society ever was known. Mrs. G. is one of the aristocracy, and intimate with everybody of fashion : quarrel with her, or even displease her, and where will we be, or who will know us? Our difficulties are already great enough. Papa's drab gaiters, and the name of Dodd, are obstacles in our way, that only great tact and first-rate management can get over. When we are swimming for our lives," said she, " let us not throw away a life-preserver." Was n't it a nice name for a woman that was going to shipwreck a whole family.

The end of it all was, however, that I was to restrain my feelings, and be satisfied to observe and watch what was going on, for as they could have no conception of my knowing anything, I might be sure to detect them.

When I agreed to this plan, I grew easier in my mind, for, as I remarked to Mary Anne, " I'm like soda-water, and when you once draw the cork, I never fret nor froth any more." So that after a cold chicken, cut up with salad, a thing Mary Anne makes to perfection, and a glass of white wine negus, I slept very soundly till late in the afternoon.

Mary Anne came twice into my room to see if I was awake, but I was lying in a dreamy kind of half-sleep, and took no notice of her, till she said that Mrs. Gore Hampton was so anxious to speak to me about something confidentially. " I think," said Mary Anne, " she wants your advice and counsel for some matter of difficulty, because she seems greatly agitated, and very impatient to be admitted." I thought at first to say I was indisposed, and could n't see any one; but Mary Anne persuaded me it was best to let her in; so I dressed myself in my brown satin with three flounces, and my jet ornaments, out of respect to poor Jones that was gone, and waited for her as composed as could be.

Mary Anne has often remarked that there's a sort of quiet dignity in my manner when I'm offended, that becomes me greatly. I suppose I'm more engaging when I am pleased. But the grander style, Mary Anne thinks, becomes me even better. Upon this occasion I conclude that I was looking my very best, for I saw that Mrs. G. made an involuntary stop as she entered, and then, as if suddenly correcting herself, rushed over to embrace me.

" Forgive my rudeness, my dear Mrs. Dodd, and although nothing can be in worse taste than to offer any remark upon a friend's dress, I must positively do it. Your cap is charming, — actually charming."

It was a bit of net, Molly, with a rosette of pink and blue ribbon on the sides, and only cost eight francs, so that I showed her that the flattery did n't succeed. "It's very simple, ma'am," said I, "and therefore more suitable to my time of life."

"Your time of life," said she, laughing, so that for several minutes she could n't continue. "Say *our* time of life, if you like, and I hope and trust it's exactly the time in which one most enjoys the world, and is really most fitted to adorn it."

I can't follow her, Molly; I don't know what she said, or did n't say, about princesses, and duchesses, and other great folk, that made no "sensation" whatever in society till they were, as she said, "like us." She is an artful creature, and has a most plausible way with her; but this I must say, that many of her remarks were strictly and undeniably true; particularly when she spoke about the dignified repose and calm suavity of womanhood. There I was with her completely, for nothing shocks me more than that giggling levity one sees in young girls, and even in some young married women.

We talked a great deal on this subject, and I agreed with her so entirely that I was in danger every moment of forgetting the cold reserve that I ought to feel towards her; but every now and then it came over me like a shudder, and I bridled up, and called her "ma'am" in a way that quite chilled her.

"Here, it's four o'clock," said she, at last, looking at her watch, "and I have n't yet said one word about what I came for. Of course you know what I mean?"

"I have not that honor, ma'am," said I, with dignity.

"Indeed! Then Mr. Dodd has not apprised you — he has mentioned nothing — "

"No, ma'am, Mr. Dodd has mentioned nothing;" and this I said with a significance, Molly, that even stone would have shrunk under.

"Men are too absurd," said she, laughing; "they recollect nothing."

"They do forget themselves at times, ma'am," said I, with a look that must have shot through her.

She was so confused, Molly, that she had to pretend to be looking for something in her bag, and held down her head for several seconds.

"Where can I have laid that letter?" said she. "I am

so very careless about letters; fortunately for me I have no secrets, is it not?"

This was too barefaced, Molly, so I only said "Humph!"

"I must have left it on my table," said she, still search-ing, "or perhaps dropped it as I came along."

"Maybe in the conservatory, ma'am," said I, with a piercing glance.

"I never go there," said she, calmly. "One is sure to catch cold in it, with all the draughts."

The audacity of this speech gave me a sick feeling all over, and I thought I 'd have fainted. "The effrontery that could carry her through that," thought I, "will sustain her in any wickedness;" and I sat there powerless before her from that minute.

"The letter," said she, "was from old Madame de Rouge-mont, who is in waiting on the Duchess, and mentions that they will reach Ems by the 24th at latest. It's full of gossip. You know the old Rougemont, what wonderful tact she has, and how well she tells everything."

She rattled along here at such a rate, Molly, that even if I knew every topic of her discourse, I could not have kept up with her. There was the Emperor of Russia, and the Queen of Greece, and Prince this of Bavaria, and Prince that of the Asturias, all moving about in little family incidents; and what between the things they were displeased at, and others that gratified them, — how this one was dis-graced, and that got the cross of St. Something, and why such a one went *here* to meet somebody who could n't go *there*, — my head was so completely addled that I was thankful to Providence when she concluded the harangue by something that I could comprehend. "Under these circum-stances, my dear Mrs. Dodd," said she, "you will, I am sure, agree with me, there is no time to be lost."

"I think not, ma'am," said I, but without an inkling of what I was saying.

"I knew you would say so," said she, clasping my hand. "You have an unerring tact upon every question, which reminds me so strongly of Lady Paddington. She and the Great Duke, you know, were said to be never in the wrong. It is therefore an unspeakable relief to me that you see this matter as I do. It will be, besides, such a pleasure to the poor dear Duchess to have us with her; for I vow to you, Mrs. Dodd, I love her for her own sake. Many people make a show of attachment to her from selfish motives, — they know how gratified our royal family feel for such attentions, — but I really love her for herself; and so will you, dearest Mrs. Dodd. Worldly folk would speculate upon the advantages to be derived from her vast influence, — the posts of honor to be conferred on sons and daughters; but I know how little these things weigh with *you*. Not, I must add, but that I give you less credit for this independence of feeling than I should accord to others. You and yours are happily placed above all the accidents of fortune in this world; and if it ever *should* occur to you to seek for anything in the power of patronage to bestow, who is there would not hasten to confer it? But to return to the dear Duchess. She says the 24th at latest, and to-day we are at the 22nd, so you see there is not any time to lose."

"Not a great deal indeed, ma'am," said I, for I suddenly remembered all about her with K. I., as she laid her hand on *my* arm exactly as I saw her do upon *his*.

"With a sympathetic soul," cried she, "how little need is there of explanation! You already see what I am pointing at. You have read in my heart my devotion and attachment to that sweet princess, and you see how I am bound by every tie of gratitude and affection to hasten to meet her."

You may be sure, Molly, that I gave my heartiest concurrence to the arrangement. The very thought of getting rid of her was the best tidings I could hear; since, besides putting an end to all her plots and devices for the future, it would give me the opportunity of settling accounts with K. I., which it would be impossible to do till I had him here alone. It was, then, with real sincerity that my "sympathetic soul" fully assented to all she said.

"I knew you would forgive me. I knew that you would not be angry with me for this sudden flight," said she.

"Not in the least, ma'am," said I, stiffly.

"This is true kindness, — this is real friendship," said she, pressing my hand.

"I hope it is, ma'am," said I, dryly; for, indeed, Molly, it was hard work for me to keep my temper under.

She never, however, gave me much time for anything, for off she went once more about her own plans; telling me how little luggage she would take, how soon we should meet again, how delighted the Duchess would be with me and Mary Anne, and twenty things more of the same sort.

At last we separated, but not till we had embraced each other three times over; and, to tell you the truth, I had it in my heart to strangle her while she was doing it.

The agitation I went through, and my passion boiling in me, and no vent for it, made me so ill that I was taking Hoffman and camphor the whole evening after; and I could n't, of course, go down to dinner, but had a light veal cutlet with a little sweet sauce, and a roast pigeon with mushrooms, in my own room.

K. I. wanted to come in and speak to me, but I refused admission, and sent him word that "I hoped I'd be equal to the task of an interview in the course of a day or so;" a message that must have made him tremble for what was in store for him. I did this on purpose, Molly, for I often remarked that there's nothing subdues K. I. so much as to keep something hanging over him. As he said once himself, "Life is n't worth having, if a man can be called up at any minute for sentence." And that shows you, Molly, what I oftentimes mentioned to you, that if you want or expect true happiness in the married state, there's only one road to it, and that is by studying the temper and the character of your husband, learning what is his weakness and which are his defects. When you know these well, my dear, the rest is easy; and it's your own fault if you don't mould him to your liking.

Whether it was the mushrooms, or a little very weak shrub punch that Mary Anne made, disagreed with me, I can't tell, but I had a nightmare every time I went to sleep, and always woke up with a screech. That's the way I spent the blessed night, and it was only as day began to break that I felt a regular drowsiness over me and went off into a good comfortable doze. Just then there came a rattling of horses' hoofs, and a cracking of whips under the

window, and Mary Anne came up to say something, but I
would n't listen, but covered my head up in the bedclothes
till she went away.

It was twenty minutes to four when I awoke, and a
gloomy day, with a thick, soft rain falling, that I knew well
would bring on one of my bad headaches, and I was just
preparing myself for suffering, when Mary Anne came to
the bedside.

"Is she gone, Mary Anne?" said I.

"Yes," said she; "they went off before six o'clock."

"Thanks be to Providence," said I. "I hope I 'll never
see one of them again."

"Oh, mamma," said she, "don't say that!"

"And why would n't I say it, Mary Anne?" said I.
"Would you have me nurse a serpent, — harbor a boa-
constrictor in my bosom?"

"But, then, papa," said she, sobbing.

"Let him come up," said I. "Let him see the wreck he
has made of me. Let him come and feast his eyes over the
ruin his own cruelty has worked."

"Sure he 's gone," said she.

"Gone! Who 's gone?"

"Papa. He 's gone with Mrs. Gore Hampton!"

With that, Molly, I gave a scream that was heard all
over the house. And so it was for two hours — screech
after screech — tearing my hair and destroying everything
within reach of me. To think of the old wretch — for I
know his age right well; Sam Davis was at school with
him forty-eight years ago, at Dr. Bell's, and that shows
he 's no chicken — behaving this way. I knew the depravity
of the man well enough. I did n't pass twenty years with
him without learning the natural wickedness of his disposition, but I never thought he 'd go the length of this. Oh,
Molly! the shock nearly killed me; and coming as it did
after the dreadful disappointment about Jones M'Carthy's
affairs, I don't know at all how I bore up against it. I must
tell you that James and Mary Anne did n't see it with my
eyes. They thought, or they pretended to think, that he
was only going as far as Ems, to accompany her, as they
call it, on a visit to the Princess, — just as if there was a

princess at all, and that the whole story was n't lies from
beginning to end.

Lord George, too, took their side, and wanted to get
angry at my unjust suspicions about Mrs. G., but I just
said, what would the world think of *me* if I went away
in a chaise and four with *him*, by way of paying a visit
to somebody that never existed? He tried to laugh it off,
Molly, and made little of it, but I would n't let him, in
particular before Mary Anne, — for whatever sins they may
lay to my charge, I believe that they can't pretend that I
did n't bring up the girls with sound principles of virtue and
morality, — and just to convince him of that, I turned to and
exposed K. I. to James and the two girls till they were well
ashamed of him.

It 's a heartless bad world we live in, Molly! and I never
knew its badness, I may say, till now. You 'll scarce
believe me, when I tell you that it was n't from my own flesh
and blood that I met comfort or sympathy, but from that
good-for-nothing creature, Betty Cobb. Mary Anne and
Caroline persisted in saying that K. I.'s journey was all
innocence and purity, — that he was only gone in a fatherly
sort of a way with her; but Betty knew the reverse, and I
must own that she seemed to know more about him than I
ever suspected.

"Ah, the ould rogue! — the ould villain!" she 'd mutter
to herself, in a fashion that showed me the character he
had in the servants' hall. If I had only a little command
of my temper, I might have found out many a thing of
him, Molly, and of his doings at Dodsborough, but how could
I at a moment like that?

And that 's how I was, Molly, with nothing but enemies
about me, in the bosom of my own family! One saying,
"Don't expose us to the world, — don't bring people 's eyes
on us;" and the other calling out, "We 'll be ruined entirely
if it gets into the papers!" so that, in fact, they wanted
to deny me the little bit of sympathy I might have attracted
towards my destitute and forlorn condition.

Had I been at home, in Dodsborough, I 'd have made
the country ring with his disgrace; but they would n't
let me utter a word here, and I was obliged to sit down, as

the poet says, "like a worm in the bud," and consume my grief in solitude.

He went away, too, without leaving a shilling behind him, and the bill of the hotel not even paid! Nothing sustained me, Molly, but the notion of my one day meeting him, and settling these old scores. I even worked myself into a half-fever at the thought of the way I'd overwhelm him. Maybe it was well for me that I was obliged to rouse my energies to activity, and provide for the future, which I did by drawing two bills on Waters for a hundred and fifty each, and, with the help of them, we mean to remove from this on Saturday, and proceed to Baden, where, according to Lord George, "there's no such things as evil speaking, lying, or slandering;" to use his own words, "It's the most charitable society in Europe, and every one can indulge his vices without note or comment from his neighbors." And, after all, one must acknowledge the great superiority in the good breeding of the Continent in this; for, as Lord G. remarks, "If there's anything a man's own, it's his private wickedness, and there's no such indelicacy as in canvassing or discussing it; and what becomes of a conscience," says he, "if everybody reviles and abuses you? Sure, doesn't it lead you to take your own part, even when you're in the wrong?"

He has a persuasive way with him, Molly, that often surprises myself how far it goes with me, and indeed, even in the midst of my afflictions and distresses, he made me laugh with his account of Baden, and the strange people that go there. We're to go to the Hôtel de Russie, the finest in the place, and say that we are expecting some friends to join us; for K. I. and madam may arrive at any moment. As I write these lines, the girls and Betty are packing up the things, so that long before it reaches you we shall be at our destination.

The worst thing in my present situation is that I mustn't mutter a syllable against K. I., or, if I do, I have them all on my back; and as to Betty, her sympathy is far worse than the silence of the others. And there's the way your poor friend is in.

To be robbed — for I know Waters is robbing me — and

cheated and deceived all at the same time, is too much
for my unanimity! Don't let on to the neighbors about
K. I.; for, as Lord G. says, "these things should never be
mentioned in the world till they're talked of in the House
of Lords;" and I suppose he's right, though I don't see
why — but maybe it's one of the prerogatives of the peerage to have the first of an ugly story.

I have done now, Molly, and I wonder how my strength
has carried me through it. I'll write you as soon as I get
to Baden, and hope to hear from you about the wool. I'm
always reading in the papers about the improvement of Ireland, and yet I get less and less out of it; but maybe that
same is a sign of prosperity; for I remember my poor
father was never so stingy as when he saved a little money;
and indeed my own conviction is that much of what we
used to call Irish hospitality was neither more nor less than
downright desperation, — we had so little in the world, it
was n't worth hoarding.

You may write to me still as Mrs. Dodd, though maybe
it will be the last time the name will be borne by your

Injured and afflicted friend,

JEMIMA.

P. S. I'm sure Paddy Byrne is in K. I.'s secret, for he
goes about grinning and snickering in the most offensive
manner, for which I am just going to give him warning.
Not, indeed, that I'm serious about discharging him, for
the journey is terribly expensive, but by way of alarming
the little blaguard. If Father Maher would only threaten
to curse them, as he used, we'd have peace and comfort
once more.

LETTER XXII.

KENNY DODD TO THOMAS PURCELL, ESQ., OF THE GRANGE, BRUFF.

EISENACH.

MY DEAR TOM, — You will be surprised at the address at the top of this letter, but not a whit more so than I am myself; how, when, and why I came here, being matters which require some explanation, nor am I quite certain of making them very intelligible to you even by that process. My only chance of success, however, lies in beginning at the very commencement, and so I shall start with my departure from Bonn, which took place eight days ago, on the morning of the 22nd.

My last letter informed you of our having formed a travelling alliance with a very attractive and charming person, Mrs. Gore Hampton. Lord George Tiverton, who introduced us to each other, represented her as being a fashionable of the first water, very highly connected, and very rich, — facts sufficiently apparent by her manners and appearance, as well as by the style in which she was travelling. He omitted, however, all mention of her immediate circumstances, so that we were profoundly ignorant as to whether she were a widow or had a husband living, and, if so, whether separated from him casually or by a permanent arrangement.

It may sound very strange that we should have formed such a close alliance while in ignorance of these circumstances, and doubtless in our own country the inquiry would have preceded the ratification of this compact, but the habits of the Continent, my dear Tom, teach very different lessons. All social transactions are carried on upon principles of unlimited credit, and you indorse every bill of passing acquaintanceship with a most reckless disregard to the day of presentation for payment. Some would, perhaps, tell you that your scruples would only prove false terrors. My own notion, however, is less favorable, and my theory is this: you get so accustomed to "raffish" intimacies, you lose all taste or desire for discrimination; in fact, there's so much false money in circulation, it would be useless to "ring a particular rap on the counter."

Not that I have the very most distant notion of applying my theory to the case in hand. I adhere to all I said of Mrs. G. in my former epistle, and notwithstanding your quizzing about my "raptures," &c., I can only repeat everything I there said about her loveliness and fascination.

Perhaps one's heart becomes, like mutton, more tender by being old; but this I must say, I never remember to have met that kind of woman when I was young. Either I must have been a very inaccurate observer, or, what I suspect to be nearer the fact, they were not the peculiar productions of that age.

When the Continent was closed to us by war, there was a home stamp upon all our manufactures; our chairs and tables, our knives, and our candlesticks, were all made after native models, solid and substantial enough, but, I believe, neither very artistic nor graceful. We were used to them, however; and as we had never seen any other, we thought them the very perfection of their kind. The Peace of '15 opened our eyes, and we discovered, to our infinite chagrin and astonishment, that, in matters of elegance and taste, we were little better than barbarians; that shape and symmetry had their claims as well as utility, and that the happy combination of these qualities was a test of civilization.

I don't think we saw this all at once, nor, indeed, for a number of years, because, somehow, it's in the nature of a people to stand up for their shortcomings and deficiencies, — that very spirit being the bone and sinew of all patriotism; but I'll tell you where we felt this discrepancy most remarkably, — in our women, Tom; the very point, of all others, that we ought never to have experienced it in.

There was a plastic elegance, — a species of soft, seductive way — about foreign women that took us wonderfully.
They did not wait for our advances, but met us half-way in
intimacy, and this without any boldness or effrontery; quite
the reverse, but with a tact and delicacy that were perfectly
captivating.

I don't doubt but that, for home purposes, we should have
found that our own answered best, and, like our other manufactures, that they would last longer, and be less liable to
damage; but, unfortunately, the spirit of imitation that
stimulated us in hardware and jewelry, set in just as violently about our wives and daughters, and a pretty dance
has it led us! From my heart and soul I wish we had limited the use of French polish to our mahogany!

I don't know how I got into this digression, Tom, nor
have I the least notion where it would conduct me; but I
feel that the Mrs. Gore Hamptons of this world took their
origin in the time and from the spirit I speak of, and a
more dangerous invention the age never made.

When you read over your notes, and sum up what I've
been saying, you'll perhaps discover the reason of what
you are pleased in your last letter to call my "extreme sensibility to the widow's charms." But you wrong us both,
for *I*'m not in love, nor is *she* a widow! And this brings
me back to my narrative.

About ten days ago, as I was sitting in my own room, in
the *otium cum dig.* of my old dressing-gown and slippers, I
received a visit from Mrs. G. in a manner which at once
proclaimed the strictest secrecy and confidence. She came,
she said, to consult me, and, as a gentleman, I am bound
to believe her; but if you want to make use of a man's
faculties, you'd certainly never begin by turning his brain.
If you wished to send him of a message, you'd surely not
set out by spraining his ankle?

They say that the French Cuirassiers puzzled our Horse
Guards greatly at Waterloo. There was no knowing where
to get a stick at them. There's a kind of dress just now
the fashion among ladies, that confuses me fully as much, —
a species of gauzy, filmy, floating costume that makes you
always feel quite near, and yet keeps you a considerable

distance off. It's a most bewitching, etherial style of costume, and especially invented, I think, for the bewilderment
of elderly gentlemen.

More than half of the effect of a royal visit to a man's
own house is in the contrast presented by an illustrious
presence to the little commonplace objects of his daily life.
Seeing a king in his own sphere, surrounded with all the
attributes and insignia of his station, is not nearly so
astounding as to see him sitting in your old leather arm-
chair, with his feet upon your fender, — mayhap, stirring
your fire with your own poker. Just the same kind of thing
is the appearance of a pretty woman within the little den,
sacred to your secret smokings and studies of the "Times"
newspaper. An angel taking off her wings in the hall, and
dropping in to take pot-luck with you, could scarcely realize
a more charming vision!

All this preliminary discourse of mine, Tom, looks as if I
were skulking the explanation that I promised. I know
well what is passing in your mind this minute, and I fancy
that I hear you mutter, "Why not tell us what she came
about, — what brought her there?" It's not so easy as you
think, Tom Purcell. When a very pretty woman, in the
most becoming imaginable toilette, comes and tells you a
long story of personal sufferings, and invokes your sympathy against the cruel treatment of a barbarous husband
and his hard-hearted family; when the narrative alternates
between traits of shocking tyranny on one side, and angelic
submission on the other; when you listen to wrongs that
make your blood boil, recounted by accents that make your
heart vibrate; when the imploring looks and tones and gesture that failed to excite pity in her "monster of a husband"
are all rehearsed before you yourself, — to you directed
those tearful glances of melting tenderness, — to you raised
up those beautiful hands of more than sculptured symmetry,
— I say, again, that your reason is never consulted on the
whole process. Your sensibility is aroused, your sympathy is evoked, and all your tenderest emotions excited,
pretty much as in hearing an Italian opera, where, without
knowing one word of the language, the tones, the gestures,
the play of feature, and the signs of passion move and melt

you into alternate horror at cruelty, and compassionate sorrow for suffering.

Make the place, instead of the stage, your own study, and the personage no *prima donna*, but a very charming creature of the real world, and the illusion is ten times more complete.

I have no more notion of Mrs. Gore Hampton's history than I should have of the plot of a novel from reading a newspaper notice of it. She was married at sixteen. She was very beautiful, very rich, — a petted, spoilt child. She thought the world a fairy tale, she said. I was going to ask, was it "Beauty and the Beast" that was in her mind? At first all was happiness and bliss; then came jealousy, not on her part, but his; disagreements and disputes followed. They went abroad to visit some royal personage, — a duchess, a grand-duchess, an archduchess of something, who figures through the whole history in a mysterious and wonderful manner, coming in at all times and places, and apparently never for any other purpose than wickedness, like Zamiel in the "Freyschutz;" but, notwithstanding, she is always called the dear, good, kind Princess, — an apparent contradiction that also assists the mystification. Then, there are letters from the husband, — reproach and condemnation; from the wife, — love, tenderness, and fidelity.

The Duchess happily writes French, so I am spared the pains of following *her* correspondence. Chancery was nothing to the confusion that comes of all this letter-writing, but I come out with the one strong fact, that the dear Princess stands by Mrs. G. through thick and thin, and takes a bold part against the husband. A shipwrecked sailor never clung to a hencoop with greater tenacity than did I grasp this one solitary fact, floating at large upon the wide ocean of uncertainty.

I assure you I almost began to feel an affection for the Duchess, from the mere feeling of relief this thought afforded. She was like a sanctuary to my poor, persecuted, hunted-down imagination!

Have you ever, in reading a three-volume novel, Tom, been on the eve of abandoning the task from pure inability

to trace out the story, when suddenly, and as it were by
chance, some little trait or incident gives, if not a clew to
the mystery, at least that small flickering of light that acts
as a guide-star to speculation?

This was what I experienced here, and I said to myself,
" I know the sentiments of the Duchess, at least, and that's
something."

Do you know that I did n't like proceeding any farther
with the story; like a tired swimmer, who had reached a
rock far out at sea, I did n't fancy trusting myself once
more to the waves. However, I was not allowed the option.
Away went the narrative again, — like an express train in a
dark tunnel. If we now and then did emerge upon a bit of
open country where we could see about us, it was to dive
the next minute into some deep cutting, or some gloomy
cavern, without light or intelligence.

It appeared to me that Mr. Gore Hampton would be a very
proper case for private assassination; but I did n't like the
notion of doing it myself, and I was considerably comforted
by finding that the course she had decided on, and for which
she was now asking my assistance, was more pacific in
character, and less dangerous. We were to seek out the
dear Princess; she was to be at Ems on the 24th, and we
were at once to throw ourselves, figuratively, into her
hands, and implore protection. The "monster" — the word
is shorter than his name, and serves equally well — had
written innumerable letters to prejudice her against his wife,
recounting the most infamous calumnies and the most incredible accusations. These we were to refute: how I
did n't exactly know, but we were to do it. With the dear
Princess on our side, the monster would be quite powerless
for further mischief; for, by some mysterious agency, it appeared that this wonderful Duchess could restore a damaged
reputation, just as formerly kings used to cure the evil.

It was a great load off my mind, Tom, to know that nothing more was expected of me. She might have wanted me
to go to England, where there are two writs out against
me, or to advance a sum of money for law when I have n't
a sixpence for living, or maybe to bully somebody that
would n't be bullied; in fact, I did n't know what impossi-

bilities might n't be passing through her brain, or what difficult tasks she might be inventing, as we read of in those
stories where people make compacts with the devil, and
always try to pose him by the terms of the bargain.

In the present instance, I certainly got off easier than I
should have done with the "Black Gentleman." All that
was required of me was to accompany a very charming
and most agreeable woman on an excursion of about two
or three days' duration through one of the most picturesque
parts of the Rhine country, in a comfortable town-built
britschka, with every appliance of ease and luxury about
it. We have an adage in Ireland, "There's worse than
this in the North," and faith, Tom, I could n't help saying
so. Mrs. G.'s motive in asking my companionship was to
show her dear Duchess that she was domesticated, and
living with a most respectable family, of which I was the
head. You may laugh at the notion, Tom, but I was to be
brought forward as a model "paterfamilias," who could
harbor nothing wrong.

I believe I smiled myself at the character assigned. But
"is n't life a stage?" and in nothing more so than the fact
that no man can choose his part, but must just take what
the great stage-manager — Fate — assigns him; and it is
just as cruel to ridicule the failures and shortcomings we
often witness in public men as to shout, in gallery-fashion,
at some poor devil actor obliged to play a gentleman with
broken boots and patched pantaloons.

There were, indeed, two difficulties, neither of them inconsiderable, in the matter. One was money. The journey
would needs be costly. Posting abroad is to the full as
expensive as at home. The other was as to Mrs. Dodd.
How would she take it? I was bound over in the very
heaviest recognizances to secrecy. Mrs. G. insisted that I
alone should be the depositary of her secret; and she was
wise there, for Mrs. D. would have revealed it to Betty
Cobb before she slept. What if she should take a jealous
turn? It was true the Mary Jane affair had made her rather
ashamed of herself, but time was wearing off the effect.
Mrs. Gore Hampton was a handsome woman, and there
would be a kind of *éclat* in such a rivalry! I knew well,

Tom, that if she once mounted this hobby, there was nothing could stop her. All her visions of fashionable introductions, all the bright charms of high society, to which Mrs. G.'s intimacy was to lead, would melt away, like a mirage, before the high wind of her angry indignation.

She would have put Mrs. G. in the dock, and arraigned her like any common offender. It was not without reason, then, that I dreaded such a catastrophe; and in a kind of semi-serious, semi-jocose way, I told Mrs. Gore of my misgivings.

She took it beautifully, Tom. She did n't laugh as if the thing was ridiculous, and as if the idea of Kenny Dodd performing "Amoroso" was a glaring absurdity. "Not at all," she gravely said; "I have been thinking over that, and, as you remark, it *is* a difficulty." Shall I own to you, Tom, that the confession sent a strange thrill through me; and like a man selected to lead a forlorn hope, I still felt that the choice redounded to my credit?

"I think, however," said she, after a pause, "if you confided the matter to *my* management, if you leave *me* to explain to Mrs. Dodd, I shall be able, without revealing more than I wish, to satisfy her as to the object of our journey."

I heartily assented to an arrangement so agreeable; I even promised not to see Mrs. D. before we started, lest any unfortunate combination of circumstances might interfere with our project.

The pecuniary embarrassment I communicated to Lord George. He quite agreed with me that I could n't possibly allude to it to Mrs. G. "In all likelihood," said he, "she will just hand you a book of blank checks, or Herries's circulars, and say, ' Pray do me the favor to take the trouble off my hands.' It is what she usually does with any of her friends with whom she is sufficiently intimate; for, as I told you, she is a ' perfect child about money.' " I might have told him that, so far as having very little of it, so was I too.

"But supposing," said I, "that, in the bustle of departure, and in the preoccupation of other thoughts, she should n't remember to do this; such is likely enough, you know?"

"Oh, nothing more so," said he, laughing. "She is the most absent creature in the world."

"In that case," said I, "one ought to be, in a measure, prepared."

"To a certain extent, assuredly," said he, coolly. "You might as well take something with you, — a hundred pounds or so."

You can imagine the choking gulp in my throat as I heard these words. Why, I had n't twenty — no, not ten; I doubt, greatly, if I had fully five pounds in my possession. I was living in the daily hope of that remittance from you, which, by the way, seems always tardier in coming in proportion as Ireland grows more prosperous.

Tiverton, however, does not limit his services to good counsel; he can act as well as think. For a bill of three thousand francs, at thirty-one days, I received, from the landlord of the hotel, something short of a hundred Napoleons, — a trifle under six hundred per cent per annum, but, of course, not meant to run for that time. Lord George said, "Everything considered, it was reasonable enough;" and if that implied that I 'd never repay a farthing of it, perhaps he was correct. "I 'm sorry," said he, "that the ' bit of stiff,' " meaning the bill, "was n't for five thousand francs, for I want a trifle of cash myself, at this moment." In this regret I did not share, Tom, for I clearly saw that the additional eighty pounds would have been out of *my* pocket!

I have now, as briefly as I am able, but, perhaps, tediously enough, told you of all the preliminary arrangements of our journey, save one, which was three lines that I left for Mrs. D. before starting, — not very explanatory, perhaps, but written in "great haste."

It was a splendid morning when we started. The sun was just topping the Drachenfels, and sending a perfect flood of golden glory over the Rhine, and that rich tract of yellow corn country along its left bank, the right being still in deep shadow. From the Kreutzberg to the Seven Mountains it was one gorgeuos panorama, with mountain and crag, and ruined castles, vine-clad cliffs, and plains of waving wheat, all seen in the calm splendor of a still summer's morning.

I never saw anything as beautiful; perhaps I never shall again. Of my rapturous enjoyment of the scene, as we whirled along with four posters at a gallop, the best criterion I can give you is that I totally forgot everything but the enchanting vision around me. Ireland, home, Dodsborough, petty sessions, police and poor-rates, county cess, Chancery, all my difficulties, down even to Mrs. D. herself, faded away, and left me in undisturbed and unbounded enjoyment.

I have often had to tell you of my disappointment with the Continent; how little it responded to my previous expectations, and how short came every trait of nationality of that striking effect I had once foreshadowed. The distinctive features of race, from which I had anticipated so much amusement, all the peculiarities of dress, custom, and manner which I had speculated on as sources of interest, had either no existence whatever, or demanded a far shrewder and nicer observation than mine to detect. These have I more than once complained of to you in my letters; and I was fast lapsing into the deep conviction that, except in being the rear-guard of civilization, and adhering to habits which have long since been superseded by improved and better modes with us, the Continent differs wonderfully little from England.

The reason of this impression was manifestly because I was always in intercourse with foreigners who live and trade upon English travellers, who make a livelihood of ministering to John Bull's national leanings in dress, cookery, and furniture; and who, so to say, get up a kind of artificial England abroad, where the Englishman is painfully reminded of all the comforts he has left behind him, without one single opportunity for remembering the compensations he is receiving in return. To this cause is attributable, mainly, the vulgar impression conveyed by a first glance at the Continent. It is a bad travesty of a homely original.

What a sudden change came over me now, as we swept along through this enchanting country, where every sight and every sound were novel and interesting! The little villages, almost escarped from the tall precipice that skirted the river, were often of Roman origin; old towers of brick, and battlemented walls, displaying the S. P. Q. R., — those wonderful letters which, from school days to old age, call up such conceptions of this mighty people. A great wagon would draw aside to let us pass; and its giant oxen, with their massive beams of timber on their necks, remind one of the old pictures in some illustrated edition of the "Georgics." The splash of oars, and the loud shouts of men, turn your eyes to the Rhine, and it is a raft, whole acres of timber, slowly floating along, the evidence of some primeval pine forest hundreds of miles away, where the night winds used to sigh in the days of the Cæsars. And now every head is bare, and every knee is bowed, for a procession moves past, on its way to some holy shrine, the zigzag path to which, up the mountain, is traceable by the white line of peasant girls, whose voices are floating down in mellow chorus. Oh, Tom! the whole scene was full of enchantment, and did n't require the consciousness that would haunt me to make it a vision of perfect enjoyment. You ask what was that same consciousness I allude to? Neither more nor less, my dear friend, than the little whisper within me, that said, "Kenny Dodd, where are you going, and for what? Is it Mrs. D. is sitting beside you? or are you quite sure it 's not some other man's wife?"

You 'll say, perhaps, these were rather disturbing reflections, and so they would have been had they ever got that far; but as mere flitting fancies, as passing shadows over the mind, they heightened the enjoyment of the moment by some strange and mysterious agency, which I am quite unable to explain, but which, I believe, is referable to the same category as the French Duchess's regret "that iced water was n't a sin, or it would be the greatest delight of existence."

If my conscience had been unmannerly enough to say, "Ain't you doing wrong, Kenny Dodd?" I 'm afraid I 'd have said "Yes," with a chuckle of satisfaction. I 'm afraid, my dear Tom, that the human heart, at least in the Irish version, is a very incomprehensible volume.

Let us strive to be good as much as we may, there is a secret sense of pleasure in doing wrong that shows what a

K. D. getting over the ground.

hold wickedness has of us. I believe we flatter ourselves that we are cheating the devil all the while, because we intend to do right at last; but the danger is that the game comes to an end before we suspect, and there we are, "cleaned out," and our hand full of trumps.

You'll say, "What has all this to say to the Rhine, or Mrs. Gore Hampton?" Nothing whatever. It only shows that, like the Reflections on a Broomstick, your point of departure bears no relation to the goal of your voyage.

"What's the name of this village, Mr. Dodd?" whispers a soft voice from the deep recesses of the britschka.

"This is Andernach, Madam," said I, opening my "John," for I find there's no doing without him. "It is one of the most ancient cities of the Rhine. It was called by the Romans —"

"Never mind what it was called by the Romans; is n't there a legend about this ancient castle? To be sure there is; pray find it."

And I go on mumbling about Drusus, and Roman camps, and vaulted portals.

"Oh, it's not that," cries she, laughing.

"There are two articles of traffic peculiar to this spot. Millstones —" She puts her hand on my lips here, and I am unable to continue my reading, while she goes on: "I remember the legend now. It was a certain Siegfried, the Count Palatine of the Rhine, who, on his return from the Crusades, was persuaded by slanderous tongues to believe his wife had been faithless to him."

"The wretch! — the Count, I mean."

"So he was. He drove her out a wanderer upon the wide world, and she fled across the Rhine into that mountain country you see yonder, which then, as now, was all impenetrable forest. There she passed years and years of solitary existence, unknown and friendless. There were no Mr. Dodds in those days, or, at least, she had not the good fortune to meet with them."

I sigh deeply under the influence of such a glance, Tom, and she resumes, —

"At last, one day, when fatigued with the chase, and separated from his companions, the cruel Count throws himself down to rest beside a fountain; a lovely creature, attired gracefully but strangely in the skins of wild beasts — ”

“She did n’t kill them herself?” said I, interrupting.

“How absurd you are! Of course she did n’t;” and she draws her own ermine mantle across her as she speaks, smoothing the soft fur with her softer hand. “The Count starts to his feet, and recognizes her in a moment, and at the same instant, too, he is so struck by the manifest protection Providence has vouchsafed her, that he listens to her tale of justification, and conducts her in triumph home, — his injured but adored wife. I think, really, people were better formerly than they are now, — more forgiving, or rather, I mean, more open to truth and its generous impulses.”

“Faith, I can’t say,” replied I, pondering; “the skins may have had something to say to it.” Here she bursts into such a fit of laughter that I join from sheer sympathy with the sound, but not guessing in the least why or at what.

We soon left Andernach behind us, and rolled along beside the rapid Rhine, on a beautiful road almost level with the river, which now for some miles becomes less bold and picturesque.

At last we arrived at Coblentz to dinner, stopping at a capital inn called the “Giant,” after which we strolled through the town to stare at the shops and the quaintly dressed peasant girls, whose embroidered head-gear, a kind of velvet cap worked in gold or silver, so pleased Mrs. G. that we bought three or four of them, as well as several of those curiously wrought silver daggers which they wear stuck through their black hair.

I soon discovered that my fair friend was a “child” about other things besides “money.” Jewelry was one of these, and for which she seemed to have the most insatiable desire, combined with a most juvenile indifference as to cost. The country girls wear massive gold earrings of the strangest fashion, and nothing would content her but buying several sets of these. Then she took a fancy to their gold chains and rosaries, and, lastly, to their uncouth shoe-buckles, all of which she assured me would be priceless in a fancy dress.

In fact, my dear Tom, these minor preparations of hers, to resemble a Rhine-land peasant, came to a little over seventeen pounds sterling, and suggested to me, more than once, the secret wish that our excursion had been through Ireland, where the habits of the natives could have been counterfeited at considerably less cost.

As "we were in for it," however, I bore myself as gallantly as might be, and pressed several trifling articles on her acceptance, but she tossed them over contemptuously, and merely said, "Oh, we shall find all these things so much better at Ems. They have such a bazaar there!" an announcement that gave me a cold shudder from head to foot. After taking our coffee, we resumed our journey, Ems being only distant some eleven or twelve miles, and, I must say, a drive of unequalled beauty.

Once more on the road, Mrs. G. became more charming and delightful than ever. The romantic glen, through which we journeyed, suggested much material for conversation, and she was legendary and lyrical, plaintive and merry by turns, now recounting some story of tragic history, now remembering some little incident of modern fashionable life, but all, no matter what the theme, touched with a grace and delicacy quite her own. In a little silence that followed one of these charming sallies, I noticed that she smiled as if at something passing in her own thoughts.

"Shall I tell you what I was thinking of?" said she, smiling.

"By all means," said I; "it is a pleasant thought, so pray let me share in it."

"I'm not quite so certain of that," said she. "It is rather puzzling than pleasant. It is simply this: 'Here we are now within a mile of Ems. It is one of the most gossiping places in Europe. How shall we announce ourselves in the Strangers' List?"

The difficulty had never occurred to me before, Tom; nor indeed, did I very clearly appreciate it even now. I thought that the name of Kenny Dodd would have sufficed for me,

and I saw no reason why Mrs. Gore Hampton should not
have been satisfied with her own appellation.

" I knew," said she, laughing, " that you never gave this
a thought. Is n't that so?" I had to confess that she was
quite correct, and she went on : " Adolphus " — this was the
familiar for Mr. Gore Hampton — " is so well known that
you could n't possibly pass for him ; besides, he is very tall,
and wears large moustaches, — the largest, I think, in the
Blues."

" That 's clean out of the question, then," said I, stroking
my smooth chin in utter despair.

" You 're very like Lord Harvey Bruce, could n't you be
him?"

" I 'm afraid not ; my passport calls me Kenny James
Dodd."

" But Lord Harvey is a kind of relative of mine ; his
mother was a Gore ; I 'm sure you could be him."

I shook my head despondently ; but somehow, whenever
a sudden fancy strikes her, the impulse to yield to it seems
perfectly irresistible.

" It 's an excellent idea," continued she, " and all you
have to do is to write the name boldly in the Travellers'
Book, and say your passport is coming with one of your
people."

" But he might be here? "

" Oh, he 's not here ; he could n't be here ! I should have
heard of it if he were here."

" There may be several who may know him personally
here."

" There need be no difficulty about that," replied she ;
" you have only to feign illness, and keep your room. I 'll
take every precaution to sustain the deception. You shall
have everything in the way of comfort, but no visitors, — not
one."

I was thunderstruck, Tom ! the notion of coming away
from home, leaving my family, and braving Mrs. D., all
that I might go to bed at Ems, and partake of low diet
under a fictitious title, actually overwhelmed me. I thought
to myself, " This is a hazardous exploit of mine ; it may be
a costly one too : at the rate we are travelling, money flies

like chaff, but at least I shall have something for it. I
shall see fashionable life under the most favorable auspices.
I shall dine in public with my beautiful travelling-com-
panion. I shall accompany her to the Cursaal, to the Promenade, to the play-tables. I shall eat ice with her under the
' Lindens,' in the ' Allée.' I shall be envied and hated by
all the puppy population of the Baths, and feel myself glorious, conquering, and triumphant." These, and similar, had
been my sustaining reflections, under all the adverse pressure
of home thoughts. These had been my compensation for
the terrors that assuredly loomed in the distance. But now,
instead of the realization, I was to seek my consolation in a
darkened room, with old newspapers and water gruel!

Anger and indignation rendered me almost speechless.
" Was it for this?" I exclaimed twice or thrice, without
being able to finish my sentence; and she gently drew her
hand within my arm, and, in the tenderest of accents,
stopped me, and said, " No; not for this! "

Ah, Tom! you know what we used to hear in the "Beg-
gar's Opera," long ago. "'T is women that seduces all
mankind." I suppose it 's true. I suppose that if nature
has made us physically strong, she has made us morally
weak.

I wanted to be resolute; injured and indignant, I did my
best to feel outraged, but it would n't do. The touch of
three taper fingers of an ungloved hand, the silvery sounds
of a soft voice, and the tenderly reproachful glance of a pair
of dark blue eyes routed all my resolves, and I was half
ashamed of myself for needing even such gentle reproof.

From that moment I was her slave; she might have sent
me to a plantation, or sold me in a market-place, resistance,
on my part, was out of the question; and is n't this a pretty
confession for the father of a family, and the husband of
Mrs. D.? Not but, if I had time, I could explain the problem, in a non-natural sense, as the fashionable phrase has it,
or even go farther, and justify my divided allegiance, like
one of our own bishops, showing the difference between submission to constituted authority, and fidelity to matters of
faith, — Mrs. D. standing to represent Queen Victoria, and
Mrs. Gore Hampton Pope Pius the Ninth!

These thoughts did n't occur to me at once, Tom; they were the fruit of many a long hour of self-examination and reflection as I lay alone in my silent chamber, thinking over all the singular things that have occurred to me in life, the strange situations I have occupied, and of this, I own, the very strangest of all.

It must be a dreadful thing to be really sick in one of these places. There seems to be no such thing as night, at least as a season of repose. The same clatter of plates, knives, and glasses goes on; the same ringing of bells, and scuffling sounds of running feet; waltzes and polkas; wagons and mule-carts; donkeys and hurdy-gurdies; whistling waiters and small puppies, with a weak falsetto, infest the air, and make up a din that would addle the spirit of Pandemonium.

Hour after hour had I to lie listening to these, taking out my wrath in curses upon Strauss and late suppers, and anathematizing the whole family of opera writers, who have unquestionably originated the bleating performances of every late bed-goer. Not a wretch toiled upstairs, at four in the morning, without yelling out " Casta Diva," or " Gib, mir wein." The half-tipsy ones were usually sentimental, and hiccuped the " Tu che al cielo," out of the " Lucia."

To these succeeded the late sitters at the play-tables, — a race who, to their honor be it recorded, never sing. Gambling is a grave passion, and, whether a man win or lose, it takes all fun out of him. A deep-muttered malediction upon bad luck, a false oath to play no more, a hearty curse against Fortune were the only soliloquies of these the last votaries of Pleasure that now sought their beds as day was breaking.

Have you ever stopped your ears, Tom, and looked at a room full of people dancing? The effect is very curious. What was so graceful but a moment back is now only grotesque. The plastic elegance of gesture becomes downright absurdity. She who tripped with such fairy-like lightness, or that other who floated with swan-like dignity, now seems to move without purpose, and, stranger still, without grace. It was the measure which gave the soul to the performance, — it was that mystic accord, like what binds mind to matter, that gave the wondrous charm to the whole; divested of this it was like motion without vitality, — abrupt, mechanical, convulsive. Exactly the same kind of effect is produced by witnessing fashionable amusements, with a spirit untuned to pleasure. You know nothing of their motives, nor incentives to enjoyment; you are not admitted to any participation in their plan or their object, and to *your* eyes it is all " dancing without music."

I need not dwell on a tiresome theme, for such would be any description of my life at Ems. Of my lovely companion I saw but little. About midday her maid would bring me a few lines, written in pencil, with kind inquiries after me. Later on I could detect the silvery music of her voice, as she issued forth to her afternoon drive. Later again I could hear her, as she passed along the corridor to her room; and then, as night wore on, she would sometimes come to my door to say a few words, — very kind ones, and in her own softest manner, but of which I could recall nothing, so occupied was I with observing her in all the splendor of evening dress.

When a bright object of this kind passes from your presence, there still lingers for a second or so a species of twilight, after which comes the black and starless night of deep despondency. Out of these dreamy delusive fits of low spirits I used to start with the sudden question, " What are you doing here, Kenny Dodd? Is it the father of a family ought to be living in this fashion? What tom-foolery is this? Is this kind of life instructive, intellectual, or even amusing? Is it respectable? I am not certain it is any one of the four. How long is it to continue, or where is it to end? Am I to go down to the grave under a false name, and are the Dodd family to put on mourning for Lord Harvey Bruce?"

One night that these thoughts had carried me to a high pitch of excitement, I was walking hurriedly to and fro in my room inveighing against the absurd folly which originally had embarked me on this journey. Anger had so far mastered my reason that I began to doubt everything and everybody. I grew sceptical that there were such people in the world as Mr. Gore Hampton or Lord Harvey Bruce, and in my heart I utterly rejected the existence of the "Princess." Up to this moment I had contented myself with hating her, as the first cause of all my calamities, but now I denied her a reality and a being. I did n't at first perceive what would come of my thus disturbing a great foundation-stone, and how inevitably the whole edifice would come tumbling down about my ears in consequence.

This terrible truth, however, now stared me in the face, and I sat down to consider it with a trembling spirit.

"May I come in?" whispered a low but well-known voice, — "may I come in?"

My first thoughts were to affect sleep and not answer, but I saw that there was an eagerness in the manner that would not brook denial, and answered, "Who's there?"

"It is I, my dear friend," said Mrs. Gore Hampton, entering, and closing the door behind her. She came forward to where I was sitting despondingly on the side of the bed, and took a chair in front of me.

"What's the matter; you are surely not ill in reality?" asked she, tenderly.

"I believe I am," replied I. "They say in Ireland 'mocking is catching,' and, faith, I half suspect I'm going to pay the price of my own deceitfulness."

"Oh, no, no! you only say that to alarm me. You will be perfectly well when you leave this; the confinement disagrees with you."

"I think it does," said I; "but when are we to go?"

"Immediately; to-night, if possible. I have just received a few lines from the dear Princess — "

"Oh, the Princess!" ejaculated I, with a faint groan.

"Why, what do you mean?" asked she, eagerly.

"Oh, nothing; go on."

"But, first tell me, what made you sigh so when I spoke of the Princess?"

"God knows," said I; "I believe my head was wandering."

"Poor, dear head!" said she, patting me as if I was a small King Charles's spaniel, "it will be better in the fresh air. The Princess writes to say that we must meet her at Eisenach, since she finds herself too ill to come on here. She urges us to lose no time about it, because the Empress

Sophia will be on a visit with her in a few days, which of course would interfere with our seeing her frequently. The letter should have been here yesterday, but she gave it to the Archduke Nicholas, and he only remembered it when he was walking with me this evening."

. These high and mighty names only made me sigh heartily, and she seemed at once to read all that was passing within me.

"I see what it is," said she, with deep emotion; "you are growing weary of me. You are beginning to regret the noble chivalry, the generous devotion you had shown me. You are asking yourself, 'What am I to her? Why should she cling to me?' Cruel question — of a still more cruel answer! But go, sir, return to your family, and leave me if you will to those heartless courtiers who mete out their sympathies by a sovereign's smiles, and only bestow their pity when royalty commands it; and yet, before we part forever, let me here, on my bended knees, thank and bless — " I can't do it, Tom; I can't write it. I find I am

blubbering away just as badly as when the scene occurred.
Blue eyes half swimming in tears, silky-brown ringlets, and
a voice broken by sobs, are shamefully unfair odds against
an Irish gentleman on the shady side of fifty-two or three.

It's all very well for you — sitting quietly at your turf
fire — with an old sleepy spaniel snoring on the hearth-rug,
and nothing younger in the house than Mrs. Shea, your late
wife's aunt — to talk about " My time of life " — " Grown-
up daughters " — and so on. " He scoffs at wounds who
never felt a scar." The fact is, I'm not a bit more susceptible than other people; I even think I am less yielding
— less open to soft influences than many of my acquaintances. I can answer for it, I never found that the strongest persuasions of a tax-gatherer disposed me to look
favorably on " county cess, or a rate-in-aid." Even the
priest acknowledges me a tough subject on the score of
Easter dues and offerings. If I know anything about my
own nature, it is that I have rather a casuistic, hair-splitting
kind of way with me, — the very reverse of your soft, submissive, easily seduced fellows. I was always known as the obstinate juryman at our assizes, that preferred starvation and
a cart to a glib verdict like the others. I am not sure that
anybody ever found it an easy task to convince me about
anything, except, perhaps, Mrs. D., and then, Tom, it was
not precisely " conviction," — *that* was something else.

I think I have now made out a sufficient defence of myself, and I'll not make the lawyer's blunder of proving
too much. Give me the same latitude that is always con-
ceded to great men when their actions will not square with
their previous sentiments. Think of the Duke and Sir
Robert, and be merciful to Kenny Dodd.

We left Ems, like a thief, in the night; the robbery,
however, was performed by the landlord, whose bill for five
days amounted to upwards of twenty-seven pounds sterling.
Whether Grégoire and Mademoiselle Virginie drank all the
champagne set down in it I cannot say; but if so, they could
never have been sober since their arrival. There are some
other curious items, too, such as maraschino and eau de
Dantzic, and a large assessment for " real Havannahs " !
Who sipped and smoked the above is more than I know.

With regard to out-of-door amusements, Mrs. G. must
have ridden, at the least, four donkeys daily, not to speak
of carriages, and a sort of sedan-chair for the evening.

I assure you I left the place with a heart even lighter
than my purse. I was falling into a very alarming kind
of melancholy, and could n't much longer have answered
for my actions.

If we loitered inactively at Ems, we certainly suffered
no grass to grow under our feet now. Four horses on the
level, six when the road was heavy or newly gravelled; bulls
at all the hills.

It 's the truth I 'm telling you, Tom, for a light London
britschka, the usual team on a rising ground was six horses
and three oxen, with about two men per quadruped, — boys
and beggars *ad libitum*. I laughed heartily at it, till it
came to paying for them, after which it became one of the
worst jokes you can imagine. Onward we went, however,
in one fashion or another, walking to "blow the cattle"
when the road was level and smooth, and keeping a very
pretty hunting-pace when the ruts were deep, and the rocks
rugged.

It seemed, to judge from our speed, that our haste was
most imminent, for we changed horses at every station
with an attempt at despatch that greatly disconcerted the
post functionaries, and probably suggested to them grievous
doubts about our respectability. After twenty-four hours
of this jolting process, I was, as you may suppose, well
wearied, — the more so, since my late confinement to bed had
made me weak and irritable. Mrs. G., however, seemed
to think nothing of it, so that for very shame' sake I could
not complain. There is either a greater fund of endurance
about women than in men, or else they have a stronger and
more impulsive will, overcoming all obstacles in its way, or
regarding them as nothing. I assure you, Tom, I 'd have
pulled up short at any of the villages we passed through and
booked myself for a ten-hours' sleep, in that horizontal
position that nature intended, but she would n't hear of it.
"We must get on, dear Mr. Dodd; " "*You* know how important time is to us; " "Do our best, and we shall be late
enough." These and such like were the propositions which

I had to assent to, without the very vaguest conception why.

That night seemed to me as if it would never end. I never could close my eyes without dreaming of bailiffs, writs, judges' warrants, and Mrs. D. Then I got the notion into my head that I had been sentenced for some crime or other to everlasting travelling, — an impression, doubtless, suggested by my hearing through my sleep how we were constantly crossing some frontier, and entering a new territory. Now it was Hesse Cassel would pry into our portmanteaus; now it was Bavaria wanted to peep at our passports. Sigmaringen insisted on seeing that we had no concealed fire-arms. Hoch Heckingen searched us for smuggled tobacco. From a deep doze, which to my ineffable shame I discovered I had been taking on my fair companion's shoulder, I was suddenly awakened at daybreak by the roll of a drum, and the clatter of presenting arms. This was a place called Heinfeld, in the Duchy of Saxe-Weimar, where the commandant, supposing us to be royal personages, from our six horses and mounted courier, turned out the guard to salute us. I gave him briefly to understand that we were *incog.*, and we passed on without further molestation.

By noon we reached Eisenach, where, descending at the "Rautenkranz," the head inn, I bolted my door, and, throwing myself on my bed, slept far into the night. When I awoke, the house was all at rest, every one had retired, and in this solitude did I begin the recital of the singular page in my history which is now before you. I felt like one of those storm-tossed mariners who, on some unknown and distant ocean, commit their sorrows to paper, and then enclosing it in a bottle, leave the address to Fortune. I know not if these lines are ever to reach you. I know not who may read them. Perhaps, like Perouse, my fate may be a mystery for future ages. I feel altogether very low about myself.

I was obliged to break off suddenly above, but I am now better. We have been two days here, and I like the place greatly. It lies in the midst of a fine mountain range — the Thuringians — with a deep forest on every side. Up

to this we have had no tidings of the Princess, but we pass
our time agreeably enough in visiting the remarkable objects
in the neighborhood, one of which is the Wartburg, where
Luther passed a year of imprisonment.

I have collected some curious materials about the life of
this Protestant champion for Father Maher, which will make
a considerable sensation at home. There is an armory, too,
in the castle of the most interesting kind; but, as usual, all
the remarkable warriors were little fellows. The robbers of
antiquity were big, but the great characters of chivalry, I
remark, were small. The Constable do Bourbon's armor
would n't fit Kenny Dodd.

I intend to send off this package to-day, by a "gentleman
of the Jewish persuasion," so he styles himself, who is
travelling "in the interest of soft soap," and will be in
England within a fortnight. Where I shall be myself, by
that time, Tom, Heaven alone can tell!

My cash is running very low. I don't think that, above
my lawful debts in this place, I could muster twelve pounds,
and, after a careful exploration of the locality, I see no spot
at all likely to "advance money on good personal security."
You must immediately remit me a hundred, or a hundred
and fifty, for present emergencies. My humiliation will be
terrible if I have to speak about pecuniary matters in a
certain quarter; and, as I said before, how long we may
remain here, or where proceed when we leave this, I know
as much as you do!

I have begun four letters to Mrs. D., but have not satisfied myself that I am on the right tack in any of them.
Writing home when you have not heard from it, is like legislation for a distant colony without any clew to the state of
public opinion. You may be trying rigorous measures with
a people ripe for rebellion, or perhaps refusing some concession that they have just wrested by force. When I think
of domestic matters, I am strongly reminded of the Caffre
war, for somehow affairs never look so badly as when they
seem to promise a peace; and, like Sandilla, Mrs. D. is
great at an ambush.

You must write to her, Tom; say that I am greatly distressed at not getting any answers to my letters; that I

wrote four, — which is true, though I never sent off any of them. Make a plausible case for my absence out of the present materials, and speak alarmingly about my health, for she knows I have sold my policy of insurance at the Phœnix, and is really uneasy when I look ill.

If I was n't in such a mess, I should be distressed about the family, for I left them at Bonn with a mere trifle. When a man has got an incurable malady, he spends little money on doctoring, and so there is nothing saves fretting so much as being irretrievably ruined. Besides, it is in the world as in the water, it is struggling that drowns you; lie quietly down on your back, don't stir hand or limb, and somebody will be sure to pull you out, though it may chance to be by the hair.

I have often thought, Tom, that life is like the game of chess. It 's a fine thing to have the " move," if you play well, but if you don't, take my word for it, it 's better to stay quiet, and not budge. This will give you the key to my system; and if I ever get into public life, this, I assure you, shall be " Dodd's Parliamentary Guide."

I have now done, and you 'll say it 's time too; but let me tell you, Tom, that when I seal and send off this, I 'll feel myself very lonely and miserable. It was a comfort to me some days back to go every now and then and dot down a line or two; it kept me from thinking, which was a great blessing. You know how Gibbon felt when he wrote the last sentence of his great history; and although the Rise and Fall of Kenny Dodd be a small matter to posterity, it has a great hold upon his own affections.

I see my pony at the door, and Mrs. G. is already mounted. We are going to some old abbey in the forest, where she is to sketch, and I am to smoke for an hour or two; so good-bye, and remember that my escape from this must depend upon your assistance. This Princess has not yet made her appearance, nor have I the slightest guide as to her future intentions.

There are a quantity of home questions I am anxious to speak about, but must defer the discussion till my next. I have not seen a newspaper since I started on this excursion. I know not who is " in " or " out." I shall learn all these things later on; so, once more, good-bye. Address me at the "Rue Garland," and believe me, faithfully, your friend,

KENNY I. DODD.

P. S. When you mention to the neighbors having heard from me, it would be as well to say nothing of this little adventure of mine. Say that the Dodds are all well, and enjoying themselves, or something like that. If Mrs. D. has written to old Molly, try and get hold of the epistle, or otherwise I might as well be in the "Hue and Cry." Indeed, I don't see why you couldn't stop her letters at the postoffice in Bruff.

LETTER XXIII.

MRS. DODD TO MISTRESS MARY GALLAGHER, DODSBOROUGH.

COUR DE BADE, BADEN-BADEN.

MY DEAR MOLLY, — It will be five weeks on Tuesday next since we saw K. I., and except a bit of a note, of which I'll speak presently, never any tidings of him has reached us! I suppose, within the memory of man, wickedness equal to this has not been heard of. To go and disgrace himself, and, what's more, disgrace *us*, at his time of life, with two daughters grown up, and a son just going into the world, is a depth of baseness to which the mind cannot ascend.

They're away in Germany, my dear, — the happy pair! I wish I was near him. I'd only ask to be for five minutes within reach of him. Faith, I don't think he'd be so seductive and captivating for a little time to come. They're off, I hear, to what they call the "Hearts Forest," — a place, I take from the name, to be the favorite resort of loving couples. From the first day, Molly, I suspected what was coming; for, though James and Mary Anne persisted in saying that he was only gone for a day or two, I went to his drawers and saw that he had taken every stitch of his clothes that was good for anything away with him.

"If he's only gone for two days," says I, "what does he want with fourteen shirts and four embroidered fronts for dress, not to speak of his new black suit and his undress Deputy-Lieutenant's coat?" I tossed and tumbled over everything, and sure enough there was little left to look at. So you see, Molly, it was all planned before, and the whole was arranged with a cold-blooded duplicity that makes me boil to think over. This wasn't all, either; but he must go and draw a bill on the landlord for a hundred and twenty pounds; and, without the slightest attention to all that we owed in the hotel, or even leaving us a sixpence, away goes my gallant Lutherian, only thinking of love and pleasure!

The half of the M'Carthy legacy is gone already to meet these demands and enable us to come on here; and even with that I could n't have done it if it had n't been for Lord George's kindness, for he knows so much about bills, and bankers, and when the exchange is good, and what is the favorable moment to draw upon London, that, as he says himself, one learns at last to "make a pound go as far as five."

As to staying any longer at Bonn, it was out of the question. The whole town was talking of K. I., and everybody used to stop us and ask, with a mournful voice, if we had n't got any tidings of Mr. Dodd?

And now we 're here, I must say it is a charming place; and for real life and enjoyment, there 's probably not its equal in Europe. And then, Molly, the great feature is certainly the universal kindness and charity that prevails. You may do what you like, wear what you like, go where you like. I was a little bit afraid at first that the story of K. I. would get abroad and damage us in society; but Lord George said: "You mistake Baden, my dear Mrs. Dodd. If there 's anything they 're peculiarly lenient to, it 's just *that*. There 's no cant, no hypocrisy here; nobody would endure such for an hour. Everybody knows that the world is not peopled with angels, and England is the only country where they affect that delusion. Here all are natural, sincere, and candid." These were his words, and I assure you they are no more than the truth; and so far from K. I.'s conduct being regarded in any spirit of unfairness towards *us*, I really believe that we have met a great deal of delicate and refined notice on account of it. As Lord G. remarks, "They know that you don't belong to that strait-laced set of humbugs that want to frown down all mankind. They see at once that you have the habits of the world, and the instincts of good society, and that you come amongst them neither to criticise nor censure, but to please and be pleased." I quote his very expressions, Molly, because, with all his wildness, his sentiments are invariably beautiful; and I must say that an ill-natured word never comes out of his mouth. If there's anything he excels in, too, it's tact. This he showed very remarkably when we arrived here. "We must do the thing handsomely," said he, "or we shall be sure to hear that Mr. D.'s absence is owing to pecuniary difficulties." And so, accordingly, he arranged to purchase a beautiful pair of gray ponies, and a small park phaeton, belonging to a young Russian, that was just ruined at the tables. We got the whole equipage for little more than half what it cost, and a tiger — as they call the little boy in buttons — goes with it.

We have taken the first apartment in the "Cour de Bade," and have put Paddy Byrne in a suit of green and gold, that always reminds me of poor Daniel O'Connell. Lord G. drives me out every day himself, and I hear all the passers-by say, "It's Tiverton and Mrs. Dodd," in a manner that shows we're as well known as the first people in the place. He is acquainted with every man, woman, and child in the town; and it is a perpetual "How are ye, Tiverton?" — "How goes it, George?" — "At the old trade, eh?" — as we drive along, that amuses me greatly. And it isn't only that he knows them personally, but he is familiar with all their private histories. It would fill a book — and a nice volume it would be! — if I were to tell you one-half of the stories he told me yesterday, going down to Lichtenthal. But the names is so confusing. How he remembers them all, I can't conceive.

We go to the rooms in the evening, full dressed, and as fine as you please; and if you saw how the company rises to meet us, and the gracious manner we are received by all the first people, you'd think we were sisters with half the room. For rank, wealth, and beauty, I never saw its equal; and the "tone," as Lord G. observes, is "so easy." Mary Anne usually dances all night, but *I* only stand up for a quadrille, though Lord George torments me to polka with him. As for James, he never quits the roulette-table, which is a kind of game where you always win thirty-six times as much as you put down, though maybe occasionally you lose your stake, for it's all chance, Molly, and,

like everything else in this wicked world, in the hands of
Fate!

I'm afraid James does n't understand the game, or forgets
to take up his winnings; for when he joins us at supper, he
looks depressed and careworn, till he has taken two or three
glasses of champagne. Caroline, as you may suppose, stays
moping at home. If there's anything distresses me more
than another, it's the way that girl goes on. Here we are,
in the very thick of the fashion, spending money, — as fast
as hops, — ruining ourselves, I may say, with expense;
and instead of taking the benefit of it while "it's going,"
she sits up in her room reading her eyes out of her head,
and studying things that no woman need know. As I say
to her, "What good is it to you? Will it ever get you a
husband, to know that Sir Humphrey Clinker invented the
safety-lamp? or do you suppose that any man will take a
fancy to you for the sake of your chemistry and eccentricity? Besides," says I, "you could do all this at home,
in Dodsborough, and who knows if we should n't be obliged
to go back and finish our days in Ireland!" And in my
heart and soul I believe it's what she'd like!

The real affliction in life is to see your children not take
after you! That is the most dreadful calamity of all.
You toil and you slave to bring them up with high notions,
to teach them to look down upon whatever is low and mean,
to avoid their poor relations, and whatever disgraces them,
and you find, the whole time, 't is looking back they are to
their humble origin, and fancying that they were happier,
for no other reason than because they were lower!

It is, maybe, the M'Carthy blood in me, but I feel as if
the higher I went the lighter I grew; and so it is, I'm sure,
with Mary Anne. I know, from her face across the room,
whether she's dancing with a "prince," or only "a gentleman from the United States"! And even in the matter of
looks it makes the greatest difference in her. In the one
case her eyes sparkle, her head is thrown back, her cheek
glows with animation; while in the other she seems half
asleep, dances out of time, and probably answers out of
place.

From all these facts, I gather, Molly, that there's nothing

so elevating to the mind as moving in a rank above your own; and I'm sure I don't forgive myself when I keep company with my equals. I believe James has less of the Dodd and more of the M'Carthy in him than the girls. He takes to the aristocracy so naturally, — calls them by their names, and makes free with them in a way that is really beautiful; and they call him "Jim," or some of them say "Jeemes," just as familiar as himself. I suppose it's no use repining, but I often feel, Molly, that if it was the Lord's will that I was to be left a widow, I'd see my children high in the world before long.

This reminds me of K. I., and here's his letter for you. I copy it word for word, without note or comma: —

"Dear Jemi, — We are waiting here for the Princess, who has not yet arrived, but is expected to-day or to-morrow at furthest. You will be sorry to hear that I was ill and confined for more than a week to my bed at Ems." Will I, indeed? "It was a kind of low fever." I read it a love fever, Molly, when I saw it first. "But I am now much better." You never were worse in your life, you old hypocrite, thinks I. "And am able to take a little exercise on horseback.

"The expense of this journey, unavoidable as it was! is very considerable, so that I reckon upon your practising the strictest economy during my absence." I thought I'd choke, Molly, when I seen this. Just think of the daring impudence of the man telling me that while he is lavishing hundreds on his vices and wickedness, the family is to starve to enable him to bear the expense. "The strictest economy during my absence." I wish I was near you when you wrote it!

Then comes in some balderdash about the scenery, and the place they're at, just as coolly described as if it was talking of Bruff or the neighborhood; the whole winding up with, "Mrs. G. H. desires me to convey her tender regards" — what she can spare, I suppose, without robbing him — "to you and the girls. No time for more, from yours sincerely,

"Kenny James Dodd."

There's an epistle for you! You'll not find the like of
it in the "Polite Letter-Writer," I'll wager. The father of
a family — and such a family too! — discoursing as easily
about the height of iniquity as if he was alluding to the
state of the weather, or the price of sheep at the last fair.
He flatters himself, maybe, that this free-and-easy way is
the best to bamboozle me, and that by seeming to make
nothing of it, I'll take the same view as himself. Is that
all he knows of me yet? Did he ever succeed in deceiving
me during the last seventeen years? Did n't I find him out
in twenty things when he did n't know himself of his own
depravity? I tell you in confidence, Molly, that if coming
abroad is an elegant thing for our sex, it's downright ruin
to men of K. I.'s time of life! When they come to fifty, or
thereabouts, in Ireland, they settle down to something
respectable, either on the Bench, or Guardians to the Union.
Their thoughts runs upon green crops and draining, and
how to raise a trifle, by way of loan, from the Board of
Works. But not having these things, abroad, to engage
them, they take to smartening themselves up with polished
boots and blackened whiskers, and what between pinching
here, and padding there, they get the notion that they're
just what they were thirty years ago! Oh dear! oh dear!
sure they've only to go upstairs a little quick, to stoop to
pick up a handkerchief, or button a boot, to detect the
mistake, and if that won't do, let them try a polka with a
young lady just out for her first season!

Of all the old fools, in this fashion, I never met a worse
than K. I.! and what adds to the disgrace, he knows it himself, and he goes on saying, "Sure I'm too old for this," or
"I'm past that;" and I always chime in with, "Of course
you are; you'd cut a nice figure;" and so on. But what's
the use of it, Molly? Their vanity and conceit sustains
them against all the snubs in the world, and till they come
down to a Bath-chair, they never believe that they can't
dance a hornpipe!

I could say a great deal more on this subject, but I must
turn to other things. You must see Purcell and tell him the
way we're left, without a fraction of money, nor knowing
where to get it. Tell him that I wrote to Waters about a

separation, which I would, only that K. I.'s affairs is in
such a state, I'd have to put up with a mere trifle. Say
that I'm going to expose him in the newspapers, and there's
"no knowing where I'll stop," for that's exactly the threat
Tom Purcell will be frightened at.

Get him to send me a remittance immediately, and describe our distress and destitution as touchingly as you can.

Here's more of it, Molly. James has just come in to say
that the Ministry is out in England, and that the new Government is giving everything away to the Irish, and that old
villain, K. I., not on the spot to ask for a place! James
tells me it's the Brigade is to have the best things; but I
don't remember if K. I. belongs to it, though I know he's
in the Yeomanry. From Lord-Lieutenant down to the letter-
carriers, they must be all Irish now, James says. We're to
have Ireland for ourselves, and as much of England as we
can, for we'll never rest till we get perfect equality, and I
must say it's time too!

K. I. isn't fit for much, but maybe he might get something. The Treasury is where he'd like to be, but I'm not
certain it would suit him. At all events, he's not to the
fore, and I don't think they'll send to look for him, as they
did for Sir Robert Peel! Till we know, however, whether
he has a chance of anything, it would be better to keep his
present conduct a profound secret, for James remarks "that
they make a great fuss about character nowadays;" and it
comes well from them, Molly, if the stories I hear be true!

Ask Purcell what's vacant in K. I.'s line? which, you
may say, goes from Lunatic Asylums to the Court of Chancery. I don't want James to have an Irish appointment,
but he says there's something in Gambia — wherever that is
— that he'd like.

As, of course, K. I. and myself can never live together
again, it would be very convenient if he was to get something that would require him to stay in Ireland, — either
a suspensory magistrate or a place in Newgate would do.
You'll wonder at my troubling myself about a man that
behaved as he did; and, indeed, I wonder at myself for it;
and what I say is, maybe this might happen, maybe the
other, and I'd be sorry afterwards; and if he was to be

taken away suddenly, I'd like to be sure to have my mind easy, and in a happy frame.

Is n't it dreadful to think that it's about these things my letter is filled, while all the enjoyment in life is going on about me? There's the band underneath my window playing the Railroad Polka, and the crowd round them is princesses and duchesses and countesses, all so elegantly dressed, and looking so sweet and amiable. Every minute the door opens, with an invitation for this or that, or maybe a nosegay of beautiful flowers that a prince with a wonderful name has sent to Mary Anne. And here's a man with the most tempting jewelry from Vienna, and another with lace and artificial flowers; and all for nothing, Molly, or next to nothing, — if one had a trifle to spend on them. And so we might, too, if K. I. had n't behaved this way.

There's to be a grand ball to-night at the Rooms, and Mary Anne is come to me about her dress; for one thing here is indispensable, — you must never appear twice in the same. For the life of me, I don't know what they do with the old gowns, but Mary Anne and myself has a stock already that would set up a moderate mantua-maker. As to shoes, and gloves too, a second night out of them is impossible, though Mary Anne tries to wear them at small tea-parties. Speaking of this, I must say that girl will be a treasure to the man that gets her; for she has so many ways of turning things to account: there's not an old lace veil, nor a bit of net, nor even a flower, that she can't find use for, somewhere or other. As to Caroline, she looks like a poor governess; there's no taste nor style whatever about her; and as to a bit of ribbon round her throat, or a cheap brooch, she never wears one! I tell her every day, "You're a Dodd, my dear, — a regular Dodd. You have no more of the M'Carthy in you than if you never saw me." And, indeed, she takes after the father in everything. She has a dry, sneering way about whatever is genteel or high-bred, and the same liking for anything low and common; but, after all, I'm lucky to have Mary Anne and James what they are! There's no position in life that they're not equal to; and if I'm not greatly mistaken, it's in the very highest rank they'll settle down at last. This opinion of mine,

Molly, is the best and shortest answer I can give to what you ask me in your last letter, — "What's the use of going abroad?" But, indeed, your question — as Lord George remarked, when I told him of it — is, "What's the use of civilization? What's the use of clothes? What's the use of cooked victuals?" You'll say, perhaps, that you have all these in Ireland; and I'll tell you, just as flatly, You have not. You stare with surprise, but I repeat to you, You have not.

An old iron shop in Pill Lane, with bits of brass, broken glass, and old crockery, is just as like Storr and Mortimer's as your Irish habits and ways are like the real world. Why, Molly, there's no breeding nor manners at all! You are all twice too familiar, or what you perhaps would call cordial, with each other; and yet you daren't, for the life of you, say what every foreigner would say to a lady the first time he ever met her. That's your notion of good manners!

As to your clothes, I get red as a turkey-cock with pure shame when I think of a Dublin bonnet, with a whole botanical garden over it; but, indeed, when one thinks of the dirty streets and the shocking climate, they forgive you for keeping all the finery for the head.

The cookery I won't speak of. There's people can eat it, and much good may it do them; and my heart bleeds when I think of their sufferings. But maybe Ireland *is* coming round, after all. What I hear is, that when everybody is sold out, matters will begin to mend. I suppose it's just as if the whole country was taking what's called the "Benefit of the Act," and that they'll start fresh again in the world without owing sixpence. If that's the meaning of the Cumbered Estates, it's the best thing ever was done for Ireland, and I only wonder they didn't think of it earlier; for my sure and certain opinion is that there's nothing distresses a man like trying to pay off old debts; and it destroys the spirits besides, for ye're always saying, "It wasn't *me* that spent *this*. *I* hadn't any fun for *that*."

James has just come in with the list of the new Ministry, and among all the Irish appointments I don't see as good a name as K. I.'s; and you may fancy how respectable they are after that! But the truth is, Molly, it's the same with politics as with the potatoes: one is satisfied to put up with anything in a famine. K. I. used to say that when he was young, his Irish name would have excluded him as much from any chance of office as if he was a Red Indian; but times is changed now, and I see two or three in the list that their colleagues will never pronounce rightly,— and that, at least, is something gained.

And just to think of it, Molly! Who knows, if K. I. was n't disgracing himself this minute, that he would n't be high in the Administration? I remember the time when it was only Lord James this, or Sir Michael that, got anything; but now you may remark that it's maybe a fellow would rob the mail is a Lord of the Treasury, and one that would take fright at his own shadow is made Clerk of the Ordnance. That's a great "step in the right direction," Molly, and it shows, besides, that we 're daily living down obscene and antiquated prejudices.

You like a long letter, you say, and I hope you 'll be satisfied with this, for I 'm four days over it; but, to be sure, half the time is spent crying over the barbarous treatment I 've met from K. I. That you may never know what it is to have a like grief, is the prayer of your affectionate friend,

JEMIMA DODD.

P. S. Mary Anne sends her love and regards, and Cary, too, desires to be remembered to you. She is longing to have old Tib here, as if a black cat would be anything remarkable on the Continent. But that's the way with her. All the Dodsborough geese are swans in *her* estimation.

LETTER XXIV.

JAMES DODD TO ROBERT DOOLAN, ESQUIRE, TRINITY COLLEGE,
DUBLIN.

BADEN-BADEN.

MY DEAR BOB, — I copy the following paragraph from the
"Galignani" of yesterday: "Considerable excitement has
been caused amongst the fashionable visitors of Baden by
the rumored elopement of the charming Mrs. G * * *
H * * * * * * with an Irish gentleman of large fortune, and
who, though considerably past the prime of life, is evidently
not beyond the age of fascination. Our readers will appreciate the reserve with which we only allude to a report, the
bare mention of which will doubtless give the deepest distress amongst a wide circle of our very highest aristocracy."

Probably all your conic sections and spherical trigo-
nometry learning would never enable you to read the riddle
aright, and so I shall save you the profitless effort by saying that the delinquent so delicately indicated in the above
is no other than the worthy governor himself. Ay, Bob,
as the old song says, —

> "No age, no profession, nor station is free,
> To sovereign beauty mankind bends the knee;"

and how should it be expected that Dodd père could resist
the soft impeachment? To be as intelligible as the circumstances permit, I must ask of you to call to mind a
certain very beautiful fellow-traveller of ours, — a Mrs.
Gore Hampton. She is the Dido of this Æneid. Not
that there is in reality any — even the remotest — shade of
truth in the newspaper paragraph; the entire event being
explicable upon far less romantic and less interesting
grounds. Mrs. G. H. having desired the protection of

my father's escort to some small town in Germany, and
not wishing to excite the inevitable hostility of my mother
to the arrangement, determined upon a night march, without beat of drum. In this way was the fortress evacuated;
and when the garrison were mustered for duty, Dodd père
was reported missing.

Tiverton, who was in the secret throughout, explained
everything to me, and I as readily imparted the explanation to the girls; but all our endeavors to convince my
mother were totally fruitless. "She knew him of old," —
"she guessed many a day since what he was," — "it was
not now that she had to read his character," — these and
similar intimations, coupled with others even stronger and
less flattering as regarded his time of life, manners, and personal advantages, were more than enough to drown all our
arguments; and I must confess that she arranged the details
of circumstantial evidence against him with a degree of art
and dexterity that might have reflected credit on a Crown
lawyer.

Of course, the first three or four days after the event were
not of the pleasantest; for, not satisfied with the sympathies
of a home circle, my mother empanelled "special juries"
of the waiters and chambermaids, and arraigned the unlucky
governor on a series of charges extending to a period far
beyond the "statute of limitations."

Under these circumstances there was nothing for it but
to leave this place at once, and establish our quarters in
some new locality. Baden offered the most advisable sphere,
whither we have come, if not to hide our sorrows, at least
to console our griefs. I am perfectly convinced that if the
governor came back to-morrow, and could only obtain a fair
hearing, he could satisfactorily explain why he went, where
he was, and everything else about his absence; but there
lies the real difficulty, Bob. He will be condemned *per con-
tumaciam*, if not actually hooted out of court with indignation. While this is undeniably true, you will be astonished
to hear how thoroughly public sympathy would be with
him, were he boldly to stand forth and tender his plea of
"Guilty." I was slow to credit this when Tiverton told me
so at first, but I now see it is perfect fact. Good society

abroad exacts something in the way of qualification, — like what certain charitable institutions require at home, — you must have sinned before you can hope for admittance! It is not enough that you express profligate opinions, — speak disparagingly of whatever is right, and praise the wrong, — you are expected to give a proof, a good, palpable, unmistakable proof of your professions, and show yourself a man of your word. The oddest thing about all this is that these evidences are not demanded on any moral or immoral grounds, but simply as requirements of good breeding, — in other words, you have no right to mix in society where your purity of character may give offence; such pretension would be a downright impertinence.

Hence you will perceive that if the governor only knew of it, he might take brevet rank as a scamp, and actually figure here as one of the " profligates of the season." Meanwhile, his absence is not without its inconveniences; and if he remain much longer away, I am sorely afraid, we shall be reduced to a paper currency, not " convertible " at will.

I have myself been terribly unlucky at " the tables," have lost heavily, and am deeply in debt. Tiverton, however, tells me never to despair, and that when pushed to the wall a man can always retrieve himself by a rich marriage. I confess the remedy is not exactly to my taste, — but what remedy ever is? If it must be so, it must. There are just now some three or four great prizes in the wheel matrimonial here, of which I will speak more fully in my next; my object in the present being rather to tell you where we are, than to communicate the *res gestæ* of

Your ever attached friend,

JAMES DODD.

P. S. Don't think of reading for the Fellowship, I beg and entreat of you. If you will take to " monkery," do it among our own fellows, who at least enjoy lives of ease and indolence. Besides, it is a downright absurdity to suppose that any man ever rallies after four years of hard study and application. As Tiverton says, " You train too fine, and there's no work in you afterwards."

LETTER XXV.

EISENACH, "THE RUE GARLAND."

MY DEAR TOM, — You may see by the address that I am
still here, although in somewhat different circumstances from
those in which I last wrote to you. No longer "mi lor,"
the occupant of the "grand suite of apartments with the
balcony," flattered by beauty, and waited on with devotion.
I am now alone; the humble tenant of a small sanded parlor, and but too happy to take a very unpretending place at
my host's table. I seek out solitary spots for my daily
walks, — I select the very cheapest "Canastre" for my
lonely pipe, — and, in a word, I am undergoing a course of
"the silent system," accompanied by thoughts of the past,
present, and the future, gloomy as ever were inflicted by
any code of penitentiary discipline.

I know not if — seeing the bulk of this formidable
despatch — you will have patience to read it: I have my
doubts that you will employ somebody to "note the brief"
for you, and only address yourself to the strong points of
the case. Be this as it may, it is a relief to me to decant
my sorrows even into my ink-bottle; and I come back at
night with a sense of consolation that shows me that, no
matter how lonely and desolate a man may be in the world,
there is a great source of comfort in the sympathy he has
for himself. This may sound like a bull, but it is not one,
as I am quite ready to show. But my poor brains are not
in order for metaphysics, and so, with your leave, I'll just
confine myself to narrative for the present, and keep all the
philosophy of my argument for another occasion.

Lest, however, you should only throw your eyes carelessly over these lines and not adventure far into the detail of my sorrows, I take this early opportunity of saying that I am living here on credit, — that I have n't five shillings left to me, — that my shoemaker lies in wait for me in the Juden-Gasse, and my washerwoman watches for me near the church. Schnaps, snuff, and cigars have encompassed me round about with small duns, and I live in a charmed circle of petty persecutions, that would drive a less good-tempered man half-crazy. Not that I am ungrateful to Providence for many blessings; I acknowledge heartily the great advantage I possess in knowing nothing whatever of the language, so that I am enabled to preserve my equanimity under what very probably may be the foulest abuse that ever was poured out upon insolvent humanity.

My wardrobe is dwindled to the " shortest span." I have " taken out" my great-coat in Kirschwasser, and converted my spare small-clothes into cigars. My hat has gone to repair my shoes; and as my razors are pledged for pen, ink, and paper, I have grown a beard that would make the fortune of an Italian refugee, or of a missionary speaker at Exeter Hall!

My host of the " Rue Garland " has n't seen a piece of my money for the last fortnight; and now, for the first time since I came abroad, am I able to say that I find the Continent cheap to live in. Ay, Tom, take my word for it, the whole secret lies in this, — " Do with little, and pay for less," and you 'll find a great economy in coming abroad to live. But if you cannot cheat yourself as well as your creditors, take my advice and stay at home. These, however, are only spare reflections; and I'll now resume my story, taking up the thread of it where I left off in my last.

It is really all like a dream to me, Tom; and many times I am unable to convince myself that it is not a dream, so strange and so novel are all the incidents that have of late befallen me, so unlike every former passage of my life, and so unsuited am I by nature, habit, and temperament for the curious series of adventures in which I have been involved.

After all, I suppose it is downright balderdash to say that

a man is not adapted for this, or suited to that. I remember people telling me that public life would n't do for me; that I was n't the kind of man for Parliament, and so on; but I see the folly of it all now. The truth is, Tom, that there is a faculty of accommodation in human nature, and wherever you are placed, under whatever circumstances situated, you 'll discover that your spirit, like your stomach, learns to digest everything; though I won't deny that it may now and then be at the cost of a heartburn in the one case as well as the other.

When I wrote to you last, I was living a kind of pastoral life, — a species of Melibœus, without sheep! If I remember aright, I left off when we were just setting out on an excursion into the forest, — one of those charming rides over the smooth sward, and under the trellised shadow of tall trees, now loitering pensively before some vista of the wood, now cantering along with merry laughter, as though with every bound we left some care behind never to overtake us. Ah, Tom, it 's no use for me to argue and reason with myself; I always find that I come back to the same point, and that whatever touches my feelings, whatever makes my heart vibrate with pleasant emotion, whatever brings back to me the ardent, confiding, trustful tone of my young days, does me good, and that I 'm a better man for it, even though "the situation," as you would call it, was rather equivocal. Don't mistake me, Tom Purcell, I don't want to go wrong; I have not the slightest inclination to break my neck. The height of my ambition is only to look over the precipice. Can't you understand that? Try and "realize" that to yourself, as the Yankees say, and you 'll at once comprehend the whole charm and fascination of my late life here. I was always "looking over the precipice," always speculating upon the terrible perils of the drop, and always half hugging myself in my sense of security. Maybe this is metaphysics again; if it is, I 'm sorry for it, but the German Diet must take the blame of it, — a course of sauerkraut would make any man flighty.

Well, I 'll spare you all description of these "Forest days," at whatever cost to my own feelings; and it is not every man that would put that much constraint upon himself, for something tells me that the theme would make me "come out strong." That, what with my descriptive powers as regards scenery, and my acute analysis on the score of emotions, I'd astonish you, and you'd be forced to exclaim, "Kenny is a very remarkable man. Faith! I never thought he had this in him." Nor did I know it myself, Tom Purcell; nor as much as suspect it. The fact is, my natural powers never had fair play. Mrs. D. kept me in a state of perpetual conflict. "Little wars," as the Duke used to say, "destroy a state;" and in the same way it's your small domesticities — to coin a word — that ruin a man's nature and fetter his genius. You think, perhaps, that I'm employing an over-ambitious phrase, but I am not. Mrs. G. H. assured me that I actually did possess "genius," and I believe in my heart that she is the only one who ever really understood me.

No man understood human nature better than Byron, and he says, in one of his letters, "that none of us ever do anything till a woman takes us in hand;" by which, of course, he means the developing of our better instincts, — the illustrating our latent capabilities, and so on; and that, let me observe to you, is exactly what our wives never do. With them, it is everlastingly some small question of domestic economy. They "take the vote on the supplies" every morning at breakfast, and they go to bed at night with thoughts of the "budget." The woman, therefore, referred to by the poet cannot be what we should call in Ireland "the woman that owns you." And here, again, my dear friend, is another illustration of my old theory, — how hard it is for a man to be good and great at the same time. Indeed, I am disposed to say that Nature never intended we should, but in all probability meant to typify, by the separation, the great manufacturing axiom, — "the division of labor."

Be this as it may, Byron is right, and if there be an infinitesimal spark of the divine essence in your nature, your female friend will detect it with the same unerring accuracy that a French chemist hunts out the ten-thousandth part of a grain of arsenic in a case of poison. It

would amaze you were I to tell you how markedly I perceived the changes going on in myself when under this
influence.   There was, so to say, a great revolution going
on within me, that embraced all my previous thoughts and
opinions on men, manners, and morals.   I felt that hitherto
I had been taking a kind of Dutch view of life from the
mere level of surrounding objects, but that now I was
elevated to a high and commanding position, from which I
looked down with calm dignity.   I must observe to you
that Mrs. G. H. was not only in the highest fashionable
circles of London, but that she was one who took a very
active part in political life.   This will doubtless surprise
you, Tom, as it did myself, for we know really nothing in
Ireland of the springs that set great events in motion.
Little do we suspect the real influence women exercise, — the
sway and control they practise over those who rule us.   I
wish you heard Mrs. G. H. talk, how she made Bustle do
this, and persuaded Pumistone do the other.   Foreign
affairs are her forte, and, indeed, she owned to me that
purely Home matters were too narrow and too local to interest her.   What she likes is a great Russian question,
with the Bosphorus and the Danubian Provinces, and the
Hospodar of Wallachia to deal with; or Italy and the Austrians, with a skirmishing dash at the Pope and the King of
Naples.   She is a Whig, for she told me that the Tories
were a set of rude barbarians, that never admitted female
influence; and " the consequence is," says she, " they never
know what is doing at foreign courts.   Now *we* knew everything : there was the Princess Sleeboffsky, at St. Petersburg ;
and the Countess von Schwarmerey, at Berlin ; and Madame
de la Tour de Force, at Florence, all in our interest.   There
was not a single impertinent allusion made to England, in
all the privacy of royal domestic life, that we had n't it
reported to us ; and we knew, besides, all the little ' ten-
dresses ' of the different statesmen of the Continent, for, in
our age, we bribe with Beauty, where formerly it was a
matter of Bank-notes.   The Tories, on the other hand,
lived with their wives, which at once accounts for the nar-
rowness of their views, and the limited range of their
speculations."

All this may read to you like a digression, my dear Tom, but it is not; for it enables me to exhibit to you some of those traits by which this fascinating creature charmed and engaged me. She opened so many new views of life to me, — explained so much of what was mystery to me before, — recounted so many amusing stories of great people, — gave me such passing glimpses of that wonderful world made up of kings and kaisers and ministers, who are, so to say, the great pieces of the chess-board, whereon *we* are but pawns, — that I actually felt as if I had been a child till I knew her.

Another grand result of this kind of information is, that, as you extend your observation beyond the narrow sphere of home, — whether it be politically or domestically, — you learn at last to think so little of what you once regarded as your own immediate and material interests, that you have as many — maybe more — sympathies with the world at large than with those actually belonging to you. Such was the progress I made in this enlightenment, that I felt far more anxious about the Bosphorus than ever I did for Bruff, and would rather have seen the Austrians expelled from Lombardy than have turned out every "squatter" off my own estate at Dodsborough. And it is not only that one acquires grander notions this way, but there are a variety of consolations in the system. You grumble at the poor-rates, and I point to the population of Milan paying ten times as much to their tyrants. You exclaim against extermination, and I reply, "Look at Poland." You complain of the priests' exactions, and I say, "Be thankful that you have n't the Pope."

Now, Tom, come back from all these speculations, and bring your thoughts to bear upon her that originated them, and don't wonder at me if I did n't know how the days were slipping past; nor could only give a mere passing, fugitive reflection to the fact that I have a wife and three children somewhere, not very abundantly furnished with the "sinews of war." I suppose, if we could only understand it, that we 'd discover our minds were like our bodies, and that we sometimes succumb to influences we could resist at other moments. Put your head out of the window at certain

periods, and you are certain to catch a cold. I conclude
that there are seasons the heart is just as susceptible.

I cannot give you a stronger illustration of the strange
delirium of my faculties than the fact that I actually forgot
the Princess whom we came expressly to meet, and never
once asked about her. It was some time in the sixth week

of our sojourn that the thought shot through my brain, —
"Was n't there a princess to be here? — did n't we expect to
see her?" How Mrs. G. H. laughed when I asked her the
question! She really could n't stop herself for ten minutes.
"But I am right," cried I; "there really *was* a princess?"

"To be sure you are, my dear Mr. Dodd," said she, wiping her eyes; "but you must have been living in a state of
trance, or you would have remembered that the poor dear

Duchess was obliged to accompany the Empress to Sicily, and that she could n't possibly count upon being here before the middle of September."

"What month are we in now?" asked I, timidly.

"July, of course!" said she, laughing.

"June, July, August, September," said I, counting on my fingers; "that will be four months!"

"What do you mean?" asked she.

"I mean," said I, "it will be four months since I saw Mrs. D. and the family."

She pressed her handkerchief to her face, and I thought I heard her sob; indeed I am certain I did. Nothing was further from my thoughts than to say a rude thing, or even an unfeeling one, and so I assured her over and over. I protested that it was the very first time since I came away that I ever as much as remembered one belonging to me; that it was impossible for a man to feel less the ties of family; that I looked upon myself — and, indeed, I hoped she also looked upon me in a way — in fact, regarded me in a light — I 'm not exactly clear, Tom, what light I said; of course, you can imagine what I intended to say, if I did n't say it.

"Is this really true?" said she, without uncovering her face, while she extended her other hand towards me.

"True!" repeated I. "If it were not true, why am I here? Why have I left — " I just caught myself in time, Tom. I was nearly "in it" again, with an allusion to Mrs. D.; but I changed it, and said, "Why am I your slave, — why am I at your feet — " Just as I said that, suiting the action to the words, the door of the room was jerked violently open, and a tall man, with a tremendous bushy pair of whiskers, poked his head in.

"Oh, heavens!" cried she; "ruined and undone!" and fled before I could see her; while the stranger, fastening the door behind him with the key, advanced towards me with an air at once so menacing and warlike that I seized the poker, an instrument about four feet six long, and stood on the defensive.

"Mr. Kenny Dodd, I believe," said he, solemnly.

"The same!" said I.

"And not Lord Harvey Bruce, at least, on this occasion," said he, with a kind of sneer.

"No," said I, "and who are you?"

"I am Lord Harvey Bruce, sir," was the answer.

I don't think I said anything in reply; indeed, I am quite sure I did not say a syllable; but I must have made

some expressive gesture, or suffered some exclamation to escape me, for he quickly rejoined, —

"Yes, sir, you have, indeed, reason to be thankful; for had it been my wretched, miserable, and injured friend instead, you would now be lying weltering in your blood."

"Might I make bold to ask the name of the wretched, miserable, and injured gentleman to whom I was about to be so much indebted?"

"The husband of your unhappy victim, sir," exclaimed he, and with such an energy of voice that I brandished the poker to show I was ready for him. "Yes, sir, Mr. Gore Hampton is now in this village, — to a mere accident you owe it that he is not in this hotel, — ay, in this very room."

And he gave a shudder at the words, as though the thoughts they suggested were enough to curdle a man's blood.

"I 'll tell you what, my Lord," said I, getting the table between us, to prevent any sudden attack on his part, "all your anger and high-flown indignation are clean thrown away. There is no victim here at all, — there is no villain; and, so far as I am concerned, your friend is not either miserable or injured. The circumstances under which I accompanied that lady to this place are all easy of explanation, and such as require a very different acknowledgment from what you seem disposed to make for them."

"If you think you are dealing with a schoolboy, sir, you are somewhat mistaken," broke he in. "I am a man of the world, and it will save us a deal of time, sir, if you will please to bear this plain fact in your memory."

"You may be that, or anything else you like, my Lord," said I; "but I 'd have you to know that I am a man well respected in the world, the father of a grown-up family. There is no occasion for that heavy groan at all, my Lord; the case is not what you suspect. I came here purely out of friendship — "

"Come, come, sir, this is sheer trifling; or, it is worse, — it is outrageous insult. The man who elopes with a woman, passes under a false name, retires with her into one of the most remote and unvisited towns of Germany, is discovered — as I lately discovered you, — only insults the understanding of him who listens to such excuses. We have tracked you, sir, — it is but fair to tell you, — from the Rhine to this village. We are prepared, when the proper time comes, to bring a host of evidence against you. In all probability, a more scandalous case has not come before the public these last twenty years. Rest assured, then, that denial, no matter how well sustained, will avail you little;

and when you have arrived at this palpable conviction, it will greatly facilitate our progress towards the termination of this unhappy business."

"Well, my Lord, let us suppose, for argument's sake, — 'without prejudice,' however, as the attorneys say, — that I see everything with your eyes, what is the nature of the termination you allude to?"

"From a gentleman coming from your side of St. George's Channel, the question is somewhat singular," observed he, with a sneer.

"Oh, I perceive," said I; "your Lordship means a duel." He bowed, and I went on: "Very well; I'm quite ready, whenever and wherever you please; and if your friend should n't make the arrangement inconvenient, it would be a great honor to me to exchange a shot with your Lordship afterwards. I have no friend by me, it is true; but maybe the landlord would oblige me so far, and I'm sure you'll not refuse me a pistol."

"As regards your polite attentions to myself, sir, I have but to say I accept them; at the same time, I fear you are paying me a French compliment. It is not a case for a formal exchange of shots; so long as Hampton lives, you can never leave the ground alive!"

"Then the best thing I can do is to shoot him," said I; and whether the speech was an unfeeling one, or the way I said it was bloodthirsty, but he certainly looked anything but easy in his mind.

"The sooner we settle the affair the better, sir," said he, haughtily.

"I think so, too, my Lord."

"With whom can I, then, communicate on your part?"

"I'll ask the landlord, and if he declines, I'll try the little barber on the Platz."

"I must say, sir, it is the first time in my life I find myself in such company. Have you no countryman of your acquaintance within a reasonable distance?"

"If Lord George Tiverton were here — "

"If he were, sir, he could not act for you, — he is the near relative of my friend."

I thought of everybody I could remember; but what was

the use of it? I could n't reach any of them, and so I was obliged to own. He seemed to ponder over this for some time, and then said, —

"The matter requires some consideration, sir. When the unhappy result gets abroad in the world, it is necessary that nothing should attach to us as men of honor and gentlemen. Your friends will have the right to ask if you were properly seconded."

"By the unhappy result, your Lordship delicately insinuates my death?"

He gave a little sigh, adjusted his cravat, and smoothed down his moustaches at the glass over the chimney.

"If it should occur as your Lordship surmises," said I, "it little matters who officiates on the occasion; indeed," added I, stroking my beard, "the barber might n't be an inappropriate friend. But I 've been ' out ' on matters of this kind a few times, and somehow I never got grazed yet; and that 's more than the man opposite me was able to say."

"You 'll stand before a man to-morrow, sir, that can hit a Napoleon at twenty paces."

Faith, Tom, I was nigh saying I wish he could find one for a mark about *me ;* but I caught myself in time, and only observed, —

"He must be an elegant shot."

"The best in the Blues, sir; but this is beside the question. The difficulty is, now, about your friend. There may be some retired officer here, — some one who has served; if you will institute inquiry, I 'll wait upon you this evening, and conclude our arrangements."

I promised I 'd do all in my power, and bowed him out of the room and downstairs with every civility, which, I am bound to say, he also returned, and we parted on excellent terms.

Now, Tom, you 'll maybe think it strange of me, with a thing of the kind on hand, but so it was, the moment he was off, I went to look for Mrs. Gore Hampton.

"The lady?" cried the waiter; "she started with extra-post half an hour ago."

"Started!" exclaimed I, — "which way?"

"On the high-road to Munich."

"She left no letter, — no note for me?"

"No, sir."

"Poor thing, — overcome, I suppose. She was crying, was n't she?"

"No, sir, she looked very much as usual, but hurried, perhaps; for she nearly forgot the ham sandwiches she had ordered to be got ready for her."

"The ham sandwiches!" exclaimed I, and they nearly choked me. "I 'm going to be shot for a woman that, in the very extremity of her ruin, has the heart to order ham sandwiches!" That was the reflection that arose to my mind, and can you fancy a more bitter one?

"Are you sure," asked I, "the sandwiches were n't for Madame Virginie, or the little dog?"

"They might, sir, but my Lady desired us to be sure and put plenty of mustard on them."

This was the damning circumstance, Tom. She was fond of mustard, — I had often remarked it; and just see, now, on what a trivial thing a man's happiness can hang. For I own to you, so long as I was strong in what I fancied to be her good graces, I could have fought the whole regiment of Blues; but when I thought to myself, "She does n't care a brass farthing for you, Kenny Dodd; she may be laughing at you this minute over the ham sandwiches," — I felt like a drowning man that had nothing to grapple on. Talk of unhappy and injured men, indeed! Was n't I in that category myself? Not even a husband's selfishness could dispute the palm of misery with *me!* In the matter of desertion we were both in the same boat, and for the life of me, I don't see what we could have to fight about. I never heard of two sailors rescued from shipwreck quarrelling as to who it was lost the vessel!

"The best thing for us to do," thought I, "would be to try and console each other; and if he be a sensible, good-hearted fellow, he 'll maybe take the same view of it. I 'll ask him and my Lord to dinner; I'll make the landlord give us some of that wonderful old Steinberger that was bottled three hundred years ago; I 'll treat them to a regular Saxon dish of venison with capers washed down with Marco-

brunner, and if we 're not brothers before morning, my name
is n't Kenny Dodd."

I was on "these hospitable thoughts intent," when Lord
Harvey Bruce was again announced. He had found out
an old sergeant-major of artillery, who for a consideration
would undertake the duties of my second, — kindly adding
that he and his family, a very large one, would also attend
my obsequies. ɪ

I interrupted his Lordship to remark that an event had
just occurred to modify the circumstances of the case, and
mentioned Mrs. Gore Hampton's departure.

"I really cannot perceive, sir," replied he, "that this in
any way affects the matter in hand. Is my friend less
injured — is his honor less tarnished because this unhappy
woman has at last awoke to a sense of her degraded and
pitiable condition?"

I thought of the sandwiches, Tom, but could say nothing.

"Are you less his greatest enemy on earth, sir?" cried he,
passionately.

"Now listen to me patiently, my Lord," said I. "I 'll
be as brief as I can, for both our sakes. I don't value it
one rush whether I go out with your friend or not. If you
want a proof of what I say, step into the little garden here
and I 'll give it to you. I 'm neither boasting nor bloodthirsty, when I say that I know how to stand at either end
of a pistol; but there 's nothing to fight about between us."

"Oh, if you renew that line of argument," cried he, interrupting me, "it is totally impossible I can listen."

"And why not?" said I. "Is it a greater satisfaction to
your friend to believe himself injured and dishonored than
to know that he is neither one nor the other?"

"Then why did you come away with her?"

"I can't tell," said I, for my head was quite confused
with all the discussion.

"And why call yourself by *my* name at Ems?"

"I cannot tell."

"Nor what do you mean by the attitude in which I found
you when I entered the room?"

"I can't tell that, either," cried I, driven to desperation
by sheer embarrassment. "It 's no use asking me any more.

I have been living for the last five or six weeks like one
under a spell of enchantment. I can no more account for
my actions than a patient in Swift's Hospital. I'm afraid
to commit my scattered thoughts to paper, lest they might
convict me of insanity. I know and feel that I am a responsible being, but somehow my notions of right and wrong are
so confused, I have learned to look on so many things
differently from what I used, that I'd cut a sorry figure
under cross-examination on any matter of morality. There's
the whole truth of it now. I'd have kept it to myself if I
could; I'm heartily ashamed at owning to it — but I can't
help it — it would come out. Therefore, don't bother me
with, ' Why did you do this?' 'What made you do that?'
for I can give you no reasons for anything."

"By Jove! this is a very singular affair," said he, leaning over the back of a chair, and staring me steadfastly in
the face. "Your age — your standing in society — your
appearance generally, Mr. Dodd, would, I feel bound to
say, rather — " Here he hesitated and faltered, as if the
right word was not forthcoming; and so I continued for
him, —

"Just so, my Lord; would rather refute than fix upon me
such an imputation. I'm not very like the kind of man
that figures usually in these sort of cases."

"As to *that*," said he, cautiously, "there is no saying.
I am now only speaking my own private sentiments, the
result of impressions made upon myself as an individual.
Courts of Law take their own views of these things; and the
House of Lords has also its own way of regarding them."

The words threw me into a cold perspiration from head
to foot, Tom! Courts of Law! and the House of Lords!
was n't that a pretty prospect for an encumbered Irish gentleman? A shot, or even two, at twelve or fourteen paces,
cannot be a very expensive thing, in a pecuniary point, to
any man, and there's an awkwardness in declining it if
others are anxious to have it, so that you appear ungracious
and disobliging. But Westminster Hall and St. Stephen's,
Tom, is mighty different. I won't speak of the disgrace
that attends such a proceeding at my time of life, nor the
hue-and-cry that the Press sets up at you, and follows you

with to your own hearth, — "the place from whence you came," and where now your wife waits for you — to perform the last sentence of the law. I won't allude to "Punch" and the "Illustrated News," that live upon you for three weeks; but I 'll just take the thing in its simplest form, — financially. Why, racing, railroads, contested elections, are nothing to it. You go to work exactly as Cobden says France and England do with their armaments: Chatham launches a seventy-four, and out comes Cherbourg with a line-of-battle ship, — "Injured Husband," secures Sir Fitz-roy Kelly; "Heartless Seducer," sends his brief to Cock-burn. It's a game of brag from that moment; and there's as much scheming and plotting to get a hold of Frank Murphy as if he was the knave of spades! It matters little or nothing what the upshot of the case may be; you may sink the enemy, or be compelled to strike your own flag; it does n't signify, in the least; the damages of the action are fatal to you.

Now, Tom, although I never speculated in all my life as to figuring in an affair like this, these considerations were often strongly impressed upon me by reading the news-papers, and I had come to the conclusion that a man should never think of defending an action of this kind, no more than he would a petition against his election, and for the same reason. Since, although not actually guilty in the one case or the other, you are certain to have committed so many indiscretions, — written, maybe, so many ridiculous letters, — and, in fact, exposed yourself so much, that if you cannot keep out of sight altogether, the next best thing is, let the judgment go by default. I say this to show you that the moment my Lord threw out the hint about law I had made up my mind from that instant.

"I sincerely wish," said he, after some deliberation, "that I could hit upon any mode of arranging this affair; for although I own you have made a strongly favorable impres-sion upon me, 'Dodd,' " — he called me Dodd here, quite like an old friend, — "we cannot expect that Hampton could concur in this view. The fact is, the whole thing has got so much blazed abroad, — they are so well known in the fashionable world, both home and foreign, — she is so very

handsome, so much admired, and he is such a charming
fellow,— the case has created a kind of European *éclat*.
Looking at the matter candidly, there may be a good deal
in what you have said, but as a man of the world, I am
forced to say that Hampton must shoot you, or sue for a
divorce. I am well aware that whichever course he adopts
many will condemn him. In the clubs there will be always
parties. There may spring up even a kind of *juste milieu*,
who will say, ' Now that poor Dodd is dead, I wonder if he
really *was* guilty? ' "

"I protest I feel very grateful to them, my Lord," said I.
But he paid no attention to my remark, and went on, —

"If vengeance be all that a man looks for, probably the
law of the land will do as much for him as the law of honor.
You ruin a fellow, irretrievably ruin him, by an action of
this kind. You probably remember Sir Gaybrook Foster,
that ran off with Lady Mudford? Well, he had a splendid
estate, did n't owe a shilling, they said, before that; they
tell me now that some one saw him the other day at Geelong,
croupier to a small ' hell.' Then there was Lackington,
whom we used to call the ' Cool of the Evening.' "

"I never knew one of them, my Lord," said I, impatiently, for I did n't care to hear all the illustrations of his
theory.

"Lackington was older than you are," continued he,
"when he bolted with that city man's wife, — what 's his
confounded name? "

"I am shamefully ill-read, my Lord, in this kind of literature," said I, "nor has it the same interest for me that it
seems to afford your Lordship. May I take the liberty of
recalling your attention to the matter before us? "

"I am giving to it, sir," said he, gravely, "my best and
most careful consideration. I am endeavoring, by the aid
of such information as is before me, to weigh the difficulties
that attach to either course, and to decide for that one
which shall secure to my friend Hampton the largest share
of the world's sympathy and approval. I have seen a
great deal of life, and all that I know of it teaches the one
lesson, — distrust, rather than yield to, first impressions.
Awhile ago, when I entered this room, I would have said to

Hampton, ' Shoot him like a dog, sir.' Now, I own to you,
Dodd, this is not the counsel I should give him. Now,
understand me well, I neither acquit nor condemn you;
circumstances are far too strong against you for the one,
and I have not the heart to do the other."

"This talking is dry work, my Lord," said I. "Shall we
have a glass of wine?"

"Willingly," said he, seating himself, and throwing his
gloves into his hat, with the air of a man quite disposed to
take his ease comfortably.

Our host produced a flask of his inimitable Steinberger,
and another of a native growth, to which he invited our
attention, and left us to ourselves once more. We filled,
touched our glasses, German fashion, drank, and resumed
our converse.

"If any man could have told me, twenty-four hours ago,
that I should be sitting where I now find myself, and with
you for my companion, I'd have told him to his face he
was a calumniator and a scoundrel! This time yesterday,
Dodd, I'd have put a bullet through you, myself."

"You don't say that, my Lord?"

"I do say, and repeat it, I believed you to be the greatest
villain the universe contained. I thought you a monster of
the foulest depravity."

"Well, I'm delighted to have undeceived you, my
Lord."

"You *have* undeceived me! — I own to it. I believe, if I
know anything, it is human nature. I have not been a deep
student in other things, but in the heart of man I have read
deeply. I know your whole history in this affair as well
as if I was present at the events. You never intended
seduction here."

"Nothing of the kind, my Lord, — never dreamed of it!"

"I know it; I know it. She got an influence over you, —
she fascinated you, — she held you captive, Dodd. She
mingled in your thoughts, — she became part of all your
most secret cogitations. With that warm, impulsive nature
of your country, you made no resistance, — you could make
none. You fell into the net at once, — don't deny it. I
like you the better for it, — upon my life I do. Don't sup-

pose that I'm Archbishop of Canterbury or Dean of Durham, man."

"I don't suspect, in the least," said I.

"I'm no humbug of that kind," said he, resolutely. "I'm a man of the world, that just takes life as he finds it, and neither fancies that human nature is one jot better or worse than it is. Hampton goes and marries a girl of sixteen; she is very beautiful and very rich. What of that? She leaves him — and what becomes of the wealth and beauty? She is ruined, — utterly ruined! He has his action at law, and gets swingeing damages, of course. What's the use of that? Will twenty thousand — will forty — would a hundred thousand pounds serve to compensate him for a lost position in life, and the affection of that charming creature? You know it would not, sir. Don't affect hesitation nor doubt about it. You know it would not."

"That wasn't what I was thinking of at all, my Lord. I was only speculating on the mighty small chance your friend would have of the money."

"Do you mean to say, sir, that the jury wouldn't give it?"

"The *jury* might, but Kenny Dodd wouldn't," said I.

"The Queen's Bench, sir, or the Court of Exchequer, would take care of that. They'd issue a 'Mandamus,' — the strongest weapon of our law; they'd sell to the last stick of your property; they'd take your wife's jewels, — the coat off your back — "

"As to the jewels of Mrs. D.," says I, "and my own wardrobe, I'm afraid they'd not go far towards the liquidation."

"They'd attach every acre of your estate."

"Much good it would do them," said I. "We're in the Encumbered Court already."

"Whatever your income may be derived from, they're sure to discover it."

"Faith!" said I, "I'd be grateful to them for the information, for it's two months now since I heard from Tom Purcell, and I don't know where I'm to get a shilling!"

"But what are damages, after all!" said he; "nothing, absolutely nothing!"

" Nothing indeed ! " said I.

" And look at the misery through which a man must wade ere he attain to them. A public trial, a rule to show cause, a motion, — three or four thousand gone for that. The case heard at Westminster Hall, — forty-seven witnesses brought over special from different parts of the Continent, at from two guineas to ten per diem, and travelling expenses, — what money could stand it; and see what it comes to : you ruin some poor devil without benefiting yourself. That 's the folly of it ! Believe me, Dodd, the only people that get any enjoyment out of these cases are the lawyers ! "

" I can believe it well, my Lord."

" I know it, — I know it, sir," said he, fiercely. " I have already told you that I 'm no humbug. I don't want to pretend to any nonsense about virtue, and all that. I was once in my life — I was young, it is true — in the same predicament you now stand in. It won't do to speak of the parties, but I suspect our cases were very similar. The friend who acted for the husband happened to be one who knew all my family and connections. He came frankly to me, and said, —

" ' Bruce, this affair will come to a trial, — the damages will be laid at ten thousand, — the costs will be about three more. Can you meet that?'

" ' No,' said I, ' I 'm a younger son, — I 've got my commission in the Guards, and eight thousand in the " Three-and-a-Half's " to live on, so that I can't.'

" ' What *can* you pay?' said he.

" ' I can stand two thousand,' said I, boldly.

" ' Say three,' said he, — ' say three.'

" And I said, ' Three be it,' and the affair was settled — an exposure escaped — a reputation rescued — and a clear saving of something like ten thousand pounds ; and this just because we chanced both of us to be ' men of the world.' For look at the thing calmly ; how should any of us have been bettered by a three days' publicity at Nisi Prius, — one's little tendernesses ridiculed by Thesiger, and their soft speeches slanged by Serjeant Wilkins. Turn it over in your mind how you may, and the same conclusion always meets you. The husband, it is true, gets less money ; but

then he has no obloquy. The wife escapes exposure; and
the 'other party' is only mulct to one-fourth of his liability, and at the same time is exempt from all the ruffian-
ism of the long robe! A vulgarly minded fellow might
have said, 'What's the woman's reputation to *me?* I'll
defend the action, — I'll prove this, that, and t'other. I'll
engage the first counsel at the bar, and fight the battle out.
I don't care a jot about being blackguarded before a jury,
lampooned in the papers, and caricatured in the windows,' he
might say; 'what signifies to *me* what character I hold before the world, — I have neither sons nor daughters to suffer
from my disgrace.' I know that all these and similar
reasons might prompt a man of a certain stamp to regret
this course, and say, 'Be it so. Let there be a trial!' But
neither *you* nor *I*, Dodd, could see the matter in this light.
There is this peculiarity about a man of the world, that not
alone he sees rightly, but he sees quickly; he judges passing
events with a kind of instinctive appreciation of what will
be the tone of society generally, and he says to himself,
'There are doubtless elements in this question that I would
wish otherwise. I would, perhaps, say *this* is not exactly to
my taste; I don't like *that;*' but whoever yet found that he
broke his leg exactly in the right place? What man ever
discovered that the toothache ever attacked the very tooth
he wanted! I take it, Dodd, that you are a man who has
seen a good deal of life; now did your heart ever bound
with delight on seeing the outside of a bill of costs? or on
hearing the well-known knock of a better known dun at
your hall door? True philosophy consists in diminishing,
so far as may be, the inevitable ills of life. Don't you
agree with me?"

"With the general proposition I do, my Lord; the question here is, how far the present case may be considered as
coming within your theory. Suppose now, just for argument's sake, I was to observe that there was no similarity
between our situations; that while *you* openly avow culpa-
bility, *I* as distinctly deny it."

"You prefer to die innocent, Dodd?" said he, puffing his
cigar coolly as he spoke.

"I prefer, my Lord, to maintain the vantage ground that

I feel under my feet. Had you been patient enough to hear
me out, I could have explained to your perfect satisfaction
how I came here, and why. I could have shown you a
reason for everything that may possibly seem strange or
mysterious — "

.'' As, for instance, the assumption of a name and title
that did not belong to you, — a fortnight's close seclusion to
avoid discovery, — the sudden departure for Ems, and headlong haste of your journey here, — and, finally, the attitude
of more than persuasive eloquence in which I myself saw
you. Of course, to a man of an ingenious and inventive
turn, all these things are capable of at least some approach
to explanation. Lawyers do the thing every day, — some,
with tears in their eyes, with very affecting appeals to
Heaven, according to the sums marked on the outside of the
briefs. If your case had been one of murder, I could have
got you a very clever fellow who would have invoked divine
vengeance on his own head in open court if he were not in
heart and soul assured of your spotless innocence ! But
now please to bear in mind that we are not in Westminster
Hall. We are here talking frankly and honestly, man to
man, — sophistry and special pleading avail nothing ; and
here I candidly tell you, that, turn the matter how you will,
the advice I have given is the only feasible and practicable
mode of escaping from this difficulty."

If you think me prolix, my dear Purcell, in narrating so
circumstantially every part of this curious interview, just
remember that I am naturally anxious to bring to bear upon
your mind the force of argument to which *mine* at last
yielded. It is very possible I may not be able to present
these reasonings with all the strength and vigor with which
they appealed to myself. I may — like a man who plays
chess with himself — favor one side a little more than the
other, or it is possible that I may seem weaker in my self-
defence than I ought to have been. However you interpret
my conduct on this trying occasion, give me the benefit of
never having for a moment forgotten the fame and fortune
of that lovely creature whose fate was in my hands, and
whom I have rescued at a heavy price.

I do not wish to impose upon you the wearisome task of

reading all that passed between my Lord and myself. The whole correspondence would fill a blue book, and be about as amusing as such folios usually are. I'll spare you, therefore, the steps of the negotiation, and merely give you the heads of the treaty: —

"Firstly, Mr. G. H., by reason and in virtue of certain compensations to be hereafter stated, binds himself to consider Mrs. G. H. in all respects as before her meeting K. I. D., regarding her with the same feelings of esteem, love, and affection as before that event, and treating her with the same 'distinguished consideration.'

"Secondly, K. I. D., on his part, agrees to give acceptances for two thousand pounds sterling, with interest at the rate of five per cent per annum on same till the time of payment. The dates to be at the convenience of K. I. D., always provided that the entire payment be completed within the term of five years from the present day.

"Thirdly, K. I. D. pledges his word of honor never to dispute or contest his liability to the above debt, by any unworthy subterfuge, such as 'no value,' 'intimidation used,' or any like artifice, legal or otherwise, but accepts these conditions in all the frankness of a gentleman."

Here follow the signatures and seals of the high contracting parties, with those of a host of witnesses on both sides. Brief as the articles read, they occupied several days in the discussion of them, during which Hampton retired to a village in the neighborhood, it not being deemed "etiquette" for us to inhabit the same town until the terms of a treaty had laid down our respective positions. These were my Lord's ideas, and you can infer from them the punctilious character of the whole negotiation. Lord Harvey dined and supped with me every day, breakfasting at Schweinstock with his principal. I thought, indeed, when all was finally settled between us, that G. H. and I might have met and dined together as friends; but my Lord negatived the notion strongly. "Come, come, Dodd, you must n't be too hard upon poor Gore; it is not generous." And although, Tom, I cannot see the force of the observation, I felt bound to yield to it, rather than appear in any invidious or unamiable

light. I, consequently, never met him during his stay in
the neighborhood.

Lord Harvey left this, about ten days ago, for Dresden.
We parted the very best of friends, for with all his zeal
for G. H., I must say that he behaved handsomely to me
throughout; and in the matter of the bills, he at once yielded
to my making the first for £500, at nine months, though he
assured me it would be a great convenience to his friend if I
could have said " six." I should have quitted this to join
the family on the same day; but when I came to pay the
hotel bill, I found that the dinners and champagne during
the week of diplomacy had not left me five dollars remaining,
so that I have been detained by sheer necessity; and partly
by my own will, and partly by my host's sense of caution,
my daily life has been gradually despoiled of its little enjoyments, till I find myself in the narrow circumstances of
which this letter makes mention at the opening.

From beginning to end, it would be difficult to imagine a
more unlucky incident; nor do I believe that any man ever
got less for two thousand pounds since the world began.
You cannot say a severe thing to me that I have not said to
myself; you cannot appeal to my age and my habits with a
more sneering insolence than I am daily in the habit of doing; your very bitterest vituperations would be mild in comparison to one of my own soliloquies, so that, as a matter of
surplusage, spare me all abuse, and rather devote your loose
ingenuities to assisting me out of my great embarrassments.

I know well, that if we don't discover a gold-mine at
Dodsborough, or fall upon a coal-shaft near Bruff, that I
have no possible prospect to pay these bills; but as the first
of them is nine months off, there is no such pressing emergency. The immediate necessity is, to send me enough to
leave this place, and join Mrs. D. and the family. Write to
me, therefore, at once, with a remittance, and mention where
they are, — if still at Bonn, where I left them.

You had also better write to Mrs. D. ; in what strain, and
to what purport, I must leave to your own ingenuity. As
for myself, I know no more how to meet her, nor what mood
to assume, than if I were about to enter the cage of one of
Van Amburgh's lions. Now I fancy that maybe a contrite,

broken-hearted look would be best; and now I rather lean
to the bold, courageous, overbearing tone! Heaven direct
me to what is best, for I never felt myself so much in want
of guidance!

When you write to me, be brief; don't worry me with
details of home, and inflict me with one of your national
epistles about famine, and fever, and faction fights. I have
no pity for anybody but myself just now, and I care no
more for what's doing in Tipperary than if it was Canton.
It will be time enough when I join the others to speculate
upon whither we shall turn our steps, but my present
thoughts tend to going back to Dodsborough. I wish from
my soul that we had never left it, nor embarked in this
infernal crusade after high society, education, and grandeur,
— the vain pursuit of which leaves me to write myself, as I
now do, your most miserable and melancholy friend,

KENNY DODD.

P. S.   I have a gold watch, made by Gaskin of Dublin
about fifty years back; but it's so big and unwieldy that
nobody would buy it, except for a town clock. The case of
it alone would n't make a bad-sized covered dish, and I'm
sure the works are as strong as a French steam-engine; but
what's the use of it all if I can't find a purchaser? I have
already parted with my tortoiseshell snuff-box, that my
grandmother swore belonged to Quintus Curtius; and the
only family relic remaining to me is a bamboo sword-cane,
the being possessed of which, if it became known, would
subject me to three months' imprisonment in a fortress, with
hard labor! If I were in Austria, the penalty is death; and
maybe that same would be a mercy in my misfortunes.

The only walk where I don't meet my duns is down by
a canal, — a lonely path, with dwarf willows along it. I
almost think I'd have jumped in yesterday, if it was n't
for the bull-frogs, — the noise they made drove me away
from the place. Depend upon it, Tom, the Humane Society
ought to get the breed for the Serpentine. It's only a most
"determined suicide" could venture into their company!
The chorus in "Robert le Diable" is a love ditty compared
to them!

LETTER XXVI.

BADEN-BADEN.

DEAR MR. PURCELL, — Your letter is now before me, and if I did n't know the mark of your hand before, I 'd scarce believe the sentiments was yours. It well becomes you, one that but *one* woman would ever accept of, to lecture the likes of me on the way I ought to treat my husband. A stingy old creature that sits croaking over an extra sod of turf on the fire, and counts out the potatoes to the kitchen, is not exactly the kind of authority to dictate laws to the respectable head of a family! I often suspected the nature of the advice you gave K. I., but I did n't think you 'd have the hardihood to come out with it *yourself*, and to *me!* How much you must have forgotten both of us, it 's mighty clear!

Where did you get all the elegant expressions about K. I.'s "unavoidably prolonged absence," "the sacrifices exacted from friendship," "the generous ardor of a chivalrous nature," and the other fine balderdash you bestow upon your friend's disgraceful behavior? Do you know what you are talking about? Have you a notion about the affair at all? Answer me that. Are you aware that he is now two months and four days away without as much as a letter, except a bit of an impertinent note, once, to ask are we alive or dead, not a sixpence in cash, not a check, nor even a bill that we might try to get protested, or whatever they call it? I don't make any illusions to why he went, and what he went for. I would n't disgrace my pen with the subject, nor myself by noticing it; but, except yourself, in the brown wig and the black satin small clothes, I don't

know one less suited to perform the "Lutherian." You are
a nice pair, and I expect nothing less than to hear of yourself next! And you have the impudence to tell me that
these are some of the "innocent freedoms of Continental
life"! What do *you* know about them, I'd beg to ask, —
you, that never was nearer the Continent than Malahide?
As to the innocent freedoms of the Continent, there's
nobody can teach me anything; I see them before me in the
day when I drive out, at the *table d'hôte* where I dine, and
at every ball where they dance. Sweet innocence it is, indeed! and particularly when practised by the father of a
grown-up family, — fifty-seven, he says, in June, but more
likely sixty odd, for I know many of his co-trumperies,
and nice young gentlemen they are too!

You assure me that you sympathize sincerely with K. I.
I 've no objection to that; he 'll need all the comfort it can
give him when he comes home again, or I 'm much mistaken.
With the help of the saints, I 'll teach him the differ between going off with a lady and living with his lawful wife.
If he did n't know the distinction before, he shall now!
And then you think to terrify me about the state of his
health. It won't do, Mr. Tom Purcell. He 'll live to disgrace us this many a year. I know well what his constitution can bear, and what he calls the gout is neither more nor
less than the outbreaks of his violent and furious temper!
Never flatter yourself, therefore, that you can make any of
us uneasy on that score; and if he comes back on a litter, it
won't save him.

Your "sincere regrets that we ever came abroad" are
very elegantly expressed, and require all my acknowledg-
ments. Is n't there anything else you are sorry for? Is n't
it grief to you that we never caught the smallpox, or that
James was n't transported for forgery? We ought to have
stayed at Bruff; and, judging from the charms of your
style, I have no doubt that we might have derived great
benefit from your vicinity.

You are eloquent, too, about expense; and add that you
always believed that there was no economy in living
abroad. Perhaps not, sir, if one unites foreign vices with
home ones; but I beg to say, when we left Dodsborough, I,

for one, never contemplated the cost of *two* establishments,
— take that, Mr. Tom Purcell!

I wonder at myself how I keep my temper, and conde-
scend to argue with you about points on which an old bachelor, or widower (for it's the same), must necessarily be
ignorant. Don't you perceive that for you to discourse
on family matters is like a deaf man describing music?

And you wind up about the privileges of old friendship,
and so on! It's a new notion of friendship that makes a
man impudent! Where did you ever hear that knowing
people a long time was a reason for insulting them? As to
your kind inquiries for the girls, I'd have liked them as well
if not coupled with those "natural fears" for the consequences of foreign contamination. Mary Anne and myself
got a hearty laugh out of your terrors; and so I forgive
your mention of them.

James is quite well; and would, he says, be better, if
that remittance you spoke of had arrived.

You tell me that the M'Carthy legacy is paid, and the
money lodged at Latouche's. But what's the use of that?
It's here I want it. Find out a safe hand, if you can, and
send it over to me; for I'm resolved to have nothing to do
with bills as long as I live.

And now I believe I have gone through the principal matters in your last, and I hope given you my ideas as clearly
as your own. It may save you some time and stationery if
I say that my mind is made up about K. I.; and if it was
Queen Victoria was interceding for him, I'd not alter my
sentiments. It's no use appealing "to the goodness of my
heart, and the feminine sweetness of my nature;" all that
you say on that head is only a warning to me not to let my
weaknesses get the upper hand of me: a lesson I will endeavor to profit by, so long as I write myself,

Your very obedient to command,

JEMIMA DODD.

LETTER XXVII.

DEAR MOLLY, — I send you herewith a letter for Tom Purcell, which you 'll take care to deliver with your own hands.
If you are by when he reads it, you 'll maybe perceive that
it 's not the "compliments of the season " I was sending him.
He says he likes plain speaking, and I trust he is satisfied
now.

You are already aware of the barbarous manner K. I. has
behaved. I 've told you how he deserted me and the family,
and the disgrace that he has brought down upon us in the
face of Europe; for I must observe to you, Molly, that
whatever is talked of here goes flying over the whole world,
and is the common talk of every Court on the Continent. I
could fill chapters if I was to describe his wickedness and
inhumanity. Well, my dear, what do you think! but in
the face of all this Mr. Tom Purcell takes the opportunity
to read me a long lecture on my "congenial" duties, and
to instruct me in what manner I am to treat K. I. on his
return.

Considering what he knows of my character, Molly, I
almost suspect that he might have spared himself this
trouble. Did he, or did any one else, ever see me posed by
a difficulty? When did any event take me unawares? Am
I by nature one of those terrified creatures that get flurried
by misfortune; or am I, by the blessing of Providence,
gifted in a remarkable manner with great powers of judgment, matured by a deep knowledge of life, and a thorough
acquaintance with the wickedness of the human heart?
That 's the whole question, — which am I? Is it after
twenty-six years' studying his disposition and pondering

over all his badness, that any one can come and teach me
how to manage him? I know K. I. as I know my old slipper; and, indeed, one is worth about as much as the other!
I have n't the patience — it would be too much to expect
from any one — to tell you how beautifully Mister Tom
discourses to me about the innocent freedoms of the Continent, and the harmless fragilities of female life abroad!
Does the old sinner believe in his heart that black is white
abroad? and would he have me think that what's murder in
Bruff was only a justifiable hom'-a-side at Brussels? If he
does n't mean that, what does he mean? Maybe, to be
sure, he 's one of the fashionable set that make out that the
husband is always driven to some kind of vice or other by
his wife's conduct! For, I must remark to you, Molly,
there 's a set of people now in the world — they call themselves "The Peace Congress," I think — that say there must
be no more wars, no fighting, domestically or nationally!

Their notion is this: everybody is right, and nobody need
quarrel with his neighbor, but settle any trifling disagree-
ment by means of arbitration. Mister Tom is, perhaps,
an arbitrator. Well, I hope he likes the office! Since I
knew anything of life myself, I always found that if there
was three people mixed up in a shindy there was no hope of
settling it, on any terms.

He says, K. I. is coming home. Let him come, says I.
Let him surrender himself, Molly, and justice will take its
course. That 's all the satisfaction I 'll give either of them.

"Don't be vindictive," says Mister Tom. Is n't that
pretty language to use to me, I ask? Is the Chief Justice
"vindictive," Molly, when he says, "Stand forward, and
hear your sentence"? Is he behaving "unlike a Christian"
when he says, "Use the little time that 's left you in making
your peace"?

The old creature then goes on to quote Scripture to me,
and talks about the prodigal son. "Very well," says I,
"be it so. K. I. may be that if he likes, but I 'll not be
the fatted calf, — that 's all!" The fact is, Molly, I 'm
immutable as the Maids and Prussians. They may talk till
they 're black in the face, but I 'll never forgive him!

Would n't it be a nice example, I ask, to the girls, if I was to overlook K. I.'s conduct, and call it a "venal" offence? And this, too, when the eyes of all Europe is staring at us. "How will Mrs. D. take it?" says the Prince of this. "What will Mrs. D. say to him?" says the Duke of that. "Does *she* know it yet?" asks the Archduke of Moravia. That's the way they go on from morning till night; so that, in fact, Molly, — as Lord George observes, — "he is less of a private culprit than a great public malefactor."

There's the way I am forced to look on the case; and think more of the good of society than of my family feelings.

Such are my sentiments, Molly, after giving to the case a most patient and careful consideration; and it's little good in Tom Purcell's trying to oppose and obstruct me.

If it were not for this unhappy event, I must own to you, Molly, that we never enjoyed ourselves anywhere more than we do here. It's a scene of pleasure and gayety all day, — and, indeed, all night long; and nothing but the anticipation of K. I.'s return could damp the ardor of our happiness. However it's managed, I can't tell; but the most elegant balls and entertainments are given here free and for nothing! Who keep up the rooms, pays for the lighting, the servants, and the refreshments, is more than I can say. All I know is, that your humble servant never contributed a sixpence to one of them. Lord George says that the Grand Duke is never happy except when the place is crammed; and that he'd spend his last shilling rather than not see people amuse themselves. And there's a Frenchman, too, — a Mr. Begasset, or Benasset, or something like that, — who is so wild about amusement that he goes to any expense about the place, and even keeps a pack of hounds for the public.

Contrast this, my dear Molly, with one of our little miserable subscription balls at home, where Dan Cassidy, the dancing-master, is driving about the country, for maybe three weeks, in his old gig, before he can scrape together a matter of six or seven pounds, to pay for mutton lights, two fiddles, and a dulcimer; and, after all, it's perhaps over the Bridewell we'd be dancing, and the shouts of the dirty creatures below would be coming up at every pause of the

music. Now, here, it's like a royal palace, — elegant lustres, with two hundred wax-lights in each of them, — a floor
like glass. Ask Mary Anne if it is n't as slippery! The
dress of the company actually magnificent! none of your
little shabby-colored muslins, or Limerick lace; none of
your gauze petticoats, worn over glazed calico, to look like
satin, but everything real, Molly, — the lace, the silk, the
satin, the jewels, the gold trimmings, the feathers, — all the
best of the kind, and fresh as they came out of the shop.
You don't see the white satin shoes with the mark of a
man's foot on them, nor the satin body with four fingers
and a thumb on the back of it, as you would at a Patrick's
Ball in Dublin! Everything is new for each night.

How Mary Anne laughs at the Irish notions of dress, of
what they call in the "Evening Post" "a beautiful lama
petticoat over a white satin slip!" or "a train of elegant
figured tabinet." Why, Molly darling, you might as well
wear a mackintosh, or go out in a suit of glazed alpaca
cloth. Mary Anne says that the ball at the Castle of Dublin
is like a tournament, where all the company dance in armor;
and, indeed, when I think of the rattling of bead bracelets,
false pearls, and Berlin necklaces, it rather reminds me of
a hornpipe in fetters!

I must confess to you, Molly, there's nothing as low anywhere as Dublin, and latterly, when anybody asks Mary
Anne or me if it's pleasant, we always say with a strong
English accent, "Our military friends say, vastly, but we
really don't know ourselves." Is n't that a pretty pass to be
reduced to? But I'm told that all the Irish, of any distinction, are obliged to do the same, and never confess to
have seen more of Ireland than one does from the Welsh
mountains. It's no want of patriotism makes me say this.
I wish, with all my heart, that Ireland was a perfect paradise; and it's no fault of mine that Providence intended
otherwise.

If I was n't writing with my head so full of Tom Purcell
and his late impudence, I'd have plenty to tell you about the
girls and James. Mary Anne is more admired than any
girl here, and so would Cary, if she'd only let herself be
so; but she has got a short, snubby, tart kind of way with

people, that never goes down abroad, where, as Lord G.
says, "every cat plays with his claws covered."

And as to Lord George himself, I wonder is it Mary Anne
or Cary that he's after. I watch him day by day, and can
make nothing of it; but sure and certain it is he means one
of the two, and that is the reason why he left this suddenly
the other morning for England, and saying, —

"There's no use letter-writing; I'll just dash over and
have a talk with my governor."

I wouldn't ask him about what, but I saw the way the
girls looked down when he spoke, and that was enough to
show me in what quarter the wind was blowing.

I wish from my heart and soul the proposal would come
before K. I. came back. I'd like to have to show the superior way I have always managed the family affairs; for I
needn't tell you, Molly, that *he* never had an eye to the
peerage for one of his daughters! but if he returns before
it's settled, he'll say that he had his share in it all! As to
James, he is everything that a fond and doting mother could
wish. Six feet two and a half, — he grew the half since he
came here, — with dark eyes, and a pair of whiskers and
moustaches that there's not the like here, dressed in the very
top of the fashion, with opal and diamond studs to his shirt
and waistcoat, and a black velvet paletot with turquoise
buttons for evening wear. The whole room turns to look at
him wherever he goes, for he walks along just for all the
world as if he owned the place. You may suppose, my
dear Molly, how little he resembles K. I.; and, indeed, I
have heard many make the same remark when we were at
Bonn.

I made Mary Anne write me down a list of the great
people here who have all called on us; but what's the use of
sending it, after all? You couldn't pronounce them if they
were before you! I send you, however, a bit I cut out of
"Galignani's Messenger," where you'll see that we are put
down amongst the distinguished visitors as "Madame
M'Carthy Dodd, family and suite!" James still thinks if
K. I. would call himself "The O'Dodd," it would serve us
greatly; and Mary Anne agrees with the opinion; and
perhaps now, when he comes back under a cloud, as one

may say, it may not be so difficult to make him give in. As
James remarks, "Print it on your card, call out and shoot
the first fellow that addresses you as Mr. — make it no
laughing matter for anybody, before your face at least, —
and the thing is done." Maybe we 'll live to see this yet,
Molly, but I fear it won't be till Providence sends for K. I.

I spoke rather sharply to Waters in my last; and I find
now that the legacy is paid into Latouche's. Will you
remind Purcell that to be of any use to me the money
ought to be here? As to the Loan Fund, I wonder how you
have the face to ask me for anything, knowing the way I 'm
in for ready cash, and that I 'd rather borrow than lend any
day. Tell Peter Belton, also, that I stop my subscription
after this year to the Dispensary; and I am quite sure the
old system of physic is nothing but legalized poisoning.
Looking to the facilities of the country, and the natural
habits of the people, I 'm convinced, Molly, that the water-
cure is what you want in Ireland; and I 've half a mind to
write a letter to one of the papers about it. Cheapness is
the first requisite in a poor country; and any one can vouch
for it, water is n't a dear commodity with you.

Father Maher's remarks upon poor Jones M'Carthy is, I
must say, very unfeeling; and I don't coincide with the
conclusions he draws from them; for if he was half as bad
as he says, masses will do him little good; and for a few
thousand years, more or less, I can't afford to pay fifty
pounds! Ask him, besides, is it reasonable that when the
price of everything is falling, with Free-trade, that the old
tariff of Purgatory is to be kept up still? That would be
downright absurd! Priests, my dear Molly, must lower
their rates, as the Protectionists do their rents: that 's "one
of the demands of the age, and can't be resisted." As
Lord George says, "The Church, like the railroad people,
fell into the mistake of lavish expenditure! Purgatory was
like a station, and ought never to be made too costly. No
one wants to live there: the most one requires is to be
decently comfortable, till you can ' go on.' What 's the use
of fine furniture, elegant chairs and carpets? they 're clean
thrown away in such a place." If Father Maher thinks that
the remarks are not uttered in a respectful spirit, tell him

he's wrong; for Lord G. and all his family are great Whigs, and intend to do more mischief to the Established Church than any party that ever was in power; and I must say, I never heard Father Maher abuse Protestants, bigotry, and intolerance more bitterly than Lord G. It is so seldom that one ever hears really liberal sentiments, or anything like justice to Ireland, I could listen to him for hours when he begins. If I'm right in my conjecture about the object of his journey to London, it will be the making of James; since, once that we are connected with the aristocracy, Molly, there's nothing we cannot have; for, you see, the way is this: if you belong to the middle classes, they expect that you ought to have some kind of fitness for the occupation you look for; and they say, "This would n't suit you at all;" "That's not your line, in the least;" but when you are one of the "higher orders," there's, so to say, a general adaptiveness about you, and you can do anything they put before you, from ranging Windsor Forest to keeping a lighthouse! When one reflects upon that, it's no wonder that one of our great poets says, "Oh, bless," or "preserve" — I forget which — "our old nobility!"

Go into any of the great public offices — the Foreign or the Colonial, for instance — and they tell me that such a set of incapable-looking creatures never was seen, with spy-glasses stuck in their eyes, airing themselves before a big fire, and reading the "Times;" and yet, Molly, — confess it we must, — the work is done somehow and by somebody. It reminds me of a paper-mill I once saw; and no matter how dirty and squalid the rags that went in, they came out "Beautiful fine wove," or "Bath extra."

As to the questions in your last, I can't answer a tithe of them. You go on, letter after letter, with the same tiresome demand, — "Are we as much in love with the Continent as we were? Is it so cheap? Is the climate as fine as they say? Is there never any rain or wind at all? Is everybody polite and agreeable? Is there no such thing as backbiting or slandering? Are all the men handsome and brave, and all the women beautiful and virtuous?" This is but a specimen taken at random out of your late inquiries; and I'd like to know that if even

you gave me "notice of a question," as they do in the
House, how could I satisfy you on these points? The
most I can do is to say that there may be some slight
exaggeration in one or two of these, — the rain, for instance,
and the virtue, — but that, generally speaking, the rest is
all true. I can be more explicit in regard to what you ask
in your last postscript, — "After living so long abroad, can
we ever come back to reside in Ireland?" Never, Molly,
never! I make neither reserve nor qualification in my answer. *That* would be clearly impossible! for it's not only
that Ireland would be insupportable to us, but, as Mary
Anne remarks, "we would be insupportable to the Irish."
Our walk, our dress, our looks, our accent, our manner with
men, and our way with women; the homage we're used to;
the respect we feel our due; the topics we discuss with
freedom, and the range of our views generally over life, —
would shock the whole population from Cape Clear to the
Causeway.

It's not easy for me to explain it to you, Molly; but,
somehow, everything abroad is different from at home.
Not only the things you talk of, but the way you talk of
them, is quite distinct; and the whole world of men, morals,
and manners have quite another standard! It is the same
with one's thoughts as with their diet; half the things we
like best are only what is called acquired tastes. Trouble
enough we often have to learn them; but when once we do so,
who'd be fool enough to go back upon his old ignorance
again? High society and genteel manners, Molly, however
you may like them when you are used to them, are just like
London porter, — mighty bitter when you first taste it. I
know there are plenty of people will tell you the contrary,
and that they took to it naturally like mother's milk; but
don't believe them, it's quite impossible it could be true.

Once for all, I beg to tell you that there's no earthly
use in tormenting and teasing us about the state the house
is in at Dodsborough; how the roof is broken here, and
the walls given way there. I trust sincerely that it may
soon become perfectly uninhabitable, for I never wish to
see it again! I often think it wouldn't be a bad plan for
K. I. to go back and reside there. I'm sure if he collected

his rents himself, instead of leaving all to Tom Purcell, it would be " telling him something." You say that the country is getting disturbed again, and that they 're likely to have a " sharp winter for the landlords ; " but if it was the will of Providence anything should happen, I hope I have Christian feelings to support me! Indeed, I 'm well used to trials now! It 's a mistake, besides, Molly, to suppose that these — I hate to call them " outrages," as the newspapers do — these little outbreaks of the boys have any deep root in the country. The Orangemen, I know, would make them out as a regular system, and say that it's an organized society for murder; but it 's no such thing. Father Maher himself told me that he spoke against it from the altar, and said : " What a pass the country has come to," says he, " that the poor laboring hard-working man has no justice to right him, except his own stout heart and strong arm ! " What could he *say more than that, Molly? But even these beautiful expressions did n't save him from the " Evening Mail " !

The English are always boasting about their bravery and their courage, and so on; and when any one says, " Why don't you buy property in Ireland? " the answer is, " We 're afraid." I have heard it myself, Molly, with my own ears. But their ignorance is even worse than their cowardness, for if they only knew the people, they 'd see there was nothing to be frightened at. Sure, I remember myself, when we lived at Cloughmanus, Sam Gill came up to the house one morning, to say that there was two men come from below Lahinch to shoot K. I.

" They have the passwords," says he, " and all the tokens, and though I 'm your honor's man, I was obliged to take them into my house and feed them."

" It 's a bad business, Sam," says he. " What are they to get for it ? "

" Five pound between them, sir, — if it 's done complete."

" Would they take three," says K. I., " and let me live ? "

" I don't know, sir ; but, if you like, I 'll ask them."

" I would like it, indeed," says K. I.

And down went Sam to the gate-house, and spoke to them. They were both decent, reasonable men, and agreed at once to the offer. The money was paid, and the two came up and ate a hearty breakfast at the house, and K. I. walked more than a mile of the road with them afterwards, — talking about the crops and the state of the country down westward,— and shook hands with them cordially at parting.

Now, Molly, this is as true as the Bible, and yet there's people and there's newspapers call the Irish "irreclaimable savages." It is as big a lie as ever was written! The real truth is, they don't know how, if they really wished, to reclaim them! And after all, how little reclaiming they need! To hear English people discuss Ireland, you'd suppose that it was the worst part of Arabia Felix they were describing. But I haven't patience to go on; I fly out the moment I hear them, and faith they're not proud of themselves when I'm done."

"I wish you were in the House, Mrs. Dodd," says one of them to me the other night.

"I wish I was," says I; "if I wouldn't make it too hot for Slowbuck, my name isn't Jemima! for he's the one that abuses us most of all!" Well, I must say, we are well repaid for all the cruel treatment we receive at home, by the kindness and "consideration," as they call it, we meet with abroad! The minute a foreigner hears we're Irish, he says, "Oh dear, how sorry we are for your sufferings; we never cease deploring your hard lot;" and to be sure, Molly, "wicked Old England," and the "Harlequin Flag," as Dan called it, come in for their share of abuse. Besides these advantages, I must remark that Catholics is greatly thought of on the Continent; for it isn't as in Ireland, where's it's only the common people to mass. Here you may see royalty at their devotions. They sit in little galleries with glass windows, which they open every now and then, to take part in the prayers; and indeed, whatever rank and fashion is in the place, you're sure to see it "at church;" mind, Molly, at church, for no educated Catholic even says "at mass."

You want to hear "all about the converts to our holy faith," you say, but this isn't the place to get you the best information; but as I hope we'll pass the winter in Italy, I'll maybe be able to give you some account of them.

Lord George tells me that the Pope makes Rome delightful
to strangers; but whether it's "dinners" or "receptions,"
I don't know. At any rate, I conclude he does n't give
" balls."

What a fuss they're making all over the world about
these " rapparees," or refugees, or whatever they call them.
My notion is, Molly, that we who harbor them have the
worst of the bargain; and as to our fighting for them, it
would be almost as sensible as to take up arms in defence
of a flea that got into your bed! Considering how plenty
blackguards are at home, I think it's nothing but greedi-
ness in us to want to take Russian and Austrian ones! We
have our own villains; and any one of moderate desires
might be satisfied with them! These are Lord G.'s sentiments, but I'm sure you like to hear the opinions of the
aristocracy on all matters.

What you say about Bony's marriage was the very
thought that occurred to myself, and it was just the turn
of a pin whether Mary Anne was n't at this moment Empress
of France! Well, who knows what's coming, Molly!
There's many a one, now in a private station, and mighty
hard up for means, that will maybe turn out a King or a
Grand-Duke before long. At any rate, no elevation to
rank or dignity will ever make me forget my old friends,
and yourself, the first of them. And with this, I subscribe
myself,

Yours ever affectionately,

JEMIMA DODD M'CARTHY.

P. S. I 'll make one of the girls write to you next week,
for I know I 'll be so much overcome by my feelings when
K. I. arrives, that I 'll be quite incapable to take up my pen.

I sometimes think that I 'll take to my bed, and be "given
over," against the day of his coming; for you see there's
nothing gives such solemnity and weight to one's reproaches
as their being last words. You can say such bitter things,
Molly, when you are supposed to be too weak to bear a reply.
But I 've done this once or twice before, and K. I. is a hardened creature.

Lord G. says: " Treat him as if it were nothing at all, —

as if you saw him yesterday: don't give him the importance of having irritated you. Be a regular woman of fashion." If my temper would permit, perhaps this would be best of all; but have I a right to acquit a " great public male-factor"? That's a " case of conscience," Molly, that per-haps only the Church could resolve. The saints direct me!

LETTER XXVIII.

JAMES DODD TO ROBERT DOOLAN, ESQUIRE, TRINITY COLLEGE,
DUBLIN.

My DEAR BOB, — It is quite true, I am a shameful correspondent, and your last three letters now before me, unanswered, comprise a tremendous indictment against me;
but reflect for a moment, and you will see that in all
complaints of this kind there is a certain amount of injustice, since it is hardly possible ever to find two people
whose tastes, habits, and present circumstances place them
on such terms of perfect equality that the interchange of
letters is as easy for one as the other. Think over this
for a moment, and you will perceive that sitting down at
your quiet desk, in "No. 2, Old Square," is a different
process from snatching a hurried moment amidst the din,
the crash, and the conflict of life at Baden; and if *your*
thoughts flow on calmly, tinctured with the solemn influences around you, *mine* as necessarily reflect an existence
checkered by every rainbow hue of good or evil fortune.

Be therefore tolerant of my silence and indulgent to my
stupidity, since to transmit one's thoughts requires previously that you should think; and who can, or ever could,
in a place like this? Imagine a winding valley, with
wooded hills rising in some places to the height of mountains, in the midst of which stands a little village — for it
is no more — nearly every house of which is a palace, some
splendid hotel of France, Russia, or England. You pass
from these by a shady alley to a little rustic bridge, over
what might be, and very possibly is, an excellent trout-
stream, and come at once in front of a magnificent structure, frescoed without and gilded and stuccoed within.
"The Rooms," the Temple of Fortune, the ordeal of des-

tiny, Bob, is held here; and the rake of the croupier is the distaff of the Fate. Hither come flocking the representatives of every nation of the world, and of almost every class in each. Royalty, princely houses, and nobility with twenty quarterings, are jostled in the indiscriminate crowd with houseless adventurers, beggared spendthrifts, and ruined debauchees. All who can contribute the clink of their Louis d'or to the music are welcome to this orchestra! And women, too, fair, delicate, and lovely, the tenderest flowers that ever were nursed within domestic care, mixed up with others, not less handsome perhaps, but whose siren beauty is almost diabolic by comparison. What a babel of tongues, and what confusion of characters! The grandee of Spain, the escaped galley-slave, the Hungarian magnate, the London " swell," the old and hoary gambler with snow-white moustaches, and the unfledged minor, anticipating manhood by ruining himself in his " teens." All these are blended and commingled by the influence of play; and, differing as they do in birth, in blood, in lineage, and condition, yet are they members of one guild, associates of one society, — the gambling-table. And what a leveller is play! He who whispers in the ear of the Crown Prince yonder is a branded felon from the Bagnes de Brest; the dark-whiskered man yonder, who leans over the lady's chair, is an escaped forger; the Carlist noble is asking friendly counsel of a Christino spy; the London pickpocket offers his jewelled snuff-box to an Archduke of Austria. "How goes the game to-day?" cries a Neapolitan prince of the blood, and the question is addressed to a red-bearded Corsican, whose livelihood is a stiletto. "Is that the beautiful Countess of Hapsburg?" asks a fresh-looking Oxford man; and his friend laughingly answers: "Not exactly; it is Mademoiselle Varenne, of the Odéon." The fine-looking man yonder is a Mexican general, who carried off the military chest from Guanaguato; the pompous little fellow beside him is a Lucchese count, who stole part of the Crown jewels of his sovereign; the long-haired, broad-foreheaded man, with open shirt-collar, so violently denouncing the wrongs of injured Italy, is a Russian spy; and the dark Arab be-

hind him is a Swiss valet, more than suspected of having
murdered his master in the Mediterranean. Our English
contingent embraces lords of the bedchamber, members of
Parliament, railroad magnates, money-lending attorneys,
legs, swells, and swindlers, and a small sprinkling of University men, out to read and be ruined, — the fair sex,
comprising women of a certain fast set in London, divorced
countesses, a long category of the widow class, some with
daughters, some without. There is an abundance of good
looks, splendid dress, and money without limit! The most
striking feature of all, however, is the reckless helter-
skelter pace at which every one is going, whether his pursuit be play, love, or mere extravagance. There is no such
thing as calculation, — no counting the cost of anything.
Life takes its tone from the tables, and where, as wealth
and beggary succeed each other, so does every possible
extreme of joy and misery, people wager their passions and
their emotions exactly as they do their bank-notes and their
gold pieces. Chance, my dear Bob, — chance is ten times
a more intoxicating liquor than champagne, and once take
to "dramming" with fortune, and you may bid a long
adieu to sobriety! I do not speak here of the terrible in-
fatuation of play, and the almost utter impossibility of
resisting it, but I allude to what is infinitely worse, the
certainty of your applying play theories and play tactics
to every event and circumstance of real life.

The whole world becomes to you but one great green
cloth, and everything in it a question of luck! Will the
bad run continue here? Will good fortune stand much
longer to you? These are the questions ever rising to your
mind. You grow to regard yourself as utterly powerless
and impassive; a football at the toe of Destiny! I think
I see your eyebrows upraised in astonishment at these profound reflections of mine. You never suspected me of mor-
alizing, nor, shall I own it, was I aware myself that I had
any genius that way. Shall I tell you the secret, Bob, —
shall I unlock the mysterious drawer of hidden motives for
you? It is this, then: I have been a tremendously heavy
loser at Rouge-et-Noir! As long as luck lasted, which
it did for three weeks or more, I enjoyed this place with

a zest I cannot describe to you. The moralists tell us that prosperity hardens the heart; I cannot believe it. I know at least, that in my brief experience I never felt such a universal tenderness for everything and everybody. I seemed to live in an atmosphere of beauty, luxury, and splendor; every one was courteous; all were amiable! It was not alone that fortune favored me, but I appeared to have the good wishes of all beholders; words of encouragement murmured around me as I won; soft bewitching glances beamed over at me, as I raked up my gold. The very banker seemed to shovel out the shining pieces to me with a sense of satisfaction! Old veterans of the tables peeped over me to watch my game, and exclamations of wonder and admiration broke forth at each new moment of my triumphs! I don't care what it may be that constitutes the subject of display: a great speech in the House, a splendid picture at the Gallery, a novel, a song, a spirited lecture, a wonderful feat of strength or horsemanship; but there is an inward sense of intoxication in being the " cynosure of all eyes " — the " one in a thousand " — that comes very nigh to madness! Many a time have I screwed up my hunter to a fence — a regular yawner — that I knew in my heart was touch-and-go with both of us, simply because some one in the crowd said, " Look how young Dodd will do it." I made some smashing ventures at the " tables," under pretty similar promptings, and, I must say, with splendid success.

" Are you always so fortunate? " asked a royal personage, with a courteous smile towards me.

" And in everything? " sighs a gentle voice, with a look of such bewitching softness that I forgot to take up my stake, and see it remain on the board to double itself the next deal.

Besides all this, there is a grand magnificence in all your notions under the access of sudden wealth. You give orders to your tradespeople with a Jove-like omnipotence. You revel in the unbounded realms of " I will." What signifies the cost of anything, — the most gorgeous entertainment? It is only adding twenty Naps. to your next bet! That rich bracelet of rubies — pshaw! — it is to be

had for the turn of a card! In a word, Bob, I felt that I
had fallen upon the "Bendigo Diggins," without even the
trouble of the search! I wanted fifty Naps. for a caprice,
and strolled in to win them, as coolly as though I were
changing a check at my banker's!

"Come, Jim, be a good fellow, and back me this time;
I'm certain to win if you do," whispers a young lord, with
fifteen thousand a year.

"Which side is Dodd on?" asked an old peer, with his
purse in his hand.

"How I should like to win eighty Louis, and buy that
roan Arab," whispers Lady Mary to her sister.

"I'd rather spend the money on that opal brooch," murmurs the other.

"Egad! if I win this time, I'll start for my regiment
to-night,' mutters a pale-looking sub., with a red spot in
one cheek, and eyes lustrous as if on fire.

Fancy the power of him who can accomplish these, and
a hundred like longings, without a particle of sacrifice on
his own part! Imagine, my dear Bob, the conscious rule
and sway thus suggested, and ask yourself what ecstasy
ever equalled it! I possessed all that Peter Schlemihl did,
and had n't to give even my "shadow" in return. During
these three glorious weeks, I gave dinners, concerts, and
suppers, commanded plays, bespoke operas, patronized humbugs of all kinds, and headed charities without number.
As to presents of jewelry, I almost fancied myself a kind
of distributing agent for Storr and Mortimer.

The hotel stables were filled with animals of all kinds
belonging to me, — dogs, donkeys, horses, Spanish mules,
and a bear; while every shape and description of equipage
crammed the coach-houses and the courtyard. One of
these, with a single wheel in front, and great facilities for
upsetting behind, was invented by a Baden artist, and most
flatteringly and felicitously called "Le Dod." Was n't that
fame for you, my boy? Think of going down to posterity
on noiseless wheels and patent axles! Fancy being trans-
mitted to remote ages on C springs and elastic cushions!
Such was the rage for my patronage that an ingenious
cutler had dubbed a newly invented forceps by my name,

and I was introduced into the world of surgery as a
torture.

Now for the obverse of the medal. It was on that unluckiest of all days — a Friday — that fortune changed with
me. I had lain all the morning abed, after being up the
whole night previous, and only went down to "the Rooms"
in the evening. As usual, I was accompanied by my train
of followers, lords, baronets, M. P.s, foreign counts and
chevaliers, — for I went to the field like a general, with his
full staff around him! You'll scarcely believe me when I
tell you, Bob, but I say it in all truth and seriousness, that
so long as my star was in the ascendant, so long as my
counsels were what Homer would call "wealth-bestowing
words," there was not an opinion of mine upon any subject,
no matter how great my ignorance of it might have been,
that was not listened to with deference and repeated with
approval. "Dodd said so yesterday," "I hear Dodd thinks
highly of it," "Dodd's opinion is unfavorable," and so
on, were phrases that rang around me from every group
I passed, and from the "odds on the Derby" to the "division on the Budget," there was a profound impression that
my sentiments were worth hearing.

The pleasantest talkers in Europe, the wittiest conversers
that ever convulsed a dinner-party with laughter, would have
been deserted and forsaken to hear *me* hold forth, whether
the theme was art, literature, law and politics, or the drama,
or any other you please to mention, and of which my ignorance was profound. My luck was unfailing. "Dodd never
loses," "Dodd has only to back it," — these were the gifts
which all could acknowledge and profit by, and these no man
undervalued or denied.

"Benasset" — this was the proprietor of the tables —
"has been employing his time profitably, Dodd, during your
absence. He has made a great morning of it, — cleared out
the old Elector, and sent the Margraf of Ragatz penniless to
his dominions." This was the speech that met me as I
entered the door, and a general all hail followed it.

"Now you'll see some smart play," whispered one to his
newly come friend. "Here's young Dodd; we shall have
some fun presently." Amid these and similar murmurings

I approached the tables, at which a place for me was speedily made, for my coming was regarded by the company as a good augury.

I could dwell long upon the sensations that then thronged my brain; they were certainly upon the whole highly pleasurable, but not unmixed with some sadness; for I already was beginning to feel a kind of contempt for my worshippers, and for myself too, as the unworthy object of their devotion. This scorn had not much leisure granted for its indulgence, for the cards were now presented to me for "the cut," and the game began.

As usual, my luck was unbroken. If I had doubled my stake, or by caprice withdrew it altogether, it was the same. Fortune seemed to wait upon my orders. Revelling in a kind of absolutism over fate, I played a thousand pranks with luck, and won, — won on, as if to lose was an impossibility. What strange fancies crossed my mind as I sat there, — vague fears, shadowy terrors of the oddest kind, wild, dreamy, and undefined! Visions of joy and misery; orgies, mad and furious with mirth, and agonizing sights of misery, thoughts of men who had made compacts with the Fiend, and the terrors that beset them in the midst of their voluptuous abandonment; Belshazzar at his feast; Faust on the Brocken, — rose to my mind, and I almost started up and fled from the table at one moment, so impressed was I by these images! Would that I had! Would that I had listened to that warning whisper of my good genius that was then admonishing me!

My revery had become such at last that I really never saw nor heard what went on about me. You can picture my condition to yourself when I say that I was only recalled to self-possession by loud and incessant laughter, that rang out on every side of me. "What's the matter, — what has happened?" cried I, in amazement. "Don't you perceive, sir," said a bystander, "that you have broken the bank, and they are waiting for a remittance to continue the play?"

So it was, Bob; I had actually won their last Napoleon, and there I sat pushing my stake mechanically into the middle of the table, and raking it up again, playing an im-

aginary game, to the amusement of that motley crowd, who
looked on at me with screams of laughter. I laughed, too,
when I came to myself. It was such a relief to me to join,
even for a moment, in any feeling that others experienced!

The money came at last. Two strongly clasped, heavily
ironed coffers were borne into the room by four powerful
men. I watched them with interest as they unlocked and
poured forth their shining stores; for in imagination they
were already my own. I believe at that moment, if any one
had offered to assure me the winning of them "for fifty
Naps.," that I should have rejected the proposal with disdain,
so impossible did it seem to me that luck could desert me!
Do you know, Bob, that what most interested me at the
time was the varied expressions displayed by the company
at sight of the gorgeous treasure before them? It was
strange to mark how little all their good breeding and fine
manners availed to repress vulgarity of thought and feeling,
for there was greed or envy or hatred, or some inordinate
passion or other, on every face around; looks of mild and
gentle meaning became dashed with a half ferocity; venerable old age grew fretful and impatient; youth lost its frank
and careless bearing; and, in fact, gain, and the lust of
gain, was the predominant and overbearing thought of every
mind, and wish of every heart! I pledge you my word,
there was more animal savagery in the expressions on all
sides than ever I saw on a pack of yelping fox-hounds when
the huntsman held up the fox in the midst of them. It was
the comparison that came to my mind at the moment, and
I repeat it, with the reservation that the dogs behaved
best.

There was an old careworn, meanly dressed man, with a
faded blue ribbon in his button-hole, seated in the place I
usually occupied, and he arose to give it to me with that
mingled air of reluctance and respect which it is so hard to
resist. His manner seemed to say, "I am too poor and too
humble to contest the matter, but I'd remain here if I could."

"So you shall, then," said I to myself, and pushed him
gently down upon the seat again.

"By Jove! the old fellow has got the lucky place," cried
one in the crowd behind me.

"Hang *me*, if Dodd has n't given up his old chair!" said another.

"I 'd rather have had *that* seat," exclaimed a third, "than one at the India Board."

But I only laughed at these absurd superstitions, — as though it were the spot, and not myself, that Fortune loved to caress! As if to resent the foolish credulity, I threw a heavy bet on the table, and lost it! Again and again I did the same, with the like result; and now a murmur ran through the room that luck had turned with me. I had given up my winning seat, and was losing at every turn of the cards.

"Let *me* have a peep at him," I heard one whisper to his friend behind. "I 'd like to see how he bears it!"

"He loses remarkably well," muttered the other.

"Admirably!" said another. "He seems neither confident nor impatient; I like the way he stands it."

"Egad, his hand trembles, though! He tore that bank-note in trying to get it out of his fingers!"

"His hand is hot, too, — see how the Louis stick to it!"

"They 'll not do so very long, depend on 't," said a close-shaved, well-whiskered fellow, with a knowing eye; and the remark met an approving smile from the bystanders.

"I have just added up his last fifteen bets," said a young man to a lady on his arm, "and what do you think he has lost? Forty-eight thousand francs, — close on two thousand pounds!"

"Quite enough for one evening!" said I, with a smile towards him, which made both himself and his friend blush deeply at being overheard; and with this I shut up my pocket-book, and strolled away from the tables into another room, where there were chess and whist players. I took a chair, and affected to watch the game with interest, my heart at the moment throbbing as though it would burst through my chest. Don't mistake, Bob, and fancy it was the accursed thirst for gold that enthralled me. I swear to you that mere gain, mere wealth, never entered into my thought at that moment. It was the gambler's lust — to be the victor, not to be beaten — that was the terrible passion that now struggled and stormed within me! I 'd like to

have staked a limb — honor — happiness — life itself —
on the issue of a chance; for I felt as though it were a duel
with destiny, and I could not quit the ground till one of us
should succumb!

How poor and unsatisfying seemed the slow combinations
of skill, as I watched the chess-players! What miserable
minuteness, what petty plottings for small results! —
nothing grand, great, or decisive! It was like being bled
to death from some wretched trickling vessel, instead of
meeting one's fate gloriously, amidst the roar of artillery
and the crash of squadrons!

I lounged into the *salons* where they dance; it was a very
brilliant and a very beautiful assembly. There were faces
and figures there that might have proved attractive to eyes
more critical than my own. My sudden appearance amongst
them, too, was rapturously welcomed. I was already a
celebrity; and I felt that amidst the soft glances and beam-
ing smiles around me, I had but to choose out her whom I
would distinguish by my attentions. My mother and the
girls came to me with pressing entreaties to take out the
beautiful Countess de B., or to be presented to the charming
Marchioness of N. There was a dowager archduchess who
vouchsafed to know me. Miss Somebody, with I forget
how many millions in the funds, told Mary Anne she might
introduce me. Already the master of the ceremonies came
to know if I preferred a mazurka or a waltz. The world
was, so to say, at my feet; and, as is usual at such
moments, I kicked it for being there. In plain English,
Bob, I saw nothing in all that bright and brilliant crowd
but scheming mammas and designing daughters; a universal
distrust, an utter disbelief in everything and everybody, had
got hold of me. Whatever I could n't explain, I discredited.
The ringlets might be false; the carnation might be rouge;
the gentle timidity of manner might be the cat-like slyness
of the tiger; the artless gayety of heart, the practised co-
quetry of a flirt, — ay, the very symmetry that seemed perfection, might it not be the staymaker's! Play had utterly
corrupted me, and there was not one healthy feeling, one
manly thought, or one generous impulse left within me! I
left the room a few minutes after I entered it. I neither

danced nor got presented to any one; but after one lounging stroll through the *salons,* I quitted the place, as though there was not one to know, not one to speak to! I have more than once witnessed the performance of this polite process by another. I have watched a fellow making the tour of a company, with a glass stuck in his eye, and his hand thrust in his pocket. I have tracked him as he passed on from group to group, examining the guests with the same coolness he bestowed on the china, and smiling his little sardonic ap-

preciation of whatever struck him as droll or ridiculous; and when he has retired, it has been all I could do not to follow him out, and kick him down the stairs at his departure. I have no doubt that my conduct on this occasion must have inspired similar sentiments; nor have I any hesitation in avowing that they were well merited.

When I reached the open air I felt a delicious sense of relief. It was so still, so calm, so tranquil! a bright starlit summer's night, with here and there a murmuring of low voices, a gentle laugh, heard amongst the trees, and the rustling sounds of silk drapery brushing through the alleys, — all those little suggestive tokens that bring up one's reminiscences of

"Those odorous hours
　　In jasmine bowers,
　　Or under the linden-tree!"

But they only came for a second, Bob, and they left not a trace behind them. The monotonous rubric of the croupier rang ever through my brain, — "Faîtes votre jeu, Messieurs!" — "Messieurs, faîtes votre jeu!" The table, the lights, the glittering gold, the clank of the rake, were all before me, and I set off at full speed to the hotel, to fetch more money, and resume my play.

I 'll not weary you with a detail, at every step of which I know that your condemnation tracks me. I re-entered the play-room, secretly and cautiously; I approached the table stealthily; I hoped to escape all observation, — at least, for a time; and with this object I betted small sums, and attracted no notice. My luck varied, — now inclining on this side, now to that. Fortune seemed as though in a half-capricious mood, and as it were undetermined how to treat me. "This comes of my own miserable timidity," thought I; "when I was bold and courageous, she favored me. It is the same in everything. To win, one must venture."

There was a vacant place in front of me; a young Hungarian had just quitted it, having lost his last "Louis." I immediately took it. The card on which he had been marking the chances of the game still lay there. I took it up, and saw that he had been playing most rashly; that no luck could possibly have carried a man safely through such a system as he had followed.

I must let you into a little secret of this game, Bob, and do not be incredulous of my theory, because my own case is a sorry illustration of it. Where all men fail at Rouge-et-Noir, is from temper. The loser makes tremendous efforts to repair his losses; the winner grows cautious with success, and diminishes his stake. Now the wise course is, play low when you see Fate against you, and back your luck to the very limit of the bank. You ask, perhaps, "How are you to ascertain either of these facts? What evidence have you that Fortune is with or against you?" As you are not a gambler, I cannot explain this to you. It is part of

the masonry of the play-table, and every one who risks
heavily on a chance knows well what are the instincts that
guide him.

I own to you, that though well aware of these facts, and
thoroughly convinced that they form the only rules of play,
I soon forgot them in the excitement of the game, and
betted on, as caprice, or rather as passion, dictated. We
Irish are bad stuff for gamblers. We have the bull-dog
resistance of the Englishman, — his stern resolve not to be
beaten, — but we have none of his caution or reserve. We
are as impassioned as the men of the South, but we are destitute of that intense selfishness that never suffers an Italian
to peril his all. In fact, as an old Belgian said to me one
night, we make bad winners and worse losers, — too lavish
in one case, too reckless in the other.

I am not seeking excuses for my failure in my nationality.
I accept the whole blame on my own shoulders. With
common prudence I might have arisen that night a large
winner; as it was, I left the table with a loss of nigh three
thousand pounds. Just fancy it, Bob, — five thousand
pounds poorer than when I strolled out after luncheon. A
sum sufficient to have started me splendidly in some career,
— the army, for instance, — gone without enjoyment, even
without credit; for already the critics were busily employed
in analyzing my "play," which they unanimously pronounced
"badly reasoned and contemptible." There remained to me
still — at home in the hotel, fortunately — about eight hundred pounds of my former winnings, and I passed the
night canvassing with myself what I should do with these.
Three or four weeks back I had never given a second thought
to the matter, — indeed, it would never have entered my head
to risk such a sum at play; but now the habit of winning
and losing heavy wages, the alternations of affluence and
want, had totally mastered all the calmer properties of reason, and I could entertain the notion without an effort. I'll
not tire you with my reasonings on this subject. Probably
you would scarcely dignify them with the name. They all
resolved themselves into this: "If I did not play, I'd never
win back what I lost; if I did, I *might*." My mind once
made up to this, I began to plot how I should proceed to

execute it. I resolved to enter the room next day just as the table opened, at twelve o'clock. The players who frequented the room at that hour were a few straggling, poor-looking people, who usually combined together to make up the solitary crown-piece they wished to venture. Of course I had no acquaintances amongst them, and therefore should be free from all the embarrassing restraints of observation by my intimates. My judgment would be calmer, my head cooler, and, in fact, I could devote myself to the game with all my energies uncramped and unimpeded.

Sharp to the moment of the clock striking twelve, I entered the room. One of the croupiers was talking to a peasant-girl at the window. The other, seated on a table, was reading the newspaper. They both looked astonished at seeing me, but bowed respectfully, not, however, making any motion to assume their accustomed places, since it never occurred to them that I could have come to play at such an hour of the morning. A little group, of the very "seediest" exterior, was waiting respectfully for when it might be the croupiers' pleasure to begin, but the functionaries never deigned to notice them.

"At what hour are the tables opened?" asked I, as if for information.

"At noon, Monsieur le Comte," said one of the croupiers, folding up his paper, and producing the keys of the strong-box; "but, except these worthy people," — this he said with a most contemptuous air of compassion, — "we have no players till four, or even five, of the afternoon."

"Come, then," said I, taking a seat, "I'll set the virtuous fashion of early hours. There go twenty Naps. for a beginning."

The dealer shuffled the cards. I cut them, and we began. We, I say; because I was the only player, the little knot of humble folk gathering around me in mute astonishment, and wondering what millionnaire they had before them. If I had not been too deeply engaged in the interest of the game, I should have experienced the very highest degree of entertainment from the remarks and comments of the bystanders, who all sympathized with me, and made common cause against the bank.

Some of them were peasants, some were small shop-keepers from distant towns, — the police regulations exclude all natives of Baden, it being the Grand-Ducal policy only to pillage the foreigner, — and one, a half-starved, decrepit old fellow, had been a professor of something somewhere, and turned out of his university to starve for having broached some liberal doctrines in a lecture. He it was who watched me with most eager intensity, following every alternation of my game with a card and a pin. At the end of about an hour I was winner of something more than two hundred pounds, and I sat betting on, my habitual stake of five, or sometimes ten "Naps." each time.

"Get up and go away now," whispered the old man in my ear. "You have done enough for once, — gained more in this brief hour than ever I did in any two years of hard labor."

"At what trade did you work?" asked I, without raising my head from my game.

"My faculty was the ' Pandects,' " replied he, gravely; "but I lectured in private on history, philology, and chemistry."

Shocked at the rudeness of my question to one in his station, I muttered some half-intelligible excuse; but he did not seem to suspect any occasion for apology, — never recognizing that he who labored with head could arrogate over him who toiled with his hands.

"There, I told you so," broke he in, suddenly. "You will lose all back again. You play rashly. The runs of the game have been ' triplets,' and *you* bet on to the fourth time of passing."

"So, then, you understand it!" said I, smiling, and still making my stake as before.

"Let the deal pass; don't bet now," whispered he, eagerly.

"Herr Ephraim, I have warned you already," cried the croupier, "that if you persist in disturbing the gentlemen who play here, you will be removed by the police."

The word "police" — so dreadful to all German ears — made the old man tremble from head to foot; and he bowed twice or thrice in hurried submission, and protested that he would be more cautious in future.

"You certainly do not exhibit such signs of good fortune on your own person," said the croupier, "that should entitle you to advise and counsel others."

"Quite true, Herr Croupier," assented he, with an attempt to smile.

"Besides that, if you reckon upon the Count's good-nature to give you a trifle when the game is over, you'll certainly merit it better by silence and respect now."

The old man's face became deep scarlet, and then as suddenly pale. He made an effort to say something; but though his hands gesticulated, and his lips moved, no sounds were audible, and with a faint sigh he tottered back and leaned against the wall. I sprang up and placed him in a chair, and, seeing that he was overcome by weakness, I called for wine, and hastily poured a glassful down his throat. I could not induce him to take a second, and he seemed, while expressing his gratitude, to be impatient to get away and leave the place.

"Shall I see you home, Herr Ephraim?" said I; "will you allow me to accompany you?"

"On no account, Herr Graf," said he, giving me the title he had heard the croupier address me by. "I can go alone; I am quite able, and — I prefer it."

"But you are too weak, far too weak to venture by yourself, — is he not so?" said I, turning to the croupier to corroborate my words. A strangely significant raising of the eyebrow, a sort of — I know not what — meaning, was all the reply he made me; and half ashamed of the possibility of being made the dupe of some practised impostor, I drew nigh the table for an explanation.

"What is it? what do you mean?" asked I, eagerly.

A shrug of the shoulders and a look of pity was his answer.

"Is he a hypocrite? — is he a cheat?" asked I.

"Perhaps not exactly *that*," said he, shuffling the cards.

"A drunkard, — does he drink, then?" asked I.

"I have never heard so," said he.

"Then what has he done? — what is he?" cried I, impatiently.

He made a sign for me to come close, and then whispered

in my ear what I have just told you, only with a voice full
of holy horror at the crime of a man who had dared to have
an opinion not in accordance with that of a Police Prefect!
That he — a man of hard study and deep reading — should
venture to draw other lessons from history than those taught
at drum-heads by corporals and petty officers!

"Is that all? — is that all?" asked I, indignantly.

"All! all!" exclaimed he; "do you want more?"

"Why, these things may possibly interest police spies,
but they have no imaginable concern for me."

"That is precisely what they have, sir," said he, hastily,
and in a still more cautious tone. "You could not show
that miserable man a kindness without its attracting the
attention of the authorities. They never could be brought
to believe mere humanity was the motive, and they would
seek for some explanation more akin to their daily habits.
As an Englishman, I know your custom is to treat these
things haughtily, and make every personal insult of this
kind a national question; but the inconvenience of this
course will track you over the whole Continent. Your
passport will be demanded here, permission refused you to
remain there. At one town your luggage will be scruti-
nized, at another, your letters opened. I conclude you come
abroad to enjoy yourself. Is this the way to do it? At all
events, he is gone now," added he, looking down the room,
"and let's think no more of him. Messieurs, faîtes votre
jeu!" and once more rang out the burden of that monotonous
injunction to ruin and beggary!

I was n't exactly in the mood for high play at the moment;
on the contrary, my thoughts were with poor Ephraim and
his sorrows; but, for very pride's sake, I was obliged to
seem indifferent and at ease. For I must tell you, Bob,
this cold, impassive bearing is the high breeding of the
play-table, and to transgress it, even for an instant, is a
gross breach of good manners. I have told you my mind
was preoccupied; the results were soon manifest in my play.
Every "coup" was ill-timed. I was always on the wrong
color, and lost without intermission.

"This is not your ' beau moment,' Monsieur le Comte,"
said the croupier to me, as he raked in a stake I had

suffered to quadruple itself by remaining. "I should almost say, wait for another time!"

"Had you said so half an hour ago," replied I, bitterly, "the counsel might have been worth heeding. There goes the last of twenty thousand francs." And there it did go, Bob! swept in by the same remorseless hand that gathered all I possessed.

I lingered for a few moments, half stunned. I felt like one that requires some seconds to recover from the effects of a severe blow, but who feels conscious that with time he shall rally and be himself again. After that I strolled out into the open air, lighted my cigar, and turned off into a steep path that led up the mountain side, under the cover of a dense pine forest. I walked for hours, without noticing the way at either side of me, and it was only when, overcome with thirst, I stooped to drink at a little fountain, that I perceived I had crossed over the crest of the mountain, and gained a little glen at its foot, watered by what I guessed must be a capital fishing-stream. Indeed, I had not long to speculate on this point, for, a few hundred yards off, I beheld a man standing knee-deep in the water, over which he threw his line, with that easy motion of the wrist that bespeaks the angler.

I must tell you that the sight of a fly-fisher is so far interesting abroad that it is only practised by the English; and although, Heaven knows, there is no scarcity of them in town and cities, the moment you wander in the least out of the beaten, frequented track of travel, you rejoice to see your countryman. I made towards him, therefore, at once, to ask what sport he had, and came up just as he had landed a good-sized fish.

"I see, sir," said I, " that the fish are not so strong as in our waters. You'd have given that fellow twenty minutes more play, had he been in a Highland tarn."

" Or in that brisk little river at Dodsborough," replied he, laughing ; and, turning round at the same time to salute me, I perceived that it was Captain Morris. You may remember him being quartered at Bruff, about two years ago, and having had some altercation with my governor on some magisterial topics. He was never much to my taste. I thought him somewhat of a military prig, very stiff and stand off; but whether it was the shooting-jacket *vice* the red coat, or change of place and scene, I know not, but now he seemed far more companionable than I could have thought him. He was a capital angler too, and spoke of shooting and deer-stalking like one passionately fond of them. I felt half ashamed at first, when he asked me my opinion of the trout streams in the neighborhood, and it was only as we warmed up that I owned to the kind of life I had been leading at Baden, and the consequences it had entailed.

" Fortunately for me, in one sense," said he, laughing, " I have always been too poor a man to play at anything; and chess, which excludes all idea of money, is the only game I know. But of this I am quite sure, that the worst of gambling is neither the time nor the money lost upon it; it is the simple fact that, if you ever win, from that moment forth you are unfitted to the pursuits by which men earn their livelihood. The slow, careworn paths of daily industry become insufferable to him who can compass a year's labor by the turn of a die. Enrich yourself but once — only once — at the play-table, and try then what it is to follow any career of patient toil."

He had seen, he said, many examples of this in his own regiment; some of the very finest fellows had been ruined by play, for, as he remarked, " it is strange enough, there are few vices so debasing, and yet the natures and temperaments most open to the seduction of the gaming-table are very far from being those originally degraded." I suppose that his tone of conversation chimed in well with my thoughts at the moment, for I listened to all he said with deep interest, and willingly accepted his invitation to eat some of his morning's sport at a little cottage, where he lived, hard by. He had taken it for the season, and was staying there with his mother, a charming old lady, who welcomed me with great cordiality.

I dined and passed the evening with them. I don't remember when I spent one so much to my satisfaction, for there was something more than courtesy, something beyond mere politeness, in their manner towards me; and I could observe in any chance allusion to the girls, there was a degree of real interest that almost savored of friendship. There was but one point on which I did not thoroughly go with Morris, and that was about Tiverton. On that I found him full of the commonest and most vulgar prejudices. He owned that there was no acquaintanceship between them, and therefore I was able to attribute much, if not all, of his impressions to erroneous information. Now I know George intimately, — nobody can know him better. He is what they call in the world " a loose fish." He's not overburdened with strict notions or rigid principles; he'd tell you himself, that to be encumbered with either would be like entering for a rowing-match in a strait waistcoat; but he is a fellow to share his last shilling with a friend, — thoroughly generous and free-hearted. These are qualities, however, that men like Morris hold cheap. They seem to argue that nobody stands in need of such attributes. I differ with them there totally. My notion is that shipwreck is so common a thing in life, it is always pleasant to think that a friend can throw you a spare hencoop when you're sinking.

We chatted till the night closed in, and then, as the moon got up, Morris strolled with me to within a mile of Baden.

"There!" said he, pointing to the little village, now all spangled with its starry lights, — " there lies the fatal spot that has blighted many a hope, and made many a heart a ruin! I wish you were miles away from it!"

"It cannot injure me much now," said I, laughing; "I am as regularly ' cleaned out' as a poor old professor I met there this morning, Herr Ephraim."

"Not Ephraim Gauss?" asked he. "Did you meet *him* ?"

"If that be his name, — a small, mean-looking man, with a white beard — "

"One of the first men in Germany — the greatest civilian — the most learned Orientalist — and a man of almost universal attainment in science — tell me of him."

I told him the little incident I have already related to you, and mentioned the caution given me by the croupier.

"Which is not the less valuable," broke he in, " because he who gave it is himself a paid spy of the police."

I started, and he went on.

"Yes, it is perfectly true; and the advice he gave you was both good and well intended. These men who act as the croupiers are always in the pay of the police. Their position affords them the very best and safest means of obtaining information; they see everybody, and they hear an immensity of gossip. Still, it is not their interest that the English, who form the great majority of play-victims, should be excluded from places of gambling resort. With them, they would lose a great part of their income; for this reason he gave you that warning, and it is by no means to be despised or undervalued."

At length we parted, — he to return over the mountain to his cottage, and I to continue my way to the hotel.

"At least promise me one thing," said he, as he shook my hand: "you'll not venture down yonder to-night;" and he pointed to the great building where the play went forward, now brilliant in all its illumination.

"That's easily done," said I, laughing, "if you mean as regards play."

"It is as regards play, I say it," replied he; "for the rest, I suppose you'll not incur much hazard."

"I say that the pledge costs little sacrifice; I have no money to wager."

"All the better, at least for the present. My advice to you would be, take your rod, or, if you haven't one, take one of mine, and set out for a week or ten days up the valley of the 'Moorg.' You'll have plenty of fishing, pretty scenery, and, above all, quiet and tranquillity to compose your mind and recover your faculties after all this fevered excitement."

He continued to urge this plan upon me with considerable show of reason, and such success that as I shook his hand for the last time it was in a promise to carry out the scheme. He'd have gone with me himself, he said, but that he could not leave his mother even for a few days; and, indeed, this I scarcely regretted, because, to own the honest fact, my dear Bob, I felt that there was a terrible gulf between us in fifty matters of thought and opinion; and, what was worse, I saw that he was more often in the right than myself. Now, wise notions of life, prudent resolves, and sage aphorisms are certain to come some time or other to everybody; but I'd as soon think of "getting up" wrinkles and crows'-feet as of assuming them at one-and-twenty. I know, at least, that's Tiverton's theory; and he, it can't be denied, does understand the world as well as most men. Not that I do not like Morris; on the contrary, I am sure he is an excellent fellow, and worthy of all respect, but somehow he does n't "go along," Bob; he's — as we used to say of a clumsy horse in heavy ground — "he's sticky." But I'm not going to abuse him, and particularly at the moment when I am indebted to his friendship.

When I reached the hotel, I was so full of my plan that I sent for the landlord, and asked him to convert all my goods and chattels, live and dead, into ready cash. After a brief and rather hot discussion the scoundrel agreed to give me two hundred "Naps." for what would have been cheap at twelve. No matter, thought I, I'll make an end of Baden, and if ever I set foot in it again — "

"Come, out with the cash, Master Müller," cried I, impatient to be off; "I'm sick of this place, and hope never to set eyes on 't more!"

"Ah, the 'Herr Graf' is going away then?" said he, in some surprise. "And the ladies, are they, too, about to leave?"

"I know nothing about their intentions, nor have you any business to make the inquiry," replied I; "pay this money, and make an end of it."

He muttered something about doing the thing regularly, not having "so much gold by him," and so on, ending with a promise that in half an hour I should have the cash sent to my room.

I accordingly hurried upstairs to put away my traps. My mother and the girls had already gone out for the evening, so that I wrote a few lines to say that I was off for a week's fishing, but would be back by Wednesday. I had just finished my short despatch, when the landlord entered with a slip of paper in one hand and a canvas bag of money in the other.

"This is the inventory of the goods, Herr Graf, which

you will please assign **over** to me, by affixing your signature."

I wrote it at once.

"This is my little account for your expenses at the hotel," said he, presenting a hateful-looking strip of a foot and a half long.

"Another time, — no leisure for looking over that now!" said I, angrily.

"Whenever you please, Herr Graf," said he, with the same imperturbable manner. "You will find it all correct, I'm sure. This is the balance!" And opening the bag he poured forth some gold and silver, which, when counted, made up twenty-seven Napoleons, fourteen francs.

"And what's this?" cried I, almost boiling over with rage.

"Your balance, Herr Graf. All that is coming to you. If you will please to look here — "

"Give me up that inventory, — that bill of sale," cried I, perfectly wild with passion.

He only gave a grim smile, while, by a significant gesture, he showed that the paper in question was in his breeches-pocket. For a second, Bob, I was so thoroughly beside myself with passion, that I determined to regain possession of it by force. To this end I went to the door, and locked it; but by the time I returned to him, I found that he had thrown up the window and addressed some words to the people in the courtyard. This brought me to my senses, so I counted over my twenty-seven Naps., placed the bill on the chimney-piece, unlocked the door, and told him to go, — an injunction which, I assure you, he obeyed with such alacrity that had I been disposed to assist his exit I could not have been in time to do it.

For both our sakes I'll not recall the state of mind in which this scene left me. As to going an excursion with such a sum, or rather with what would have remained of it after paying waiters, porters, and such-like, it was too absurd to think of, so that I coolly put it in my pocket, walked over to "the Rooms," threw it on the green cloth of the gaming-table — and — lost it! There ends the episode of my last fortnight's existence, — as dreary and dis-

reputable a one as need be. As to how I have passed the
last four days I 'm not quite so clear! I have walked some
twenty-five or thirty miles in each, dining at little wayside
inns, and returning late at night to Baden.

Passing through picturesque glens, and along mountain
ridges of boldest outline, I have marked little. I remember still less. Still the play-fever is abating. I can sleep
without dreaming of the croupier's chant, and I awake without starting at any imaginary loss! I feel as though great
bodily exertion and fatigue would ultimately antagonize
the excessive tension of nerves too long and too painfully
on the stretch, and I am steadily pursuing this system for
a cure.

When I come home — after midnight — I add some pages
to this long epistle, which I sometimes doubt if I shall
ever have courage to send you! for there is this poignant
misery about one's play misfortunes, you never can expect
a friend's sympathy, no matter how severe your sufferings
be. The losses at play are thoroughly selfish ills; they
appeal to nothing for consolation!

You will have remarked how I have avoided all mention
of the family in this epistle. The truth is, I scarcely ever
see my mother or Mary Anne. Caroline occasionally comes
to me before I 'm up of a morning; but it is to sorrow over
domestic griefs of one kind or other. My father is still
away, and, strangely too, we do not hear from him; and,
in fact, we are a most ill-ordered, broken-up household,
each going his own road, and that being — in almost every
case, I fear — a bad one.

This recital — if it be ever destined to come to hand —
may possibly tend to reconcile you to home life, and the
want of those advantages which you are so thoroughly convinced pertain to foreign travel. I know that in my present
mood I am very far from being an impartial witness, and
I am also aware that I am open to the reproach of not having cultivated those arts which give to Continental residence
its peculiar value; but let me tell you, Bob, the ignorance
with which I left home — the utter neglect of education in
youth — left me unable to derive profit from what lay so
seemingly accessible. You do not plate over cast-iron, and

the thin lacquer of gold or silver would never even hide
the base metal beneath. I have n't courage to go over
and see Morris; and here I live, perfectly isolated and
companionless.

Tiverton writes me word that he 'll be back in a few days.
He went over to speak on the Jew Bill. He says that his
liberal speech on that measure "stood to him " very handsomely in Lombard Street. He has forwarded the report of
his oration, but I have n't read it. His chief argument in
favor of admitting them into Parliament is, "There are so
few of them." It 's very like the lady's plea, — of the
child being a little one. However, I don't think it signifies
much one way or t'other; but it seems strange to exclude
men from legislation who claim for their ancestor the first
Lawgiver.

I shall be all eagerness to hear what success you have had
for the scholarship. You are a happy fellow to have heart
and energy for an honorable ambition; and that you may
have "luck " — for that is requisite, too — is the sincere
wish of your attached friend,

                                        JAMES DODD.

LETTER XXIX.

CAROLINE DODD TO MISS COX AT MISS MINCING'S ACADEMY,
BLACK ROCK, IRELAND.

THE MOORG THAL.

MY DEAR MISS COX, — How happy would you be if only seated in the spot where I now write these lines! I am at an open window, the sill of which is a great rock, all covered with red-brown moss, and beneath, again, at some thirty feet lower, runs the clear stream of the Moorg River. Two gigantic mountains, clad in pine forests to the summits, enclose the valley, the view of which, however, extends to full two miles, showing little peeps of farmhouses and mills along the river's bank, and high upon a great bold crag, the ducal castle of Eberstein. The day is hot but not sultry, for a light summer breeze is playing over the water, and, high up, the clouds move slowly on, now casting broad masses of mellow shadow over the deep-tinted forest.

The stream here falls over some masses of rock with a pleasant gushing music that harmonizes well with the songs of the peasant girls, who are what we should in Ireland call "beetling" their clothes in the water. On the opposite bank some mowers are seated at their dinner, under the shadow of a leafy horsechestnut-tree, and, far away in the distance, a wagon of the newly cut hay is traversing the river; the horses stop to drink, and the merry children are screaming their laughter from the top of the load. I hear them even here.

That you may learn where I am, and how I have come hither, let me tell you that I am on a visit with Mrs. Morris, the mother of Captain M., at a little cottage they have taken for the season, about twelve miles from Baden, in a

valley called the Moorg Thal. If its situation be the very
perfection of picturesque choice, it contains within quite
enough of accommodation for those who occupy it. The
furniture, too, most simple though it be, is of that nice old
walnut-wood, so bright and mellow-looking; and our little
drawing-room is even handsomely ornamented by a richly
carved cabinet and a centre-table, the support of which is a
grotesque dwarf with four heads. Then we have a piano, a
reasonably well-filled book-shelf, and a painter's easel, to
which I turn at intervals, as I write, to give a passing touch
of light to those trees now waving in the summer's wind,
and which I destine, when finished, for my dear, dear governess. All the externals of rural life in Germany are
highly picturesque, — I might almost call them poetic. The
cottages, the costume, the little phrases in use amongst the
people, their devotional offices, and, above all, their music,
make up an ideal of country life such as I scarcely conceived possible to exist.

There is, too, I am told, — for my imperfect knowledge
of the language does not permit me to state the fact of
myself, — an amount of information amongst the people
seldom found in a similar class throughout the rest of
Europe. I do not mean the peasantry here, but the dwellers
in the small villages, — those, for instance, who follow
handicrafts and small trades, and who are usually great
readers and very acute thinkers. Denied almost entirely all
access to that daily literature of newspapers on which our
people feed, they fall back upon a very different class of
writing, and are conversant with the works of their great
prose and verse writers. Their thoughts are thus idealized
to a degree; they themselves become assuredly less work-a-
day and practical, but their hopes, their aspirations, and
their ambitions take a higher flight than we could ever think
possible from such humble resting-places. Mrs. Morris,
who knew Germany many years ago, tells me that those
fatal years of '48 and '49 have done them great injury.
Suddenly called upon to act, in events and contingencies of
which they derived all their knowledge from some parallels
in remote history, they rushed into the excesses of a mediæval period, as the natural consequences of the position;

and all the atrocities of bygone centuries were re-enacted by a people who are unquestionably the most docile and law-obeying of the whole Continent. They are now calming down again, and there is every reason to think that, if, unshaken by troubles from without or within, Germany will again be the happy land it used to be.

Forgive me, my dear Miss Cox, if I grow tiresome to you, by a theme which now fills all my thoughts, and occupies so much of our daily talking. Captain M. has gone to England on some important matter of business, and the old lady is my only companion.

Oh, how you would like her! and how capable you would be of appreciating traits and features of her mind, of which I, in my insufficiency, can but dimly catch the meaning. She is within a year or two of eighty, and yet with a freshness of heart and a brightness of intellect that would shame one of *my* age.

The mellow gayety of heart that, surviving all the trials of life, lives on to remote age, hopeful in the midst of disappointments, trusting even when betrayed, is the most captivating trait that can adorn our poor nature. The spirit that can extract its pleasant memories from the past, forgetting all their bitterness, is truly a happy one. This she seems to do in all gratitude for what blessings remain to her, after a life not devoid of misfortune. She is devotedly attached to her son, who, in return, adores her. Probably no picture of domestic affection is more touching than that subsisting between a man already past youth and his aged and widowed mother, — the little tender attentions, the watchful kindnesses on both sides, those graceful concessions which each knows how and when to make of their own comfort, and, above all, that blending of tastes by which, at last, each learns to adopt some of the other's likings, and, even in prejudices, to become more companionable.

To me, the happiness of my present life is greater than I can describe to you. The peaceful quietude of an existence on which no shocks obtrude is unspeakably delightful. If the weather forbid us to venture abroad, which on fine days we do for hours together, our home resources are numerous. The little cares of a household, amusing as they

are, associated with so many little peculiar traits of nationality, help the morning to pass; after which I draw, or
write, or play, or read aloud, mostly German, to the old
lady.   Whatever my occupation, be it at the easel, the desk,
or the pianoforte, her criticisms are always good and just;
for, strange to say, even on subjects of which she professes
to know nothing, there is an instinctive appreciation of the
right; and this would seem to result from an intense study,
and deep love of nature.   She herself was the first to show
me that this was a charm which the Bible possessed in the
most remarkable manner, and, unlike other literature, gave
it the most uncommon value in the eyes of the humblest
classes, who are from the very accidents of fortune the deep
students of nature.   The language whose illustrations are
taken from objects and incidents that every peasant can
confirm, has a direct appeal to a lowly heart; and there is
a species of flattery to his intelligence in the fact that inspi-
ration could not typify more strongly its conception than by
analogies open to the lowliest son of labor.

After this, she places Shakspeare, whose actual knowledge
is miraculous, and whose immortality is based upon that
very fact, since the true will be true to all ages and people;
and, however men's minds may differ about the forms of
expression, the fact will remain imperishable.   According
to her theory, Shakspeare understood human nature as
learned men do an exact science, — where certain results
must follow certain premises and combinations inevitably
and of necessity.   How otherwise explain that intimate acquaintance with the habits and modes of thought of classes
of which he never made one?   How account for the delinea-
tion of kingly feelings by him who scarcely saw the steps of
a throne?   "And yet," said Mrs. M., "Louis Philippe himself told me, that Shakspeare's kings were as true as his
lovers.   His Majesty once amused me much," said she,
"by alluding to a passage in ' Hamlet,' which assuredly
would never have occurred to me to notice.   It is where the
King and Queen are dismissing their attendants from further
waiting.   His Majesty says, ' Thanks, Rosenkrantz, and
gentle Guildenstern;' on which the Queen adds, ' Thanks,
Guildenstern, and gentle Rosenkrantz.'   ' Now,' said Louis

Philippe, ' one almost should have been a queen to know that it was needful to balance the seeming preference of the Royal epithet, by inverting the phrase.' "

While I ramble on thus, I may seem to be forgetting the subjects on which more properly I ought to dwell, — home and family. Our pursuit of greatness still continues, my dear Miss Cox. We are determined to be fine people; and I suppose, after all, that our shortcomings and disappointments are not greater than usually fall to the lot of those who aspire to what is beyond or above them. In England the gradations of rank are as fixed as the degrees of a service; and we, being who and what we are, could no more pretend to something else than could a subaltern pass off for a colonel to his own regiment. Here, however, there is a general scramble for position, and each seems to have the same privilege to call himself what he likes, that he exercises over the mere spelling of his name. I judge this to be the case from the anecdotes I have heard in society about the Count this, and the Baron that. Since papa's absence in the interior of Germany, whither he accompanied Mrs. Gore Hampton, to visit, I believe, some crowned head of her acquaintance, mamma has pursued a kind of royal progress towards greatness. Our style of living has been most expensive, — I might almost call it splendid. We have servants, horses, equipage, — everything, in fact, that appertains to a certain station, but one, and that one thing, unfortunately, is the grand requisite of all, — the air that belongs to it. The truth is, Miss Cox, as the old lawyer one day said at dinner to papa, "You prove too much, Mr. Dodd." That is exactly what mamma is doing. She dresses magnificently for small occasions; she insists too eagerly upon what she deems her due; and she is far too exclusive with respect to those who seek her acquaintanceship. Would you believe it, that though I am permitted to accept the kind hospitality which I at this moment enjoy, it is upon the condition that neither mamma nor Mary Anne are to "be dragged into the mire of low intimacies;" that Mrs. Morris is to be "Cary's friend." Proud am I, indeed, if she will deign to consider me such!

I must acknowledge that mamma's "Wednesdays" col-

lected all that was high and distinguished at Baden. We
had the old Kurfürst of something, with a long white moustache, and thirty orders; an archduchess with a humpback,
and a mediatized prince with one eye. There were generals, marshals, ministers, envoys, and plenipos without
end, — "your Highness" and "your Excellency" were
household words round our tea-table. But I often asked
myself, "Are not these great folk paying off in falsehood
the imposition we are practising upon *them?* Are they not
laughing at the ' Dodds,' and their thousand solecisms in
good breeding?" These would be very unworthy suspicions
of mine if I did not feel convinced they were well founded;
but more than once I have overheard chance words and
phrases that have suffused my cheeks with "shame-red," as
the Germans call it, for an hour after. Is it not an indignity to accept hospitality and requite it by ridicule? Is it
not base to receive attentions, and repay them in scorn?

Whether it is from feeling as I do on the subject or not, I
cannot say, but James rarely or never appears at mamma's
receptions. He is among what is called "a fast set;" but
I always incline to think that his nature is not corrupted,
though doubtless sullied, by the tone of society around us.

You ask me about Mary Anne's appearance, and here I
can speak without reserve or qualification. She is, indeed,
the handsomest girl I ever saw; tall and well-proportioned,
and with a carriage and a style about her that might grace
a princess. A critic inclined to severity might say there
was perhaps a slight tendency to haughtiness in the expression of the features, especially the mouth; the head, too,
is a little, a very little, too much thrown back; but somehow
these might be defects in another, and yet in her they seem
to give a peculiar stamp and character to her beauty. All
her gestures are grace itself, and her courtesy, save that it
is a little too low, perfect. She speaks French and German
fluently, and knows the precise title of some hundred acquaintances, every one of whom would be distracted if
defrauded in the smallest coin of his rank. I need not say
how superior all these gifts make her to your humble and
unlettered correspondent. Yes, my dear Miss Cox, the
French "irregulars" are the same puzzle to me they used to

be, and my mind will no more carry me on to the verb at the end of the German sentence than will my feet bear me over fifty miles a day. I am the stupid Caroline of long ago, and what renders the case so hopeless is, with the best of dispositions to do otherwise.

I am, however, improved in my painting, particularly in my use of color. I begin at last to recognize the merits of harmony in tint, and see how Nature herself always contrives to be correct. I hope you will like the little sketch that accompanies this; the rock in the foreground is the spot on which I sit at every sunset. Would that I had you beside me there, to counsel, to guide, and to correct me!

When Captain Morris returns, I shall leave this, as Mrs. M. will not require my companionship any longer, although she is already planning twenty things we are to do then.

Pray, therefore, write to me, as before, to Baden; and with my most affectionate regards to all who may remember me, and my dearest love to yourself,

Believe me, yours ever,

CAROLINE DODD.

LETTER XXX.

MISS MARY ANNE DODD TO MISS DOOLAN, OF BALLYDOOLAN.

My dearest Kitty, — It *was* our names you saw in the "Morning Post"! We are "The Dodd M'Carthys." It was no use deferring the decision for papa's return; and, as I observed to mamma, circumstances are often stronger than ourselves; for, in all likelihood, Louis Napoleon would not have declared the Empire so soon if it were not for the "Rouges," or the Orleanists, or the others. Events, in fact, pressed us from behind, — go forward we must; and so, like the distinguished authority I have mentioned, we accepted greatness, in the shape of our present designation.

We took the great step on Monday evening last, and issued one hundred and thirty-eight cards for our Wednesday at home, as Madame Dodd M'Carthy. Of course, I conclude the new title was amply discussed and criticised; but, as James remarked, the *coup d'état* succeeded perfectly. He sent me three different bulletins during the day from "the Rooms," where he was engaged at play. The first was briefly: "Great excitement, and much curiosity as to the reasons. Causes assigned, — vague, various, and contradictory. Strict silence on *my* part." The second ran: "Funds rising rapidly, — confidence restored." The third was: "Victory — opposition crushed, annihilated — dynasty secure. Send a card at once to the Crown Prince of Dalmatia, at the 'Lion.' He is just come."

Mamma's nervous tremors during this eventful day were dreadful. Nothing sustained her but a high consciousness, and some excellent curaçoa. Every cry in the street, every chance commotion, the slightest assemblage, beneath our windows, she took for popular demonstrations. You know, my dearest Kitty, we live in really eventful times, and

nobody can answer for how the mere populace will receive
any attempts to recover ancient feudal privileges. I own
to you, frankly, the attempt was a bold one. We, so to
say, stemmed the foamy torrent of Democracy at its highest
flood; but the moment was also propitious. Now or never
was the time for nobility to raise its head again; and *we*,
I am proud to say, have given the initiative to astonished
Europe.

From the hour that we took the great step, Kitty, I felt
my heart rise with the occasion. My spirit seemed to say,
"Swell to the magnitude of those grand proportions around
you;" and I really felt myself, as it were, disenthralled from
the narrow limits of a mere Dodd, and expanding to the
wide realms of a M'Carthy! If you only knew the sufferings and heart-burnings that plebeian appellation has cost
us! The hateful monosyllable seemed to drop down like a
shell in the midst of a company; and often has it needed a
fortnight's dinners and evening parties, in a new place, to
overcome the horrid impression caused by the name of Dodd!

Now, as it stands at present, it serves to give vigor and
energy to the name. Dodd M'Carthy is like Gorman
O'Moore, Grogan O'Dwyer, or any other of the patronymics
of ancient Ireland.

From the deep interest caused by this decisive step, I was
obliged at once to turn to the details of our great reception
to be held on the Wednesday following, for it was necessary
that in splendor and distinction it should eclipse all that
had preceded it. Happily for us, dearest Caroline was
absent as well as papa; she had gone to spend a week
with a tiresome old lady some miles away, and we were
therefore relieved from the annoyance of that vexatious
restraint imposed by the mere presence of those whose
thoughts and ideas are never yours. I have already told
you that she has taken up a completely mistaken line, and
utterly destroyed any natural advantages she possessed. I
told her so myself over and over; I reasoned and argued the
question deliberately. "I see," said I, "your tastes are
not those of high and fashionable society. You do not feel
the instinctive fascination that comes of being admired by
the distinguished classes. Your ambitions do not soar to

those aristocratic regions whose atmosphere breathes of
royalty.   Be it so; there is another path open to you, — the
sentimental and the romantic.   Your hair suits it, your com-
plexion, your figure, your style generally, will easily adapt
themselves to the character.   If not a part that attracts general admiration, it is one which never fails, in every society,
to secure some favorable notice; and elder sons, educated
either ' at home or in clergymen's families,' are constantly
captured by its fascination."   This, I must remark to you,
Kitty, is perfectly true, and it is of great consequence frequently to have a woman that suits shy men, and saves
them the much-dreaded exhibition of themselves by talking
aloud.   I told her all this, and I even condescended to use
arguments derived from her own narrow views of life, by
showing that it is a style requiring little expense in the way
of dress, — ringlets and a white muslin "peignoir" of a
morning, a broad-leaved straw hat for the promenade, —
something, in short, of the very simplest kind, and no ornaments.   No! my dearest Kitty, it was of no use!   She is
one of those self-opinionated girls that reason never appeals
to.   She coolly replied to me, that all this would be unreal
and unnatural, — "a mere piece of acting," as she said, and,
consequently, unworthy of her, and unbecoming.   I repeat
the very words of her reply, to show you the great benefits
she has derived from foreign travel!   Why, dearest Kitty,
nobody is real, — nobody pretends to be real abroad; if they
were to do so, they 'd be shunned like wild beasts.   What
is it, I ask, that constitutes the very essence of high breeding?   Conventional usages, forms of expression, courtesies,
attentions, flatteries, and observances, — all stimulated, all
put on, to please and captivate.   Reject this theory, and
instead of society, you have a mob; instead of a *salon*, you
have a wild-beast "menagerie."   Caroline says she is Irish;
she might as well say she was Cochin-Chinese.   Nobody can
recognize any trait in that nationality but its uniform "savagery;" for I must tell you, Kitty, that Ireland itself —
though politically deplored, pitied, and wept over, abroad —
is encumbered by geographical doubts and difficulties like
the North-West Passage.   Many suppose it to be a town in
the West of England; others fancy it a barren tract along

the coast; and a few, whose sympathies are more acute for suffering nations, fancy it to be a species of penal settlement in an unknown latitude.

If Caroline even developed the character — if she had, as the French say, *créé le rôle* of an Irish girl, what with eccentricities of dress, manner, and Moore's melodies, something might be made of it. It admits of all those extravagances that are occasionally admired, and any amount of liberty with the male sex. Cary's reading of the part was very different; it was neither poetic nor pictorial; in fact, it was a mere vulgar piece of commonplace devotion to home and its tiresome associations, and a clinging attachment to whatever recalled memories of our former obscurity, — these "national traits" being eked out with a most insolent contempt for the foreigner, and a compassionate sorrow for the patience with which *we* endured him.

Pardon me, my dearest friend, if I weary you with this unpleasant theme; but I wish to satisfy your mind that if my sisterly affection be strong, it still does not tyrannize over my reason, and that increased powers of judgment, if they elevate the understanding, are frequently exercised at the cost of our tenderest feelings.

To come back to the point whence I started, "our Wednesday" — and this, by the way, enables me to answer some of the questions in your last. You ask about my admirers; you shall have the catalogue as lately revised and corrected, though I scarcely flatter myself that the names will admit of vocal repetition. First, then, there is the Neapolitan Prince Sierra d'Aquila Nero, whom I already mentioned to you in one of my letters from Brussels. In my then innocence of the Continent I thought him charming, so impassioned, so poetical, and so perfumed. Now, Kitty, I find him an intolerable old bore; he is upwards of seventy, but so painted, patched, and plastered as to pass off panoramically for five-and-forty. He affects all the habits and even the vices of young men. He keeps saddle-horses that he dare not ride, and hires a "chasse," though he never fires a gun; and lastly, issues from his hairdresser's shop, at intervals, with a wig of shortened proportions, coolly alleging that he has just had his hair cut! When he drives out of an evening, the whole Allée reeks of "Bergamot," and the flutter of his handkerchief is a tornado in the Spice Islands. Need I say that *his* chance is at zero? Count Rastuche-witsky, a Russian Pole, comes next, — at least, in order of seniority; a short, stern-looking man, of about fifty, with a snow-white beard and moustache, with abrupt manners, and an unpleasant voice. I believe that he only pays me any attention because he sees the Prince do so, for he hates all Italians, and tries to thwart them in everything. The Count's great claim to distinction rests upon his father, or mother, I forget which, having helped to assassinate the Emperor Paul, — a piece of chivalry that he dwells on unceasingly.

The Chevalier de Courcelles makes "No. Three," and thirty years ago he might have been very presentable; but he belongs to a school even older than his time. He is of the Richelieu order, and seems to be always in a terrible fright about the effect of his own powers of fascination: his constant effort being to show you that he really is not fond of making victims. There is a German Graf von Herren-shausen, a large, yellow-bearded, blear-eyed monster, with a frogged coat and a huge pipe-stick projecting from the hindpocket, who kisses my hand whenever we meet, and leers at me from the whist-table — for, happily, he is past dancing — like a Ghoul in an Eastern tale. There are a vast number of others, one or two of whom I reserve for favorable mention hereafter; but these are the true "préten-dants," of which number, I believe, I might select the one which pleases me best.

Amongst "home productions," as you term them, I may mention the Honorable Sackville Cavendish, — a thin, pale, white-eyebrowed babe of diplomacy, that smallest of For-eign Office infants yclept an "unpaid attaché." He has just emerged from the "nursery" at Downing Street, and is really not strong enough to go alone. I have supported him in an occasional polka, and "hustled him," as James called it, through a waltz, and have in turn received the meed of his admiration as expressed in the most lack-lustre eyes that ever glittered out of a doll's head; and, lastly, there is Mister Milo Blake O'Dwyer, who formerly —

O'Connell regnante — represented the town of Tralee in Parliament, and who now, with altered fortunes, performs the duty of Foreign Correspondent to that great newspaper, "THE SLEDGE HAMMER OF FREEDOM."

Perhaps I'm not strictly correct in enrolling him amongst the number of my worshippers; with more rigid justice, I believe he belongs to mamma; at least he's in constant attendance upon her, and continually assures me, with upturned eyes and a smack of the lip, that she is a "gorgeous woman," and "wonderfully preserved!" This worthy individual is really a curiosity; since being in manner, exterior, knowledge, and fortune totally deficient of all those aids which achieve success in society, he has actually contrived, by the bare force of impudence, to move with, and be received by, persons in the very first ranks. Foreigners, I must tell you, Kitty, conceive the most ridiculous notions of England; one of the most popular of which is that more than one-half of our government is carried on by newspaper writing, the minister contributing his sentiments one day, some individual of the public replying the next. Now, the illustrious Milo takes every opportunity of propping up this fallacy, while he represents himself as the very bone and sinew of all English opinion on the Continent. To believe him, no foreign prince or potentate could raise a sixpence on loan till he subscribes the scheme. How many an appropriation of territory have his warnings arrested? From what cruelties has he saved the Poles? What a crisis did his pen achieve in the fortunes of Hungary! And then the bushels of diamond snuff-boxes that he has thrown from him with disgust, the "heaps of orders that he has rejected with proud scorn!" As he says himself, "Have n't I more power than them all? When I send off my article to the 'Sledge,' don't I see them trembling and shaking for what's coming? Ay, says I to myself, haughty enough you look to-day, but won't I expose your Majesty, won't I lay bare the cruelties of your prisons and the infamy of your spies! And your Eminence, too, how silky you are; but I know you well, and I 've a copy of the last rescript you sent over to Ireland! Don't be afraid, my little darling; never mind the puppies that hissed you at Parma, I 'll make your fortune in London. A word from me to Lumley, and it's as good as five thousand pounds in the bank!"

It really gives me a great notion of the glut of genius that we possess in England, when you see a man whose qualifications are great in war and peace; whose knowledge ranges over the world of politics, religion, literature, fine arts, and the drama; who knows mankind to perfection, and understands statecraft to a miracle, with no higher nor prouder position than that of writing for the "Sledge." It is but fair to own that he has been of great service to us here. The hardest thing to find in the world is some person of pushing habits and impudent address, who will speak of you at all times and in all companies, doing for you, socially, what, in the world of trade, is accomplished by huge advertisements and red-lettered placards. Now, one really cannot stick up on the walls great announcements of "unrivalled attraction," the "positively last night but one" of Mrs. Dodd's great *soirées*, and so on, but you can come pretty nigh the same result by a little tact and management. A few insignificant commissions about camellias, a change of arrangement about the fiddles, intrusted to him, and Milo was prepared to go forth, trumpet in hand, for us, from day to dark. Woe to the luckless wight that hadn't got a card for our "Evening"! the obligation Milo would place him under was a bond debt for life. Then he contrived to know everybody; and though he made sad hash of their names, they only smiled at his blunders.

I have heard that a great English minister one day confessed that the only exaction of office he never could thoroughly reconcile himself to, was the nature of those persons he was occasionally obliged to employ as subordinates. I suppose that, without being leader of a cabinet, everybody must have experienced something or other of this kind in life.

I think I hear you ask, "Where is the Ritter von Wolfenshäfer all this time? What has become of *him?*" you say. You really are very tiresome, dearest Kitty, with your little poisonous allusions to "old loves," former attachments, and so on. As to the Ritter, however, I heard from him yesterday; he cannot, it seems, come to Baden; his father is not

on terms with the Grand-Duke, and he strictly charges me
not to mention their names to any one. His letter repeats
the invitation to us all to spend some weeks at the " Schloss,"
— an arrangement which might, very possibly, suit our
plans well, since, when the season ends here, it is still too
early to go into winter quarters; and one is sorely puzzled
what to do with the late autumn, which is as wearisome as
the time one passes in the drawing-room before dinner. Of
course we must await pa's return, to reply to this invitation ;
and I incline to say we shall accept it. Why will you be so
silly as to remind me of the follies of my childhood? Are
there no naughtinesses of the nursery you can rake up to
record? You know as well, if not better than myself, that
the attentions you allude to could never have been seriously
meant! nor could Dr. B. believe them such, if not totally
deficient in those qualities of good sense and judgment for
which I always have given him credit. I will not say that,
in the artless gayety of infancy, I have not amused myself
with the mock devotion he proffered; but you might as
well reproach me with fickleness for not taking a child's
interest any longer in the nursery games that once delighted
me, as for not sustaining my share in this absurd illusion !

I plainly perceive one thing, Kitty, — the gentleman in
question has very little pride; but even *that*, in your eyes,
may be an excellence, for you have discovered innumerable
merits in his character under circumstances which, I am constrained to own, have failed to impress me with a suitable
degree of interest. The subject is so very unpleasant, however, that I must beg it may never be reopened between us ;
and if you really feel for him so acutely as you say, I can
only suggest that you should hit upon some plan of consolation perfectly independent of any aid from your attached
friend,

MARY ANNE.

LETTER XXXI.

MARY ANNE DODD TO MISS DOOLAN, OF BALLYDOOLAN.

My dearest Kitty, — Another delay, and more "last words"! I had thought that my poor epistle was already miles on the way towards you, wafted by the sighs of my heaving heart, but I now discover that Mr. Cavendish will not send off his bag to the Foreign Office before Saturday, as the Grand-Duke wants to send over some guinea-pigs to the royal children, so that I shall detain this till that day, and perhaps be able to tell you of a great "picnic" we are planning to the Castle of Eberstein for Thursday next. It is one of the things everybody does here, and of course we must not omit it. James talks of the expense as terrific, which really comes with an ill grace from one who wagers fifty, or even sixty, Napoleons on a card! Besides, a "picnic" is an association, and the whole cost cannot fall to the share of an individual. The Great Milo begs that we will leave everything to him, and I feel assured that it is the wisest course we can adopt, not to speak of the advantage of seeing the whole festivity glowingly described in the columns of the "Sledge." The Princess Sloboffsky has just driven to the door, so I must conclude for the present.

I come back to say that the picnic is fixed for Thursday, the number to be, by special request of the Princess, limited to forty, — the list to be made out this evening. "Mammas" to go in open carriages, — young ladies horseback or ass-back, — men indiscriminately; no more at present decided on. I am wild with delight at the pleasure before us. Would you were one of us, dearest Kitty!

Thursday Morning.

Oh, Kitty, what a day! It might be December in London. The rain is swooping down the mountain sides, and

the wind howling fearfully. It is now seven o'clock, and
my maid, Augustine, has called me to get up and dress.
Mamma has had two notes already, which, being in French,
she is waiting for me to read and reply to. I'll hasten to
see what they mean.

One of the "billets" is from the Duchesse de Sargance,
merely asking the question, "Que faire?" The other is
from the Princess Sloboffsky, who, in consideration "for all
the trouble mamma has been put to," deems it better to go
at all events, and that we can dine at the Grand-Ducal
Schloss, instead of on the grass. This reads ominously in
one sense, Kitty, and seems to imply that *we* are giving the
entertainment ourselves; but I must keep this suspicion to
myself, or we should have a terrible exposure. When an
evil becomes inevitable, patient submission is the true
philosophy.

Ten o'clock.

What an animated, I might almost call it a stormy, debate
we have just had in the drawing-room! The assembled
lieges have been all discussing the proposed excursion, — if
that can be called discussion, where everybody screamed
out his own opinion, and nobody listened to his neighbor.
The two parties for and against going divided themselves
into the two sexes, — the men being for staying where we
are, the ladies as clamorously declaring for the road. Of
course the "Ayes" had it, and we are now putting the
whole house in requisition for cloaks, mantles, and mack-
intoshes. The half-dozen men for whom no place can be
made in coach or "calèche" are furious at having to ride.
I half suspect that some attachments whose fidelity has
hitherto defied time and years, will yield to-day before the
influence of mere water. The truth is, Kitty, foreigners
dread it in every shape. They mix a little of it now and
then with their wine, and they rather like to see it in foun-
tains and "jets d'eau," but there ends all the acquaintance
they ever desire to maintain with the pure element.

I must confess that the aspect of the "outsiders" is suggestive of anything rather than amusement. They stand to
be muffled and waterproofed like men who, having resigned
themselves to an inevitable fate, have lost all interest in the

preliminaries that conduct to it. They are, as it were, bound for the scaffold, and they have no care for the shape of the "hurdle" that is to draw them thither. The others, who have secured inside places, are overwhelmingly civil, and profuse in all the little attentions that cost nothing, nor exact any sacrifice. I have seen no small share of national character this morning, and if I had time could let you into some secrets about it.

The arrangement of the company — that is, who is to go with whom — is our next difficulty. There are such intricacies of family history, such subtle questions of propriety to be solved, we 'd not get away under a year were we to enter upon half of them. As a general rule, however, ladies ought not to be packed up in the same coach with the husbands from whom they have been for years separated, nor people with deadly feuds between them to be placed *vis-à-vis*. As to the attractive principles, the cohesionary elements, Kitty, are more puzzling still, since none but the parties themselves know where the minds are simulated and where real.

Milo has taken a great part of this arrangement upon his own hands, and, from what I can see, with his accustomed want of success in all matters of tact and delicacy. Of this, however, he is most beautifully unconscious, and goes about in the midst of muttered execrations with the implicit belief of being a benefactor of the human race. I wish you could see the self-satisfied chuckle of his greasy laugh, or could hear his mumbled " Maybe I don't know what ye 'r after, my old lady. Have n't I put the little Count with the green spectacles next you ; don't I understand the cross looks ye 'r giving me ? Ah, Mademoiselle, never fear me, I have in my eye for you, — a wink is enough for Milo Blake any day. Yes, my darling, I 'm looking for him this minute." These and such-like mutterings will show you the spirit of his ministering ; and when I repeat that he makes nothing but blunders, you may picture to yourself the man. He has appointed himself on mamma's staff ; and as I go with the Princess and the Count Boldourouki, I shall see no more of him for a while.

It is quite clear, Kitty, that we are the entertainers,

though how it came to be so, I cannot even guess. Some blunder, I suspect, of this detestable Milo; and James will do nothing whatever. He is still in bed, and, to all my entreaties to get up, merely says that he'll be with us at dinner. The hampers of proggery will fill two carriages, and a charette with the champagne in ice is already sent forward. Three cooks — for such, I am told, are three gentlemen in black coats and white neckcloths — are to accompany us; and the whole preparations are evidently got up in the "very first style," and "totally regardless of expense."

Twelve o'clock.

Another dilemma. There is only one "bus" in the town; and as none of the band will sit outside in this terrible weather, what is to be done? Milo proposes billeting them, singly, here and there, through the carriages; but the bare mention has excited a rebellion amongst the equestrians, who will not consent to be treated worse than the fiddlers! The Commissary of Police has just sent to know if we have obtained "a ministerial permission to assemble in vast numbers and for objects unnamed." I have got one of the German nobles to settle this difficulty, which, in Milo's hands, — if he only heard of it, — might become formidable.

Happily, he is now engaged "telling off" the band, and selecting from the number such as we can find room to accommodate. The permission has been accorded, the carriages are drawing up, the guests are taking their seats, we are ready, — we are off.

Saturday Morning.

DEAREST KITTY, — Mr. Cavendish has just sent me word that the courier will start in half an hour, so that I have only time for a few lines. Gloomily as the day broke yesterday, its setting at evening was infinitely sadder and more sorrowful. Never did a prospect of pleasure prove more delusive; never did a scene of enjoyment terminate more miserably.

Tears of anguish, of passion, and of shame blot my words as I write them. You must not ask me to describe the course of events, when my mind has but room for the sad catastrophe that closed them; but in a few brief lines I will endeavor to convey to you what occurred.

Our journey to Eberstein, from being all up hill and over roads terribly cut up by the weather, was a slow process. The procession, some of the riders remarked, had a most funereal look, winding along up the zig-zags of the mountain, and on a day which assuredly suggested few thoughts of pleasure. I can only answer for my own companions; but they, I am bound to say, were in the very worst of tempers the whole way, discussing the whole plot of the excursion with — considering mamma's share in it — a far greater degree of candor than politeness. They ridiculed picnics in general; pronounced them vulgar, tiresome, and usually "failures." They insinuated that they were the resources of people who felt more at ease in the semi-civilized scramble of a country party than amid the more correct courtesies of daily life! As to the "dîner sur l'herbe" itself, it was a shocking travesty of a real dinner. Spiders and cockroaches settled in your soup, black beetles bathed in your champagne, wasps contested your fruit with you, and you were lucky if you did not carry back a scorpion or a snake in your pocket. Then the company came in for its share of comment. So many people crept in that nobody knew, nobody acknowledged, and apparently nobody had invited. You always, they said, found that all your objectionable acquaintances dated from these parties. Lastly, they were excursions which no weather suited, no toilet became! If it were hot, the sufferings of sun-scorching and mosquitoes were insufferable. If it proved bad and rainy, they were in the sad situation of that very moment! As to dress, who could fix upon a costume to be becoming in the morning, graceful in the afternoon, and fresh and radiant at night? In a word, Kitty, they said so much, and so forcibly, that nothing but great constraint upon my feelings saved me from asking, "Why, in Heaven's name, could they have consented to come upon an excursion every detail of which was a sorrow, and every step a suffering?"

No other theme, however, divided attention with this calamitous one; and as we toiled languidly up the mountain side, you can fancy with what pleasant feelings the way was beguiled.

At last we reached the castle; but fresh disappointment here awaited us. Although parties were admitted to see the Schloss and the grounds, they could not obtain leave to dine anywhere within the precincts. We begged hard for a room in the porter's lodge, the laundry, the stable, even the hayloft! but all without success. We at length capitulated for a moss-house, where the rain came filtering down through a network of foliage and birds'-nests; but even this was refused. What was to be done? The army was now little short of mutiny; a violent debate was carried on from carriage windows; and strong partisans of particular opinions went slopping about, with tucked-up trousers and huge umbrellas, trying to enforce their own views! Some were for an equitable distribution of the eatables on the spot,— " Food Commissaries," as the Germans expressed it, being chosen, to allot the victuals to each coach; some were for a forcible entry into the castle, and an occupation by dint of arms; others voted for a return to Baden; and lastly, a small section, which gradually grew in power and persuasiveness, suggested that, by descending the opposite side of the mountain, we should reach a little inn in the Moorg Thal, much frequented by fishermen, and where we were sure to find shelter at least, if not something more. The " Anglers' Rest" was now adopted as our goal; and thither we started, with some slight tinge of renewed hope and pleasure.

Our journey *down* was nearly as slow as that *up* the mountain; for the steep descent required the greatest caution, with heavily laden and jaded horses. It was, therefore, already dark when we reached the " Anglers' Rest." All that I could see of this " hostel," from the rain-streaked glasses of the carriage, was a small one-storied house, built over the stream of a small but rapid river. Mountains, half wrapped in mists, and seeming to smoke with the steam of hot rain, environed the spot on all sides, which probably, in fine weather, would have been picturesque and even pretty.

" We are destined to be unlucky to-day, Princess," said a

young French marquis, approaching our carriage. "This miserable 'guinguette,' it seems, is full of people, who are by no means disposed to yield the place to us."

"Who are they, — what are they?" asked she, in haughty astonishment at their contumacy.

"They are, I believe, some young tradesfolk, on what is called in Germany the 'Wander-Jahre,' — that travelling probation that municipal law dictates to native handicraft."

"But, surely, when they hear who we are —"

"Graf Adelberger has been eloquently explaining that to them the last ten minutes, and the Baron von Badenschwill has told them of his eighteen quarterings; but though they have consented to drink his health, they will not abdicate the territory."

Here was a pretty proof of what the years '48 and '49 had done for the Continent of Europe, and maybe Blum, Kossuth, Mazzini, and Co., did n't come in for their share! To think of creatures — shoemakers, who could assure us they were, might be tailors — daring to proclaim that they preferred their own ease and comfort to that of carriages full of unknown but titled individuals!

"It 's impossible!" "Incredible!" "Fabulous!" "Infamous!" "Monstrous!" were expressions screamed from carriage to carriage, while telegraphic signs of horror and amazement were exchanged from window to window. "Did they know who we were?" "Do they know who I am?" were the questions incessantly pouring forth. Alas! they had heard it all. There was not a claim we could prefer to greatness that they had not before them, and, alas! they remained inexorable!

Deputations of various nations went in, and came back baffled and unsuccessful. The "Burschen," as they were called, were at that very moment impatiently waiting for their own supper, and seemed to verify the adage of the ill result of arguing with hungry men. Milder and more practicable counsels now began to prevail amongst us, and some even of the most conservative hinted at compromise and accommodation. What if we were to share with some of the vast abundance that we had with us? What if we tried bribery? The "Food Commissaries" assured us that even after the most liberal allowance for our wants we could feed a moderately sized village.

The proposal was therefore framed, and two Germans of high rank persuaded — sorely against their prejudices and inclination — to convey it to "Das Volk," — the populace. It seemed as though the memorable years I have referred to had taught some curious lessons in popular force; for the demands of the masses indicated strength and power. They stipulated, first, that they should hold the kitchen; secondly, that the meats assigned them should be set before them uncut; and lastly, that none of our servants were to be quartered on the table. Here was the "Monarchy of the Middle Classes" proudly enunciated; and, I assure you, many excellent things were said by all of us, — not only upon the past and the present, but on "what we were coming to!"

If I weary you with this detail, Kitty, it is that you may sympathize with me in the fatigue the long discussion inflicted. We were fully three-quarters of an hour at the door ere the treaty was concluded. Then came the descent from the carriages, the unpacking of the eatables, the unrolling of the life-mummies that were to consume them, which, wrapped up as they were in soaked drapery, was a long process. I shall not delay you with an account of the distribution of the proggery, but content myself with stating that the two deputies accredited by the "Trades'" union to receive their share, acknowledged that we behaved not only well, but with munificence; since not only did we bestow upon them the grosser material of a meal, but many of the higher refinements of a great entertainment; in particular, a large game pasty, representing a feudal fortress, with a flag waving over it, on which the enthusiastic cook had inscribed the words, "Hoch Lebe die Dodd," or "the Dodd forever." It was a vulgar dish, Kitty, and by my own special diplomacy was it consigned to the second table.

At length we were seated at table, but only for new disappointment. Milo, in telling off the band, had made the irreparable blunder of leaving all the flute, clarionet, and horn players behind; and there we were, with kettle-drums, trombones, and ophocleides enough to have stunned a garrison. They could beat a " générale," it is true, but there ended their orchestral powers. This stupid mistake, however, gave room for laughter, and, in spite of our annoyance, we laughed at it long and heartily.

I am spared the painful task of recording the catastrophe of our story, by a message from Mr. Cavendish, to say that the courier is starting. Indeed, his carriage is now at the door, and I must say, Kitty, that the handsomest men in our diplomacy are the Mercuries. They dress so becomingly too,— something between a hussar and Lord Byron; their pelisses of rich furs, their slashed frocks, and Polish caps harmonizing beautifully with their mingled air of intrepidity and gentleness.

Mr. Dudley Vignerton, who takes this, is remarkably good-looking,— something of George Canning, with a dash of Count d'Orsay. I wish, however, he would let me finish these few lines in peace, for he keeps on complimenting me about my hair, and my handwriting, and I don't know what besides. He offers also to bring me shoes from Paris, for really Germany is too bad!

He is a strange man, Kitty, and I regret not to see more of him; he looks at once so bland and so determined. He tells me that the adventurous nature of the life he leads makes a man at once daring and enduring, — about equal parts lamb and lion. Don't you wish to see him?

Yours, in great haste,

M. A. D.

LETTER XXXII.

JAMES DODD TO ROBERT DOOLAN, ESQ., TRINITY COLLEGE,
DUBLIN.

"The Fox," Lichtenthal.

My dear Bob, — I promised to give you the earliest intelligence of the governor's return; and this is to inform you
that the agreeable incident in question occurred on Wednesday last, accompanied, however, by circumstances which I
must call "atténuantes," that is to say, considerably im-
pairing the felicitous character of the event. We — that is,
the Dodd M'Carthy portion of the family, for so we had
already constituted ourselves — had organized a most stunning picnic; one of those entertainments which are the great
facts of the season, just as certain battles are the grand
incidents of a campaign: we had secured everything that
Baden contained of company and *cuisine*, and we did not
leave a turkey, a truffle, nor a titled individual in the whole
village.

La Mère Dodd had, in fact, resolved on one of those
great *coups de tête*, which, in the social as in the political
world, are needed to terminate a difficult position, and, as
the journalists say in France, "legitimize the situation."
How I love a phrase that permits one to escape the pettiness
of a personal detail by some grand and sweeping generality!

The picnic is to the fashionable world what a general
election is in that of politics. It is a brief orgie, in which
each condescends to acquaintanceship, or even intimacy,
without in the slightest degree pledging himself to future
consequences. You, as it were, pass out of the conventional
limits of ordinary life, and take a "day rule" for indiscretions. The natural consequence is that people will come
to you in this way that no efforts could seduce into your

house; and the great lady, who would scorn your attentions
on a Turkey carpet, will suffer you to carve her chicken,
and fill her champagne glass, when seated on the grass.
"Oh! I don't know him. I saw him somewhere, — on a
steamer, or at a picnic, perhaps." This spoken, with a
stare of ineffable unconcern, is the extent of the recognition
accorded to you after. At first, when you call to mind the
way you struggled to get her sherry, how you fought for the
lobster, and descended to actual meanness for the mustard,
you are disposed to fancy yourself the most injured, and
her the most ingrate of mankind; but you soon learn to perceive that this is the law of these cases, and that you are
not worse treated than your fellows.

I leave you to conjecture why we deemed a picnic an
essential stroke of policy. I assure you it was a question
well and maturely discussed in our cabinet. We knew it to
be a measure from which there was no retreating when once
entered upon; we also knew that the governor's return
would utterly render such a course impossible. It was now
or never with us. Would that it had been never! But to
proceed. Everything, even from the start, promised badly;
the day broke in torrents of rain; it was like one of those
days of Irish picnic at the "Dargle," where a drowned family
squat under a hedge to eat soaked sandwiches. We set out,
in bad humor, determined to "take our pleasure excursion"
under difficulties; a proceeding about as sensible as that of
a man who, having sprained his ankle on his way to a ball,
still insists upon waltzing. At Eberstein, where we had
purposed to dine, they would not admit us. It is a royal
residence, and although usually there was no permission necessary for parties wishing to pass the day there, an order
from the court had closed the castle against all picnicaries,
— a fact not made more palatable to us by the information
that it was the misconduct of some interesting individuals
of the family of the Simkins, the Popkins, or the Perkins,
which had provoked the edict in question. And here I must
say, Bob, — and I say it in deep sorrow, — that we are either
grossly calumniated abroad, or else very grievous faults
attach to us, since every scratched picture, every noseless
statue, every chipped relic, and every flawed marble is sure

of being assigned to the work of English fingers. I repeat,
I have no means of knowing if the accusation be wrongful
or not; at all events, I conclude it to be greatly exaggerated
beyond truth. If scratching and mutilating, "the chalking
and maiming acts" against works of art, be popular practices
of travellers generally, it follows that, as we English supply
a very large majority of the earth's vagabonds, a vast number of these offences must fall to our share; but I sincerely
hope we do not deserve our wholesale reputation, nor possess any exclusive patent for barbarism. I argue the point
as the priest used to do at home about Catholics and Protestants, when he triumphantly asked, "Why white-faced
sheep eat more than black-faced?" and having puzzled us
all, answered, "Because there are more of them!" And
that's the reason the English commit more breaches of
decorum than their neighbors. Rely upon it, Bob, the
simple illustration is very widely applicable; and whenever
you hear of our derelictions abroad, please to remember it.

As we could not gain admittance to Eberstein, it became
a grand subject of debate what to do. The prudent said,
"Go back." Is it not strange, Bob? but there is an almost
stereotyped uniformity in wise counsellors, and that whenever a difficulty arises in life, they all cry out, "Go back!"
I conclude that this is the whole secret of the Tory party,
and that all the reputation they have acquired of "safe,"
"prudent," and so forth, has no other basis than this simple
maxim. Upon the present occasion, "the Progresistas"
carried the day, — we went on!

A little wayside inn — the resort of a few summer visitors
— was to be our destination; but when we arrived there, it
was to find the house crammed with a most motley rabble,
— a set of those wandering artisans which, from some singular notion of her own upon the virtues of vagabondism,
Germany sends forth broadcast over her whole land; the
law requiring that each tradesman should travel for a year,
or, in some states, two years, before he can obtain permission from the municipality of his own town to reside at
home. Now, as these individuals are rarely or never persons of independent fortune, but rather of scanty and preca-
rious means, the "Wander-Jahre," as the year of travel is

called, is usually a series of events vibrating between
roguery and begging, and at all events little conducive to
those habits of orderly, patient industry which, in England at least, are deemed the highest qualities of a laboring
man.

Wherever you travel in Germany you are certain to find
droves of these people on the road, their heavy knapsacks
covered with an undressed calf-skin, and usually decorated
at either extremity by a Wellington boot, "pendant," but
not "proper," their long pipes and longer beards, their well-
tuned voices, — for they always sing, — and, lastly, their
unblushing appeals to your charity, proclaim them to be
"Lehre-Junge," or apprentices. But you must not fall into
the absurd mistake of one of our well-known English writers
on Germany, who has called them travelling students, and
thereupon moralized long and learnedly on the poverty of
life and the cheapness of education in that country. Occasionally, it is true, a student of the very humblest class will
associate himself with the "youths;" but even he will be
the exception, and the university to which he belongs one
of the very lowest in rank. I should ask your forgiveness
for this long and wide digression, my dear Bob, were it not
that I know that whenever I speak of matters which are
new and unfamiliar to you, I am at least as interesting as
by any purely personal history. You would like to hear a
thousand traits of foreign life and manners, far better than
I am capable of communicating them.

Our inn, as I have said, was full of these "gents," and
no persuasion of ours, no threats, nor any flatteries, could
induce them to vacate the territory in our favor. In fact,
they presumed to reason upon the case, on the absurd presumption that rain would wet and wind chill them, and positively resisted all our assurances to the contrary.

We ended by a compromise; they gave us the parlor, and
retired to the kitchen, we purchasing the concession by
sundry articles of consumption, such as fowls, ham, preserves, and a pasty, to be by them devoured as their own
proper and peculiar prog. The selection, which was made
by a special commission named by both sides, was rather
an amusing process, though probably prolonged a little

beyond the limits of ordinary patience. At length the
treaty was concluded, the price paid, the territory evacuated, and we sat down ourselves to table, I will not say in
the very happiest of humors, for throughout the whole of the
negotiation our pride and self-esteem were at each moment
receiving the very rudest buffets, princes, dukes, counts,
and barons as we were! It was a sore lesson we were acquiring; and as a great man of our party remarked, "The
canaille had apparently been taught little or nothing by
the last two years," — a fact not so difficult to entertain
when one remembers that those whose education is conducted by grape and musketry are seldom left to evidence
the advantages of the system, and the survivors are the
"naughty boys who have learned nothing."

Our first disappointment was rather a laughable one,
though certes in itself a bore. In the hurry of leaving
Baden, a selection of the town band of musicians was made,
as we had not carriage-room for the whole; but by ill-luck
it was the rejected we had taken, and there we were with
drums, cymbals, trombones, and an ophocleide, but not a
flute, flageolet, or a French horn! You may fancy the
attempt to perform the overture to "William Tell" with
such appliances. Crash after crash it went, drowned in our
own uproarious laughter, or louder cries of horror and disgust. We had scarcely rallied, some from the amusement,
others from the annoyance produced by this event, when a
tremendous uproar outside the door attracted our attention.
It sounded like an attempt being made to establish a forcible
entry into our apartment, and vigorous resistance offered.
So it proved, by the account of certain wounded and disabled who fell back to tell us of the affray. "The Trades"
were in reality in open insurrection, and marching upon us,
"headed," as the trombone said, "by a stout, elderly man
of savage appearance." To organize a resistance would
have been impossible, with countesses fainting on every
side, duchesses in hysterics. The men of our party, too,
avowed that without an armory of guns, pistols, and cut-
lasses they were powerless. As to smashing up a chair,
or seizing a table-leg, they had no idea of it; so that I saw
myself the only combatant in a room full of people, who,

by way of fitting me for my task, threw themselves around my neck and on my back in a fashion far more flattering than favorable.

By great exertions I wrested myself free from my "backers," and, bounding over the table with a formidable old tongs in my hand, I reached the door just as it gave way to the assaulting party, and came flat down off the hinges, discovering the forlorn hope of the enemy led on by — oh, shame and disgrace ineffable! — no other than my father himself! There he was, Bob, without his coat, with a large saucepan in one hand for a shield, and a kitchen cleaver in the other. He vociferously cheered on his followers to the breach. I own to you that, what with his patched and poor attire, his long beard, and his moustaches, I scarcely knew him. His voice, however, there was no mistaking; and, at the first word he uttered, I grounded my arms in surrender.

It turned out that some infernal device in pastry had communicated to him the intelligence that it was Mrs. D. was the entertainer of the gorgeous company, the crumbs from whose sumptuous table he and his friends were then consuming. Maddened with the indignity of *his* position, and outraged at *her* extravagance, he tossed off two tumblers of sherry to give him courage, and cried out to his partisans "to charge!" I have often heard that no description can convey even the faintest notion of the horrors of a town taken by assault. I now believed it. For the same good reason, you will not expect of me to portray what I own to be beyond my pictorial powers. I can, it is true, give you the ingredients, as Lord Macartney did those of a plum-pudding to the Chinese cook, but you must yourself know how to mingle and combine them. Take thirty ladies of various ages, from sixteen to sixty, and of all nations of Europe, with gents to match; throw them into strong convulsions of fright, horror, fun, or laughter, amidst smashed crockery, broken glass, upset viands, and drinkables; beat them up with some ten or twelve travellers of unwashed appearance, neither civil of speech nor ceremonious in conduct; dash the mixture with Dodd père in a state of frenzied passion, to which he gave short and *per saltum* utterance in such phrases as "Spitzbuben!" "Coquins!" "Canaille!" "Scoundrels!" "Gueux!" "Blackguards!" &c., — a vocabulary that, even without a labored context, seemed sufficiently intelligible. The company took Lady Macbeth's hint; they did n't stand upon the order of their going, "they went at once." I do not believe that a party ever separated with greater despatch and less useless ceremony. A few of the "greatly overcome" were, indeed, led out between friends, "unconscious;" but the mass fled with a laudable precipitancy, leaving the field to my father and the rest of the Dodd family, — a group, I beg to say, that nothing but a painter could properly render. That it may one day be thought worthy of a fresco, let me record it.

Foreground, and principal figure, Dodd père, seated Marius-like amidst the ruins, cravat in one hand, turban of a spoiled countess inadvertently grasped in the other; countenance strongly marked with intense perplexity, a kind of universal doubt of everything; prevailing impression of the figure, power, but power weakened by incredulity.

Middle distance, Mary Anne Dodd, dishevelled and weeping, gracefully draped, and the attitude well chosen.

Extreme distance, Dodd mère, seated on the floor, with a student's cap stuck on over her own toque, evidently horror-struck and unconscious, as seen by the wild stare of her eyes, and the half-open lips. Dodd fils, dimly detected in the shadow of left foreground, mixing brandy-and-water.

There 's the tableau; the smaller details are, a universal smashery, with occasional vestiges of that part of the creation consigned to hairdressers, tailors, and milliners, of which the ground displays various curious specimens, in scalps, fronts, ringlets, and tufts, scraps of lace, tuckers, and trinkets, with skirts of coats, cravats, and a false calf! Had these been all that the company left behind them, Bob, it might have been bearable; but, alas! they had bequeathed to us other relics, — their contempt, their very lowest contempt. Even my father's French was intelligible enough to show what he claimed, and what we could not deny him, to be. You can fancy, therefore, the impression they must have conceived of us!

One of the worst features of this unlucky occurrence was that it happened at Baden. Baden is, so to say, one of those great banking-houses at which a note is sure to be presented at some period or other of its circulation, and here we were now, — declared a "forgery," pronounced "not negotiable."

These were the bitter thoughts which each of us had now to revolve in secret, tormenting our several ingenuities to find a remedy for the evil. The governor was apparently the first of us to rally, for he turned round at last to the table, cleared a small spot for his operations at a corner, helped himself to some of a game pie, and began to eat like one who had not relished such delicacies for some time back.

"May I give you a glass of champagne, sir?" said I, seeing that he was "going in" with an air of determination.

"With all my heart," responded he; "but I think you might as well open a fresh bottle." I did so, Bob, and followed it by another, of which I partook also.

"There are some excellent fellows out there in the kitchen," said the governor. "There is a little lame tailor from Anspach, and an ivory-turner from the town of Lindau, both as agreeable companions as ever I journeyed with. Take them out that pie, James, and let the waiter fetch them half a dozen bottles of this red wine. Pay Jacob — he's the tailor — four florins that I borrowed from him; and beg of Herman, a little Jewish rogue, with an Astracan cap, to keep my tobacco-bag, out of remembrance of me. Tell the assembled company that I'll see them all by and by, for at present I have some family affairs to look after. Be civil and courteous with them, James, they all have been so to me; and if you'll sit down at the table for half an hour, and converse with them, take my word for it, boy, you'll not rise to go away without being both wiser and humbler."

I set about my mission with a willing heart. I was glad to do anything which should give the governor even a momentary satisfaction; and I was well pleased, also, to mark the calm, dispassionate tone of his language.

The "Lehr-Jungen" received me with a most respectful

courtesy, in which, however, there was not the very slightest taint of subserviency or meanness. They showed me that they really felt kindly, and even affectionately, towards my father, who had been their companion for the last nine days on foot. They enjoyed in a high degree the dry humor which he possesses, and they relished his remarks on the country, and the people, through which they travelled, savoring as they did of a caustic shrewdness perfectly new to them. In fact, I soon saw that his frank temperament, enriched by that native quaintness every Irishman has his share of, had made him a prime favorite with them, and they were equally disposed to be flattered by his acquaintance-ship as attached to himself. I sat with them till past midnight. Indeed, when I heard that our family had ordered bedrooms and retired for the night, I was not sorry to dissipate my cares, even in much humbler society than I had left home to foregather with.

It is not necessary I should make any confession to you of my unlettered ignorance, nor own how deplorably deficient I am in every branch of knowledge or acquirement. I was a stupid schoolboy, and an idle one, and the result is not very difficult to imagine; and yet, with all these disadvantages, I have a lazy man's craving for information, if I only could obtain it easily. I'd like to be cured, if the doctor would only make the physic palatable. Now, will you believe me, Bob, when I say that these poor travelling tradesfolk, patched and threadbare as they were, talked upon subjects of a very high character, and discussed them, too, with a shrewdness and propriety perfectly astonishing? I had been living in Germany for some six or eight months, and yet now, for the first time, did I hear mention made of the popular literature of the day, — who were the writers most in vogue, and what modifications public taste was undergoing, and how the mystical and the imaginative were giving way before a practical common-sense and common-place spirit more adapted to the exigencies of our age. This, I must observe, they entirely ascribed to the influence of England, which they described as being paramount on the Continent since the peace. Not alone that the vast hordes of our nation flooded every land of Europe, but

that our mechanical arts, our inventions, and our literature
pervaded every nook and crevice of the Continent.

As the tailor said, "It is not alone that we conform to
your notions in dress, and endeavor to make our coats loose
and square-skirted, to look English, but there is an Anglo-
mania in all things, even where we will not confess it.   Our
novelists, too, have followed the fashion, and instead of
those dreamy conceptions, where the possible and impossible were always in conflict, we have now domestic stories,
ay, even before we have domesticity itself."

I do not quote my friend Jacob for anything remarkable
in the sentiment itself, though I believe it to be just and
true; but to show the general tone of a conversation maintained for hours by a set of poor artisans, not one of whom
would not be well contented could he earn a shilling a day.

Perhaps you will ask me, if, in their several trades, these
fellows were the equals of our own?   In all probability they
were not.   The likelihood is, they were greatly inferior, as
in every detail of the useful and the practical Germany is
far behind us; but it is strange to speculate on what such a
people may or might become, if their institutions should
ever conform to the development of their natural intelligence.   This, again, is the tailor's remark, — and I could
"cabbage" from him for hours together.

I thought a hundred times of *you*, Bob.   How *you* would
have enjoyed this strange fraternity.   What amusement —
not to say something better and higher — you would have
abstracted from them.   What traits of native humor, —
what studies of character!   As for *me*, much, by far the
greater part, was lost upon me for want of previous knowledge of the subjects they discussed.   Of the kingdoms
whose politics they canvassed I scarcely knew the names;
of the books, I had not even heard the titles!   I have no
doubt many of their opinions were incorrect; much of what
they uttered might have been illogical or inaccurate; but
making a wide allowance for this, I was struck by the
general acuteness of their remarks, and the tone of moderation and forbearance that characterized all they said.

This brief intercourse has at least taught me one thing, —
which is not to look down with any depreciating pity on the

troops of these wayfarers we pass on the road, still less to ridicule their absurd appearance, or make a jest of their varied costume. I now know that amidst those motley figures are men of shrewd intelligence and cultivated minds, content to follow the very humblest callings, and quite satisfied if their share of this world's good things never rises higher than black bread and a cup of sour wine. I should like greatly to see something more of the gypsy life they lead, and if ever the opportunity offer, shall certainly not suffer it to escape me.

We left the inn of the Moorg Thal at daybreak, my mother and Mary Anne in one carriage, the governor and myself in a little open calèche. He spoke little, and seemed deep in thought all the way. From an occasional expression he dropped, I dreaded to surmise that he had resolved on returning to Ireland. One remark which he made of more than ordinary bitterness was: " If we go on as we are doing, we shall at length close every town of Europe against us. We left Brussels in shame, and now we quit Baden in disgrace: the sooner this ends the better."

We did not proceed the whole way to Baden, but stopped about a mile from it, at a village called Lichtenthal, where we found a comfortable inn, with moderate charges. From this I was despatched to our hotel, after nightfall, to arrange our affairs, settle our bill, fetch away our baggage, and make all necessary arrangements for departure.

I am free to own that I entered on my mission with no common sense of shame. I knew, of course, how our story had by this time become the table-talk of Baden, and how, from the prince to the courier, " the Dodds" were the only topic. Such notoriety as this is no boon, and I confess, Bob, that I believe I could have submitted my hand to the knife with less shrinking of the spirit than I raised it to pull the door-bell of the Hôtel de Russie.

When a man has to encounter an anticipated humiliation, he usually puts on an extra amount of offensive armor. I suppose mine, on this occasion, must have been of unquestionable strength, None seemed willing to put it to the proof. The host was humble, — the waiters cringing, — the very porter fawned on me! The secretary — at your flash hotels abroad they always have a secretary, usually a Pole, who has an immense estate under sequestration somewhere, — this dread functionary, who, in presenting you the bill, ever gives you to understand that he is quite prepared to afford you personal satisfaction for any item in the score, — even he, I say, was bland, courteous, and gentle. I little knew at the moment to what circumstance I owed all this unexpected politeness, and that this silky courtesy was a very different testimony from what I suspected; it being neither more nor less than the joyful astonishment of the household at seeing one of us again, and an amazement, rising to enthusiastic delight, at the bare possibility of our paying our bill! Already in their estimation the "Dodd family" had been pronounced swindlers, and various speculations were abroad as to the value of the several trunks, imperials, and valises we had left behind us.

My mother, in her abject misery, — you may imagine the amount of it from the circumstance, — had given me her bank-book, with full liberty to deal with the balance in her favor. In fact, such was her dread of encountering one of her former acquaintances, that I verily believe she would have agreed to an exile to Siberia rather than pass one more week at Baden. Our bill was a swingeing one. With all the external show of politeness, I plainly saw that they treated us just as Napoleon used to treat a conquered nation whose imputed misconduct had outlawed it! For *us* there was no appeal; *we* could not threaten the indignation of powerful friends, — the terrors of fashionable exposure, — not even the hackneyed expedient of a letter in the "Times"! Alas! we had ceased to be "reasonable and sufficient bail" for any statement.

Such charges never were seen before, I'd swear. Dinners and suppers figured as unimportant matters. It was the "extraordinaries" that ruined us; for your hotel-keeper is obliged, for very shame's sake, to observe a semblance of decorum in his demands for recognized items. It is in the indefinable that he revels; just as your geographer indulges every caprice of his imagination when laying down the limits of land and water at the Pole!

It would not amuse, nor could it instruct you, were I to

give the details of this iniquitous demand. I shall therefore spare you all, save the grand fact of the total, wherein
something less than six weeks' living of four people, with as
many servants, amounts to a fraction under three hundred
pounds sterling! Meanwhile, the price of rooms, breakfasts,
beds, &c., were all reasonable enough. It was "Éclairage,"
" Service," " Réceptions, Mardi," "Mercredi," and " Jeudi."
These were the heavy artillery, to which all the rest was a light-
dropping fire. This bill-settling is indeed an awful process;
for when you rally from the first horror-stricken feelings that
the sum total calls up, and are blandly asked by the smirking
secretary, " To what is it that Monsieur objects?" you are
totally powerless and prostrated. Your natural impulse would
be to say, " To the whole of it, — to that infamous row of
figures at the bottom! "

In all probability, you never made an hotel bill in your
life. The wretches know this, and they feel the full force
of your unhappy situation. Just fancy a surgeon saying,
" What particular part of the operation do you dislike,
sir? It can't be the first incision; I made it in Cooper's
method, — one sweep of the knife. You surely have no
complaint about the arteries, — I took them up in eighteen
seconds by a stop-watch." " What do I care for all this?"
you answer. " I know nothing about science, but I am fully
open to the impression of pain." Nothing, however, kills me
like the fellow saying, " If Monsieur thinks the lemonade too
dear, we 'll take off half a franc." Two-and-sixpence deducted from a bill of three hundred pounds!

I went through all this, and more. I went through special
appeal cases, from twenty subordinates, on peculiar infrac-
tions of broken heads, smashed crockery, and damaged furniture, which each assured me in turn " would be charged
against *him*," if Monsieur had not the " honorable consideration " — that 's the formula — to pay it. I satisfied some,
I compromised with others; I resisted none. No, Bob.
There was no " locus standi," as you would call it, for
opposition. None of the Dodds could come into court,
and claim to be heard as witnesses.

This agreeable function concluded, I drove off to the Police
Commissary about our passport. The " authorities " had fin-

ished the duties of the day. The bureau was closed. I asked
where the "authorities" lived, and was told the street and
the number. I went there, but the "authorities" were at
their *café*. They liked "their dominos and their beer;"
and why should they not have their weaknesses?

I hastened to the *café;* not one of those brilliantly
decorated and lighted establishments where foreigners of
all nations foregather, but a dim-looking, musty, sanded-
floored, smoke-dried den, filled with a company to suit.
There was that mysterious half-light, and that low whispering sound which seemed to form a fit atmosphere for spies
and eavesdroppers, of which I need scarcely tell you government officials are composed.

By the guidance of the waiter, I reached the table where
the Herr von Schureke was seated at his dominos. He was
a beetle-browed, scowling, ill-conditioned-looking gent of
about fifty, who had a trick of coughing a hard dry cough
between every word he uttered.

"Ah," said he, after I explained the object of my visit,
"you want your passport. You wish to leave Baden, and
you come here, to give your orders to the Polizey Beamten
as if you were the Grand-Duke!"

I deprecated this intention in my politest German; but he
went on.

"Es geht nicht" — literally, "It's no go" — "my worthy
friend. We are not the officials of England. We are
Badeners. We are the functionaries of an independent
sovereign. You can't bully us here with your line-of-battle
ships, your frigates, and bomb-boats."

"No. Gott bewahr!" echoed the company; "that will
do elsewhere, — but Baden is free!"

The enthusiasm the sentiment evoked brought all the
guests from the several tables to swarm around us.

I assured the meeting that Cobden and Co. were not
more pacifically minded than I was; that as to anything
like threat, menace, or insolence towards the Grand-Duchy,
it never came within thousands of miles of my thoughts; that
I came to make the civilest of requests, in the very humblest
of manner; and if by ill-luck the distinguished functionary

I had the honor to address should not deem either the time opportune, or the place suitable —

" You 'll make it an affair for your House of Commons," broke he in.

" Or your ' Ti-mes ' newspaper ! " cried another, converting the title of the Thunderer into a strange dissyllable.

" Or your Secretary of State will tell us that you are a ' Civis Romanus,' " wheezed out a small man, that I heard was Archivist of something, somewhere.

" Britannia rule de waves, but do not rule de Grand-Duchy," muttered a fourth, in English, to show that he was thoroughly imbued, not alone with our language, but the spirit of our Constitution.

" Really, gentlemen," said I, " I am quite at a loss for any reason for this audible outburst of nationality. I disclaim the very remotest idea of offending Baden, or anything belonging to it. I entertain no intention of converting my case into a question of international dispute. I simply wait my passport, and free permission to leave the Grand-Duchy and all belonging to it."

This declaration was unanimously pronounced insolent, offensive, and insulting; and a vast number of unpleasant remarks poured down upon England and Englishmen, which, I need not tell you, are not worth repetition. The end of all was that I lost temper too, — the wonder is how I kept it so long, — and ventured to hint that people of my country had sometimes the practice of righting themselves, when wronged, instead of tormenting their Government or pestering the " Times " newspaper; and that if they had any curiosity as to the *how*, I should be most happy to favor any one with the information that would follow me into the street.

There was a perfect Babel of angry vociferation as I said this; the meaning of which I might guess, though the words were unintelligible; and as I issued forth into the street, expressions of angry indignation and insult were actually showered upon me. I reached Lichtenthal late at night; the governor was in bed, and I hastened to " report myself " to him. This done, I sat down to give you this full narration of our doings; and only regret that I must conclude without telling you anything of our future plans, of which I know actually nothing. I should have spared you the uninteresting scene with the authorities, if you had not asked me, in your last, "Whether the respect felt towards England by every foreign nation did not invest the travelling Englishman with many privileges and immunities unknown to others?" I have heard that such was once the case. I believe, indeed, there was a time that any absurdity or excess of John Bull would have been set down as mere eccentricity, — a dash of that folly ascribable to our insular tastes and habits; but this is all changed now! Partly from our own conduct, in part from real and sometimes merely imputed acts of our rulers, and partly from the tone of our Press, which no foreigner can ever be brought to understand aright, we have got to be thought a set of spendthrift, wealthy, reckless misers, lavish and economical by turns, socially proud and exclusive, but politically red republican and levelling, — tyrants in our families, and democrats in the world; in fact, a sort of living mass of contradictory qualities, not rendered more endurable by coarse tastes and rude manners! This, at least, Morris told me, and he is a shrewd observer, like many of those sleepy-eyed, quiet "coves" one meets with. Not that he reads individuals like Tiverton! No: George is unequalled in ready dissection of a man's motives, and will detect a dodge before another begins to suspect it. I wish he were back; I feel frequently so helpless without his counsel and advice. The turf is, surely, a wonderful school for sharpening a man's faculties, and it gives you the habit of connecting words with motives, and asking yourself, "What does So-and-so mean by that?" "What is he up to now?" that at last you decipher character, let its lines be written in the very faintest ink!

Our post leaves at daybreak, so that I shall just have time for this. When I write next, I'll answer — that is, if I can — all your questions about myself, what I mean to do, and when to begin it.

Not, indeed, that they are themes I like to touch upon, for somehow all the quiet pursuits of life look wonderfully slow and tiresome affairs in comparison with the panoramic effects of travel. The perpetual change of scene, actors, and incidents supplies in itself that amount of excitement which, under other circumstances, calls for so much exertion and effort. There is another thing, also, which has always given me great discouragement. It is that the humbler walks of life require not only an amount of labor, but of actual ability, that are never called for in higher positions. Think of the work a fellow does as a doctor or a lawyer; and think of the brains, too, he has to bring to these careers, and then picture to yourself a man in a Government situation, some snug colonial governorship, or something at home, — say, he 's Secretary-at-War, or has something in the household. He writes his name at the foot of an occasional report or a despatch, and he puts on his blue ribbon, or his grand cross, as it may be, on birthdays. There 's the whole of it! As Tiverton says, " One needs more blood and bone nowadays for the hack stakes than the Derby; " he means, of course, in allusion to real life, and not to the turf! Don't fancy that I take it in ill part any remarks you make upon my idleness, nor its probable consequences. We are old friends, Bob; but even were we not, I accept them as sincere evidence of true interest and regard, though I may not profit by them as I ought. The Dodds are an impracticable race, and in nothing more so than by fully appreciating all their faults, and yet never making an effort for their eradication.

Some people are civil enough to say how very Irish this is; but I think it is only so in half, inasmuch as our perceptions are sharp enough to show us even in ourselves those blemishes which your blear-eyed Saxon would never have discovered anywhere. Do you agree with me? Whether or not, my dear Bob, continue to esteem and believe me ever your affectionate friend,

JAMES DODD.

Though I am totally innocent as to our future, it is better not to write till you hear again from me, for of course we shall leave this at once; but where for? that 's the question.

LETTER XXXIII.

KENNY JAMES DODD TO MR. PURCELL, OF THE GRANGE, BRUFF.

MY DEAR TOM, — I am not in a humor for letter-writing,
nor, indeed, for anything else that I know of. I am sick,
sore, and sorry, — sick of the world, sore in my feet, and
sorry of heart that I ever consented to come out upon this
touring expedition, every step and mile of which is marked
by its own misery and misfortune. I got back — I won't
say home, for it would be an abuse of the word — on
Wednesday last. I travelled all the way on foot, with something less than one-and-fourpence English for my daily expenses, and arrived to find my wife entertaining, at a picnic,
all Baden and its vicinity, with pheasants and champagne
enough to feast the London Corporation, and an amount of
cost and outlay that would have made Dodsborough brilliant during a whole Assizes.

I broke up the meeting, perhaps less ceremoniously than
a Cabinet Council is dissolved at Osborne House, where the
Ministers, after luncheon, embark — as the "Court Journal"
tells — on board the "Fairy," to meet the express train for
London: valuable facts, that we never weary of reading! I
routed them without even reading the Riot Act, and saw
myself "master of the situation;" and a very pretty situation it was.

Now, Tom, when the best of two evils at a man's choice
is to expose his family as vulgar pretenders and adventurers,
— to show them up to the fine world of their fashionable
acquaintances as a humbug and a sham, — let me tell you
that the other side of the medal cannot have been very
attractive. This was precisely the case here. "It is not
pleasant," said I to myself, "to bring all the scandal and
slander of professional bad tongues upon an unfortunate

family, but ruin is worse still!" There was the whole sum
and substance of my calculation, — "Ruin is worse still!"
The picnic cost above a hundred pounds; the hotel expenses
at Baden amounted to three hundred more; there are bills
to be paid at nearly every shop in the town; and here we
are, economizing, as usual, at a large hotel, at, to say the
least, the rate of some five or six pounds per day. That I
am able to sit down and write these items in a clear and
legible hand, I take to be as fine an example of courage as
ever was given to the world. Talk of men in a fire — an
earthquake — a shipwreck — or even the "last collision on
the South-Eastern" — I give the palm to the man who can
be calm in the midst of duns, and be *collected* when his
debts cannot be. To be credited when you can no longer
pay, — to drink champagne when you have n't small change
for small beer, is enough to shake the boldest nerves; it is
exactly like dancing on a tight rope, from which you know
in your heart you must ultimately come down with a crash.

When one reads of any sudden calamity having befallen a
man who has incurred voluntary peril, the natural question
at once rises, "What did he want to do? What was he
trying for?" Now, suppose this question to be addressed
to the Dodd family, and that any one should ask, "What
did we want to do?" I am sadly afraid, Tom, that we
should be puzzled for the answer. I have no doubt that my
wife would sustain a long and harassing cross-examination
before the truth would come out. I am well aware of all
the specious illusions she would evoke, and what sagacious
notions she would scatter about education, accomplishments,
modern languages, and maybe — mother-like — great matches
for the girls, but the truth would out, at last, — we came
abroad to be something — whatever it might be — that we
could n't be at home; we changed our theatre, that we might
take a new line of parts. We wanted, in short, to be in a
world that we never were in before, and we have had our
wish. I am not going to rail at fashionable life and high
society. I am sure that, to those brought up in their ways,
they are both pleasant and agreeable; but they never were
our ways, and we were too old when we began to learn
them. The grand world, to people like us, is like going up

Mont Blanc, — fatigue, peril, expense, injury to health, and ruin to pocket, just to have the barren satisfaction of saying, "I was up there last August — I was at the top in June." "What did you get for your pains, Kenny Dodd? What did you see for all the trouble you had? Are you wiser?" "No." "Are you happier?" "No." "Are you better informed?" "No." "Are you pleasanter company for your old friends?" "No." "Are you richer?" "Upon my conscience, I am not! All I know is, that we were there, and that we came down again." Ay, Tom, there's the moral of the whole story, — we came *down* again! Had we limited our ambition, when we came abroad, to things reasonably attainable, — had we been satisfied to know and to associate with people like ourselves, — had we sought out the advantages which certainly the Continent possesses in certain matters of taste and accomplishment, we might have got something, at least, for our money, and not paid too dearly for it. But, no; the great object with us seemed always to be, swimming for our lives in the great ocean of fashion. And, let me tell you a secret, Tom; this grovelling desire to be amongst a set that we have no pretension to, is essentially and entirely English. No foreigner, so far as I have seen, has the vulgar vice of what is called "tuft-hunting." When I see my countrymen abroad, I am forcibly reminded of what I once witnessed at a show of wild beasts. It was a big cage full of monkeys, that were eating their dinner at a long trough, but none of them would taste what was before himself, but was always eating out of his neighbor's dish. It gave them the oddest look in the world; but it is exactly what you see on the Continent; and I'll tell you what fosters this taste more strongly than all. Our titled classes at home are a close borough, that men like you and myself never trespass upon. We see a lord as we see a prize bull at a cattle show, once and away in our lives; but here the aristocracy is plentiful, — barons, counts, and even princes abound, and can be obtained at the "shortest notice, and sent to any part of the town." Think of the fascination of this; fancy the delight of a family like the Dodds, surrounded with dukes and marquises!

One of the very first things that strikes a man on coming

abroad is the abundance of that kind of fruit that we only see at home in our hot-houses. Every ragged urchin is munching a peach or a melon, and picking the big grapes off a bunch that he speedily flings away. The astonishment of the Englishman is great, and he naturally thinks it all paradise. But wait a bit. He soon discovers that the melon has no more flavor than a mangel-wurzel, and that the apricot tastes like a turnip radish. If they are plenty, they are totally deficient in every excellence of their kind; and it is just the same with the aristocracy. The climate is favorable to them, and the same sun and soil rears princes and ripens pineapples; but they 're not like our own, Tom, — not a bit of it. Like the fruit, they are poor, sapless, tasteless productions, and the very utmost they do for you is to give you a downright indifference to the real article. I know how it reads in the newspapers, in a letter dated from some far-away land, on a Christmas-day, — "As I write, my window is open; the garden is one sea of blossoms, and the perfume of the rose and the jasmine fills the room." Just the same is the effect of those wonderful paragraphs of distinguished and illustrious guests at Mrs. Somebody's *soirée*. They are the common products of the soil, and they do not rise to the rank of luxuries with even the poor! Don't mistake me; I am not depreciating what is called high society, no more than I would condemn a particular climate. All that I would infer is, simply, that it does not suit *my* constitution. It 's a very common remark, how much more easily women conform to the habits and customs of a class above their own than men, and, so far as I have seen, the observation is a just one; but, let me tell you, Tom, the price they pay for this same plastic quality is more than the value of the article, for they lose all self-guidance and judgment by the change. Your quietly disposed, domestic ones turn out gadders, your thrifty housekeepers grow lavish and wasteful, your safe and cautious talkers become evil speakers and slanderers. It is not that these are the characteristics of the new sect they have adopted, but that, like all converts, they always begin their imitation with the vices of the faith they conform to, and by way of laying a good foundation, they start from the bottom!

If I say these things in bitterness, it is because I feel them in sincerity. Poor old Giles Langrishe used to say that all the expenses of contested elections, all the bribery and treating, all the cost of a Parliamentary life, would never have embarrassed him, if it was n't for his wife going to London. "It was n't only what she spent," said he, "while there; but Molly brought Piccadilly back with her to the county Clare! She turned up her nose at all our old neighbors, because they did n't know the Prussian ambassador, or Chevalier Somebody from the Brazils. The only man that could fit her in shoes lived in Bond Street; and as to getting her hair dressed, except by a French scoundrel that made wigs for the aristocracy, it was clearly impossible." And I 'll tell you another thing, Tom, our wives get a kind of smattering of political knowledge by this trip to town, that makes them unbearable. They hear no other talk all the morning than the cant of the House and the slang of the Lobby. It 's a dodge of Sir James, or a sly trick of Lord John, that forms the gossip at breakfast; and all the little rogueries of political life, all the tactics of party, are discussed before them, and when they take to that line of talk they become perfectly odious.

Have n't they their own topics? Is n't dancing, dress, the drama, enough for them, I ask? — without even speaking of divorce cases, — that they won't leave bills, motions, and debates to their husbands? Whenever I see Mrs. Roney, of Bally Roney, or Mrs. Miles MacDermot, of Castle Brack, in the "Morning Post," among the illustrious company at Lady Wheedleham's party, I say to myself, "I wish your neighbors joy of you when you go home again, that 's all!"

And yet all this would have been better for me than this coming abroad! I might have been member for Bruff for half the cost of this unlucky expedition! And this was economy, forsooth! Do you know how much we spent, hard cash, since March last? I am fairly ashamed to tell you, Tom; and though money lies mighty close to my heart, I don't regret the loss as much as I do that of many a good trait that we brought away with us, and have contrived to lose on the road. All this running about the world, this eternal change of place and people, imparts such an "Old Soldierism," if I may make the word, to a family, that they lose all that quiet charm of domesticity that forms the fascination of a home.

Fathers and mothers are worldly, as a matter of course. It comes upon them just like chronic rheumatism, or baldness, or any other infirmity of time and years, but it's hateful to see young people calculating and speculating; planning for this, and plotting for that. You ask, perhaps, "What has this to do with foreign travel?" and I say, "Everything." Your young lady that has polka'd at Paris, galloped up the Rhine, waltzed at Vienna, and bolero'd at Madrid, has about as much resemblance to an English or Irish girl brought up at home as the show-off horse of a circus has to a thoroughbred hunter. It's all training and teaching, — very graceful, perhaps, and pretty to look at, — but only fit for display, and worth nothing without lamps, sawdust, and spectators. Now, these things are not native to us, partly from climate, partly from old habit, prejudice, and natural inclination. We like to have a home. Our fireside has a kind of religious estimation in our eyes, associated as it is with that family grouping that includes everything from two years and a half to eighty, — from the pleasant prattle of infancy to the harmless murmurings of grandpapa. The foreigner — I don't care of what nation, they are all alike — has no idea of this. His own house to him is only one remove above a prison. He has little light, and less fire; neither comfort nor companionship! For him, life means society, plenty of well-dressed people, handsome *salons*, wax-lights, movement, bustle, and confusion, the din of five hundred tongues that only wag for scandal, and the sparkle of eyes that are only brilliant for wickedness.

These foreigners are really wonderful people, so frivolous about all that is grave or serious, so sober-minded in every folly and absurdity, we never rightly understand them, and that is one reason why all our imitation of them is so ludicrous.

Have you ever seen a fellow in a circus, Tom, whose feat was to jump from a horse's back through some half-dozen

hoops a little bigger than his body? He has kept this performance for his finish, for it is his *chef d'œuvre*, and he
wants to "sink in full glory resplendent." Somehow or
other, though, he can't summon up pluck for the effort.
Now the horse goes wrong leg, now it's the fault of the
fellows that hold the hoops, now the pace is not fast
enough; in fact, nothing goes right with him, and there he
spins round and round, wishing with all his heart it was
done and over. I'm pretty much in the same plight this
moment, Tom, at least as regards hesitation and indecision;
for while I have been rambling on about foreign life and
manners, my mind was full of a very different theme; but
from downright shame have I kept off it, for I'm tired of
recording all our miseries and misfortunes. Here goes,
however, for the spring,—I can't defer it any longer.

Since I came back, I have n't exchanged ten words with
Mrs. D. It is an armed truce between us, and each stands
ready, and only waiting for the attack. If, however, I consign to oblivion all remembrance of *her* extravagance, the
chance is that she is to keep blind to my infidelity! In a
word, the picnic and Mrs. G. are to be buried together.
Of course the terms of our convention prevented my learning much of the family doings in my absence. Even had
I moved for any papers or correspondence on the subject, I
should have been met by a flat refusal; and, in fact, I was
left, the way poor Curran used to say of himself, to pick up
my facts from the opposite counsel's statement. I was not
long destined to the bliss of ignorance. Such a hurricane
of bills and accounts I never withstood before. James,
however, by what arts of flattery I know not, succeeded in
getting hold of his mother's bank-book, and went out, a few
evenings ago, and paid everything; and, that we might
escape at once from this den of iniquity, went immediately
to the Prefecture for our passport. The Commissary was at
his *café*, whither James followed him, and, somehow or
other, an angry discussion got up between them, and they
separated, after exchanging something that was not the
compliments of the season.

I'm so used to rows and shindies that I went fast asleep
while he was telling me of it; but the following morning I

was to have a jog to my memory that I did n't expect, —
no less than two gendarmes, with their carbines on their
arms, having arrived to escort me to the "Bureau of the
Police." I dressed accordingly, and set out alone; for
although James might have been useful in many ways, I
was too much afraid of his rashness and hot temper to take
him. We arrived before the door was open, and spent
twenty minutes in the street, surrounded by a mixed assemblage, who commented upon me and my supposed crime
with great freedom and impartiality.

After another long wait in a dirty ante-room, I was
ushered into a large chamber, where the great functionary
was seated at a table covered with papers, and at a smaller
one, close by, sat what I perceived to be his clerk, or private
secretary. Of course I imagined it was for something that
James had said the previous evening that I was thus
arraigned, and though I thought it was like reading the
passage in the Decalogue backwards, to make the father
suffer for the children, I resolved to be patient and submissive throughout.

"Your name?" said the Commissary, bluntly, but never
offering me a seat, nor even noticing my "Good-morning."

"Dodd," said I, as shortly.

"Christian name?"

"Kenny James."

"Where born?"

"At Bruff, in Ireland."

"How old?"

"Upwards of fifty, — not certain for a year, more or
less."

"Religion?"

"Catholic."

"Married or single?"

"Married."

"With children, — how many?"

"Three, — a boy and two girls."

"Do you follow any trade or profession?"

"No."

"Living upon private means?"

"Yes."

These, and a vast number of similar queries — they filled five sheets of long post — followed, touching where we came from, how we had travelled, our object in the journey, and twenty things of the like kind, till I began to feel that the examination in itself was not a small penalty for a light transgression. At last, after a close scrutiny into all my family matters, my money resources, and my habits, he entered upon another chapter, which I own I thought was pushing the matter rather far, by saying, "Apparently, Herr Dodd, you are one of those who think that the monarchies of Europe are obsolete systems of government, ill suited to the spirit and requirements of the age. Is it not so?"

If I had only a moment's time for reflection, I should have said, "What is it to you how I think on these subjects? I don't belong to your country, and will render no account of my private sentiments to you;" but, unfortunately, a discussion on politics is always "nuts" to me, — I can't resist it, — and in I went, with that kind of specious generality that lays down a broad and wide foundation for any edifice you like afterwards to rear.

"Kings," said I, "are pretty much like other men,— good, bad, or indifferent, and, like other men, they are not bettered by being left to the sway of their own unbridled passions and tempers. Wherever, therefore, there is no constitution to bind them, the chances are that they make ducks and drakes of their subjects."

I must tell you, Tom, that we conducted our interview in English, which the Commissary spoke fluently.

"The divine right of kings, then, you utterly overlook?"

"I deny it, — I laugh it to scorn," said I. "Look at the fellows we see on thrones, — one is a creature fit for Bedlam; another ought to be in Norfolk Island. If they possessed any of this divine right you talk of, should we have seen them scuttling away as they did the other day, because there was a row in their capitals?"

"That will do, — quite enough," said he, stopping me short. "Your sentiments are sufficiently clear and explicit. You are a worthy disciple of your friend Gauss."

"I never heard of him till now," said I.

"Nor of Isaac Henkenstrom? — nor Reichard Blitzler? — nor Johann von Darg?"

"Not one of them."

"This you swear?"

"This I swear," said I, firmly; but the words were not well out, when the door was opened at a signal made by the Commissary, and an old man, with a very white beard and in shabby black, was led forward.

"Do you know the Herr Professor now?" asked the Commissary of me.

"No," said I, stoutly, — "never saw him before."

"Bring in the others," said he; and, to my astonishment, came forward three of the young fellows I had travelled with on foot from Saxony, but whose names I had not heard, or, if I heard, had forgotten.

"Are these men known to you?" asked the Prefect, with a sneer.

"Yes," said I; "we travelled in company for some days."

"Ah! you acknowledge them at last?" said he, "although you swore you had never seen them."

"Are you so stupid," said I, "as not to distinguish between a man's knowledge of an individual and his remembrance of a name?"

"You yourself might be a puzzle in that respect," replied he, not heeding my taunt. "You assumed one appellation at Bonn, another at Ems, and your family are living under a third here."

"I deny it!" cried I, indignantly.

"Here's the proof," said he. "Is this your wife's handwriting? 'Mrs. Dodd M'Carthy requests the favor of having two gendarmes stationed at the hotel on each Wednesday evening, to keep order in the line of carriages at her receptions.' Is that authentic?"

What a shell exploded beneath me, as I saw that I was tracked by the spies of the police from town to village up the Rhine, and half across Germany! The three youths with whom I was confronted were already condemned to prison. One had a tobacco bag, with a picture of Blum on it; the other was detected with a case-knife, whose blade exceeded the regulation length by half an inch; and the third was heard to say, "Germany forever," as he tossed off a tumbler of beer; and I was the associate and trusted comrade of this combined Socialism and Democracy. It came out that amongst our fraternity of the road there had been a paid spy of the police, who kept a regular journal of all our wayside conversation; and from the singularity of an Englishman's presence in such a party, it was inferred that his object was to spread those infamous doctrines by which it is now well known England sustains her position in Europe.

The absurdity I could laugh at, but there were some things in the matter not to be treated lightly. With my name at Ems they had no possible concern. Ems was in Nassau, not Baden. What could have persuaded my wife to call herself Dodd M'Carthy? We were always Dodd; we never had any other name. I could n't explain this, nor even give it a coloring; but I grew angry, Tom, vexed and irritated by the pestering impertinence of this pumping scoundrel. I said a vast number of things which had been better unsaid. I gave a great deal of good advice, too, about legislation generally, that I might have known would not have been accepted; and, in fact, I was what would be called generally indiscreet; the more, since all my remarks were committed to paper as fast as I made them, the whole being courteously submitted to me for signature, as if I had been purposely making a confession of my political belief.

"Give me my passport," cried I, at last, "and let me quit your little rascally territory of spies and sharpers. I promise you sacredly I 'll never put foot in it again."

"Not so fast, my worthy friend," said he. "We must first know under which of your aliases you are to travel; meanwhile, we shall take the liberty of committing you to prison as Herr Dodd!"

"To prison! — for what crime?" cried I, nearly choking with passion.

"You 'll hear it all time enough," was the only response, as, ringing his bell, he summoned the gendarmes, who, advancing one to either side of me, led me away like a common malefactor.

The prison is a kind of Bridewell, over a livery-stable, and only meant as a "station" before being forwarded to the larger establishment at Carlsruhe. I suppose, had they wished it, they could not have accorded me any place of separate confinement; for there was but scanty space, and many occupants. As it was, my lot was to be put in the same cell with two fellows just apprehended for a murder, and who obligingly entered into a full narrative of their crime, believing that *my* revelations would be equally interesting. I lost no time in writing a note to James, and another to our English Chargé d'Affaires, a young attaché, I believe, of the Legation at Stuttgard.

James and the sucking diplomatist were both out, so that I had no answer from either till evening. During this interval I had much meditation over the state of politics in Germany, and the probable future of that country, of which I shall take another occasion to tell you.

At six o'clock came the following, enclosed in a very large envelope, and sealed with a very spacious impression of the English Arms: —

"The undersigned Attaché of H. B. M.'s Legation at the Court of Stuttgard has the honor to acknowledge receipt of Mr. Kenny J. Dodd's communication of this morning's date, and will lay it under the consideration of H. B. M.'s Principal Secretary of State for Foreign Affairs."

This was pleasant, forsooth! And was I to remain in jail till the despatch had reached London, a deliberation formed on it, and an answer returned? I was boiling over with rage at this thought, when James entered. He had just been with our illustrious Chargé d'Affaires, who received him with that diplomatic reserve so peculiar amongst the small fry of the Foreign Office. At the same time James saw a lurking satisfaction in his manner at the thought of having got up a case of international dispute, which might have his name mentioned in the House, and possibly a despatch with his signature printed in a Blue Book. He was dying for an opportunity of distinguishing himself, as Baden offered nothing to his ambition; and all his fear was, that the authorities might liberate me too soon. James perceived all this, — for the lad is not wanting in shrewdness, and

his Continental life, if it has not bettered his morals, has
certainly sharpened his wit; but all his arguments were
unavailing, and all his reasonings useless. The despatch
was already begun, and it was too good a grievance to let
slip unprofitably.

James next called on a friend of his, a certain Mr. Milo
Blake O'Dwyer, who is the correspondent of a great London
paper called the "Sledge Hammer of Freedom;" but instead
of advice and guidance, the worthy news-gatherer was taking down all the particulars for a grand letter to his journal;
and he, too, it was plain to see, wished that some outrageous
treatment of me by the authorities would make his communication the great event of that day's post in London. "I
wish they 'd put him in irons, — in heavy irons," said he.
"Are you sure that his cell is not eight feet below the surface of the earth? Be particular, I beg of you, about the
depth. You saw how Gladstone destroyed that elegant
case of Poerio, all for want of a little accuracy in his meas-
urements; for, I must observe to you, in all our ' correspondence,' names, dates, and distances require to be true as
the Bible. Facts admit of varnishing. They can be always
stretched a little this way or that. Now, for instance, we 'll
call the conduct of the authorities in this case brutal, cowardly, and disgraceful. We 'll appeal to the universally
acknowledged right of Englishmen to do everything everywhere, and we 'll wind up with a grand peroration about
Despotism and the glorious privileges of the British
Constitution."

The fellow chuckled over my case with unfeigned satisfaction. He would n't listen to the real, plain facts of the
matter at all. They were poor, meagre, and insignificant
in themselves, till they had acquired the touch of genius to
illustrate them; and though I was a gem, as he owned, yet,
like the Koh-i-noor, I was nothing without cutting. He
appears, besides, to think that he has a kind of vested
interest in me, now that my case is to figure in his newspaper, and he contradicts my own statements flatly wherever
they don't suit him.

I have just despatched James to assure him that I don't
care a rush about the sympathy of the whole British public;

that I have no taste for martyrdom; and that, as to expending any hopes in redress from our Foreign Office, I'd as soon make an investment in Poyais Scrip, or Irish Canal Debentures. I trust that he will be induced to leave me alone, and neither make me matter for the Press nor a speech in Parliament.

These reporters, or correspondents, or whatever they call them, are, in my mind, the greatest disturbers of the peace of Europe. The moment they assert anything, they set about looking for proofs of it; and they don't know how to praise themselves enough, whenever they are driven to confess that they were in the wrong; and then, if you mind, Tom, it is not to the public they excuse themselves, — not a bit of it; it's the King of Naples, or the Emperor of Russia, or the Bey of Tiflis, that "they sincerely hope will not be offended by statements made after mature reflection and painful consideration of the topic." They throw out sly hints of all the Royal attentions that have been bestowed upon them, and the intimate habits they have enjoyed of confidence with the Queen of this, and the Crown Prince of that. Vulgar rapscallions! they have never seen more of Royalty than what a church or an opera admits; and though Majesty now and then may feel the sting, take my word for it, he never notices the mosquito.

If you, then, see me in print, — and be on the look-out, — just write a letter in my name from Dodsborough, to say that I am well and hearty on my paternal acres, and know nothing of politics, police, or reporters, and would rather the Government would reduce the county cess than prosecute every Grand-Duke in Europe.

I will write again to-morrow. Yours ever,

K. I. DODD.

LETTER XXXIV.

KENNY JAMES DODD TO THOMAS PURCELL, ESQ., OF THE
GRANGE, BRUFF.

"THE FOX."

My DEAR TOM, — However Morris managed it I know not,
but an order came for my liberation that same evening,
with the assurance that my passport was to be made out
for wherever I pleased to name, and the Prefect was to
express to me his regrets and apologies for an inadvertence
which he deeply deplored.

It seemed that, but for diplomacy, I'd not have been
detained half an hour; but our worthy representative of
Great Britain had asked for copies of all the charges
against me so formally, had requested the names, ages,
and station in life of the several witnesses so circumstantially, and had, in fact, imparted such a mock importance
to a police impertinence, that the Grand-Ducal authorities
began to suspect that they had caught a first-rate revolu-
tionist, with a whole trunkful of Kossuth and Mazzini correspondence. This comes of setting school-boys to write
despatches! The greedy appetite for notoriety — to be up
and doing — to be before the world in some public capacity
— of these juveniles, brings England into more trouble,
and Englishmen into more embarrassment, than you could
believe. If they'd be satisfied with recording Royal dinner-
parties and Court scandal, — who got the Order of the
Guinea-pig, and who is to receive the "Tortoise," they
could n't do much harm; but the moment they get hold of
an international grievance, and quote Puffendorf, we have
no peace on the Continent for six months after.

"You wish to leave Baden," said Morris; "where will
you go?"

" I have not the slightest notion," said I. " I 'm wait-ing for letters from Ireland," — yours, my dear Tom, the chief of them, — " and therefore it must be somewhere in the vicinity."

" Go over to Rastadt, then," said he, " and amuse your-self with the fortifications: they are now in course of con-struction, and when completed will be some of the strongest in Europe. I 'll give you a letter to the Commandant, who will show all that can interest you, and explain everything that you may wish to know." Rastadt is only twenty miles away; it is, however, in all that regards intercourse with Baden, fully two hundred distant. It is cheap, rarely visited by strangers, has no " fashionables," and, in fact, just the kind of model-prison residence that I was wishing for to discipline the family, and get them once more " in hand."

Thither, therefore, we remove to-morrow morning, if nothing unforeseen should occur in the interim. Morris, as you may observe, behaved most kindly in this affair; and, indeed, showed a strong interest in James, from cer-tain remarks the boy himself has let drop; but he seems cold, Tom, — one of those excellent fellows that are always doing the right thing for its own sake, and not for yours. I don't want to disparage principle, no more than I do a great balance at Coutts's, or anything else that I don't possess myself; but I mean to say that, somehow or other, one likes to feel that it is to yourself, as an individual, — to your own proper identity,— a service is rendered, and not to a mere fraction of that great biped race that wear cloth clothes and eat cooked victuals.

That's the way with the English, however, all over the globe, and I have often felt more grateful to an Irishman for helping me on with my surtout than I have to John Bull for a real downright piece of service. I suppose the fault is more mine than his; but the fact is true, and so I give it to you. I suppose, besides, that an impartial observer of both of us would say that we make too much of every favor, and the Englishman too little; we exact all the obligation of a debt for it, they treat the whole thing lightly, as if the service rendered, and those to whom it was done, were not worthy of further consideration. However

we strike the balance between us, Tom,— in our favor or
against us, — I own to you I like our own way best; and
though nothing could be truly more kind and considerate
than Morris, it was quite a relief to me when he gave me his
cold shake-hands, and said " Good-bye ! "

And so it will ever be, so long as human actions are
swayed by human emotions. The man who recognizes your
feelings, who regards you with some touch of sympathy,
is more your friend than the benevolent machine who bestows
upon you his mechanical philanthropy.

"THE GOLDEN OX," RASTADT.

We left Lichtenthal like a thief in the night; and here
we are now in the " Golden Ox " at Rastadt, which, I own
to you, seems a most comfortable house. James and I —
for we are now *two* parties domestically, Mrs. D. and Mary
Anne living very much to themselves, and Cary still on a
visit with Morris's mother — had a most excellent breakfast
of fresh trout, a roast partridge, a venison steak with capers
— a capital dish — and chocolate, with abundance of good
white wine of the place, and on calling for the bill, out of
curiosity, I see we are charged something under a florin for
two of us, — about tenpence each. Tom, this will do.
You may therefore look upon me as a citizen of Rastadt for
the next month to come. I have kept my letter by me
hitherto, to give you a bulletin of this place before closing it,
and I have still some time at my disposal before the post
leaves.

I'm not sure, though, I'd exactly recommend this town
to a patient laboring under nervous headaches, or to a
university man reading for honors. Indeed, up to this
— I suppose I'll get used to it later on — the din has so
addled me that I have often to stand two minutes reflecting over what I had to say, and then own that I have
forgotten it. We are — that is, the " Ox " is — in the quiet-
est spot in the town, and yet close under my bedroom there
are, from early morning till dusk, twelve drummers at
practice, with a head drummer to teach them. In the
green, before the door, two companies of recruits are at
drill. The foot artillery limbers and unlimbers all day

in the "Platz" close by, and what should be our garden
is a riding-school for the cadets. These several educational
establishments have their peculiar tumult, which accompany
me through my sleep; and for all the requirements of quiet
and reflection, I might as well have taken up my abode in
a kettle-drum. Liège was a Trappist monastery in comparison! As it is, the routine tramp of feet has made me
conform to the step, and I march "quick" or "orderly,"
exactly as the fellows are doing it outside. I swallow my
soup to the sound of a trumpet, and take off my clothes to
the roll of the drum. James is in ecstasy with it all; I
never saw him enjoy himself so much. He is out looking
at them the entire day, and I'm greatly mistaken but Mary
Anne passes a large portion of her time at the green
"jalousie" that opens over the riding-school.

I am always asking myself — that is, whenever I can
summon composure even for so much — what do the Germans
want with all these soldiers? Surely they 're not going to in-
vade France, nor Russia; and yet their armies are maintained
in a strength that might imply it! As to any occasion for
them at home in their own land, it 's downright balderdash
to talk of it! Do you know, Tom, that whenever I think of
Germany and her rulers, I am strongly reminded of poor
old Dr. Drake, that lived at Dronestown, and the flea-bitten
mare he used to drive in his gig. She was forty if she was
an hour; she was quiet and docile from the day she was
foaled: all the whipping in the world could n't shake her
into five miles an hour, and yet the doctor had her surrounded with every precaution and appliance that would
have suited a regular runaway. There were safety-reins,
and kicking-straps, and double traces without end, — and
all to restrain a poor old beast that only wanted to be let
alone, and drag out her tiresome existence in the jog-trot
she was used to! "Ah, you don't know as well as I do,"
Drake would say; "she 's a devil at heart, and if she did n't
feel it was useless to resist, she 'd smash everything behind
her. She looks quiet enough, but *that* does n't impose upon
me." These were the kind of reflections he indulged in, and
I suppose they are about the same in use in the Cabinets
of Austria, Prussia, and Bavaria. I was often malicious

enough for a half wish that Drake should have a spicy devil in
the shafts, just for once, to show him a trick or two; and in
the same spirit, Tom, I cannot help saying that I'd like to
see John Bull "put to" in this fashion! Would n't he kick
up, — would n't he soon knock the whole concern to atoms!
Ah, Tom, it's all alike, believe me; and whether you have
to drive a nag or a nation, take my word for it, the kicking-
straps are only efficacious when the beast has n't a kick in
him! At all events, such are not the popular notions here;
and on they go, building fortresses, strengthening garrisons,
and reinforcing army corps, till at last the military will be
more numerous than the nation, and every prisoner will
have two jailers to restrain him. "Who is to pay?" becomes the question; but indeed that is the very question that
puzzles me now. Who pays for all this at present? Is
it possible that a people will suffer itself to be taxed that
it may be bullied? I'm unable to continue this theme, for
there go the drums again, — there are forty of them at it now!
What's in the wind I can't guess. Oh, here's the explanation. It is the Herr Commandant — be sure you accent the
last syllable — is come to pay me a visit, and the guard has
turned out to drum him upstairs!

Four o'clock.

He is gone at last, — I thought he never would, — and I
have only time to say that he has appointed to-morrow
after breakfast, to show me the fortress, and as I am too
late for the post, I'll be able to add a line or two before
this leaves me. Mary Anne has come to say that her
mother's head is distracted, and that she cannot endure the
uproar of the place. My reply is, "Mine is exactly in the
same way; but I cannot go any further, — I've no money."
Mrs. D. "thinks she'll go mad!" If she means it in
earnest, this is as cheap a place to do it in as any I know.
We are only to pay two pounds a week each, and I suppose
whether we preserve our senses or not makes no difference in
the expense! This would sound very unfeelingly, Tom,
but that you are well aware of Mrs. D.'s system, and that
she gives notice of a motion without any intention of going
to a debate, much less of pressing for a "division." Mary

Anne is very urgent that I should see her mother, but I am not quite equal to it yet. Maybe after visiting the fortress to-morrow I'll be in a more martial mood; and now here's dinner, and a most savory odor preludes it.

Tuesday.

This must go as it is, Tom, — I'm dead beat! That old veteran would n't let me off a casemate nor a bomb-proof, and I have walked twenty miles this blessed morning! Nor is that all; but I have handled shot, lifted cannon-balls, adjusted mortars, and peeped out of embrasures, till my back is half broken with straining and fatigue. Just to judge from what I'm suffering, a siege must be a dreadful thing! He says he showed me everything; and, upon my conscience, I can well believe it! There was a great deal of it, too, that I saw in the dark, for there was no end of galleries without a single loophole, and many of the passages seemed only four feet high; for, though a short man, I had to stoop. I ought to have a great deal to say about this place, if I could remember it, or if I could be sure it would interest you. It appears that Rastadt is built upon an entirely new principle, quite distinct from any hitherto in use. It must be attacked *en ricochet*, and not directly; a hint, I suppose, they stole from our common law, where they fire into *you*, by pretending to assail John Doe or Richard Roe. The Commandant sneered at the old system, but I'd rather trust myself in Gibraltar, notwithstanding all he said. It stands to reason, Tom, that if you are up in a window you have a great advantage over a fellow down in the street. Now, all these modern fortresses are what is called "*à fleur d'eau*," quite level, and not raised in the least over the attacking force. Put me up high, say I; if on a parapet, so much the better; and besides, Tom, nothing gives a man such coolness as to know that he is all as one as out of danger! Of course, I did n't make this remark to the Commandant, because in talking with military people it is good tact always to assume that being shot at is rather pleasant than otherwise; and so I have observed that they themselves generally make use of some jocular phrase or other to express being killed and wounded; "he was knocked over," "he got an ugly poke," being the more popular mode of recording what finished a man's existence, or made the remainder of it miserable.

Soldiering has always struck me as an insupportable line of life. I have no objection in the world to fight the man who has injured *me*, nor to give satisfaction where I have been the offender; but to go patiently to work to learn how to destroy somebody I never saw and never heard of, *does* seem absurd and unchristianlike altogether. You say, "He is the enemy of my country, and, consequently, mine." Let me see that; let me be sure of it. If he invades us, I know that he is an enemy; but if he is only occupied about his own affairs, — if he is simply hunting out a nest of old squatters that he is tired of, — if he is merely changing the sign of his house, and instead of the "Lily" prefers to live under the "Cock," or maybe the "Drone-bee," what have I to say to that? So long as he stays at home, and only "gets drunk on the premises," I have no right to meddle with him. It's all very well to say that nobody likes to have a disorderly house in his neighborhood. Very true; but you ought n't to go in and murder the residents to keep them quiet. There's the mail gone by, and I have forgotten to send this off. It's a wonderful thing how living in Germany makes a man long-winded and tiresome. It must be the air, at least with me, or the cookery, for I am perfectly innocent of the language. The "mysterious gutturals," as Macaulay calls them, will ever be mysteries to *me!* At all events, to prevent further indiscretions, I'll close this and seal it now. And so, with my sincere regards, believe me, dear Tom, ever yours,

KENNY I. DODD.

Address me, "Golden Ox," — I mean at the sign of, — Rastadt, for you 're sure of finding me here for the next four weeks at least.

"The Golden Ox," Rastadt.

My dearest Kitty, — I have only time for a few and very hurried lines, written with trembling fingers and a heart audible in its palpitations! Yes, dearest, an eventful moment has arrived, — the dread instant has come, on which my whole future destiny must depend. It was last night, just as I was making papa's tea, that a servant arrived on horseback at the inn with a letter addressed to the Right Honorable and Reverend the Lord Dodd de Dodsborough. This, of course, could only mean papa, and so he opened and read it, for it was in English, dearest, or at least in imitation of that language.

I refrain from quoting the precise expressions, lest in circumstances so serious a smile of passing levity should cross those dear features, now all tension with anxiety for your own Mary Anne. The letter was from Adolf von Wolfenschäfer, making me an offer of his hand, title, and fortune! I swooned away when I heard it, and only recovered to hear papa still spelling out the strange phraseology of the letter.

I wish he had not written in English, Kitty. It is provoking that an event so naturally serious in itself should be alloyed with the dross of grammatical absurdities; besides that, really, our tongue does not lend itself to those delicate and half-vanishing allusions to future bliss so germane to such a proposal. Papa, and James, too, I must say, evinced a want of regard to my feelings, and an absence of that fine sympathy which I should have looked for at a moment like this. They actually screamed with laughter, Kitty, at

little lapses of orthography, when the subject might reasonably have imposed far different emotions.

"Why, it's a proposal of marriage!" exclaimed papa,
"and I thought it a summons from the police."

"Egad, so it is!" cried James. "It's an offer to you,
Mary Anne. 'The Baron Adolf von Wolfenschäfer, Frei-
herr von Schweinbraten and Ritter of the Order of the Cock
of Tubingen, maketh hereby, and not the less, that with

future-coming-time-to-be-proved-and-experienced affection,
the profound humility of an offer of himself, with all his to-
be-named-and-enumerated belongings, both in effects and
majorats, to the lovely and very beautiful Miss, the first
daughter of the Venerable and very Honorable the Lord
Dodd de Dodsborough.' "

"Pray stop, James," said I; "this is scarcely a fitting
matter for coarse jesting, nor is my heart to be made the
theme for indelicate banter."

"The letter is a gem," said he, and went on: "'The so-
named A. von W., overflowing with a mild but in-heaven-

soaring and never-to-earth-descending love, expecteth, in all the pendulating anxieties of a never-at-any-moment-to-be-distrusted devotion — ' "

"Papa, I really beg and request that I may not be trifled with in this unfeeling manner. The Baron's intentions are sufficiently clear and explicit, nor are we now engaged in the work of correcting his English epistolary style."

This I said haughtily, Kitty; and Mister James at last thought proper to recover some respect for my feelings.

"Why, I never suspected you could take the thing seriously, dear Mary Anne," said he. "If I only thought — "

"And pray, why not, James? I'm sure the Baron's ancient birth — his rank, his fortune — his position, in fact — "

"Of all of which we know nothing," broke in papa.

"But of which you may know everything," said I; "for here, at the postscript, is an invitation to us all to pass some weeks at the Schloss, in the Black Forest, his ancestral seat."

"Or, as he styles it," broke in James, impertinently, " ' the very old castle, where for numerous centuries his high-blooded and on-lofty-eminence-standing ancestors did sit,' and where now ' his with-years-bestricken but not-the-less-on-that-account-sharp-with-intelligence-begifted parent father doth reside.' "

"Read that again, James," said papa.

"Pray allow me, sir," said I, taking the letter. "The invitation is a most hospitable request that we should go and pass some time at his chateau, and name the earliest day our convenience will permit for the visit."

"He spoke of capital shooting there!" cried James. "He told me that the Auer-Hahn, a kind of black-cock, abounds in that country."

"And I remember, too, that he mentioned some wonderful Steinberger, — a cabinet wine, full two hundred years in wood!" chimed in papa.

I wished, dearest Kitty, that they could have entertained the subject-matter of the letter without these "contingent remainders," and not mix up my future fate with either wine or wild fowl; but they really were so carried away by

the pleasures so peculiarly adapted to their own feelings
that they at once said, and in a breath too, "Write him
word ' Yes,' by all means! "

"Do you mean for his offer of marriage, papa?" asked I,
with struggling indignation.

"By George, I had forgotten all about that," said he.
"We must deliberate a bit. Your mother, too, will expect
to be consulted. Take the letter upstairs to her; or, better
still, just say that I want to speak to her myself."

As papa and mamma had not met nor spoken together
since his return, I willingly embraced this opportunity of
restoring them to intercourse with each other.

"Don't go away, Mary Anne," said James, as I was about
to seek my own room, for I dreaded being left alone, and
exposed to his unfeeling banter; "I want to speak to you."
This he said with a tone of kindness and interest which at
once decided me to remain. He wore a look of seriousness,
Kitty, that I have seldom, if ever, seen in his features, and
spoke in a tone that, to my ears, was new from him.

"Let me be your friend, Mary Anne," said he, "and the
better to be so, let me talk to you in all frankness and
sincerity. If I say one single word that can hurt your
feelings, put it down to the true account, — that I 'd rather
do even such than suffer you to take the most eventful
step in all your life without weighing every consequence
of it. Answer me, then, two or three questions that I shall
ask you, but as truly and unreservedly as though you were
at confession."

I sat down beside him, and with my hand in his.

"Now, first of all, Mary Anne," said he, "do you love
this Baron von Wolfenschäfer? "

Who ever could answer such a question in one word,
Kitty? How seldom does it occur in life that all the circumstances of any man's position respond to the ambitious
imaginings of a girl's heart! He may be handsome, and
yet poor; he may be rich, and yet low-born; intellectual,
and yet his great gifts may be alloyed with infirmities of
temper; he may be coldly natured, secret, self-contained,
uncommunicative, — a hundred things that one does not like,
— and yet, with all these drawbacks, what the world calls
an "excellent match."

I believe very few people marry the person they wish to marry. I fancy that such instances are the rarest things imaginable. It is a question of compensation throughout, — you accept this, notwithstanding that; you put up with *that*, for the sake of this! Of course, dearest, I am rejecting here all belief in the "greatest happiness principle" as a stupid fallacy, that only imposes upon elderly gentlemen when they marry their housekeeper. I speak of the considerations which weigh with a young girl who has moved in society, who knows its requirements, and can estimate all that contributes to what is called a "position."

This little digression of mine will give you to understand what was passing in my mind as James sat waiting for my reply.

"So, then," said he, at last, "the question is not so easily answered as I suspected; and we will now pass to another one. Are your affections already engaged elsewhere?"

What could I say, Kitty, but "No! decidedly not." The embarrassment, however, so natural to an inquiry like this, made me blush and seem confused; and James, perceiving it, said, —

"Poor fellow, it will be a sad blow to *him*, for I know he loved you."

I tried to look astonished, angry, unconscious, — anything, in fact, which should convey displeasure and surprise together; but with that want of tact so essentially fraternal, he went on, —

"It was almost the last thing he said to me at parting, 'Don't let her forget me!'"

"May I venture to inquire," said I, haughtily, "of whom you are speaking?"

Simple and inoffensive as the words were, Kitty, they threw him into an ungovernable passion; he stamped, and stormed, and swore fearfully. He called me "a heartless coquette," "an unfeeling flirt," and a variety of epithets equally mellifluous as well merited.

I drew my embroidery-frame before me quite calmly under this torrent of abuse, and worked away at my pattern of the "Faithful Shepherd," singing to myself all the time.

"Are you really as devoid of feeling as this, Mary Anne?" asked he.

"My dear brother," said I, "don't you wish excessively for a commission in a regiment of Hussars or Lancers? Well, as your great merits have not been recognized at the Horse Guards, would you feel justified in refusing an appointment to the Rifle Brigade?"

"What has all this to say to what we are discussing?" cried he, angrily.

"Just everything," replied I; "but as you cannot make the application, you must excuse *me* if I decline the task also."

"And so you mean to be a baroness?" said he, rudely.

I courtesied profoundly to him, and he flung out of the room with a bang that nearly brought the door down. In a moment after, mamma was in my arms, overcome with tenderness and emotion.

"I have carried the day, my dearest child," said she. "We are to accept the invitation, at all events, and we set out to-morrow."

I have no time for more, Kitty, for all our preparations for departure have yet to be made. What fate awaits me I know not, nor can I even fancy what may be the future of your ever attached and devoted friend,

MARY ANNE DODD.

LETTER XXXVI.

SCHLOSS, WOLFENFELS.

MY DEAR MOLLY, — It is only since we came to the elegant place, the hard name of which I have written at the top of this letter, that my feelings have subsided into the calm sereniousness adapted to epistolary correspondence. From the day that K. I. returned, my life has been like the parallax of a fever! The man was never possessed of any refined or exalted sentiments; but the woman, this Mrs. G. H. — I could n't write the name in full if you were to give me twenty pounds for it — made him far worse with self-conceit and vanity. If you knew the way my time is passed, "taking it out of him," Molly, showing him how ridiculous he is, and why everybody is laughing at him, you 'd pity me. As to gratitude, my dear, he has n't a notion of it; and he feels no more thankful to me for what I 've gone through than if I was indulging him in all his nefarious propensities. It is a weary task; and the only wonder is how I 'm able to go on with it.

"Have n't you done yet, Mrs. D. ?" said he, the other morning. "Don't you think that you might grant me a little peace now?"

"I wish to the saints I had," said I; "it 's bringing me to the grave, it is; but I have a duty to perform, and as long as my tongue can wag, I 'll do it! When I 'm gone, K. I.," said I, — "when I 'm gone, you 'll not have to say, ' It was her fault, — it was all her doing. Jemima never said this; she never told me that.' " I vow and declare to you here, Molly, that there is n't a thing a woman could say to a man, that I have n't said to him; and as I remarked yesterday, "If I have n't taken the self-conceit out of you now, it is

because it's grained in your nature," — I believe, indeed, I
said, "in your filthy nature."

When we left Baden, we came to a place called Rastadt,
a great fortification that they're making, as they tell me, to
defend the Rhine; but, between ourselves, it's as far from
the river as our house at Dodsborough is from Kelly's
mills. There we stopped three weeks, — I believe in the
confident hope of K. I. that I could n't survive the uproarious tumult. They were drilling or training horses, or firing
guns, or flogging recruits under our windows, from sunrise
to sunset; and although at first the novelty was amusing,
you grew, at last, so tormented and teased with the noise
that your very brain ached from it.

"I wonder," said I, one night, "that you never thought
of taking furnished apartments in Barrack Street! It ought
to be to your taste."

"It's not unlikely, ma'am, that I may end my days in
that neighborhood," said he, tartly, "for I believe it's very
convenient to the sheriff's prison."

"I was alluding to your military tastes," said I. "One
might suppose you were meant for a great general."

"I might have claim to the character, ma'am," said he,
"if being always under fire signified anything, — always
exposed to attack."

"Oh, but," said I, "you forget she has retired her forces,"
— I meant Mrs. G., Molly; "she took pity on your poor
unprotected situation!"

"Look now, Mrs. D.," said he, with a blow of his fist on
the table, "if there's another word — one syllable more on
this matter, may I never sign my name K. I. again, if I
don't walk you back, every one of you, to Dodsborough!
It was an evil hour that saw us leave it, but it would be a
joyous one that brings us back again."

When he grows so brutal as that, Molly, I never utter a
word. 'T is n't to-day nor yesterday that I learned to be a
martyr; so that all I did was to wait a minute or two, and
then go off in strong hysterics! and, indeed, I don't know
anything that provokes him more.

I give you this as a slight sample of the way we lived,
with occasional diversions on the subject of expense, the

extravagance of James, his idleness, and so forth; pleasant topics, and amusing for a family circle. Indeed, Molly, I'm ashamed to own that my natural spirit was beginning to break down under it. I felt that all the blood of the M'Carthys was weak to resist such inhuman cruelty; and whether it was the climate, or what, I don't know, but crying did n't give me the same relief it used. I suppose the fact is that one exhausts the natural resources of one's constitution; but I think I'm not so old but that a good hearty cry ought to be a comfort to me.

This is how affairs was, when, about a week ago, came a servant on horseback, with a letter for K. I. I was sitting up at my window, with the blinds down, when I saw the man get off and enter the inn, and the first thought that struck me was that it was Mrs. G. herself sent him. "I've caught you," says I to myself; and throwing on my dressing-gown, I slipped downstairs. It was K. I. and James were together talking, so I just waited a second at the door to listen. "If I had a voice in the family," — it was K. I. said this, — "if I had a voice in the family," said he, "I'd refuse. These kind of things always turn out ill, — people calculate so much upon affection; but the truth is, marrying for love is like buying a pair of Russia-duck trousers to wear through the year. They'll do beautifully in summer, and even an odd day in the autumn; but in the cold and rainy reason they'll be downright ridiculous."

"Still," said James, "the offer sounds like a great one."

"All glitter, maybe. I distrust them all, James. At any rate, say nothing about it to your mother till I think it over a bit."

"And why not say anything to his mother?" says I, bouncing into the room. "Am I nobody in the family?"

"Bedad you are!" said K. I., with a heavy sigh.

"Have n't I an opinion of my own, eh?"

"That you have!" said he.

"And don't I stand to it, too! — eh, Kenny James?"

"Your worst enemy could n't deny it!" said he, shaking his head.

"Then what's all this about?" said I, snatching the letter out of his hands. But though I tried with my double eye-glass, Molly, it was no use, for the writing was in a German hand, not to say anything of the language.

"Well, ma'am," said K. I., with a grin, "I hope the contents are pleasing to you?" And before I could fly out at him, James broke in: "It's a proposal for Mary Anne, mother. The young Baron that we met at Bonn makes her an offer of his hand and fortune, and invites us all to his castle in the Black Forest as a preliminary step."

"Isn't that to your taste, Mrs. D.?" said K. I., with another grin. "High connection — nobility — great family, — eh?"

"I don't think," said I, "that, considering the step I took myself in life, anybody can reproach me with prejudices of that kind." The step I took! Molly, I said the words with a sneer that made him purple.

"What's his fortune, James?" said I.

"Heaven knows! but he must have a stunning income. This Castle of Wolfenfels is in all the print-shops of the town. It's a thing as large as Windsor, and surrounded by miles of forest."

"My poor child," said I, "I always knew where you'd be at last; and it's only two nights ago I had a dream of taking grease out of my yellow satin. I thought I was rubbing and scrubbing at it with all my might."

"And what did that portend, ma'am?" said K. I., with his usual sneer.

"Can't you guess?" said I. "Mightn't it mean an effort to get rid of the stain of a low connection?" Wasn't that a home-thrust, Molly? Faith, he felt it so!

"Mrs. D.," said he, gravely, and as if after profound thought, "this is a question of our child's happiness for life-long, and if we are to discuss it at all, let it be without any admixture of attack or recrimination."

"Who began it?" said I.

"You did, my dear," said he.

"I didn't," said I; "and I'm not 'your dear.' Oh, you needn't sigh that way; your case isn't half so bad as you think it, but, like all men, you fancy yourself cruelly treated whenever the slightest bar is placed to your bad passions. You argue as if wickedness was good for your constitution."

"Have you done?" said he.

"Not yet," said I, taking a chair in front of him.

"When you have, then," said he, "call me, for I'll go out and sit on the stairs." But I put my back to the door, Molly, so that he had nothing for it but to resume his seat. "Let us move the order of the day, Mrs. D.," said he, — "this business of Mary Anne. My opinion of it is told in few words. These mixed marriages seldom succeed. Even with long previous intimacy, suitable fortune, and equality of station, there is that in a difference of nationality that opens a hundred discrepancies in taste, feeling —"

"Bother!" said I, "we have just as much when we come from the same stock."

"Sometimes," said he, sighing.

"Here's what he says, mother," said James, and read out the letter, which I am bound to say, Molly, was a curiosity in its way; for though it had such a strange look, it turned out to be in English, or at least what the Baron thought was such. Happily there was no mistaking the meaning; and as I said to K. I., "At least there's one thing in the Baron's favor, — there's neither deceit nor subterfuge about him. He makes his proposal like a man!" And let me tell you, Molly, we live in an age when even that same is a virtue; for really, with the liberties that's allowed, and the way girls goes on, there's no saying what intentions men have at all!

Some mothers make a point of never seeing anything; but that may be carried too far, particularly abroad, my dear. Others are for always being dragons, but that is sure to scare off the men; and as I say, what's the use of birdlime if you're always shouting and screaming!

My notion is, Molly, that a moderate degree of what the French call "surveillance" is the right thing, — a manner that seems to say, "I'm looking at you: I'm not against innocent enjoyments, and so forth, but I won't stand any nonsense, nor falling in love." Many's the time the right man is scared away by a new flirtation, that meant nothing. "She's too gay for *me* — she has a look in her eye, or a toss of the head, or a — Heaven knows — I don't like."

"Does she care for him?" said K. I. "Does Mary Anne care for him? — that's the question."

"Of course she does," said I. "If a girl's affections are not engaged in some other quarter, she always cares for the man that proposes for her. Is n't he a good match?"

"He as much as says so himself."

"And a Baron?"

"Yes."

"And has an elegant place, with a park of miles round it?"

"So he says."

"Well, then, I 'm sure I see nothing to prevent her being attached to him."

"At all events, let us speak to her," said he, and sent James upstairs to fetch her down.

Short as the time was that he was away, it was enough for K. I. to get into one of his passions, just because I gave him the friendly caution that he ought to be delicate and guarded in the way he mentioned the matter to Mary Anne.

"Is n't she my daughter?" said he, with a stamp of his foot; and just for that, Molly, I would n't give him the satisfaction to say she is.

"I ask you," cried he again, "is n't she my daughter?"

Not a syllable would I answer him.

"Well, maybe she is n't," said he; "but my authority over her is all the same."

"Oh, you can be as cruel and tyrannical as you please," said I.

"Look now, Mrs. D. — " said he; but, fortunately, Molly, just at that moment James and his sister came in, and he stopped suddenly.

"Oh, dearest papa," cried Mary Anne, falling at his feet, and hiding her face in her hands, "how can I leave you, and dear, dear mamma?"

"That's what we are going to talk over, my dear," said he, quite dryly, and taking a pinch of snuff.

"Your father is never overpowered by his commotions, my love," said I.

"To forsake my happy home!" sobbed Mary Anne, as if her heart was breaking. "Oh, what an agony to think of!"

"To be sure it is," said K. I., in the same hard, husky

voice; " but it's what we see done every day. Ask your mother — "

" Don't ask me to justify it," said I. " *My* experiences go all the other way."

" At any rate you ventured on the experiment," said he, with a grin. Then, turning to Mary Anne, he went on : " I see that James has informed you on this affair, and it only remains for me now to ask you what your sentiments are."

" Oh, my poor heart! " said she, pressing her hand to her side, " how can I divide its allegiance ? "

" Don't try that, at all events," said he, " for though I never thought him a suitable match for you, my dear, if you really do feel an attachment to Peter Belton — "

" Of course I do not, papa."

" Of course she does not — never did — never could," said I.

" So much the better," said he ; " and now for this Baron von — I never can remember his name — do you think you could be happy with him? Or do you know enough of his temper, tastes, and disposition to answer that question ? "

" I 'm sure he is a most amiable person ; he is exceedingly clever and accomplished — "

" I don't care a brass bodkin for all that," broke in K. I. " A man may be as wise as the bench of bishops, and be a bad husband."

" Let *me* talk to Mary Anne," said I. It's only a female heart, Molly, understands these cases ; for men discuss them as if they were matters of reason ! And with that I marched her off with me to my own room.

I need n't tell you all I said, nor what she replied to me ; but this much I will say, a more sensible girl I never saw. She took in the whole of our situation at once. She perceived that there was no saying how long K. I. might be induced to remain abroad ; it might be, perhaps, to-morrow, or next day, that he 'd decide to go back to Ireland. What a position we 'd be in, then ! " I don't doubt," says she, " but if time were allowed me, I could do better than this. With the knowledge I have now of life, I feel very confident ; but if we are to be marched off before the campaign begins, mamma, how are we to win our laurels?" Them's her words, Molly, and they express her meaning beautifully.

We agreed at last that the best thing was to accept the invitation to the castle, and when we saw the place, and the way of living, we could then decide on the offer of marriage.

If I could only repeat to you the remarks Mary Anne made about this, you'd see what a girl she was, and what a wonderful degree of intelligence she possesses. Even on the point that K. I. himself raised a doubt, — the difference of nationality and language, — she summed up the whole question in a few words. Her observation was, that this very circumstance was rather an advantage than otherwise, "as offering a barrier against the over-intimacy and over-familiarity that is the bane of married life."

"The fact is, mamma," said she, "people do not conform to each other. They make a show of doing so, and they become hypocrites, — great or little ones, as their talents decide for them, — but their real characters remain at bottom unchanged. Now, married to a foreigner, a woman need not even affect to assume his tastes and habits. She may always follow her own, and set them down, whatever they be, to the score of her peculiar nationality."

She is really, Molly, an astonishing girl, and in all that regards life and knowledge of mankind, I never met her equal. As to Caroline, she never could have made such a remark. The advantages of the Continent are clean thrown away on her; she knows no more of the world than the day we left Dodsborough. Indeed, I sometimes half regret that we didn't leave her behind with the Doolans; for I observe that whenever foreign travel fails in inculcating new refinement and genteel notions, it is sure to strengthen all old prejudices, and suggest a most absurd attachment to one's own country; and when that happens to be Ireland, Molly, I need scarcely say how injurious the tendency is! It's very dreadful, my dear, but it's equally true, whenever anything is out of fashion, in bad taste, vulgar, or common, you're sure to hear it called Irish, though, maybe, it never crossed the Channel; and out of self-defence one is obliged to adopt the custom.

On one point Mary Anne and myself were both agreed. It is next to impossible for any one but a banker's daughter, or in the ballet, to get a husband in the peerage at home. The nobility, with us, are either very cunning or very foolish. As to the gentry class, they never think of them at all. The consequence is, that a girl who wishes for a title must take a foreigner. Now, Molly, German nobility is mightily like German silver, — it has only a look of the real article; but if you can't afford the right thing, it is better than the vulgar metal!

Mary Anne has declared, over and over again, that nothing would induce her to be Mrs. Anybody. As she says, "Your whole life is passed in a struggle, if not heralded by a designation, even though it only be 'Madame.'" And sure nobody knows this better than I do. Has n't the odious name weighed me down for years past?

"Take him, then, my dear child," said I, — "take him, then, and may you have luck in your choice! It will be a consolation to me, in all my troubles and trials, to know that one of my girls at least sustains the honor of her mother's family. You 'll be a baroness, at all events."

She pressed my hand affectionately, Molly, but said nothing. I saw that the poor dear child was n't doing it all without some sacrifice or other; but I was too prudent to ask questions. There 's nothing, in my opinion, does such mischief as the system of probing and poking into wounds of the affections; it 's the sure way to keep them open, and prevent their healing; so that I kept on, never minding, and only talked of "the Baron."

"It will kill the Davises," said she, at last; "they 'll die of spite when they hear it."

"That they will," said I; "and they 'll deny it to all the neighbors, till it 's copied into the country papers out of the 'Morning Post.' What will become of all their sneering remarks about going abroad now, I wonder! Faith, my dear, you might live long enough at Bruff without seeing a baron."

"I think Mr. Peter, too, will at last perceive the outrageous absurdity of his pretensions," said she. "The Castle of Wolfenfels is not exactly like the village dispensary."

In a word, my dear Molly, we considered the question in all its bearings, and agreed that though we had rather he was a viscount, with a fine estate at home, yet that the thing was still too good to refuse. "It's a fine position," said Mary Anne, "and I'll see if I can't improve it." We agreed, as Caroline was so happy where she was, — on a visit with this Mrs. Morris, — that we'd leave her there a little longer; for, as Mary Anne remarked, " She's so natural and so frank and so very confiding, she'll just tell everything about us, and spoil all!" And it is true, Molly. That girl has no more notion of the difficulties it costs us to be what we are, and where we are, than if she was n't one of the family. She's a regular Dodd, and no more need be said.

The next day, you may be sure, was n't an idle one. We had to pack all our things, to get a new livery made for Paddy Byrne, and to hire a travelling-carriage, so that we might make our appearance in a style becoming us. Betty, too, had to be drilled how she was to behave in a great house full of servants, and taught not to expose us by any of her outlandish ways. Mary Anne had her up to eat before her, and teach her various politenesses; but the saints alone can tell how the lesson will prosper.

We started from Rastadt in great style, — six posters, and a riding courier in front, to order relays on the road. Even the sight of it, Molly, and the tramp of the horses, and the jingle of the bells on the harness, all did me good, for I'm of a susceptible nature; and what between my sensations at the moment, and the thought of all before us, I cried heartily for the first two stages.

"If it overcomes you so much," said K. I., "don't you think you'd better turn back?"

Did you ever hear brutality like that speech, Molly? I ask you, in all your experience of life, did you ever know of any man that could make himself so odious? You may be sure I did n't cry much after that! I made it so comfortable to him that he was glad to exchange places with Betty, and get into the rumble for the remainder of the journey.

Betty herself, too, was in one of her blessed tempers, all

because Mary Anne would n't let her stick all the old artificial flowers, that were thrown away, over her bonnet. As
Mary Anne said to her, "she only wanted wax-candles to
be like a Christmas-tree." The consequence was that she
cried and howled all the way, till we dined; after that she
slept and snored awfully. To mend matters, Paddy got
very drunk, and had to be tied on the box, and drew a
crowd round us, at every place we changed horses, by his
yells. In other respects the journey was agreeable.

We supped at a place called Offenburg; and, indeed, I
thought we 'd never get away from it, for K. I. found out
that the landlord could speak English, and was, besides, a
great farmer; and, in spite of Mary Anne and myself, he
had the man in to supper, and there they sat, smoking,
and drinking, and prosing about clover and green crops
and flax, and such things, till past midnight. However, it
did one thing, — it made K. I. good-humored for the rest
of the way; for the truth is, Molly, the nature of the man
is unchanged, and, I believe, unchangeable. Do what we
will, take him where we may, give him all the advantages
of high life and genteel society, but his heart will still cling
to yearling heifers and ewes; and he 'd rather be at Ballinasloe than a ball at Buckingham Palace.

We ought to have been at Freyburg in time to sleep,
but we did n't get there till breakfast hour. I 'm mighty
particular about all the names of these places, Molly, for
it will amuse you to trace our journey on the celestial globe
in the schoolroom, and then you 'll perceive how we are
going " round the world " in earnest.

After breakfast we went to see the cathedral of the town.
It is really a fine sight; and the carving that 's thrown away
in dark, out-of-the-way places, would make two other
churches. The most beautiful thing of all, however, is an
image of the Virgin, sheltering under her cloak more than
a dozen cardinals and bishops. She is looking down at the
creatures — for they are all made small in comparison —
with an angelical smile, as much as to say, " Keep quiet, and
nobody will see you." I suppose she wants to get them
into heaven " unknownst; " or, as James rather irreverently
expressed it, "going to do it by a dodge." To judge by

their faces, they are not quite at their ease; they seem to
think that their case is n't too good, and that it will go
hard with them if they 're found out! And I suppose, my
dear Molly, that 's the way with the best of us. Sure, with
all our plotting and scheming for the good of our children,
after lives of every kind of device, ain't we often masses
of corruption? — is n't our very best thoughts, sometimes,
wicked enough? Them was exactly my own meditations,
as I sat alone in a dark corner of the church, musing and
reflecting, and only brought to myself as I heard K. I.
fighting with one of the " beagles " — I think they call them
— about a bad groschen in change!

" I 'm never in a heavenly frame of mind, K. I." said I
to him, " that you don't bring me back to earthly feelings
with your meanness."

" If you told me you were going to heaven, Mrs. D.," said
he, " I would n't have brought you out of it for worlds! "

It did n't need the grin that he gave, to show me what
the meaning of this speech was. The old wretch said as
much as that he wished me dead and buried; so I just gave
him a look, and passed out of the church with contempt.
Oh, Molly, Molly, whatever may be your spire in life,
never descend from it for a husband!

You 'll laugh when I tell you that we left this place by
the Valley of Hell. That 's the name of it; and so far as
gloom and darkness goes, not a bad name either. It is a
deep, narrow glen, with only room for a narrow road at the
bottom of it, and over your head the rocks seem ready to
tumble down and crush you to atoms. Instead, too, of
getting through it as fast as we could, K. I. used to stop
the carriage, and get out to " examine the position," as he
called it; for it seems that a great French general once
made a wonderful retreat through this same pass years ago.
K. I. and James had bought a map, and this they used to
spread out on the ground; and sometimes they got into
disputing about the name of this place or that, so that the
Valley of Hell had its share of torments for me and Mary
Anne before we got out of it.

At a little lake called the " Titi See " — be sure you look
for it on the globe, and you 'll know it by a small island in

it with willow-trees — we found that the Baron had sent
horses to meet us, and eight miles more brought us to the
place of our destiny. I own to you, Molly, that I could
have cried with sheer disappointment, when I found we
were in the demesne without knowing it. I was always
looking out for a grand entrance, — maybe an archway
between two towers, like Nockslobber Castle, or an elegant cut-stone building, with a lodge at each side, like
Dolly Mount; but there we were, Molly, driving through
deep clay roads, with great fields of maize at each side of
us, and neither a gate nor a hedge, — not a bit of paling
to be seen anywhere. There were trees enough, but they
were ugly pines and firs, or beech, with all the lower
branches lopped away for firewood. We had two miles
or more of this interesting landscape, and then we came
out upon a great wide space planted with mangel and beet-
root, and all cut up with little drains, or canals of running
water; and in the middle of this, like a great, big, black,
dirty jail, stood the Castle of Wolfenfels. I give you my
first impressions honestly, Molly, because, on nearer acquaintance, I have lived to see them changed.

I must say our reception drove all other thoughts away.
The old Baron was confined to his room with the gout, and
could n't come down to meet us; but the discharge of cannon,
the sounds of music, and the joyful shouts of the people —
of whom there were some hundreds assembled — was really
imposing.

The young Baron, too, looked far more awake and alive
than he used to do at Bonn; and he was dressed in a
kind of uniform that rather became him. He was overjoyed at our arrival, and kissed K. I. and James on both
cheeks, and made them look very much ashamed before all
the people.

"Never was my poor castle so much honored," said he,
"since the King of — somewhere I forget — came to pass
the night here with my ancestor, Conrad von Wolfenscha-
fer; and that was in the sixth century."

"Begad, it's easy to see you have had no encumbered
estates court," said K. I., "or you would n't be here to tell
us that."

"My ancestor did not hold from the King," said he. "He was not what you call a vessel!"

K. I. laughed, and only said, "Faith, there's many of us mighty weak vessels, and very leaky besides."

After that he conducted us through two lines of his menials.

"I do detest to have so many 'detainers'" — he meant retainers. "I hope you are less annoyed in this respect."

"You don't dislike them more than I do," said K. I.; "the very name makes me shudder."

"How your fader and I agree!" said he to Mary Anne. "We are one family already."

And we all laughed heartily as we went to our rooms. Every country has its own ways and habits, but I must say, Molly, that the furniture of these castles is very mean. There were two children's beds for K. I. and myself, — at least they did not look longer than the beds in the nursery at home, — with what K. I. called a swansdown poultice for coverlid; no curtains of any kind, and the pillows as big as a small mattress. Four oak chairs, and a looking-glass the size of your face, and a chest of drawers that wouldn't open, and that K. I. had to make serviceable by lifting off

the marble slab on the top, — this was all our room contained.
There were old swords and pikes hung up in abundance,
and a tree of the family history, framed and glazed, over
the chimney, — but these had little to do towards making
the place comfortable.

"He's a good farmer, anyhow," said K. I., looking out
of the window. "I did n't see such turnips since I left
England."

"I suppose he has a good steward," said I, for I began
to fear that K. I. would make some blunder, and speak to
the Baron about crops, and so forth.

"Them drills are as neat as ever I seen," said he, half to
himself.

"Look now, K. I.," said I to him, gravely, "make your
own remarks on whatever you like, but remember where we
are, and that it's exactly the same as if we were on a visit
to the Duke of Leinster at home. If you must ask questions about farming, always say, 'How does your steward
do this?' 'What does he think of that?' Keep in mind
that the aristocracy does n't dirty its fingers abroad as it
does in England, with agricultural pursuits, and that they
have neither prizes for cows nor cottagers!"

"Mrs. D.," said he, turning on me like a tiger, "are you
going to teach me polite breeding and genteel manners?"

"I wish to the saints I could," said I, "if the lesson was
only good for a week."

"Look now," said he, "if I detect the slightest appearance
of any drilling or training of me, — if I ever find out that
you want to impose me on the world for anything but what
I am, — may I never do any good if I don't disgrace you all
by my behavior!"

"Can you be worse?" said I.

"I can," said he; "a devilish deal worse."

And with that he went out of the room with a bang that
nearly tore the door off its hinges, and never came back till
late in the evening.

We apologized for his not appearing at dinner by saying
that he felt fatigued, and requested that he might be permitted to sleep on undisturbed; and as, happily, he did go
to bed when he returned, the excuse succeeded.

So that you see, Molly, even in the midst of splendor and greatness, that man's temper, and the mean ways he has, keeps me in perpetual hot water. I know, besides, that when he is downright angry, he never cares for consequences, nor counts the damage of anything. He 'd just go down and tell the Baron that we had n't a sixpence we could call our own; that Dodsborough was mortgaged for three times its value; and that, maybe, to-morrow or next day we 'd be sold out in the Cumbered Court. He 'd expose me and Mary Anne without the slightest compunctuation, and there 's not a family secret he would n't publish in the servants' hall!

Don't I remember well, when the 55th was quartered at Bruff, he used to boast at the mess that he could n't give his daughters a farthing of fortune, when any man with proper feelings, and a respect for his position, would have made it seem that the girls had a snug thing quite at their own disposal. Is n't the world ready enough, Molly, to detect one's little failings and shortcomings, without our going about to put them in the "Hue and Cry"? But that was always the way with K. I. He used to say, "It 's no disgrace to us if we can't do this;" "It 's no shame if we 're not rich enough for that." But I say, it is both a shame and a disgrace if *it 's found out*, Molly. That 's the whole of it!

I used to think that coming abroad might have taught him something, — that he 'd see the way other people lived, and similate himself to their manners and customs. Not a bit of it. He grows worse every day. He 's more of a Dodd now than the hour he left home. The consequence is that the whole responsibility of supporting the credit of the family is thrown upon me and Mary Anne. I don't mean to say that we are unequal to the task, but surely the whole burden need n't be laid upon our shoulders. That we are on the spot from which I write these lines is all my own doing. When we first met the young Baron at Bonn, K. I. tried to prejudice us against him; he used to ridicule him to James and the girls, and went so far as to say that he was sure he was a low fellow!

What an elegant blunder we 'd have made if we 'd took his

advice! It's all very fine saying he does n't "look like this "
— or he has n't an "air of that;" sure nobody can be taken
by his appearance abroad.   The scrubbiest old snuffy creatures that go shambling about with shoes too big for them,
airing their pocket-handkerchiefs in the sun, are dukes or
marquises, and the elegantly dressed men in light blue
frocks, all frogs and velvet, are just bagmen or watering-
place doctors.   It takes time, and great powers of discrim-
inality, Molly, to divide the sheep from the goats; but I
have got to that point at last, and I 'm proud to say that
he must be a really shrewd hand that imposes upon your
humble servant.

Long as this letter is, I 'd have made it longer if I had
time, for though we 're only a short time here, I have made
many remarks to myself about the ways and manners of
foreign country life.   The post, however, only goes out once
a week, and I don't wish to lose the occasion of giving you
the first intelligence of where we are, what we are doing,
and what 's — with the Virgin's help — before us!

Up to this, it has been all hospitalities and the honors of
the house, and I suppose, until the old Baron is up and able
to see us, we 'll hear no more about the marriage.   At all
events, you may mention the matter in confidence to Father
John and Mrs. Clancey; and if you like to tell the Davises,
and Tom Kelly, and Margaret, I 'm sure it will be safe with
them.   You can state that the Baron is one of the first families in Europe, and the richest.   His great-grandfather, or
mother, I forget which, was half-sister to the Empress of
Poland, and he is related, in some way or other, to either
the Grand Turk, or the Grand-Duke of Moravia, — but
either will do to speak of.

All the cellars under the castle are, they say, filled with
gold, in the rough, as it came out of his mines, and as he
lives in what might be called an unostensible manner, his
yearly savings is immense.   I suppose while the old man
lives the young couple will have to conform to his notions,
and only keep a moderate establishment; but when the Lord
takes him, I don't know Mary Anne if she 'll not make the
money fly.   That I may be spared to witness that blessed
day, and see my darling child in the enjoyment of every

happiness, and all the pleasures of wealth, is the constant prayer of your faithful friend,

JEMIMA DODD.

P. S. If Mary Anne has finished her sketch of the castle, I'll send it with this. She'd have done it yesterday, but, unfortunately, she had n't a bit of red she wanted for a fisherman's small-clothes, — for it seems they always wear red in a picture, — and had to send down to the town, eleven miles, for it.

Address me still here when you write, and let it be soon.

LETTER XXXVII.

KENNY JAMES DODD TO THOMAS PURCELL, ESQ., OF THE
GRANGE, BRUFF.

THE CASTLE OF WOLFENFELS.

MY DEAR TOM, — I'm glad old Molly has shown you Mrs.
D.'s epistle, which, independent of its other claims, saves
me all the trouble of explaining where we are, and how we
came there. We arrived on Wednesday last, and since that
have been living in a very quiet, humdrum kind of monotonous life, which, were it in Ireland, we should call, honestly, tiresome; but as the scene is Germany and the Black
Forest, I suppose should be chronicled as highly romantic
and interesting. To be plain, Tom, we inhabit a big house
— they call it a castle — in the midst of a large expanse of
maize and turnips, backed by a dense wood of pines.
We eat and drink in a very plain sort of over-abundant
and greasy fashion. We sleep in a thing like the drawer
of a cabinet, with a large pincushion on our stomachs for
covering. We smoke a home-grown weed, that has some
of the bad properties of tobacco; and we ponder — at
least I do — of how long it would take of an existence like
this to make a man wish himself a member of the vegetable
creation. Don't fancy that I'm growing exorbitant in my
demands for pleasure and amusement, nor believe that I
have forgotten the humdrum uniformity of my life at home.
I remember it all, and well. I can recall the lazy hours
passed in the sunshine of our few summer days; I can
bring back to mind the wearisome watching of the rain as it
poured down for a spell of two months together, when we
asked each other every morning, "What's to become of the
wheat? How are we to get in the turf, if this lasts?" The
newspapers, too, only alternated their narratives of outrage

with flood, and spoke of bridges, mills, and mail-coaches being carried away in all directions. I mention these to show you that, though "far from the land," not a trait of it is n't green in my memory. But still, Tom, there was, so to say, a tone and a keeping in the picture which is wanting here. Our home dulness impressed itself as a matter of necessity, not choice. We looked out of our window at a fine red-brick mansion, two miles away, — where we 've drunk many a bottle of claret, and in younger days danced the "White Cockade" till morning, — and we see it a police-station, or mayhap a union. A starved dog dashes past the door with a hen in his mouth; we recognize him as the last remnant of poor Fetherstone's foxhounds, now broken up and gone. The smoke does n't rise from the midst of the little copses of beech and alder, along the river side; no, the cabins are all roofless, and their once inhabitants are now in Australia, or toiling to enrich the commonwealth of America.

There is a stir and a movement going forward, it is true; but, unlike that which betokens the march of prosperity and gain, it only implies transition. Ay, Tom, all is changing around us. The gentry are going, the middle classes are going, and the peasant is going,— some of their free will, more from hard necessity. I know that the general opinion is favorable to all this, — in England, at least. The cry is ever, "Ireland is improving, — Ireland will be better." But my notion is that by Ireland we should understand not alone the soil, the rocks, and the rivers, but the people, — the heart and soul and life-blood that made the island the generous, warm-hearted, social spot we once knew it. Take away these, and I no longer recognize it as my country. What matters it to me if the Scotchman or the Norfolk farmer is to prosper where we only could exist? My sympathies are not with *him*. You might as well try and console me for the death of my child by showing me how comfortably some other man's boy could sleep in his bed. I want to see Ireland prosper with Irishmen; and I wish it, because I know in my heart the thing is possible and practicable.

I 'm old enough — and, indeed, so are you — to remember

when the English used to be satisfied to laugh at our blunders and our bulls, and ridicule our eccentricities; but the spirit of the times is changed, and now they 've taken to rail at us, and abuse us, as if we were the greatest villains in Europe. They assume the very tone the Yankee adopts to the Red Man, and frankly say, "You must be extirpated!" Hence the general flight that you now witness. Men naturally say, "Why cling to a land that is no longer secure to us? Why link our destinies to a soil that may be denied to us to-morrow?" And the English will be sorry for this yet. Take my word for it, Tom, they 'll rue it! Paddy, by reason of his poverty and his taste for adventure, and a touch of romance in his nature, was always ready to enlist. He did n't know what might not turn out of it. He knew that Wellington was an Irishman, and, faith, he had only to read very little to learn that most of the best men came from the same country. Luck might, then, stand to him, and, at all events, it was n't a bad change from fourpence a day, stone-breaking!

Now, John Bull took another view of it. *He* was better off at home. He had n't a spark of adventure about him. His only notion of worldly advancement led through money. You 'll not catch him becoming a soldier. Every year will make him less and less disposed to the life. Cheapen food and luxuries, reduce tariffs and the cost of foreign produce, and the laborer will think twice before he 'll give up home and its comforts, to be, as the song says, —

> "Proud as a goat,
>   With a fine scarlet coat,
>   And a long cap and feather."

Turn over these things in your mind, Tom, and see if England has not made a great mistake in eradicating the very class she might have reckoned upon in any warlike emergency. Take my word for it, it is a fine thing to have at your disposal a hundred thousand fellows who can esteem a shilling a day a high premium, and who are not too well off in the world to be afraid of leaving it! How did I come here at all? What has led me into this digression? I protest to you solemnly, Tom, I don't know. I can only

say that my hand trembles, and my head throbs with indignation, as I think over this insolent cant that tells us that
Ireland has no chance of prosperity save in ceasing to be
Irish. It is worse than a lie, — it is a mean, cowardly
slander!

I must leave off this till my brain is calmer: besides,
whether it is the light wines I'm drinking, or my anger has
brought it on, but I've just got a terrible twinge of gout in
my right foot.

Tuesday Evening.

I have passed a miserable twenty-four hours. They've
all the incentives to gout in this country, and yet they
don't appear to have the commonest remedies against it.
I sent Belton's recipe to be made up at the apothecaries',
and they had never as much as heard of one of the ingredients! They told me to regulate my diet, and be careful to
avoid acids, — and this, while I was bellowing like a bull
with pain. It was like replying to my request for a shirt,
by saying that they were going to sow flax in August. It's
their confounded cookery, and the vinegar we wash it down
with, has given me this!

The old housekeeper at last took compassion on my sufferings, and made me up a kind of broth of herbs that nearly
finished me. She assured me that they all grew wild in the
fields, and were freely eaten by the cattle. I can only say
it's well that Nebuchadnezzar was n't put out to graze here!
Sea-sickness was a mild nausea compared to it. I'm better
now; but so low and so depressed, and with such loss of
energy, that in a discussion with Mrs. D. about Mary
Anne's "trousseau," as they call it, I gave in to everything!

Since this attack seized me, events have made a great
progress; indeed, a suspiciously minded person would n't
scruple to say that a mild poison had been administered to
me to forward the course of negotiations; and in my heart
and soul I believe that another bowl of the same broth
would make me consent to my daughter's union with the
Bey of Tunis! The poor old Dean of Lurra used to say of
the Baths of Kreutznach, "I've lost enough flesh in three
weeks to make a curate!" — and, indeed, when I look at

myself in the glass, I turn involuntarily around to see where's the rest of me!

Meanwhile, as I said, all has been arranged and settled, and the marriage is fixed for an early day in the coming week. I suppose it's all for the best. I take it that the match is a very great one; but I own to you frankly, Tom, I'd have fewer misgivings if the dear child was going to be the wife of some respectable man of her own country, though he had neither a castle to live in nor a title to bestow.

Foreigners are essentially and totally different from us in everything; and marrying one of them is, to my thinking, the very next thing to being united to some strange outlandish beast, as one reads of in fairy tales. I suppose that my prejudice is a very mean and narrow-minded one; but I can't get rid of it. It looks churlish and cold-hearted in me that I cannot show the same joy on the occasion that the others display; but, with all my efforts, and the very best will, I can't do it, Tom. The bridegroom, too, is not to my taste: he is one of those moping, dreamy, moonstruck fellows, that pass their lives in an imaginary sphere of thought and action; and, to *my* thinking, these people are distasteful to the world at large, and insufferable to their wives.

I think I see that Mary Anne already anticipates he will prove a stubborn subject. Her mother, however, gives her courage and support. She gently insinuates, too, that worse cases have been treated successfully. Lord help us, it's a strange world!

As to the material features of the affair, — I mean as regards means and fortune, — he appears to have more than enough, yet not so much as to prevent his giving a very palpable hint to me about what I intended to give my daughter. He made the overture with a most laudable candor, though, I own, with no excess of delicacy. James, however, had in a manner prepared me for it, and mentioned that I was indebted for this gratification, as I am for a variety of others, to Mrs. D. It seems that, by way of giving a very imposing notion of our possessions, she had cut the county map out of O'Kelly's old Gazetteer, and passed it off for the survey of our estate. Of course I could n't disavow the statement, and have been reduced to the pleasant alternative of settling on my daughter about five baronies and twenty townlands of Tipperary, with no inconsiderable share of villages and hamlets. Some old leases, an insurance policy, and a writ against myself have served me for title-deeds; and though the young Baron pores over them for hours with a dictionary, thanks to the figurative language of the law, they have defied detection!

The father is still too ill to receive me, but each day I am promised an interview with him. Of what benefit to either of us it is to prove, may be guessed from the fact that we cannot speak to each other. You will perceive from all this, Tom, that I am by no means enamored of our approaching greatness; and it is but fair to state that James is even less so. He calls the Baron a "snob;" and probably, in all the fashionable vocabulary of an enlightened age, a more depreciatory epithet could not be discovered. What a sham and a humbug is all the parade we make of our parental affection, and what a gross cheat, too, do we practise upon ourselves by it! We train up a girl from infancy with every care and devotedness, — we surround her with all the luxuries our means can compass, and every affection of our hearts, — and we give her away, for "better and for worse," to the first fellow that offers with what seems a reasonable chance of being able to support her!

Many of us would n't take a butler with the scanty knowledge we accept a son-in-law. His moral qualities, his disposition, the habits he has been reared in, — what do we know of them? Less than nothing! And yet, while we ask about these, and twenty more, of the man to whom we are about to confide the key of our cellar, we intrust the happiness of our child to an unknown individual, the only ascertained fact about whom — if even that be so — is his income!

As I should like to tell you every step I take in this affair, I 'll not send off my letter till I can give you the latest information. Meanwhile let me impress upon you that it is now three months since I received a shilling from Ireland. James has just informed me that there is not fifty pounds left of the M'Carthy legacy, of which his mother only gave

him permission to draw for three hundred. The debate
upon this, when it comes, will be strong. What I intend is
that immediately after Mary Anne's marriage we should
return to Ireland; but of course I reserve the declaration
for a fitting opportunity, since I well know how it will be
received. Cary would never marry a foreigner, nor would
anything induce me to consent to her doing so. James is
only frittering away his best years here in idleness and dissipation; and if I can get nothing for him from the Government, he must emigrate to Australia or New Zealand. As
for Mrs. D., the sooner she gets home to Dodsborough the
better for her health, her means, and her morals!

I am afraid to say a word about Ireland and Irish affairs,
for as sure as I do I stick fast there; still I must say that I
think you 're wrong for abusing those members that have
accepted office from Government. Put it to yourself, my
dear Tom; if anybody offered you fifty pounds for the old
gray mare you drive into market of a Saturday, would you
set about explaining that she was blind of an eye, and a
roarer, with a splint before, and a spavin behind? Would n't
you rather expatiate upon her blood and breeding, her endurance of fatigue, and her fine trotting action? I don't know
you if you would n't! Well, it 's just the same with these
fellows. Briefless lawyers and distressed gentlemen as they
are, why should they say to the Ministry, "You 're giving
too much for us; we can neither speak for you nor write for
you; we have neither influence at home, nor power abroad;
we are a noisy, riotous, disorderly set of devils, always
quarrelling amongst ourselves, and never agreeing, except
when there 's a bit of robbery or roguery to be done; don't
think of buying *us;* it is a clear waste of public money;
we 'd only disgrace and not benefit you"? If anybody is to
be blamed, it is the Ministers that bought them, Tom.

As to all your disputed questions of education, tenant-
right, and taxation, take my word for it you have no chance
of settling them amicably; and for this reason: a great
number of excellent men, on both sides, have pledged themselves so strongly to particular opinions that they cannot
decently recant, and yet they begin to see many points in a
different view, and would, were the matter to come fresh

before them, treat it in another fashion. If you really wish to see Ireland better, try and get people to let her alone for some fifteen or twenty years. She is nearly ruined by doctoring. Just wait a bit, and see if the natural goodness of constitution won't do more for her than all your nostrums.

James has just interrupted me, to say that he has shot "the partridge," for it seems there was only one in the country. That's the fruits of revolution. Before the year '48, this part of Germany abounded in game of every sort — partridges, hares, and quails, in immense abundance, besides plenty of deer on the hills, and that excellent bird the "Auer-Hahn," which is like the black-cock we have at home. When the troubles came, the peasants shot everything; and now the whole breed of game is extinct. They tell me it is the same throughout Bohemia and Hungary, — the two best sporting countries in all Europe. Foreigners were never oppressed with game-laws as we are; there was a far wider liberty enjoyed by them in this respect, and, in consequence, the privileges were less abused; so that really the wholesale destruction is much to be regretted. But is it not exactly what always follows in every case of popular domination? The masses love excess, and are never satisfied with anything short of it. I don't pretend to say that the Germans had not good and valid reasons for being dissatisfied with their Governments. I believe, in my heart, it would be difficult to imagine a more stupid piece of ingenuous blundering than a German Administration; and this is the less excusable when one thinks of the people over whom they rule.

The excesses of that same year of '48 will be the stock-in-trade for these grinding Governments for many a day to come. It is like a "barring out" to a cruel schoolmaster; the excuse for any violence he may wish to indulge in. At the same time I say this, I tell you frankly that none of the foreigners I have yet seen are fit for the system of a representative Government. From whatever causes I know not, but they are less patient, less given to calm investigation, than the English. Their perceptions are as quick — perhaps quicker — but they will not weigh the consequences of conflicting interests, and, above all, they will

not put any restrictions upon their own liberty for the
benefit of the community at large. Their origin, climate,
traditions, and so forth, of course influence them greatly;
but I have a notion, Tom, that our domesticity has a very
considerable share in the formation of that temperate and
obedient spirit so observable amongst us. I think I see the
sly dimple that's deepening in the corner of your mouth as
you murmur to yourself, "Kenny James is thinking of his
Mrs. D. He's pondering over the natural results of home
discipline." But that is not what I mean, at least it is not
the whole of it. My theory is that a family is the best
training-school for the virtues that prosper in a well-ordered
State, and that the little incidents of home life have a wonderful bearing upon, and similarity to, the great events that
stir mankind.

I was going to become very abstruse and incomprehensible, I've no doubt, on this theme, but Mrs. D. just
dropped in with a small catalogue of some three hundred and
twenty-one articles Mary Anne requires for her wedding.

I ventured to hint that her mother entered the connubial state with a more modest preparation; and hereupon
arose one of those lively discussions now so frequent
between us, in which, amidst other desultory and miscellaneous remarks, she drew a graphic contrast between
marrying a man of rank and title, and "making a low connection that has forever served to alienate the affection of
one's family."

Will you tell me what peculiarity there is in the atmosphere, or the food, or the electric influences abroad, that
have made a woman that was at least occasionally reasonable at home a most unmanageable fury on the Continent?
I don't want to deny that we had our little differences at
Dodsborough, but they were "tiffs," — mere skirmishes, —
but here they are downright pitched battles, Tom. She
will have it so, too. She won't exchange a few shots and
retire, but she comes up in line, with her heavy artillery,
and seems resolved to have a day of it! If this blessed
tour brought me no other pleasures than these, I'd have
reason to thank it! You, of course, are quite ready to
assert that the fault is as much mine as hers, — that I pro-

voke contradiction, — that I even invite conflict! There
you are perfectly in the wrong! I do, I acknowledge,
intrench myself in a strong position, and only fire an
occasional shot at any tempting exposure of the enemy;
but she comes on by storm and escalade, and, sparing
neither age nor sex, never stops till she's in the very
heart of the citadel. That I come out maimed, crippled,
and disabled from such encounters, is not to be wondered
at.

Amongst the other signs of progress of our enlightened
age, a very remarkable one is the habit, now become a law,
for everybody with any pretensions to the rank of a gentleman, to live in the same style, or, at least, with as close
an imitation as he can of it, as persons of large fortune.
Men like myself were formerly satisfied with giving their
friends a little sherry and port at dinner, continued afterwards, till some considerate friend begged, " as a favor,"
for a glass of punch. Now we start with Madeira after the
soup, if you haven't had oysters and chablis before, hock
with your first *entrée*, and champagne afterwards, graduat-
ing into Chambertin with " the roast," and Pacquarete with
the dessert, claret, at double the price it costs in Ireland,
closing the entertainment. Why, a duke cannot do more
than Kenny Dodd at this rate! To be sure the cookery
will be more refined, and the wines in higher condition.
Moët will be iced to its due point, and Chateau Margaux
will be served in a carefully aired decanter; but the cost,
the outlay, will be fully as much in one case as the other.
Have we — that is to say, humble men like myself — gained
by this in an intellectual or social point of view? Not a
bit of it! We have lost all that easy cordiality that was
native to us in our former condition, and we have not become as coldly polite and elegantly tiresome as the grand
folk.

The same system obtains in other matters. *My* daughter
must be dressed on her wedding-day like Lady Olivia or
Lady Jemima, who has a father a marquis, and fifty thousand pounds settled on her for pin-money.

The globe has to become tributary to the marriage of
Mary Anne! Cashmere sends a shawl; Lyons, silk; and

Genoa, velvet; furs from Hudson's Bay, and feathers from Mexico; Valenciennes and Brussels contribute lace; Paris reserving for her peculiar share the architectural skill that is to combine these costly materials, and construct out of them that artistic being they call a " bride." Taking a wife with nothing " but the clothes on her back " used to be the expression of a most disinterested marriage. Now it might mean anything between Swan and Edgar's and Howell and James's, or, to state it differently, between moderate embarassment aud irretrievable ruin!

If you ask me how I am to pay for all this, or when, I tell you honestly and fairly, I don't know. As well as I can make out the last accounts you sent me, we're getting deeper into debt every day; but as figures always distract and puzzle me, I'd rather you'd put the case into something like a statement in words, just saying when we may expect a remittance, and how much it will be. I find that I shall lose the mail if I don't cease at once; but I'll send you a few lines by to-morrow's post, as I have something important to say, but can't remember it now.

Yours, ever sincerely,

KENNY JAMES DODD.

LETTER XXXVIII.

MY DEAR TOM, — The post had n't left this five minutes
yesterday, when I remembered what I wanted to say to you.
Wednesday, the 26th, is fixed for the happy occasion; and
if nothing should intervene, you may insert the following
paragraph in the " Tipperary Press," under the accustomed
heading of " Marriage in High Life " : " The Baron Adolf
Heinrich Conrad Hapsburg von Wolfenschäfer, Lord of the
Manors of Hohendeken, Kalbsbratenhausen, and Schwein-
kraut, to Mary Anne, eldest daughter of Kenny James Dodd,
Esq., of Dodsborough, in this county." Faith, Tom, I was
near saying " universally regretted by a large circle of
afflicted survivors," for I was just wishing myself dead and
buried! But you must put it in the usual formula of " beautiful and accomplished," and take care it is not applied to
the bridegroom, for, upon my conscience, his claim to the
first epithet could n't be settled by even a Parliamentary
title! My heart is heavy about it all, and I wish it was
over!

If anything exemplifies the vanity of human wishes, it
is our efforts to marry our daughters, and our regrets when
the plans succeed. Tom goes to India, and Billy to sea,
and there is scarcely a gap in the family circle. " The
boys " were seldom at home, — they were shooting in Scot-
land, or hunting in England, or fishing in Norway. They
never, so to say, made part of the effective garrison of the
house; they came and went with that rackety good-humor
that even in quiet families is pleasurable; but your girls are
household gods : lose *them*, even one of them, and the altar
is despoiled. The thousand little unobtrusive duties, noise-

less cares, that make home better a hundred-fold than anywhere else, be it ever so rich and splendid, the unasked
solicitude, the watchful attention that provides for your
little daily wants and habits, are all *their* province.   And
just fancy, then, what scheming and intriguing we practise
to get rid of them!   You'll say that this shows we are
above the selfishness of only considering our own enjoyment, and that we sacrifice all for their happiness.   There
you mistake; our sole aim is a rich man, — our one notion
of a good marriage is that the husband be wealthy.   It's
not a man like myself, who has sometimes paid fifty, ay,
sixty per cent for money, that can afford to sneer at and
despise it; but this I will say, that the mere possession of it
will not suffice for happiness.   I know fellows with fifteen
thousand a year that have not the heart to spend five hundred.   I know others that, with as much, are always over
head and ears in debt, raising cash everywhere and anyhow!
What kind of life must a girl lead that marries either of
these?   And yet would you or I think of refusing such a
match for a daughter?   Let me tell you, Tom, that for
people of small fortune, the nunneries were fine things!
What signifies serge and simple diet to the wearisome
drudgery of a governess!   If I was a woman, I think I'd
rather sit in my quiet cell, working an embroidered suit of
body clothes for Father O'Leary, than I'd be snubbed by
the family of some vulgar citizen, tortured by the brats, and
insulted by the servants.

I don't suppose that it signifies a straw one way or other,
but I feel some compunctions of conscience at the way I
have been assigning imaginary estates, mines, woods, and
collieries to Mary Anne for the last three days.   I know
it's mere greed makes the Baron so eager on the subject,
since he is enormously wealthy.   James and I rode twelve
miles, this morning, through a forest that belongs to the
castle, and the arable land stretches more than that distance
in another direction; but who knows how he'll behave when
he discovers she has nothing!   To be sure, we can always
ascribe our ruin to political causes, and, in verification, exhibit ourselves as poor as need be; but still I don't like it.
And this is one of the blessed results of a false position, —

one step in a wrong direction very frequently necessitates a
long journey. Yesterday I protested to my affluence;
to-day I vouched for the nobility of my family. Heaven
only can tell what I won't swear to to-morrow! . And again
I am interrupted by Mrs. D., who has just come to inform
me that though the bride's finery can all be had at Paris, —
whither the happy couple are to repair for the honeymoon,
— there are certain indispensables must be obtained at once
from Baden; and she begs that I will privately write a few
lines to Morris, who will, of course, undertake the commission. It is not without shame that I enclose a list of purchases to make, which, to a man who knew what we were in
Ireland, will appear preposterous; but the false position we
have attained to is surrounded with interminable mortifica-
tions of the same kind.

Ah, Tom! I remember the time when, if a bride changed
her smart white silk and muslin that she wore at the altar
for a good brown or blue satin pelisse to travel in, we
thought her a miracle of fashion and finery; but now the
millinery of a wedding is the principal thing. There is a
stereotyped formula, out of which there is no hope of conjugal happiness; and the bride that begins life without
Brussels lace. enters upon her career with gloomy omens!
Now, a scarf of this alone costs thirty guineas; you may, if
you like, go as high as a hundred and fifty. Why can't
people wait for the ruin that is so sure to overtake them,
without forestalling it in this way? Twenty pounds for
clothes, and a trip to Castle Connel or Kilkee for the
honeymoon, would have satisfied every wish of Mary Anne's
heart in Ireland; and if she drove away in a post-chaise
with four horses for the first stage, she'd have been the envy
of all the marriageable girls for miles round.

But now I have had to ask Morris to buy a travelling-
carriage, because Mrs. D., in one of those expansions of
splendor that occasionally attack her, said to the Baron,
"Oh, take one of our carriages, we have left several of
them at Baden." The excellent woman cannot be brought
to perceive that romance of this kind is a most expensive
amusement. I have drawn a bill on you for four hundred at
three months, to meet these, and sent it to Morris to "get

done." I hope he 'll succeed, and I hope you 'll pay it when it comes due; so that come what will, Tom, my intentions are honorable!

If Mrs. D. and myself had been upon better terms, we might have discussed this marriage question more fully and confidentially, but there are now so many cabinet difficulties that we rarely hold a council, and when we do, we are sure to disagree. This is another blessed result of our continent-alizing. Home had its duties, and with them came that spirit of concord and agreement so essential to family happi-ness; but in this vagabond kind of existence, where every-thing is feigned, unreal, and unnatural, all concert and confidence is completely lost.

Now I have told you frankly and fairly everything about us, and don't take advantage of my candor by giving advice, for there is nothing in this world I have so little taste for. There 's no man above the condition of an idiot that is n't thoroughly aware of his failings and shortcomings, but all that knowledge does n't bring him an inch nearer the cure of them. Do you think I 'm not fully alive to everything you could say of my wasteful habits, my improvidence, indolence, irritability, and so forth? I know them all better than you do, — ay, and I feel them acutely, too, for I know them to be incurable! Reformation, indeed! Do you know when a man gives up dancing, Tom? When he 's too stiff in the knees for it. There 's the whole philosophy of life. When we grow wiser, as they are pleased to call it, it is always in spite of ourselves!

I find that by enclosing this to Morris, he can forward it to you by the bag of the Legation. Once more let me remind you of our want of cash, and believe me, very faith-fully your friend,

KENNY I. DODD.

P. S. Address me " Freyburg, to be forwarded to the Schloss, Wolfenfels."

LETTER XXXIX.

BETTY COBB TO MRS. SHUSAN O'SHEA, PRIEST'S HOUSE, BRUFF.

DEAR MRS. SHUSAN, — I was meaning to write to you for the last week, but could n't by reason of the conflagration I was in, for sure any poor girl might feel it, seeing that I was far away among furriners, and had nobody to advise, barrin' the evil counsels of my wicked heart. We cam here two weeks gone, on a visit to the father of the young man that's going to marry "Mary Anne." It's a great big ould place, like the jail at Limerick, only darker, with little windows, and a flite of stairs out of every corner in it. And the furnishing is n't a bit newer. It's a bit of rag here and a rag there, an ould cabbinet, a hard sofia, and maybe four wooden chairs that would take a ladder to get into! Eatin' and drinkin' likewise the same. Biled beef — biled first for the broth, and sarved afterwards with cow-comers, sliced and steeped in oil — the Heavens preserve us! Then a dish of roast vale, with rasberry jam and musheroons, for they tries the human stomich with every ingradiant they can think of!

But the great favorite of all is a salad made out of potatoes, biled hard, sliced and pickled the same way as the cow-comers! A bowl of that, Mrs. Shusan, after a long dinner, makes you feel as full as a tick, and if the house was afire I could n't run! To be sure, when the meal is over everybody sits down to coffee, and does n't distress themselves about anything for a matter of two hours. And, indeed, I must make the remark that "manials" is n't as badly treated anywhere in the whole 'versal globe as in Ireland, and if it was n't that I hear the people is runnin' away o' themselves, I 'd write a letter to the papers about it! 'T is exactly like pigs you are, no better; potatoes and buttermilk all the year round! deny it if you can. Could you offer a pig less wages than four pound a year?

I must say, too, Shusan, that eatin' one's fill molly-fies ther nature, and subdues ther hasty dispositions in a wonderful way; I know it myself; and that after a strong supper now I can bear more from the mistress than I used at home, only giving a sigh now and then out of the fulness of my heart. But it's not them things I wanted to tell you, but of the state of my infections. Don't be angry with me, Mrs. Shusan. I don't forget the iligant lessons you gave me long ago, about thrusting the men; I know well how thrue every word you said is. They're base, and wicked, and deceatful! Flatterin' us when we're young and beautiful, and gibin' and jeerin' when we're ould as yourself! But what's the use of fiting agin the will of Providence? Sure, if he intended us to have better husbands it's not them craytures he'd have left us to! My sentiments is these, Shusy: 'T is a way of chastezin' us is marriage! The throubles and tumults we have with a man are our crosses, and it's only cowardly to avoid them. Meet your feat, say I, whatever it be, — whether it be a man or the measles, don't be afraid!

I'm shure and sartain it's nothing but fear makes young girls go and be nuns; they're afraid, and no wonder, of the wickedness of the world; but somehow, Shusan, like everything else in this life, one gets used to it. I know it well, there's many a thing I see now, without minding, that long ago I dared not look at. "Live and learn," they say, and there's nothing so thrue! And talking of that, you'd be shocked to see how Mary Anne goes on wid the young Baron. She, that would scarce let poor Doctor Belton spake to her alone. We meet them walkin' in the lonesomest places together; and Taddy and I never goes into the far part of the wood without seeing them! And that's not all of it, my dear, but she must get the mistress to give me a lecture about going off myself with a man.

"Does n't your daughter do it, ma'am?" says I. "Is all the wickedness of this world," says I, "to be kept for one's betters?"

"Do you call marriage wickedness?" says she.

" Sometimes it is, ma'am," says I, with a look she understood well.

" You 're a huzzy," says she; " and I 'll give you warnin' next Saturday."

" I 'll take it now," says I, " ma'am, for I 'm going to better myself."

If ye saw her face, Shusy, as I said this! She knows in her heart that she could n't get on at all without me. Not a word of a furrin lingo can she say; and I 'm obleeged to traduce her meanin' to all the other sarvants! And, indeed, that 's the way I become such an iligant linguist; and it 's no differ to me now between talkin' French and Jarman, — I make them just the same!

I was n't in my room when Mary Anne was after me.

" Ain't you a fool, Betty?" says she, puttin' a hand on my shoulder.

" Maybe I am, miss," says I; " but there 's others fools as well as me ! "

" But I mean," says she, " is n't it silly to fall out with mamma, — that was always so good, and so kind, and so fond of you?"

I saw at once, Shusy, how the wind was, and so I just went on folding up my collars and settling my things without a word.

"I 'm sure," says she, "you could n't leave her in a faraway country like this!"

"The dearest friends must part, miss," says I.

"Not to speak of your own desolate and deserted condition," says she.

"There 's them that won't lave me dissolute and disconsoled, miss," says I. And with that, Shusy, I told her that Taddy Hetzler had made me honorable proposals.

"But you 'd not think of Taddy," says she. "He 's only a herd," says she.

"We must take what we can get, miss," says I, "and be thankful in this life."

And she blushed red up to the eyes, Shusy; for she knew well what I meant by *that!*

"But a nice girl, and a purty girl like you, Betty," says she, *"sleudering"* me, "is n't it throwing yourself away?

Sure, ye have only to wait a little to make an iligant match here on the Continent. Don't be precipitouous," says she, "but see the effect you'll make with that beautiful pink gownd;" and here, Shusan, she gave me all as one as a bran new silk of the mistress's, with five flounces, and lace trimmins down the front! It's what they call glassy silk, and shines like it!

"I'm sorry, miss," says I, "that as I took the mistress's warnin', I'm obleeged to refuse you."

"Nonsense, Betty," says she; "I'll arrange all that."

"But my feelins, miss, — my feelins."

"Well, I'll even engage to smoothe these," says she, laughing.

And so, Shusy, I had to laugh too; for my nature is always to be easy and compliyant; and when anybody means well to me, they can do what they plaze with me. It's a weak part in my character, but I can't help it. "I'm not able to be selfish, Miss Mary Anne," says I.

"No, Betty, *that* you are not," says she, patting my cheek.

But for all that, Shusy, I'm not going to give up Taddy till I know why, — tho' I didn't say so to her. So I just put up the pink gownd in my drawer, and went up and told the mistress I'd stay; but begged she wouldn't try my nerves that way another time, for my constitution wouldn't bear repated shocks. I saw she was burstin' to say something, but dar'n't, Shusy, and she tore a lace cuff to tatters while I was talkin'. Well, well, there's no denyin' it, anyhow; manials has many troubles, but they can give a great deal of annoyance and misery if they set about it right. You'd like to hear about Taddy, and I'll be candid and own that he isn't what would be called handsome in Ireland, though here he is reckoned a fine-looking man. He is six foot four and a half, without shoes, a little bent in the shoulders, has long red hair, and sore eyes; that cums from the snow, for he's out in all weathers — after the pigs. You're surprised at that, and well you may; for instead of keeping the craytures in a house as we do, and giving them all the filth we can find to eat, they turns them out wild into the woods, to eat beech-nuts, and acorns, and chestnuts;

and the beasts grow so wicked that it's not safe for a stranger to go near them; and even the man that guides them they call a "swine-fearer."[1] Taddy is one of these; and when he's dressed in a goat-skin coat and cap, leather gaiters buttoned on his legs, and reachin' to the hips, and a long pole, with an iron hook and a hatchet at the end of it, and a naked knife, two feet long, at his side, you'd think the pigs would be more likely to be afraid of *him !* Indeed, the first time I saw him come into the kitchen, with a great hairy dog they call a fang-hound at his heels, I schreeched out with frite, for I thought them — God forgive me! — the ugliest pare I ever set eyes on. To be sure, the green shade he wore over his eyes, and the beard that grew down to his breast, did n't improve him; but I've trimmed him up since that; and it's only a slight squint, and two teeth that sticks out at the side of his mouth, that I can't remedy at all !

Paddy Byrne spends his time mockin' him, and makin' pictures of him on the servants' hall with a bit of charcoal. It well becomes a dirty little spalpeen like him to make fun of a man four times his size. His notion of manly beauty is four foot eight, short legs, long breeches and gaiters, with a waistcoat over the hips, and a Jim Crow! A monkey is graceful compared to it!

Taddy is not much given to talkin', but he has told me that he has been on the estate, "with the pigs," he calls it, since he was eight years old; and as he said, another time, that "he was nine-and-twenty years a herd," you can put the two together, and it makes him out thirty-three or thirty-four years of age. He never had any father or mother, which is a great advantage, and, as he remarks, "it's the same to him if there came another Flood and drowned all the world to-morrow ! "

Our plans is to live here till we can go and take a bit of land for ourselves; and as Taddy has saved something, and has very good idais about his own advantage, I trust, with the blessin' of the Virgin, that we'll do very well. This that

---

[1] Perhaps the accomplished Betty has been led into this pardonable mistake from the sound of the German epithet " Schwein-führer." — *Editor of " Dodd Correspondence."*

I tell you now, Shusan, is all in confidence, because to the neighbors, and to Sam Healey, you can say that I am going to be married to a rich farmer that has more pigs — and that's thrue — than ye'd see in Ballinasloe Fair.

What distresses me most of all is, I can't make out what religion he's of, if he has any at all! I try him very hard about penance and 'tarnal punishments, but all he says is, "When we're married I'll know all about that."

As the mistress writ all about Mary Anne's marriage to Mrs. Galagher, at the house, I don't say anything about it; but he's an ugly crayture, Shusan dear, and there's a hang-dog, treach'rous look about him I wonder any young girl could like. The servants, too, knows more of him than they lets on, but, by rayson of their furrin language, there's no coming at it.

Between ourselves, she does n't take to the marriage at all, for I seen her twice cryin' in her room over some ould letters; but she bundled them up whin she seen me, and tried to laugh.

"I wonder, Betty," says she, "will I ever see Dodsborough again!"

"Who knows, miss?" said I; "but it would be a pity if you did n't, and so many there that's fond of you!"

"I don't believe it," says she, sharp. "I don't believe there's one cares a bit about me!"

"Baithershin!" says I, mocking.

"Who does?" says she; "can ye tell me even one?"

"Sure there's Miss Davis," says I, "and the Kellys, and there's Miss Kitty Doolan, and ould Molly, not to spake of Dr. Bel—"

"There, do not speak of him," says she, getting red; "the very names of the people make me shudder. I hope I'll never see one of them."

Now, Shusan dear, I told you all that it's in my mind, and hope you'll write to me the same. If you could send me the gray cloak with the blue linin', and the bayver bonnet I wore last winter two years, they'd be useful to me here, and you could tell the neighbors that it was new clothes you were sendin' me for my weddin'. Be sure ye tell me how

Sam Healey bears it. Tell him from me, with my regards, that I hope he won't take to drink, and desthroy his constitution.

You can write to me still as before, to your attached and true friend,

BETTY COBB.

LETTER XL.

KENNY I. DODD TO THOMAS PURCELL, ESQ., OF THE GRANGE, BRUFF.

CONSTANCE, SWITZERLAND.

MY DEAR TOM, — Before passion gets the better of me, and I forget all about it, let me acknowledge the welcome arrival of your post bill for one hundred, but for which, Heaven knows in what additional embarrassment I might now be in. You will see, by the address, that I am in Switzerland. How we came here I'll try and explain, if Providence grants me patience for the effort; this being the third time I have addressed myself to the task unsuccessfully.

I need not refer to the situation in which my last letter to you left us. You may remember that I told you of the various preparations that were then in progress for a certain auspicious event, whose accomplishment was fixed for the ensuing week. Amongst others, I wrote to Morris for some articles of dress and finery to be procured at Baden, and for, if possible, a comfortable travelling-carriage, with a suffi- ciency of boxes and imperials.

Of course in doing so it was necessary, or at least it was fitting, that I should make mention of the cause for these extraordinary preparations, and I did so by a very brief allusion to the coming event, and to the rank of my future son-in-law, the youthful Baron and heir of Wolfenfels. I am not aware of having said much more than this, for my letter was so crammed with commissions, and catalogues of purchases, that there was little space disposable for more intelligence. I wrote on a Monday, and on the following Wednesday evening I was taking a stroll with James through the park, chatting over the approaching event in our family, when a mounted postboy galloped up with a letter, which being marked "Most pressing and immediate," the postmaster had very properly forwarded to me with all expedition. It was in Morris's hand, and very brief. I give it to you verbatim: —

"My dear Sir, — For Heaven's sake do not advance another step in this affair. You have been grossly imposed upon. As soon as I can procure horses I will join you, and expose the most scandalous trick that has ever come to the knowledge of yours truly,

"E. Morris.

"Post-House, Tite See. 2 o'clock p.m. Wednesday."

You may imagine — *I* cannot attempt to describe — the feelings with which James and I read and re-read these lines. I suppose we had passed the letter back and forwards to each other fully a dozen times, ere either of us could summon composure to speak.

"Do you understand it, James?" said I.

"No," said he. "Do *you*?"

"Not unless the scoundrel is married already," said I.

"That was exactly what had occurred to *me*," replied he. "'Most scandalous trick,' are the words; and they can only mean that."

"Morris is such a safe fellow, — so invariably sure of whatever he says."

"Precisely the way I take it," cried James. "He is far too cautious to make a grave charge without ample evidence to sustain it! We may rely upon it that he knows what he is about."

"But bigamy is a crime in Germany. They send a fellow to the galleys for it," said I. "Is it likely that he'd put himself in such peril?"

"Who knows!" said James, "if he thought he was going to get an English girl of high family, and with a pot of money!"

Shall I own to you, Tom, that remark of James's nearly stunned me, — carelessly and casually as it fell from *him*, it almost overwhelmed *me*, and I asked myself, Why should he think she was of high family? Why should he suppose she had a large fortune? Who was it that propagated these delusions? and if there really was a "scandalous trick," as Morris said, could I affirm that all the roguery was on one side? Could I come into court with clean hands, and say, "Mrs. Dodd has not been cheating, neither has Kenny James"? Where are these broad acres of arable and pasture,— these verdant forests and swelling lawns, that I have been bestowing with such boundless munificence? How shall we prove these fourteen quarterings that we have been quoting incessantly for the past three weeks? "No matter for *that*," thought I, at length. "If the fellow has got another wife, I 'll break every bone in his skin!" I must have pondered this sentiment aloud, for James echoed it even more forcibly, adding, by way of sequel, "And kick him from this to Rotterdam!"

I mention this in detail to show that we both jumped at once to the same conclusion, and, having done so, never disputed the correctness of our guess. We now proceeded to discuss our line of action,— James advising that he should be "brought to book" at once; I overruling the counsel by showing that we could do nothing whatever till Morris arrived.

"But to-morrow is fixed for the wedding!" exclaimed James.

"I know it," said I, "and Morris will be here to-night. At all events, the marriage shall not take place till he comes."

"I 'd charge him with it on the spot," cried James. "I 'd tell him, in plain terms, the information had come to me from an authority of unimpeachable veracity, and to refute it if he could."

"Refute what?" said I. "Don't you see, boy, that we really are not in possession of any single fact, — we have not even an allegation?"

I assure you, Tom, that I had to make him read the note over again, word by word, before he was convinced of the case.

As we walked back to the castle, we talked over the affair, and turned it in every possible shape, both of us agreeing

that we could not, with any safety, intrust our intelligence
to the womankind.

"We 'll watch him," said James; "we 'll keep an eye on
him, and wait for Morris."

I own to you my feelings distressed me to that degree I
could scarcely enter the house, and as to appearing at supper it was clean out of the question. How could I bring
myself to accept the shelter of a man's roof against whom I
harbored the very worst suspicions! Could I be Judas
enough to sit down at table with one against whom I was
hatching exposure and shame! It was bad enough to think
that my wife and daughter were there. As for James, he
took his place at the board with such an expression in his
features that I verily believe Banquo looked a pleasanter
guest at Macbeth's banquet. I betook myself to the terrace, and walked there till midnight, watching with eye and
ear towards the road that led from Freyburg.

"Night or Blücher!" said the Duke, on the memorable
field at Waterloo; but there was the blessing of an alternative in *his* case. *Mine* had none. It was Morris or nothing
with *me*. And now I began anathematizing to myself those
crusty, secret, cautious natures that are always satisfied
when they cry "Stop!" without taking the trouble to say
wherefore. What may be a precipice to one man, thought
I, is only a step to another! How does *he* know that *his*
notions of roguery would tally with *mine*? There 's many a
thing they call a cheat in England we might think a practical joke in Ireland. The national prejudices are constantly in opposition; look, for instance, at the opposite
view they take of the "Income tax"! Morris, besides, is a
strait-laced fellow that would be shocked at a trifle. Maybe
it 's some tomfoolery about his ancestors, some flaw in the
'scutcheon of Conrad, or Leopold, that lived in the year
nine. Egad! I wonder what the Dodds were doing in that
century? Or perhaps it is his politics he 's hinting at, for
I believe the Baron is a bit of a Radical! For that matter,
so am I, — at least, occasionally, and when the Whigs are
in power; for, as I observed to you once, Tom, "always
be a shade more liberal than the Government." It was
years and years before I came to see the good policy of that

simple rule, but, believe me, it's well worth remembering. Be a Whig to the Tories; be a Radical to the Whigs; and when Cobden and that batch come in, as they are sure to do sooner or later, there will be yet some lower depth to descend to and cry, "Take me out!"

I was remarking that Morris is quite capable of being shocked at the Baron's politics, and fancying that I am giving my daughter to one of those Organization of Labor and Rights of Man humbugs that are always getting up rows and running away from them. Now, Tom, I hold these fellows mighty cheap. A patriot without pluck is like a steam-engine wanting a boiler. Why, it's the very essence and vitality of the whole; but still I am not sure that, as the world goes, I'd be right in refusing him my daughter because he put his faith in Kossuth, and thought the Austrian Empire an unclean thing!

I tell you these ruminations and reasonings of mine that you may perceive how I turned the matter over with myself in a candid spirit, and was led away neither by prejudice nor passion. From ten o'clock till eleven — from eleven till midnight — I walked the terrace up and down, like the Ghost in "Hamlet," — I hope I'm right in my quotation, — but neither sight nor sound indicated Morris's arrival! "What if he should not come!" thought I. "How can I frame a pretext for putting off the wedding?" There was no opening for delay that I could think of. I had signed no end of deeds and parchments; I had written my name to "acts" of every possible shape and description. The solemnity of the church and my paternal blessing were alone wanting to complete the fifth act of the drama. I racked my brain to invent a plausible, or even an intelligible cause for postponement. Had I been a condemned felon, I could not have tortured my imagination more intensely to find a pretext for a reprieve. But one issue of escape presented itself. I could be dangerously ill, — a sudden attack; at my age a man can always have gout in the stomach! My daughter, of course, could not be married if I was at death's door; and as, happily, there was no doctor in the neighborhood, the feint attack ran no risk of being converted into a serious action. Since the memorable experiment of my mock ill-

ness at Ems, I own I had no fancy for the performance,
nor could I divest my mind of the belief that all these things
are, in a measure, a tempting of Providence. But what
else could I do? There was not, so far as I could see,
another road open to me.

I was just, therefore, turning back into the house, to
take to my bed in a dangerous condition, when I heard the
clattering of whips, in that crack-crack fashion your German postilion always announces an arrival. I at once hastened down to the door, and arrived at the same moment
that four posters, hot and smoking, drew up a travelling-
barouche to the spot. Morris sprang out at once, and, seizing my hand, with what for him expressed great warmth,
said, —

"Not too late, I hope and trust?"

"No," said I; "thanks to your note, I was fully warned."

By this time a stranger had also descended from the carriage, and stood beside us.

"First of all, let me introduce my friend, Count Adelberg,
who, I rejoice to say, speaks English as well as ourselves."

We bowed, and shook hands.

"By the greatest good luck in the world," continued Morris, "the Count happened to be with me when your letter
arrived, and, seeing the post-mark, observed, 'I see you
have got a correspondent in my part of the world, — who
can he be?' Anxious to obtain information from him, I
immediately mentioned the circumstances to which your note
referred, when he stopped me suddenly, exclaiming, 'Is this
possible, — can you really assure me that this is so?'"

But, my dear Purcell, I cannot go over a scene which
nearly overcame me at the time, and now, in recollection,
is scarcely endurable. The torture and humiliation of
that moment I hope never to go through again. In three
words, let me tell my tale. Count Adelberg was the owner
and lord of Wolfsberg, the Wolfenschäfers being his stewards. This pretended Baron was a young swindling rascal,
who had gone to Bonn less for education than to seek his
fortune. The popular notion in Germany, that every English girl is an heiress of immense wealth, had suggested to
him the idea of passing himself off for a noble of ancient

family and possessions, and thus securing the hand of some rich girl ambitious of a foreign rank and title. He had considerable difficulties to encounter in the prosecution of his scheme, but he surmounted or evaded them all. He absented himself from Baden, for instance, where recognition would have been inevitable, under the pretext of his political opinions; and he, with equal tact, avoided the exposure of his father's vulgarity, by keeping the worthy individual confined to bed. Of the servants and retainers of the castle, the shrewd ones were his accomplices, the less intelligent his dupes. In a word, Tom, an artful plot was well laid and carried out, to impose upon people whose own short-sightedness and vulgar pretensions made them ready victims for even a less ingenious artifice.

I was very nigh crazy as I heard this explanation. They had to hold me twice or thrice by main force to prevent my rushing into the house and wreaking a personal vengeance on the scoundrel. Morris reasoned and argued with me for above an hour. The Count, too, showed that our whole aim should be to prevent the affair getting rumored abroad, and to suppress all notoriety of the transaction. He alluded with consummate delicacy to our want of knowledge of Germany and its people as an explanation of our blunder, and condoled with me on the outrage to our feelings with all the tact of a well-bred gentleman. Any slight pricks of conscience I had felt before, from our own share in the deception, were totally merged in my sense of insulted honor, and I utterly forgot everything about the imaginary townlands and villages I had so generously laid apart for Mary Anne's dowry.

The next question was, what to do? The Count, with great politeness and hospitality, entreated that we should remain, at least for some days, at the castle. He insisted that no other course could so effectually suppress any gossip the affair might give rise to. He supported this view, besides, by many arguments, equally ingenious as polite. But Morris agreed perfectly with me, that the best thing was to get away at once; that, in fact, it would be utterly impossible for us to pass another day under that roof.

The next step was to break the matter to Mrs. D. I

suppose, Tom, that even to as old a friend as yourself I
ought not to make the confession; but I can't help it, — it
will out, in spite of me; and I frankly admit it would have
amply compensated to me for all the insult, outrage, and
humiliation I experienced, if I were permitted just to lay a
plain statement of the case before Mrs. D., and compliment
her upon the talents she exercises for the advancement of her
children, and the proud successes they have achieved.   In
my heart and soul I believe that, in the disposition I then
felt myself, and with as good a cause to handle, I could
very nearly have driven her stark mad with rage, shame,
and disappointment.   Morris, however, declared positively
against this.   He took upon himself the whole duty of the
explanation, and even made me give a solemn pledge not in
any way to interfere in the matter.   He went further, and
compelled me to forego my plans of vengeance against the
young rascal who had so grossly outraged us.

I have not patience to repeat the arguments he employed.
They, however, just came to this: that the paramount question was to hush up the whole affair, and escape at once
from the scene in which it occurred.   I don't think I'll ever
forgive myself for my compliance on this head!   I have an
accommodating conscience with respect to many debts; but
to know and feel that I owe a fellow a horse-whipping,
and to experience in my heart the conviction that I
don't intend to pay it, lowers me in my own esteem to a
degree I have no power to express.   I explained this to
Morris.   I showed him that in yielding to his views I was
storing up a secret source of misery for many a solitary
reflection.   I even proposed to be satisfied with ten minutes'
thrashing of him in secret; none to be the wiser but our two
selves!   He would not hear of it.   And now, Tom, I own
to you that if the story gets abroad in the world, this is the
part of it that will most acutely afflict me.   I really can't
tell you why I permitted him to over-persuade me, and
make me do an act at once contrary to my country, my
nature, and my instincts.   The only explanation I can give
is this: it is the air of the Continent.   Bring an English
bull-dog abroad, feed him with raw beef as you would at
home, treat him exactly the same — but he loses his courage,

and would n't face a terrier. I 'm convinced it 's the same
with a man; and you 'll see fellows put up with slights and
offences here that in their own land they 'd travel a hundred
miles to resent. One comfort I have, however, and it is
this, — I have never been well since I yielded this point.
My appetite is gone; I can't sleep without starting up, and
I have a fluttering about my heart that distresses me greatly;
and although these are more or less disagreeable, they show
me that, under fair circumstances, K. I. could be himself
again; and that though the Continent has breached, it has
not utterly destroyed, his natural good constitution.

To be brief, our plan of procedure was this: I was to
remain with the Count in his apartment, while Morris went
on his mission to Mrs. D. The explanation being made,
we were to take the Count's carriage to Constance, where
we could remain for a week or so, until we had decided
which way to turn our steps; and gave also time to Caroline, who was still with Morris's mother, to join us.

I told M. that I did n't like to go far, that my remittances
might possibly miss me, and so on; and the poor fellow at
once said, that if a couple of hundred pounds could be of the
slightest convenience to me, they were heartily at my service.
Of course, Tom, I said no, that I was not in the least in
want of money. It was the first time in my life I refused a
loan; but I could n't take it. I could have found it easier to
rob a church at that moment! He flushed deeply when I
declined the offer, and stammered out something about his
deep regret if he could have offended me; and, indeed, I
had some trouble to prove that I was n't a bit annoyed or
provoked.

Although all the conversation I have alluded to took place
outside the castle, we were not well inside the door when we
perceived that Count Adelberg's arrival had already been
made known to the household. Troops of servants hastened
to receive him, amongst whom, however, neither the steward
nor his son were to be found.

" Send Wolfenschäfer to the library," said he to a foot·
man, as we went along, and then conducted me to a small
and favorite chamber of which he always kept the key himself. He made me promise not to quit this till he returned,

and then left me to my own not over-gratifying reflections in perfect solitude as they were; Morris having departed on his embassy.

I was speculating on the various emotions each of us was likely to experience at the discovery of this catastrophe, when Morris entered the room, with an amount of agitation in his manner I had never witnessed before.

"Well," said I, "you've told her, — how does she bear it?"

"I confess," said he, stammeringly, "Mrs. Dodd does not appear to place too much reliance upon my mere word, — I mean, not that kind of confidence which could be called implicit."

"Why, you showed her that we have been infamously deceived, grossly insulted?"

"I endeavored to do so," said he, still hesitating. "I tried in the most delicate manner to explain by what vile artifices you had been tricked; and that, on my detection of the scheme, I had hastened over from Baden, fortunately in sufficient time to prevent the accomplishment of this nefarious plot. She scarcely would hear me out, however; for, without paying any regard to the proofs I was giving of my statement, she flew into a passion about my habit of obtruding myself into family affairs, and the impertinent interference which I had practised more than once in matters which did not concern me. In a word, she utterly disbelieved every word I said, attributed my interested feelings to very unworthy motives, and made a few personal remarks of a nature the reverse of complimentary."

"Was my daughter present?" asked I.

"Miss Dodd had gone to her room a short time previously, but Mrs. Dodd sent for her as I was leaving the chamber."

I could not any longer master my impatience, but, without waiting for more, rushed upstairs and into my wife's room. A glance assured me that the work of persuasion was already accomplished; for she was lying half-fainting in a large chair, while Mary Anne and Betty were bathing her temples and using the usual restoratives for suspended animation.

I had abundant time to observe Mary Anne during these proceedings, and, to my excessive wonderment do I own it, the girl was as calm, as self-possessed, and as collected as ever I saw her. I defy the very shrewdest to say that they could detect one trait of anxiety or discomposure about her; so that, though I saw Mrs. D. had yielded to the convictions of truth, I really could not say whether or not Mary Anne had yet heard of the story. I thought, however, I 'd explore the way by an artificial path, and said: " If she 's well enough to be carried downstairs, Mary Anne, we ought to do it. The great matter is to quit this place at once."

" Of course, papa," said she, without the slightest touch of emotion.

" After what has occurred," said I, " every moment I remain is a fresh insult."

" Quite so," said she, composedly.

Ah, Tom, these women are out and out beyond us! Neither physiologists nor novel-writers know a bit about them. The stock themes with these fellows are their tender susceptibility, gentleness, and so forth. Take my word for it, it is in strength of character, in downright power of endurance, that they excel us. They possess a quality of submission that rises to actual heroism, and they can summon an amount of energy to resist an insult to their pride of which we men have no conception whatever.

Instead of any attempt to condole with Mary Anne, or to comfort her, the best I could do was to try to imitate the dignified calm of her composure.

" Don't you think," said I to her, " that we could be off by daybreak?"

" Easily," said she. " Augustine is packing up, and when mamma is a little better I 'll assist her."

" *She* knows it all?" said I, with a gesture towards my wife.

" Everything! "

" And believes it at last?"

A nod was the reply.

Egad, Tom, this coolness completely took me aback. I could do nothing but stare at the girl with amazement, and ask myself, " Does she really know what has happened?"

In utter indifference to my scrutiny, she continued her attentions to her mother, whispering orders from time to time
to Betty Cobb.

"Had n't you better give some directions about your
trunks, papa?" said she to me.

And thus recalled to myself, I hastened to follow the
advice. Paddy, as is customary with him at any great
emergency, was drunk, and, with the usual consequence,
engaged in active conflict with the rest of the servants'
hall. As for James, I sought for him everywhere in vain,
but at last learned that he was seen to saddle and bridle
a horse for himself about half an hour before, which done,
he mounted and rode off at speed towards the forest, which
direction, it appeared, the young Baron! had taken some
time before. I should have felt uncommonly uneasy for
the result had they not assured me that there was not the
very slightest chance of his overtaking the fugitive.

Morris told me, too, that the old steward had been turned
out of doors already, so that we had at least the satisfaction of a very heavy vengeance. The Count never ceased
to show us every attention in his power; and, so far as
politeness and good manners could atone to us, everything
was done that could be imagined. With Morris's aid I got
my things together, and before daybreak the carriage stood
fully loaded at the door. There was, it is true, "an awful
sacrifice" exacted by this hurried packing; and the frail
finery of the trousseau found but scanty tenderness, as it
was bundled up into valises and even carpet-bags! However, I was determined to march, even at the loss of all
my baggage, if necessary!

While these active operations went forward, Mrs. D.
"improved the occasion" by some sharp attacks of hysterics, which providentially ended in a loss of voice at last;
and thus a happy calm was permitted us, in which to take
a slight breakfast before starting.

If I call it slight, Tom, it was not with reference to the
preparations, which were really on the most sumptuous
scale, and all laid out in the large dinner-room with great
taste. The Count had told Morris that if his presence
might not be thought intrusive, he would feel it a great

honor to be permitted to pay his respects to the ladies;
and when I mentioned this to Mary Anne, to my no small
astonishment she replied, "Oh, with pleasure! I really
think we owe it to him for all his attentions." Ay! Tom,
and what is more, down came my wife, who had passed the
night in screaming and sobbing, looking all smiles and
blandnesses, leaning on Mary Anne, who, by the way, had
dressed herself in the most becoming fashion, and seemed
quite bent on a conquest. Oh, these woman, these women!
— read them if you can, Tom Purcell! for, upon my conscience, they are far above the humble intelligence of your
friend K. I.

I don't think you'd believe me if I was to give you an
account of that same breakfast. If ever there was an incident calculated to overwhelm with shame and confusion,
it was precisely that which had just occurred to us. It was
not possible to conceive a situation more painful than we
were placed in; and with all that, I vow and declare that,
except Morris and myself, none seemed to feel it. Mrs. D.
ate and drank, and bowed and smiled and gesticulated, and
ogled the Count to her heart's content; and Mary Anne chatted and laughed with him in all the ease of intimate acquaintanceship; and as he evidently was struck by her beauty,
she appeared to accept the homage of his admiration as a
very satisfactory compliment. As for me, I tried to behave
with the same good breeding as the others, but it was no
use! — every mouthful I ate almost choked me; every time
I attempted to be jocose, I broke down, with a lamentable
failure. Rage, shame, and indignation were all at work
within me; and even the ease and indifference displayed
by the womenkind increased my sense of humiliation. It
might very probably have been far less well-mannered and
genteel; but I tell you frankly, I'd have been better pleased
with them both if they had cried heartily, and made no
secret of their suffering. I half suspect Morris was of the
same mind too; for he could not keep his eyes off them,
and evidently in profound astonishment. But for him, indeed, I don't know how I should have got through that morning, for Mrs. D. and her daughter were far too intent upon
fresh conquests to waste a thought on recent defeats, and

it was evident that Count Adelberg was received by them
both with all the credit due to the "real article." This
threw me completely on Morris for all counsel and guidance; and I must say he behaved admirably, making all
the arrangements for our departure with a ready promptitude that showed old habits of discipline.

In the Count's *calèche* there was no room for servants;
but our own was to follow with them and the baggage, and
also bring up James, — all of which details M. was to look
after, as well as the care of forwarding to me any letters
that might arrive after I was gone.

It was nigh eight o'clock before we started, though breakfast was over a little after six; and, indeed, when all was
ready, horses harnessed, and postilions in the saddle, the
Count insisted on the "ladies" ascending the great watch-
tower of the castle to see the sun rise. He assured them
people came from all parts of the world for that view, which
was considered one of the finest in Europe; and in proof of
his assertion pointed to a long string of inscriptions on
marble tablets in the wall. Here it was the Kur Furst of
this; and there the Landgravine of that. Dukes, arch-
dukes, and field-marshals figured in the catalogue, and
amidst the illustrious of foreign lands a distinguished place
was occupied by Milor Stubbs, who made the ascent on a
day in the year recorded. That Mrs. Dodd and Mary Anne
are destined to a like immortality, I have no doubt whatever.

At last we got into the carriage, but not until the Count
had saluted me on both cheeks, and embraced me tenderly
in stage fashion; he kissed Mrs. D.'s hand, and Mary
Anne's also, with such a touching devotion that, for the
first time during that memorable morning, they both wiped
their eyes. The sight of Morris, however, seemed to recall
them to the sober realities of life; they shook hands with
him, and away we went at that tearing gallop which, though
very little more than six miles an hour, has all the apparent
speed and the real peril of a special train.

"Where's my fur cloak? Is my muff put in? I don't see
the gray shawl. Mary Anne, what has become of the rug?
I'm certain half our things are left behind. How could it
be otherwise, seeing the absurd haste in which we came

away!" These are a few specimens of Mrs. D.'s lucubra-
tions, given *per saltum* as we bumped through the deep ruts
of the road, and will explain, as well as a chapter on the
subject, the train in which her thoughts were proceeding.

Ay, Tom! for all the disgrace and ignominy of that miserable night and morning, she had no other sentiment of
sorrow than for the absurd haste in which we came away.   I
had firmly determined not to recur to this unpleasant affair,
and to let it sleep amongst the archives of similar disagreeable reminiscences, but this provocation was really too
strong for me!   Were they women? — were they human
beings, and could reason this way? — were the questions
that struggled for an answer within me!   I tried to repress
the temptation, but I could not, and so I resolved, if I
could do no more, at least to discipline my emotions, and
hold them within certain limits.   I waited till we were out
of the grounds, — I delayed till we were some miles on the
high-road, — and then, with a voice subdued to a mere whisper, and in a manner that vouched for the most complete
subjection, said, —

"Mrs. Dodd, may I be permitted to inquire — and I
premise that the object of my question is neither any personal nor a mere vulgar curiosity, but simply to investigate
what might be termed a physiological fact, namely, whether
females really feel less than the males of the human
species?"

My dear Tom, the calm tone of my exordium availed me
nothing.   To no end was it that I propounded the purely
scientific basis of my investigation.   She flew at me at once
like a tigress.   The abstract question that I had submitted
for discussion she flung indignantly to the winds, and boldly
asked me if I thought "to escape that way."   "Escape " —
that way!   I was thunderstruck, stupefied, dumfoundered!
Did the woman want to infer — could she by any diabolical
ingenuity or perverseness imply — that I was possibly to
blame for our late calamity?   You'll not credit it; nobody
could, but it is the truth, notwithstanding.   *That* was
exactly the charge she now preferred against me.   If *I* had
taken proper steps to investigate the "Baron's" real pretensions, — if *I* had made due and fitting inquiries about him, —

if *I* had been commonly intelligent, and displayed the most
ordinary knowledge of the world, — in fact, if, instead of
being a bull-headed, blundering old Irish country gentleman, I had been a cross between a foreign prefect and a
London detective, the chances were that we had been spared
the mortification of exhibiting ourselves as endeavoring to
dupe people who were already successfully engaged in dup-
ing us! This was n't all, Tom, but she boldly propounded
the startling declaration that she and Mary Anne both
had suspected the Baron to be an imposition and a cheat!
and although his low manners and vulgar tone imposed upon
me, they had always regarded him as shockingly underbred!
It was *I*, however, who had rushed into the whole misadventure,— it was *I* concocted the entire scheme,— *I* planned the
visit, — *I* made up the match. My stupid cupidity, my
blundering anxiety for a grand alliance, were the causes of
all the evil! The mock munificence of my settlements was
hurled at me as proof positive of the eagerness of my
duplicity, and I was overwhelmed with a mass of accusations which I verily believe would have obtained a verdict
against me at the hands of any honest and impartial jury of
my countrymen.

I have more than once had to acknowledge, that when perfectly assured in my own conscience of my innocence, Mrs.
D. has contrived to shake my doubts about myself, and at
last succeeded in·making me believe that I might have been
culpable without knowing it. I suppose in these cases I
may have been morally innocent and legally guilty, but I 'll
not puzzle my head by any subtlety of explanation; enough
if I own that a less enviable predicament no man need
covet!

I sat under this new allegation sad, silent, and abashed;
and although Mary Anne said but little, yet her occasional
"You must admit, papa," "You will surely acknowledge,"
or "You cannot possibly forget," chimed in, and swelled
the full chorus of accusation against me. If I said nothing,
I thought the more. My reflections took this shape: Here
is another blessed fruit of our coming abroad. Such an
incident never could have befallen us at home. Why, then,
should we continue to live on exposed to similar casualties?

Why reside in a land where we cannot distinguish the man of rank from his scullion, and where all the forms that constitute good breeding and, maybe, good grammar, are quite beyond our appreciation? Every dilettante scribbler for the magazines who sketches his rambles in Spain or Switzerland, grows jocose over some eccentricity or absurdity of his countrymen. Their blunders in language, dress, or demeanor are duly chronicled and relied upon as subjects for a droll chapter; but let me tell you, Tom, that the difficulties of foreign residence are very considerable indeed, and, except to the man who issues from England with a certain well-proved and admitted station, social or political, the society into which he may be thrown is a downright lottery. The first error he commits, and it is almost inevitable, is to mistake the common forms of hat-lifting and bowing for acquaintanceship. "Bull" thinks that the gentleman desires to know him, and obligingly condescends to accept his overtures. The foreigner, somewhat amused to see the veriest commonplace of politeness received as evidence of acquaintance, profits by the admission, chats, and comes to tea. Now, Tom, whether it be cheap soup, cheap clothing, cheap travelling, or cheap friendship, I have a strong prejudice against them all. My notion is that the real article is not to be had without some cost and trouble.

These were some of my ruminations as we rattled along; and although the road was interesting, and the day a fine bracing autumnal one, my mind was not attuned to pleasure or enjoyment. We stopped to bait at Donaueschingen, for we were obliged, by some accident or other, to take the same horses on, and found a most comfortable little inn at the sign of the "Sharpshooter." After dinner we took a stroll in the garden of the palace of the mediatized Prince of Fürstenberg; for, of course, there is a palace and a mediatized prince wherever there is a town of three thousand inhabitants throughout Germany. By the way, Napoleon treated these people pretty much like our own Encumbered Estates Court at home. He sold them out without any ceremony, and got rid of the feudal privileges and the seignorial rights with a bang of the auctioneer's hammer. Of course, as with us, there was often a great deal of individual hardship, but these little principalities were large evils, and half the disturbances of Europe grew out of their corrupt administration.

There is, I often fancy, a natural instinctive kind of corruption incidental to the dominion of a small state. They are too small and too insignificant to attract any attention from the world without, and within their own narrow limits there is no such thing as a public opinion. The ruler, consequently, is free to follow the caprices of his folly, his cruelty, or his wastefulness. He has neither to dread a parliament nor a newspaper. If he send his small contingent — a "commander-in-chief and a drummer of great experience" — to the great army of the Confederation he belongs to, he may tax his subjects, or hang them, to his heart's content! Now, I cannot imagine a worse state of things than this, nor any more likely to foster that spirit of discontent which every hour is adding to the feeling of the Continent.

While I am following this theme, I am forgetting what was uppermost a few minutes back in my mind. In the garden of the same palace, which belongs to a certain Count Fürstenberg, there is a singularly beautiful little spring; it bubbles up amidst flowers and grass, and overruns the greensward in many a limpid streamlet. There is something in the unadorned simplicity of this tiny well, rippling through the yellow daffodils and "starry river buds," wonderfully pleasing; but what an interest fills the mind as we hear that this is the source of the Danube! "The mighty river that sweeps along through the rocky gorges of Upper Austria, washes the foundations of the Imperial Vienna, and flows on, ever swelling and widening and deepening, to the Black Sea, — that giant stream, so romantic in its associations with the touching tale of our own Richard, — so picturesque in its windings, so teeming with interest to the poet, the painter, the merchant, and the politician, there it is, a little crystal rivulet, whose destiny might well seem limited to the flowery borders, and blossoming beds around it." This isn't mine, Tom, though it's exactly what I would have said if the words occurred to me, but I copy it out of the Visitors' Book, where strangers write their names, and, so to say, leave their cards upon the infant Danube.

Truisms are only tiresome to the hearer; they are a delightful recreation to the man that tells them, so that I am sorely tempted to mention some of those that suggested themselves to my mind as I stood beside that little spring, — all the analogies that at once arose to my fancy, between human life and the course of a mighty river, between the turnings and twinings and aberrations of childhood, the headlong current of youth, the mature force of manhood, and the trackless issue, at last, into the great ocean of eternity! One lesson we may assuredly gather from the contemplation: not to predicate from small beginnings against the likelihood of a glorious future!

I left the place regretfully; the tranquil quietude of my two hours' ramble through the garden restored me to a serene and peaceful frame of mind. The little village itself, the tidy, unpretending inn, clean, comfortable, and a model of cheapness, were all to my fancy, and I could very well have liked to linger on there for a week or so. After all, what a commentary is it upon all pursuits of pleasure and amusement, to think that we really find our greatest happiness in those little, out-of-the-way, isolated spots, remote from all the attractions and blandishments of the gay world! I don't mean to say that Mrs. D. quite concurred with me, for she grew very impatient at my delay, and wondered excessively "what peculiar attraction the garden of the palace might have possessed, to make me forget myself." But it's not so easy a thing to do as she thinks! Forgetting oneself, Tom, implies so many other oblivions. It means forgetting one's tenants that have been over-rented, one's banker overdrawn, one's horses overworked, one's house out of repair, one's estate out at elbows; forgetting the duns that torment, the creditors that torture you, — the latitats, the writs, the mortgages, the bonds, — all the inflictions, in fact, consequent to parchment, signed, sealed, and delivered over to your persecuting angel! Oh dear, oh dear! what a thirsty swig would I take of Lethe if I could! and how happy would I be to start fresh in life without any

one of the "liabilities," as they call them, that attach to
Kenny Dodd!

I remember, when I was a schoolboy, no day of the week
had such terrors for me as Saturday, because we were
obliged to answer a repetition of the whole week's work.
That carrying up of the past was a load that always destroyed me! My notion was to let bygones be bygones,
and it was downright cruelty to take me over the old ground
of my former calamities. The same prejudice has tracked
me through life. I can face a new misfortune as well as
my neighbors; what kills me is going back over the old
ones. Let me tell you, too, that there is a great deal of
balderdash talked in the world about experience, — that
with experience you'll do this, that, and t' other better.
Don't believe a word of it. You might as well tell me that
having the typhus will teach a man patience the next time
he catches a fever! Take my word for it, be as fresh as
you can against the ills of life, — know as little of them as
you can, — think as little of them! Keep your constitution
— whether it be moral or physical — as intact as you are
able, and rely on it you'll not fare the worse when it comes
to the trial!

It was a fine evening, with a thin rim of a new moon in
the sky, when we got ready to leave Donaueschingen. The
bill for dinner came to about five shillings for three of us,
wine included, and no charge for rooms, so that when I gave
as much more to the servants, the enthusiasm of the household knew no bounds. The housemaid, indeed, in an excess
of enthusiasm, would kiss my hand, and got rebuked by my
wife as a "forward hussy, that ought to be well looked
after." From this incident, however, our attention was
soon diverted by the arrival of our second carriage, but
without James! A note from Morris explained that he did
not like to detain the servants, lest it should prove inconvenient to us, and that he would take care James should join
us at Constance, — probably early on the next day. This
note was handed to me by the post-boy, — a circumstance
speedily accounted for, as I got out and saw that the whole
company, consisting of Betty, Augustine, the courier, Paddy
Byrne, and a fifth, unknown, were all very drunk and

unable to speak, closely wedged in the britschka! Of course it was no time to ask for any explanations, and we came on to this place, which we reached by midnight.

As I have given you a somewhat full narrative of what befell us, I may as well, ere I conclude, add some words of explanation of the state of our amiable followers. Betty Cobb, it appears, was seized with connubial symptoms while we were at the castle, and, yielding to the soft impeachment, and not being deterred by any discovery of false rank or pretensions, actually bestowed her hand on a distinguished swineherd that pertained to the place. The wedding took place after we left, the convivial festivities being continued all along the road till they overtook us. Had the unlucky girl married a New Zealand chief, or a Kaffir, her choice could not have fallen upon a more thoroughly savage specimen of the human race. The fellow is a Black Forest Caliban of the worst description. The question is now what to do with him, for Mrs. D. will not consent to part with Betty, nor will Betty separate from her liege lord; so that amongst my other blessings I may number that of carrying about the world a scoundrel that would disgrace a string of galley-slaves! Just imagine, Tom, in the rumble of a travelling-carriage a fellow six foot and a half high, dressed in a cowhide, with an ox goad in his hand, and a long naked knife in his girdle, speaking no intelligible tongue, nor capable of any function save the herding of wild animals, — the most uncultivated specimen of brute nature I ever heard, saw, or even read of! Fancy, I say, the pleasure of "lugging" this creature over the Continent of Europe, feeding, housing, and clothing him, his sole claim being that he is the husband of that precious bargain, Betty Cobb!

Why, he'd bring shame on a beast caravan! The best of it is, too, he holds to his "caste" like a Hindoo, and refuses all other occupation save the charge of swine. He would not aid to unload the carriage, — would not lift a trunk, nor carry a carpet-bag; and when admonished by Paddy for his laziness, showed two inches of a broad knife up his sleeve with a grin meant to imply that he knew how to resist any assault on his dignity! That the scoundrel has no respect for law, is clear enough; so that my hope is he will commit some terrible infraction, and that we may be able to send him to the galleys for the rest of his days. How I 'm to keep him and Paddy apart is more than yet appears to me. I suppose, in the end, one of them will kill the other. From what I see here, the expense of keeping this beast

— at an hotel at least — will be equal to the cost of three ordinary servants; for he has no regular meal-times, but has food cooked for him "promiscuously," and eats — if I 'm to credit the landlord — either a kid or a lamb *per diem*. A bear would n't be half the expense, and a far more companionable beast besides. It is but fair to say that Betty seems to adore him; she crams the monster all day with stolen victuals, and appears to have no other care in life than in watching after him.

What induces Mrs. D. to feel this sudden attachment to
Betty herself, I can't imagine.   Up to this she railed at her
unceasingly, and deplored the day and the hour she took her
from home.   But now, when this alliance really makes her
insupportable, she won't hear of parting with her, and sub-
mits to a degree of tyranny from this woman that is utterly
inexplicable.   It's another of those feminine anomalies,
Tom, that neither you nor I, nor maybe anybody else, will
ever be able to reconcile.

You will probably wonder how, at a moment like this,
smarting as I am under the combined effects of insult and
disappointment, I can turn my attention to a matter of this
trifling nature; but I confess to you that the admission of
this uncivilized element into the circle of my family in-
spires me with feelings of disgust, not unmixed with terror;
for what he may do in any access of fury the infernal gods
alone can say.   So long as we are here, in this remote and
little-visited town, the notice he attracts is confined to a
troop of street loungers who follow him; but I have yet to
learn how we are ever to make our appearance in a regular
city in his company.

Now to another matter, Tom, and the most essential of
all.   What are we to do for money? for, whether we go
on or go back, we must have it.   I haven't the heart to
go over the accounts; nor would it put sixpence more in
my pockets, if I was like Babbage's calculating-machine!
Screw up the tenants, and make them pay the arrears.
Healey owes us at least two hundred pounds.   Try if he
can't pay half.   See, besides, if you cannot find a tenant
for the place, even for a year.   This Exhibition in Dublin
will fill the country with strangers; and a good advertisement of Dodsborough, with an account of the "shooting and
fishing, capital society, and two packs of hounds in the
neighborhood," might take the notice of some aspiring
Cockney.   From what I see in the papers, Ireland is going
to be the fashion this summer.   I suppose that she is starved
down to the pitch to be "thin and genteel," and that's the
reason of it.

Tell me what you think of this great display of "industrial
products;" as they call it.   Are we as wonderful as the Irish

papers say, or are we really as backward as the "Times" pronounces us? My own notion is that the whole thing proceeds on a misconception of the country and its capabilities. These Exhibitions are essentially dependent on manufacturing skill for their excellence. Now, we are not a manufacturing people. We are agriculturists, and so are the Yankees; and consequently the utmost we can do is to show off the clever inventions and cunning products of our neighbors. Writing, as I do, confidentially to yourself, I will own, too, that I am not one of those sanguine admirers of these raree-shows, nor do I see in them the seeds of all that progress that others prophesy. Looking at a wonderful mechanical invention will no more teach me to imitate it, than going to Batty's Circus will enable me to jump through a hoop, or ride on my head! Amusement, pleasure, interest, there is in one as much as the other; but as for any educational advantage, Tom, I don't believe in it. To the scientific man these things are all familiar, — to the peasant they are all miraculous; and though the Electric Telegraph be really a wonderful thing, after one sees the miracles of the Church it ceases to surprise you! At all events, give me some account of the place and the people in your next, and write soon.

I have kept this a day back, hoping to announce James's arrival here, but up to this there is no tidings of him.

Yours, ever faithfully,

KENNY JAMES DODD.

P. S. I find now that this town is not in Switzerland, but in Baden, for the police have been here to know " who we are?" and " why we have come?"— two questions that would take longer to answer than they suspect. How absurd these little bits of national prejudice sound, when the symbol of nationality is only a blue post or a white one, and no geographical limit announces a new country. Droll enough, too, they are most importunate in their inquiries after James; as if the appearance of his name in the passport requires that he should be forthcoming when asked for. Ah, Tom! if the fellows that knocked old Europe about in '48 had resolutely set their faces against these stumbling-blocks to civilization,

— passports, police spies, town dues, and gate imposts, — they 'd have won the sympathy of millions, who do not care a rush about Universal Suffrage and the Liberty of the Press, — and, what is more, the concessions could never have been revoked nor recalled !

To myself, individually, the system presents few annoyances ; for I sit serene behind my ignorance of all continental languages, and say to myself, "Touch me if you dare.". Maybe they half suspect the substance of my meditations, for they show the greatest deference towards my condition of passive resistance. The Brigadier has just bowed himself out of the room, with what sounded like a hearty curse, but what Mary Anne assures me was a sincere protestation of his sentiment of "high consideration and esteem." And now to dinner.

LETTER XLI.

MARY ANNE DODD TO MISS DOOLAN, OF BALLYDOOLAN.

CONSTANCE ON THE LAKE.

DEAREST KITTY, — With what rapture do I once more throw myself into the arms of your affection! How devotedly do I seek the sanctuary of my dearest Kitty's heart! It is all over, my sweet friend, — all over! I see you start, — your cheek is bloodless, and your lips tremble, — but reassure yourself, Kitty, and hear me. If there be anything against which I am weak and powerless, — if there be aught in life to oppose which I have neither strength nor energy, — it is the reproach of one I love! Already do I stand accused before you, even now have you arraigned me, and my condemnation is trembling on your lips. Avow it, — own it, dear girl. Your heart, at least, has said the words of my sentence: "All over! so then Mary Anne has jilted him, — changed her mind in the last hour, — trifled with his affections, and made a sport of his feelings." Yes, such is the charge against me; and, trembling as I stand before you, I syllable the word "Guilty." "Guilty, but with extenuating circumstances." Be calm then, be patient; and, above all, be merciful, while I plead before you.

I deny nothing, I evade nothing. I cannot even pretend that my altered feelings originated in any long process of reason or reflection. I will not affect to say that I struggled against conflicting doubts, and only yielded when powerless to resist them. No, dearest, I am above every such shallow artifice; and I own that it was on the very morning your letter arrived — at the moment when my hot tears were falling over the characters traced by your hand — as, enraptured, I kissed the lines that breathed your love — then there suddenly broke upon me a light illumining the dark

horizon around me.   Space became peopled with forms and
images, voices and warnings floated around and above me,
and as I read your words — " If, then, your whole heart be
his " — I trembled, Kitty, my eyes grew dim, my bosom
heaved in agony, and, in my heart-wrung misery, I cried
aloud, " Oh, save me from this perfidy, — save me from
myself ! "

Save that the letter which my fingers grasped convul-
sively was the offspring of friendship and not of love
betrayed, the scene was precisely like that which closes
the second act of the " Lucia di Lammermoor."   Mamma,
the Baron, James, even to the priest, all were there ; and,
like Lucia, dressed in my bridal robe, the orange-flowers
in my hair, and such a love of a Brussels veil fastened
mantilla-wise to the back of the head, I stood pale, trembling, and conscience-stricken ! the awful words of your
question ringing in my ears, like the voice of an angel come
to call me to judgment, " ' If your whole heart be his ! '
But it is not," cried I, aloud, — " it is not, it never can
be ! "   I know not in what wild rhapsody my emotions found
utterance.   I have no memory of that gushing cataract in
which overwrought feelings found their channel.   I spoke in
that rapt enthusiasm in which, as we are told, the ancient
priestesses delivered their dream-revealings, for I, too, was
as one inspired, as agony alone can inspire.   Of myself I
know nothing, but I have since heard that the scene was
harrowing to a degree that no words can convey.   The
Baron, mounted on his fastest courser, fled into the woods ;
James, spirited on by some imagined sense of injury, thirst-
ing for a vengeance on he knew not what or whom, pursued
him ; mamma was seized with frantic screaming ; and even
papa himself, whose lethargic humor stands him like an
armor of proof, — even he swore and imprecated in a
manner that called forth a most impressive rebuke from the
chaplain.

The scene changes, — we are away !   The castle and its
deep woods grow dim behind us ; the wild mountains of
the Schwartz Wald rise before and around us.   The dark
pines wave their stately tops, the wood-pigeon cries his
plaintive note ; rocky glen and rugged precipice, foaming

waterfalls and wooded slopes, pass swiftly by, and on we hasten, — on and on; but, with all our speed, dark, brooding care can still outstrip us, and sorrow follows faster than the wind.

We arrived at Constance by midnight, when I soon betook me to bed, and cried myself to sleep. Sweet — sweet tears were they, flowing like the crystal drops from the margin of an overcharged fountain; for such was the heart of your afflicted Mary Anne.

It is not by any casuistry about the injustice I should have done, had I bestowed a moiety where I had promised a whole heart. It is not by any pretence that I felt this to be an unworthy artifice, that I now appeal to your merciful consideration. It is simply as one suddenly awakened to the terrible conviction that she cannot be loved as she is capable of loving; or, in other words, that she despairs of ever inspiring that passion which alone could requite her for the agony of love. Oh, Kitty, it is an agony, and such a one as no torture of human wickedness ever equalled. May you never feel it in that intensity of suffering which is alike its ecstasy and its woe!

Do not reproach me, Kitty; my heart has already done so, bitterly, — terribly! Again and again have I asked myself, "Who and what are you, that dare to reject rank, wealth, station, glorious lineage, and a noble name? If these and the most devoted love cannot move you, what are the ambitions that rise before you?" Over and over do I interrogate myself thus, and yet the only reply is, a heart-heaved sigh, — the spirit-wrung voice of inward suffering! You, dearest, who know your friend, will not accuse her of exaggerated or overwrought vanity. None so well as you are aware that these are not my characteristic failings.

An excess of humility may depreciate me, even to the lowliest condition of humble fortune; and if happiness be but there, I will not deem the choice a mean one! You will judge of the sincerity of my words, when I tell you that I have just been unpacking all my things, and putting them away in drawers and wardrobes; and oh, Kitty, if you could but see them! Papa was really splendid, and allowed

me to order everything I could fancy. Of course his generosity fettered rather than stimulated my extravagance, so
that I merely took the absolute *nécessaire.* Of these I may
mention two cashmeres and three Brussels scarfs, one a
perfect love; twelve morning, eighteen evening dresses, of
which one for the altar is covered with Valenciennes, looped
up with pearls and brilliants; the corsage ornamented down
the front with a bouquet of the same stones, arranged to
represent lilies of the valley, with dewdrops, — a pretty device, and quite simple, to suit the occasion. The presentation robe is actually magnificent, and only needs a diamond
parure to be queenly. How I dote, too, on these dear little
bonnets! I never weary of trying them on; they sit so
coquettishly on the back of the head, and make one look sly
and modest, and gentle and saucy, all at once! In this
walk of art the French are incomparably above us. Dress
with them observes all the harmony of color and the keeping
of a great picture. No lilac bonnets and blue shawls, — no
scarlets and pinks alternately killing and marring each other,
— none of that false heraldry of costume by which your
Englishwoman displays her vulgar wealth and ill-assorted
finery. All is graceful, well toned, and harmonious. Your
mise is, so to say, the declaration of your sentiments, just
as the signal of a man-of-war proclaims her intention; and
how ingenious to think that your stately cashmere suggests
homage, your ermined mantle watchful devotion, your
muslin peignoir confidence and intimate intercourse.

Now, your "English" must *look* all these to be intelligible, and constantly converts herself into a great staring,
ogling, leering machine, very shocking to contemplate.

I need scarcely remark to you, dearest, that the step I
have just taken has made my position in the family like that
of the young lady who refused Louis Napoleon before
Europe. Our situations, if you come to consider them, are
wonderfully alike; and there are extraordinary points of
resemblance between the gentlemen, to which I cannot at
present more fully allude. The ungenerous observations
and slighting allusions to which I am exposed would actually
wring your heart. Even James remarked that the whole
affair reminded him of Joe Hudson, who, after accepting an

Indian appointment, refused to sail when he had obtained
the outfit. "Mary Anne only wanted the kit," was the
vulgar impertinence by which he closed this piece of flattery;
and this was in allusion to the *trousseau!* Men are so
shallow, so meanly minded, Kitty, and, above all, so ungenerous in the measure of our motives. They really think
that we value dress for itself, and not as a means to an end,
— that end being their own subjection! Mamma, I must
say, is truly kind; she regrets, naturally enough you will
think, the loss of a great alliance. She had pictured to herself the quartering of the M'Carthys with the house of W——,
and ranged in imagination over various remote but ambitious
contingencies; but, with true maternal affection, she has
effaced all these memories from her heart, only to think of
me and of my emotions. I have also been able to supply
her with a consolation, no less great than unexpected, in
this wise: papa, from one cause or other, had been of late
seriously meditating a return to Ireland; I shame to say,
Kitty, that he never valued, never understood the Continent;
its habits, its ways, and its wines, all disagreed with him;
financial reasons, too, influenced him; for somehow, up to
this, we have been forced to overlook the claims of economy,
and only regard those which refer to the station we are to
maintain in society. Now, from all these causes, he had
brought himself to think the only safety lay in a speedy retreat! Mamma had ascertained this beyond a doubt by
some passages in Mr. Purcell's letters to papa; how obtained
I know not. From these she gathered that at any moment
he was capable of abandoning the campaign, and embarking
the whole army! The misery such a course would entail
upon us I have no need to enlarge upon; nor could I, if I
tried, find words to depict the condition of suffering that
would be ours if again domesticated in that dreadful island.
Forgive me, dearest, if I wound one susceptibility of your
tender heart, — I would not ruffle even a rose-leaf of your
gentle nature; but I cannot refrain from saying that Ireland
is very dreadful! Philosophers affect to tell us, Kitty, that
from the chemical properties of meteoric stones we can predicate the nature of the planets from which they have fallen,
and the most ingenious theories as to the structure, size,

and conformation of their bodies are built upon such slender materials. Now, would it be too wide a stretch of ingenuity to apply this theory to home affairs, and argue, from the specimen one sees of the dear country, what must be the land that has reared them? And oh, Kitty, if so, what a sentence we should be condemned to pass!

But to the consolation of which I spoke, and which in this diversion I was nigh forgetting. Papa, as I mentioned, was bent on going home; and now these costly preparations of wedding finery offer the means of opposing him, for of what use could they possibly be at Dodsborough, Kitty? To what end that enormous outlay, if brought back to the regions of Bruff? Here is an expensive armament, — all the *matériel* of a campaign provided; who would counsel the consigning it to rust and decay? who would advise giving over to moths what might be made the adornment of some brilliant capital? Whether we consider the question morally, financially, or strategically, we arrive at the same conclusion. Such a display as this, if exhibited at home, would revolutionize the whole neighborhood, disgust them with home-grown gowns and bonnets, and lead to irrepressible extravagance, debt, and ruin. So far for moral considerations. Financially, the cost is incurred, and it only remains to make the outlay profitable; this, it is needless to say, cannot be done at Dodsborough. And now for the strategy, the tactical part, Kitty. We all know that whenever a marriage is broken off, scandal seizes the occasion for any reports she likes to circulate, and the good-natured world always agrees in condemning "the lady." If her character or conduct be unimpeachable, then they make searches as to her temper. She was a termagant that ruled her whole family, scolded her sisters, bullied her brothers, and was the terror of every one. If this indictment cannot be sustained, they find a flaw in her fortune; her twenty thousand was "only ten;" ten, Irish currency; perhaps on an Irish mortgage of an Irish property, mayhap charged with Heaven knows what of annuities to Irish relations! Now, Kitty, it is essential to avoid every one of these evil imputations, and I have supplied mamma with so good a brief in the cause, so carefully drawn up, and so well argued, that I don't think papa will let the case go to a jury, or, in other words, that he will give in his submission at once. I have much more to tell you, and will write again to-morrow.

Ever yours in affection,

MARY ANNE DODD.

LETTER XLII.

MARY ANNE DODD TO MISS DOOLAN, OF BALLYDOOLAN.

LAKE OF CONSTANCE.

MY DEAREST KITTY, — True to my pledge, I sit down to continue the revelations, the first volume of which is already before you; and as I left off in a chapter of *désagréables*, let me finish the theme ere I proceed to pleasanter paths and greener pastures.

Betty Cobb has gone and taken to herself a husband; and such a husband as really I did not fancy could be found nearer us than the Waterkloof, if that be the correct spelling of the pleasant locality in Kaffirland where some of the something — Fifth or Eighth — are always getting surprised and cut to pieces. The creature is a swineherd, — one of those dreadful semi-savages that Germany rears out of respect to its ancient traditions about wood demons and kobolds. So terrific an object I never beheld, and his "get up," as James would call it, equals his natural advantages.

You may remember the wretches who are thrusting the page into the furnace in Retsch's illustrations of Schiller's poem, "Der Gang auf den Eisenhammer," — one of these is a flattering likeness of him. Betty, however, whose taste in manly beauty is not formed on the Antinous model, believes him to be perfection. At all events, no promise of double wages, presents, or other seductions could warp her allegiance from this seductive object; and as mamma suddenly discovered that she was quite indispensable to her, the consequence is that we have to accept the company and companionship of the graceful "Taddy," who is now part of our legation as a swineherd unattached. You must know, Kitty, that these worthy people, who are brought up

from infancy to regard pigs as the most important part of
the creation, are impressed with a profound contempt for
the human species; that all their habits are imbued with
swinish tastes, modes, and prejudices,— that they love to
live in woods, sleep on the ground, and grunt their sentiments, when they have any. Whether these be the characteristics of conjugalism, or the features which, as the book
says, "make home happy," time and Betty alone can tell.
I must say that fear and disgust are, for the present, the
impressions his appearance suggests to me; but Betty is
clearly of a different mind.

Meanwhile, as regards ourselves, he is really a most
embarrassing element of the state. He is totally unac-
quainted with all laws, divine and human, and only sufficiently gifted with speech to convey his commonest wishes;
and, from what I can learn, Caspar Hauser was a man of the
world in comparison to him. Papa is, of course, frantic at
the thought of his pertaining to us, — but what is to be
done? Betty has declared that she will follow him to Jericho;
by which she means to some fabulous land of unreal geography; and mamma will not part with Betty. To-morrow,
or next day, I expect to hear that Taddy protests he can't
live without his pigs, and that a legion of swine become part
of our travelling equipment. Already has his presence on
our staff called for the attention of the authorities, who are,
very naturally, curious to know what we mean by such a
functionary. Papa, on his side, thinks it part of an Englishman's birthright to resist, oppose, and torment the police;
and, of course, will give no information whatever as to
why he is here, but avows his determination to retain him
in his service just on that account.

These complications — to give them a mild name — have
so absorbed me that I have forgotten to tell you about our
present place of sojourn. The Lake of Constance sounds
pretty, dearest. It seems to address itself at once to our
sense of the beautiful, and our moral attachment to the true.
As we approached it, I looked eagerly from the carriage, at
each turning of the mountain road, for some glimpses of
the scenery; but night fell suddenly, and closed all in darkness. Early on the following morning I arose, and taking

Augustine with my sketch-book, hurried down to the border
of the lake; for our most quaint and ancient "hostelry"
stands in the very centre of the town, and fully fifteen minutes' walk from the water. We reached it suddenly, on
turning the angle of a narrow lane, and came out upon a
small stone pier projecting into the water, and this was the
lake, — the Lake of Constance! Only think, Kitty, of a
great wide expanse of bleak water, with low shores; no
glaciers, no Alps, no sublimity! I could have cried with
disappointment. The custom-house people — very nice-
looking men, with a becoming uniform of green and gold —
assured me that at the upper end of the lake I should see the
mountains of the Vorarlberg, and also the range of the
Swiss Alps, and have abundant material for my pencil.
Meanwhile they made an old boatman sit while I sketched
him; he was mending his net, and with his long blue night-
cap, and scarf of the same color, his snow-white beard, and
fine Rembrandt color, he really made a charming study.
The chief officer of the customs — a remarkably handsome
man, with the very blackest moustaches — was in downright
enthusiasm at the success of my little sketch; and really,
as it was utterly valueless, I could not resist Augustine's
entreaty to tear it out of my book and give it to him.

You can't think, Kitty, with what a graceful mixture of
gratitude and dignity he accepted my worthless present.
He might, so far as breeding went, have been a captain of
hussars. He accompanied us all the way back to the hotel,
having previously placed his boat and his boat's crew at
my disposal during our stay here. Ah, Kitty, what a
charm there is in the amiable tone of foreigners! How
striking the contrast between their cultivated politeness
and the rude barbarism of our own people! Fancy for a
moment what is our home notion of a custom-house official!
— a shabby genteel individual, with a week's beard and a
brandy-and-water eye, that pokes into your trunk after
French gloves, and searches your brother's pocket for
cheroots. Imagine *him* beside one of these magnificently
dressed and really splendid-looking men, with all the air of
an aide-de-camp to the Queen! How naturally we are led
to estimate the style in which people live by the dress and

appointment of their household; and should we not pass a similar judgment on states, and argue, from the appropriate costume of the functionaries, to their own completeness and perfection of system?

I said nothing to mamma of our newly made acquaintance; for as I entered the inn I learned that James and another gentleman had just arrived, but so tired and fatigued that they both had given orders that they should not be disturbed on any account. You may be sure, Kitty, I was intensely curious to know who the stranger was; but all my inquiries were only so many additional provocatives to my eagerness, without any satisfaction! I learned, indeed, that he was young, handsome, tall, and spoke French and German fluently; so much so, indeed, that the waiter hesitated whether to call him English or not! James and his fellow-traveller had arrived by the diligence from Schaffhausen, so that there was really nothing by which we could catch a clew to his friend; and I was left to my patience and my conjectures till breakfast time.

I own to you, Kitty, the trial was too much for my nerves, overstrung as they have been by late events. I fancied a thousand things. I imagined incidents, events, casualties, of which, even to you, dearest, I cannot give the interpretation. Unable, at last, to resist the working of a curiosity that had risen to a torture, I took the resolution to awake James, and ask who was his friend. I traversed the corridor with stealthy footsteps, and sought out the number of his room. It was 43, the waiter said, and the last on the gallery; and so I found it. I turned the handle noiselessly, and entered. The window-curtains were closely drawn, and all was in deep shadow. In one corner of the chamber stood the bed, from which the deep respirations of the sleeper issued; and, poor fellow, it must have been more than common fatigue and weariness that could have caused such sounds. As with cat-like stillness I stole across the chamber, my eyes, growing accustomed to the dim half-light, began to discover objects on each side of me. For instance, I perceived a splendid dressing-gown of amber-colored silk, lined with pale blue, and gorgeously embroidered; a cap of the same colors, with a silver tassel of a foot in length, lay beside it. Slippers of costly embroidery in silver thread, and a most magnificent meerschaum, with a mounting of gold and rubies, was on the table, beside a pair of pistols, whose carved stocks were inlaid with a tracery of the finest workmanship. These I knew to be James's, for I had seen them with him; and there were various other articles equally splendid and costly, all new to me, — such as card-cases, tablets, cigar-holders, and a most gorgeous dressing-case of gold and Bohemian glass, from which, really, I could scarcely tear myself away. I was well aware that James had set no limit to his personal extravagance; but these, and the display of rings, pins, buttons, shirt-studs, chains, and trinkets of all kinds, perfectly astounded me. And here let me remark, Kitty, that the young men of the present day far exceed us in all that pertains to this taste for ornamental jewelry. As my eyes ranged over these attractive and beautiful objects, I was particularly struck with an opal brooch, representing a parrot in the midst of palm-leaves. It was a most beautiful piece of enamel work, studded with gems of every brilliant hue.

It was, as you may imagine, far too pretty for a man's wear, and I resolved to profit by the occasion, to appropriate, or, as the Americans say, to "annex" it to my own possessions. I had just fastened it in the front of my dress, when the handle of the door turned, and — oh, Kitty! conceive my agony as I heard James's voice speaking from without! It was, therefore, not *his* chamber where I was standing, nor could the sleeper be *he!* Escape and concealment were my first thought, and I sprang behind a screen at the very moment the door opened. Should I live a hundred years, I shall never cease to remember the intense misery of that moment. You need only picture my situation to your own mind, to see how distressing it must have been. The certainty of being discovered if I made the slightest noise saved me from fainting, but I almost fancied that the loud beating of my heart might have betrayed me.

James came in without any peculiar deference for the sleeper's nerves, and, upsetting a chair or two, stumbled across the room towards the bed, on which he seated him-

self, calling out "George — Tiverton — old fellow! don't
you mean to get up at all to-day?"

Oh, Kitty! fancy my trembling terror as I heard that I
was in the chamber of Lord George Tiverton. The very
utmost I could do was to refrain from a scream; nor do I
now know how I succeeded in repressing it.

It was not till after repeated efforts that James succeeded
in awaking his friend, who at length, with a long-drawn
sigh, exclaimed, "By Jove, Jemmy! I'm glad you routed
me up. I've had a horrid dream. Only think, I imagined
that I was still in the House of Lords listening to that confounded case! I fancied that Scratchley addressing
their Lordships in reply, and pledging himself to show that
gross neglect, and even cruelty, could be proved against me.

The old scoundrel's harsh voice is still ringing in my ears, and I hear him tearing me to very tatters!"

"Was there anything of that sort?" said James, as he struck a light to his cigar and began smoking.

"Why, I must say, he was *not* complimentary. These fellows, you are aware, have a vocabulary of their own, and when setting up a defence for a pretty woman, married at seventeen, they pitch into one's little frailties at a very cruel rate. Not exactly that the narrative is very detrimental to a man's future prospects; what really damages you is what they call cruelty, and your wife's maid — particularly if she be a Frenchwoman — can always prove this."

"Indeed!" exclaimed James, in some astonishment.

"To be sure she can. Why, everything that thwarts her mistress in anything — good, bad, or indifferent — is cruelty in the French sense. You are rather given to fast acquaintances; you bring home with you to supper, some three or four times a week, detachments of that respectable company one meets at Tattersall's Yard, or in the Turf Club; chicken hazard and the *coulisses* of the opera are amongst your weaknesses; you have a taste for sport, and would rather take the odds against the favorite than lay out your spare cash at Howell and James's. That's cruelty! When regularly done up in town, you make a bolt for Boulogne, or rush down to your shooting-box in the Highlands. That's more cruelty, and neglect besides! Terribly pressed for money, you try to bully your wife's uncle, one of the trustees to her settlement, and threaten to kick him downstairs. Gross cruelty! Harder up again, you pledge her diamonds. Shocking cruelty! Cleared out and sold up, you suggest the propriety of her sending away the French maid, and travelling up to Paris alone. That's monstrous cruelty! And, in fact, all together establish a clear justification for anything that may befall you. Besides this, Jemmy, if you marry a girl of good family, she is sure to have either a father, an uncle, or a brother, or perhaps some three or four cousins in the Lords; now, whatever comes off, they oppose your bill, and as their Lordships only want to hear your story, to listen to the piquant narrative of domestic differences and conjugal jarrings, nobody cares a straw whether you succeed or not. Give me a light, Jim."

They both continued to puff their cigars for some time in silence, during which my sufferings rose to absolute torture; for, in addition to the shocking circumstances of my own situation, was now the fact of my having overheard a most private conversation.

"So they threw out your bill?" asked James, after a pause.

"Deferred judgment!" replied the other, puffing, "which comes to pretty nigh the same thing. Asked for further evidence, explanations, what not! Cursed cigars! don't draw at all."

"They 're Bollard's best Havannahs."

"Well, perhaps I 've been unlucky in my choice; if so, it 's not the first time, Jem; " and he laughed heartily at the notion. "I say, take care and don't say anything about this affair of mine."

"But it will be in all the papers. The ' Times ' will give it to-morrow or next day."

"Not a bit of it, — had a private hearing, old fellow. Too many good names compromised to have the thing made town talk, — you understand."

"Ah, that 's it!" said James.

"Yes, it 's one of the few privileges remaining to what Lord Grey calls ' our order,' except, perhaps, the judgments of the London magistrates. To do *them* justice, the fellows do know what a lord is, and ' they act accordingly.' There, it 's out at last," — and he threw away his cigar, — "and I suppose I may as well think of getting up. Just draw that curtain, Jem, and open the shutter."

Oh, Kitty dearest, can you form to yourself any idea of my situation! James had already risen from the bedside, and was groping his way to the window. Another moment, and the flood of light would pour into the room and inevitably discover me. My agitation almost choked me; it was like a sense of drowning, and at the same time accompanied by the terrible thought that I must not dare to cry for succor. James was busy with the button of the window-fastening, — another instant and it would be too late, — and with the energy of utter despair I sprang from behind the screen, and then, pushing it with all my force, upset it over the toilet-table, the whole tumbling against James with a horrid crash, and laying him prostrate beneath the ruins. I dashed from the room with the speed of lightning; I know not how I flew along the gallery, up the stairs, and gained my own chamber, but, as I turned the key inside, all consciousness left me, and I fell fainting on the floor. The noise of many footsteps on the corridor outside, and the sound of voices, aroused me. The fragments I could collect showed me that all were discussing the late catastrophe, and none able to explain it. Oh, Kitty, what a gush of delight rushed through me to hear that I had escaped unseen, unknown, unsuspected!

The general voice attributed the accident to James's awkwardness, and I could perceive that he had not escaped without some bruises.

It was a long time, too, ere I could turn my thoughts from my late peril to think of the strange revelation I had been witness to; nor was it without a certain shock to my feelings that I learned Lord George was married. His attentions to me were certainly particular, Kitty. No girl, with any knowledge of life, makes any mistake on the subject, because, if she entertains a doubt, she knows how at once to resolve it, by tests as unerring as those a chemist employs to discover arsenic.

Now, I had submitted him to one or two of these at times, and they all showed him to be "infallibly affected." With what a sense of disappointment, then, was I to hear that he was already married, the only alleviation being that he was seeking to dissolve the tie! Poor fellow! how completely did this unhappy circumstance explain many expressions whose meaning had hitherto puzzled me! How I saw through clouds and mists that once obscured the atmosphere of my hopes! And how readily did I forgive him for vacillation and uncertainty, which, before, had often distressed and displeased me. Until free, it was, of course, impossible that he could avow his sentiments undisguisedly, and now I recognized the noble character of the struggle that he had maintained with himself. Oh, Kitty, it is not only that "the course of true love never did run smooth," but it really could not be true love if it did so. The sluggish stream of common affection flows lazily along between the muddy banks and sedgy sides of ordinary life, but the boiling torrent of passionate love requires the rocks of difficulty to dam its course and impart that character of foamy impetuosity that sweeps away every obstacle and dashes onward to its goal regardless of danger! I'm sure I feel quite convinced that such is the nature of Lord G.'s passion; and that now these stupid "Lords" have rejected his plea for a divorce, if he be not rescued by the hand of devoted affection, he may rush madly into every excess, and dissipate the great talents with which he is so remarkably gifted.

Be candid now, my darling Kitty, and confess frankly that you are greatly shocked at these doctrines, and your dear little Irish prudery blushes crimson at the bare thought of feeling even an interest in a man already married, and horrified at the notion of his hypothetical attentions. Yes, I see it all; your sweetly dimpled mouth is pursed up with conscious propriety, and you are arranging your features into all the sternness of judicial severity; but hear me for one moment in defence, if not in justification. All these things seem very dreadful to you in the solitudes of Tipperary, simply because of their infrequency. The man who has separated from his wife, or the woman divorced from her husband, are great criminals to your home-bred notions, and by your social code they are sentenced at once to a life of solitude and isolation; but in the real world, my dear Kitty, on the great stage of life, this severity would be downright absurdity; the category so mercilessly condemned by you is exactly that which contains the true salt of society; these are the very people that everybody calls charming, fascinating, delightful! All the elastic, buoyant natures, the joyous spirits, the invariable good tempers, the generous hearts one meets with, are amongst them. Why such happily gifted creatures should not have made their homes a paradise, is a problem none can solve. It is like the squaring of the circle, — the cause of Irish misery, — or anything else you can think of equally inscrutable; but the

fact is as I tell you; and if you will just run your eye over
any list of fashionable company, and select such as I speak
of, believe me you will have extracted all the plums from
the pudding. As for Lord George himself, a more delightful creature does not exist; and one has only to know him
to be convinced that the woman who could not be happy
with him must be a demon. Of the generous character he
possesses, and at the same time the consummate tact of his
manner, an instance grew out of the little event I have just
related. In my confusion and embarrassment after escaping from the room, I totally forgot the brooch which I had
placed in my dress, and actually came down to breakfast
with it still there. Guess my shame and horror, Kitty, when
James called out, across the table, "I say, Mary Anne, what
a smart pin you 've got there, — one of the neatest things
I have seen." I grew scarlet, then pale, and felt as if I
was going to faint; when Lord George cried out, "It is,
really, very tasty. I had one myself something like it, but
the stones were emeralds, not rubies; and I think Miss
Dodd's is prettier."

The man who could rescue one at such a conjuncture,
Kitty, is worthy of all confidence, and so I told him by a
glance. Meanwhile he gave the conversation another turn
by proposing a fishing excursion on the lake, and immediately after breakfast we all sallied forth to the water.

Notwithstanding his agreeability, — and he never displayed it to greater advantage, — I was silent and abstracted
during the entire day. The embarrassment of my position
was almost unendurable; and it was only as he took my arm,
to conduct me back to the hotel, that I regained anything
like courage.

"Why are you so serious?" said he. "Mind, I don't
want a confession; only, that I have a secret for *your* ear,
whenever you will trust *me* with one of yours."

I made him no answer, Kitty, but walked along in silence,
and with my veil down.

I write all these things to my dearest friend with less
reserve than I could recall them to my own memory in solitude. I tell her everything; and she is the true partner of
my joys, my sorrows, my hopes, and my terrors. Yet must

I leave much to her imagination to picture forth the state of my affections, and the troubled sea of my heart's emotions. And, oh! dearest, kindest, tenderest of all friends, do not mistake, do not misconstrue the feelings of your ever attached and devoted

MARY ANNE.

I wanted to tell you something of our future destination, and I have detained this for that purpose, but still everything is uncertain and undecided. Papa received a large packet, like law papers and leases, from Mr. Purcell yesterday, and has been occupied in perusing them ever since. We are in terror lest he should decide on going back; and every time he enters the room we are trembling in dread of the announcement. Mamma has had an hysterical attack in preparation for the moment, for the last twenty-four hours, and even if "no cause be shown," I fancy she will not throw away so much good agony for nothing, but take it out for what Sir Boyle Roach fought his duel, "miscellaneous reasons."

Cary is still staying with the Morrises. How she endures it I can't conceive; a half-pay lover and a half-pay *ménage* are two things that, to *me* at least, would be insupportable. The girl is really totally destitute of all proper pride, and makes the silly mistake of supposing that a spirit of independence is the best form of self-esteem. I suppose it will end by the "Captain's" proposing for her; but up to this, I believe, it is all friendship, regard, and so on.

END OF VOL. I.